THE
THE BLACK

A CHRONICLE OF 1830

by

STENDHAL

COMPASS CIRCLE

The Red And The Black.
Written by Stendhal.
Translated by Horace B. Samuel.
Current edition published by Compass Circle in 2019.

Published by Compass Circle
A Division of Garcia & Kitzinger Pty Ltd
Cover copyright ©2019 by Compass Circle.

Note:
All efforts have been made to preserve original spellings and punctuation of the original edition which may include old-fashioned English spellings of words and archaic variants.

This book is a product of its time and does not reflect the same views on race, gender, sexuality, ethnicity, and interpersonal relations as it would if it were written today.

For information contact :
information@compass-circle.com

A novel is a mirror walking along a main road.

STENDHAL

SECRET WISDOM OF THE AGES SERIES

Life presents itself, it advances in a fast way. Life indeed never stops. It never stops until the end. The most diverse questions peek and fade in our minds. Sometimes we seek for answers. Sometimes we just let time go by.

The book you have now in your hands has been waiting to be discovered by you. This book may reveal the answers to some of your questions.

Books are friends. Friends who are always by your side and who can give you great ideas, advice or just comfort your soul.

A great book can make you see things in your soul that you have not yet discovered, make you see things in your soul that you were not aware of.

Great books can change your life for the better. They can make you understand fascinating theories, give you new ideas, inspire you to undertake new challenges or to walk along new paths.

Literature Classics like the one of *The Red And The Black* are indeed a secret to many, but for those of us lucky enough to have discovered them, by one way or another, these books can enlighten us. They can open a wide range of possibilities to us. Because achieving greatness requires knowledge.

The series SECRET WISDOM OF THE AGES presented by Compass Circle try to bring you the great timeless masterpieces of literature, autobiographies and personal development,.

We welcome you to discover with us fascinating works by Nathaniel Hawthorne, Sir Arthur Conan Doyle, Edith Wharton, among others.

INTRODUCTION

Some slight sketch of the life and character of Stendhal is particularly necessary to an understanding of *Le Rouge et Le Noir* (*The Red and the Black*) not so much as being the formal stuffing of which introductions are made, but because the book as a book stands in the most intimate relation to the author's life and character. The hero, Julien, is no doubt, viewed superficially, a cad, a scoundrel, an assassin, albeit a person who will alternate the moist eye of the sentimentalist with the ferocious grin of the beast of prey. But Stendhal so far from putting forward any excuses makes a specific point of wallowing defiantly in his own alleged wickedness. "Even assuming that Julien is a villain and that it is my portrait," he wrote shortly after the publication of the book, "why quarrel with me. In the time of the Emperor, Julien would have passed for a very honest man. I lived in the time of the Emperor. So—but what does it matter?"

Henri Beyle was born in 1783 in Grenoble in Dauphiny, the son of a royalist lawyer, situated on the borderland between the gentry and that bourgeoisie which our author was subsequently to chastise with that malice peculiar to those who spring themselves from the class which they despise. The boy's character was a compound of sensibility and hard rebelliousness, virility and introspection. Orphaned of his mother at the age of seven, hated by his father and unpopular with his schoolmates, he spent the orthodox unhappy childhood of the artistic temperament. Winning a scholarship at the Ecole Polytechnique at the age of sixteen he proceeded to Paris, where with characteristic independence he refused to attend the college classes and set himself to study privately in his solitary rooms.

In 1800 the influence of his relative M. Daru procured him a commission in the French Army, and the Marengo campaign gave him an opportunity of practising that Napoleonic worship to which throughout his life he remained consistently faithful, for the operation of the philosophical materialism of the French sceptics on an essentially logical and mathematical mind soon swept away all competing claimants for his religious adoration. Almost from his childhood, moreover, he had abominated the Jesuits, and "Papism is the source of all crimes," was throughout his life one of his favourite maxims.

After the army's triumphant entry into Milan, Beyle returned to Grenoble on furlough, whence he dashed off to Paris in pursuit of a young woman to whom he was paying some attention, resigned his commission in the army and set himself to study "with the view of becoming a great man." It is in this period that we find the most marked development in Beyle's enthusiasm of psychology. This tendency sprang primarily no doubt from his own introspection. For throughout his life Beyle enjoyed the indisputable and at times dubious luxury of a double consciousness. He invariably carried inside his brain a psychological mirror which reflected every phrase of his emotion with scientific accuracy. And simultaneously, the critical spirit, half-genie, half-demon inside his brain, would survey in the semi-detached mood of a keenly interested spectator, the actual emotion itself, applaud or condemn it as the case might be, and ticket the verdict with ample commentations in the psychological register of its own analysis.

But this trend to psychology, while as we have seen, to some extent, the natural development of mere self-analysis was also tinged with the spirit of self-preservation. With a mind, which in spite of its natural physical courage was morbidly susceptible to ridicule and was only too frequently the dupe of the fear of being duped, Stendhal would scent an enemy in every friend, and as a mere matter of self-protection set himself to penetrate the secret of every character with which he came into contact. One is also justified in taking into account an honest intellectual enthusiasm which found its vent in deciphering the rarer and more precious manuscripts of the "human document."

With the exception of a stay in Marseilles, with his first mistress Mélanie Guilhert ("a charming actress who had the most refined sentiments and to whom I never gave a sou,") and a subsequent sojourn in Grenoble, Stendhal remained in Paris till 1806, living so far as was permitted by the modest allowance of his niggard father the full life of the literary temperament. The essence, however, of his character was that he was at the same time a man of imagination and a man of action. We consequently find him serving in the Napoleonic campaigns of 1806, 1809 and 1812. He was present at the Battle of Jena, came several times into personal contact with Napoleon, discharged with singular efficiency the administration of the State of Brunswick, and retained his sangfroid and his bravery during the whole of the panic-stricken retreat of the Moscow campaign.

It is, moreover, to this period that we date Stendhal's liaison with Mme. Daru the wife of his aged relative, M. Daru. This particular intrigue has, moreover, a certain psychological importance in that Mme. Daru constituted the model on whom Mathilde de la Mole was drawn in *The Red and the Black*. The student and historian consequently who is anxious to check how far the novelist is drawing on his experience and how far on his imagination can compare with profit the description of the Mathilde episode in *The Red and the Black* with those sections in Stendhal's Journal entitled the *Life and Sentiments of Silencious Harry*, *Memoirs of my Life during my Amour with Countess Palfy*, and also with the posthumous fragment, *Le Consultation de Banti*, a piece of methodical deliberation on the pressing question. "Dois-je ou ne dois-je pas avoir la duchesse?" written with all the documentary coldness of a Government report. It is characteristic that both Bansi and Julien decide in the affirmative as a matter of abstract principle. For they both feel that they must necessarily reproach themselves in after life if they miss so signal an opportunity.

Disgusted by the Restoration, Stendhal migrated in 1814 to Milan, his favourite town in Europe, whose rich and varied life he savoured to the full from the celebrated ices in the entreates of the opera, to the reciprocated interest of Mme. Angelina Pietragrua (the Duchesse de Sansererina of the Chartreuse of Parma), "a sublime wanton à la Lucrezia Borgia" who would appear to have deceived him systematically. It was in Milan that Stendhal first began to write for publication, producing in 1814 *The Lives of Haydn and Mozart*, and in 1817 a series of travel sketches, *Rome, Naples, Florence*, which was published in London.

It was in Milan also than Stendhal first nursed the abstract thrills of his grand passion for Métilde Countess Dunbowska, whose angelic sweetness would seem to have served at any rate to some extent as a prototype to the character of Mme. de Rênal. In 1821 the novelist was expelled from Milan on the apparently unfounded accusation of being a French spy. It is typical of that mixture of brutal sensuality and rarefied sentimentalism which is one of the most fascinating features of Stendhal's character, that even though he had never loved more than the lady's heart, he should have remained for three years faithful to this mistress of his ideal.

In 1822 Stendhal published his treatise, *De l'Amour*, a practical scientific treatise on the erotic emotion by an author who possessed the unusual advantage of being at the same time an acute psychologist and a brilliant man of the world, who could test abstract theories by concrete practice and could co-ordinate what he had felt in himself and observe in others into broad general principles.

In 1825 Stendhal plunging vigorously into the controversy between the Classicists and the Romanticists, published his celebrated pamphlet, *Racine and Shakespeare*, in which he vindicated with successful crispness the claims of live verse against stereotyped couplets and of modern analysis against historical tradition. His next work was the *Life of Rossini*, whom he had known personally in Milan, while in 1827 he published his first novel *Armance*, which, while not equal to the author's greatest work, give none the less good promise of that analytical dash which he was subsequently to manifest. After *Armance* come the well-known *Promenades Rome*, while the Stendhalian masterpiece *Le Rouge et Le Noir* was presented in 1830 to an unappreciative public.

Enthusiasm for this book is the infallible test of your true Stendhalian. Some critics may prefer, possibly, the more Jamesian delicacy of

Armance, and others fortified by the example of Goethe may avow their predilection for *The Chartreuse de Parme* with all the *jeune premier* charm of its amiable hero. But in our view no book by Stendhal is capable of giving the reader such intellectual thrills as that work which has been adjudged to be his greatest by Balzac, by Taine, by Bourget. Certainly no other book by Stendhal than that which has conjured up *Rougistes* in all countries in Europe has been the object of a cult in itself. We doubt, moreover, if there is any other modern book whether by Stendhal or any one else, which has actually been learnt by heart by its devotees, who, if we may borrow the story told by M. Paul Bourget, are accustomed to challenge the authenticity of each other's knowledge by starting off with some random passage only to find it immediately taken up, as though the book had been the very Bible itself.

The more personal appeal of what is perhaps the greatest romance of the intellect ever written lies in the character of Julien, its villain-hero. In view of the identification of Julien with Stendhal himself to which we have already alluded, it is only fair to state that Stendhal does not appear to have ever been a tutor in a bourgeois family, nor does history relate his ever having made any attempt at the homicide of a woman. So far, in fact, as what we may call the external physical basis of the story is concerned, the material is supplied not by the life of the author, but by the life of a young student of Besançon, of the name of Berthet, who duly expiated on the threshold that crime which supplied the plot of this immortal novel. But the soul, the brain of Julien is not Berthet but Beyle. And what indeed is the whole book if not a vindication of *beylisme*, if we may use the word, coined by the man himself for his own outlook on life? For the procedure of Stendhal would seem to have placed his own self in his hero's shoes, to have lived in imagination his whole life, and to have recorded his experience with a wealth of analytic detail, which in spite of some arrogance, is yet both honest and scientific.

And the life of this scoundrel, this ingrate, this assassin, certainly seems to have been eminently worth living. In its line, indeed, it constitutes a veritable triumph of idealism, a positive monument of "self-help." For judged by the code of the Revolution, when the career was open to talents, the goodness or badness of a man was determined by the use he made of his opportunities. Efficiency was the supreme test of virtue, as was failure the one brand of unworthiness. And measured by these values Julien ranks high as an ethical saint. For does he not sacrifice everything to the forgiving of his character and the hammering out of his career? He is by nature nervous, he forces himself to be courageous, fighting a duel or capturing a woman, less out of thirst for blood or hunger for flesh, than because he thinks it due to his own *parvenu* self-respect to give himself some concrete proof on his own moral force.

"Pose and affection" will sneer those enemies whom he will have to-day as assuredly as he had them in his lifetime, the smug bourgeois and Valenods of our present age. But the spirit of Julien will retort, "I made myself master of my affectation and I succeeded in my pose." And will he not have logic on his side? For what after all is pose but the pursuit of a subjective ideal, grotesque no doubt in failure, but dignified by its success. And as M. Gaultier has shown in his book on *Bovarysme*, is not all human progress simply the deliberate change from what one is, into what one is not yet, but what nevertheless one has a tendency to be? Viewed from this standpoint Julien's character is what one feels justified in calling a *bonâ fide* pose. For speaking broadly his character is two-fold, half-sensitive tenderness, half ferocious ambition, and his pose simply consists in the subordination of his softer qualities for the more effective realization of his harder. Considered on these lines *Le Rouge et Le Noir* stands pre-eminent in European literature as the tragedy of energy and ambition, the epic of the struggle for existence, the modern Bible of Nietzschean self-discipline. And from the sheer romantic aspect also the book has its own peculiar charm. How truly poetic, for instance, are the passages where Julien takes his own mind alone into the mountains, plots out his own fate, and symbolizes his own solitary life in the lonely circlings of a predatory hawk.

Julien's enemies will no doubt taunt him with his introspection, while they point to a character distorted, so they say, by the eternal mirror of its own consciousness. Yet it should be remembered that Julien lived in an age when introspection had, so to speak, been only recently invented, and Byronism and Wertherism were the stock food of artistic tempera-ments. In the case of Julien, moreover, even though his own criticisms on his own acts were to some extent as important to him as the actual acts themselves, his introspection was more a strength than a weakness and never blunted the edge of his drastic action. Compare, for instance, the character of Julien with the character of Robert Greslou, the hero of Bourget's *Le Disciple*, and the nearest analogue to Julien in *fin de siècle* literature, and one will appreciate at once the difference between health and decadence, virility and hysteria.

One of the most essential features of the book, however, is the swing of the pendulum between Julien's ambition and Julien's tenderness. For our hunter is quite frequently caught in his own traps, so that he falls genuinely in love with the woman whom, as a matter of abstract princi-ple, he had specifically set himself to conquer. The book consequently as a romance of love, ranks almost as high as it does as a romance of ambition. The final idyll in prison with Mme. de Rênal, in particular, is one of the sweetest and purest in literature, painted in colours too true ever to be florid, steeped in a sentiment too deep ever to be mawkish.

As moreover, orthodox and suburban minds tend to regard all French novels as specifically devoted to obscene wallowings, it seems only relevant to mention that Stendhal at any rate never finds in sensualism any inspiration for ecstatic rhapsodies, and that he narrates the most specific episodes in the chastest style imaginable.

Though too the sinister figure of the carpenter's son looms large over the book, the characterization of all the other personages is portrayed with consummate brilliancy. For Stendhal standing first outside his characters with all the sceptical scrutiny of a detached observer, then goes deep inside them so that he describes not merely what they do, but why they do it, not merely what they think, but why they think it, while he assigns their respective share to innate disposition, accident, and environment, and criticizes his creations with an irony that is only occasionally benevolent. For it must be confessed that Stendhal approves of extremely few people. True scion of the middle-classes he hates the bourgeois because he is bourgeois, and the aristocrat because he is aristocrat. Nevertheless, as a gallery of the most varied characters, patricians and plebeians, prudes and profligates, Jesuits and Jansenists, Kings and coachmen, bishops and bourgeois, whose mutual difference acts as a most effective foil to each other's reality, *Le Rouge et Le Noir* will beat any novel outside Balzac.

We would mention in particular those two contrasted figures, Mme. de Rênal the *bourgeoise passionée*, and Matilde de la Mole the noble damozel who enters into her intrigue out of a deliberate wish to emulate the exploits of a romantic ancestress. But after all these individuals stand out not so much because their characterization is better than that of their fellow-personages, but because it is more elaborate. Even such minor characters, for instance, as de Frilair, the lascivious Jesuit, Noiraud, the avaricious gaoler, Mme. de Fervaques, the amoristic prude, are all in their respective ways real, vivid, convincing, no mere padded figures of the imagination, but observed actualities swung from the lived life on the written page.

The style of Stendhal is noticeable from its simplicity, clear and cold, devoid of all literary artifice, characteristic of his analytic purpose. He is strenuous in his avoidance of affection. Though, however, he never holds out his style as an aesthetic delight in itself, he reaches occasionally passages of a rare and simple beauty. We would refer in particular to the description of Julien in the mountains, which we have already mentioned, and to the short but impressive death scene. His habit, however, of using language as a means and never as an end, occasionally revenges itself upon him in places where the style, though intelligible, is none the less slovenly, anacoluthic, almost Thucydidean.

After the publication of *Le Rouge et Le Noir* Stendhal was forced by his financial embarrassment to leave Paris and take up the post of consul at Trieste. Driven from this position by the intrigues of a vindictive Church he was transferred to Civita Vecchia where he remained till 1835, solacing his ennui by the compilation of his autobiography and thinking seriously of marriage with the rich and highly respectable daughter of his laundress. He then returned to Paris where he remained till 1842, where he died suddenly at the age of fifty-nine in the full swing of all his mental and physical activities.

His later works included, *La Chartreuse de Parme, Lucien, Leuwen* and *Lamiel*, of which the *Chartreuse* is the most celebrated, but *Lamiel* certainly the most sprightly. But it is on *Le Rouge et Le Noir* that his fame as a novelist is the most firmly based. It is with this most personal document, this record of his experiences and emotions that he lives identified, just as D'Annunzio will live identified with *Il Fuoco* or Mr. Wells with the *New Machiavelli. Le Rouge et Le Noir* is the greatest novel of its age and one of the greatest novels of the whole nineteenth century. It is full to the brim of intellect and adventure, introspection and action, youth, romance, tenderness, cynicism and rebellion. It is in a word the intellectual quintessence of the Napoleonic era.

HORACE B. SAMUEL,

TEMPLE,
Oct., 1913.

I

A SMALL TOWN

Put thousands together less bad,
But the cage less gay.—*Hobbes.*

The little town of Verrières can pass for one of the prettiest in Franche-Comté. Its white houses with their pointed red-tiled roofs stretch along the slope of a hill, whose slightest undulations are marked by groups of vigorous chestnuts. The Doubs flows to within some hundred feet above its fortifications, which were built long ago by the Spaniards, and are now in ruins.

Verrières is sheltered on the north by a high mountain which is one of the branches of the Jura. The jagged peaks of the Verra are covered with snow from the beginning of the October frosts. A torrent which rushes down from the mountains traverses Verrières before throwing itself into the Doubs, and supplies the motive power for a great number of saw mills. The industry is very simple, and secures a certain prosperity to the majority of the inhabitants who are more peasant than bourgeois. It is not, however, the wood saws which have enriched this little town. It is the manufacture of painted tiles, called Mulhouse tiles, that is responsible for that general affluence which has caused the façades of nearly all the houses in Verrières to be rebuilt since the fall of Napoleon.

One has scarcely entered the town, before one is stunned by the din of a strident machine of terrifying aspect. Twenty heavy hammers which fall with a noise that makes the paved floor tremble, are lifted up by a wheel set in motion by the torrent. Each of these hammers manufactures every day I don't know how many thousands of nails. The little pieces of iron which are rapidly transformed into nails by these enormous hammers, are put in position by fresh pretty young girls. This labour so rough at first sight is one of the industries which most surprises the traveller who penetrates for the first time the mountains which separate France and Helvetia. If when he enters Verrières, the traveller asks who owns this fine nail factory which deafens everybody who goes up the Grande-Rue, he is answered in a drawling tone "*Eh! it belongs to M. the Mayor.*"

And if the traveller stops a few minutes in that Grande-Rue of Verrières which goes on an upward incline from the bank of the Doubs to nearly as far as the summit of the hill, it is a hundred to one that he will see a big man with a busy and important air.

When he comes in sight all hats are quickly taken off. His hair is grizzled and he is dressed in grey. He is a Knight of several Orders, has a large forehead and an aquiline nose, and if you take him all round, his features are not devoid of certain regularity. One might even think on the first inspection that it combines with the dignity of the village mayor that particular kind of comfortableness which is appropriate to the age of forty-eight or fifty. But soon the traveller from Paris will be shocked by a certain air of self-satisfaction and self-complacency mingled with an almost indefinable narrowness and lack of inspiration. One realises at last that this man's talent is limited to seeing that he is paid exactly what he is owed, and in paying his own debts at the latest possible moment.

Such is M. de Rênal, the mayor of Verrières. After having crossed the road with a solemn step, he enters the mayoral residence and disappears from the eye of the traveller. But if the latter continues to walk a hundred steps further up, he will perceive a house with a fairly fine appearance, with some magnificent gardens behind an iron grill belonging to the house. Beyond that is an horizon line formed by the hills of Burgundy, which seem ideally made to delight the eyes. This view causes the traveller to forget that pestilential atmosphere of petty money-grubbing by which he is beginning to be suffocated.

He is told that this house belongs to M. de Rênal. It is to the profits which he has made out of his big nail factory that the mayor of Verrières owes this fine residence of hewn stone which he is just finishing. His family is said to be Spanish and ancient, and is alleged to have been established in the country well before the conquest of Louis XIV.

Since 1815, he blushes at being a manufacturer: 1815 made him mayor of Verrières. The terraced walls of this magnificent garden which descends to the Doubs, plateau by plateau, also represent the reward of M. de Rênal's proficiency in the iron-trade. Do not expect to find in France those picturesque gardens which surround the manufacturing towns of Germany, like Leipsic, Frankfort and Nurenburgh, etc. The more walls you build in Franche-Comté and the more you fortify your estate with piles of stone, the more claim you will acquire on the respect of your neighbours. Another reason for the admiration due to M. de Rênal's gardens and their numerous walls, is the fact that he has purchased, through sheer power of the purse, certain small parcels of the ground on which they stand. That saw-mill, for instance, whose singular position on the banks of the Doubs struck you when you entered Verrières, and where you notice the name of SOREL written in gigantic characters on the chief beam of the roof, used to occupy six years ago that precise space on which is now reared the wall of the fourth terrace in M. de Rênal's gardens.

Proud man that he was, the mayor had none the less to negotiate with that tough, stubborn peasant, old Sorel. He had to pay him in good solid golden louis before he could induce him to transfer his workshop elsewhere. As to the *public*stream which supplied the motive power for the saw-mill, M. de Rênal obtained its diversion, thanks to the influence which he enjoyed at Paris. This favour was accorded him after the election of 182-.

He gave Sorel four acres for every one he had previously held, five hundred yards lower down on the banks of the Doubs. Although this position was much more advantageous for his pine-plank trade, father Sorel (as he is called since he has become rich) knew how to exploit the impatience and *mania for landed ownership* which animated his neighbour to the tune of six thousand francs.

It is true that this arrangement was criticised by the wiseacres of the locality. One day, it was on a Sunday four years later, as M. de Rênal was coming back from church in his mayor's uniform, he saw old Sorel smiling at him, as he stared at him some distance away surrounded by his three sons. That smile threw a fatal flood of light into the soul of the mayor. From that time on, he is of opinion that he could have obtained the exchange at a cheaper rate.

In order to win the public esteem of Verrières it is essential that, though you should build as many walls as you can, you should not adopt some plan imported from Italy by those masons who cross the passes of the Jura in the spring on their way to Paris. Such an innovation would bring down upon the head of the imprudent builder an eternal reputation for *wrongheadedness*, and he will be lost for ever in the sight of those wise, well-balanced people who dispense public esteem in Franche-Comté.

As a matter of fact, these prudent people exercise in the place the most offensive despotism. It is by reason of this awful word, that anyone who has lived in that great republic which is called Paris, finds living in little towns quite intolerable. The tyranny of public opinion (and what public opinion!) is as *stupid* in the little towns of France as in the United States of America.

II
A MAYOR

Importance! What is it, sir after all? The respect of fools, the wonder of children, the envy of the rich, the contempt of the wise man.—*Barnave*

Happily for the reputation of M. de Rênal as an administrator an immense wall of support was necessary for the public promenade which goes along the hill, a hundred steps above the course of the Doubs. This admirable position secures for the promenade one of the most picturesque views in the whole of France. But the rain water used to make furrows in the walk every spring, caused ditches to appear, and rendered it generally impracticable. This nuisance, which was felt by the whole town, put M. de Rênal in the happy position of being compelled to immortalise his administration by building a wall twenty feet high and thirty to forty yards long.

The parapet of this wall, which occasioned M. de Rênal three journeys to Paris (for the last Minister of the Interior but one had declared himself the mortal enemy of the promenade of Verrières), is now raised to a height of four feet above the ground, and as though to defy all ministers whether past or present, it is at present adorned with tiles of hewn stone.

How many times have my looks plunged into the valley of the Doubs, as I thought of the Paris balls which I had abandoned on the previous night, and leant my breast against the great blocks of stone, whose beautiful grey almost verged on blue. Beyond the left bank, there wind five or six valleys, at the bottom of which I could see quite distinctly several small streams. There is a view of them falling into the Doubs, after a series of cascades. The sun is very warm in these mountains. When it beats straight down, the pensive traveller on the terrace finds shelter under some magnificent plane trees. They owe their rapid growth and their fine verdure with its almost bluish shade to the new soil, which M. the mayor has had placed behind his immense wall of support for (in spite of the opposition of the Municipal Council) he has enlarged the promenade by more than six feet (and although he is an Ultra and I am a Liberal, I praise him for it), and that is why both in his opinion and in that of M. Valenod, the fortunate Director of the workhouse of Verrières, this terrace can brook comparison with that of Saint-Germain en Laye.

I find personally only one thing at which to cavil in the COURS DE LA FIDELITE, (this official name is to be read in fifteen to twenty places on those immortal tiles which earned M. de Rênal an extra cross.) The grievance I find in the Cours de la Fidélité is the barbarous manner in which the authorities have cut these vigorous plane trees and clipped them to the quick. In fact they really resemble with their dwarfed, rounded and flattened heads the most vulgar plants of the vegetable garden, while they are really capable of attaining the magnificent development of the English plane trees. But the wish of M. the mayor is despotic, and all the trees belonging to the municipality are ruthlessly pruned twice a year. The local Liberals suggest, but they are probably exaggerating, that the hand of the official gardener has become much more severe, since M. the Vicar Maslon started appropriating the clippings. This young ecclesiastic was sent to Besançon some years ago to keep watch on the abbé Chélan and some cures in the neighbouring districts. An old Surgeon-Major of Napoleon's Italian Army, who was living in retirement at Verrières, and who had been in his time described by M. the mayor as both a Jacobin and a Bonapartiste, dared to complain to the mayor one day of the periodical mutilation of these fine trees.

"I like the shade," answered M. de Rênal, with just a tinge of that hauteur which becomes a mayor when he is talking to a surgeon, who is a member of the Legion of Honour. "I like the shade, I have *my* trees clipped in order to give shade, and I cannot conceive that a tree can have any other purpose, provided of course *it is not bringing in any profit*, like the useful walnut tree."

This is the great word which is all decisive at Verrières. "BRINGING IN PROFIT," this word alone sums up the habitual trend of thought of more than three-quarters of the inhabitants.

Bringing in profit is the consideration which decides everything in this little town which you thought so pretty. The stranger who arrives in the town is fascinated by the beauty of the fresh deep valleys which surround it, and he imagines at first that the inhabitants have an appreciation of the beautiful. They talk only too frequently of the beauty of their country, and it cannot be denied that they lay great stress on it, but the reason is that it attracts a number of strangers, whose money enriches the inn-keepers, a process which *brings in profit* to the town, owing to the machinery of the octroi.

It was on a fine, autumn day that M. de Rênal was taking a promenade on the Cours de la Fidélité with his wife on his arm. While listening to her husband (who was talking in a somewhat solemn manner) Madame de Rênal followed anxiously with her eyes the movements of three little boys. The eldest, who might have been eleven years old, went too frequently near the parapet and looked as though he was going to climb up it. A sweet voice then pronounced the name of Adolphe and the child gave up his ambitious project. Madame de Rênal seemed a woman of thirty years of age but still fairly pretty.

"He may be sorry for it, may this fine gentleman from Paris," said M. de Rênal, with an offended air and a face even paler than usual. "I am not without a few friends at court!" But though I want to talk to you about the provinces for two hundred pages, I lack the requisite barbarity to make you undergo all the long-windedness and circumlocutions of a provincial dialogue.

This fine gentleman from Paris, who was so odious to the mayor of Verrières, was no other than the M. Appert, who had two days previously managed to find his way not only into the prison and workhouse of Verrières, but also into the hospital, which was gratuitously conducted by the mayor and the principal proprietors of the district.

"But," said Madame de Rênal timidly, "what harm can this Paris gentleman do you, since you administer the poor fund with the utmost scrupulous honesty?"

"He only comes to *throw* blame and afterwards he will get some articles into the Liberal press."

"You never read them, my dear."

"But they always talk to us about those Jacobin articles, all that distracts us and prevents us from doing good.[1] Personally, I shall never forgive the curé."

III
THE POOR FUND

A virtuous curé who does not intrigue is a providence for the village.—*Fleury*

It should be mentioned that the curé of Verrières, an old man of ninety, who owed to the bracing mountain air an iron constitution and an iron character, had the right to visit the prison, the hospital and the workhouse at any hour. It had been at precisely six o'clock in the morning that M. Appert, who had a Paris recommendation to the curé, had been shrewd enough to arrive at a little inquisitive town. He had immediately gone on to the curé's house.

The curé Chélan became pensive as he read the letter written to him by the M. le Marquis de La Mole, Peer of France, and the richest landed proprietor of the province.

"I am old and beloved here," he said to himself in a whisper, "they would not dare!" Then he suddenly turned to the gentleman from Paris, with eyes, which in spite of his great age, shone with that sacred fire which betokens the delight of doing a fine but slightly dangerous act.

"Come with me, sir," he said, "but please do not express any opinion of the things which we shall see, in the presence of the jailer, and above all not in the presence of the superintendents of the workhouse."

M. Appert realised that he had to do with a man of spirit. He followed the venerable curé, visited the hospital and workhouse, put a lot of questions, but in spite of somewhat extraordinary answers, did not indulge in the slightest expression of censure.

This visit lasted several hours; the curé invited M. Appert to dine, but the latter made the excuse of having some letters to write; as a matter of fact, he did not wish to compromise his generous companion to any further extent. About three o'clock these gentlemen went to finish their inspection of the workhouse and then returned to the prison. There they found the jailer by the gate, a kind of giant, six feet high, with bow legs. His ignoble face had become hideous by reason of his terror.

"Ah, monsieur," he said to the curé as soon as he saw him, "is not the gentleman whom I see there, M. Appert?"

"What does that matter?" said the curé.

"The reason is that I received yesterday the most specific orders, and M. the Prefect sent a message by a gendarme who must have galloped during the whole of the night, that M. Appert was not to be allowed in the prisons."

"I can tell you, M. Noiroud," said the curé, "that the traveller who is with me is M. Appert, but do you or do you not admit that I have the right to enter the prison at any hour of the day or night accompanied by anybody I choose?"

"Yes, M. the curé," said the jailer in a low voice, lowering his head like a bull-dog, induced to a grudging obedience by fear of the stick, "only, M. the curé, I have a wife and children, and shall be turned out if they inform against me. I only have my place to live on."

"I, too, should be sorry enough to lose mine," answered the good curé, with increasing emotion in his voice.

"What a difference!" answered the jailer keenly. "As for you, M. le curé, we all know that you have eight hundred francs a year, good solid money."

Such were the facts which, commented upon and exaggerated in twenty different ways, had been agitating for the last two days all the odious passions of the little town of Verrières.

At the present time they served as the text for the little discussion which M. de Rênal was having with his wife. He had visited the curé earlier in the morning accompanied by M. Valenod, the director of the workhouse, in order to convey their most emphatic displeasure. M. Chélan had no protector, and felt all the weight of their words.

"Well, gentlemen, I shall be the third curé of eighty years of age who has been turned out in this district. I have been here for fifty-six years. I have baptized nearly all the inhabitants of the town, which was only a hamlet when I came to it. Every day I marry young people whose grandparents I have married in days gone by. Verrières is my family, but I said to myself when I saw the stranger, 'This man from Paris may as a matter of fact be a Liberal, there are only too many of them about, but what harm can he do to our poor and to our prisoners?'"

The reproaches of M. de Rênal, and above all, those of M. Valenod, the director of the workhouse, became more and more animated.

"Well, gentlemen, turn me out then," the old curé exclaimed in a trembling voice; "I shall still continue to live in the district. As you know, I inherited forty-eight years ago a piece of land that brings in eight hundred francs a year; I shall live on that income. I do not save anything out of my living, gentlemen; and that is perhaps why, when you talk to me about it, I am not particularly frightened."

M. de Rênal always got on very well with his wife, but he did not know what to answer when she timidly repeated the phrase of M. le curé, "What harm can this Paris gentleman do the prisoners?" He was on the point of quite losing his temper when she gave a cry. Her second son had mounted the parapet of the terrace wall and was running along it, although the wall was raised to a height of more than twenty feet above the vineyard on the other side. The fear of frightening her son and making him fall prevented Madame de Rênal speaking to him. But at last the child, who was smiling at his own pluck, looked at his mother, saw her pallor, jumped down on to the walk and ran to her. He was well scolded.

This little event changed the course of the conversation.

"I really mean to take Sorel, the son of the sawyer, into the house," said M. de Rênal; "he will look after the children, who are getting too naughty for us to manage. He is a young priest, or as good as one, a good Latin scholar, and will make the children get on. According to the curé, he has a steady character. I will give him three hundred francs a year and his board. I have some doubts as to his morality, for he used to be the favourite of that old Surgeon-Major, Member of the Legion of Honour, who went to board with the Sorels, on the pretext that he was their cousin. It is quite possible that that man was really simply a secret agent of the Liberals. He said that the mountain air did his asthma good, but that is something which has never been proved. He has gone through all *Buonaparte's* campaigns in Italy, and had even, it was said, voted against the Empire in the plebiscite. This Liberal taught the Sorel boy Latin, and left him a number of books which he had brought with him. Of course, in the ordinary way, I should have never thought of allowing a carpenter's son to come into contact with our children, but the curé told me, the very day before the scene which has just estranged us for ever, that Sorel has been studying theology for three years with the intention of entering a seminary. He is, consequently, not a Liberal, and he certainly is a good Latin scholar.

"This arrangement will be convenient in more than one way," continued M. de Rênal, looking at his wife with a diplomatic air. "That Valenod is proud enough of his two fine Norman horses which he has just bought for his carriage, but he hasn't a tutor for his children."

"He might take this one away from us."

"You approve of my plan, then?" said M. de Rênal, thanking his wife with a smile for the excellent idea which she had just had. "Well, that's settled."

"Good gracious, my dear, how quickly you make up your mind!"

"It is because I'm a man of character, as the curé found out right enough. Don't let us deceive ourselves; we are surrounded by Liberals in this place. All those cloth merchants are jealous of me, I am certain of it; two or three are becoming rich men. Well, I should rather fancy it for them to see M. de Rênal's children pass along the street as they go out for their walk, escorted by *their tutor*. It will impress people. My grandfather often used to tell us that he had a tutor when he was young. It may run me into a hundred crowns, but that ought to be looked upon as an expense necessary for keeping up our position."

This sudden resolution left Madame de Rênal quite pensive. She was a big, well-made woman, who had been the beauty of the country, to use the local expression. She had a certain air of simplicity and youthfulness in her deportment. This naive grace, with its innocence and its vivacity, might even have recalled to a Parisian some suggestion of the sweets he had left behind him. If she had realised this particular phase of her success, Madame de Rênal would have been quite ashamed of it. All coquetry, all affectation, were absolutely alien to her temperament. M. Valenod, the rich director of the workhouse, had the reputation of having paid her court, a fact which had cast a singular glamour over her virtue; for this M. Valenod, a big young man with a square, sturdy frame, florid face, and big, black whiskers, was one of those coarse, blustering, and noisy people who pass in the provinces for a "fine man."

Madame de Rênal, who had a very shy, and apparently a very uneven temperament, was particularly shocked by M. Valenod's lack of repose, and by his boisterous loudness. Her aloofness from what, in the Verrières' jargon, was called "having a good time," had earned her the reputation of being very proud of her birth. In fact, she never thought about it, but she had been extremely glad to find the inhabitants of the town visit her less frequently. We shall not deny that she passed for a fool in the eyes of *their* good ladies because she did not wheedle her husband, and allowed herself to miss the most splendid opportunities of getting fine hats from Paris or Besançon. Provided she was allowed to wander in her beautiful garden, she never complained. She was a naïve soul, who had never educated herself up to the point of judging her husband and confessing to herself that he bored her. She supposed, without actually formulating the thought, that there was no greater sweetness in the relationship between husband and wife than she herself had experienced. She loved M. de Rênal most when he talked about his projects for their children. The elder he had destined for the army, the second for the law, and the third for the Church. To sum up, she found M. de Rênal much less boring than all the other men of her acquaintance.

This conjugal opinion was quite sound. The Mayor of Verrières had a reputation for wit, and above all, a reputation for good form, on the strength of half-a-dozen "chestnuts" which he had inherited from an uncle. Old Captain de Rênal had served, before the Revolution, in the infantry regiment of M. the Duke of Orleans, and was admitted to the Prince's salons when he went to Paris. He had seen Madame de Montesson, the famous Madame de Genlis, M. Ducret, the inventor, of the Palais-Royal. These personages would crop up only too frequently in M. de Rênal's anecdotes. He found it, however, more and more of a strain to remember stories which required such delicacy in the telling, and for some time past it had only been on great occasions that he would trot out his anecdotes concerning the House of Orleans. As, moreover, he was extremely polite, except on money matters, he passed, and justly so, for the most aristocratic personage in Verrières.

IV
A FATHER AND A SON

E sara mia colpa
Se cosi è?
—*Machiavelli.*

"My wife really has a head on her shoulders," said the mayor of Verrières at six o'clock the following morning, as he went down to the saw-mill of Father Sorel. "It had never occurred to me that if I do not take little Abbé Sorel, who, they say, knows Latin like an angel, that restless spirit, the director of the workhouse, might have the same idea and snatch him away from me, though of course I told her that it had, in order to preserve my proper superiority. And how smugly, to be sure, would he talk about his children's tutor!... The question is, once the tutor's mine, shall he wear the cassock?"

M. de Rênal was absorbed in this problem when he saw a peasant in the distance, a man nearly six feet tall, who since dawn had apparently been occupied in measuring some pieces of wood which had been put down alongside the Doubs on the towing-path. The peasant did not look particularly pleased when he saw M. the Mayor approach, as these pieces of wood obstructed the road, and had been placed there in breach of the rules.

Father Sorel (for it was he) was very surprised, and even more pleased at the singular offer which M. de Rênal made him for his son Julien. None the less, he listened to it with that air of sulky discontent and apathy which the subtle inhabitants of these mountains know so well how to assume. Slaves as they have been since the time of the Spanish Conquest, they still preserve this feature, which is also found in the character of the Egyptian fellah.

Sorel's answer was at first simply a long-winded recitation of all the formulas of respect which he knew by heart. While he was repeating these empty words with an uneasy smile, which accentuated all the natural disingenuousness, if not, indeed, knavishness of his physiognomy, the active mind of the old peasant tried to discover what reason could induce so important a man to take into his house his good-for-nothing of a son. He was very dissatisfied with Julien, and it was for Julien that M. de Rênal offered the undreamt-of salary of 300 fcs. a year, with board and even clothing. This latter claim, which Father Sorel had had the genius to spring upon the mayor, had been granted with equal suddenness by M. de Rênal.

This demand made an impression on the mayor. It is clear, he said to himself, that since Sorel is not beside himself with delight over my proposal, as in the ordinary way he ought to be, he must have had offers made to him elsewhere, and whom could they have come from, if not from Valenod. It was in vain that M. de Rênal pressed Sorel to clinch the matter then and there. The old peasant, astute man that he was, stubbornly refused to do so. He wanted, he said, to consult his son, as if in the provinces, forsooth, a rich father consulted a penniless son for any other reason than as a mere matter of form.

A water saw-mill consists of a shed by the side of a stream. The roof is supported by a framework resting on four large timber pillars. A saw can be seen going up and down at a height of eight to ten feet in the middle of the shed, while a piece of wood is propelled against this saw by a very simple mechanism. It is a wheel whose motive-power is supplied by the stream, which sets in motion this double piece of mechanism, the mechanism of the saw which goes up and down, and the mechanism which gently pushes the piece of wood towards the saw, which cuts it up into planks.

Approaching his workshop, Father Sorel called Julien in his stentorian voice; nobody answered. He only saw his giant elder sons, who, armed with heavy axes, were cutting up the pine planks which they had to carry to the saw. They were engrossed in following exactly the black mark traced on each piece of wood, from which every blow of their axes threw off enormous shavings. They did not hear their father's voice. The latter made his way towards the shed. He entered it and looked in vain for Julien in the place where he ought to have been by the side of the saw. He saw him five or six feet higher up, sitting astride one of the rafters of the roof. Instead of watching attentively the action of the machinery, Julien was reading. Nothing was more anti-pathetic to old Sorel. He might possibly have forgiven Julien his puny physique, ill adapted as it was to manual labour, and different as it was from that of his elder brothers; but he hated this reading mania. He could not read himself.

It was in vain that he called Julien two or three times. It was the young man's concentration on his book, rather than the din made by the saw, which prevented him from hearing his father's terrible voice. At last the latter, in spite of his age, jumped nimbly on to the tree that was undergoing the action of the saw, and from there on to the cross-bar that supported the roof. A violent blow made the book which Julien held, go flying into the stream; a second blow on the head, equally violent, which took the form of a box on the ears, made him lose his balance. He was on the point of falling twelve or fifteen feet lower down into the middle of the levers of the running machinery which would have cut him to pieces, but his father caught him as he fell, in his left hand.

"So that's it, is it, lazy bones! always going to read your damned books are you, when you're keeping watch on the saw? You read them in the evening if you want to, when you go to play the fool at the curé's, that's the proper time."

Although stunned by the force of the blow and bleeding profusely, Julien went back to his official post by the side of the saw. He had tears in his eyes, less by reason of the physical pain than on account of the loss of his beloved book.

"Get down, you beast, when I am talking to you," the noise of the machinery prevented Julien from hearing this order. His father, who had gone down did not wish to give himself the trouble of climbing up on to the machinery again, and went to fetch a long fork used for bringing down nuts, with which he struck him on the shoulder. Julien had scarcely reached the ground, when old Sorel chased him roughly in front of him and pushed him roughly towards the house. "God knows what he is going to do with me," said the young man to himself. As he passed, he looked sorrowfully into the stream into which his book had fallen, it was the one that he held dearest of all, the *Memorial of St. Helena*.

He had purple cheeks and downcast eyes. He was a young man of eighteen to nineteen years old, and of puny appearance, with irregular but delicate features, and an aquiline nose. The big black eyes which betokened in their tranquil moments a temperament at once fiery and reflective were at the present moment animated by an expression of the most ferocious hate. Dark chestnut hair, which came low down over his brow, made his forehead appear small and gave him a sinister look during his angry moods. It is doubtful if any face out of all the innumerable varieties of the human physiognomy was ever distinguished by a more arresting individuality.

A supple well-knit figure, indicated agility rather than strength. His air of extreme pensiveness and his great pallor had given his father the idea that he would not live, or that if he did, it would only be to be a burden to his family. The butt of the whole house, he hated his brothers and his father. He was regularly beaten in the Sunday sports in the public square.

A little less than a year ago his pretty face had begun to win him some sympathy among the young girls. Universally despised as a weakling, Julien had adored that old Surgeon-Major, who had one day dared to talk to the mayor on the subject of the plane trees.

This Surgeon had sometimes paid Father Sorel for taking his son for a day, and had taught him Latin and History, that is to say the 1796 Campaign in Italy which was all the history he knew. When he died, he had bequeathed his Cross of the Legion of Honour, his arrears of half pay, and thirty or forty volumes, of which the most precious had just fallen into the public stream, which had been diverted owing to the influence of M. the Mayor.

Scarcely had he entered the house, when Julien felt his shoulder gripped by his father's powerful hand; he trembled, expecting some blows.

"Answer me without lying," cried the harsh voice of the old peasant in his ears, while his hand turned him round and round, like a child's hand turns round a lead soldier. The big black eyes of Julien filled with tears, and were confronted by the small grey eyes of the old carpenter, who looked as if he meant to read to the very bottom of his soul.

V
A NEGOTIATION

Cunctando restituit rem.—*Ennius.*

"Answer me without lies, if you can, you damned dog, how did you get to know Madame de Rênal? When did you speak to her?"

"I have never spoken to her," answered Julien, "I have only seen that lady in church."

"You must have looked at her, you impudent rascal."

"Not once! you know, I only see God in church," answered Julien, with a little hypocritical air, well suited, so he thought, to keep off the parental claws.

"None the less there's something that does not meet the eye," answered the cunning peasant. He was then silent for a moment. "But I shall never get anything out of you, you damned hypocrite," he went on. "As a matter of fact, I am going to get rid of you, and my saw-mill will go all the better for it. You have nobbled the curate, or somebody else, who has got you a good place. Run along and pack your traps, and I will take you to M. de Rênal's, where you are going to be tutor to his children."

"What shall I get for that?"

"Board, clothing, and three hundred francs salary."

"I do not want to be a servant."

"Who's talking of being a servant, you brute, do you think I want my son to be a servant?"

"But with whom shall I have my meals?"

This question discomforted old Sorel, who felt he might possibly commit some imprudence if he went on talking. He burst out against Julien, flung insult after insult at him, accused him of gluttony, and left him to go and consult his other sons.

Julien saw them afterwards, each one leaning on his axe and holding counsel. Having looked at them for a long time, Julien saw that he could find out nothing, and went and stationed himself on the other side of the saw in order to avoid being surprised. He wanted to think over this unexpected piece of news, which changed his whole life, but he felt himself unable to consider the matter prudently, his imagination being concentrated in wondering what he would see in M. de Rênal's fine mansion.

"I must give all that up," he said to himself, "rather than let myself be reduced to eating with the servants. My father would like to force me to it. I would rather die. I have fifteen francs and eight sous of savings. I will run away to-night; I will go across country by paths where there are no gendarmes to be feared, and in two days I shall be at Besançon. I will enlist as a soldier there, and, if necessary, I will cross into Switzerland. But in that case, no more advancement, it will be all up with my being a priest, that fine career which may lead to anything."

This abhorrence of eating with the servants was not really natural to Julien; he would have done things quite, if not more, disagreeable in order to get on. He derived this repugnance from the *Confessions* of Rousseau. It was the only book by whose help his imagination endeavoured to construct the world. The collection of the Bulletins of the Grand Army, and the *Memorial of St. Helena* completed his Koran. He would have died for these three works. He never believed in any other. To use a phrase of the old Surgeon-Major, he regarded all the other books in the world as packs of lies, written by rogues in order to get on.

Julien possessed both a fiery soul and one of those astonishing memories which are so often combined with stupidity.

In order to win over the old curé Chélan, on whose good grace he realized that his future prospects depended, he had learnt by heart the New Testament in Latin. He also knew M. de Maistre's book on The Pope, and believed in one as little as he did in the other.

Sorel and his son avoided talking to each other to-day as though by mutual consent. In the evening Julien went to take his theology lesson at the curé's, but he did not consider that it was prudent to say anything to him about the strange proposal which had been made to his father. "It is possibly a trap," he said to himself, "I must pretend that I have forgotten all about it."

Early next morning, M. de Rênal had old Sorel summoned to him. He eventually arrived, after keeping M. de Rênal waiting for an hour-and-a-half, and made, as he entered the room, a hundred apologies interspersed with as many bows. After having run the gauntlet of all kinds of objections, Sorel was given to understand that his son would have his meals with the master and mistress of the house, and that he would eat alone in a room with the children on the days when they had company. The more clearly Sorel realized the genuine eagerness of M. the Mayor, the more difficulties he felt inclined to raise. Being moreover full of mistrust and astonishment, he asked to see the room where his son would sleep. It was a big room, quite decently furnished, into which the servants were already engaged in carrying the beds of the three children.

This circumstance explained a lot to the old peasant. He asked immediately, with quite an air of assurance, to see the suit which would be given to his son. M. de Rênal opened his desk and took out one hundred francs.

"Your son will go to M. Durand, the draper, with this money and will get a complete black suit."

"And even supposing I take him away from you," said the peasant, who had suddenly forgotten all his respectful formalities, "will he still keep this black suit?"

"Certainly!"

"Well," said Sorel, in a drawling voice, "all that remains to do is to agree on just one thing, the money which you will give him."

"What!" exclaimed M. de Rênal, indignantly, "we agreed on that yesterday. I shall give him three hundred francs, I think that is a lot, and probably too much."

"That is your offer and I do not deny it," said old Sorel, speaking still very slowly; and by a stroke of genius which will only astonish those who do not know the Franche-Comté peasants, he fixed his eyes on M. de Rênal and added, "We shall get better terms elsewhere."

The Mayor's face exhibited the utmost consternation at these words. He pulled himself together however and after a cunning conversation of two hours' length, where every single word on both sides was carefully weighed, the subtlety of the peasant scored a victory over the subtlety of the rich man, whose livelihood was not so dependent on his faculty of cunning. All the numerous stipulations which were to regulate Julien's new existence were duly formulated. Not only was his salary fixed at four hundred francs, but they were to be paid in advance on the first of each month.

"Very well, I will give him thirty-five francs," said M. de Rênal.

"I am quite sure," said the peasant, in a fawning voice, "that a rich, generous man like the M. mayor would go as far as thirty-six francs, to make up a good round sum."

"Agreed!" said M. de Rênal, "but let this be final." For the moment his temper gave him a tone of genuine firmness. The peasant saw that it would not do to go any further.

Then, on his side, M. de Rênal managed to score. He absolutely refused to give old Sorel, who was very anxious to receive it on behalf of his son, the thirty-six francs for the first month. It had occurred to M. de Rênal that he would have to tell his wife the figure which he had cut throughout these negotiations.

"Hand me back the hundred francs which I gave you," he said sharply. "M. Durand owes me something, I will go with your son to see about a black cloth suit."

After this manifestation of firmness, Sorel had the prudence to return to his respectful formulas; they took a good quarter of an hour. Finally, seeing that there was nothing more to be gained, he took his leave. He finished his last bow with these words:

"I will send my son to the Château." The Mayor's officials called his house by this designation when they wanted to humour him.

When he got back to his workshop, it was in vain that Sorel sought his son. Suspicious of what might happen, Julien had gone out in the middle of the night. He wished to place his Cross of the Legion of Honour and his books in a place of safety. He had taken everything to a young wood-merchant named Fouqué, who was a friend of his, and who lived in the high mountain which commands Verrières.

"God knows, you damned lazy bones," said his father to him when he re-appeared, "if you will ever be sufficiently honourable to pay me back the price of your board which I have been advancing to you for so many years. Take your rags and clear out to M. the Mayor's."

Julien was astonished at not being beaten and hastened to leave. He had scarcely got out of sight of his terrible father when he slackened his pace. He considered that it would assist the rôle played by his hypocrisy to go and say a prayer in the church.

The word hypocrisy surprises you? The soul of the peasant had had to go through a great deal before arriving at this horrible word.

Julien had seen in the days of his early childhood certain Dragoons of the 6th[2] with long white cloaks and hats covered with long black plumed helmets who were returning from Italy, and tied up their horses to the grilled window of his father's house. The sight had made him mad on the military profession. Later on he had listened with ecstasy to the narrations of the battles of Lodi, Arcola and Rivoli with which the old surgeon-major had regaled him. He observed the ardent gaze which the old man used to direct towards his cross.

But when Julien was fourteen years of age they commenced to build a church at Verrières which, in view of the smallness of the town, has some claim to be called magnificent. There were four marble columns in particular, the sight of which impressed Julien. They became celebrated in the district owing to the mortal hate which they raised between the Justice of the Peace and the young vicar who had been sent from Besançon and who passed for a spy of the congregation. The Justice of the Peace was on the point of losing his place, so said the public opinion at any rate. Had he not dared to have a difference with the priest who went every fortnight to Besançon; where he saw, so they said, my Lord the Bishop.

In the meanwhile the Justice of the Peace, who was the father of a numerous family, gave several sentences which seemed unjust: all these sentences were inflicted on those of the inhabitants who read the "*Constitutionnel*." The right party triumphed. It is true it was only a question of sums of three or five francs, but one of these little fines had to be paid by a nail-maker, who was god-father to Julien. This man exclaimed in his anger "What a change! and to think that for more than twenty years the Justice of the Peace has passed for an honest man."

The Surgeon-Major, Julien's friend, died. Suddenly Julien left off talking about Napoleon. He announced his intention of becoming a priest, and was always to be seen in his father's workshop occupied in learning by heart the Latin Bible which the curé had lent him. The good old man was astonished at his progress, and passed whole evenings in teaching him theology. In his society Julien did not manifest other than pious sentiments. Who could not possibly guess that beneath this girlish face, so pale and so sweet, lurked the unbreakable resolution to risk a thousand deaths rather than fail to make his fortune. Making his fortune primarily meant to Julien getting out of Verrières: he abhorred his native country; everything that he saw there froze his imagination.

He had had moments of exultation since his earliest childhood. He would then dream with gusto of being presented one day to the pretty women of Paris. He would manage to attract their attention by some dazzling feat: why should he not be loved by one of them just as Buonaparte, when still poor, had been loved by the brilliant Madame de Beauharnais. For many years past Julien had scarcely passed a single year of his life without reminding himself that Buonaparte, the obscure and penniless lieutenant, had made himself master of the whole world by the power of his sword. This idea consoled him for his misfortune, which he considered to be great, and rendered such joyful moments as he had doubly intense.

The building of the church and the sentences pronounced by the Justice of the Peace suddenly enlightened him. An idea came to him which made him almost mad for some weeks, and finally took complete possession of him with all the magic that a first idea possesses for a passionate soul which believes that it is original.

"At the time when Buonaparte got himself talked about, France was frightened of being invaded; military distinction was necessary and fashionable. Nowadays, one sees priests of forty with salaries of 100,000 francs, that is to say, three times as much as Napoleon's famous generals of a division. They need persons to assist them. Look at that Justice of the Peace, such a good sort and such an honest man up to the present and so old too; he sacrifices his honour through the fear of incurring the displeasure of a young vicar of thirty. I must be a priest."

On one occasion, in the middle of his new-found piety (he had already been studying theology for two years), he was betrayed by a sudden burst of fire which consumed his soul. It was at M. Chélan's. The good curé had invited him to a dinner of priests, and he actually let himself praise Napoleon with enthusiasm. He bound his right arm over his breast, pretending that he had dislocated it in moving a trunk of a pine-tree and carried it for two months in that painful position. After this painful penance, he forgave himself. This is the young man of eighteen with a puny physique, and scarcely looking more than seventeen at the outside, who entered the magnificent church of Verrières carrying a little parcel under his arm.

He found it gloomy and deserted. All the transepts in the building had been covered with crimson cloth in celebration of a feast. The result was that the sun's rays produced an effect of dazzling light of the most impressive and religious character. Julien shuddered. Finding himself alone in the church, he established himself in the pew which had the most magnificent appearance. It bore the arms of M. de Rênal.

Julien noticed a piece of printed paper spread out on the stool, which was apparently intended to be read, he cast his eyes over it and saw:— "*Details of the execution and the last moments of Louis Jenrel, executed at Besançon the....*" The paper was torn. The two first words of a line were legible on the back, they were, "*The First Step.*"

"Who could have put this paper there?" said Julien. "Poor fellow!" he added with a sigh, "the last syllable of his name is the same as mine," and he crumpled up the paper. As he left, Julien thought he saw blood near the Host, it was holy water which the priests had been sprinkling on it, the reflection of the red curtains which covered the windows made it look like blood.

Finally, Julien felt ashamed of his secret terror. "Am I going to play the coward," he said to himself: "*To Arms!*" This phrase, repeated so often in the old Surgeon-Major's battle stories, symbolized heroism to Julien. He got up rapidly and walked to M. de Rênal's house. As soon as he saw it twenty yards in front of him he was seized, in spite of his fine resolution, with an overwhelming timidity. The iron grill was open. He thought it was magnificent. He had to go inside.

Julien was not the only person whose heart was troubled by his arrival in the house. The extreme timidity of Madame de Rênal was fluttered when she thought of this stranger whose functions would necessitate his coming between her and her children. She was accustomed to seeing her sons sleep in her own room. She had shed many tears that morning, when she had seen their beds carried into the apartment intended for the tutor. It was in vain that she asked her husband to have the bed of Stanislas-Xavier, the youngest, carried back into her room.

Womanly delicacy was carried in Madame de Rênal to the point of excess. She conjured up in her imagination the most disagreeable personage, who was coarse, badly groomed and encharged with the duty of scolding her children simply because he happened to know Latin, and only too ready to flog her sons for their ignorance of that barbarous language.

VI
ENNUI

Non so piú cosa son
Cosa facio.
MOZART (*Figaro*).

Madame de Rênal was going out of the salon by the folding window which opened on to the garden with that vivacity and grace which was natural to her when she was free from human observation, when she noticed a young peasant near the entrance gate. He was still almost a child, extremely pale, and looked as though he had been crying. He was in a white shirt and had under his arm a perfectly new suit of violet frieze.

The little peasant's complexion was so white and his eyes were so soft, that Madame de Rênal's somewhat romantic spirit thought at first that it might be a young girl in disguise, who had come to ask some favour of the M. the Mayor. She took pity on this poor creature, who had stopped at the entrance of the door, and who apparently did not dare to raise its hand to the bell. Madame de Rênal approached, forgetting for the moment the bitter chagrin occasioned by the tutor's arrival. Julien, who was turned towards the gate, did not see her advance. He trembled when a soft voice said quite close to his ear:

"What do you want here, my child."

Julien turned round sharply and was so struck by Madame de Rênal's look, full of graciousness as it was, that up to a certain point he forgot to be nervous. Overcome by her beauty he soon forgot everything, even what he had come for. Madame de Rênal repeated her question.

"I have come here to be tutor, Madame," he said at last, quite ashamed of his tears which he was drying as best as he could.

Madame de Rênal remained silent. They had a view of each other at close range. Julien had never seen a human being so well-dressed, and above all he had never seen a woman with so dazzling a complexion speak to him at all softly. Madame de Rênal observed the big tears which had lingered on the cheeks of the young peasant, those cheeks which had been so pale and were now so pink. Soon she began to laugh with all the mad gaiety of a young girl, she made fun of herself, and was unable to realise the extent of her happiness. So this was that tutor whom she had imagined a dirty, badly dressed priest, who was coming to scold and flog her children.

"What! Monsieur," she said to him at last, "you know Latin?"

The word "Monsieur" astonished Julien so much that he reflected for a moment.

"Yes, Madame," he said timidly.

Madame de Rênal was so happy that she plucked up the courage to say to Julien, "You will not scold the poor children too much?"

"I scold them!" said Julien in astonishment; "why should I?"

"You won't, will you, Monsieur," she added after a little silence, in a soft voice whose emotion became more and more intense. "You will be nice to them, you promise me?"

To hear himself called "Monsieur" again in all seriousness by so well dressed a lady was beyond all Julien's expectations. He had always said to himself in all the castles of Spain that he had built in his youth, that no real lady would ever condescend to talk to him except when he had a fine uniform. Madame de Rênal, on her side, was completely taken in by Julien's beautiful complexion, his big black eyes, and his pretty hair, which was more than usually curly, because he had just plunged his head into the basin of the public fountain in order to refresh himself. She was over-joyed to find that this sinister tutor, whom she had feared to find so harsh and severe to her children, had, as a matter of fact, the timid manner of a girl. The contrast between her fears and what she now saw, proved a great event for Madame de Rênal's peaceful temperament. Finally, she recovered from her surprise. She was astonished to find herself at the gate of her own house talking in this way and at such close quarters to this young and somewhat scantily dressed man.

"Let us go in, Monsieur," she said to him with a certain air of embarrassment.

During Madame de Rênal's whole life she had never been so deeply moved by such a sense of pure pleasure. Never had so gracious a vision followed in the wake of her disconcerting fears. So these pretty children of whom she took such care were not after all to fall into the hands of a dirty grumbling priest. She had scarcely entered the vestibule when she turned round towards Julien, who was following her trembling. His astonishment at the sight of so fine a house proved but an additional charm in Madame de Rênal's eyes. She could not believe her own eyes. It seemed to her, above all, that the tutor ought to have a black suit.

"But is it true, Monsieur," she said to him, stopping once again, and in mortal fear that she had made a mistake, so happy had her discovery made her. "Is it true that you know Latin?" These words offended Julien's pride, and dissipated the charming atmosphere which he had been enjoying for the last quarter of an hour.

"Yes, Madame," he said, trying to assume an air of coldness, "I know Latin as well as the curé, who has been good enough to say sometimes that I know it even better."

Madame de Rênal thought that Julien looked extremely wicked. He had stopped two paces from her. She approached and said to him in a whisper:

"You won't beat my children the first few days, will you, even if they do not know their lessons?"

The softness and almost supplication of so beautiful a lady made Julien suddenly forget what he owed to his reputation as a Latinist. Madame de Rênal's face was close to his own. He smelt the perfume of a woman's summer clothing, a quite astonishing experience for a poor peasant. Julien blushed extremely, and said with a sigh in a faltering voice:

"Fear nothing, Madame, I will obey you in everything."

It was only now, when her anxiety about her children had been relieved once and for all, that Madame de Rênal was struck by Julien's extreme beauty. The comparative effeminacy of his features and his air of extreme embarrassment did not seem in any way ridiculous to a woman who was herself extremely timid. The male air, which is usually considered essential to a man's beauty, would have terrified her.

"How old are you, sir," she said to Julien.

"Nearly nineteen."

"My elder son is eleven," went on Madame de Rênal, who had completely recovered her confidence. "He will be almost a chum for you.

You will talk sensibly to him. His father started beating him once. The child was ill for a whole week, and yet it was only a little tap."

What a difference between him and me, thought Julien. Why, it was only yesterday that my father beat me. How happy these rich people are. Madame de Rênal, who had already begun to observe the fine nuances of the workings in the tutor's mind, took this fit of sadness for timidity and tried to encourage him.

"What is your name, Monsieur?" she said to him, with an accent and a graciousness whose charm Julien appreciated without being able to explain.

"I am called Julien Sorel, Madame. I feel nervous of entering a strange house for the first time in my life. I have need of your protection and I want you to make many allowances for me during the first few days. I have never been to the college, I was too poor. I have never spoken to anyone else except my cousin who was Surgeon-Major, Member of the Legion of Honour, and M. the curé Chélan. He will give you a good account of me. My brothers always used to beat me, and you must not believe them if they speak badly of me to you. You must forgive my faults, Madame. I shall always mean everything for the best."

Julien had regained his confidence during this long speech. He was examining Madame de Rênal. Perfect grace works wonders when it is natural to the character, and above all, when the person whom it adorns never thinks of trying to affect it. Julien, who was quite a connoisseur in feminine beauty, would have sworn at this particular moment that she was not more than twenty. The rash idea of kissing her hand immediately occurred to him. He soon became frightened of his idea. A minute later he said to himself, it will be an act of cowardice if I do not carry out an action which may be useful to me, and lessen the contempt which this fine lady probably has for a poor workman just taken away from the saw-mill. Possibly Julien was a little encouraged through having heard some young girls repeat on Sundays during the last six months the words "pretty boy."

During this internal debate, Madame de Rênal was giving him two or three hints on the way to commence handling the children. The strain Julien was putting on himself made him once more very pale. He said with an air of constraint.

"I will never beat your children, Madame. I swear it before God." In saying this, he dared to take Madame de Rênal's hand and carry it to his lips. She was astonished at this act, and after reflecting, became shocked. As the weather was very warm, her arm was quite bare underneath the shawl, and Julien's movement in carrying her hand to his lips entirely uncovered it. After a few moments she scolded herself. It seemed to her that her anger had not been quick enough.

M. de Rênal, who had heard voices, came out of his study, and assuming the same air of paternal majesty with which he celebrated marriages at the mayoral office, said to Julien:

"It is essential for me to have a few words with you before my children see you." He made Julien enter a room and insisted on his wife being present, although she wished to leave them alone. Having closed the door M. Rênal sat down.

"M. the curé has told me that you are a worthy person, and everybody here will treat you with respect. If I am satisfied with you I will later on help you in having a little establishment of your own. I do not wish you to see either anything more of your relatives or your friends. Their tone is bound to be prejudicial to my children. Here are thirty-six francs for the first month, but I insist on your word not to give a sou of this money to your father."

M. de Rênal was piqued against the old man for having proved the shrewder bargainer.

"Now, Monsieur, for I have given orders for everybody here to call you Monsieur, and you will appreciate the advantage of having entered the house of real gentle folk, now, Monsieur, it is not becoming for the children to see you in a jacket." "Have the servants seen him?" said M. de Rênal to his wife.

"No, my dear," she answered, with an air of deep pensiveness.

"All the better. Put this on," he said to the surprised young man, giving him a frock-coat of his own. "Let us now go to M. Durand's the draper."

When M. de Rênal came back with the new tutor in his black suit more than an hour later, he found his wife still seated in the same place. She felt calmed by Julien's presence. When she examined him she forgot to be frightened of him. Julien was not thinking about her at all. In spite of all his distrust of destiny and mankind, his soul at this moment was as simple as that of a child. It seemed as though he had lived through years since the moment, three hours ago, when he had been all atremble in the church. He noticed Madame de Rênal's frigid manner and realised that she was very angry, because he had dared to kiss her hand. But the proud consciousness which was given to him by the feel of clothes so different from those which he usually wore, transported him so violently and he had so great a desire to conceal his exultation, that all his movements were marked by a certain spasmodic irresponsibility. Madame de Rênal looked at him with astonishment.

"Monsieur," said M. de Rênal to him, "dignity above all is necessary if you wish to be respected by my children."

"Sir," answered Julien, "I feel awkward in my new clothes. I am a poor peasant and have never wore anything but jackets. If you allow it, I will retire to my room."

"What do you think of this 'acquisition?'" said M. de Rênal to his wife.

Madame de Rênal concealed the truth from her husband, obeying an almost instinctive impulse which she certainly did not own to herself.

"I am not as fascinated as you are by this little peasant. Your favours will result in his not being able to keep his place, and you will have to send him back before the month is out."

"Oh, well! we'll send him back then, he cannot run me into more than a hundred francs, and Verrières will have got used to seeing M. de Rênal's children with a tutor. That result would not have been achieved if I had allowed Julien to wear a workman's clothes. If I do send him back, I shall of course keep the complete black suit which I have just ordered at the draper's. All he will keep is the ready-made suit which I have just put him into at the tailor's."

The hour that Julien spent in his room seemed only a minute to Madame de Rênal. The children who had been told about their new tutor began to overwhelm their mother with questions. Eventually Julien appeared. He was quite another man. It would be incorrect to say that he was grave—he was the very incarnation of gravity. He was introduced to the children and spoke to them in a manner that astonished M. de Rênal himself.

"I am here, gentlemen, he said, as he finished his speech, to teach you Latin. You know what it means to recite a lesson. Here is the Holy Bible, he said, showing them a small volume in thirty-two mo., bound in black. It deals especially with the history of our Lord Jesus Christ and is the part which is called the New Testament. I shall often make you recite your lesson, but do you make me now recite mine."

Adolphe, the eldest of the children, had taken up the book. "Open it anywhere you like," went on Julien and tell me the first word of any verse, "I will then recite by heart that sacred book which governs our conduct towards the whole world, until you stop me."

Adolphe opened the book and read a word, and Julien recited the whole of the page as easily as though he had been talking French. M. de Rênal looked at his wife with an air of triumph The children, seeing the astonishment of their parents, opened their eyes wide. A servant came to the door of the drawing-room; Julien went on talking Latin. The servant first remained motionless, and then disappeared. Soon Madame's house-maid, together with the cook, arrived at the door. Adolphe had already opened the book at eight different places, while Julien went on reciting all the time with the same facility. "Great heavens!" said the cook, a good and devout girl, quite aloud, "what a pretty little priest!" M. de Rênal's self-esteem became uneasy. Instead of thinking of examining the tutor, his mind was concentrated in racking his memory for some other Latin words. Eventually he managed to spout a phrase of Horace. Julien knew no other Latin except his Bible. He answered with a frown. "The holy ministry to which I destine myself has forbidden me to read so profane a poet."

M. de Rênal quoted quite a large number of alleged verses from Horace. He explained to his children who Horace was, but the admiring children, scarcely attended to what he was saying: they were looking at Julien.

The servants were still at the door. Julien thought that he ought to prolong the test—"M. Stanislas-Xavier also," he said to the youngest of the children, "must give me a passage from the holy book."

Little Stanislas, who was quite flattered, read indifferently the first word of a verse, and Julien said the whole page.

To put the finishing touch on M. de Rênal's triumph, M. Valenod, the owner of the fine Norman horses, and M. Charcot de Maugiron, the sub-prefect of the district came in when Julien was reciting. This scene earned for Julien the title of Monsieur; even the servants did not dare to refuse it to him.

That evening all Verrières flocked to M. de Rênal's to see the prodigy. Julien answered everybody in a gloomy manner and kept his own distance. His fame spread so rapidly in the town that a few hours afterwards M. de Rênal, fearing that he would be taken away by somebody else, proposed to that he should sign an engagement for two years.

"No, Monsieur," Julien answered coldly, "if you wished to dismiss me, I should have to go. An engagement which binds me without involving you in any obligation is not an equal one and I refuse it."

Julien played his cards so well, that in less than a month of his arrival at the house, M. de Rênal himself respected him. As the curé had quarrelled with both M. de Rênal and M. Valenod, there was no one who could betray Julien's old passion for Napoleon. He always spoke of Napoleon with abhorrence.

VII
THE ELECTIVE AFFINITIES

They only manage to touch the heart by wounding it.—*A Modern.*

The children adored him, but he did not like them in the least. His thoughts were elsewhere. But nothing which the little brats ever did made him lose his patience. Cold, just and impassive, and none the less liked, inasmuch his arrival had more or less driven ennui out of the house, he was a good tutor. As for himself, he felt nothing but hate and abhorrence for that good society into which he had been admitted; admitted, it is true at the bottom of the table, a circumstance which perhaps explained his hate and his abhorrence. There were certain 'full-dress' dinners at which he was scarcely able to control his hate for everything that surrounded him. One St. Louis feast day in particular, when M. Valenod was monopolizing the conversation of M. de Rênal, Julien was on the point of betraying himself. He escaped into the garden on the pretext of finding the children. "What praise of honesty," he exclaimed. "One would say that was the only virtue, and yet think how they respect and grovel before a man who has almost doubled and trebled his fortune since he has administered the poor fund. I would bet anything that he makes a profit even out of the monies which are intended for the foundlings of these poor creatures whose misery is even more sacred than that of others. Oh, Monsters! Monsters! And I too, am a kind of foundling, hated as I am by my father, my brothers, and all my family."

Some days before the feast of St. Louis, when Julien was taking a solitary walk and reciting his breviary in the little wood called the Belvedere, which dominates the *Cours de la Fidélité*, he had endeavoured in vain to avoid his two brothers whom he saw coming along in the distance by a lonely path. The jealousy of these coarse workmen had been provoked to such a pitch by their brother's fine black suit, by his air of extreme respectability, and by the sincere contempt which he had for them, that they had beaten him until he had fainted and was bleeding all over.

Madame de Rênal, who was taking a walk with M. de Rênal and the sub-prefect, happened to arrive in the little wood. She saw Julien lying on the ground and thought that he was dead. She was so overcome that she made M. Valenod jealous.

His alarm was premature. Julien found Madame de Rênal very pretty, but he hated her on account of her beauty, for that had been the first danger which had almost stopped his career.

He talked to her as little as possible, in order to make her forget the transport which had induced him to kiss her hand on the first day.

Madame de Rênal's housemaid, Elisa, had lost no time in falling in love with the young tutor. She often talked about him to her mistress. Elisa's love had earned for Julien the hatred of one of the men-servants. One day he heard the man saying to Elisa, "You haven't a word for me now that this dirty tutor has entered the household." The insult was undeserved, but Julien with the instinctive vanity of a pretty boy redoubled his care of his personal appearance. M. Valenod's hate also increased. He said publicly, that it was not becoming for a young abbé to be such a fop.

Madame de Rênal observed that Julien talked more frequently than usual to Mademoiselle Elisa. She learnt that the reason of these interviews was the poverty of Julien's extremely small wardrobe. He had so little linen that he was obliged to have it very frequently washed outside the house, and it was in these little matters that Elisa was useful to him. Madame de Rênal was touched by this extreme poverty which she had never suspected before. She was anxious to make him presents, but she did not dare to do so. This inner conflict was the first painful emotion that Julien had caused her. Till then Julien's name had been synonymous with a pure and quite intellectual joy. Tormented by the idea of Julien's poverty, Madame de Rênal spoke to her husband about giving him some linen for a present.

"What nonsense," he answered, "the very idea of giving presents to a man with whom we are perfectly satisfied and who is a good servant. It will only be if he is remiss that we shall have to stimulate his zeal."

Madame de Rênal felt humiliated by this way of looking at things, though she would never have noticed it in the days before Julien's arrival. She never looked at the young abbé's attire, with its combination of simplicity and absolute cleanliness, without saying to herself, "The poor boy, how can he manage?"

Little by little, instead of being shocked by all Julien's deficiencies, she pitied him for them.

Madame de Rênal was one of those provincial women whom one is apt to take for fools during the first fortnight of acquaintanceship. She had no experience of the world and never bothered to keep up the conversation. Nature had given her a refined and fastidious soul, while that instinct for happiness which is innate in all human beings caused her, as a rule, to pay no attention to the acts of the coarse persons in whose midst chance had thrown her. If she had received the slightest education, she would have been noticeable for the spontaneity and vivacity of her mind, but being an heiress, she had been brought up in a Convent of Nuns, who were passionate devotees of the *Sacred Heart of Jesus* and animated by a violent hate for the French as being the enemies of the Jesuits. Madame de Rênal had had enough sense to forget quickly all the nonsense which she had learned at the convent, but had substituted nothing for it, and in the long run knew nothing. The flatteries which had been lavished on her when still a child, by reason of the great fortune of which she was the heiress, and a decided tendency to passionate devotion, had given her quite an inner life of her own. In spite of her pose of perfect affability and her elimination of her individual will which was cited as a model example by all the husbands in Verrières and which made M. de Rênal feel very proud, the moods of her mind were usually dictated by a spirit of the most haughty discontent.

Many a princess who has become a bye-word for pride has given infinitely more attention to what her courtiers have been doing around her than did this apparently gentle and demure woman to anything which her husband either said or did. Up to the time of Julien's arrival she had never really troubled about anything except her children. Their little maladies, their troubles, their little joys, occupied all the sensibility of that soul, who, during her whole life, had adored no one but God, when she had been at the Sacred Heart of Besançon.

A feverish attack of one of her sons would affect her almost as deeply as if the child had died, though she would not deign to confide in anyone. A burst of coarse laughter, a shrug of the shoulders, accompanied by some platitude on the folly of women, had been the only welcome her husband had vouchsafed to those confidences about her troubles, which the need of unburdening herself had induced her to make during the first years of their marriage. Jokes of this kind, and above all, when they were directed at her children's ailments, were exquisite torture to Madame de Rênal. And these jokes were all she found to take the place of those exaggerated sugary flatteries with which she had been regaled at the Jesuit Convent where she had passed her youth. Her education had been given her by suffering. Too proud even to talk to her friend, Madame Derville, about troubles of this kind, she imagined that all men were like her husband, M. Valenod, and the sub-prefect, M. Charcot de Maugiron. Coarseness, and the most brutal callousness to everything except financial gain, precedence, or orders, together with blind hate of every argument to which they objected, seemed to her as natural to the male sex as wearing boots and felt hats.

After many years, Madame de Rênal had still failed to acclimatize herself to those monied people in whose society she had to live.

Hence the success of the little peasant Julien. She found in the sympathy of this proud and noble soul a sweet enjoyment which had all the glamour and fascination of novelty.

Madame de Rênal soon forgave him that extreme ignorance, which constituted but an additional charm, and the roughness of his manner which she succeeded in correcting. She thought that he was worth listening to, even when the conversation turned on the most ordinary events, even in fact when it was only a question of a poor dog which had been crushed as he crossed the street by a peasant's cart going at a trot. The sight of the dog's pain made her husband indulge in his coarse laugh, while she noticed Julien frown, with his fine black eyebrows which were so beautifully arched.

Little by little, it seemed to her that generosity, nobility of soul and humanity were to be found in nobody else except this young abbé. She felt for him all the sympathy and even all the admiration which those virtues excite in well-born souls.

If the scene had been Paris, Julien's position towards Madame de Rênal would have been soon simplified. But at Paris, love is a creature of novels. The young tutor and his timid mistress would soon have found the elucidation of their position in three or four novels, and even in the couplets of the Gymnase Theatre. The novels which have traced out for them the part they would play, and showed them the model which they were to imitate, and Julien would sooner or later have been forced by his vanity to follow that model, even though it had given him no pleasure and had perhaps actually gone against the grain.

If the scene had been laid in a small town in Aveyron or the Pyrenees, the slightest episode would have been rendered crucial by the fiery condition of the atmosphere. But under our more gloomy skies, a poor young man who is only ambitious because his natural refinement makes him feel the necessity of some of those joys which only money can give, can see every day a woman of thirty who is sincerely virtuous, is absorbed in her children, and never goes to novels for her examples of conduct. Everything goes slowly, everything happens gradually, in the provinces where there is far more naturalness.

Madame de Rênal was often overcome to the point of tears when she thought of the young tutor's poverty. Julien surprised her one day actually crying.

"Oh Madame! has any misfortune happened to you?"

"No, my friend," she answered, "call the children, let us go for a walk."

She took his arm and leant on it in a manner that struck Julien as singular. It was the first time she had called Julien "My friend."

Towards the end of the walk, Julien noticed that she was blushing violently. She slackened her pace.

"You have no doubt heard," she said, without looking at him, "that I am the only heiress of a very rich aunt who lives at Besançon. She loads me with presents.... My sons are getting on so wonderfully that I should like to ask you to accept a small present as a token of my gratitude. It is only a matter of a few louis to enable you to get some linen. But—" she added, blushing still more, and she left off speaking—

"But what, Madame?" said Julien.

"It is unnecessary," she went on lowering her head, "to mention this to my husband."

"I may not be big, Madame, but I am not mean," answered Julien, stopping, and drawing himself up to his full height, with his eyes shining with rage, "and this is what you have not realised sufficiently. I should be lower than a menial if I were to put myself in the position of concealing from M de. Rênal anything at all having to do with my money."

Madame de Rênal was thunderstruck.

"The Mayor," went on Julien, "has given me on five occasions sums of thirty-six francs since I have been living in his house. I am ready to show any account-book to M. de Rênal and anyone else, even to M. Valenod who hates me."

As the result of this outburst, Madame de Rênal remained pale and nervous, and the walk ended without either one or the other finding any pretext for renewing the conversation. Julien's proud heart had found it more and more impossible to love Madame de Rênal.

As for her, she respected him, she admired him, and she had been scolded by him. Under the pretext of making up for the involuntary humiliation which she had caused him, she indulged in acts of the most tender solicitude. The novelty of these attentions made Madame de Rênal happy for eight days. Their effect was to appease to some extent Julien's anger. He was far from seeing anything in them in the nature of a fancy for himself personally.

"That is just what rich people are," he said to himself—"they snub you and then they think they can make up for everything by a few monkey tricks."

Madame de Rênal's heart was too full, and at the same time too innocent, for her not too tell her husband, in spite of her resolutions not to do so, about the offer she had made to Julien, and the manner in which she had been rebuffed.

"How on earth," answered M. de Rênal, keenly piqued, "could you put up with a refusal on the part of a servant,"—and, when Madame de Rênal protested against the word "Servant," "I am using, madam, the words of the late Prince of Condé, when he presented his Chamberlains to his new wife. 'All these people' he said 'are servants.' I have also read you this passage from the Memoirs of Besenval, a book which is indispensable on all questions of etiquette. 'Every person, not a gentleman, who lives in your house and receives a salary is your servant.' I'll go and say a few words to M. Julien and give him a hundred francs."

"Oh, my dear," said Madame De Rênal trembling, "I hope you won't do it before the servants!"

"Yes, they might be jealous and rightly so," said her husband as he took his leave, thinking of the greatness of the sum.

Madame de Rênal fell on a chair almost fainting in her anguish. He is going to humiliate Julien, and it is my fault! She felt an abhorrence for her husband and hid her face in her hands. She resolved that henceforth she would never make any more confidences.

When she saw Julien again she was trembling all over. Her chest was so cramped that she could not succeed in pronouncing a single word. In her embarrassment she took his hands and pressed them.

"Well, my friend," she said to him at last, "are you satisfied with my husband?"

"How could I be otherwise," answered Julien, with a bitter smile, "he has given me a hundred francs."

Madame de Rênal looked at him doubtfully.

"Give me your arm," she said at last, with a courageous intonation that Julien had not heard before.

She dared to go as far as the shop of the bookseller of Verrières, in spite of his awful reputation for Liberalism. In the shop she chose ten louis worth of books for a present for her sons. But these books were those which she knew Julien was wanting. She insisted on each child writing his name then and there in the bookseller's shop in those books which fell to his lot. While Madame de Rênal was rejoicing over the kind reparation which she had had the courage to make to Julien, the latter was overwhelmed with astonishment at the quantity of books which he saw at the bookseller's. He had never dared to enter so profane a place. His heart was palpitating. Instead of trying to guess what was passing in Madame de Rênal's heart he pondered deeply over the means by which a young theological student could procure some of those books. Eventually it occurred to him that it would be possible, with tact, to persuade M. de Rênal that one of the proper subjects of his sons' curriculum would be the history of the celebrated gentlemen who had been born in the province. After a month of careful preparation Julien witnessed the success of this idea. The success was so great that he actually dared to risk mentioning to M. de Rênal in conversation, a matter which the noble mayor found disagreeable from quite another point of view. The suggestion was to contribute to the fortune of a Liberal by taking a subscription at the bookseller's. M. de Rênal agreed that it would be wise to give his elder son a first hand acquaintance with many works which he would hear mentioned in conversation when he went to the Military School.

But Julien saw that the mayor had determined to go no further. He suspected some secret reason but could not guess it.

"I was thinking, sir," he said to him one day, "that it would be highly undesirable for the name of so good a gentleman as a Rênal to appear on a bookseller's dirty ledger." M. de Rênal's face cleared.

"It would also be a black mark," continued Julien in a more humble tone, "against a poor theology student if it ever leaked out that his name had been on the ledger of a bookseller who let out books. The Liberals might go so far as to accuse me of having asked for the most infamous books. Who knows if they will not even go so far as to write the titles of those perverse volumes after my name?" But Julien was getting off the track. He noticed that the Mayor's physiognomy was re-assuming its expression of embarrassment and displeasure. Julien was silent. "I have caught my man," he said to himself.

It so happened that a few days afterwards the elder of the children asked Julien, in M. de Rênal's presence, about a book which had been advertised in the *Quotidienne*.

"In order to prevent the Jacobin Party having the slightest pretext for a score," said the young tutor, "and yet give me the means of answering M. de Adolphe's question, you can make your most menial servant take out a subscription at the booksellers."

"That's not a bad idea," said M. de Rênal, who was obviously very delighted.

"You will have to stipulate all the same," said Julien in that solemn and almost melancholy manner which suits some people so well when they see the realization of matters which they have desired for a long time past, "you will have to stipulate that the servant should not take out any novels. Those dangerous books, once they got into the house, might corrupt Madame de Rênal's maids, and even the servant himself."

"You are forgetting the political pamphlets," went on M. de Rênal with an important air. He was anxious to conceal the admiration with which the cunning "middle course" devised by his children's tutor had filled him.

In this way Julien's life was made up of a series of little acts of diplomacy, and their success gave him far more food for thought than the marked manifestation of favouritism which he could have read at any time in Madame de Rênal's heart, had he so wished.

The psychological position in which he had found himself all his life was renewed again in the mayor of Verrières' house. Here in the same way as at his father's saw-mill, he deeply despised the people with whom he lived, and was hated by them. He saw every day in the conversation of the sub-perfect, M. Valenod and the other friends of the family, about things which had just taken place under their very eyes, how little ideas corresponded to reality. If an action seemed to Julien worthy of admiration, it was precisely that very action which would bring down upon itself the censure of the people with whom he lived. His inner mental reply always was, "What beasts or what fools!" The joke was that, in spite of all his pride, he often understood absolutely nothing what they were talking about.

Throughout his whole life he had only spoken sincerely to the old Surgeon-Major.

The few ideas he had were about Buonaparte's Italian Campaigns or else surgery. His youthful courage revelled in the circumstantial details of the most terrible operations. He said to himself.

"I should not have flinched."

The first time that Madame de Rênal tried to enter into conversation independently of the children's education, he began to talk of surgical operations. She grew pale and asked him to leave off. Julien knew nothing beyond that.

So it came about that, though he passed his life in Madame de Rênal's company, the most singular silence would reign between them as soon as they were alone.

When he was in the salon, she noticed in his eyes, in spite of all the humbleness of his demeanour, an air of intellectual superiority towards everyone who came to visit her. If she found herself alone with him for a single moment, she saw that he was palpably embarrassed. This made her feel uneasy, for her woman's instinct caused her to realise that this embarrassment was not inspired by any tenderness.

Owing to some mysterious idea, derived from some tale of good society, such as the old Surgeon-Major had seen it, Julien felt humiliated whenever the conversation languished on any occasion when he found himself in a woman's society, as though the particular pause were his own special fault. This sensation was a hundred times more painful in *tête-à-tête*. His imagination, full as it was of the most extravagant and most Spanish ideas of what a man ought to say when he is alone with a woman, only suggested to the troubled youth things which were absolutely impossible. His soul was in the clouds. Nevertheless he was unable to emerge from this most humiliating silence. Consequently, during his long walks with Madame de Rênal and the children, the severity of his manner was accentuated by the poignancy of his sufferings. He despised himself terribly. If, by any luck, he made himself speak, he came out with the most absurd things. To put the finishing touch on his misery, he saw his own absurdity and exaggerated its extent, but what he did not see was the expression in his eyes, which were so beautiful and betokened so ardent a soul, that like good actors, they sometimes gave charm to something which is really devoid of it.

Madame de Rênal noticed that when he was alone with her he never chanced to say a good thing except when he was taken out of himself by some unexpected event, and consequently forgot to try and turn a compliment. As the friends of the house did not spoil her by regaling her with new and brilliant ideas, she enjoyed with delight all the flashes of Julien's intellect.

After the fall of Napoleon, every appearance of gallantry has been severely exiled from provincial etiquette. People are frightened of losing their jobs. All rascals look to the religious order for support, and hypocrisy has made firm progress even among the Liberal classes. One's ennui is doubled. The only pleasures left are reading and agriculture.

Madame de Rênal, the rich heiress of a devout aunt, and married at sixteen to a respectable gentleman, had never felt or seen in her whole life anything that had the slightest resemblance in the whole world to love. Her confessor, the good curé Chélan, had once mentioned love to her, in discussing the advances of M. de Valenod, and had drawn so loathsome a picture of the passion that the word now stood to her for nothing but the most abject debauchery. She had regarded love, such as she had come across it, in the very small number of novels with which chance had made her acquainted, as an exception if not indeed as something absolutely abnormal. It was, thanks to this ignorance, that Madame de Rênal, although incessantly absorbed in Julien, was perfectly happy, and never thought of reproaching herself in the slightest.

VIII
LITTLE EPISODES

"Then there were sighs, the deeper for suppression,
And stolen glances sweeter for the ft,
And burning blushes, though for no transgression."
Don Juan, c. I, st. 74.

It was only when Madame de Rênal began to think of her maid Elisa that there was some slight change in that angelic sweetness which she owed both to her natural character and her actual happiness. The girl had come into a fortune, went to confess herself to the curé Chélan and confessed to him her plan of marrying Julien. The curé was truly rejoiced at his friend's good fortune, but he was extremely surprised when Julien resolutely informed him that Mademoiselle Elisa's offer could not suit him.

"Beware, my friend, of what is passing within your heart," said the curé with a frown, "I congratulate you on your mission, if that is the only reason why you despise a more than ample fortune. It is fifty-six years since I was first curé of Verrières, and yet I shall be turned out, according to all appearances. I am distressed by it, and yet my income amounts to eight hundred francs. I inform you of this detail so that you may not be under any illusions as to what awaits you in your career as a priest. If you think of paying court to the men who enjoy power, your eternal damnation is assured. You may make your fortune, but you will have to do harm to the poor, flatter the sub-prefect, the mayor, the man who enjoys prestige, and pander to his passion; this conduct, which in the world is called knowledge of life, is not absolutely incompatible with salvation so far as a layman is concerned; but in our career we have to make a choice; it is a question of making one's fortune either in this world or the next; there is no middle course. Come, my dear friend, reflect, and come back in three days with a definite answer. I am pained to detect that there is at the bottom of your character a sombre passion which is far from indicating to me that moderation and that perfect renunciation of earthly advantages so necessary for a priest; I augur well of your intellect, but allow me to tell you," added the good curé with tears in his eyes, "I tremble for your salvation in your career as a priest."

Julien was ashamed of his emotion; he found himself loved for the first time in his life; he wept with delight; and went to hide his tears in the great woods behind Verrières.

"Why am I in this position?" he said to himself at last, "I feel that I would give my life a hundred times over for this good curé Chélan, and he has just proved to me that I am nothing more than a fool. It is especially necessary for me to deceive him, and he manages to find me out. The secret ardour which he refers to is my plan of making my fortune. He thinks I am unworthy of being a priest, that too, just when I was imagining that my sacrifice of fifty louis would give him the very highest idea of my piety and devotion to my mission."

"In future," continued Julien, "I will only reckon on those elements in my character which I have tested. Who could have told me that I should find any pleasure in shedding tears? How I should like some one to convince me that I am simply a fool!"

Three days later, Julien found the excuse with which he ought to have been prepared on the first day; the excuse was a piece of calumny, but what did it matter? He confessed to the curé, with a great deal of hesitation, that he had been persuaded from the suggested union by a reason he could not explain, inasmuch as it tended to damage a third party. This was equivalent to impeaching Elisa's conduct. M. Chélan found that his manner betrayed a certain worldly fire which was very different from that which ought to have animated a young acolyte.

"My friend," he said to him again, "be a good country citizen, respected and educated, rather than a priest without a true mission."

So far as words were concerned, Julien answered these new remonstrances very well. He managed to find the words which a young and ardent seminarist would have employed, but the tone in which he pronounced them, together with the thinly concealed fire which blazed in his eye, alarmed M. Chélan.

You must not have too bad an opinion of Julien's prospects. He invented with correctness all the words suitable to a prudent and cunning hypocrisy. It was not bad for his age. As for his tone and his gestures, he had spent his life with country people; he had never been given an opportunity of seeing great models. Consequently, as soon as he was given a chance of getting near such gentlemen, his gestures became as admirable as his words.

Madame de Rênal was astonished that her maid's new fortune did not make her more happy. She saw her repeatedly going to the curé and coming back with tears in her eyes. At last Elisa talked to her of her marriage.

Madame de Rênal thought she was ill. A kind of fever prevented her from sleeping. She only lived when either maid or Julien were in sight. She was unable to think of anything except them and the happiness which they would find in their home. Her imagination depicted in the most fascinating colours the poverty of the little house, where they were to live on their income of fifty louis a year. Julien could quite well become an advocate at Bray, the sub-prefecture, two leagues from Verrières. In that case she would see him sometimes. Madame de Rênal sincerely believed she would go mad. She said so to her husband and finally fell ill. That very evening when her maid was attending her, she noticed that the girl was crying. She abhorred Elisa at that moment, and started to scold her; she then begged her pardon. Elisa's tears redoubled. She said if her mistress would allow her, she would tell her all her unhappiness.

"Tell me," answered Madame de Rênal.

"Well, Madame, he refuses me, some wicked people must have spoken badly about me. He believes them."

"Who refuses you?" said Madame de Rênal, scarcely breathing.

"Who else, Madame, but M. Julien," answered the maid sobbing. "M. the curé had been unable to overcome his resistance, for M. the curé thinks that he ought not to refuse an honest girl on the pretext that she has been a maid. After all, M. Julien's father is nothing more than a carpenter, and how did he himself earn his living before he was at Madame's?"

Madame de Rênal stopped listening; her excessive happiness had almost deprived her of her reason. She made the girl repeat several times the assurance that Julien had refused her, with a positiveness which shut the door on the possibility of his coming round to a more prudent decision.

"I will make a last attempt," she said to her maid. "I will speak to M. Julien."

The following day, after breakfast, Madame de Rênal indulged in the delightful luxury of pleading her rival's cause, and of seeing Elisa's hand and fortune stubbornly refused for a whole hour.

Julien gradually emerged from his cautiously worded answers, and finished by answering with spirit Madame de Rênal's good advice. She could not help being overcome by the torrent of happiness which, after so many days of despair, now inundated her soul. She felt quite ill. When she had recovered and was comfortably in her own room she sent everyone away. She was profoundly astonished.

"Can I be in love with Julien?" she finally said to herself. This discovery, which at any other time would have plunged her into remorse and the deepest agitation, now only produced the effect of a singular, but as it were, indifferent spectacle. Her soul was exhausted by all that she had just gone through, and had no more sensibility to passion left.

Madame de Rênal tried to work, and fell into a deep sleep; when she woke up she did not frighten herself so much as she ought to have. She was too happy to be able to see anything wrong in anything. Naive and innocent as she was, this worthy provincial woman had never tortured her soul in her endeavours to extract from it a little sensibility to some new shade of sentiment or unhappiness. Entirely absorbed as she had been before Julien's arrival with that mass of work which falls to the lot of a good mistress of a household away from Paris, Madame de Rênal thought of passion in the same way in which we think of a lottery: a certain deception, a happiness sought after by fools.

The dinner bell rang. Madame de Rênal blushed violently. She heard the voice of Julien who was bringing in the children. Having grown somewhat adroit since her falling in love, she complained of an awful headache in order to explain her redness.

"That's just like what all women are," answered M. de Rênal with a coarse laugh. "Those machines have always got something or other to be put right."

Although she was accustomed to this type of wit, Madame de Rênal was shocked by the tone of voice. In order to distract herself, she looked at Julien's physiognomy; he would have pleased her at this particular moment, even if he had been the ugliest man imaginable.

M. de Rênal, who always made a point of copying the habits of the gentry of the court, established himself at Vergy in the first fine days of the spring; this is the village rendered celebrated by the tragic adventure of Gabrielle. A hundred paces from the picturesque ruin of the old Gothic church, M. de Rênal owns an old château with its four towers and a garden designed like the one in the Tuileries with a great many edging verges of box and avenues of chestnut trees which are cut twice in the year. An adjacent field, crowded with apple trees, served for a promenade. Eight or ten magnificent walnut trees were at the end of the orchard. Their immense foliage went as high as perhaps eighty feet.

"Each of these cursed walnut trees," M. de Rênal was in the habit of saying, whenever his wife admired them, "costs me the harvest of at least half an acre; corn cannot grow under their shade."

Madame de Rênal found the sight of the country novel: her admiration reached the point of enthusiasm. The sentiment by which she was animated gave her both ideas and resolution. M. de Rênal had returned to the town, for mayoral business, two days after their arrival in Vergy. But Madame de Rênal engaged workmen at her own expense. Julien had given her the idea of a little sanded path which was to go round the orchard and under the big walnut trees, and render it possible for the children to take their walk in the very earliest hours of the morning without getting their feet wet from the dew. This idea was put into execution within twenty-four hours of its being conceived. Madame de Rênal gaily spent the whole day with Julien in supervising the workmen.

When the Mayor of Verrières came back from the town he was very surprised to find the avenue completed. His arrival surprised Madame de Rênal as well. She had forgotten his existence. For two months he talked with irritation about the boldness involved in making so important a repair without consulting him, but Madame de Rênal had had it executed at her own expense, a fact which somewhat consoled him.

She spent her days in running about the orchard with her children, and in catching butterflies. They had made big hoods of clear gauze with which they caught the poor *lepidoptera*. This is the barbarous name which Julien taught Madame de Rênal. For she had had M. Godart's fine work ordered from Besançon, and Julien used to tell her about the strange habits of the creatures.

They ruthlessly transfixed them by means of pins in a great cardboard box which Julien had prepared.

Madame de Rênal and Julien had at last a topic of conversation; he was no longer exposed to the awful torture that had been occasioned by their moments of silence.

They talked incessantly and with extreme interest, though always about very innocent matters. This gay, full, active life, pleased the fancy of everyone, except Mademoiselle Elisa who found herself overworked. Madame had never taken so much trouble with her dress, even at carnival time, when there is a ball at Verrières, she would say; she changes her gowns two or three times a day.

As it is not our intention to flatter anyone, we do not propose to deny that Madame de Rênal, who had a superb skin, arranged her gowns in such a way as to leave her arms and her bosom very exposed. She was extremely well made, and this style of dress suited her delightfully.

"You have never been *so young*, Madame," her Verrières friends would say to her, when they came to dinner at Vergy (this is one of the local expressions).

It is a singular thing, and one which few amongst us will believe, but Madame de Rênal had no specific object in taking so much trouble. She found pleasure in it and spent all the time which she did not pass in hunting butterflies with the children and Julien, in working with Elisa at making gowns, without giving the matter a further thought. Her only expedition to Verrières was caused by her desire to buy some new summer gowns which had just come from Mulhouse.

She brought back to Vergy a young woman who was a relative of hers. Since her marriage, Madame de Rênal had gradually become attached to Madame Derville, who had once been her school mate at the *Sacré Cœur*.

Madame Derville laughed a great deal at what she called her cousin's mad ideas: "I would never have thought of them alone," she said. When Madame de Rênal was with her husband, she was ashamed of those sudden ideas, which, are called sallies in Paris, and thought them quite silly: but Madame Derville's presence gave her courage. She would start to telling her thoughts in a timid voice, but after the ladies had been alone for a long time, Madame de Rênal's brain became more animated, and a long morning spent together by the two friends passed like a second, and left them in the best of spirits. On this particular journey, however, the acute Madame Derville thought her cousin much less merry, but much more happy than usual.

Julien, on his side, had since coming to the country lived like an absolute child, and been as happy as his pupils in running after the butterflies. After so long a period of constraint and wary diplomacy, he was at last alone and far from human observation; he was instinctively free from any apprehension on the score of Madame de Rênal, and abandoned himself to the sheer pleasure of being alive, which is so keen at so young an age, especially among the most beautiful mountains in the world.

Ever since Madame Derville's arrival, Julien thought that she was his friend; he took the first opportunity of showing her the view from the end of the new avenue, under the walnut tree; as a matter of fact it is equal, if not superior, to the most wonderful views that Switzerland and the Italian lakes can offer. If you ascend the steep slope which commences some paces from there, you soon arrive at great precipices fringed by oak forests, which almost jut on to the river. It was to the peaked summits of these rocks that Julien, who was now happy, free, and king of the household into the bargain, would take the two friends, and enjoy their admiration these sublime views.

"To me it's like Mozart's music," Madame Derville would say.

The country around Verrières had been spoilt for Julien by the jealousy of his brothers and the presence of a tyranous and angry father. He was free from these bitter memories at Vergy; for the first time in his life, he failed to see an enemy. When, as frequently happened, M. de Rênal was in town, he ventured to read; soon, instead of reading at night time, a procedure, moreover, which involved carefully hiding his lamp at the bottom of a flower-pot turned upside down, he was able to indulge in sleep; in the day, however, in the intervals between the children's lessons, he would come among these rocks with that book which was the one guide of his conduct and object of his enthusiasm. He found in it simultaneously happiness, ecstasy and consolation for his moments of discouragement.

Certain remarks of Napoleon about women, several discussions about the merits of the novels which were fashionable in his reign, furnished him now for the first time with some ideas which any other young man of his age would have had for a long time.

The dog days arrived. They started the habit of spending the evenings under an immense pine tree some yards from the house. The darkness was profound. One evening, Julien was speaking and gesticulating, en-joying to the full the pleasure of being at his best when talking to young women; in one of his gestures, he touched the hand of Madame de Rênal which was leaning on the back of one of those chairs of painted wood, which are so frequently to be seen in gardens.

The hand was quickly removed, but Julien thought it a point of duty to secure that that hand should not be removed when he touched it. The idea of a duty to be performed and the consciousness of his stultifica-tion, or rather of his social inferiority, if he should fail in achieving it, immediately banished all pleasure from his heart.

IX
AN EVENING IN THE COUNTRY

M. Guérin's Dido, a charming sketch!—*Strombeck*.

His expression was singular when he saw Madame de Rênal the next day; he watched her like an enemy with whom he would have to fight a duel. These looks, which were so different from those of the previous evening, made Madame de Rênal lose her head; she had been kind to him and he appeared angry. She could not take her eyes off his.

Madame Derville's presence allowed Julien to devote less time to conversation, and more time to thinking about what he had in his mind. His one object all this day was to fortify himself by reading the inspired book that gave strength to his soul.

He considerably curtailed the children's lessons, and when Madame de Rênal's presence had effectually brought him back to the pursuit of his ambition, he decided that she absolutely must allow her hand to rest in his that evening.

The setting of the sun which brought the crucial moment nearer and nearer made Julien's heart beat in a strange way. Night came. He noticed with a joy, which took an immense weight off his heart, that it was going to be very dark. The sky, which was laden with big clouds that had been brought along by a sultry wind, seemed to herald a storm. The two friends went for their walk very late. All they did that night struck Julien as strange. They were enjoying that hour which seems to give certain refined souls an increased pleasure in loving.

At last they sat down, Madame de Rênal beside Julien, and Madame Derville near her friend. Engrossed as he was by the attempt which he was going to make, Julien could think of nothing to say. The conversation languished.

"Shall I be as nervous and miserable over my first duel?" said Julien to himself; for he was too suspicious both of himself and of others, not to realise his own mental state.

In his mortal anguish, he would have preferred any danger whatsoever. How many times did he not wish some matter to crop up which would necessitate Madame de Rênal going into the house and leaving the garden! The violent strain on Julien's nerves was too great for his voice not to be considerably changed; soon Madame de Rênal's voice became nervous as well, but Julien did not notice it. The awful battle raging between duty and timidity was too painful, for him to be in a position to observe anything outside himself. A quarter to ten had just struck on the château clock without his having ventured anything. Julien was indignant at his own cowardice, and said to himself, "at the exact moment when ten o'clock strikes, I will perform what I have resolved to do all through the day, or I will go up to my room and blow out my brains."

After a final moment of expectation and anxiety, during which Julien was rendered almost beside himself by his excessive emotion, ten o'clock struck from the clock over his head. Each stroke of the fatal clock reverberated in his bosom, and caused an almost physical pang.

Finally, when the last stroke of ten was still reverberating, he stretched out his hand and took Madame de Rênal's, who immediately withdrew it. Julien, scarcely knowing what he was doing, seized it again. In spite of his own excitement, he could not help being struck by the icy coldness of the hand which he was taking; he pressed it convulsively; a last effort was made to take it away, but in the end the hand remained in his.

His soul was inundated with happiness, not that he loved Madame de Rênal, but an awful torture had just ended. He thought it necessary to say something, to avoid Madame Derville noticing anything. His voice was now strong and ringing. Madame de Rênal's, on the contrary, betrayed so much emotion that her friend thought she was ill, and suggested her going in. Julien scented danger, "if Madame de Rênal goes back to the salon, I shall relapse into the awful state in which I have been all day. I have held the hand far too short a time for it really to count as the scoring of an actual advantage."

At the moment when Madame Derville was repeating her suggestion to go back to the salon, Julien squeezed vigorously the hand that was abandoned to him.

Madame de Rênal, who had started to get up, sat down again and said in a faint voice,

"I feel a little ill, as a matter of fact, but the open air is doing me good."

These words confirmed Julien's happiness, which at the present moment was extreme; he spoke, he forgot to pose, and appeared the most charming man in the world to the two friends who were listening to him. Nevertheless, there was a slight lack of courage in all this eloquence which had suddenly come upon him. He was mortally afraid that Madame Derville would get tired of the wind before the storm, which was beginning to rise, and want to go back alone into the salon. He would then have remained *tête-à-tête* with Madame de Rênal. He had had, almost by accident that blind courage which is sufficient for action; but he felt that it was out of his power to speak the simplest word to Madame de Rênal. He was certain that, however slight her reproaches might be, he would nevertheless be worsted, and that the advantage he had just won would be destroyed.

Luckily for him on this evening, his moving and emphatic speeches found favour with Madame Derville, who very often found him as clumsy as a child and not at all amusing. As for Madame de Rênal, with her hand in Julien's, she did not have a thought; she simply allowed herself to go on living.

The hours spent under this great pine tree, planted by Charles the Bold according to the local tradition, were a real period of happiness. She listened with delight to the soughing of the wind in the thick foliage of the pine tree and to the noise of some stray drops which were beginning to fall upon the leaves which were lowest down. Julien failed to notice one circumstance which, if he had, would have quickly reassured him; Madame de Rênal, who had been obliged to take away her hand, because she had got up to help her cousin to pick up a flower-pot which the wind had knocked over at her feet, had scarcely sat down again before she gave him her hand with scarcely any difficulty and as though it had already been a pre-arranged thing between them.

Midnight had struck a long time ago; it was at last necessary to leave the garden; they separated. Madame de Rênal swept away as she was, by the happiness of loving, was so completely ignorant of the world that she scarcely reproached herself at all. Her happiness deprived her of her sleep. A leaden sleep overwhelmed Julien who was mortally fatigued by the battle which timidity and pride had waged in his heart all through the day.

He was called at five o'clock on the following day and scarcely gave

Madame de Rênal a single thought.

He had accomplished his duty, and a heroic duty too. The consciousness of this filled him with happiness; he locked himself in his room,
and abandoned himself with quite a new pleasure to reading exploits of
his hero.

When the breakfast bell sounded, the reading of the Bulletins of the
Great Army had made him forget all his advantages of the previous day.
He said to himself flippantly, as he went down to the salon, "I must tell
that woman that I am in love with her." Instead of those looks brimful of
pleasure which he was expecting to meet, he found the stern visage of
M. de Rênal, who had arrived from Verrières two hours ago, and did not
conceal his dissatisfaction at Julien's having passed the whole morning
without attending to the children. Nothing could have been more sordid
than this self-important man when he was in a bad temper and thought
that he could safely show it.

Each harsh word of her husband pierced Madame de Rênal's heart.

As for Julien, he was so plunged in his ecstasy, and still so engrossed by
the great events which had been passing before his eyes for several hours,
that he had some difficulty at first in bringing his attention sufficiently
down to listen to the harsh remarks which M. de Rênal was addressing
to him. He said to him at last, rather abruptly,

"I was ill."

The tone of this answer would have stung a much less sensitive man
than the mayor of Verrières. He half thought of answering Julien by
turning him out of the house straight away. He was only restrained
by the maxim which he had prescribed for himself, of never hurrying
unduly in business matters.

"The young fool," he said to himself shortly afterwards, "has won a
kind of reputation in my house. That man Valenod may take him into
his family, or he may quite well marry Elisa, and in either case, he will
be able to have the laugh of me in his heart."

In spite of the wisdom of these reflections, M. de Rênal's dissatisfaction did not fail to vent itself any the less by a string of coarse insults
which gradually irritated Julien. Madame de Rênal was on the point of
bursting into tears. Breakfast was scarcely over, when she asked Julien
to give her his arm for a walk. She leaned on him affectionately. Julien
could only answer all that Madame de Rênal said to him by whispering.

"*That's what rich people are like!*"

M. de Rênal was walking quite close to them; his presence increased
Julien's anger. He suddenly noticed that Madame de Rênal was leaning
on his arm in a manner which was somewhat marked. This horrified
him, and he pushed her violently away and disengaged his arm.

Luckily, M. de Rênal did not see this new piece of impertinence; it was only noticed by Madame Derville. Her friend burst into tears. M. de Rênal now started to chase away by a shower of stones a little peasant girl who had taken a private path crossing a corner of the orchard. "Monsieur Julien, restrain yourself, I pray you. Remember that we all have our moments of temper," said madame Derville rapidly.

Julien looked at her coldly with eyes in which the most supreme contempt was depicted.

This look astonished Madame Derville, and it would have surprised her even more if she had appreciated its real expression; she would have read in it something like a vague hope of the most atrocious vengeance. It is, no doubt, such moments of humiliation which have made Robespierres.

"Your Julien is very violent; he frightens me," said Madame Derville to her friend, in a low voice.

"He is right to be angry," she answered. "What does it matter if he does pass a morning without speaking to the children, after the astonishing progress which he has made them make. One must admit that men are very hard."

For the first time in her life Madame de Rênal experienced a kind of desire for vengeance against her husband. The extreme hatred of the rich by which Julien was animated was on the point of exploding. Luckily, M. de Rênal called his gardener, and remained occupied with him in barring by faggots of thorns the private road through the orchard. Julien did not vouchsafe any answer to the kindly consideration of which he was the object during all the rest of the walk. M. de Rênal had scarcely gone away before the two friends made the excuse of being fatigued, and each asked him for an arm.

Walking as he did between these two women whose extreme nervousness filled their cheeks with a blushing embarrassment, the haughty pallor and sombre, resolute air of Julien formed a strange contrast. He despised these women and all tender sentiments.

"What!" he said to himself, "not even an income of five hundred francs to finish my studies! Ah! how I should like to send them packing."

And absorbed as he was by these stern ideas, such few courteous words of his two friends as he deigned to take the trouble to understand, displeased him as devoid of sense, silly, feeble, in a word—feminine.

As the result of speaking for the sake of speaking and of endeavouring to keep the conversation alive, it came about that Madame de Rênal mentioned that her husband had come from Verrières because he had made a bargain for the May straw with one of his farmers. (In this district it is the May straw with which the bed mattresses are filled).

"My husband will not rejoin us," added Madame de Rênal; "he will occupy himself with finishing the re-stuffing of the house mattresses with the help of the gardener and his valet. He has put the May straw this morning in all the beds on the first storey; he is now at the second."

Julien changed colour. He looked at Madame de Rênal in a singular way, and soon managed somehow to take her on one side, doubling his pace. Madame Derville allowed them to get ahead.

"Save my life," said Julien to Madame de Rênal; "only you can do it, for you know that the valet hates me desperately. I must confess to you, madame, that I have a portrait. I have hidden it in the mattress of my bed."

At these words Madame de Rênal in her turn became pale.

"Only you, Madame, are able at this moment to go into my room, feel about without their noticing in the corner of the mattress; it is nearest the window. You will find a small, round box of black cardboard, very glossy."

"Does it contain a portrait?" said Madame de Rênal, scarcely able to hold herself upright.

Julien noticed her air of discouragement, and at once proceeded to exploit it.

"I have a second favour to ask you, madame. I entreat you not to look at that portrait; it is my secret."

"It is a secret," repeated Madame de Rênal in a faint voice.

But though she had been brought up among people who are proud of their fortune and appreciative of nothing except money, love had already instilled generosity into her soul. Truly wounded as she was, it was with an air of the most simple devotion that Madame de Rênal asked Julien the questions necessary to enable her to fulfil her commission.

"So" she said to him as she went away, "it is a little round box of black cardboard, very glossy."

"Yes, Madame," answered Julien, with that hardness which danger gives to men.

She ascended the second storey of the château as pale as though she had been going to her death. Her misery was completed by the sensation that she was on the verge of falling ill, but the necessity of doing Julien a service restored her strength.

"I must have that box," she said to herself, as she doubled her pace.

She heard her husband speaking to the valet in Julien's very room. Happily, they passed into the children's room. She lifted up the mattress, and plunged her hand into the stuffing so violently that she bruised her fingers. But, though she was very sensitive to slight pain of this kind, she was not conscious of it now, for she felt almost simultaneously the smooth surface of the cardboard box. She seized it and disappeared.

She had scarcely recovered from the fear of being surprised by her husband than the horror with which this box inspired her came within an ace of positively making her feel ill.

"So Julien is in love, and I hold here the portrait of the woman whom he loves!"

Seated on the chair in the ante-chamber of his apartment, Madame de Rênal fell a prey to all the horrors of jealousy. Her extreme ignorance, moreover, was useful to her at this juncture; her astonishment mitigated her grief. Julien seized the box without thanking her or saying a single word, and ran into his room, where he lit a fire and immediately burnt it. He was pale and in a state of collapse. He exaggerated the extent of the danger which he had undergone.

"Finding Napoleon's portrait," he said to himself, "in the possession of a man who professes so great a hate for the usurper! Found, too, by M. de Rênal, who is so great an *ultra*, and is now in a state of irritation, and, to complete my imprudence, lines written in my own handwriting on the white cardboard behind the portrait, lines, too, which can leave no doubt on the score of my excessive admiration. And each of these transports of love is dated. There was one the day before yesterday."

"All my reputation collapsed and shattered in a moment," said Julien to himself as he watched the box burn, "and my reputation is my only asset. It is all I have to live by—and what a life to, by heaven!"

An hour afterwards, this fatigue, together with the pity which he felt for himself made him inclined to be more tender. He met Madame de Rênal and took her hand, which he kissed with more sincerity than he had ever done before. She blushed with happiness and almost simultaneously rebuffed Julien with all the anger of jealousy. Julien's pride which had been so recently wounded made him act foolishly at this juncture. He saw in Madame de Rênal nothing but a rich woman, he disdainfully let her hand fall and went away. He went and walked about meditatively in the garden. Soon a bitter smile appeared on his lips.

"Here I am walking about as serenely as a man who is master of his own time. I am not bothering about the children! I am exposing myself to M. de Rênal's humiliating remarks, and he will be quite right." He ran to the children's room. The caresses of the youngest child, whom he loved very much, somewhat calmed his agony.

"He does not despise me yet," thought Julien. But he soon reproached himself for this alleviation of his agony as though it were a new weakness. The children caress me just in the same way in which they would caress the young hunting-hound which was bought yesterday.

X

A GREAT HEART AND A SMALL FORTUNE

But passion most disembles, yet betrays,
Even by its darkness, as the blackest sky
Foretells the heaviest tempest.
Don Juan, c. 4, st. 75.

M. De Rênal was going through all the rooms in the château, and he came back into the children's room with the servants who were bringing back the stuffings of the mattresses. The sudden entry of this man had the effect on Julien of the drop of water which makes the pot overflow.

Looking paler and more sinister than usual, he rushed towards him. M. de Rênal stopped and looked at his servants.

"Monsieur," said Julien to him, "Do you think your children would have made the progress they have made with me with any other tutor? If you answer 'No,'" continued Julien so quickly that M. de Rênal did not have time to speak, "how dare you reproach me with neglecting them?"

M. de Rênal, who had scarcely recovered from his fright, concluded from the strange tone he saw this little peasant assume, that he had some advantageous offer in his pocket, and that he was going to leave him.

The more he spoke the more Julien's anger increased, "I can live without you, Monsieur," he added.

"I am really sorry to see you so upset," answered M. de Rênal shuddering a little. The servants were ten yards off engaged in making the beds.

"That is not what I mean, Monsieur," replied Julien quite beside himself. "Think of the infamous words that you have addressed to me, and before women too."

M. de Rênal understood only too well what Julien was asking, and a painful conflict tore his soul. It happened that Julien, who was really mad with rage, cried out,

"I know where to go, Monsieur, when I leave your house."

At these words M. de Rênal saw Julien installed with M. Valenod. "Well, sir," he said at last with a sigh, just as though he had called in a surgeon to perform the most painful operation, "I accede to your request. I will give you fifty francs a month. Starting from the day after to-morrow which is the first of the month."

Julien wanted to laugh, and stood there dumbfounded. All his anger had vanished.

"I do not despise the brute enough," he said to himself. "I have no doubt that that is the greatest apology that so base a soul can make."

The children who had listened to this scene with gaping mouths, ran into the garden to tell their mother that M. Julien was very angry, but that he was going to have fifty francs a month.

Julien followed them as a matter of habit without even looking at M. de Rênal whom he left in a considerable state of irritation.

"That makes one hundred and sixty-eight francs," said the mayor to himself, "that M. Valenod has cost me. I must absolutely speak a few strong words to him about his contract to provide for the foundlings."

A minute afterwards Julien found himself opposite M. de Rênal.

"I want to speak to M. Chélan on a matter of conscience. I have the honour to inform you that I shall be absent some hours."

"Why, my dear Julien," said M. de Rênal smiling with the falsest expression possible, "take the whole day, and to-morrow too if you like, my good friend. Take the gardener's horse to go to Verrières."

"He is on the very point," said M. de Rênal to himself, "of giving an answer to Valenod. He has promised me nothing, but I must let this hot-headed young man have time to cool down."

Julien quickly went away, and went up into the great forest, through which one can manage to get from Vergy to Verrières. He did not wish to arrive at M. Chélan's at once. Far from wishing to cramp himself in a new pose of hypocrisy he needed to see clear in his own soul, and to give audience to the crowd of sentiments which were agitating him.

"I have won a battle," he said to himself, as soon as he saw that he was well in the forest, and far from all human gaze. "So I have won a battle."

This expression shed a rosy light on his situation, and restored him to some serenity.

"Here I am with a salary of fifty francs a month, M. de Rênal must be precious afraid, but what of?"

This meditation about what could have put fear into the heart of that happy, powerful man against whom he had been boiling with rage only an hour back, completed the restoration to serenity of Julien's soul. He was almost able to enjoy for a moment the delightful beauty of the woods amidst which he was walking. Enormous blocks of bare rocks had fallen down long ago in the middle of the forest by the mountain side. Great cedars towered almost as high as these rocks whose shade caused a delicious freshness within three yards of places where the heat of the sun's rays would have made it impossible to rest.

Julien took breath for a moment in the shade of these great rocks, and then he began again to climb. Traversing a narrow path that was scarcely marked, and was only used by the goat herds, he soon found himself standing upon an immense rock with the complete certainty of being far away from all mankind. This physical position made him smile. It symbolised to him the position he was burning to attain in the moral sphere. The pure air of these lovely mountains filled his soul with serenity and even with joy. The mayor of Verrières still continued to typify in his eyes all the wealth and all the arrogance of the earth; but Julien felt that the hatred that had just thrilled him had nothing personal about it in spite of all the violence which he had manifested. If he had left off seeing M. de Rênal he would in eight days have forgotten him, his castle, his dogs, his children and all his family. "I forced him, I don't know how, to make the greatest sacrifice. What? more than fifty crowns a year, and only a minute before I managed to extricate myself from the greatest danger; so there are two victories in one day. The second one is devoid of merit, I must find out the why and the wherefore. But these laborious researches are for to-morrow."

Standing up on his great rock, Julien looked at the sky which was all afire with an August sun. The grasshoppers sang in the field about the rock; when they held their peace there was universal silence around him. He saw twenty leagues of country at his feet. He noticed from time to time some hawk, which launching off from the great rocks over his head was describing in silence its immense circles. Julien's eye followed the bird of prey mechanically. Its tranquil powerful movements struck him. He envied that strength, that isolation.

"Would Napoleon's destiny be one day his?"

XI
AN EVENING

Yet Julia's very coldness still was kind,
And tremulously gently her small hand
Withdrew itself from his, but left behind
A little pressure, thrilling, and so bland,
And slight, so very slight that to the mind,
'Twas but a doubt.
Don Juan, c. I. st, 71.

It was necessary, however, to put in an appearance at Verrières. As Julien left the curé house he was fortunate enough to meet M. Valenod, whom he hastened to tell of the increase in his salary.

On returning to Vergy, Julien waited till night had fallen before going down into the garden. His soul was fatigued by the great number of violent emotions which had agitated him during the day. "What shall I say to them?" he reflected anxiously, as he thought about the ladies. He was far from realising that his soul was just in a mood to discuss those trivial circumstances which usually monopolise all feminine interests.

Julien was often unintelligible to Madame Derville, and even to her friend, and he in his turn only half understood all that they said to him. Such was the effect of the force and, if I may venture to use such language, the greatness of the transports of passion which overwhelmed the soul of this ambitious youth. In this singular being it was storm nearly every day.

As he entered the garden this evening, Julien was inclined to take an interest in what the pretty cousins were thinking. They were waiting for him impatiently. He took his accustomed seat next to Madame de Rênal. The darkness soon became profound. He attempted to take hold of a white hand which he had seen some time near him, as it leant on the back of a chair. Some hesitation was shewn, but eventually the hand was withdrawn in a manner which indicated displeasure. Julien was inclined to give up the attempt as a bad job, and to continue his conversation quite gaily, when he heard M. de Rênal approaching.

The coarse words he had uttered in the morning were still ringing in Julien's ears. "Would not taking possession of his wife's hand in his very presence," he said to himself, "be a good way of scoring off that creature who has all that life can give him. Yes! I will do it. I, the very man for whom he has evidenced so great a contempt."

From that moment the tranquillity which was so alien to Julien's real character quickly disappeared. He was obsessed by an anxious desire that Madame de Rênal should abandon her hand to him.

M. de Rênal was talking politics with vehemence; two or three commercial men in Verrières had been growing distinctly richer than he was, and were going to annoy him over the elections. Madame Derville was listening to him. Irritated by these tirades, Julien brought his chair nearer Madame de Rênal. All his movements were concealed by the darkness. He dared to put his hand very near to the pretty arm which was left uncovered by the dress. He was troubled and had lost control of his mind. He brought his face near to that pretty arm and dared to put his lips on it.

Madame de Rênal shuddered. Her husband was four paces away. She hastened to give her hand to Julien, and at the same time to push him back a little. As M. de Rênal was continuing his insults against those ne'er-do-wells and Jacobins who were growing so rich, Julien covered the hand which had been abandoned to him with kisses, which were either really passionate or at any rate seemed so to Madame de Rênal. But the poor woman had already had the proofs on that same fatal day that the man whom she adored, without owning it to herself, loved another! During the whole time Julien had been absent she had been the prey to an extreme unhappiness which had made her reflect.

"What," she said to herself, "Am I going to love, am I going to be in love? Am I, a married woman, going to fall in love? But," she said to herself, "I have never felt for my husband this dark madness, which never permits of my keeping Julien out of my thoughts. After all, he is only a child who is full of respect for me. This madness will be fleeting. In what way do the sentiments which I may have for this young man concern my husband? M. de Rênal would be bored by the conversations which I have with Julien on imaginative subjects. As for him, he simply thinks of his business. I am not taking anything away from him to give to Julien."

No hypocrisy had sullied the purity of that naïve soul, now swept away by a passion such as it had never felt before. She deceived herself, but without knowing it. But none the less, a certain instinct of virtue was alarmed. Such were the combats which were agitating her when Julien appeared in the garden. She heard him speak and almost at the same moment she saw him sit down by her side. Her soul was as it were transported by this charming happiness which had for the last fortnight surprised her even more than it had allured. Everything was novel for her. None the less, she said to herself after some moments, "the mere presence of Julien is quite enough to blot out all his wrongs." She was frightened; it was then that she took away her hand.

His passionate kisses, the like of which she had never received before, made her forget that perhaps he loved another woman. Soon he was no longer guilty in her eyes. The cessation of that poignant pain which suspicion had engendered and the presence of a happiness that she had never even dreamt of, gave her ecstasies of love and of mad gaiety. The evening was charming for everyone, except the mayor of Verrières, who was unable to forget his *parvenu*manufacturers. Julien left off thinking about his black ambition, or about those plans of his which were so difficult to accomplish. For the first time in his life he was led away by the power of beauty. Lost in a sweetly vague reverie, quite alien to his character, and softly pressing that hand, which he thought ideally pretty, he half listened to the rustle of the leaves of the pine trees, swept by the light night breeze, and to the dogs of the mill on the Doubs, who barked in the distance.

But this emotion was one of pleasure and not passion. As he entered his room, he only thought of one happiness, that of taking up again his favourite book. When one is twenty the idea of the world and the figure to be cut in it dominate everything.

He soon, however, laid down the book. As the result of thinking of the victories of Napoleon, he had seen a new element in his own victory. "Yes," he said to himself, "I have won a battle. I must exploit it. I must crush the pride of that proud gentleman while he is in retreat. That would be real Napoleon. I must ask him for three days' holiday to go and see my friend Fouqué. If he refuses me I will threaten to give him notice, but he will yield the point."

Madame de Rênal could not sleep a wink. It seemed as though, until this moment, she had never lived. She was unable to distract her thoughts from the happiness of feeling Julian cover her hand with his burning kisses.

Suddenly the awful word adultery came into her mind. All the loathesomeness with which the vilest debauchery can invest sensual love presented itself to her imagination. These ideas essayed to pollute the divinely tender image which she was fashioning of Julien, and of the happiness of loving him. The future began to be painted in terrible colours. She began to regard herself as contemptible.

That moment was awful. Her soul was arriving in unknown countries. During the evening she had tasted a novel happiness. Now she found herself suddenly plunged in an atrocious unhappiness. She had never had any idea of such sufferings; they troubled her reason. She thought for a moment of confessing to her husband that she was apprehensive of loving Julien. It would be an opportunity of speaking of him. Fortunately her memory threw up a maxim which her aunt had once given her on the eve of her marriage. The maxim dealt with the danger of making confidences to a husband, for a husband is after all a master. She wrung her hands in the excess of her grief. She was driven this way and that by clashing and painful ideas. At one moment she feared that she was not loved. The next the awful idea of crime tortured her, as much as if she had to be exposed in the pillory on the following day in the public square of Verrières, with a placard to explain her adultery to the populace.

Madame de Rênal had no experience of life. Even in the full possession of her faculties, and when fully exercising her reason, she would never have appreciated any distinction between being guilty in the eyes of God, and finding herself publicly overwhelmed with the crudest marks of universal contempt.

When the awful idea of adultery, and of all the disgrace which in her view that crime brought in its train, left her some rest, she began to dream of the sweetness of living innocently with Julien as in the days that had gone by.

She found herself confronted with the horrible idea that Julien loved another woman. She still saw his pallor when he had feared to lose her portrait, or to compromise her by exposing it to view. For the first time she had caught fear on that tranquil and noble visage. He had never shewn such emotion to her or her children. This additional anguish reached the maximum of unhappiness which the human soul is capable of enduring. Unconsciously, Madame de Rênal uttered cries which woke up her maid. Suddenly she saw the brightness of a light appear near her bed, and recognized Elisa. "Is it you he loves?" she exclaimed in her delirium.

Fortunately, the maid was so astonished by the terrible trouble in which she found her mistress that she paid no attention to this singular expression. Madame de Rênal appreciated her imprudence. "I have the fever," she said to her, "and I think I am a little delirious." Completely woken up by the necessity of controlling herself, she became less unhappy. Reason regained that supreme control which the semi-somnolent state had taken away. To free herself from her maid's continual stare, she ordered her maid to read the paper, and it was as she listened to the monotonous voice of this girl, reading a long article from the *Quotidienne* that Madame de Rênal made the virtuous resolution to treat Julien with absolute coldness when she saw him again.

XII
A JOURNEY

> Elegant people are to be found in Paris. People of character
> may exist in the provinces.—Sièyes

At five o'clock the following day, before Madame de Rênal was visible, Julien obtained a three days' holiday from her husband. Contrary to his expectation Julien found himself desirous of seeing her again. He kept thinking of that pretty hand of hers. He went down into the garden, but Madame de Rênal kept him waiting for a long time. But if Julien had loved her, he would have seen her forehead glued to the pane behind the half-closed blinds on the first floor. She was looking at him. Finally, in spite of her resolutions, she decided to go into the garden. Her habitual pallor had been succeeded by more lively hues. This woman, simple as she was, was manifestly agitated; a sentiment of constraint, and even of anger, altered that expression of profound serenity which seemed, as it were, to be above all the vulgar interests of life and gave so much charm to that divine face.

Julien approached her with eagerness, admiring those beautiful arms which were just visible through a hastily donned shawl. The freshness of the morning air seemed to accentuate still more the brilliance of her complexion which the agitation of the past night rendered all the more susceptible to all impressions. This demure and pathetic beauty, which was, at the same time, full of thoughts which are never found in the inferior classes, seemed to reveal to Julien a faculty in his own soul which he had never before realised. Engrossed in his admiration of the charms on which his greedy gaze was riveted, Julien took for granted the friendly welcome which he was expecting to receive. He was all the more astonished at the icy coldness which she endeavoured to manifest to him, and through which he thought he could even distinguish the intention of putting him in his place.

The smile of pleasure died away from his lips as he remembered his rank in society, especially from the point of view of a rich and noble heiress. In a single moment his face exhibited nothing but haughtiness and anger against himself. He felt violently disgusted that he could have put off his departure for more than an hour, simply to receive so humiliating a welcome.

"It is only a fool," he said to himself, "who is angry with others; a stone falls because it is heavy. Am I going to be a child all my life? How on earth is it that I manage to contract the charming habit of showing my real self to those people simply in return for their money? If I want to win their respect and that of my own self, I must shew them that it is simply a business transaction between my poverty and their wealth, but that my heart is a thousand leagues away from their insolence, and is situated in too high a sphere to be affected by their petty marks of favour or disdain."

While these feelings were crowding the soul of the young tutor, his mobile features assumed an expression of ferocity and injured pride. Madame de Rênal was extremely troubled. The virtuous coldness that she had meant to put into her welcome was succeeded by an expression of interest—an interest animated by all the surprise brought about by the sudden change which she had just seen. The empty morning platitudes about their health and the fineness of the day suddenly dried up. Julien's judgment was disturbed by no passion, and he soon found a means of manifesting to Madame de Rênal how light was the friendly relationship that he considered existed between them. He said nothing to her about the little journey that he was going to make; saluted her, and went away.

As she watched him go, she was overwhelmed by the sombre haughtiness which she read in that look which had been so gracious the previous evening. Her eldest son ran up from the bottom of the garden, and said as he kissed her,

"We have a holiday, M. Julien is going on a journey."

At these words, Madame de Rênal felt seized by a deadly coldness. She was unhappy by reason of her virtue, and even more unhappy by reason of her weakness.

This new event engrossed her imagination, and she was transported far beyond the good resolutions which she owed to the awful night she had just passed. It was not now a question of resisting that charming lover, but of losing him for ever.

It was necessary to appear at breakfast. To complete her anguish, M. de Rênal and Madame Derville talked of nothing but Julien's departure.

The mayor of Verrières had noticed something unusual in the firm tone in which he had asked for a holiday.

"That little peasant has no doubt got somebody else's offer up his sleeve, but that somebody else, even though it's M. Valenod, is bound to be a little discouraged by the sum of six hundred francs, which the annual salary now tots up to. He must have asked yesterday at Verrières for a period of three days to think it over, and our little gentleman runs off to the mountains this morning so as not to be obliged to give me an answer. Think of having to reckon with a wretched workman who puts on airs, but that's what we've come to."

"If my husband, who does not know how deeply he has wounded Julien, thinks that he will leave us, what can I think myself?" said Madame de Rênal to herself. "Yes, that is all decided." In order to be able at any rate to be free to cry, and to avoid answering Madame Derville's questions, she pleaded an awful headache, and went to bed.

"That's what women are," repeated M. de Rênal, "there is always something out of order in those complicated machines," and he went off jeering.

While Madame de Rênal was a prey to all the poignancy of the terrible passion in which chance had involved her, Julien went merrily on his way, surrounded by the most beautiful views that mountain scenery can offer. He had to cross the great chain north of Vergy. The path which he followed rose gradually among the big beech woods, and ran into infinite spirals on the slope of the high mountain which forms the northern boundary of the Doubs valley. Soon the traveller's view, as he passed over the lower slopes bounding the course of the Doubs towards the south, extends as far as the fertile plains of Burgundy and Beaujolais. However insensible was the soul of this ambitious youth to this kind of beauty, he could not help stopping from time to time to look at a spectacle at once so vast and so impressive.

Finally, he reached the summit of the great mountain, near which he had to pass in order to arrive by this cross-country route at the solitary valley where lived his friend Fouqué, the young wood merchant. Julien was in no hurry to see him; either him, or any other human being. Hidden like a bird of prey amid the bare rocks which crowned the great mountain, he could see a long way off anyone coming near him. He discovered a little grotto in the middle of the almost vertical slope of one of the rocks. He found a way to it, and was soon ensconced in this retreat. "Here," he said, "with eyes brilliant with joy, men cannot hurt me." It occurred to him to indulge in the pleasure of writing down those thoughts of his which were so dangerous to him everywhere else. A square stone served him for a desk; his pen flew. He saw nothing of what was around him. He noticed at last that the sun was setting behind the distant mountains of Beaujolais.

"Why shouldn't I pass the night here?" he said to himself. "I have bread, and I am free." He felt a spiritual exultation at the sound of that great word. The necessity of playing the hypocrite resulted in his not being free, even at Fouqué's. Leaning his head on his two hands, Julien stayed in the grotto, more happy than he had ever been in his life, thrilled by his dreams, and by the bliss of his freedom. Without realising it, he saw all the rays of the twilight become successively extinguished. Surrounded by this immense obscurity, his soul wandered into the contemplation of what he imagined that he would one day meet in Paris. First it was a woman, much more beautiful and possessed of a much more refined temperament than anything he could have found in the provinces. He loved with passion, and was loved. If he separated from her for some instants, it was only to cover himself with glory, and to deserve to be loved still more.

A young man brought up in the environment of the sad truths of Paris society, would, on reaching this point in his romance, even if we assume him possessed of Julien's imagination, have been brought back to himself by the cold irony of the situation. Great deeds would have disappeared from out his ken together with hope of achieving them and have been succeeded by the platitude. "If one leave one's mistress one runs alas! the risk of being deceived two or three times a day." But the young peasant saw nothing but the lack of opportunity between himself and the most heroic feats.

But a deep night had succeeded the day, and there were still two leagues to walk before he could descend to the cabin in which Fouqué lived. Before leaving the little cave, Julien made a light and carefully burnt all that he had written. He quite astonished his friend when he knocked at his door at one o'clock in the morning. He found Fouqué engaged in making up his accounts. He was a young man of high stature, rather badly made, with big, hard features, a never-ending nose, and a large fund of good nature concealed beneath this repulsive appearance.

"Have you quarelled with M. de Rênal then that you turn up unexpectedly like this?" Julien told him, but in a suitable way, the events of the previous day.

"Stay with me," said Fouqué to him. "I see that you know M. de Rênal, M. Valenod, the sub-prefect Maugron, the curé Chélan. You have understood the subtleties of the character of those people. So there you are then, quite qualified to attend auctions. You know arithmetic better than I do; you will keep my accounts; I make a lot in my business. The impossibility of doing everything myself, and the fear of taking a rascal for my partner prevents me daily from undertaking excellent business. It's scarcely a month since I put Michaud de Saint-Amand, whom I haven't seen for six years, and whom I ran across at the sale at Pontarlier in the way of making six thousand francs. Why shouldn't it have been you who made those six thousand francs, or at any rate three thousand. For if I had had you with me that day, I would have raised the bidding for that lot of timber and everybody else would soon have run away. Be my partner."

This offer upset Julien. It spoilt the train of his mad dreams. Fouqué showed his accounts to Julien during the whole of the supper—which the two friends prepared themselves like the Homeric heroes (for Fouqué lived alone) and proved to him all the advantages offered by his timber business. Fouqué had the highest opinion of the gifts and character of Julien.

When, finally, the latter was alone in his little room of pinewood, he said to himself: "It is true I can make some thousands of francs here and then take up with advantage the profession of a soldier, or of a priest, according to the fashion then prevalent in France. The little hoard that I shall have amassed will remove all petty difficulties. In the solitude of this mountain I shall have dissipated to some extent my awful ignorance of so many of the things which make up the life of all those men of fashion. But Fouqué has given up all thoughts of marriage, and at the same time keeps telling me that solitude makes him unhappy. It is clear that if he takes a partner who has no capital to put into his business, he does so in the hopes of getting a companion who will never leave him."

"Shall I deceive my friend," exclaimed Julien petulantly. This being who found hypocrisy and complete callousness his ordinary means of self-preservation could not, on this occasion, endure the idea of the slightest lack of delicate feeling towards a man whom he loved.

But suddenly Julien was happy. He had a reason for a refusal. What! Shall I be coward enough to waste seven or eight years. I shall get to twenty-eight in that way! But at that age Bonaparte had achieved his greatest feats. When I shall have made in obscurity a little money by frequenting timber sales, and earning the good graces of some rascally under-strappers who will guarantee that I shall still have the sacred fire with which one makes a name for oneself?

The following morning, Julien with considerable sangfroid, said in answer to the good Fouqué, who regarded the matter of the partnership as settled, that his vocation for the holy ministry of the altars would not permit him to accept it. Fouqué did not return to the subject.

"But just think," he repeated to him, "I'll make you my partner, or if you prefer it, I'll give you four thousand francs a year, and you want to return to that M. de Rênal of yours, who despises you like the mud on his shoes. When you have got two hundred louis in front of you, what is to prevent you from entering the seminary? I'll go further: I will undertake to procure for you the best living in the district, for," added Fouqué, lowering his voice, I supply firewood to M. le ——, M. le ——, M. ——. I provide them with first quality oak, but they only pay me for plain wood, but never was money better invested.

Nothing could conquer Julien's vocation. Fouqué finished by thinking him a little mad. The third day, in the early morning, Julien left his friend, and passed the day amongst the rocks of the great mountain. He found his little cave again, but he had no longer peace of mind. His friend's offers had robbed him of it. He found himself, not between vice and virtue, like Hercules, but between mediocrity coupled with an assured prosperity, and all the heroic dreams of his youth. "So I have not got real determination after all," he said to himself, and it was his doubt on this score which pained him the most. "I am not of the stuff of which great men are made, because I fear that eight years spent in earning a livelihood will deprive me of that sublime energy which inspires the accomplishment of extraordinary feats."

XIII
THE OPEN WORK STOCKINGS

A novel: a mirror which one takes out on one's walk
along the high road.—*Saint-Réal.*

When Julien perceived the picturesque ruins of the old church at Vergy, he noticed that he had not given a single thought to Madame de Rênal since the day before yesterday. The other day, when I took my leave, that woman made me realise the infinite distance which separated us; she treated me like a labourer's son. No doubt she wished to signify her repentance for having allowed me to hold her hand the evening before.

... It is, however very pretty, is that hand. What a charm, what a nobility is there in that woman's expression!

The possibility of making a fortune with Fouqué gave a certain facility to Julien's logic. It was not spoilt quite so frequently by the irritation and the keen consciousness of his poverty and low estate in the eyes of the world. Placed as it were on a high promontory, he was able to exercise his judgment, and had a commanding view, so to speak, of both extreme poverty and that competence which he still called wealth. He was far from judging his position really philosophically, but he had enough penetration to feel different after this little journey into the mountain.

He was struck with the extreme uneasiness with which Madame de Rênal listened to the brief account which she had asked for of his journey.

Fouqué had had plans of marriage, and unhappy love affairs, and long confidences on this subject had formed the staple of the two friends' conversation. Having found happiness too soon, Fouqué had realised that he was not the only one who was loved. All these accounts had astonished Julien. He had learnt many new things. His solitary life of imagination and suspicion had kept him remote from anything which could enlighten him.

During his absence, life had been nothing for Madame de Rênal but a series of tortures, which, though different, were all unbearable. She was really ill.

"Now mind," said Madame Derville to her when she saw Julien arrive, "you don't go into the garden this evening in your weak state; the damp air will make your complaint twice as bad."

Madame Derville was surprised to see that her friend, who was always scolded by M. de Rênal by reason of the excessive simplicity of her dress, had just got some open-work stockings and some charming little shoes which had come from Paris. For three days Madame de Rênal's only distraction had been to cut out a summer dress of a pretty little material which was very fashionable, and get it made with express speed by Elisa. This dress could scarcely have been finished a few moments before Julien's arrival, but Madame de Rênal put it on immediately. Her friend had no longer any doubt. "She loves," unhappy woman, said Madame Derville to herself. She understood all the strange symptoms of the malady.

She saw her speak to Julien. The most violent blush was succeeded by pallor. Anxiety was depicted in her eyes, which were riveted on those of the young tutor. Madame de Rênal expected every minute that he would give an explanation of his conduct, and announce that he was either going to leave the house or stay there. Julien carefully avoided that subject, and did not even think of it. After terrible struggles, Madame de Rênal eventually dared to say to him in a trembling voice that mirrored all her passion:

"Are you going to leave your pupils to take another place?"

Julien was struck by Madame de Rênal's hesitating voice and look. "That woman loves me," he said to himself! "But after this temporary moment of weakness, for which her pride is no doubt reproaching her, and as soon as she has ceased fearing that I shall leave, she will be as haughty as ever." This view of their mutual position passed through Julien's mind as rapidly as a flash of lightning. He answered with some hesitation,

"I shall be extremely distressed to leave children who are so nice and so well-born, but perhaps it will be necessary. One has duties to oneself as well."

As he pronounced the expression, "well-born" (it was one of those aristocratic phrases which Julien had recently learnt), he became animated by a profound feeling of antipathy.

"I am not well-born," he said to himself, "in that woman's eyes."

As Madame de Rênal listened to him, she admired his genius and his beauty, and the hinted possibility of his departure pierced her heart. All her friends at Verrières who had come to dine at Vergy during Julien's absence had complimented her almost jealously on the astonishing man whom her husband had had the good fortune to unearth. It was not that they understood anything about the progress of children. The feat of knowing his Bible by heart, and what is more, of knowing it in Latin, had struck the inhabitants of Verrières with an admiration which will last perhaps a century.

Julien, who never spoke to anyone, was ignorant of all this. If Madame de Rênal had possessed the slightest presence of mind, she would have complimented him on the reputation which he had won, and Julien's pride, once satisfied, he would have been sweet and amiable towards her, especially as he thought her new dress charming. Madame de Rênal was also pleased with her pretty dress, and with what Julien had said to her about it, and wanted to walk round the garden. But she soon confessed that she was incapable of walking. She had taken the traveller's arm, and the contact of that arm, far from increasing her strength, deprived her of it completely.

It was night. They had scarcely sat down before Julien, availing himself of his old privilege, dared to bring his lips near his pretty neighbour's arm, and to take her hand. He kept thinking of the boldness which Fouqué had exhibited with his mistresses and not of Madame de Rênal; the word "well-born" was still heavy on his heart. He felt his hand pressed, but experienced no pleasure. So far from his being proud, or even grateful for the sentiment that Madame de Rênal was betraying that evening by only too evident signs, he was almost insensible to her beauty, her elegance, and her freshness. Purity of soul, and the absence of all hateful emotion, doubtless prolong the duration of youth. It is the face which ages first with the majority of women.

Julien sulked all the evening. Up to the present he had only been angry with the social order, but from that time that Fouqué had offered him an ignoble means of obtaining a competency, he was irritated with himself. Julien was so engrossed in his thoughts, that, although from time to time he said a few words to the ladies, he eventually let go Madame de Rênal's hand without noticing it. This action overwhelmed the soul of the poor woman. She saw in it her whole fate.

If she had been certain of Julien's affection, her virtue would possibly have found strength to resist him. But trembling lest she should lose him for ever, she was distracted by her passion to the point of taking again Julien's hand, which he had left in his absent-mindedness leaning on the back of the chair. This action woke up this ambitious youth; he would have liked to have had for witnesses all those proud nobles who had regarded him at meals, when he was at the bottom of the table with the children, with so condescending a smile. "That woman cannot despise me; in that case," he said to himself. "I ought to shew my appreciation of her beauty. I owe it to myself to be her lover." That idea would not have occurred to him before the naive confidences which his friend had made.

The sudden resolution which he had just made formed an agreeable distraction. He kept saying to himself, "I must have one of those two women;" he realised that he would have very much preferred to have paid court to Madame Derville. It was not that she was more agreeable, but that she had always seen him as the tutor distinguished by his knowledge, and not as the journeyman carpenter with his cloth jacket folded under his arm as he had first appeared to Madame de Rênal.

It was precisely as a young workman, blushing up to the whites of his eyes, standing by the door of the house and not daring to ring, that he made the most alluring appeal to Madame de Rênal's imagination.

As he went on reviewing his position, Julien saw that the conquest of Madame Derville, who had probably noticed the taste which Madame de Rênal was manifesting for him, was out of the question. He was thus brought back to the latter lady. "What do I know of the character of that woman?" said Julien to himself. "Only this: before my journey, I used to take her hand, and she used to take it away. To-day, I take my hand away, and she seizes and presses it. A fine opportunity to pay her back all the contempt she had had for me. God knows how many lovers she has had, probably she is only deciding in my favour by reason of the easiness of assignations."

Such, alas, is the misfortune of an excessive civilisation. The soul of a young man of twenty, possessed of any education, is a thousand leagues away from that *abandon* without which love is frequently but the most tedious of duties.

"I owe it all the more to myself," went on the petty vanity of Julien, "to succeed with that woman, by reason of the fact that if I ever make a fortune, and I am reproached by anyone with my menial position as a tutor, I shall then be able to give out that it was love which got me the post."

Julien again took his hand away from Madame de Rênal, and then took her hand again and pressed it. As they went back to the drawing-room about midnight, Madame de Rênal said to him in a whisper.

"You are leaving us, you are going?"

Julien answered with a sigh.

"I absolutely must leave, for I love you passionately. It is wrong ... how wrong indeed for a young priest?" Madame de Rênal leant upon his arm, and with so much abandon that her cheek felt the warmth of Julien's.

The nights of these two persons were quite different. Madame de Rênal was exalted by the ecstacies of the highest moral pleasure. A coquettish young girl, who loves early in life, gets habituated to the trouble of love, and when she reaches the age of real passion, finds the charm of novelty lacking. As Madame de Rênal had never read any novels, all the refinements of her happiness were new to her. No mournful truth came to chill her, not even the spectre of the future. She imagined herself as happy in ten years' time as she was at the present moment. Even the idea of virtue and of her sworn fidelity to M. de Rênal, which had agitated her some days past, now presented itself in vain, and was sent about its business like an importunate visitor. "I will never grant anything to Julien," said Madame de Rênal; "we will live in the future like we have been living for the last month. He shall be a friend."

XIV
THE ENGLISH SCISSORS

A young girl of sixteen had a pink complexion, and
yet used red rouge.—*Polidori.*

Fouqué's offer had, as a matter of fact, taken away all Julien's happiness; he could not make up his mind to any definite course. "Alas! perhaps I am lacking in character. I should have been a bad soldier of Napoleon. At least," he added, "my little intrigue with the mistress of the house will distract me a little."

Happily for him, even in this little subordinate incident, his inner emotions quite failed to correspond with his flippant words. He was frightened of Madame de Rênal because of her pretty dress. In his eyes, that dress was a vanguard of Paris. His pride refused to leave anything to chance and the inspiration of the moment. He made himself a very minute plan of campaign, moulded on the confidences of Fouqué, and a little that he had read about love in the Bible. As he was very nervous, though he did not admit it to himself, he wrote down this plan.

Madame de Rênal was alone with him for a moment in the drawing-room on the following morning.

"Have you no other name except Julien," she said.

Our hero was at a loss to answer so nattering a question. This circumstance had not been anticipated in his plan. If he had not been stupid enough to have made a plan, Julien's quick wit would have served him well, and the surprise would only have intensified the quickness of his perception.

He was clumsy, and exaggerated his clumsiness, Madame de Rênal quickly forgave him. She attributed it to a charming frankness. And an air of frankness was the very thing which in her view was just lacking in this man who was acknowledged to have so much genius.

"That little tutor of yours inspires me with a great deal of suspicion," said Madame Derville to her sometimes. "I think he looks as if he were always thinking, and he never acts without calculation. He is a sly fox."

Julien remained profoundly humiliated by the misfortune of not having known what answer to make to Madame de Rênal.

"A man like I am ought to make up for this check!" and seizing the moment when they were passing from one room to another, he thought it was his duty to give Madame de Rênal a kiss.

Nothing could have been less tactful, nothing less agreeable, and nothing more imprudent both for him and for her. They were within an inch of being noticed. Madame de Rênal thought him mad. She was frightened, and above all, shocked. This stupidity reminded her of M. Valenod.

"What would happen to me," she said to herself, "if I were alone with him?" All her virtue returned, because her love was waning.

She so arranged it that one of her children always remained with her. Julien found the day very tedious, and passed it entirely in clumsily putting into operation his plan of seduction. He did not look at Madame de Rênal on a single occasion without that look having a reason, but nevertheless he was not sufficiently stupid to fail to see that he was not succeeding at all in being amiable, and was succeeding even less in being fascinating.

Madame de Rênal did not recover from her astonishment at finding him so awkward and at the same time so bold. "It is the timidity of love in men of intellect," she said to herself with an inexpressible joy. "Could it be possible that he had never been loved by my rival?"

After breakfast Madame de Rênal went back to the drawing-room to receive the visit of M. Charcot de Maugiron, the sub-prefect of Bray. She was working at a little frame of fancy-work some distance from the ground. Madame Derville was at her side; that was how she was placed when our hero thought it suitable to advance his boot in the full light and press the pretty foot of Madame de Rênal, whose open-work stockings, and pretty Paris shoe were evidently attracting the looks of the gallant sub-prefect.

Madame de Rênal was very much afraid, and let fall her scissors, her ball of wool and her needles, so that Julien's movement could be passed for a clumsy effort, intended to prevent the fall of the scissors, which presumably he had seen slide. Fortunately, these little scissors of English steel were broken, and Madame de Rênal did not spare her regrets that Julien had not succeeded in getting nearer to her. "You noticed them falling before I did—you could have prevented it, instead, all your zealousness only succeeding in giving me a very big kick." All this took in the sub-perfect, but not Madame Derville. "That pretty boy has very silly manners," she thought. The social code of a provincial capital never forgives this kind of lapse.

Madame de Rênal found an opportunity of saying to Julien, "Be prudent, I order you."

Julien appreciated his own clumsiness. He was upset. He deliberated with himself for a long time, in order to ascertain whether or not he ought to be angry at the expression "I order you." He was silly enough to think she might have said "I order you," if it were some question concerning the children's education, but in answering my love she puts me on an equality. It is impossible to love without equality ... and all his mind ran riot in making common-places on equality. He angrily repeated to himself that verse of Corneille which Madame Derville had taught him some days before.

"L'amour
les égalités, et ne les cherche pas."

Julien who had never had a mistress in his whole life, but yet insisted on playing the rôle of a Don Juan, made a shocking fool of himself all day. He had only one sensible idea. Bored with himself and Madame de Rênal, he viewed with apprehension the advance of the evening when he would have to sit by her side in the darkness of the garden. He told M. de Rênal that he was going to Verrières to see the curé. He left after dinner, and only came back in the night.

At Verrières Julien found M. Chélan occupied in moving. He had just been deprived of his living; the curate Maslon was replacing him. Julien helped the good curé, and it occurred to him to write to Fouqué that the irresistible mission which he felt for the holy ministry had previously prevented him from accepting his kind offer, but that he had just seen an instance of injustice, and that perhaps it would be safer not to enter into Holy Orders.

Julien congratulated himself on his subtlety in exploiting the dismissal of the curé of Verrières so as to leave himself a loop-hole for returning to commerce in the event of a gloomy prudence routing the spirit of heroism from his mind.

XV
THE COCK'S SONG

Amour en latin faict amour;
Or done provient d'amour la mart,
Et, par avant, souley qui moreq,
Deuil, plours, pieges, forfailz, remord.
BLASON D'AMOUR.

If Julien had possessed a little of that adroitness on which he so gratuitously plumed himself, he could have congratulated himself the following day on the effect produced by his journey to Verrières. His absence had caused his clumsiness to be forgotten. But on that day also he was rather sulky. He had a ludicrous idea in the evening, and with singular courage he communicated it to Madame de Rênal. They had scarcely sat down in the garden before Julien brought his mouth near Madame de Rênal's ear without waiting till it was sufficiently dark and at the risk of compromising her terribly, said to her,

"Madame, to-night, at two o'clock, I shall go into your room, I must tell you something."

Julien trembled lest his request should be granted. His rakish pose weighed him down so terribly that if he could have followed his own inclination he would have returned to his room for several days and refrained from seeing the ladies any more. He realised that he had spoiled by his clever conduct of last evening all the bright prospects of the day that had just passed, and was at his wits' end what to do.

Madame de Rênal answered the impertinent declaration which Julien had dared to make to her with indignation which was real and in no way exaggerated. He thought he could see contempt in her curt reply. The expression "for shame," had certainly occurred in that whispered answer.

Julien went to the children's room under the pretext of having something to say to them, and on his return he placed himself beside Madame Derville and very far from Madame de Rênal. He thus deprived himself of all possibility of taking her hand. The conversation was serious, and Julien acquitted himself very well, apart from a few moments of silence during which he was cudgelling his brains.

"Why can't I invent some pretty manœuvre," he said to himself which will force Madame de Rênal to vouchsafe to me those unambiguous signs of tenderness which a few days ago made me think that she was mine.

Julien was extremely disconcerted by the almost desperate plight to which he had brought his affairs. Nothing, however, would have embarrassed him more than success.

When they separated at midnight, his pessimism made him think that he enjoyed Madame Derville's contempt, and that probably he stood no better with Madame de Rênal.

Feeling in a very bad temper and very humiliated, Julien did not sleep. He was leagues away from the idea of giving up all intriguing and planning, and of living from day to day with Madame de Rênal, and of being contented like a child with the happiness brought by every day.

He racked his brains inventing clever manœuvres, which an instant afterwards he found absurd, and, to put it shortly, was very unhappy when two o'clock rang from the castle clock.

The noise woke him up like the cock's crow woke up St. Peter. The most painful episode was now timed to begin—he had not given a thought to his impertinent proposition, since the moment when he had made it and it had been so badly received.

"I have told her that I will go to her at two o'clock," he said to himself as he got up, "I may be inexperienced and coarse, as the son of a peasant naturally would be. Madame Derville has given me to understand as much, but at any rate, I will not be weak."

Julien had reason to congratulate himself on his courage, for he had never put his self-control to so painful a test. As he opened his door, he was trembling to such an extent that his knees gave way under him, and he was forced to lean against the wall.

He was without shoes; he went and listened at M. de Rênal's door, and could hear his snoring. He was disconsolate, he had no longer any excuse for not going to her room. But, Great Heaven! What was he to do there? He had no plan, and even if he had had one, he felt himself so nervous that he would have been incapable of carrying it out.

Eventually, suffering a thousand times more than if he had been walking to his death, he entered the little corridor that led to Madame de Rênal's room. He opened the door with a trembling hand and made a frightful noise.

There was light; a night light was burning on the mantelpiece. He had not expected this new misfortune. As she saw him enter, Madame de Rênal got quickly out of bed. "Wretch," she cried. There was a little confusion. Julien forgot his useless plans, and turned to his natural role. To fail to please so charming a woman appeared to him the greatest of misfortunes. His only answer to her reproaches was to throw himself at her feet while he kissed her knees. As she was speaking to him with extreme harshness, he burst into tears.

When Julien came out of Madame de Rênal's room some hours afterwards, one could have said, adopting the conventional language of the novel, that there was nothing left to be desired. In fact, he owed to the love he had inspired, and to the unexpected impression which her alluring charms had produced upon him, a victory to which his own clumsy tactics would never have led him.

But victim that he was of a distorted pride, he pretended even in the sweetest moments to play the role of a man accustomed to the subjugation of women: he made incredible but deliberate efforts to spoil his natural charm. Instead of watching the transports which he was bringing into existence, and those pangs of remorse which only set their keenness into fuller relief, the idea of duty was continually before his eyes. He feared a frightful remorse, and eternal ridicule, if he departed from the ideal model he proposed to follow. In a word, the very quality which made Julien into a superior being was precisely that which prevented him from savouring the happiness which was placed within his grasp. It's like the case of a young girl of sixteen with a charming complexion who is mad enough to put on rouge before going to a ball.

Mortally terrified by the apparition of Julien, Madame de Rênal was soon a prey to the most cruel alarm. The prayers and despair of Julien troubled her keenly.

Even when there was nothing left for her to refuse him she pushed Julien away from her with a genuine indignation, and straightway threw herself into his arms. There was no plan apparent in all this conduct. She thought herself eternally damned, and tried to hide from herself the sight of hell by loading Julien with the wildest caresses. In a word, nothing would have been lacking in our hero's happiness, not even an ardent sensibility in the woman whom he had just captured, if he had only known how to enjoy it. Julien's departure did not in any way bring to an end those ecstacies which thrilled her in spite of herself, and those troubles of remorse which lacerated her.

"My God! being happy—being loved, is that all it comes to?" This was Julien's first thought as he entered his room. He was a prey to the astonishment and nervous anxiety of the man who has just obtained what he has long desired. He has been accustomed to desire, and has no longer anything to desire, and nevertheless has no memories. Like a soldier coming back from parade. Julien was absorbed in rehearsing the details of his conduct. "Have I failed in nothing which I owe to myself? Have I played my part well?"

And what a part! the part of a man accustomed to be brilliant with women.

XVI
THE DAY AFTER

He turned his lips to hers and with his hand
Called back the tangles of her wandering hair.
Don Juan, c. I, st. 170.

Happily for Julien's fame, Madame de Rênal had been too agitated and too astonished to appreciate the stupidity of the man who had in a single moment become the whole to world her.

"Oh, my God!" she said to herself, as she pressed him to retire when she saw the dawn break, "if my husband has heard the noise, I am lost." Julien, who had had the time to make up some phrases, remembered this one,

"Would you regret your life?"

"Oh, very much at a moment like this, but I should not regret having known you."

Julien thought it incumbent on his dignity to go back to his room in broad daylight and with deliberate imprudence.

The continuous attention with which he kept on studying his slightest actions with the absurd idea of appearing a man of experience had only one advantage. When he saw Madame de Rênal again at breakfast his conduct was a masterpiece of prudence.

As for her, she could not look at him without blushing up to the eyes, and could not live a moment without looking at him. She realised her own nervousness, and her efforts to hide it redoubled. Julien only lifted his eyes towards her once. At first Madame de Rênal admired his prudence: soon seeing that this single look was not repealed, she became alarmed. "Could it be that he does not love me?" she said to herself. "Alas! I am quite old for him. I am ten years older than he is."

As she passed from the dining-room to the garden, she pressed Julien's hand. In the surprise caused by so singular a mark of love, he regarded her with passion, for he had thought her very pretty over breakfast, and while keeping his eyes downcast he had passed his time in thinking of the details of her charms. This look consoled Madame de Rênal. It did not take away all her anxiety, but her anxiety tended to take away nearly completely all her remorse towards her husband.

The husband had noticed nothing at breakfast. It was not so with Madame Derville. She thought she saw Madame de Rênal on the point of succumbing. During the whole day her bold and incisive friendship regaled her cousin with those innuendoes which were intended to paint in hideous colours the dangers she was running.

Madame de Rênal was burning to find herself alone with Julien. She wished to ask him if he still loved her. In spite of the unalterable sweetness of her character, she was several times on the point of notifying her friend how officious she was.

Madame Derville arranged things so adroitly that evening in the garden, that she found herself placed between Madame de Rênal and Julien. Madame de Rênal, who had thought in her imagination how delicious it would be to press Julien's hand and carry it to her lips, was not able to address a single word to him.

This hitch increased her agitation. She was devoured by one pang of remorse. She had so scolded Julien for his imprudence in coming to her room on the preceding night, that she trembled lest he should not come to-night. She left the garden early and went and ensconced herself in her room, but not being able to control her impatience, she went and glued her ear to Julien's door. In spite of the uncertainty and passion which devoured her, she did not dare to enter. This action seemed to her the greatest possible meanness, for it forms the basis of a provincial proverb.

The servants had not yet all gone to bed. Prudence at last compelled her to return to her room. Two hours of waiting were two centuries of torture.

Julien was too faithful to what he called his duty to fail to accomplish stage by stage what he had mapped out for himself.

As one o'clock struck, he escaped softly from his room, assured himself that the master of the house was soundly asleep, and appeared in Madame de Rênal's room. To-night he experienced more happiness by the side of his love, for he thought less constantly about the part he had to play. He had eyes to see, and ears to hear. What Madame de Rênal said to him about his age contributed to give him some assurance.

"Alas! I am ten years older than you. How can you love me?" she repeated vaguely, because the idea oppressed her.

Julien could not realise her happiness, but he saw that it was genuine and he forgot almost entirely his own fear of being ridiculous.

The foolish thought that he was regarded as an inferior, by reason of his obscure birth, disappeared also. As Julien's transports reassured his timid mistress, she regained a little of her happiness, and of her power to judge her lover. Happily, he had not, on this occasion, that artificial air which had made the assignation of the previous night a triumph rather than a pleasure. If she had realised his concentration on playing a part that melancholy discovery would have taken away all her happiness for ever. She could only have seen in it the result of the difference in their ages.

Although Madame de Rênal had never thought of the ories of love, difference in age is next to difference in fortune, one of the great commonplaces of provincial witticisms, whenever love is the topic of conversation.

In a few days Julien surrendered himself with all the ardour of his age, and was desperately in love.

"One must own," he said to himself, "that she has an angelic kindness of soul, and no one in the world is prettier."

He had almost completely given up playing a part. In a moment of abandon, he even confessed to her all his nervousness. This confidence raised the passion which he was inspiring to its zenith. "And I have no lucky rival after all," said Madame de Rênal to herself with delight. She ventured to question him on the portrait in which he used to be so interested. Julien swore to her that it was that of a man.

When Madame de Rênal had enough presence of mind left to reflect, she did not recover from her astonishment that so great a happiness could exist; and that she had never had anything of.

"Oh," she said to herself, "if I had only known Julien ten years ago when I was still considered pretty."

Julien was far from having thoughts like these. His love was still akin to ambition. It was the joy of possessing, poor, unfortunate and despised as he was, so beautiful a woman. His acts of devotion, and his ecstacies at the sight of his mistress's charms finished by reassuring her a little with regard to the difference of age. If she had possessed a little of that knowledge of life which the woman of thirty has enjoyed in the more civilised of countries for quite a long time, she would have trembled for the duration of a love, which only seemed to thrive on novelty and the intoxication of a young man's vanity. In those moments when he forgot his ambition, Julien admired ecstatically even the hats and even the dresses of Madame de Rênal. He could not sate himself with the pleasure of smelling their perfume. He would open her mirrored cupboard, and remain hours on end admiring the beauty and the order of everything that he found there. His love leaned on him and looked at him. He was looking at those jewels and those dresses which had had been her wedding presents.

"I might have married a man like that," thought Madame de Rênal sometimes. "What a fiery soul! What a delightful life one would have with him?"

As for Julien, he had never been so near to those terrible instruments of feminine artillery. "It is impossible," he said to himself "for there to be anything more beautiful in Paris." He could find no flaw in his happiness. The sincere admiration and ecstacies of his mistress would frequently make him forget that silly pose which had rendered him so stiff and almost ridiculous during the first moments of the intrigue. There were moments where, in spite of his habitual hypocrisy, he found an extreme delight in confessing to this great lady who admired him, his ignorance of a crowd of little usages. His mistress's rank seemed to lift him above himself. Madame de Rênal, on her side, would find the sweetest thrill of intellectual voluptuousness in thus instructing in a number of little things this young man who was so full of genius, and who was looked upon by everyone as destined one day to go so far. Even the sub-prefect and M. Valenod could not help admiring him. She thought it made them less foolish. As for Madame Derville, she was very far from being in a position to express the same sentiments. Rendered desperate by what she thought she divined, and seeing that her good advice was becoming offensive to a woman who had literally lost her head, she left Vergy without giving the explanation, which her friend carefully refrained from asking. Madame de Rênal shed a few tears for her, and soon found her happiness greater than ever. As a result of her departure, she found herself alone with her lover nearly the whole day.

Julien abandoned himself all the more to the delightful society of his sweetheart, since, whenever he was alone, Fouqué's fatal proposition still continued to agitate him. During the first days of his novel life there were moments when the man who had never loved, who had never been loved by anyone, would find so delicious a pleasure in being sincere, that he was on the point of confessing to Madame de Rênal that ambition which up to then had been the very essence of his existence. He would have liked to have been able to consult her on the strange temptation which Fouqué's offer held out to him, but a little episode rendered any frankness impossible.

XVII
THE FIRST DEPUTY

Oh, how this spring of love resembleth
The uncertain glory of an April day,
Which now shows all the beauty of the sun,
And by and by a cloud takes all away.
Two Gentlemen of Verona.

One evening when the sun was setting, and he was sitting near his love, at the bottom of the orchard, far from all intruders, he meditated deeply. "Will such sweet moments" he said to himself "last for ever?" His soul was engrossed in the difficulty of deciding on a calling. He lamented that great attack of unhappiness which comes at the end of childhood and spoils the first years of youth in those who are not rich.

"Ah!" he exclaimed, "was not Napoleon the heaven-sent saviour for young Frenchmen? Who is to replace him? What will those unfortunate youths do without him, who, even though they are richer than I am, have only just the few crowns necessary to procure an education for themselves, but have not at the age of twenty enough money to buy a man and advance themselves in their career." "Whatever one does," he added, with a deep sigh, "this fatal memory will always prevent our being happy."

He suddenly saw Madame de Rênal frown. She assumed a cold and disdainful air. She thought his way of looking at things typical of a servant. Brought up as she was with the idea that she was very rich, she took it for granted that Julien was so also. She loved him a thousand times more than life and set no store by money.

Julien was far from guessing these ideas, but that frown brought him back to earth. He had sufficient presence of mind to manipulate his phrases, and to give the noble lady who was sitting so near him on the grass seat to understand that the words he had just repeated had been heard by him during his journey to his friend the wood merchant. It was the logic of infidels.

"Well, have nothing to do with those people," said Madame de Rênal, still keeping a little of that icy air which had suddenly succeeded an expression of the warmest tenderness.

This frown, or rather his remorse for his own imprudence, was the first check to the illusion which was transporting Julien. He said to himself, "She is good and sweet, she has a great fancy for me, but she has been brought up in the enemy's camp. They must be particularly afraid of that class of men of spirit who, after a good education, have not enough money to take up a career. What would become of those nobles if we had an opportunity of fighting them with equal arms. Suppose me, for example, mayor of Verrières, and as well meaning and honest as M. de Rênal is at bottom. What short shrift I should make of the vicaire, M. Valenod and all their jobberies! How justice would triumph in Verrières. It is not their talents which would stop me. They are always fumbling about."

That day Julien's happiness almost became permanent. Our hero lacked the power of daring to be sincere. He ought to have had the courage to have given battle, and on the spot; Madame de Rênal had been astonished by Julien's phrase, because the men in her circle kept on repeating that the return of Robespierre was essentially possible by reason of those over-educated young persons of the lower classes. Madame de Rênal's coldness lasted a longish time, and struck Julien as marked. The reason was that the fear that she had said something in some way or other disagreeable to him, succeeded her annoyance for his own breach of taste. This unhappiness was vividly reflected in those features which looked so pure and so naïve when she was happy and away from intruders.

Julien no longer dared to surrender himself to his dreams. Growing calmer and less infatuated, he considered that it was imprudent to go and see Madame de Rênal in her room. It was better for her to come to him. If a servant noticed her going about the house, a dozen different excuses could explain it.

But this arrangement had also its inconveniences. Julien had received from Fouqué some books, which he, as a theology student would never have dared to ask for in a bookshop. He only dared to open them at night. He would often have found it much more convenient not to be interrupted by a visit, the very waiting for which had even on the evening before the little scene in the orchard completely destroyed his mood for reading.

He had Madame de Rênal to thank for understanding books in quite a new way. He had dared to question her on a number of little things, the ignorance of which cuts quite short the intellectual progress of any young man born out of society, however much natural genius one may choose to ascribe to him.

This education given through sheer love by a woman who was extremely ignorant, was a piece of luck. Julien managed to get a clear insight into society such as it is to-day. His mind was not bewildered by the narration of what it had been once, two thousand years ago, or even sixty years ago, in the time of Voltaire and Louis XV. The scales fell from his eyes to his inexpressible joy, and he understood at last what was going on in Verrières.

In the first place there were the very complicated intrigues which had been woven for the last two years around the prefect of Besançon. They were backed up by letters from Paris, written by the cream of the aristocracy. The scheme was to make M. de Moirod (he was the most devout man in the district) the first and not the second deputy of the mayor of Verrières.

He had for a competitor a very rich manufacturer whom it was essential to push back into the place of second deputy.

Julien understood at last the innuendoes which he had surprised, when the high society of the locality used to come and dine at M. de Rênal's. This privileged society was deeply concerned with the choice of a first deputy, while the rest of the town, and above all, the Liberals, did not even suspect its possibility. The factor which made the matter important was that, as everybody knows, the east side of the main street of Verrières has to be put more than nine feet back since that street has become a royal route.

Now if M. de Moirod, who had three houses liable to have their frontage put back, succeeded in becoming first deputy and consequently mayor in the event of M. de Rênal being elected to the chamber, he would shut his eyes, and it would be possible to make little imperceptible repairs in the houses projecting on to the public road, as the result of which they would last a hundred years. In spite of the great piety and proved integrity of M. de Moirod, everyone was certain that he would prove amenable, because he had a great many children. Among the houses liable to have their frontage put back nine belonged to the cream of Verrières society.

In Julien's eyes this intrigue was much more important than the history of the battle of Fontenoy, whose name he now came across for the first time in one of the books which Fouqué had sent him. There had been many things which had astonished Julien since the time five years ago when he had started going to the curé's in the evening. But discretion and humility of spirit being the primary qualities of a theological student, it had always been impossible for him to put questions.

One day Madame de Rênal was giving an order to her husband's valet who was Julien's enemy.

"But, Madame, to-day is the last Friday in the month," the man answered in a rather strange manner.

"Go," said Madame de Rênal.

"Well," said Julien, "I suppose he's going to go to that corn shop which was once a church, and has recently been restored to religion, but what is he going to do there? That's one of the mysteries which I have never been able to fathom."

"It's a very literary institution, but a very curious one," answered Madame de Rênal. "Women are not admitted to it. All I know is, that everybody uses the second person singular. This servant, for instance, will go and meet M. Valenod there, and the haughty prig will not be a bit offended at hearing himself addressed by Saint-Jean in that familiar way, and will answer him in the same way. If you are keen on knowing what takes place, I will ask M. de Maugiron and M. Valenod for details. We pay twenty francs for each servant, to prevent their cutting our throats one fine day."

Time flew. The memory of his mistress's charms distracted Julien from his black ambition. The necessity of refraining from mentioning gloomy or intellectual topics since they both belonged to opposing parties, added, without his suspecting it, to the happiness which he owed her, and to the dominion which she acquired over him.

On the occasions when the presence of the precocious children reduced them to speaking the language of cold reason, Julien looking at her with eyes sparkling with love, would listen with complete docility to her explanations of the world as it is. Frequently, in the middle of an account of some cunning piece of jobbery, with reference to a road or a contract, Madame de Rênal's mind would suddenly wander to the very point of delirium. Julien found it necessary to scold her. She indulged when with him in the same intimate gestures which she used with her own children. The fact was that there were days when she deceived herself that she loved him like her own child. Had she not repeatedly to answer his naïve questions about a thousand simple things that a well-born child of fifteen knows quite well? An instant afterwards she would admire him like her master. His genius would even go so far as to frighten her. She thought she should see more clearly every day the future great man in this young abbé. She saw him Pope; she saw him first minister like Richelieu. "Shall I live long enough to see you in your glory?" she said to Julien. "There is room for a great man; church and state have need of one."

XVIII
A KING AT VERRIÈRES

*Do you not deserve to be thrown aside like a plebeian
corpse which has no soul and whose blood flows no
longer in its veins.*
Sermon of the Bishop at the Chapel of Saint Clement.

On the 3rd of September at ten o'clock in the evening, a gendarme woke up the whole of Verrières by galloping up the main street. He brought the news that His Majesty the King of —— would arrive the following Sunday, and it was already Tuesday. The prefect authorised, that is to say, demanded the forming of a guard of honour. They were to exhibit all possible pomp. An express messenger was sent to Vergy. M. de Rênal arrived during the night and found the town in a commotion. Each individual had his own pretensions; those who were less busy hired balconies to see the King.

Who was to command the Guard of Honour? M. de Rênal at once realised how essential it was in the interests of the houses liable to have their frontage put back that M. de Moirod should have the command. That might entitle him to the post of first deputy-mayor. There was nothing to say against the devoutness of M. de Moirod. It brooked no comparison, but he had never sat on a horse. He was a man of thirty-six, timid in every way, and equally frightened of falling and of looking ridiculous. The mayor had summoned him as early as five o'clock in the morning.

"You see, monsieur, I ask your advice, as though you already occupy that post to which all the people on the right side want to carry you. In this unhappy town, manufacturers are prospering, the Liberal party is becoming possessed of millions, it aspires to power; it will manage to exploit everything to its own ends. Let us consult the interests of the king, the interest of the monarchy, and above all, the interest of our holy religion. Who do you think, monsieur, could be entrusted with the command of the guard of honour?"

In spite of the terrible fear with which horses inspired him, M. de Moirod finished by accepting this honour like a martyr. "I shall know how to take the right tone," he said to the mayor. There was scarcely time enough to get ready the uniforms which had served seven years ago on the occasion of the passage of a prince of the blood.

At seven o'clock, Madame de Rênal arrived at Vergy with Julien and the children. She found her drawing room filled with Liberal ladies who preached the union of all parties and had come to beg her to urge her husband to grant a place to theirs in the guard of honour. One of them actually asserted that if her husband was not chosen he would go bankrupt out of chagrin. Madame de Rênal quickly got rid of all these people. She seemed very engrossed.

Julien was astonished, and what was more, angry that she should make a mystery of what was disturbing her, "I had anticipated it," he said bitterly to himself. "Her love is being over-shadowed by the happiness of receiving a King in her house. All this hubbub overcomes her. She will love me once more when the ideas of her caste no longer trouble her brain."

An astonishing fact, he only loved her the more.

The decorators began to fill the house. He watched a long time for the opportunity to exchange a few words. He eventually found her as she was coming out of his own room, carrying one of his suits. They were alone. He tried to speak to her. She ran away, refusing to listen to him. "I am an absolute fool to love a woman like that, whose ambition renders her as mad as her husband."

She was madder. One of her great wishes which she had never confessed to Julien for fear of shocking him, was to see him leave off, if only for one day, his gloomy black suit. With an adroitness which was truly admirable in so ingenuous a woman, she secured first from M. de Moirod, and subsequently, from M. the sub-perfect de Maugiron, an assurance that Julien should be nominated a guard of honour in preference to five or six young people, the sons of very well-off manufacturers, of whom two at least, were models of piety. M. de Valenod, who reckoned on lending his carriage to the prettiest women in the town, and on showing off his fine Norman steeds, consented to let Julien (the being he hated most in the whole world) have one of his horses. But all the guards of honour, either possessed or had borrowed, one of those pretty sky-blue uniforms, with two silver colonel epaulettes, which had shone seven years ago. Madame de Rênal wanted a new uniform, and she only had four days in which to send to Besançon and get from there the uniform, the arms, the hat, etc., everything necessary for a Guard of Honour. The most delightful part of it was that she thought it imprudent to get Julien's uniform made at Verrières. She wanted to surprise both him and the town.

Having settled the questions of the guards of honour, and of the public welcome finished, the mayor had now to organise a great religious ceremony. The King of —— did not wish to pass through Verrières without visiting the famous relic of St. Clement, which is kept at Bray-le-Haut barely a league from the town. The authorities wanted to have a numerous attendance of the clergy, but this matter was the most difficult to arrange. M. Maslon, the new curé, wanted to avoid at any price the presence of M. Chélan. It was in vain that M. de Rênal tried to represent to him that it would be imprudent to do so. M. the Marquis de La Mole whose ancestors had been governors of the province for so many generations, had been chosen to accompany the King of ——. He had known the abbé Chélan for thirty years. He would certainly ask news of him when he arrived at Verrières, and if he found him disgraced he was the very man to go and route him out in the little house to which he had retired, accompanied by all the escort that he had at his disposition. What a rebuff that would be?

"I shall be disgraced both here and at Besançon," answered the abbé Maslon, "if he appears among my clergy. A Jansenist, by the Lord."

"Whatever you can say, my dear abbé," replied M. de Rênal, "I'll never expose the administration of Verrières to receiving such an affront from M. de la Mole. You do not know him. He is orthodox enough at Court, but here in the provinces, he is a satirical wit and cynic, whose only object is to make people uncomfortable. He is capable of covering us with ridicule in the eyes of the Liberals, simply in order to amuse himself."

It was only on the night between the Saturday and the Sunday, after three whole days of negotiations that the pride of the abbé Maslon bent before the fear of the mayor, which was now changing into courage. It was necessary to write a honeyed letter to the abbé Chélan, begging him to be present at the ceremony in connection with the relic of Bray-le-Haut, if of course, his great age and his infirmity allowed him to do so. M. Chélan asked for and obtained a letter of invitation for Julien, who was to accompany him as his sub-deacon.

From the beginning of the Sunday morning, thousands of peasants began to arrive from the neighbouring mountains, and to inundate the streets of Verrières. It was the finest sunshine. Finally, about three o'clock, a thrill swept through all this crowd. A great fire had been perceived on a rock two leagues from Verrières. This signal announced that the king had just entered the territory of the department. At the same time, the sound of all the bells and the repeated volleys from an old Spanish cannon which belonged to the town, testified to its joy at this great event. Half the population climbed on to the roofs. All the women were on the balconies. The guard of honour started to march, The brilliant uniforms were universally admired; everybody recognised a relative or a friend. They made fun of the timidity of M. de Moirod, whose prudent hand was ready every single minute to catch hold of his saddle-bow. But one remark resulted in all the others being forgotten; the first cavalier in the ninth line was a very pretty, slim boy, who was not recognised at first. He soon created a general sensation, as some uttered a cry of indignation, and others were dumbfounded with astonishment. They recognised in this young man, who was sitting one of the Norman horses of M. Valenod, little Sorel, the carpenter's son. There was a unanimous out-cry against the mayor, above all on the part of the Liberals. What, because this little labourer, who masqueraded as an abbé, was tutor to his brats, he had the audacity to nominate him guard of honour to the prejudice of rich manufacturers like so-and-so and so-and-so! "Those gentlemen," said a banker's wife, "ought to put that insolent gutter-boy in his proper place."

"He is cunning and carries a sabre," answered her neighbour. "He would be dastardly enough to slash them in the face."

The conversation of aristocratic society was more dangerous. The ladies began to ask each other if the mayor alone was responsible for this grave impropriety. Speaking generally, they did justice to his contempt for lack of birth.

Julien was the happiest of men, while he was the subject of so much conversation. Bold by nature, he sat a horse better than the majority of the young men of this mountain town. He saw that, in the eyes of the women, he was the topic of interest.

His epaulettes were more brilliant than those of the others, because they were new. His horse pranced at every moment. He reached the zenith of joy.

His happiness was unbounded when, as they passed by the old rampart, the noise of the little cannon made his horse prance outside the line. By a great piece of luck he did not fall; from that moment he felt himself a hero. He was one of Napoleon's officers of artillery, and was charging a battery.

One person was happier than he. She had first seen him pass from one of the folding windows in the Hôtel de Ville. Then taking her carriage and rapidly making a long detour, she arrived in time to shudder when his horse took him outside the line. Finally she put her carriage to the gallop, left by another gate of the town, succeeded in rejoining the route by which the King was to pass, and was able to follow the Guard of Honour at twenty paces distance in the midst of a noble dust. Six thousand peasants cried "Long live the King," when the mayor had the honour to harangue his Majesty. An hour afterwards, when all the speeches had been listened to, and the King was going to enter the town, the little cannon began again to discharge its spasmodic volleys. But an accident ensued, the victim being, not one of the cannoneers who had proved their mettle at Leipsic and at Montreuil, but the future deputy-mayor, M. de Moirod. His horse gently laid him in the one heap of mud on the high road, a somewhat scandalous circumstance, inasmuch as it was necessary to extricate him to allow the King to pass. His Majesty alighted at the fine new church, which was decked out to-day with all its crimson curtains. The King was due to dine, and then afterwards take his carriage again and go and pay his respects to the celebrated relic of Saint Clement. Scarcely was the King in the church than Julien galloped towards the house of M. de Rênal. Once there he doffed with a sigh his fine sky-blue uniform, his sabre and his epaulettes, to put on again his shabby little black suit. He mounted his horse again, and in a few moments was at Bray-le-Haut, which was on the summit of a very pretty hill. "Enthusiasm is responsible for these numbers of peasants," thought Julien. It was impossible to move a step at Verrières, and here there were more than ten thousand round this ancient abbey. Half ruined by the vandalism of the Revolution, it had been magnificently restored since the Restoration, and people were already beginning to talk of miracles. Julien rejoined the abbé Chélan, who scolded him roundly and gave him a cassock and a surplice. He dressed quickly and followed M. Chélan, who was going to pay a call on the young bishop of Agde. He was a nephew of M. de la Mole, who had been recently nominated, and had been charged with the duty of showing the relic to the King. But the bishop was not to be found.

The clergy began to get impatient. It was awaiting its chief in the sombre Gothic cloister of the ancient abbey. Twenty-four curés had been brought together so as to represent the ancient chapter of Bray-le-Haut, which before 1789 consisted of twenty-four canons. The curés, having deplored the bishop's youth for three-quarters of an hour, thought it fitting for their senior to visit Monseigneur to apprise him that the King was on the point of arriving, and that it was time to betake himself to the choir. The great age of M. Chélan gave him the seniority. In spite of the bad temper which he was manifesting to Julien, he signed him to follow. Julien was wearing his surplice with distinction. By means of some trick or other of ecclesiastical dress, he had made his fine curling hair very flat, but by a forgetfulness, which redoubled the anger of M.

Chélan, the spurs of the Guard of Honour could be seen below the long folds of his cassock.

When they arrived at the bishop's apartment, the tall lackeys with their lace-frills scarcely deigned to answer the old curé to the effect that Monseigneur was not receiving. They made fun of him when he tried to explain that in his capacity of senior member of the chapter of Bray-le-Haut, he had the privilege of being admitted at any time to the officiating bishop.

Julien's haughty temper was shocked by the lackeys' insolence. He started to traverse the corridors of the ancient abbey, and to shake all the doors which he found. A very small one yielded to his efforts, and he found himself in a cell in the midst of Monseigneur's valets, who were dressed in black suits with chains on their necks. His hurried manner made these gentlemen think that he had been sent by the bishop, and they let him pass. He went some steps further on, and found himself in an immense Gothic hall, which was extremely dark, and completely wainscotted in black oak. The ogive windows had all been walled in with brick except one. There was nothing to disguise the coarseness of this masonry, which offered a melancholy contrast to the ancient magnificence of the woodwork. The two great sides of this hall, so celebrated among Burgundian antiquaries, and built by the Duke, Charles the Bold, about 1470 in expiation of some sin, were adorned with richly sculptured wooden stalls. All the mysteries of the Apocalypse were to be seen portrayed in wood of different colours.

This melancholy magnificence, debased as it was by the sight of the bare bricks and the plaster (which was still quite white) affected Julien. He stopped in silence. He saw at the other extremity of the hall, near the one window which let in the daylight, a movable mahogany mirror. A young man in a violet robe and a lace surplice, but with his head bare, was standing still three paces from the glass. This piece of furniture seemed strange in a place like this, and had doubtless been only brought there on the previous day. Julien thought that the young man had the appearance of being irritated. He was solemnly giving benedictions with his right hand close to the mirror.

"What can this mean," he thought. "Is this young priest performing some preliminary ceremony? Perhaps he is the bishop's secretary. He will be as insolent as the lackeys. Never mind though! Let us try." He advanced and traversed somewhat slowly the length of the hall, with his gaze fixed all the time on the one window, and looking at the young man who continued without any intermission bestowing slowly an infinite number of blessings.

The nearer he approached the better he could distinguish his angry manner. The richness of the lace surplice stopped Julien in spite of himself some paces in front of the mirror. "It is my duty to speak," he said to himself at last. But the beauty of the hall had moved him, and he was already upset by the harsh words he anticipated.

The young man saw him in the mirror, turned round, and suddenly discarding his angry manner, said to him in the gentlest tone,

"Well, Monsieur, has it been arranged at last?"

Julien was dumbfounded. As the young man began to turn towards him, Julien saw the pectoral cross on his breast. It was the bishop of Agde. "As young as that," thought Julien. "At most six or eight years older than I am!"

He was ashamed of his spurs.

"Monseigneur," he said at last, "I am sent by M. Chélan, the senior of the chapter."

"Ah, he has been well recommended to me," said the bishop in a polished tone which doubled Julien's delight, "But I beg your pardon, Monsieur, I mistook you for the person who was to bring me my mitre. It was badly packed at Paris. The silver cloth towards the top has been terribly spoiled. It will look awful," ended the young bishop sadly, "And besides, I am being kept waiting."

"Monseigneur, I will go and fetch the mitre if your grace will let me." Julien's fine eyes did their work.

"Go, Monsieur," answered the bishop, with charming politeness. "I need it immediately. I am grieved to keep the gentlemen of the chapter waiting."

When Julien reached the centre of the hall, he turned round towards the bishop, and saw that he had again commenced giving benedictions.

"What can it be?" Julien asked himself. "No doubt it is a necessary ecclesiastical preliminary for the ceremony which is to take place." When he reached the cell in which the valets were congregated, he saw the mitre in their hands. These gentlemen succumbed in spite of themselves to his imperious look, and gave him Monseigneur's mitre.

He felt proud to carry it. As he crossed the hall he walked slowly. He held it with reverence. He found the bishop seated before the glass, but from time to time, his right hand, although fatigued, still gave a blessing. Julien helped him to adjust his mitre. The bishop shook his head.

"Ah! it will keep on," he said to Julien with an air of satisfaction. "Do you mind going a little way off?"

Then the bishop went very quickly to the centre of the room, then approached the mirror, again resumed his angry manner, and gravely began to give blessings.

Julien was motionless with astonishment. He was tempted to understand, but did not dare. The bishop stopped, and suddenly abandoning his grave manner looked at him and said:

"What do you think of my mitre, monsieur, is it on right?"

"Quite right, Monseigneur."

"It is not too far back? That would look a little silly, but I mustn't on the other hand wear it down over the eyes like an officer's shako."

"It seems to me to be on quite right."

"The King of —— is accustomed to a venerable clergy who are doubtless very solemn. I should not like to appear lacking in dignity, especially by reason of my youth."

And the bishop started again to walk about and give benedictions.

"It is quite clear," said Julien, daring to understand at last, "He is practising giving his benediction."

"I am ready," the bishop said after a few moments. "Go, Monsieur, and advise the senior and the gentlemen of the chapter."

Soon M. Chélan, followed by the two oldest curés, entered by a big magnificently sculptured door, which Julien had not previously noticed. But this time he remained in his place quite at the back, and was only able to see the bishop over the shoulders of ecclesiastics who were pressing at the door in crowds.

The bishop began slowly to traverse the hall. When he reached the threshold, the curés formed themselves into a procession. After a short moment of confusion, the procession began to march intoning the psalm. The bishop, who was between M. Chélan and a very old curé, was the last to advance. Julien being in attendance on the abbé Chélan managed to get quite near Monseigneur. They followed the long corridors of the abbey of Bray-le-Haut. In spite of the brilliant sun they were dark and damp. They arrived finally at the portico of the cloister. Julien was dumbfounded with admiration for so fine a ceremony. His emotions were divided between thoughts of his own ambition which had been reawakened by the bishop's youth and thoughts of the latter's refinement and exquisite politeness. This politeness was quite different to that of M. de Rênal, even on his good days. "The higher you lift yourself towards the first rank of society," said Julien to himself, "the more charming manners you find."

They entered the church by a side door; suddenly an awful noise made the ancient walls echo. Julien thought they were going to crumble. It was the little piece of artillery again. It had been drawn at a gallop by eight horses and had just arrived. Immediately on its arrival it had been run out by the Leipsic cannoneers and fired five shots a minute as though the Prussians had been the target.

But this admirable noise no longer produced any effect on Julien. He no longer thought of Napoleon and military glory. "To be bishop of Agde so young," he thought. "But where is Agde? How much does it bring in? Two or three hundred thousand francs, perhaps."

Monseigneur's lackeys appeared with a magnificent canopy. M. Chélan took one of the poles, but as a matter of fact it was Julien who carried it. The bishop took his place underneath. He had really succeeded in looking old; and our hero's admiration was now quite unbounded. "What can't one accomplish with skill," he thought.

The king entered. Julien had the good fortune to see him at close quarters. The bishop began to harangue him with unction, without forgetting a little nuance of very polite anxiety for his Majesty. We will not repeat a description of the ceremony of Bray-le-Haut. They filled all the columns of the journals of the department for a fortnight on end. Julien learnt from the bishop that the king was descended from Charles the Bold.

At a later date, it was one of Julien's duties to check the accounts of the cost of this ceremony. M. de la Mole, who had succeeded in procuring a bishopric for his nephew, had wished to do him the favour of being himself responsible for all the expenses. The ceremony alone of Bray-le-Haute cost three thousand eight hundred francs.

After the speech of the bishop, and the answer of the king, his Majesty took up a position underneath the canopy, and then knelt very devoutly on a cushion near the altar. The choir was surrounded by stalls, and the stalls were raised two steps from the pavement. It was at the bottom of these steps that Julien sat at the feet of M. de Chélan almost like a train-bearer sitting next to his cardinal in the Sixtine chapel at Rome. There was a *Te Deum*, floods of incense, innumerable volleys of musketry and artillery; the peasants were drunk with happiness and piety. A day like this undoes the work of a hundred numbers of the Jacobin papers.

Julien was six paces from the king, who was really praying with devotion. He noticed for the first time a little man with a witty expression, who wore an almost plain suit. But he had a sky-blue ribbon over this very simple suit. He was nearer the king than many other lords, whose clothes were embroidered with gold to such an extent that, to use Julien's expression, it was impossible to see the cloth. He learnt some minutes later that it was Monsieur de la Mole. He thought he looked haughty, and even insolent.

"I'm sure this marquis is not so polite as my pretty bishop," he thought. "Ah, the ecclesiastical calling makes men mild and good. But the king has come to venerate the relic, and I don't see a trace of the relic. Where has Saint Clement got to?"

A little priest who sat next to him informed him that the venerable relic was at the top of the building in a *chapelle ardente*.

"What is a *chapelle ardente*," said Julien to himself.

But he was reluctant to ask the meaning of this word. He redoubled his attention.

The etiquette on the occasion of a visit of a sovereign prince is that the canons do not accompany the bishop. But, as he started on his march to the *chapelle ardente,* my lord bishop of Agde called the abbé Chélan. Julien dared to follow him. Having climbed up a long staircase, they reached an extremely small door whose Gothic frame was magnificently gilded. This work looked as though it had been constructed the day before.

Twenty-four young girls belonging to the most distinguished families in Verrières were assembled in front of the door. The bishop knelt down in the midst of these pretty maidens before he opened the door. While he was praying aloud, they seemed unable to exhaust their admiration for his fine lace, his gracious mien, and his young and gentle face. This spectacle deprived our hero of his last remnants of reason. At this moment he would have fought for the Inquisition, and with a good conscience. The door suddenly opened. The little chapel was blazing with light. More than a thousand candles could be seen before the altar, divided into eight lines and separated from each other by bouquets of flowers. The suave odour of the purest incense eddied out from the door of the sanctuary. The chapel, which had been newly gilded, was extremely small but very high. Julien noticed that there were candles more than fifteen feet high upon the altar. The young girls could not restrain a cry of admiration. Only the twenty-four young girls, the two curés and Julien had been admitted into the little vestibule of the chapel. Soon the king arrived, followed by Monsieur de la Mole and his great Chamberlain. The guards themselves remained outside kneeling and presenting arms.

His Majesty precipitated, rather than threw himself, on to the stool. It was only then that Julien, who was keeping close to the gilded door, perceived over the bare arm of a young girl, the charming statue of St. Clement. It was hidden under the altar, and bore the dress of a young Roman soldier. It had a large wound on its neck, from which the blood seemed to flow. The artist had surpassed himself. The eyes, which though dying were full of grace, were half closed. A budding moustache adored that charming mouth which, though half closed, seemed notwithstanding to be praying. The young girl next to Julien wept warm tears at the sight. One of her tears fell on Julien's hand.

After a moment of prayer in the profoundest silence, that was only broken by the distant sound of the bells of all the villages within a radius of ten leagues, the bishop of Agde asked the king's permission to speak. He finished a short but very touching speech with a passage, the very simplicity of which assured its effectiveness:

"Never forget, young Christian women, that you have seen one of the greatest kings of the world on his knees before the servants of this

Almighty and terrible God. These servants, feeble, persecuted, assassinated as they were on earth, as you can see by the still bleeding wounds of Saint Clement, will triumph in Heaven. You will remember them, my young Christian women, will you not, this day for ever, and will detest the infidel. You will be for ever faithful to this God who is so great, so terrible, but so good?"

With these words the bishop rose authoritatively.

"You promise me?" he said, lifting up his arm with an inspired air.

"We promise," said the young girls melting into tears.

"I accept your promise in the name of the terrible God," added the bishop in a thunderous voice, and the ceremony was at an end.

The king himself was crying. It was only a long time afterwards that Julien had sufficient self-possession to enquire "where were the bones of the Saint that had been sent from Rome to Philip the Good, Duke of Burgundy?" He was told that they were hidden in the charming waxen figure.

His Majesty deigned to allow the young ladies who had accompanied him into the chapel to wear a red ribbon on which were embroidered these words, "HATE OF THE INFIDEL. PERPETUAL ADORATION."

Monsieur de la Mole had ten thousand bottles of wine distributed among the peasants. In the evening at Verrières, the Liberals made a point of having illuminations which were a hundred times better than those of the Royalists. Before leaving, the king paid a visit to M. de Moirod.

XIX
THINKING PRODUCES SUFFERING

> The grotesqueness of every-day events conceals the real
> unhappiness of the passions.—*Barnave.*

As he was replacing the usual furniture in the room which M. de la Mole had occupied, Julien found a piece of very strong paper folded in four. He read at the bottom of the first page "To His Excellency M. le Marquis de la Mole, peer of France, Chevalier of the Orders of the King, etc. etc." It was a petition in the rough hand-writing of a cook.

"Monsieur le Marquis, I have had religious principles all my life. I was in Lyons exposed to the bombs at the time of the siege, in '93 of execrable memory. I communicate, I go to Mass every Sunday in the parochial church. I have never missed the paschal duty, even in '93 of execrable memory. My cook used to keep servants before the revolution, my cook fasts on Fridays. I am universally respected in Verrières, and I venture

THINKING PRODUCES SUFFERING

to say I deserve to be so. I walk under the canopy in the processions at the side of the curé and of the mayor. On great occasions I carry a big candle, bought at my own expense.

"I ask Monsieur the marquis for the lottery appointment of Verrières, which in one way or another is bound to be vacant shortly as the beneficiary is very ill, and moreover votes on the wrong side at elections, etc.

De Cholin."

In the margin of this petition was a recommendation signed "de Moirod" which began with this line, "I have had the honour, the worthy person who makes this request."

"So even that imbecile de Cholin shows me the way to go about things," said Julien to himself.

Eight days after the passage of the King of —— through Verrières, the one question which predominated over the innumerable falsehoods, foolish conjectures, and ridiculous discussions, etc., etc., which had had successively for their object the king, the Marquis de la Mole, the ten thousand bottles of wine, the fall of poor de Moirod, who, hoping to win a cross, only left his room a week after his fall, was the absolute indecency of having *foisted* Julien Sorel, a carpenter's son, into the Guard of Honour. You should have heard on this point the rich manufacturers of printed calico, the very persons who used to bawl themselves hoarse in preaching equality, morning and evening in the café. That haughty woman, Madame de Rênal, was of course responsible for this abomination. The reason? The fine eyes and fresh complexion of the little abbé Sorel explained everything else.

A short time after their return to Vergy, Stanislas, the youngest of the children, caught the fever; Madame de Rênal was suddenly attacked by an awful remorse. For the first time she reproached herself for her love with some logic. She seemed to understand as though by a miracle the enormity of the sin into which she had let herself be swept. Up to that moment, although deeply religious, she had never thought of the greatness of her crime in the eyes of God.

In former times she had loved God passionately in the Convent of the Sacred Heart; in the present circumstances, she feared him with equal intensity. The struggles which lacerated her soul were all the more awful in that her fear was quite irrational. Julien found that the least argument irritated instead of soothing her. She saw in the illness the language of hell. Moreover, Julien was himself very fond of the little Stanislas.

It soon assumed a serious character. Then incessant remorse deprived Madame de Rênal of even her power of sleep. She ensconced herself in a gloomy silence: if she had opened her mouth, it would only have been to confess her crime to God and mankind.

"I urge you," said Julien to her, as soon as they got alone, "not to speak to anyone. Let me be the sole confidant of your sufferings. If you still love me, do not speak. Your words will not be able to take away our Stanislas' fever." But his consolations produced no effect. He did not know that Madame de Rênal had got it into her head that, in order to appease the wrath of a jealous God, it was necessary either to hate Julien, or let her son die. It was because she felt she could not hate her lover that she was so unhappy.

"Fly from me," she said one day to Julien. "In the name of God leave this house. It is your presence here which kills my son. God punishes me," she added in a low voice. "He is just. I admire his fairness. My crime is awful, and I was living without remorse," she exclaimed. "That was the first sign of my desertion of God: I ought to be doubly punished."

Julien was profoundly touched. He could see in this neither hypocrisy nor exaggeration. "She thinks that she is killing her son by loving me, and all the same the unhappy woman loves me more than her son. I cannot doubt it. It is remorse for that which is killing her. Those sentiments of hers have real greatness. But how could I have inspired such a love, I who am so poor, so badly-educated, so ignorant, and sometimes so coarse in my manners?"

One night the child was extremely ill. At about two o'clock in the morning, M. de Rênal came to see it. The child consumed by fever, and extremely flushed, could not recognise its father. Suddenly Madame de Rênal threw herself at her husband's feet; Julien saw that she was going to confess everything and ruin herself for ever.

Fortunately this extraordinary proceeding annoyed M. de Rênal.

"Adieu! Adieu!" he said, going away.

"No, listen to me," cried his wife on her knees before him, trying to hold him back. "Hear the whole truth. It is I who am killing my son. I gave him life, and I am taking it back. Heaven is punishing me. In the eyes of God I am guilty of murder. It is necessary that I should ruin and humiliate myself. Perhaps that sacrifice will appease the Lord."

If M. de Rênal had been a man of any imagination, he would then have realized everything.

"Romantic nonsense," he cried, moving his wife away as she tried to embrace his knees. "All that is romantic nonsense! Julien, go and fetch the doctor at daybreak," and he went back to bed. Madame de Rênal fell on her knees half-fainting, repelling Julien's help with a hysterical gesture.

Julien was astonished.

"So this is what adultery is," he said to himself. "Is it possible that those scoundrels of priests should be right, that they who commit so many sins themselves should have the privilege of knowing the true theory of sin? How droll!"

For twenty minutes after M. de Rênal had gone back to bed, Julien saw the woman he loved with her head resting on her son's little bed, motionless, and almost unconscious. "There," he said to himself, "is a woman of superior temperament brought to the depths of unhappiness simply because she has known me."

"Time moves quickly. What can I do for her? I must make up my mind. I have not got simply myself to consider now. What do I care for men and their buffooneries? What can I do for her? Leave her? But I should be leaving her alone and a prey to the most awful grief. That automaton of a husband is more harm to her than good. He is so coarse that he is bound to speak harshly to her. She may go mad and throw herself out of the window."

"If I leave her, if I cease to watch over her, she will confess everything, and who knows, in spite of the legacy which she is bound to bring him, he will create a scandal. She may confess everything (great God) to that scoundrel of an abbé who makes the illness of a child of six an excuse for not budging from this house, and not without a purpose either. In her grief and her fear of God, she forgets all she knows of the man; she only sees the priest."

"Go away," said Madame de Rênal suddenly to him, opening her eyes.

"I would give my life a thousand times to know what could be of most use to you," answered Julien. "I have never loved you so much, my dear angel, or rather it is only from this last moment that I begin to adore you as you deserve to be adored. What would become of me far from you, and with the consciousness that you are unhappy owing to what I have done? But don't let my suffering come into the matter. I will go—yes, my love! But if I leave you, dear; if I cease to watch over you, to be incessantly between you and your husband, you will tell him everything. You will ruin yourself. Remember that he will hound you out of his house in disgrace. Besançon will talk of the scandal. You will be said to be absolutely in the wrong. You will never lift up your head again after that shame."

"That's what I ask," she cried, standing up. "I shall suffer, so much the better."

"But you will also make him unhappy through that awful scandal."

"But I shall be humiliating myself, throwing myself into the mire, and by those means, perhaps, I shall save my son. Such a humiliation in the eyes of all is perhaps to be regarded as a public penitence. So far as my weak judgment goes, is it not the greatest sacrifice that I can make to God?—perhaps He will deign to accept my humiliation, and to leave me my son. Show me another sacrifice which is more painful and I will rush to it."

"Let me punish myself. I too am guilty. Do you wish me to retire to the Trappist Monastery? The austerity of that life may appease your God. Oh, heaven, why cannot I take Stanislas's illness upon myself?"

"Ah, do you love him then," said Madame de Rênal, getting up and throwing herself in his arms.

At the same time she repelled him with horror.

"I believe you! I believe you! Oh, my one friend," she cried falling on her knees again. "Why are you not the father of Stanislas? In that case it would not be a terrible sin to love you more than your son."

"Won't you allow me to stay and love you henceforth like a brother? It is the only rational atonement. It may appease the wrath of the Most High."

"Am I," she cried, getting up and taking Julien's head between her two hands, and holding it some distance from her. "Am I to love you as if you were a brother? Is it in my power to love you like that?" Julien melted into tears.

"I will obey you," he said, falling at her feet. "I will obey you in whatever you order me. That is all there is left for me to do. My mind is struck with blindness. I do not see any course to take. If I leave you you will tell your husband everything. You will ruin yourself and him as well. He will never be nominated deputy after incurring such ridicule. If I stay, you will think I am the cause of your son's death, and you will die of grief. Do you wish to try the effect of my departure. If you wish, I will punish myself for our sin by leaving you for eight days. I will pass them in any retreat you like. In the abbey of Bray-le-Haut, for instance. But swear that you will say nothing to your husband during my absence. Remember that if you speak I shall never be able to come back."

She promised and he left, but was called back at the end of two days.

"It is impossible for me to keep my oath without you. I shall speak to my husband if you are not constantly there to enjoin me to silence by your looks. Every hour of this abominable life seems to last a day."

Finally heaven had pity on this unfortunate mother. Little by little Stanislas got out of danger. But the ice was broken. Her reason had realised the extent of her sin. She could not recover her equilibrium again. Her pangs of remorse remained, and were what they ought to have been in so sincere a heart. Her life was heaven and hell: hell when she did not see Julien; heaven when she was at his feet.

"I do not deceive myself any more," she would say to him, even during the moments when she dared to surrender herself to his full love. "I am damned, irrevocably damned. You are young, heaven may forgive you, but I, I am damned. I know it by a certain sign. I am afraid, who would not be afraid at the sight of hell? but at the bottom of my heart I do not repent at all. I would commit my sin over again if I had the opportunity. If heaven will only forbear to punish me in this world and through my children, I shall have more than I deserve. But you, at any rate, my Julien," she would cry at other moments, "are you happy? Do you think I love you enough?"

The suspiciousness and morbid pride of Julien, who needed, above all, a self-sacrificing love, altogether vanished when he saw at every hour of the day so great and indisputable a sacrifice. He adored Madame de Rênal. "It makes no difference her being noble, and my being a labourer's son. She loves me.... she does not regard me as a valet charged with the functions of a lover." That fear once dismissed, Julien fell into all the madness of love, into all its deadly uncertainties.

"At any rate," she would cry, seeing his doubts of her love, "let me feel quite happy during the three days we still have together. Let us make haste; perhaps to-morrow will be too late. If heaven strikes me through my children, it will be in vain that I shall try only to live to love you, and to be blind to the fact that it is my crime which has killed them. I could not survive that blow. Even if I wished I could not; I should go mad."

"Ah, if only I could take your sin on myself as you so generously offered to take Stanislas' burning fever!"

This great moral crisis changed the character of the sentiment which united Julien and his mistress. His love was no longer simply admiration for her beauty, and the pride of possessing her.

Henceforth their happiness was of a quite superior character. The flame which consumed them was more intense. They had transports filled with madness. Judged by the worldly standard their happiness would have appeared intensified. But they no longer found that delicious serenity, that cloudless happiness, that facile joy of the first period of their love, when Madame de Rênal's only fear was that Julien did not love her enough. Their happiness had at times the complexion of crime.

In their happiest and apparently their most tranquil moments, Madame de Rênal would suddenly cry out, "Oh, great God, I see hell," as she pressed Julien's hand with a convulsive grasp. "What horrible tortures! I have well deserved them." She grasped him and hung on to him like ivy onto a wall.

Julien would try in vain to calm that agitated soul. She would take his hand, cover it with kisses. Then, relapsing into a gloomy reverie, she would say, "Hell itself would be a blessing for me. I should still have some days to pass with him on this earth, but hell on earth, the death of my children. Still, perhaps my crime will be forgiven me at that price. Oh, great God, do not grant me my pardon at so great a price. These poor children have in no way transgressed against You. I, I am the only culprit. I love a man who is not my husband."

Julien subsequently saw Madame de Rênal attain what were apparently moments of tranquillity. She was endeavouring to control herself; she did not wish to poison the life of the man she loved. They found the days pass with the rapidity of lightning amid these alternating moods of love, remorse, and voluptuousness. Julien lost the habit of reflecting.

Mademoiselle Elisa went to attend to a little lawsuit which she had at Verrières. She found Valenod very piqued against Julien. She hated the tutor and would often speak about him.

"You will ruin me, Monsieur, if I tell the truth," she said one day to Valenod. "All masters have an understanding amongst themselves with regard to matters of importance. There are certain disclosures which poor servants are never forgiven."

After these stereotyped phrases, which his curiosity managed to cut short, Monsieur Valenod received some information extremely mortifying to his self-conceit.

This woman, who was the most distinguished in the district, the woman on whom he had lavished so much attention in the last six years, and made no secret of it, more was the pity, this woman who was so proud, whose disdain had put him to the blush times without number, had just taken for her lover a little workman masquerading as a tutor. And to fill the cup of his jealousy, Madame de Rênal adored that lover.

"And," added the housemaid with a sigh, "Julien did not put himself out at all to make his conquest, his manner was as cold as ever, even with Madame."

Elisa had only become certain in the country, but she believed that this intrigue dated from much further back. "That is no doubt the reason," she added spitefully, "why he refused to marry me. And to think what a fool I was when I went to consult Madame de Rênal and begged her to speak to the tutor."

The very same evening, M. de Rênal received from the town, together with his paper, a long anonymous letter which apprised him in the greatest detail of what was taking place in his house. Julien saw him pale as he read this letter written on blue paper, and look at him with a malicious expression. During all that evening the mayor failed to throw off his trouble. It was in vain that Julien paid him court by asking for explanations about the genealogy of the best families in Burgundy.

XX
ANONYMOUS LETTERS

Do not give dalliance
Too much the rein; the strongest oaths are straw
To the fire i' the blood.—*Tempest.*

As they left the drawing-room about midnight, Julien had time to say to his love,

"Don't let us see each other to-night. Your husband has suspicions. I would swear that that big letter he read with a sigh was an anonymous letter."

Fortunately, Julien locked himself into his room. Madame de Rênal had the mad idea that this warning was only a pretext for not seeing her. She absolutely lost her head, and came to his door at the accustomed hour. Julien, who had heard the noise in the corridor, immediately blew out his lamp. Someone was trying to open the door. Was it Madame de Rênal? Was it a jealous husband?

Very early next morning the cook, who liked Julien, brought him a book, on the cover of which he read these words written in Italian: *Guardate alla pagina* 130.

Julien shuddered at the imprudence, looked for page 130, and found pinned to it the following letter hastily written, bathed with tears, and full of spelling mistakes. Madame de Rênal was usually very correct. He was touched by this circumstance, and somewhat forgot the awfulness of the indiscretion.

"So you did not want to receive me to-night? There are moments when I think that I have never read down to the depths of your soul. Your looks frighten me. I am afraid of you. Great God! perhaps you have never loved me? In that case let my husband discover my love, and shut me up in a prison in the country far away from my children. Perhaps God wills it so. I shall die soon, but you will have proved yourself a monster.

"Do you not love me? Are you tired of my fits of folly and of remorse, you wicked man? Do you wish to ruin me? I will show you an easy way. Go and show this letter to all Verrières, or rather show it to M. Valenod. Tell him that I love you, nay, do not utter such a blasphemy, tell him I adore you, that it was only on the day I saw you that my life commenced; that even in the maddest moments of my youth I never even dreamt of the happiness that I owe to you, that I have sacrificed my life to you and that I am sacrificing my soul. You know that I am sacrificing much more. But does that man know the meaning of sacrifice? Tell him, I say, simply to irritate him, that I will defy all evil tongues, that the only misfortune for me in the whole world would be to witness any change in the only man who holds me to life. What a happiness it would be to me to lose my life, to offer it up as a sacrifice and to have no longer any fear for my children.

"Have no doubt about it, dear one, if it is an anonymous letter, it comes from that odious being who has persecuted me for the last six years with his loud voice, his stories about his jumps on horseback, his fatuity, and the never ending catalogue of all his advantages.

"Is there an anonymous letter? I should like to discuss that question with you, you wicked man; but no, you acted rightly. Clasping you in my arms perhaps for the last time, I should never have been able to argue as coldly as I do, now that I am alone. From this moment our happiness will no longer be so easy. Will that be a vexation for you? Yes, on those days when you haven't received some amusing book from M. Fouqué. The sacrifice is made; to-morrow, whether there is or whether there is not any anonymous letter, I myself will tell my husband I have received an anonymous letter and that it is necessary to give you a golden bridge at once, find some honourable excuse, and send you back to your parents without delay.

"Alas, dear one, we are going to be separated for a fortnight, perhaps a month! Go, I will do you justice, you will suffer as much as I, but anyway, this is the only means of disposing of this anonymous letter. It is not the first that my husband has received, and on my score too. Alas! how I used to laugh over them!

"My one aim is to make my husband think that the letter comes from M. Valenod; I have no doubt that he is its author. If you leave the house, make a point of establishing yourself at Verrières; I will manage that my husband should think of passing a fortnight there in order to prove to the fools there was no coldness between him and me. Once at Verrières, establish ties of friendship with everyone, even with the Liberals. I am sure that all their ladies will seek you out.

"Do not quarrel with M. Valenod, or cut off his ears, as you said you would one day. Try, on the contrary, to ingratiate yourself with him. The essential point is that it should be notorious in Verrières that you are going to enter the household either of Valenod or of someone else to take charge of the children's education.

"That is what my husband will never put up with. If he does feel bound to resign himself to it, well, at any rate, you will be living in Verrières and I shall be seeing you sometimes. My children, who love you so much, will go and see you. Great God! I feel that I love my children all the more because they love you. How is all this going to end? I am wandering.... Anyway you understand your line of conduct. Be nice, polite, but not in any way disdainful to those coarse persons. I ask you on my knees; they will be the arbiters of our fate. Do not fear for a moment but that, so far as you are concerned, my husband will conform to what public opinion lays down for him.

"It is you who will supply me with the anonymous letter. Equip yourself with patience and a pair of scissors, cut out from a book the words which you will see, then stick them with the mouth-glue on to the leaf of loose paper which I am sending you. It comes to me from M. Valenod. Be on your guard against a search in your room; burn the pages of the book which you are going to mutilate. If you do not find the words ready-made, have the patience to form them letter by letter. I have made the anonymous letter too short.

ANONYMOUS LETTER.

> 'MADAME,
>
> All your little goings-on are known, but the persons interested in stopping have been warned. I have still sufficient friendship left for you to urge you to cease all relations with the little peasant. If you are sensible enough to do this, your husband will believe that the notification he has received is misleading, and he will be left in his illusion. Remember that I have your secret; tremble, unhappy woman, you must now *walk straight* before me.'

"As soon as you have finished glueing together the words that make up this letter (have you recognised the director's special style of speech) leave the house, I will meet you.

"I will go into the village and come back with a troubled face. As a matter of fact I shall be very much troubled. Great God! What a risk I run, and all because you thought you guessed an anonymous letter. Finally, looking very much upset, I shall give this letter to my husband and say that an unknown man handed it to me. As for you, go for a walk with the children, on the road to the great woods, and do not come back before dinner-time.

"You will be able to see the tower of the dovecot from the top of the rocks. If things go well for us, I will place a white handkerchief there, in case of the contrary, there will be nothing at all.

"Ungrateful man, will not your heart find out some means of telling me that you love me before you leave for that walk. Whatever happens, be certain of one thing: I shall never survive our final separation by a single day. Oh, you bad mother! but what is the use of my writing those two words, dear Julien? I do not feel them, at this moment I can only think of you. I have only written them so as not to be blamed by you, but what is the good of deception now that I find myself face to face with losing you? Yes, let my soul seem monstrous to you, but do not let me lie to the man whom I adore. I have already deceived only too much in this life of mine. Go! I forgive you if you love me no more. I have not the time to read over my letter. It is a small thing in my eyes to pay for the happy days that I have just passed in your arms with the price of my life. You know that they will cost me more."

XXI
DIALOGUE WITH A MASTER

Alas, our frailty is the cause, not we;
For such as we are made of, such we be.—*Twelfth Night*.

It was with a childish pleasure that for a whole hour Julien put the words together. As he came out of his room, he met his pupils with their mother. She took the letter with a simplicity and a courage whose calmness terrified him.

"Is the mouth-glue dry enough yet?" she asked him.

"And is this the woman who was so maddened by remorse?" he thought. "What are her plans at this moment?" He was too proud to ask her, but she had never perhaps pleased him more.

"If this turns out badly," she added with the same coolness, "I shall be deprived of everything. Take charge of this, and bury it in some place of the mountain. It will perhaps one day be my only resource."

She gave him a glass case in red morocco filled with gold and some diamonds.

"Now go," she said to him.

She kissed the children, embracing the youngest twice. Julien remained motionless. She left him at a rapid pace without looking at him.

From the moment that M. de Rênal had opened the anonymous letter his life had been awful. He had not been so agitated since a duel which he had just missed having in 1816, and to do him justice, the prospect of receiving a bullet would have made him less unhappy. He scrutinised the letter from every standpoint. "Is that not a woman's handwriting?" he said to himself. In that case, what woman had written it? He reviewed all those whom he knew at Verrières without being able to fix his suspicions on any one. Could a man have dictated that letter? Who was that man? Equal uncertainty on this point. The majority of his acquaintances were jealous of him, and, no doubt, hated him. "I must consult my wife," he said to himself through habit, as he got up from the arm-chair in which he had collapsed.

"Great God!" he said aloud before he got up, striking his head, "it is she above all of whom I must be distrustful. At the present moment she is my enemy," and tears came into his eyes through sheer anger.

By a poetic justice for that hardness of heart which constitutes the provincial idea of shrewdness, the two men whom M. de Rênal feared the most at the present moment were his two most intimate friends.

"I have ten friends perhaps after those," and he passed them in review, gauging the degree of consolation which he could get from each one. "All of them, all of them," he exclaimed in a rage, "will derive the most supreme pleasure from my awful experience."

As luck would have it, he thought himself envied, and not without reason. Apart from his superb town mansion in which the king of — — had recently spent the night, and thus conferred on it an enduring honour, he had decorated his chateau at Vergy extremely well. The façade was painted white and the windows adorned with fine green shutters. He was consoled for a moment by the thought of this magnificence. The fact was that this château was seen from three or four leagues off, to the great prejudice of all the country houses or so-called châteaux of the neighbourhood, which had been left in the humble grey colour given them by time.

There was one of his friends on whose pity and whose tears M. de Rênal could count, the churchwarden of the parish; but he was an idiot who cried at everything. This man, however, was his only resource. "What unhappiness is comparable to mine," he exclaimed with rage. "What isolation!"

"Is it possible?" said this truly pitiable man to himself. "Is it possible that I have no friend in my misfortune of whom I can ask advice? for my mind is wandering, I feel it. Oh, Falcoz! oh, Ducros!" he exclaimed with bitterness. Those were the names of two friends of his childhood whom he had dropped owing to his snobbery in 1814. They were not noble, and he had wished to change the footing of equality on which they had been living with him since their childhood.

One of them, Falcoz, a paper-merchant of Verrières, and a man of intellect and spirit, had bought a printing press in the chief town of the department and undertaken the production of a journal. The priestly congregation had resolved to ruin him; his journal had been condemned, and he had been deprived of his printer's diploma. In these sad circumstances he ventured to write to M. de Rênal for the first time for ten years. The mayor of Verrières thought it his duty to answer in the old Roman style: "If the King's Minister were to do me the honour of consulting me, I should say to him, ruin ruthlessly all the provincial printers, and make printing a monopoly like tobacco." M. de Rênal was horrified to remember the terms of this letter to an intimate friend whom all Verrières had once admired, "Who would have said that I, with my rank, my fortune, my decorations, would ever come to regret it?" It was in these transports of rage, directed now against himself, now against all his surroundings, that he passed an awful night; but, fortunately, it never occurred to him to spy on his wife.

"I am accustomed to Louise," he said to himself, "she knows all my affairs. If I were free to marry to-morrow, I should not find anyone to take her place." Then he began to plume himself on the idea that his wife was innocent. This point of view did not require any manifestation of character, and suited him much better. "How many calumniated women has one not seen?"

"But," he suddenly exclaimed, as he walked about feverishly, "shall I put up with her making a fool of me with her lover as though I were a man of no account, some mere ragamuffin? Is all Verrières to make merry over my complaisance? What have they not said about Charmier (he was a husband in the district who was notoriously deceived)? Was there not a smile on every lip at the mention of his name? He is a good advocate, but whoever said anything about his talent for speaking? 'Oh, Charmier,' they say, 'Bernard's Charmier,' he is thus designated by the name of the man who disgraces him."

"I have no daughter, thank heaven," M. de Rênal would say at other times, "and the way in which I am going to punish the mother will consequently not be so harmful to my children's household. I could surprise this little peasant with my wife and kill them both; in that case the tragedy of the situation would perhaps do away with the grotesque element." This idea appealed to him. He followed it up in all its details. "The penal code is on my side, and whatever happens our congregation and my friends on the jury will save me." He examined his hunting-knife which was quite sharp, but the idea of blood frightened him.

"I could thrash this insolent tutor within an inch of his life and hound him out of the house; but what a sensation that would make in Verrières and even over the whole department! After Falcoz' journal had been condemned, and when its chief editor left prison, I had a hand in making him lose his place of six hundred francs a year. They say that this scribbler has dared to show himself again in Besançon. He may lampoon me adroitly and in such a way that it will be impossible to bring him up before the courts. Bring him up before the courts! The insolent wretch will insinuate in a thousand and one ways that he has spoken the truth. A well-born man who keeps his place like I do, is hated by all the plebeians. I shall see my name in all those awful Paris papers. Oh, my God, what depths. To see the ancient name of Rênal plunged in the mire of ridicule. If I ever travel I shall have to change my name. What! abandon that name which is my glory and my strength. Could anything be worse than that?

"If I do not kill my wife but turn her out in disgrace, she has her aunt in Besançon who is going to hand all her fortune over to her. My wife will go and live in Paris with Julien. It will be known at Verrières, and I shall be taken for a dupe." The unhappy man then noticed from the paleness of the lamplight that the dawn was beginning to appear. He went to get a little fresh air in the garden. At this moment he had almost determined to make no scandal, particularly in view of the fact that a scandal would overwhelm with joy all his good friends in Verrières.

The promenade in the garden calmed him a little. "No," he exclaimed, "I shall not deprive myself of my wife, she is too useful to me." He imagined with horror what his house would be without his wife. The only relative he had was the Marquise of R—— old, stupid, and malicious.

A very sensible idea occurred to him, but its execution required a strength of character considerably superior to the small amount of character which the poor man possessed. "If I keep my wife," he said to himself, "I know what I shall do one day; on some occasion when she makes me lose patience, I shall reproach her with her guilt. She is proud, we shall quarrel, and all this will happen before she has inherited her aunt's fortune. And how they will all make fun of me then! My wife loves her children, the result will be that everything will go to them. But as for me, I shall be the laughing-stock of Verrières. 'What,' they will say, 'he could not even manage to revenge himself on his wife!' Would it not be better to leave it and verify nothing? In that case I tie my hands, and cannot afterwards reproach her with anything."

An instant afterwards M. de Rênal, once more a prey to wounded vanity, set himself laboriously to recollect all the methods of procedure mentioned in the billiard-room of the *Casino* or the *Nobles' Club* in Verrières, when some fine talker interrupted the pool to divert himself at the expense of some deceived husband. How cruel these pleasantries appeared to him at the present moment!

"My God, why is my wife not dead! then I should be impregnable against ridicule. Why am I not a widower? I should go and pass six months in Paris in the best society. After this moment of happiness occasioned by the idea of widowerhood, his imagination reverted to the means of assuring himself of the truth. Should he put a slight layer of bran before the door of Julien's room at midnight after everyone had gone to bed? He would see the impression of the feet in the following morning.

"But that's no good," he suddenly exclaimed with rage. "That inquisitive Elisa will notice it, and they will soon know all over the house that I am jealous."

In another *Casino* tale a husband had assured himself of his misfortune by tying a hair with a little wax so that it shut the door of the gallant as effectually as a seal.

After so many hours of uncertainty this means of clearing up his fate seemed to him emphatically the best, and he was thinking of availing himself of it when, in one of the turnings of the avenue he met the very woman whom he would like to have seen dead. She was coming back from the village. She had gone to hear mass in the church of Vergy. A tradition, extremely doubtful in the eyes of the cold philosopher, but in which she believed, alleges that the little church was once the chapel of the château of the Lord of Vergy. This idea obsessed Madame de Rênal all the time in the church that she had counted on spending in prayer. She kept on imagining to herself the spectacle of her husband killing Julien when out hunting as though by accident, and then making her eat his heart in the evening.

"My fate," she said to herself, "depends on what he will think when he listens to me. It may be I shall never get another opportunity of speaking to him after this fatal quarter of an hour. He is not a reasonable person who is governed by his intellect. In that case, with the help of my weak intelligence, I could anticipate what he will do or say. He will decide our common fate. He has the power. But this fate depends on my adroitness, on my skill in directing the ideas of this crank, who is blinded by his rage and unable to see half of what takes place. Great God! I need talent and coolness, where shall I get it?"

She regained her calmness as though by magic, and she entered the garden and saw her husband in the distance. His dishevelled hair and disordered dress showed that he had not slept.

She gave him a letter with a broken seal but folded. As for him, without opening it, he gazed at his wife with the eyes of a madman.

"Here's an abominable thing," she said to him, "which an evil-looking man who makes out that he knows you and is under an obligation to you, handed to me as I was passing behind the notary's garden. I insist on one thing and that is that you send back this M. Julien to his parents and without delay." Madame de Rênal hastened to say these words, perhaps a little before the psychological moment, in order to free herself from the awful prospect of having to say them.

She was seized with joy on seeing that which she was occasioning to her husband. She realised from the fixed stare which he was rivetting on her that Julien had surmised rightly.

"What a genius he is to be so brilliantly diplomatic instead of succumbing to so real a misfortune," she thought. "He will go very far in the future! Alas, his successes will only make him forget me."

This little act of admiration for the man whom she adored quite cured her of her trouble.

She congratulated herself on her tactics. "I have not been unworthy of Julien," she said to herself with a sweet and secret pleasure.

M. de Rênal kept examining the second anonymous letter which the reader may remember was composed of printed words glued on to a paper verging on blue. He did not say a word for fear of giving himself away. "They still make fun of me in every possible way," said M. de Rênal to himself, overwhelmed with exhaustion. "Still more new insults to examine and all the time on account of my wife." He was on the point of heaping on her the coarsest insults. He was barely checked by the prospects of the Besançon legacy. Consumed by the need of venting his feelings on something, he crumpled up the paper of the second anonymous letter and began to walk about with huge strides. He needed to get away from his wife. A few moments afterwards he came back to her in a quieter frame of mind.

"The thing is to take some definite line and send Julien away," she said immediately, "after all it is only a labourer's son. You will compensate him by a few crowns and besides he is clever and will easily manage to find a place, with M. Valenod for example, or with the sub-prefect De Maugiron who both have children. In that way you will not be doing him any wrong...." "There you go talking like the fool that you are," exclaimed M. de Rênal in a terrible voice. "How can one hope that a woman will show any good sense? You never bother yourself about common sense. How can you ever get to know anything? Your indifference and your idleness give you no energy except for hunting those miserable butterflies, which we are unfortunate to have in our houses."

Madame de Rênal let him speak and he spoke for a long time. *He was working off his anger*, to use the local expression.

"Monsieur," she answered him at last, "I speak as a woman who has been outraged in her honour, that is to say, in what she holds most precious."

Madame de Rênal preserved an unalterable sang-froid during all this painful conversation on the result of which depended the possibility of still living under the same roof as Julien. She sought for the ideas which she thought most adapted to guide her husband's blind anger into a safe channel. She had been insensible to all the insulting imputations which he had addressed to her. She was not listening to them, she was then thinking about Julien. "Will he be pleased with me?"

"This little peasant whom we have loaded with attentions, and even with presents, may be innocent," she said to him at last, "but he is none the less the occasion of the first affront that I have ever received. Monsieur, when I read this abominable paper, I vowed to myself that either he or I should leave your house."

"Do you want to make a scandal so as to dishonour me and yourself as well? You will make things hum in Verrières I can assure you."

"It is true, the degree of prosperity in which your prudent management has succeeded in placing you yourself, your family and the town is the subject of general envy.... Well, I will urge Julien to ask you for a holiday to go and spend the month with that wood-merchant of the mountains, a fit friend to be sure for this little labourer."

"Mind you do nothing at all," resumed M. de Rênal with a fair amount of tranquillity. "I particularly insist on your not speaking to him. You will put him into a temper and make him quarrel with me. You know to what extent this little gentleman is always spoiling for a quarrel."

"That young man has no tact," resumed Madame de Rênal. "He may be learned, you know all about that, but at bottom he is only a peasant. For my own part I never thought much of him since he refused to marry Elisa. It was an assured fortune; and that on the pretext that sometimes she had made secret visits to M. Valenod."

"Ah," said M. de Rênal, lifting up his eyebrows inordinately. "What, did Julien tell you that?"

"Not exactly, he always talked of the vocation which calls him to the holy ministry, but believe me, the first vocation for those lower-class people is getting their bread and butter. He gave me to understand that he was quite aware of her secret visits."

"And I—I was ignorant," exclaimed M. de Rênal, growing as angry as before and accentuating his words. "Things take place in my house which I know nothing about.... What! has there been anything between Elisa and Valenod?"

"Oh, that's old history, my dear," said Madame de Rênal with a smile, "and perhaps no harm has come of it. It was at the time when your good friend Valenod would not have minded their thinking at Verrières that a perfectly platonic little affection was growing up between him and me."

"I had that idea once myself," exclaimed M. de Rênal, furiously striking his head as he progressed from discovery to discovery, "and you told me nothing about it."

"Should one set two friends by the ears on account of a little fit of vanity on the part of our dear director? What society woman has not had addressed to her a few letters which were both extremely witty and even a little gallant?"

"He has written to you?"

"He writes a great deal."

"Show me those letters at once, I order you," and M. de Rênal pulled himself up to his six feet.

"I will do nothing of the kind," he was answered with a sweetness verging on indifference. "I will show you them one day when you are in a better frame of mind."

"This very instant, odds life," exclaimed M. de Rênal, transported with rage and yet happier than he had been for twelve hours.

"Will you swear to me," said Madame de Rênal quite gravely, "never to quarrel with the director of the workhouse about these letters?"

"Quarrel or no quarrel, I can take those foundlings away from him, but," he continued furiously, "I want those letters at once. Where are they?"

"In a drawer in my secretary, but I shall certainly not give you the key."

"I'll manage to break it," he cried, running towards his wife's room.

He did break in fact with a bar of iron a costly secretary of veined mahogany which came from Paris and which he had often been accustomed to wipe with the nap of his coat, when he thought he had detected a spot.

Madame de Rênal had climbed up at a run the hundred and twenty steps of the dovecot. She tied the corner of a white handkerchief to one of the bars of iron of the little window. She was the happiest of women. With tears in her eyes she looked towards the great mountain forest. "Doubtless," she said to herself, "Julien is watching for this happy signal."

She listened attentively for a long time and then she cursed the monotonous noise of the grasshopper and the song of the birds. "Had it not been for that importunate noise, a cry of joy starting from the big rocks could have arrived here." Her greedy eye devoured that immense slope of dark verdure which was as level as a meadow.

"Why isn't he clever enough," she said to herself, quite overcome, "to invent some signal to tell me that his happiness is equal to mine?" She only came down from the dovecot when she was frightened of her husband coming there to look for her.

She found him furious. He was perusing the soothing phrases of M. de Valenod and reading them with an emotion to which they were but little used.

"I always come back to the same idea," said Madame de Rênal seizing a moment when a pause in her husband's ejaculations gave her the possibility of getting heard. "It is necessary for Julien to travel. Whatever talent he may have for Latin, he is only a peasant after all, often coarse and lacking in tact. Thinking to be polite, he addresses inflated compliments to me every day, which are in bad taste. He learns them by heart out of some novel or other."

"He never reads one," exclaimed M. de Rênal. "I am assured of it. Do you think that I am the master of a house who is so blind as to be ignorant of what takes place in his own home."

"Well, if he doesn't read these droll compliments anywhere, he invents them, and that's all the worse so far as he is concerned. He must have talked about me in this tone in Verrières and perhaps without going so far," said Madame Rênal with the idea of making a discovery, "he may have talked in the same strain to Elisa, which is almost the same as if he had said it to M. Valenod."

"Ah," exclaimed M. de Rênal, shaking the table and the room with one of the most violent raps ever made by a human fist. "The anonymous printed letter and Valenod's letters are written on the same paper."

"At last," thought Madame de Rênal. She pretended to be over-whelmed at this discovery, and without having the courage to add a single word, went and sat down some way off on the divan at the bottom of the drawing-room.

From this point the battle was won. She had a great deal of trouble in preventing M. de Rênal from going to speak to the supposed author of the anonymous letter. "What, can't you see that making a scene with M. Valenod without sufficient proof would be the most signal mistake? You are envied, Monsieur, and who is responsible? Your talents: your wise management, your tasteful buildings, the dowry which I have brought you, and above all, the substantial legacy which we are entitled to hope for from my good aunt, a legacy, the importance of which is inordinately exaggerated, have made you into the first person in Verrières."

"You are forgetting my birth," said M. de Rênal, smiling a little.

"You are one of the most distinguished gentlemen in the province," replied Madame de Rênal emphatically. "If the king were free and could give birth its proper due, you would no doubt figure in the Chamber of Peers, etc. And being in this magnificent position, you yet wish to give the envious a fact to take hold of."

"To speak about this anonymous letter to M. Valenod is equivalent to proclaiming over the whole of Verrières, nay, over the whole of Besançon, over the whole province that this little bourgeois who has been admitted perhaps imprudently to intimacy *with a Rênal*, has managed to offend him. At the time when those letters which you have just taken prove that I have reciprocated M. Valenod's love, you ought to kill me. I should have deserved it a hundred times over, but not to show him your anger. Remember that all our neighbours are only waiting for an excuse to revenge themselves for your superiority. Remember that in 1816 you had a hand in certain arrests.

"I think that you show neither consideration nor love for me," exclaimed M. de Rênal with all the bitterness evoked by such a memory, "and I was not made a peer."

"I am thinking, my dear," resumed Madame de Rênal with a smile, "that I shall be richer than you are, that I have been your companion for twelve years, and that by virtue of those qualifications I am entitled to have a voice in the council and, above all, in to-day's business. If you prefer M. Julien to me," she added, with a touch of temper which was but thinly disguised, "I am ready to go and pass a winter with my aunt." These words proved a lucky shot. They possessed a firmness which endeavoured to clothe itself with courtesy. It decided M. de Rênal, but following the provincial custom, he still thought for a long time, and went again over all his arguments; his wife let him speak. There was still a touch of anger in his intonation. Finally two hours of futile rant exhausted the strength of a man who had been subject during the whole night to a continuous fit of anger. He determined on the line of conduct he was going to follow with regard to M. Valenod, Julien and even Elisa.

Madame de Rênal was on the point once or twice during this great scene of feeling some sympathy for the very real unhappiness of the man who had been so dear to her for twelve years. But true passions are selfish. Besides she was expecting him every instant to mention the anonymous letter which he had received the day before and he did not mention it. In order to feel quite safe, Madame de Rênal wanted to know the ideas which the letter had succeeding in suggesting to the man on whom her fate depended, for, in the provinces the husbands are the masters of public opinion. A husband who complains covers himself with ridicule, an inconvenience which becomes no less dangerous in France with each succeeding year; but if he refuses to provide his wife with money, she falls to the status of a labouring woman at fifteen sous a day, while the virtuous souls have scruples about employing her.

An odalisque in the seraglio can love the Sultan with all her might. He is all-powerful and she has no hope of stealing his authority by a series of little subtleties. The master's vengeance is terrible and bloody but martial and generous; a dagger thrust finishes everything. But it is by stabbing her with public contempt that a nineteenth-century husband kills his wife. It is by shutting against her the doors of all the drawing-rooms.

When Madame de Rênal returned to her room, her feeling of danger was vividly awakened. She was shocked by the disorder in which she found it. The locks of all the pretty little boxes had been broken. Many planks in the floor had been lifted up. "He would have no pity on me," she said to herself. "To think of his spoiling like this, this coloured wood floor which he likes so much; he gets red with rage whenever one of his children comes into it with wet shoes, and now it is spoilt for ever." The spectacle of this violence immediately banished the last scruples which she was entertaining with respect to that victory which she had won only too rapidly.

Julien came back with the children a little before the dinner-bell. Madame de Rênal said to him very drily at dessert when the servant had left the room:

"You have told me about your wish to go and spend a fortnight at Verrières. M. de Rênal is kind enough to give you a holiday. You can leave as soon as you like, but the childrens' exercises will be sent to you every day so that they do not waste their time."

"I shall certainly not allow you more than a week," said M. de Rênal in a very bitter tone. Julien thought his visage betrayed the anxiety of a man who was seriously harassed.

"He has not yet decided what line to take," he said to his love during a moment when they were alone together in the drawing-room.

Madame de Rênal rapidly recounted to him all she had done since the morning.

"The details are for to-night," she added with a smile.

"Feminine perversity," thought Julien, "What can be the pleasure, what can be the instinct which induces them to deceive us."

"I think you are both enlightened and at the same time blinded by your love," he said to her with some coldness. "Your conduct to-day has been admirable, but is it prudent for us to try and see each other to-night? This house is paved with enemies. Just think of Elisa's passionate hatred for me."

"That hate is very like the passionate indifference which you no doubt have for me."

"Even if I were indifferent I ought to save you from the peril in which I have plunged you. If chance so wills it that M. de Rênal should speak to Elisa, she can acquaint him with everything in a single word. What is to prevent him from hiding near my room fully armed?"

"What, not even courage?" said Madame de Rênal, with all the haughtiness of a scion of nobility.

"I will never demean myself to speak about my courage," said Julien, coldly, "it would be mean to do so. Let the world judge by the facts. But," he added, taking her hand, "you have no idea how devoted I am to you and how over-joyed I am of being able to say good-bye to you before this cruel separation."

XXII

MANNERS OF PROCEDURE IN 1830

Speech has been given to man to conceal his thought.
R.P. Malagrida.

Julien had scarcely arrived at Verrières before he reproached himself with his injustice towards Madame de Rênal. "I should have despised her for a weakling of a woman if she had not had the strength to go through with her scene with M. de Rênal. But she has acquitted herself like a diplomatist and I sympathise with the defeat of the man who is my enemy. There is a bourgeois prejudice in my action; my vanity is offended because M. de Rênal is a man. Men form a vast and illustrious body to which I have the honour to belong. I am nothing but a fool." M. Chélan had refused the magnificent apartments which the most important Liberals in the district had offered him, when his loss of his living had necessitated his leaving the parsonage. The two rooms which he had rented were littered with his books. Julien, wishing to show Verrières what a priest could do, went and fetched a dozen pinewood planks from his father, carried them on his back all along the Grande-Rue, borrowed some tools from an old comrade and soon built a kind of book-case in which he arranged M. Chélan's books.

"I thought you were corrupted by the vanity of the world," said the old man to him as he cried with joy, "but this is something which well redeems all the childishness of that brilliant Guard of Honour uniform which has made you so many enemies."

M. de Rênal had ordered Julien to stay at his house. No one suspected what had taken place. The third day after his arrival Julien saw no less a personage than M. the sub-prefect de Maugiron come all the way up the stairs to his room. It was only after two long hours of fatuous gossip and long-winded lamentations about the wickedness of man, the lack of honesty among the people entrusted with the administration of the public funds, the dangers of his poor France, etc. etc., that Julien was at last vouchsafed a glimpse of the object of the visit. They were already on the landing of the staircase and the poor half disgraced tutor was escorting with all proper deference the future prefect of some prosperous department, when the latter was pleased to take an interest in Julien's fortune, to praise his moderation in money matters, etc., etc. Finally M. de Maugiron, embracing him in the most paternal way, proposed that he should leave M. de Rênal and enter the household of an official who had children to educate and who, like King Philippe, thanked Heaven not so much that they had been granted to him, but for the fact that they had been born in the same neighbourhood as M. Julien. Their tutor would enjoy a salary of 800 francs, payable not from month to month, which is not at all aristocratic, said M. de Maugiron, but quarterly and always in advance.

It was Julien's turn now. After he had been bored for an hour and a half by waiting for what he had to say, his answer was perfect and, above all, as long as a bishop's charge. It suggested everything and yet said nothing clearly. It showed at the same time respect for M. de Rênal, veneration for the public of Verrières and gratitude to the distinguished sub-prefect. The sub-prefect, astonished at finding him more Jesuitical than himself, tried in vain to obtain something definite. Julien was delighted, seized the opportunity to practise, and started his answer all over again in different language. Never has an eloquent minister who wished to make the most of the end of a session when the Chamber really seemed desirous of waking up, said less in more words.

M. de Maugiron had scarcely left before Julien began to laugh like a madman. In order to exploit his Jesuitical smartness, he wrote a nine-page letter to M. de Rênal in which he gave him an account of all that had been said to him and humbly asked his advice. "But the old scoundrel has not told me the name of the person who is making the offer. It is bound to be M. Valenod who, no doubt, sees in my exile at Verrières the result of his anonymous letter."

Having sent off his despatch and feeling as satisfied as a hunter who at six o'clock in the morning on a fine autumn day, comes out into a plain that abounds with game, he went out to go and ask advice of M. Chélan. But before he had arrived at the good curé's, providence, wishing to shower favours upon him, threw in his path M. de Valenod, to whom he owned quite freely that his heart was torn in two; a poor lad such as he was owed an exclusive devotion to the vocation to which it had pleased Heaven to call him. But vocation was not everything in this base world. In order to work worthily at the vine of the Lord, and to be not totally unworthy of so many worthy colleagues, it was necessary to be educated; it was necessary to spend two expensive years at the seminary of Besançon; saving consequently became an imperative necessity, and was certainly much easier with a salary of eight hundred francs paid quarterly than with six hundred francs which one received monthly. On the other hand, did not Heaven, by placing him by the side of the young de Rênals, and especially by inspiring him with a special devotion to them, seem to indicate that it was not proper to abandon that education for another one.

Julien reached such a degree of perfection in that particular kind of eloquence which has succeeded the drastic quickness of the empire, that he finished by boring himself with the sound of his own words.

On reaching home he found a valet of M. Valenod in full livery who had been looking for him all over the town, with a card inviting him to dinner for that same day.

Julien had never been in that man's house. Only a few days before he had been thinking of nothing but the means of giving him a sound thrashing without getting into trouble with the police. Although the time of the dinner was one o'clock, Julien thought it was more deferential to present himself at half-past twelve at the office of M. the director of the workhouse. He found him parading his importance in the middle of a lot of despatch boxes. His large black whiskers, his enormous quantity of hair, his Greek bonnet placed across the top of his head, his immense pipe, his embroidered slippers, the big chains of gold crossed all over his breast, and the whole stock-in-trade of a provincial financier who considers himself prosperous, failed to impose on Julien in the least: They only made him think the more of the thrashing which he owed him.

He asked for the honour of being introduced to Madame Valenod. She was dressing and was unable to receive him. By way of compensation he had the privilege of witnessing the toilet of M. the director of the workhouse. They subsequently went into the apartment of Madame Valenod, who introduced her children to him with tears in her eyes. This lady was one of the most important in Verrières, had a big face like a man's, on which she had put rouge in honour of this great function. She displayed all the maternal pathos of which she was capable.

Julien thought all the time of Madame de Rênal. His distrust made him only susceptible to those associations which are called up by their opposites, but he was then affected to the verge of breaking down. This tendency was increased by the sight of the house of the director of the workhouse. He was shown over it. Everything in it was new and magnificent, and he was told the price of every article of furniture. But Julien detected a certain element of sordidness, which smacked of stolen money into the bargain. Everybody in it, down to the servants, had the air of setting his face in advance against contempt.

The collector of taxes, the superintendent of indirect taxes, the officer of gendarmerie, and two or three other public officials arrived with their wives. They were followed by some rich Liberals. Dinner was announced. It occurred to Julien, who was already feeling upset, that there were some poor prisoners on the other side of the dining-room wall, and that an illicit profit had perhaps been made over their rations of meat in order to purchase all that garish luxury with which they were trying to overwhelm him.

"Perhaps they are hungry at this very minute," he said to himself. He felt a choking in his throat. He found it impossible to eat and almost impossible to speak. Matters became much worse a quarter of an hour afterwards; they heard in the distance some refrains of a popular song that was, it must be confessed, a little vulgar, which was being sung by one of the inmates. M. Valenod gave a look to one of his liveried servants who disappeared and soon there was no more singing to be heard. At that moment a valet offered Julien some Rhine wine in a green glass and Madame Valenod made a point of asking him to note that this wine cost nine francs a bottle in the market. Julien held up his green glass and said to M. Valenod,

"They are not singing that wretched song any more."

"Zounds, I should think not," answered the triumphant governor. "I have made the rascals keep quiet."

These words were too much for Julien. He had the manners of his new position, but he had not yet assimilated its spirit. In spite of all his hypocrisy and its frequent practice, he felt a big tear drip down his cheek.

He tried to hide it in the green glass, but he found it absolutely impossible to do justice to the Rhine wine. "Preventing singing he said to himself: Oh, my God, and you suffer it."

Fortunately nobody noticed his ill-bred emotion. The collector of taxes had struck up a royalist song. "So this," reflected Julien's conscience during the hubbub of the refrain which was sung in chorus, "is the sordid prosperity which you will eventually reach, and you will only enjoy it under these conditions and in company like this. You will, perhaps, have a post worth twenty thousand francs; but while you gorge yourself on meat, you will have to prevent a poor prisoner from singing; you will give dinners with the money which you have stolen out of his miserable rations and during your dinners he will be still more wretched. Oh, Napoleon, how sweet it was to climb to fortune in your way through the dangers of a battle, but to think of aggravating the pain of the unfortunate in this cowardly way."

I own that the weakness which Julien had been manifesting in this soliloquy gives me a poor opinion of him. He is worthy of being the accomplice of those kid-gloved conspirators who purport to change the whole essence of a great country's existence, without wishing to have on their conscience the most trivial scratch.

Julien was sharply brought back to his role. He had not been invited to dine in such good company simply to moon dreamily and say nothing.

A retired manufacturer of cotton prints, a corresponding member of the Academy of Besançon and of that of Uzès, spoke to him from the other end of the table and asked him if what was said everywhere about his astonishing progress in the study of the New Testament was really true.

A profound silence was suddenly inaugurated. A New Testament in Latin was found as though by magic in the possession of the learned member of the two Academies. After Julien had answered, part of a sentence in Latin was read at random. Julien then recited. His memory proved faithful and the prodigy was admired with all the boisterous energy of the end of dinner. Julien looked at the flushed faces of the ladies. A good many were not so plain. He recognised the wife of the collector, who was a fine singer.

"I am ashamed, as a matter of fact, to talk Latin so long before these ladies," he said, turning his eyes on her. "If M. Rubigneau," that was the name of the member of the two Academies, "will be kind enough to read a Latin sentence at random instead of answering by following the Latin text, I will try to translate it impromptu." This second test completed his glory.

Several Liberals were there, who, though rich, were none the less the happy fathers of children capable of obtaining scholarships, and had consequently been suddenly converted at the last mission. In spite of this diplomatic step, M. de Rênal had never been willing to receive them in his house. These worthy people, who only knew Julien by name and from having seen him on horseback on the day of the king of ——'s entry, were his most noisy admirers. "When will those fools get tired of listening to this Biblical language, which they don't understand in the least," he thought. But, on the contrary, that language amused them by its strangeness and made them smile. But Julien got tired.

As six o'clock struck he got up gravely and talked about a chapter in Ligorio's New Theology which he had to learn by heart to recite on the following day to M. Chélan, "for," he added pleasantly, "my business is to get lessons said by heart to me, and to say them by heart myself."

There was much laughter and admiration; such is the kind of wit which is customary in Verrières. Julien had already got up and in spite of etiquette everybody got up as well, so great is the dominion exercised by genius. Madame Valenod kept him for another quarter of an hour. He really must hear her children recite their catechisms. They made the most absurd mistakes which he alone noticed. He was careful not to point them out. "What ignorance of the first principles of religion," he thought. Finally he bowed and thought he could get away; but they insisted on his trying a fable of La Fontaine.

"That author is quite immoral," said Julien to Madame Valenod. A certain fable on Messire Jean Chouart dares to pour ridicule on all that we hold most venerable. He is shrewdly blamed by the best commentators. Before Julien left he received four or five invitations to dinner. "This young man is an honour to the department," cried all the guests in chorus. They even went so far as to talk of a pension voted out of the municipal funds to put him in the position of continuing his studies at Paris.

While this rash idea was resounding through the dining-room Julien had swiftly reached the front door. "You scum, you scum," he cried, three or four times in succession in a low voice as he indulged in the pleasure of breathing in the fresh air.

He felt quite an aristocrat at this moment, though he was the very man who had been shocked for so long a period by the haughty smile of disdainful superiority which he detected behind all the courtesies addressed to him at M. de Rênal's. He could not help realising the extreme difference. Why let us even forget the fact of its being money stolen from the poor inmates, he said to himself as he went away, let us forget also their stopping the singing. M. de Rênal would never think of telling his guests the price of each bottle of wine with which he regales them, and as for this M. Valenod, and his chronic cataloguing of his various belongings, he cannot talk of his house, his estate, etc., in the presence of his wife without saying, "Your house, your estate."

This lady, who was apparently so keenly alive to the delights of decorum, had just had an awful scene during the dinner with a servant who had broken a wine-glass and spoilt one of her dozens; and the servant too had answered her back with the utmost insolence.

"What a collection," said Julien to himself; "I would not live like they do were they to give me half of all they steal. I shall give myself away one fine day. I should not be able to restrain myself from expressing the disgust with which they inspire one."

It was necessary, however, to obey Madame de Rênal's injunction and be present at several dinners of the same kind. Julien was the fashion; he was forgiven his Guard of Honour uniform, or rather that indiscretion was the real cause of his successes. Soon the only question in Verrières was whether M. de Rênal or M. the director of the workhouse would be the victor in the struggle for the clever young man. These gentlemen formed, together with M. Maslon, a triumvirate which had tyrannised over the town for a number of years. People were jealous of the mayor, and the Liberals had good cause for complaint, but, after all, he was noble and born for a superior position, while M. Valenod's father had not left him six hundred francs a year. His career had necessitated a transition from pitying the shabby green suit which had been so notorious in his youth, to envying the Norman horses, his gold chains, his Paris clothes, his whole present prosperity.

Julien thought that he had discovered one honest man in the whirlpool of this novel world. He was a geometrist named Gros, and had the reputation of being a Jacobin. Julien, who had vowed to say nothing but that which he disbelieved himself, was obliged to watch himself carefully when speaking to M. Gros. He received big packets of exercises from Vergy. He was advised to visit his father frequently, and he fulfilled his unpleasant duty. In a word he was patching his reputation together pretty well, when he was thoroughly surprised to find himself woken up one morning by two hands held over his eyes.

It was Madame de Rênal who had made a trip to the town, and who, running up the stairs four at a time while she left her children playing with a pet rabbit, had reached Julien's room a moment before her sons. This moment was delicious but very short: Madame de Rênal had disappeared when the children arrived with the rabbit which they wanted to show to their friend. Julien gave them all a hearty welcome, including the rabbit. He seemed at home again. He felt that he loved these children and that he enjoyed gossiping with them. He was astonished at the sweetness of their voices, at the simplicity and dignity of their little ways; he felt he needed to purge his imagination of all the vulgar practices and all the unpleasantnesses among which he had been living in Verrières. For there everyone was always frightened of being scored off, and luxury and poverty were at daggers drawn.

The people with whom he would dine would enter into confidences over the joint which were as humiliating for themselves as they were nauseating to the hearer.

"You others, who are nobles, you are right to be proud," he said to Madame de Rênal, as he gave her an account of all the dinners which he had put up with.

"You're the fashion then," and she laughed heartily as she thought of the rouge which Madame Valenod thought herself obliged to put on each time she expected Julien. "I think she has designs on your heart," she added.

The breakfast was delicious. The presence of the children, though apparently embarrassing, increased as a matter of fact the happiness of the party. The poor children did not know how to give expression to the joy at seeing Julien again. The servants had not failed to tell them that he had been offered two hundred francs a year more to educate the little Valenods.

Stanislas-Xavier, who was still pale from his illness, suddenly asked his mother in the middle of the breakfast, the value of his silver cover and of the goblet in which he was drinking.

"Why do you want to know that?"

"I want to sell them to give the price to M. Julien so that he shan't be *done* if he stays with us."

Julien kissed him with tears in his eyes. His mother wept unrestrainedly, for Julien took Stanislas on his knees and explained to him that he should not use the word "done" which, when employed in that meaning was an expression only fit for the servants' hall. Seeing the pleasure which he was giving to Madame de Rênal, he tried to explain the meaning of being "done" by picturesque illustrations which amused the children.

"I understand," said Stanislas, "it's like the crow who is silly enough to let his cheese fall and be taken by the fox who has been playing the flatterer."

Madame de Rênal felt mad with joy and covered her children with kisses, a process which involved her leaning a little on Julien.

Suddenly the door opened. It was M. de Rênal. His severe and discontented expression contrasted strangely with the sweet joy which his presence dissipated. Madame de Rênal grew pale, she felt herself incapable of denying anything. Julien seized command of the conversation and commenced telling M. the mayor in a loud voice the incident of the silver goblet which Stanislas wanted to sell. He was quite certain this story would not be appreciated. M. de Rênal first of all frowned mechanically at the mere mention of money. Any allusion to that mineral, he was accustomed to say, is always a prelude to some demand made upon my purse. But this was something more than a mere money matter. His suspicions were increased. The air of happiness which animated his family during his absence was not calculated to smooth matters over with a man who was a prey to so touchy a vanity. "Yes, yes," he said, as his wife started to praise to him the combined grace and cleverness of the way in which Julien gave ideas to his pupils. "I know, he renders me hateful to my own children. It is easy enough for him to make himself a hundred times more loveable to them than I am myself, though after all, I am the master. In this century everything tends to make *legitimate* authority unpopular. Poor France!"

Madame de Rênal had not stopped to examine the fine shades of the welcome which her husband gave her. She had just caught a glimpse of the possibility of spending twelve hours with Julien. She had a lot of purchases to make in the town and declared that she positively insisted in going to dine at the tavern. She stuck to her idea in spite of all her husband's protests and remonstrances. The children were delighted with the mere word tavern, which our modern prudery denounces with so much gusto.

M. de Rênal left his wife in the first draper's shop which she entered and went to pay some visits. He came back more morose than he had been in the morning. He was convinced that the whole town was busy with himself and Julien. As a matter of fact no one had yet given him any inkling as to the more offensive part of the public gossip. Those items which had been repeated to M. the mayor dealt exclusively with the question of whether Julien would remain with him with six hundred francs, or would accept the eight hundred francs offered by M. the director of the workhouse.

The director, when he met M. de Rênal in society, gave him the cold shoulder. These tactics were not without cleverness. There is no impulsiveness in the provinces. Sensations are so rare there that they are never allowed to be wasted.

M. le Valenod was what is called a hundred miles from Paris a *faraud*; that means a coarse imprudent type of man. His triumphant existence since 1815 had consolidated his natural qualities. He reigned, so to say, in Verrières subject to the orders of M. de Rênal; but as he was much more energetic, was ashamed of nothing, had a finger in everything, and was always going about writing and speaking, and was oblivious of all snubs, he had, although without any personal pretensions, eventually come to equal the mayor in reputation in the eyes of the ecclesiastical authorities. M. Valenod had, as it were, said to the local tradesmen "Give me the two biggest fools among your number;" to the men of law "Show me the two greatest dunces;" to the sanitary officials "Point out to me the two biggest charlatans." When he had thus collected the most impudent members of each separate calling, he had practically said to them, "Let us reign together."

The manners of those people were offensive to M. de Rênal. The coarseness of Valenod took offence at nothing, not even the frequency with which the little abbé Maslon would give the lie to him in public.

But in the middle of all this prosperity M. Valenod found it necessary to reassure himself by a number of petty acts of insolence on the score of the crude truths which he well realised that everybody was justified in addressing to him. His activity had redoubled since the fears which the visit of M. Appert had left him. He had made three journeys to Besançon. He wrote several letters by each courier; he sent others by unknown men who came to his house at nightfall. Perhaps he had been wrong in securing the dismissal of the old curé Chélan. For this piece of vindictiveness had resulted in his being considered an extremely malicious man by several pious women of good birth. Besides, the rendering of this service had placed him in absolute dependence on M. the Grand Vicar de Frilair from whom he received some strange commissions. He had reached this point in his intrigues when he had yielded to the pleasure of writing an anonymous letter, and thus increasing his embarrassment. His wife declared to him that she wanted to have Julien in her house; her vanity was intoxicated with the idea.

Such being his position M. Valenod imagined in advance a decisive scene with his old colleague M. de Rênal. The latter might address to him some harsh words, which he would not mind much; but he might write to Besançon and even to Paris. Some minister's cousin might suddenly fall down on Verrières and take over the workhouse. Valenod thought of coming to terms with the Liberals. It was for that purpose that several of them had been invited to the dinner when Julien was present. He would have obtained powerful support against the mayor but the elections might supervene, and it was only too evident that the directorship of the workhouse was inconsistent with voting on the wrong side. Madame de Rênal had made a shrewd guess at this intrigue, and while she explained it to Julien as he gave her his arm to pass from one shop to another, they found themselves gradually taken as far as the *Cours de la Fidélité* where they spent several hours nearly as tranquil as those at Vergy.

At the same time M. Valenod was trying to put off a definite crisis with his old patron by himself assuming the aggressive. These tactics succeeded on this particular day, but aggravated the mayor's bad temper. Never has vanity at close grips with all the harshness and meanness of a pettifogging love of money reduced a man to a more sorry condition than that of M. de Rênal when he entered the tavern. The children, on the other hand, had never been more joyful and more merry. This contrast put the finishing touch on his pique.

"So far as I can see I am not wanted in my family," he said as he entered in a tone which he meant to be impressive.

For answer, his wife took him on one side and declared that it was essential to send Julien away. The hours of happiness which she had just enjoyed had given her again the ease and firmness of demeanour necessary to follow out the plan of campaign which she had been hatching for a fortnight. The finishing touch to the trouble of the poor mayor of Verrières was the fact that he knew that they joked publicly in the town about his love for cash. Valenod was as generous as a thief, and on his side had acquitted himself brilliantly in the last five or six collections for the Brotherhood of St. Joseph, the congregation of the Virgin, the congregation of the Holy Sacrament, etc., etc.

M. de Rênal's name had been seen more than once at the bottom of the list of gentlefolk of Verrières, and the surrounding neighbourhood who were adroitly classified in the list of the collecting brethren according to the amount of their offerings. It was in vain that he said that he was *not making money*. The clergy stands no nonsense in such matters.

XXIII
SORROWS OF AN OFFICIAL

Il piacere di alzar la testa tutto l'anno, è ben pagato da certi
quarti d'ora che bisogna passar.—*Casti.*

Let us leave this petty man to his petty fears; why did he take a man of spirit into his household when he needed someone with the soul of a valet? Why can't he select his staff? The ordinary trend of the nineteenth century is that when a noble and powerful individual encounters a man of spirit, he kills him, exiles him and imprisons him, or so humiliates him that the other is foolish enough to die of grief. In this country it so happens that it is not merely the man of spirit who suffers. The great misfortunes of the little towns of France and of representative governments, like that of New York, is that they find it impossible to forget the existence of individuals like M. de Rênal. It is these men who make public opinion in a town of twenty thousand inhabitants, and public opinion is terrible in a country which has a charter of liberty. A man, though of a naturally noble and generous disposition, who would have been your friend in the natural course of events, but who happens to live a hundred leagues off, judges you by the public opinion of your town which is made by those fools who have chanced to be born noble, rich and conservative. Unhappy is the man who distinguishes himself.

Immediately after dinner they left for Vergy, but the next day but one Julien saw the whole family return to Verrières. An hour had not passed before he discovered to his great surprise that Madame de Rênal had some mystery up her sleeve. Whenever he came into the room she would break off her conversation with her husband and would almost seem to desire that he should go away. Julien did not need to be given this hint twice. He became cold and reserved. Madame de Rênal noticed it and did not ask for an explanation. "Is she going to give me a successor," thought Julien. "And to think of her being so familiar with me the day before yesterday, but that is how these great ladies are said to act. It's just like kings. One never gets any more warning than the disgraced minister who enters his house to find his letter of dismissal." Julien noticed that these conversations which left off so abruptly at his approach, often dealt with a big house which belonged to the municipality of Verrières, a house which though old was large and commodious and situated opposite the church in the most busy commercial district of the town. "What connection can there be between this house and a new lover," said Julien to himself. In his chagrin he repeated to himself the pretty verses of Francis I. which seemed novel to him, for Madame de Rênal had only taught him them a month before:

> Souvent femme varie
> Bien fol est qui s'y fie.

M. de Rênal took the mail to Besançon. This journey was a matter of two hours. He seemed extremely harassed. On his return he threw a big grey paper parcel on the table.

"Here's that silly business," he said to his wife. An hour afterwards Julien saw the bill-poster carrying the big parcel. He followed him eagerly. "I shall learn the secret at the first street corner." He waited impatiently behind the bill-poster who was smearing the back of the poster with his big brush. It had scarcely been put in its place before Julien's curiosity saw the detailed announcement of the putting up for public auction of that big old house whose name had figured so frequently in M. de Rênal's conversations with his wife. The auction of the lease was announced for to-morrow at two o'clock in the Town Hall after the extinction of the third fire. Julien was very disappointed. He found the time a little short. How could there be time to apprise all the other would-be purchasers. But, moreover, the bill, which was dated a fortnight back, and which he read again in its entirety in three distinct places, taught him nothing.

He went to visit the house which was to let. The porter, who had not seen him approach, was saying mysteriously to a neighbour:

"Pooh, pooh, waste of time. M. Maslon has promised him that he shall have it for three hundred francs; and, as the mayor kicked, he has been summoned to the bishop's palace by M. the Grand Vicar de Frilair."

Julien's arrival seemed very much to disconcert the two friends who did not say another word. Julien made a point of being present at the auction of the lease.

There was a crowd in the badly-lighted hall, but everybody kept quizzing each other in quite a singular way. All eyes were fixed on a table where Julien perceived three little lighted candle-ends on a tin plate. The usher was crying out "Three hundred francs, gentlemen."

"Three hundred francs, that's a bit too thick," said a man to his neighbour in a low voice. Julien was between the two of them. "It's worth more than eight hundred, I will raise the bidding." "It's cutting off your nose to spite your face. What will you gain by putting M. Maslon, M. Valenod, the Bishop, this terrible Grand Vicar de Frilair and the whole gang on your track."

"Three hundred and twenty francs," shouted out the other.

"Damned brute," answered his neighbour. "Why here we have a spy of the mayor," he added, designating Julien.

Julien turned sharply round to punish this remark, but the two, Franc-comtois, were no longer paying any attention to him. Their coolness gave him back his own. At that moment the last candle-end went out and the usher's drawling voice awarded the house to M. de St. Giraud of the office of the prefecture of —— for a term of nine years and for a rent of 320 francs.

As soon as the mayor had left the hall, the gossip began again.

"Here's thirty francs that Grogeot's recklessness is landing the municipality in for," said one—"But," answered another, "M. de Saint Giraud will revenge himself on Grogeot."

"How monstrous," said a big man on Julien's left. "A house which I myself would have given eight hundred francs for my factory, and I would have got a good bargain."

"Pooh!" answered a young manufacturer, "doesn't M. de St. Giraud belong to the congregation? Haven't his four children got scholarships? poor man! The community of Verrières must give him five hundred francs over and above his salary, that is all."

"And to say that the mayor was not able to stop it," remarked a third. "For he's an ultra he is, I'm glad to say, but he doesn't steal."

"Doesn't he?" answered another. "Suppose it's simply a mere game of 'snap'³ then. Everything goes into a big common purse, and everything is divided up at the end of the year. But here's that little Sorel, let's go away."

Julien got home in a very bad temper. He found Madame de Rênal very sad.

"You come from the auction?" she said to him.

"Yes, madam, where I had the honour of passing for a spy of M. the Mayor."

"If he had taken my advice, he would have gone on a journey."

At this moment Monsieur de Rênal appeared: he looked very dismal. The dinner passed without a single word. Monsieur de Rênal ordered Julien to follow the children to Vergy.

Madame de Rênal endeavoured to console her husband.

"You ought to be used to it, my dear."

That evening they were seated in silence around the domestic hearth. The crackle of the burnt pinewood was their only distraction. It was one of those moments of silence which happen in the most united families. One of the children cried out gaily,

"Somebody's ringing, somebody's ringing!"

"Zounds! supposing it's Monsieur de Saint Giraud who has come under the pretext of thanking me," exclaimed the mayor. "I will give him a dressing down. It is outrageous. It is Valenod to whom he'll feel under an obligation, and it is I who get compromised. What shall I say if those damned Jacobin journalists get hold of this anecdote, and turn me into a M. Nonante Cinque."

A very good-looking man, with big black whiskers, entered at this moment, preceded by the servant.

"Monsieur the mayor, I am Signor Geronimo. Here is a letter which M. the Chevalier de Beauvoisis, who is attached to the Embassy of Naples, gave me for you on my departure. That is only nine days ago, added Signor Geronimo, gaily looking at Madame de Rênal. Your cousin, and my good friend, Signor de Beauvoisis says that you know Italian, Madame."

The Neapolitan's good humour changed this gloomy evening into a very gay one. Madame de Rênal insisted upon giving him supper. She put the whole house on the go. She wanted to free Julien at any price from the imputation of espionage which she had heard already twice that day.

Signor Geronimo was an excellent singer, excellent company, and had very gay qualities which, at any rate in France, are hardly compatible with each other. After dinner he sang a little duet with Madame de Rênal, and told some charming tales. At one o'clock in the morning the children protested, when Julien suggested that they should go to bed.

"Another of those stories," said the eldest.

"It is my own, Signorino," answered Signor Geronimo.

"Eight years ago I was, like you, a young pupil of the Naples Conservatoire. I mean I was your age, but I did not have the honour to be the son of the distinguished mayor of the pretty town of Verrières." This phrase made M. de Rênal sigh, and look at his wife.

"Signor Zingarelli," continued the young singer, somewhat exaggerating his action, and thus making the children burst into laughter, "Signor Zingarelli was an excellent though severe master. He is not popular at the Conservatoire, but he insists on the pretence being kept up that he is. I went out as often as I could. I used to go to the little Theatre de San Carlino, where I used to hear divine music. But heavens! the question was to scrape together the eight sous which were the price of admission to the parterre? An enormous sum," he said, looking at the children and watching them laugh. "Signor Giovannone, director of the San Carlino, heard me sing. I was sixteen. 'That child is a treasure,' he said.

"'Would you like me to engage you, my dear boy?' he said.

"'And how much will you give me?'

"'Forty ducats a month.' That is one hundred and sixty francs, gentlemen. I thought the gates of heaven had opened.

"'But,' I said to Giovannone, 'how shall I get the strict Zingarelli to let me go out?'

"'*Lascia fare a me.*'"

"Leave it to me," exclaimed the eldest of the children.

"Quite right, my young sir. Signor Giovannone he says to me, 'First sign this little piece of paper, my dear friend.' I sign.

"He gives me three ducats. I had never seen so much money. Then he told me what I had to do.

"Next day I asked the terrible Zingarelli for an audience. His old valet ushered me in.

"'What do you want of me, you naughty boy?' said Zingarelli.

"'Maestro,' I said, 'I repent of all my faults. I will never go out of the Conservatoire by passing through the iron grill. I will redouble my diligence.'

"'If I were not frightened of spoiling the finest bass voice I have ever heard, I would put you in prison for a fortnight on bread and water, you rascal.'

"'Maestro,' I answered, 'I will be the model boy of the whole school, *credete a me*, but I would ask one favour of you. If anyone comes and asks permission for me to sing outside, refuse. As a favour, please say that you cannot let me.'

"'And who the devil do you think is going to ask for a ne'er-do-well like you? Do you think I should ever allow you to leave the Conservatoire? Do you want to make fun of me? Clear out! Clear out!' he said, trying to give me a kick, 'or look out for prison and dry bread.'"

One thing astonished Julien. The solitary weeks passed at Verrières in de Rênal's house had been a period of happiness for him. He had only experienced revulsions and sad thoughts at the dinners to which he had been invited. And was he not able to read, write and reflect, without being distracted, in this solitary house? He was not distracted every moment from his brilliant reveries by the cruel necessity of studying the movement of a false soul in order to deceive it by intrigue and hypocrisy.

"To think of happiness being so near to me—the expense of a life like that is small enough. I could have my choice of either marrying Mademoiselle Elisa or of entering into partnership with Fouqué. But it is only the traveller who has just scaled a steep mountain and sits down on the summit who finds a perfect pleasure in resting. Would he be happy if he had to rest all the time?"

Madame de Rênal's mind had now reached a state of desperation. In spite of her resolutions, she had explained to Julien all the details of the auction. "He will make me forget all my oaths!" she thought.

She would have sacrificed her life without hesitation to save that of her husband if she had seen him in danger. She was one of those noble, romantic souls who find a source of perpetual remorse equal to that occasioned by the actual perpetration of a crime, in seeing the possibility of a generous action and not doing it. None the less, there were deadly days when she was not able to banish the imagination of the excessive happiness which she would enjoy if she suddenly became a widow, and were able to marry Julien.

He loved her sons much more than their father did; in spite of his strict justice they were devoted to him. She quite realised that if she married Julien, it would be necessary to leave that Vergy, whose shades were so dear to her. She pictured herself living at Paris, and continuing to give her sons an education which would make them admired by everyone. Her children, herself, and Julien! They would be all perfectly happy!

Strange result of marriage such as the nineteenth century has made it! The boredom of matrimonial life makes love fade away inevitably, when love has preceded the marriage. But none the less, said a philosopher, married life soon reduces those people who are sufficiently rich not to have to work, to a sense of being utterly bored by all quiet enjoyments. And among women, it is only arid souls whom it does not predispose to love.

The philosopher's reflection makes me excuse Madame de Rênal, but she was not excused in Verrières, and without her suspecting it, the whole town found its sole topic of interest in the scandal of her intrigue. As a result of this great affair, the autumn was less boring than usual.

The autumn and part of the winter passed very quickly. It was necessary to leave the woods of Vergy. Good Verrières society began to be indignant at the fact that its anathemas made so little impression on Monsieur de Rênal. Within eight days, several serious personages who made up for their habitual gravity of demeanour by their pleasure in fulfilling missions of this kind, gave him the most cruel suspicions, at the same time utilising the most measured terms.

M. Valenod, who was playing a deep game, had placed Elisa in an aristocratic family of great repute, where there were five women. Elisa, fearing, so she said, not to find a place during the winter, had only asked from this family about two-thirds of what she had received in the house of the mayor. The girl hit upon the excellent idea of going to confession at the same time to both the old curé Chélan, and also to the new one, so as to tell both of them in detail about Julien's amours.

The day after his arrival, the abbé Chélan summoned Julien to him at six o'clock in the morning.

"I ask you nothing," he said. "I beg you, and if needs be I insist, that you either leave for the Seminary of Besançon, or for your friend Fouqué, who is always ready to provide you with a splendid future. I have seen to everything and have arranged everything, but you must leave, and not come back to Verrières for a year."

Julien did not answer. He was considering whether his honour ought to regard itself offended at the trouble which Chélan, who, after all, was not his father, had taken on his behalf.

"I shall have the honour of seeing you again to-morrow at the same hour," he said finally to the curé.

Chélan, who reckoned on carrying so young a man by storm, talked a great deal. Julien, cloaked in the most complete humbleness, both of demeanour and expression, did not open his lips.

Eventually he left, and ran to warn Madame de Rênal whom he found in despair. Her husband had just spoken to her with a certain amount of frankness. The weakness of his character found support in the prospect of the legacy, and had decided him to treat her as perfectly innocent. He had just confessed to her the strange state in which he had found public opinion in Verrières. The public was wrong; it had been misled by jealous tongues. But, after all, what was one to do?

Madame de Rênal was, for the moment, under the illusion that Julien would accept the offer of Valenod and stay at Verrières. But she was no longer the simple, timid woman that she had been the preceding year. Her fatal passion and remorse had enlightened her. She soon realised the painful truth (while at the same time she listened to her husband), that at any rate a temporary separation had become essential.

When he is far from me, Julien will revert to those ambitious projects which are so natural when one has no money. And I, Great God! I am so rich, and my riches are so useless for my happiness. He will forget me. Loveable as he is, he will be loved, and he will love. You unhappy woman. What can I complain of? Heaven is just. I was not virtuous enough to leave off the crime. Fate robs me of my judgment. I could easily have bribed Elisa if I had wanted to; nothing was easier. I did not take the trouble to reflect for a moment. The mad imagination of love absorbed all my time. I am ruined.

When Julien apprised Madame de Rênal of the terrible news of his departure, he was struck with one thing. He did not find her put forward any selfish objections. She was evidently making efforts not to cry.

"We have need of firmness, my dear." She cut off a strand of her hair. "I do no know what I shall do," she said to him, "but promise me if I die, never to forget my children. Whether you are far or near, try to make them into honest men. If there is a new revolution, all the nobles will have their throats cut. Their father will probably emigrate, because of that peasant on the roof who got killed. Watch over my family. Give me your hand. Adieu, my dear. These are our last moments. Having made this great sacrifice, I hope I shall have the courage to consider my reputation in public."

Julien had been expecting despair. The simplicity of this farewell touched him.

"No, I am not going to receive your farewell like this. I will leave you now, as you yourself wish it. But three days after my departure I will come back to see you at night."

Madame de Rênal's life was changed. So Julien really loved her, since of his own accord he had thought of seeing her again. Her awful grief became changed into one of the keenest transports of joy which she had felt in her whole life. Everything became easy for her. The certainty of seeing her lover deprived these last moments of their poignancy. From that moment, both Madame de Rênal's demeanour and the expression of her face were noble, firm, and perfectly dignified.

M. de Rênal soon came back. He was beside himself. He eventually mentioned to his wife the anonymous letter which he had received two months before.

"I will take it to the Casino, and shew everybody that it has been sent by that brute Valenod, whom I took out of the gutter and made into one of the richest tradesmen in Verrières. I will disgrace him publicly, and then I will fight him. This is too much."

"Great Heavens! I may become a widow," thought Madame de Rênal, and almost at the same time she said to herself,

"If I do not, as I certainly can, prevent this duel, I shall be the murderess of my own husband."

She had never expended so much skill in honoring his vanity. Within two hours she made him see, and always by virtue of reasons which he discovered himself, that it was necessary to show more friendship than ever to M. Valenod, and even to take Elisa back into the household.

Madame de Rênal had need of courage to bring herself to see again the girl who was the cause of her unhappiness. But this idea was one of Julien's. Finally, having been put on the track three or four times, M. de Rênal arrived spontaneously at the conclusion, disagreeable though it was from the financial standpoint, that the most painful thing that could happen to him would be that Julien, in the middle of the effervescence of popular gossip throughout Verrières, should stay in the town as the tutor of Valenod's children. It was obviously to Julien's interest to accept the offer of the director of the workhouse. Conversely, it was essential for M. de Rênal's prestige that Julien should leave Verrières to enter the seminary of Besançon or that of Dijon. But how to make him decide on that course? And then how is he going to live?

M. de Rênal, seeing a monetary sacrifice looming in the distance, was in deeper despair than his wife. As for her, she felt after this interview in the position of a man of spirit who, tired of life, has taken a dose of stramonium. He only acts mechanically so to speak, and takes no longer any interest in anything. In this way, Louis XIV. came to say on his death-bed, "When I was king." An admirable epigram.

Next morning, M. de Rênal received quite early an anonymous letter. It was written in a most insulting style, and the coarsest words applicable to his position occurred on every line. It was the work of some jealous subordinate. This letter made him think again of fighting a duel with Valenod. Soon his courage went as far as the idea of immediate action. He left the house alone, went to the armourer's and got some pistols which he loaded.

"Yes, indeed," he said to himself, "even though the strict administration of the Emperor Napoleon were to become fashionable again, I should not have one sou's worth of jobbery to reproach myself with; at the outside, I have shut my eyes, and I have some good letters in my desk which authorise me to do so."

Madame de Rênal was terrified by her husband's cold anger. It recalled to her the fatal idea of widowhood which she had so much trouble in repelling. She closeted herself with him. For several hours she talked to him in vain. The new anonymous letter had decided him. Finally she succeeded in transforming the courage which had decided him to box Valenod's ears, into the courage of offering six hundred francs to Julien, which would keep him for one year in a seminary.

M. de Rênal cursed a thousand times the day that he had had the ill-starred idea of taking a tutor into his house, and forgot the anonymous letter.

He consoled himself a little by an idea which he did not tell his wife. With the exercise of some skill, and by exploiting the romantic ideas of the young man, he hoped to be able to induce him to refuse M. Valenod's offer at a cheaper price.

Madame de Rênal had much more trouble in proving to Julien that inasmuch as he was sacrificing the post of six hundred francs a year in order to enable her husband to keep up appearances, he need have no shame about accepting the compensation. But Julien would say each time, "I have never thought for a moment of accepting that offer. You have made me so used to a refined life that the coarseness of those people would kill me."

Cruel necessity bent Julien's will with its iron hand. His pride gave him the illusion that he only accepted the sum offered by M. de Rênal as a loan, and induced him to give him a promissory note, repayable in five years with interest.

Madame de Rênal had, of course, many thousands of francs which had been concealed in the little mountain cave.

She offered them to him all a tremble, feeling only too keenly that they would be angrily refused.

"Do you wish," said Julien to her, "to make the memory of our love loathsome?"

Finally Julien left Verrières. M. de Rênal was very happy, but when the fatal moment came to accept money from him the sacrifice proved beyond Julien's strength. He refused point blank. M. de Rênal embraced him around the neck with tears in his eyes. Julien had asked him for a testimonial of good conduct, and his enthusiasm could find no terms magnificent enough in which to extol his conduct.

Our hero had five louis of savings and he reckoned on asking Fouqué for an equal sum.

He was very moved. But one league from Verrières, where he left so much that was dear to him, he only thought of the happiness of seeing the capital of a great military town like Besançon.

During the short absence of three days, Madame de Rênal was the victim of one of the cruellest deceptions to which love is liable. Her life was tolerable, because between her and extreme unhappiness there was still that last interview which she was to have with Julien.

Finally during the night of the third day, she heard from a distance the preconcerted signal. Julien, having passed through a thousand dangers, appeared before her. In this moment she only had one thought—"I see him for the last time." Instead of answering the endearments of her lover, she seemed more dead than alive. If she forced herself to tell him that she loved him, she said it with an embarrassed air which almost proved the contrary. Nothing could rid her of the cruel idea of eternal separation. The suspicious Julien thought for the moment that he was already forgotten. His pointed remarks to this effect were only answered by great tears which flowed down in silence, and by some hysterical pressings of the hand.

"But," Julien would answer his mistress's cold protestations, "Great Heavens! How can you expect me to believe you? You would show one hundred times more sincere affection to Madame Derville to a mere acquaintance."

Madame de Rênal was petrified, and at a loss for an answer.

"It is impossible to be more unhappy. I hope I am going to die. I feel my heart turn to ice."

Those were the longest answers which he could obtain.

When the approach of day rendered it necessary for him to leave Madame de Rênal, her tears completely ceased. She saw him tie a knotted rope to the window without saying a word, and without returning her kisses. It was in vain that Julien said to her.

"So now we have reached the state of affairs which you wished for so much. Henceforward you will live without remorse. The slightest indisposition of your children will no longer make you see them in the tomb."

"I am sorry that you cannot kiss Stanislas," she said coldly.

Julien finished by being profoundly impressed by the cold embraces of this living corpse. He could think of nothing else for several leagues. His soul was overwhelmed, and before passing the mountain, and while he could still see the church tower of Verrières he turned round frequently.

XXIV
A CAPITAL

What a noise, what busy people! What ideas for the
future in a brain of twenty! What distraction offered by
love.—*Barnave.*

Finally he saw some black walls near a distant mountain. It was the citadel of Besançon. "How different it would be for me," he said with a sigh, "if I were arriving at this noble military town to be sub-lieutenant in one of the regiments entrusted with its defence." Besançon is not only one of the prettiest towns in France, it abounds in people of spirit and brains. But Julien was only a little peasant, and had no means of approaching distinguished people.

He had taken a civilian suit at Fouqué's, and it was in this dress that he passed the drawbridge. Steeped as he was in the history of the siege of 1674, he wished to see the ramparts of the citadel before shutting himself up in the seminary. He was within an ace two or three times of getting himself arrested by the sentinel. He was penetrating into places which military genius forbids the public to enter, in order to sell twelve or fifteen francs worth of corn every year.

The height of the walls, the depth of the ditches, the terrible aspect of the cannons had been engrossing him for several hours when he passed before the great café on the boulevard. He was motionless with wonder; it was in vain that he read the word *café*, written in big characters above the two immense doors. He could not believe his eyes. He made an effort to overcome his timidity. He dared to enter, and found himself in a hall twenty or thirty yards long, and with a ceiling at least twenty feet high. To-day, everything had a fascination for him.

Two games of billiards were in progress. The waiters were crying out the scores. The players ran round the tables encumbered by spectators. Clouds of tobacco smoke came from everybody's mouth, and enveloped them in a blue haze. The high stature of these men, their rounded shoulders, their heavy gait, their enormous whiskers, the long tailed coats which covered them, everything combined to attract Julien's attention. These noble children of the antique Bisontium only spoke at the top of their voice. They gave themselves terrible martial airs. Julien stood still and admired them. He kept thinking of the immensity and magnificence of a great capital like Besançon. He felt absolutely devoid of the requisite courage to ask one of those haughty looking gentlemen, who were crying out the billiard scores, for a cup of coffee.

But the young lady at the bar had noticed the charming face of this young civilian from the country, who had stopped three feet from the stove with his little parcel under his arm, and was looking at the fine white plaster bust of the king. This young lady, a big *Franc-comtoise*, very well made, and dressed with the elegance suitable to the prestige of the café, had already said two or three times in a little voice not intended to be heard by any one except Julien, "Monsieur, Monsieur." Julien's eyes encountered big blue eyes full of tenderness, and saw that he was the person who was being spoken to.

He sharply approached the bar and the pretty girl, as though he had been marching towards the enemy. In this great manœuvre the parcel fell.

What pity will not our provincial inspire in the young lycée scholars of Paris, who, at the early age of fifteen, know already how to enter a café with so distinguished an air? But these children who have such style at fifteen turn commonplace at eighteen. The impassioned timidity which is met with in the provinces, sometimes manages to master its own nervousness, and thus trains the will. "I must tell her the truth," thought Julien, who was becoming courageous by dint of conquering his timidity as he approached this pretty girl, who deigned to address him.

"Madame, this is the first time in my life that I have come to Besançon. I should like to have some bread and a cup of coffee in return for payment."

The young lady smiled a little, and then blushed. She feared the ironic attention and the jests of the billiard players might be turned against this pretty young man. He would be frightened and would not appear there again.

"Sit here near me," she said to him, showing him a marble table almost completely hidden by the enormous mahogany counter which extended into the hall.

The young lady leant over the counter, and had thus an opportunity of displaying a superb figure. Julien noticed it. All his ideas changed. The pretty young lady had just placed before him a cup, some sugar, and a little roll. She hesitated to call a waiter for the coffee, as she realised that his arrival would put an end to her *tête-à-tête* with Julien.

Julien was pensively comparing this blonde and merry beauty with certain memories which would often thrill him. The thought of the passion of which he had been the object, nearly freed him from all his timidity. The pretty young woman had only one moment to save the situation. She read it in Julien's looks.

"This pipe smoke makes you cough; come and have breakfast tomorrow before eight o'clock in the morning. I am practically alone then."

"What is your name?" said Julien, with the caressing smile of happy timidity.

"Amanda Binet."

"Will you allow me to send you within an hour's time a little parcel about as big as this?"

The beautiful Amanda reflected a little.

"I am watched. What you ask may compromise me. All the same, I will write my address on a card, which you will put on your parcel. Send it boldly to me."

"My name is Julien Sorel," said the young man. "I have neither relatives nor acquaintances at Besançon."

"Ah, I understand," she said joyfully. "You come to study law."

"Alas, no," answered Julien, "I am being sent to the Seminary."

The most complete discouragement damped Amanda's features. She called a waiter. She had courage now. The waiter poured out some coffee for Julien without looking at him.

Amanda was receiving money at the counter. Julien was proud of having dared to speak: a dispute was going on at one of the billiard tables. The cries and the protests of the players resounded over the immense hall, and made a din which astonished Julien. Amanda was dreamy, and kept her eyes lowered.

"If you like, Mademoiselle," he said to her suddenly with assurance, "I will say that I am your cousin."

This little air of authority pleased Amanda. "He's not a mere nobody," she thought. She spoke to him very quickly, without looking at him, because her eye was occupied in seeing if anybody was coming near the counter.

"I come from Genlis, near Dijon. Say that you are also from Genlis and are my mother's cousin."

"I shall not fail to do so."

"All the gentlemen who go to the Seminary pass here before the café every Thursday in the summer at five o'clock."

"If you think of me when I am passing, have a bunch of violets in your hand."

Amanda looked at him with an astonished air. This look changed Julien's courage into audacity. Nevertheless, he reddened considerably, as he said to her. "I feel that I love you with the most violent love."

"Speak in lower tones," she said to him with a frightened air.

Julien was trying to recollect phrases out of a volume of the *Nouvelle Héloise* which he had found at Vergy. His memory served him in good stead. For ten minutes he recited the *Nouvelle Héloise* to the delighted Mademoiselle Amanda. He was happy on the strength of his own bravery, when suddenly the beautiful Franc-contoise assumed an icy air. One of her lovers had appeared at the café door. He approached the bar, whistling, and swaggering his shoulders. He looked at Julien. The latter's imagination, which always indulged in extremes, suddenly brimmed over with ideas of a duel. He paled greatly, put down his cup, assumed an assured demeanour, and considered his rival very attentively. As this rival lowered his head, while he familiarly poured out on the counter a glass of brandy for himself, Amanda ordered Julien with a look to lower his eyes. He obeyed, and for two minutes kept motionless in his place, pale, resolute, and only thinking of what was going to happen. He was truly happy at this moment. The rival had been astonished by Julien's eyes. Gulping down his glass of brandy, he said a few words to Amanda, placed his two hands in the pockets of his big tail coat, and approached the billiard table, whistling, and looking at Julien. The latter got up transported with rage, but he did not know what to do in order to be offensive. He put down his little parcel, and walked towards the billiard table with all the swagger he could muster.

It was in vain that prudence said to him, "but your ecclesiastical career will be ruined by a duel immediately on top of your arrival at Besançon."

"What does it matter. It shall never be said that I let an insolent fellow go scot free."

Amanda saw his courage. It contrasted prettily with the simplicity of his manners. She instantly preferred him to the big young man with the tail coat. She got up, and while appearing to be following with her eye somebody who was passing in the street, she went and quickly placed herself between him and the billiard table.

"Take care not to look askance at that gentleman. He is my brother-in-law."

"What does it matter? He looked at me."

"Do you want to make me unhappy? No doubt he looked at you, why it may be he is going to speak to you. I told him that you were a relative of my mother, and that you had arrived from Genlis. He is a Franc-contois, and has never gone beyond Dôleon the Burgundy Road, so say what you like and fear nothing."

Julien was still hesitating. Her barmaid's imagination furnished her with an abundance of lies, and she quickly added.

"No doubt he looked at you, but it was at a moment when he was asking me who you were. He is a man who is boorish with everyone. He did not mean to insult you."

Julien's eye followed the pretended brother-in-law. He saw him buy a ticket for the pool, which they were playing at the further of the two billiard tables. Julien heard his loud voice shouting out in a threatening tone, "My turn to play."

He passed sharply before Madame Amanda, and took a step towards the billiard table. Amanda seized him by the arm.

"Come and pay me first," she said to him.

"That is right," thought Julien. "She is frightened that I shall leave without paying." Amanda was as agitated as he was, and very red. She gave him the change as slowly as she could, while she repeated to him, in a low voice,

"Leave the café this instant, or I shall love you no more, and yet I do love you very much."

Julien did go out, but slowly. "Am I not in duty bound," he repeated to himself, "to go and stare at that coarse person in my turn?" This uncertainty kept him on the boulevard in the front of the café for an hour; he kept looking if his man was coming out. He did not come out, and Julien went away.

He had only been at Besançon some hours, and already he had over-come one pang of remorse. The old surgeon-major had formerly given him some fencing lessons, in spite of his gout. That was all the science which Julien could enlist in the service of his anger. But this embarrass-ment would have been nothing if he had only known how to vent his temper otherwise than by the giving of a blow, for if it had come to a matter of fisticuffs, his enormous rival would have beaten him and then cleared out.

"There is not much difference between a seminary and a prison," said Julien to himself, "for a poor devil like me, without protectors and without money. I must leave my civilian clothes in some inn, where I can put my black suit on again. If I ever manage to get out of the seminary for a few hours, I shall be able to see Mdlle. Amanda again in my lay clothes." This reasoning was all very fine. Though Julien passed in front of all the inns, he did not dare to enter a single one.

Finally, as he was passing again before the Hôtel des Ambassadeurs, his anxious eyes encountered those of a big woman, still fairly young, with a high colour, and a gay and happy air. He approached her and told his story.

"Certainly, my pretty little abbé," said the hostess of the Ambassadeurs to him, "I will keep your lay clothes for you, and I will even have them regularly brushed. In weather like this, it is not good to leave a suit of cloth without touching it." She took a key, and conducted him herself to a room, and advised him to make out a note of what he was leaving.

"Good heavens. How well you look like that, M. the abbé Sorel," said the big woman to him when he came down to the kitchen. I will go and get a good dinner served up to you, and she added in a low voice, "It will only cost twenty sous instead of the fifty which everybody else pays, for one must really take care of your little purse strings."

"I have ten louis," Julien replied with certain pride.

"Oh, great heavens," answered the good hostess in alarm. "Don't talk so loud, there are quite a lot of bad characters in Besançon. They'll steal all that from you in less than no time, and above all, never go into the café s, they are filled with bad characters."

"Indeed," said Julien, to whom those words gave food for thought.

"Don't go anywhere else, except to my place. I will make coffee for you. Remember that you will always find a friend here, and a good dinner for twenty sous. So now you understand, I hope. Go and sit down at table, I will serve you myself."

"I shan't be able to eat," said Julien to her. "I am too upset. I am going to enter the seminary, as I leave you." The good woman, would not allow him to leave before she had filled his pockets with provisions. Finally Julien took his road towards the terrible place. The hostess was standing at the threshold, and showed him the way.

XXV
THE SEMINARY

Three hundred and thirty-six dinners at eighty-five centimes.
Three hundred and thirty-six suppers at fifty centimes. Chocolate to those who are entitled to it. How much profit can be
made on the contract?—*Valenod of Besançon.*

He saw in the distance the iron gilt cross on the door. He approached
slowly. His legs seemed to give way beneath him. "So here is this hell
upon earth which I shall be unable to leave."

Finally he made up his mind to ring. The noise of the bell reverberated as though through a solitude. At the end of ten minutes a pale man,
clothed in black, came and opened the door. Julien looked at him, and
immediately lowered his eyes. This porter had a singular physiognomy.
The green projecting pupils of his eyes were as round as those of a cat.
The straight lines of his eyebrows betokened the impossibility of any
sympathy. His thin lips came round in a semicircle over projecting teeth.
None the less, his physiognomy did not so much betoken crime as rather
that perfect callousness which is so much more terrifying to the young.
The one sentiment which Julien's rapid gaze surmised in this long and
devout face was a profound contempt for every topic of conversation
which did not deal with things celestial. Julien raised his eyes with an
effort, and in a voice rendered quavering by the beating of his heart
explained that he desired to speak to M. Pirard, the director of the Seminary. Without saying a word the man in black signed to him to follow.
They ascended two stories by a large staircase with a wooden rail, whose
warped stairs inclined to the side opposite the wall, and seemed on the
point of falling. A little door with a big cemetery cross of white wood
painted black at the top was opened with difficulty, and the porter made
him enter a dark low room, whose whitewashed walls were decorated
with two big pictures blackened by age. In this room Julien was left alone.
He was overwhelmed. His heart was beating violently. He would have
been happy to have ventured to cry. A silence of death reigned over the
whole house.

At the end of a quarter of an hour, which seemed a whole day to
him, the sinister looking porter reappeared on the threshold of a door
at the other end of the room, and without vouchsafing a word, signed
to him to advance. He entered into a room even larger than the first,
and very badly lighted. The walls also were whitened, but there was no
furniture. Only in a corner near the door Julien saw as he passed a white

wooden bed, two straw chairs, and a little pinewood armchair without any cushions. He perceived at the other end of the room, near a small window with yellow panes decorated with badly kept flower vases, a man seated at a table, and covered with a dilapidated cassock. He appeared to be in a temper, and took one after the other a number of little squares of paper, which he arranged on his table after he had written some words on them. He did not notice Julien's presence. The latter did not move, but kept standing near the centre of the room in the place where the porter, who had gone out and shut the door, had left him.

Ten minutes passed in this way: the badly dressed man kept on writing all the time. Julien's emotion and terror were so great that he thought he was on the point of falling. A philosopher would have said, possibly wrongly, "It is a violent impression made by ugliness on a soul intended by nature to love the beautiful."

The man who was writing lifted up his head. Julien only perceived it after a moment had passed, and even after seeing it, he still remained motionless, as though struck dead by the terrible look of which he was the victim. Julien's troubled eyes just managed to make out a long face, all covered with red blotches except the forehead, which manifested a mortal pallor. Two little black eyes, calculated to terrify the most courageous, shone between these red cheeks and that white forehead. The vast area of his forehead was bounded by thick, flat, jet black hair.

"Will you come near, yes or no?" said the man at last, impatiently.

Julien advanced with an uneasy step, and at last, paler than he had ever been in his life and on the point of falling, stopped three paces from the little white wooden table which was covered with the squares of paper.

"Nearer," said the man.

Julien advanced still further, holding out his hand, as though trying to lean on something.

"Your name?"

"Julien Sorel."

"You are certainly very late," said the man to him, as he rivetted again on him that terrible gaze.

Julien could not endure this look. Holding out his hand as though to support himself, he fell all his length along the floor.

The man rang. Julien had only lost the use of his eyes and the power of movement. He heard steps approaching.

He was lifted up and placed on the little armchair of white wood. He heard the terrible man saying to the porter,

"He has had an epileptic fit apparently, and this is the finishing touch."

When Julien was able to open his eyes, the man with the red face was going on with his writing. The porter had disappeared. "I must have courage," said our hero to himself, "and above all, hide what I feel." He felt violently sick. "If anything happens to me, God knows what they will think of me."

Finally the man stopped writing and looked sideways at Julien.

"Are you in a fit state to answer me?"

"Yes, sir," said Julien in an enfeebled voice.

"Ah, that's fortunate."

The man in black had half got up, and was looking impatiently for a letter in the drawer of his pinewood table, which opened with a grind. He found it, sat down slowly, and looking again at Julien in a manner calculated to suck out of him the little life which he still possessed, said,

"You have been recommended to me by M. Chélan. He was the best curé in the diocese; he was an upright man if there ever was one, and my friend for thirty years."

"Oh. It's to M. Pirard then that I have the honour of speaking?" said Julien in a dying voice.

"Apparently," replied the director of the seminary, as he looked at him disagreeably.

The glitter of his little eyes doubled and was followed by an involuntary movement of the muscles of the corner of the mouth. It was the physiognomy of the tiger savouring in advance the pleasure of devouring its prey.

"Chélan's letter is short," he said, as though speaking to himself. "*Intelligenti pauca*. In the present time it is impossible to write too little." He read aloud:—

"I recommend to you Julien Sorel of this parish, whom I baptized nearly twenty years ago, the son of a rich carpenter who gives him nothing. Julien will be a remarkable worker in the vineyard of the Lord. He lacks neither memory nor intelligence; he has some faculty for reflection. Will he persevere in his calling? Is he sincere?"

"Sincere," repeated the abbé Pirard with an astonished air, looking at Julien. But the abbé's look was already less devoid of all humanity. "Sincere," he repeated, lowering his voice, and resuming his reading:—

"I ask you for a stipend for Julien Sorel. He will earn it by passing the necessary examinations. I have taught him a little theology, that old and good theology of the Bossuets, the Arnaults, and the Fleury's. If the person does not suit you, send him back to me. The director of the workhouse, whom you know well, offers him eight hundred to be tutor to his children. My inner self is tranquil, thanks to God. I am accustoming myself to the terrible blow, 'Vale et me ama.'"

The abbé Pirard, speaking more slowly as he read the signature, pronounced with a sigh the word, "Chélan."

"He is tranquil," he said, "in fact his righteousness deserves such a recompense. May God grant it to me in such a case." He looked up to heaven and made the sign of the cross. At the sight of that sacred sign Julien felt an alleviation of the profound horror which had frozen him since his entry into the house.

"I have here three hundred and twenty-one aspirants for the most holy state," said the abbé Pirard at last, in a tone, which though severe, was not malicious; "only seven or eight have been recommended to me by such men as the abbé Chélan; so you will be the ninth of these among the three hundred and twenty-one. But my protection means neither favour nor weakness, it means doubled care, and doubled severity against vice. Go and lock that door."

Julian made an effort to walk, and managed not to fall. He noticed that a little window near the entrance door looked out on to the country. He saw the trees; that sight did him as much good as the sight of old friends.

"'Loquerisne linquam latinam?'" (Do you speak Latin?) said the abbé Pirard to him as he came back.

"'Ita, pater optime,'" (Yes, excellent Father) answered Julien, recovering himself a little. But it was certain that nobody in the world had ever appeared to him less excellent than had M. Pirard for the last half hour.

The conversation continued in Latin. The expression in the abbé's eyes softened. Julien regained some self-possession. "How weak I am," he thought, "to let myself be imposed on by these appearances of virtue. The man is probably nothing more than a rascal, like M. Maslon," and Julien congratulated himself on having hidden nearly all his money in his boots.

The abbé Pirard examined Julien in theology; he was surprised at the extent of his knowledge, but his astonishment increased when he questioned him in particular on sacred scriptures. But when it came to questions of the doctrines of the Fathers, he perceived that Julien scarcely even knew the names of Saint Jerome, Saint Augustin, Saint Bonaventure, Saint Basile, etc., etc.

"As a matter of fact," thought the abbé Pirard, "this is simply that fatal tendency to Protestantism for which I have always reproached Chélan. A profound, and only too profound knowledge of the Holy Scriptures."

(Julien had just started speaking to him, without being questioned on the point, about the real time when Genesis, the Pentateuch, etc., has been written).

"To what does this never-ending reasoning over the Holy Scriptures lead to?" thought the abbé Pirard, "if not to self-examination, that is to say, the most awful Protestantism. And by the side of this imprudent knowledge, nothing about the Fathers to compensate for that tendency."

But the astonishment of the director of the seminary was quite unbounded when having questioned Julien about the authority of the Pope, and expecting to hear the maxims of the ancient Gallican Church, the young man recited to him the whole book of M. de Maistre "Strange man, that Chélan," thought the abbé Pirard. "Did he show him the book simply to teach him to make fun of it?"

It was in vain that he questioned Julien and endeavoured to guess if he seriously believed in the doctrine of M. de Maistre. The young man only answered what he had learnt by heart. From this moment Julien was really happy. He felt that he was master of himself. After a very long examination, it seemed to him that M. Pirard's severity towards him was only affected. Indeed, the director of the seminary would have embraced Julien in the name of logic, for he found so much clearness, precision and lucidity in his answers, had it not been for the principles of austere gravity towards his theology pupils which he had inculcated in himself for the last fifteen years.

"Here we have a bold and healthy mind," he said to himself, "but corpus debile" (the body is weak).

"Do you often fall like that?" he said to Julien in French, pointing with his finger to the floor.

"It's the first time in my life. The porter's face unnerved me," added Julien, blushing like a child. The abbé Pirard almost smiled.

"That's the result of vain worldly pomp. You are apparently accustomed to smiling faces, those veritable theatres of falsehood. Truth is austere, Monsieur, but is not our task down here also austere? You must be careful that your conscience guards against that weakness of yours, too much sensibility to vain external graces."

"If you had not been recommended to me," said the abbé Pirard, resuming the Latin language with an obvious pleasure, "If you had not been recommended by a man, by the abbé Chélan, I would talk to you the vain language of that world, to which it would appear you are only too well accustomed. I would tell you that the full stipend which you solicit is the most difficult thing in the world to obtain. But the fifty-six years which the abbé Chélan has spent in apostolic work have stood him in poor stead if he cannot dispose of a stipend at the seminary."

After these words, the abbé Pirard recommended Julien not to enter any secret society or congregation without his consent.

"I give you my word of honour," said Julien, with all an honest man's expansion of heart. The director of the seminary smiled for the first time.

"That expression is not used here," he said to him. "It is too reminiscent of that vain honour of worldly people, which leads them to so many errors and often to so many crimes. You owe me obedience by virtue of paragraph seventeen of the bull Unam Eccesiam of St. Pius the Fifth. I am your ecclesiastical superior. To hear in this house, my dear son, is to obey. How much money, have you?"

("So here we are," said Julien to himself, "that was the reason of the 'my very dear son')."

"Thirty-five francs, my father."

"Write out carefully how you use that money. You will have to give me an account of it."

This painful audience had lasted three hours. Julien summoned the porter.

"Go and install Julien Sorel in cell No. 103," said the abbé Pirard to the man.

As a great favour he let Julien have a place all to himself. "Carry his box there," he added.

Julien lowered his eyes, and recognised his box just in front of him. He had been looking at it for three hours and had not recognised it.

As he arrived at No. 103, which was a little room eight feet square on the top story of the house, Julien noticed that it looked out on to the ramparts, and he perceived beyond them the pretty plain which the Doubs divides from the town.

"What a charming view!" exclaimed Julien. In speaking like this he did not feel what the words actually expressed. The violent sensations which he had experienced during the short time that he had been at Besançon had absolutely exhausted his strength. He sat down near the window on the one wooden chair in the cell, and fell at once into a profound sleep. He did not hear either the supper bell or the bell for benediction. They had forgotten him. When the first rays of the sun woke him up the following morning, he found himself lying on the floor.

XXVI
THE WORLD, OR WHAT THE RICH LACK

I am alone in the world. No one deigns to spare me a thought.
All those whom I see make their fortune, have an insolence
and hardness of heart which I do not feel in myself. They
hate me by reason of kindness and good-humour. Oh, I shall
die soon, either from starvation or the unhappiness of seeing
men so hard of heart.—*Young*.

He hastened to brush his clothes and run down. He was late. Instead
of trying to justify himself Julien crossed his arms over his breast.

"Peccavi pater optime (I have sinned, I confess my fault, oh, my
father)," he said with a contrite air.

This first speech was a great success. The clever ones among the
seminarists saw that they had to deal with a man who knew something
about the elements of the profession. The recreation hour arrived,
and Julien saw that he was the object of general curiosity, but he only
manifested reserved silence. Following the maxims he had laid down
for himself, he considered his three hundred and twenty-one comrades
as enemies. The most dangerous of all in his eyes was the abbé Pirard. A
few days afterwards Julien had to choose a confessor, and was given a
list.

"Great heavens! what do they take me for?" he said to himself. "Do
they think I don't understand what's what?" Then he chose the abbé
Pirard.

This step proved decisive without his suspecting it.

A little seminarist, who was quite young and a native of Verrières,
and who had declared himself his friend since the first day, informed
him that he would probably have acted more prudently if he had chosen
M. Castanède, the sub-director of the seminary.

"The abbé Castanède is the enemy of Pirard, who is suspected of
Jansenism," added the little seminarist in a whisper. All the first steps of
our hero were, in spite of the prudence on which he plumed himself, as
much mistakes as his choice of a confessor. Misled as he was by all the
self-confidence of a man of imagination, he took his projects for facts,
and believed that he was a consummate hypocrite. His folly went so far
as to reproach himself for his success in this kind of weakness.

"Alas, it is my only weapon," he said to himself. "At another period I
should have earned my livelihood by eloquent deeds in the face of the
enemy."

Satisfied as he was with his own conduct, Julien looked around him.
He found everywhere the appearance of the purest virtue.

Eight or ten seminarists lived in the odour of sanctity, and had visions like Saint Theresa, and Saint Francis, when he received his stigmata on Mount *Vernia* in the Appenines. But it was a great secret and their friends concealed it. These poor young people who had visions were always in the infirmary. A hundred others combined an indefatigable application to a robust faith. They worked till they fell ill, but without learning much. Two or three were distinguished by a real talent, amongst others a student of the name of Chazel, but both they and Julien felt mutually unsympathetic.

The rest of these three hundred and twenty-one seminarists consisted exclusively of coarse persons, who were by no means sure of understanding the Latin words which they kept on repeating the live-long day. Nearly all were the sons of peasants, and they preferred to gain their livelihood by reciting some Latin words than by ploughing the earth. It was after this examination of his colleagues that Julien, during the first few days, promised himself a speedy success.

"Intelligent people are needed in every service," he said to himself, "for, after all, there is work to be done. I should have been a sergeant under Napoleon. I shall be a grand vicar among these future curés."

"All these poor devils," he added, "manual labourers as they have been since their childhood, have lived on curded milk and black bread up till they arrived here. They would only eat meat five or six times a year in their hovels. Like the Roman soldiers who used to find war the time of rest, these poor peasants are enchanted with the delights of the seminary."

Julien could never read anything in their gloomy eyes but the satisfaction of physical craving after dinner, and the expectation of sensual pleasure before the meal. Such were the people among whom Julien had to distinguish himself; but the fact which he did not know, and which they refrained from telling him, was that coming out first in the different courses of dogma, ecclesiastical history, etc., etc., which are taken at the seminary, constituted in their eyes, neither more nor less than a splendid sin.

Since the time of Voltaire and two-chamber Government, which is at bottom simply distrust and personal self-examination, and gives the popular mind that bad habit of being suspicious, the Church of France seems to have realised that books are its real enemies. It is the submissive heart which counts for everything in its eyes. It suspects, and rightly so, any success in studies, even sacred ones. What is to prevent a superior man from crossing over to the opposite side like Sièyes or Gregory. The trembling Church clings on to the Pope as its one chance of safety. The Pope alone is in a position to attempt to paralyse all personal self-examination, and to make an impression by means of the pompous piety of his court ceremonial on the bored and morbid spirit of fashionable society.

Julien, as he began to get some glimpse of these various truths, which are none the less in total contradiction to all the official pronouncements of any seminary, fell into a profound melancholy. He worked a great deal and rapidly succeeded in learning things which were extremely useful to a priest, extremely false in his own eyes, and devoid of the slightest interest for him. He felt there was nothing else to do.

"Am I then forgotten by the whole world," he thought. He did not know that M. Pirard had received and thrown into the fire several letters with the Dijon stamp in which the most lively passion would pierce through the most formal conventionalism of style. "This love seems to be fought by great attacks of remorse. All the better," thought the abbé Pirard. "At any rate this lad has not loved an infidel woman."

One day the abbé Pirard opened a letter which seemed half-blotted out by tears. It was an adieu for ever. "At last," said the writer to Julien, "Heaven has granted me the grace of hating, not the author of my fall, but my fall itself. The sacrifice has been made, dear one, not without tears as you see. The safety of those to whom I must devote my life, and whom you love so much, is the decisive factor. A just but terrible God will no longer see His way to avenge on them their mother's crimes. Adieu, Julien. Be just towards all men." The end of the letter was nearly entirely illegible. The writer gave an address at Dijon, but at the same time expressed the hope that Julien would not answer, or at any rate would employ language which a reformed woman could read without blushing. Julien's melancholy, aggravated by the mediocre nourishment which the contractor who gave dinners at thirteen centimes per head supplied to the seminary, began to affect his health, when Fouqué suddenly appeared in his room one morning.

"I have been able to get in at last. I have duly been five times to Besançon in order to see you. Could never get in. I put someone by the door to watch. Why the devil don't you ever go out?"

"It is a test which I have imposed on myself."

"I find you greatly changed, but here you are again. I have just learned from a couple of good five franc pieces that I was only a fool not to have offered them on my first journey."

The conversation of the two friends went on for ever. Julien changed colour when Fouqué said to him,

"Do you know, by the by, that your pupils' mother has become positively devout."

And he began to talk in that off-hand manner which makes so singular an impression on the passionate soul, whose dearest interests are being destroyed without the speaker having the faintest suspicion of it.

"Yes, my friend, the most exalted devoutness. She is said to make pilgrimages. But to the eternal shame of the abbé Maslon, who has played the spy so long on that poor M. Chélan, Madame de Rênal would have nothing to do with him. She goes to confession to Dijon or Besançon."

"She goes to Besançon," said Julien, flushing all over his forehead.

"Pretty often," said Fouqué in a questioning manner.

"Have you got any *Constitutionnels* on you?"

"What do you say?" replied Fouqué.

"I'm asking if you've got any *Constitutionnels?*" went on Julien in the quietest tone imaginable. "They cost thirty sous a number here."

"What!" exclaimed Fouqué. "Liberals even in the seminary! Poor France," he added, assuming the abbé Maslon's hypocritical voice and sugary tone.

This visit would have made a deep impression on our hero, if he had not been put on the track of an important discovery by some words addressed to him the following day by the little seminarist from Verrières. Julien's conduct since he had been at the seminary had been nothing but a series of false steps. He began to make bitter fun of himself.

In point of fact the important actions in his life had been cleverly managed, but he was careless about details, and cleverness in a seminary consists in attention to details. Consequently, he had already the reputation among his comrades of being a *strong-minded person*. He had been betrayed by a number of little actions.

He had been convicted in their eyes of this enormity, *he thought and judged for himself* instead of blindly following authority and example. The abbé Pirard had been no help to him. He had not spoken to him on a single occasion apart from the confessional, and even there he listened more than he spoke. Matters would have been very different if he had chosen the abbé Castanède. The moment that Julien realised his folly, he ceased to be bored. He wished to know the whole extent of the evil, and to effect this emerged a little from that haughty obstinate silence with which he had scrupulously rebuffed his comrades. It was now that they took their revenge on him. His advances were welcomed by a contempt verging on derision. He realised that there had not been one single hour from the time of his entry into the seminary, particularly during recreation time, which had not resulted in affecting him one way or another, which had not increased the number of his enemies, or won for him the goodwill of some seminarist who was either sincerely virtuous or of a fibre slightly less coarse than that of the others. The evil to repair was infinite, and the task very difficult. Henceforth, Julien's attention was always on guard. The problem before him was to map out a new character for himself.

The moving of his eyes for example, occasioned him a great deal of trouble. It is with good reason that they are carried lowered in these places.

"How presumptuous I was at Verrières," said Julien to himself. "I thought I lived; I was only preparing for life, and here I am at last in the world such as I shall find it, until my part comes to an end, surrounded by real enemies. What immense difficulties," he added, "are involved in keeping up this hypocrisy every single minute. It is enough to put the labours of Hercules into the shade. The Hercules of modern times is the Pope Sixtus Quintus, who deceived by his modesty fifteen years on end forty Cardinals who had seen the liveliness and haughtiness of his whole youth.

"So knowledge is nothing here," he said to himself with disgust. "Progress in doctrine, in sacred history, etc., only seem to count. Everything said on those subjects is only intended to entrap fools like me. Alas my only merit consists in my rapid progress, and in the way in which I grasp all their nonsense. Do they really value those things at their true worth? Do they judge them like I do. And I had the stupidity to be proud of my quickness. The only result of my coming out top has been to give me inveterate enemies. Chazel, who really knows more than I do, always throws some blunder in his compositions which gets him put back to the fiftieth place. If he comes out first, it is only because he is absent-minded. O how useful would one word, just one word, of M. Pirard, have been to me."

As soon as Julien was disillusioned, the long exercises in ascetic piety, such as the attendances in the chapel five times a week, the intonation of hymns at the chapel of the Sacré Cœur, etc., etc., which had previously seemed to him so deadly boring, became his most interesting opportunities for action. Thanks to a severe introspection, and above all, by trying not to overdo his methods, Julien did not attempt at the outset to perform significant actions (that is to say, actions which are proof of a certain Christian perfection) like those seminarists who served as a model to the rest.

Seminarists have a special way, even of eating a poached egg, which betokens progress in the devout life.

The reader who smiles at this will perhaps be good enough to remember all the mistakes which the abbé Delille made over the eating of an egg when he was invited to breakfast with a lady of the Court of Louis XVI.

Julien first tried to arrive at the state of *non culpa*, that is to say the state of the young seminarist whose demeanour and manner of moving his arms, eyes, etc. while in fact without any trace of worldliness, do not yet indicate that the person is entirely absorbed by the conception of the other world, and the idea of the pure nothingness of this one.

Julien incessantly found such phrases as these charcoaled on the walls of the corridors. "What are sixty years of ordeals balanced against an eternity of delights or any eternity of boiling oil in hell?" He despised them no longer. He realised that it was necessary to have them incessantly before his eyes. "What am I going to do all my life," he said to himself. "I shall sell to the faithful a place in heaven. How am I going to make that place visible to their eyes? By the difference between my appearance and that of a layman."

After several months of absolutely unremitting application, Julien still had the appearance of thinking. The way in which he would move his eyes and hold his mouth did not betoken that implicit faith which is ready to believe everything and undergo everything, even at the cost of martyrdom. Julien saw with anger that he was surpassed in this by the coarsest peasants. There was good reason for their not appearing full of thought.

What pains did he not take to acquire that facial expression of blindly fervent faith which is found so frequently in the Italian convents, and of which Le Guerchin has left such perfect models in his Church pictures for the benefit of us laymen.

On feast-days, the seminarists were regaled with sausages and cabbage. Julien's table neighbours observed that he did not appreciate this happiness. That was looked upon as one of his paramount crimes. His comrades saw in this a most odious trait, and the most foolish hypocrisy. Nothing made him more enemies.

"Look at this bourgeois, look at this stuck-up person," they would say, "who pretends to despise the best rations there are, sausages and cabbage, shame on the villain! The haughty wretch, he is damned for ever."

"Alas, these young peasants, who are my comrades, find their ignorance an immense advantage," Julien would exclaim in his moments of discouragement. "The professor has not got to deliver them on their arrival at the seminary from that awful number of worldly ideas which I brought into it, and which they read on my face whatever I do."

Julien watched with an attention bordering on envy the coarsest of the little peasants who arrived at the seminary. From the moment when they were made to doff their shabby jackets to don the black robe, their education consisted of an immense and limitless respect for *hard liquid cash* as they say in Franche-Comté.

That is the consecrated and heroic way of expressing the sublime idea of current money.

These seminarists, like the heroes in Voltaire's novels, found their happiness in dining well. Julien discovered in nearly all of them an innate respect for the man who wears a suit of good cloth. This sentiment appreciates the distributive justice, which is given us at our courts, at its value or even above its true value. "What can one gain," they would often repeat among themselves, "by having a law suit with 'a big man?'"

That is the expression current in the valleys of the Jura to express a rich man. One can judge of their respect for the richest entity of all—the government. Failure to smile deferentially at the mere name of M. the Prefect is regarded as an imprudence in the eyes of the Franche-Comté peasant, and imprudence in poor people is quickly punished by lack of bread.

After having been almost suffocated at first by his feeling of contempt, Julien eventually experienced a feeling of pity; it often happened that the fathers of most of his comrades would enter their hovel in winter evenings and fail to find there either bread, chestnuts or potatoes.

"What is there astonishing then?" Julien would say to himself, "if in their eyes the happy man is in the first place the one who has just had a good dinner, and in the second place the one who possesses a good suit? My comrades have a lasting vocation, that is to say, they see in the ecclesiastical calling a long continuance of the happiness of dining well and having a warm suit."

Julien happened to hear a young imaginative seminarist say to his companion.

"Why shouldn't I become Pope like Sixtus Quintus who kept pigs?"

"They only make Italians Popes," answered his friend. "But they will certainly draw lots amongst us for the great vicarships, canonries and perhaps bishoprics. M. P—— Bishop of Châlons, is the son of a cooper. That's what my father is."

One day, in the middle of a theology lesson, the Abbé Pirard summoned Julien to him. The young fellow was delighted to leave the dark, moral atmosphere in which he had been plunged. Julien received from the director the same welcome which had frightened him so much on the first day of his entry.

"Explain to me what is written on this playing card?" he said, looking at him in a way calculated to make him sink into the earth.

Julien read:

"Amanda Binet of the Giraffe Café before eight o'clock. Say you're from Genlis, and my mother's cousin."

Julien realised the immense danger. The spies of the abbé Castanède had stolen the address.

"I was trembling with fear the day I came here," he answered, looking at the abbé Pirard's forehead, for he could not endure that terrible gaze. "M. Chélan told me that this is a place of informers and mischief-makers of all kinds, and that spying and tale-bearing by one comrade on another was encouraged by the authorities. Heaven wishes it to be so, so as to show life such as it is to the young priests, and fill them with disgust for the world and all its pomps."

"And it's to me that you make these fine speeches," said the abbé Pirard furiously. "You young villain."

"My brothers used to beat me at Verrières," answered Julien coldly, "When they had occasion to be jealous of me."

"Indeed, indeed," exclaimed M. Pirard, almost beside himself.

Julien went on with his story without being in the least intimidated:—

"The day of my arrival at Besançon I was hungry, and I entered a café. My spirit was full of revulsion for so profane a place, but I thought that my breakfast would cost me less than at an inn. A lady, who seemed to be the mistress of the establishment, took pity on my inexperience. 'Besançon is full of bad characters,' she said to me. 'I fear something will happen to you, sir. If some mishap should occur to you, have recourse to me and send to my house before eight o'clock. If the porters of the seminary refuse to execute your errand, say you are my cousin and a native of Genlis.'"

"I will have all this chatter verified," exclaimed the abbé Pirard, unable to stand still, and walking about the room.

"Back to the cell."

The abbé followed Julien and locked him in. The latter immediately began to examine his trunk, at the bottom of which the fatal cards had been so carefully hidden. Nothing was missing in the trunk, but several things had been disarranged. Nevertheless, he had never been without the key. What luck that, during the whole time of my blindness, said Julien to himself, I never availed myself of the permission to go out that Monsieur Castanède would offer me so frequently, with a kindness which I now understand. Perhaps I should have had the weakness to have changed my clothes and gone to see the fair Amanda, and then I should have been ruined. When they gave up hope of exploiting that piece of information for the accomplishment of his ruin, they had used it to inform against him. Two hours afterwards the director summoned him.

"You did not lie," he said to him, with a less severe look, "but keeping an address like that is an indiscretion of a gravity which you are unable to realise. Unhappy child! It may perhaps do you harm in ten years' time."

XXVII
FIRST EXPERIENCE OF LIFE

The present time, Great God! is the ark of the Lord; cursed be he who touches it.—*Diderot.*

The reader will kindly excuse us if we give very few clear and definite facts concerning this period of Julien's life. It is not that we lack facts; quite the contrary. But it may be that what he saw in the seminary is too black for the medium colour which the author has endeavoured to preserve throughout these pages. Those of our contemporaries who have suffered from certain things cannot remember them without a horror which paralyses every other pleasure, even that of reading a tale.

Julien achieved scant success in his essays at hypocritical gestures. He experienced moments of disgust, and even of complete discouragement. He was not a success, even in a vile career. The slightest help from outside would have sufficed to have given him heart again, for the difficulty to overcome was not very great, but he was alone, like a derelict ship in the middle of the ocean. "And when I do succeed," he would say to himself, "think of having to pass a whole lifetime in such awful company, gluttons who have no thought but for the large omelette which they will guzzle at dinner-time, or persons like the abbé Castanède, who finds no crime too black! They will attain power, but, great heavens! at what cost.

"The will of man is powerful, I read it everywhere, but is it enough to overcome so great a disgust? The task of all the great men was easy by comparison. However terrible was the danger, they found it fine, and who can realise, except myself, the ugliness of my surroundings?"

This moment was the most trying in his whole life. It would have been so easy for him to have enlisted in one of the fine regiments at the garrison of Besançon. He could have become a Latin master. He needed so little for his subsistence, but in that case no more career, no more future for his imagination. It was equivalent to death. Here is one of his sad days in detail:

"I have so often presumed to congratulate myself on being different from the other young peasants! Well, I have lived enough to realise that *difference engenders hate*," he said to himself one morning. This great truth had just been borne in upon him by one of his most irritating failures. He had been working for eight days at teaching a pupil who lived in an odour of sanctity. He used to go out with him into the courtyard and listen submissively to pieces of fatuity enough to send one to sleep standing. Suddenly the weather turned stormy. The thunder growled, and the holy pupil exclaimed as he roughly pushed him away.

"Listen! Everyone for himself in this world. I don't want to be burned by the thunder. God may strike you with lightning like a blasphemer, like a Voltaire."

"I deserve to be drowned if I go to sleep during the storm," exclaimed Julien, with his teeth clenched with rage, and with his eyes opened towards the sky now furrowed by the lightning. "Let us try the conquest of some other rogue."

The bell rang for the abbé Castanède's course of sacred history. That day the abbé Castanède was teaching those young peasants already so frightened by their father's hardships and poverty, that the Government, that entity so terrible in their eyes, possessed no real and legitimate power except by virtue of the delegation of God's vicar on earth.

"Render yourselves worthy, by the holiness of your life and by your obedience, of the benevolence of the Pope. Be *like a stick in his hands*," he added, "and you will obtain a superb position, where you will be far from all control, and enjoy the King's commands, a position from which you cannot be removed, and where one-third of the salary is paid by the Government, while the faithful who are moulded by your preaching pay the other two-thirds."

Castanède stopped in the courtyard after he left the lesson-room. "It is particularly appropriate to say of a curé," he said to the pupils who formed a ring round him, "that the place is worth as much as the man is worth. I myself have known parishes in the mountains where the surplice fees were worth more than that of many town livings. There was quite as much money, without counting the fat capons, the eggs, fresh butter, and a thousand and one pleasant details, and there the curé is indisputably the first man. There is not a good meal to which he is not invited, fêted, etc."

Castanède had scarcely gone back to his room before the pupils split up into knots. Julien did not form part of any of them; he was left out like a black sheep. He saw in every knot a pupil tossing a coin in the air, and if he managed to guess right in this game of heads or tails, his comrades would decide that he would soon have one of those fat livings.

Anecdotes ensued. A certain young priest, who had scarcely been ordained a year, had given a tame rabbit to the maidservant of an old curé, and had succeeded in being asked to be his curate. In a few months afterwards, for the curé had quickly died, he had replaced him in that excellent living. Another had succeeded in getting himself designated as a successor to a very rich town living, by being present at all the meals of an old, paralytic curé, and by dexterously carving his poultry. The seminarists, like all young people, exaggerated the effect of those little devices, which have an element of originality, and which strike the imagination.

"I must take part in these conversations," said Julien to himself. When they did not talk about sausages and good livings, the conversation ran on the worldly aspect of ecclesiastical doctrine, on the differences of bishops and prefects, of mayors and curés. Julien caught sight of the conception of a second god, but of a god who was much more formidable and much more powerful than the other one. That second god was the Pope. They said among themselves, in a low voice, however, and when they were quite sure that they would not be heard by Pirard, that the reason for the Pope not taking the trouble of nominating all the prefects and mayors of France, was that he had entrusted that duty to the King of France by entitling him a senior son of the Church.

It was about this time that Julien thought he could exploit, for the benefit of his own reputation, his knowledge of De Maistre's book on the Pope. In point of fact, he did astonish his comrades, but it was only another misfortune. He displeased them by expounding their own opinions better than they could themselves. Chélan had acted as imprudently for Julien as he had for himself. He had given him the habit of reasoning correctly, and of not being put off by empty words, but he had neglected to tell him that this habit was a crime in the person of no importance, since every piece of logical reasoning is offensive.

Julien's command of language added consequently a new crime to his score. By dint of thinking about him, his colleagues succeeded in expressing the horror with which he would inspire them by a single expression; they nicknamed him Martin Luther, "particularly," they said, "because of that infernal logic which makes him so proud."

Several young seminarists had a fresher complexion than Julien, and could pass as better-looking, but he had white hands, and was unable to conceal certain refined habits of personal cleanliness. This advantage proved a disadvantage in the gloomy house in which chance had cast him. The dirty peasants among whom he lived asserted that he had very abandoned morals. We fear that we may weary our reader by a narration of the thousand and one misfortunes of our hero. The most vigorous of his comrades, for example, wanted to start the custom of beating him. He was obliged to arm himself with an iron compass, and to indicate, though by signs, that he would make use of it. Signs cannot figure in a spy's report to such good advantage as words.

XXVIII
A PROCESSION

All hearts were moved. The presence of God seemed to have descended into these narrow Gothic streets that stretched in every direction, and were sanded by the care of the faithful.—
Young.

It was in vain that Julien pretended to be petty and stupid. He could not please; he was too different. Yet all these professors, he said to himself, are very clever people, men in a thousand. Why do they not like my humility? Only one seemed to take advantage of his readiness to believe everything, and apparently to swallow everything. This was the abbé Chas-Bernard, the director of the ceremonies of the cathedral, where, for the last fifteen years, he had been given occasion to hope for a canonry. While waiting, he taught homiletics at the seminary. During the period of Julien's blindness, this class was one of those in which he most frequently came out top. The abbé Chas had used this as an opportunity to manifest some friendship to him, and when the class broke up, he would be glad to take him by the arm for some turns in the garden.

"What is he getting at," Julien would say to himself. He noticed with astonishment that, for hours on end, the abbé would talk to him about the ornaments possessed by the cathedral. It had seventeen lace chasubles, besides the mourning vestments. A lot was hoped from the old wife of the judge de Rubempré. This lady, who was ninety years of age, had kept for at least seventy years her wedding dress of superb Lyons material, embroidered with gold.

"Imagine, my friend," the abbé Chas would say, stopping abruptly, and staring with amazement, "that this material keeps quite stiff. There is so much gold in it. It is generally thought in Besançon that the will of the judge's wife will result in the cathedral treasure being increased by more than ten chasubles, without counting four or five capes for the great feast. I will go further," said the abbé Chas, lowering his voice, "I have reasons for thinking the judge's wife will leave us her magnificent silver gilt candlesticks, supposed to have been bought in Italy by Charles the Bold, Duke of Burgundy, whose favourite minister was one of the good lady's ancestors."

"But what is the fellow getting at with all this old clothes business," thought Julien. "These adroit preliminaries have been going on for centuries, and nothing comes of them. He must be very suspicious of me. He is cleverer than all the others, whose secret aim can be guessed so easily in a fortnight. I understand. He must have been suffering for fifteen years from mortified ambition."

Julien was summoned one evening in the middle of the fencing lesson to the abbé Pirard, who said to him.

"To-morrow is the feast of Corpus Domini (the Fête Dieu) the abbé Chas-Bernard needs you to help him to decorate the cathedral. Go and obey." The abbé Pirard called him back and added sympathetically. "It depends on you whether you will utilise the occasion to go into the town."

"Incedo per ignes," answered Julien. (I have secret enemies).

Julien went to the cathedral next morning with downcast eyes. The sight of the streets and the activity which was beginning to prevail in the town did him good. In all quarters they were extending the fronts of the houses for the procession.

All the time that he had passed in the seminary seemed to him no more than a moment. His thoughts were of Vergy, and of the pretty Amanda whom he might perhaps meet, for her café was not very far off. He saw in the distance the abbé Chas-Bernard on the threshold of his beloved cathedral. He was a big man with a jovial face and a frank air. To-day he looked triumphant. "I was expecting you, my dear son," he cried as soon as he saw Julien in the distance. "Be welcome. This day's duty will be protracted and arduous. Let us fortify ourselves by a first breakfast. We will have the second at ten o'clock during high mass."

"I do not wish, sir," said Julien to him gravely, "to be alone for a single instant. Deign to observe," he added, showing him the clock over their heads, "that I have arrived at one minute to five."

"So those little rascals at the seminary frightened you. It is very good of you to think of them," said the abbé. "But is the road less beautiful because there are thorns in the hedges which border it. Travellers go on their way, and leave the wicked thorns to wait in vain where they are. And now to work my dear friend, to work."

The abbé Chas was right in saying that the task would be arduous. There had been a great funeral ceremony at the cathedral the previous day. They had not been able to make any preparations. They had consequently only one morning for dressing all the Gothic pillars which constitute the three naves with a kind of red damask cloth ascending to a height of thirty feet. The Bishop had fetched by mail four decorators from Paris, but these gentry were not able to do everything, and far from giving any encouragement to the clumsiness of the Besançon colleagues, they made it twice as great by making fun of them.

Julien saw that he would have to climb the ladder himself. His agility served him in good stead. He undertook the direction of the decorators from town. The Abbé Chas was delighted as he watched him flit from ladder to ladder. When all the pillars were dressed in damask, five enormous bouquets of feathers had to be placed on the great baldachin above the grand altar. A rich coping of gilded wood was supported by eight big straight columns of Italian marble, but to reach the centre of the baldachin above the tabernacle involved walking over an old wooden cornice which was forty feet high and possibly worm-eaten.

The sight of this difficult crossing had extinguished the gaiety of the Parisian decorators, which up till then had been so brilliant. They looked at it from down below, argued a great deal, but did not go up. Julien seized hold of the bouquets of feathers and climbed the ladder at a run. He placed it neatly on the crown-shaped ornament in the centre of the baldachin. When he came down the ladder again, the abbé Chas-Bernard embraced him in his arms.

"Optime" exclaimed the good priest, "I will tell this to Monseigneur."

Breakfast at ten o'clock was very gay. The abbé Chas had never seen his church look so beautiful.

"Dear disciple," he said to Julien. "My mother used to let out chairs in this venerable building, so I have been brought up in this great edifice. The Terror of Robespierre ruined us, but when I was eight years old, that was my age then, I used to serve masses in private houses, so you see I got my meals on mass-days. Nobody could fold a chasuble better than I could, and I never cut the fringes. After the re-establishment of public worship by Napoleon, I had the good fortune to direct everything in this venerable metropolis. Five times a year do my eyes see it adorned with these fine ornaments. But it has never been so resplendent, and the damask breadths have never been so well tied or so close to the pillars as they are to-day."

"So he is going to tell me his secret at last," said Julien. "Now he is going to talk about himself. He is expanding." But nothing imprudent was said by the man in spite of his evident exaltation.

"All the same he has worked a great deal," said Julien to himself. "He is happy. What a man! What an example for me! He really takes the cake." (This was a vulgar phrase which he had learned from the old surgeon).

As the sanctus of high mass sounded, Julien wanted to take a surplice to follow the bishop in the superb procession. "And the thieves, my friend! And the thieves," exclaimed the abbé Chas. "Have you forgotten them? The procession will go out, but we will watch, will you and I. We shall be very lucky if we get off with the loss of a couple of ells of this fine lace which surrounds the base of the pillars. It is a gift of Madame de Rubempré. It comes from her great-grandfather the famous Count. It is made of real gold, my friend," added the abbé in a whisper, and with evident exaltation. "And all genuine. I entrust you with the watching of the north wing. Do not leave it. I will keep the south wing and the great nave for myself. Keep an eye on the confessional. It is there that the women accomplices of the thieves always spy. Look out for the moment when we turn our backs."

As he finished speaking, a quarter to twelve struck. Immediately afterwards the sound of the great clock was heard. It rang a full peal. These full solemn sounds affected Julien. His imagination was no longer turned to things earthly. The perfume of the incense and of the rose leaves thrown before the holy sacrament by little children disguised as St. John increased his exaltation.

Logically the grave sounds of the bell should only have recalled to Julien's mind the thought of the labour of twenty men paid fifty-four centimes each, and possibly helped by fifteen or twenty faithful souls. Logically, he ought to have thought of the wear and tear of the cords and of the framework and of the danger of the clock itself, which falls down every two centuries, and to have considered the means of diminishing the salary of the bell-ringers, or of paying them by some indulgence or other grace dispensed from the treasures of the Church without diminishing its purse.

Julien's soul exalted by these sounds with all their virile fulness, instead of making these wise reflections, wandered in the realm of imagination. He will never turn out a good priest or a good administrator. Souls which get thrilled so easily are at the best only capable of producing an artist. At this moment the presumption of Julien bursts out into full view. Perhaps fifty of his comrades in the seminary made attentive to the realities of life by their own unpopularity and the Jacobinism which they are taught to see hiding behind every hedge, would have had no other thought suggested by the great bell of the cathedral except the wages of the ringers. They would have analysed with the genius of Bareme whether the intensity of the emotion produced among the public was worth the money which was given to the ringers. If Julien had only tried to think of the material interests of the cathedral, his imagination would have transcended its actual object and thought of economizing forty francs on the fabric and have lost the opportunity of avoiding an expense of twenty-five centimes.

While the procession slowly traversed Besançon on the finest day imaginable, and stopped at the brilliant altar-stations put up by the authorities, the church remained in profound silence. There prevailed a semi-obscurity, an agreeable freshness. It was still perfumed with the fragrance of flowers and incense.

The silence, the deep solitude, the freshness of the long naves sweetened Julien's reverie. He did not fear being troubled by the abbé Chas, who was engaged in another part of the building. His soul had almost abandoned its mortal tenement, which was pacing slowly the north wing which had been trusted to his surveillance. He was all the more tranquil when he had assured himself that there was no one in the confessional except some devout women. His eyes looked in front of him seeing nothing.

His reverie was almost broken by the sight of two well-dressed women, one in the Confessional, and the other on a chair quite near her. He looked without seeing, but noticed, however, either by reason of some vague appreciation of his duties or admiration for the aristocratic but simple dress of the ladies, that there was no priest in the Confessional.

"It is singular," he thought, "that if these fair ladies are devout, they are not kneeling before some altar, or that if they are in society they have not an advantageous position in the first row of some balcony. How well cut that dress is! How graceful!"

He slackened his pace to try and look at them. The lady who was kneeling in the Confessional turned her head a little hearing the noise of Julien's step in this solemn place. Suddenly she gave a loud cry, and felt ill.

As the lady collapsed and fell backwards on her knees, her friend who was near her hastened to help her. At the same time Julien saw the shoulders of the lady who was falling backwards. His eyes were struck by a twisted necklace of fine, big pearls, which he knew well. What were his emotions when he recognised the hair of Madame de Rênal? It was she! The lady who was trying to prevent her from falling was Madame Derville. Julien was beside himself and hastened to their side. Madame de Rênal's fall would perhaps have carried her friend along with her, if Julien had not supported them. He saw the head of Madame de Rênal, pale and entirely devoid of consciousness floating on his shoulder. He helped Madame Derville to lean that charming head up against a straw chair. He knelt down.

Madame Derville turned round and recognised him.

"Away, monsieur, away!" she said to him, in a tone of the most lively anger. "Above all, do not let her see you again. The sight of you would be sure to horrify her. She was so happy before you came. Your conduct is atrocious. Flee! Take yourself off if you have any shame left."

These words were spoken with so much authority, and Julien felt so weak, that he did take himself off. "She always hated me," he said to himself, thinking of Madame Derville. At the same moment the nasal chanting of the first priests in the procession which was now coming back resounded in the church. The abbé Chas-Bernard called Julien, who at first did not hear him, several times. He came at last and took his arm behind a pillar where Julien had taken refuge more dead than alive. He wanted to present him to the Bishop.

"Are you feeling well, my child?" said the abbé to him, seeing him so pale, and almost incapable of walking. "You have worked too much."

The abbé gave him his arm. "Come, sit down behind me here, on the little seat of the dispenser of holy water; I will hide you."

They were now beside the main door.

"Calm yourself. We have still a good twenty minutes before Monseigneur appears. Try and pull yourself together. I will lift you up when he passes, for in spite of my age, I am strong and vigorous."

Julien was trembling so violently when the Bishop passed, that the abbé Chas gave up the idea of presenting him.

"Do not take it too much to heart," he said. "I will find another opportunity."

The same evening he had six pounds of candles which had been saved, he said, by Julien's carefulness, and by the promptness with which he had extinguished them, carried to the seminary chapel. Nothing could have been nearer the truth. The poor boy was extinguished himself. He had not had a single thought after meeting Madame de Rênal.

XXIX
THE FIRST PROMOTION

He knew his age, he knew his department, and he is rich.
— *The Forerunner*.

Julien had not emerged from the deep reverie in which the episode in the cathedral had plunged him, when the severe abbé Pirard summoned him.

"M. the abbé Chas-Bernard has just written in your favour. I am on the whole sufficiently satisfied with your conduct. You are extremely imprudent and irresponsible without outward signs of it. However, up to the present, you have proved yourself possessed of a good and even generous heart. Your intellect is superior. Taking it all round, I see in you a spark which one must not neglect.

"I am on the point of leaving this house after fifteen years of work. My crime is that I have left the seminarists to their free will, and that I have neither protected nor served that secret society of which you spoke to me at the Confessional. I wish to do something for you before I leave. I would have done so two months earlier, for you deserve it, had it not been for the information laid against you as the result of the finding in your trunk of Amanda Binet's address. I will make you New and Old Testament tutor. Julien was transported with gratitude and evolved the idea of throwing himself on his knees and thanking God. He yielded to a truer impulse, and approaching the abbé Pirard, took his hand and pressed it to his lips.

"What is the meaning of this?" exclaimed the director angrily, but Julien's eyes said even more than his act.

The abbé Pirard looked at him in astonishment, after the manner of a man who has long lost the habit of encountering refined emotions. The attention deceived the director. His voice altered.

"Well yes, my child, I am attached to you. Heaven knows that I have been so in spite of myself. I ought to show neither hate nor love to anyone. I see in you something which offends the vulgar. Jealousy and calumny will pursue you in whatever place Providence may place you. Your comrades will never behold you without hate, and if they pretend to like you, it will only be to betray you with greater certainty. For this there is only one remedy. Seek help only from God, who, to punish you for your presumption, has cursed you with the inevitable hatred of your comrades. Let your conduct be pure. That is the only resource which I can see for you. If you love truth with an irresistible embrace, your enemies will sooner or later be confounded."

It had been so long since Julien had heard a friendly voice that he must be forgiven a weakness. He burst out into tears.

The abbé Pirard held out his arms to him. This moment was very sweet to both of them. Julien was mad with joy. This promotion was the first which he had obtained. The advantages were immense. To realise them one must have been condemned to pass months on end without an instant's solitude, and in immediate contact with comrades who were at the best importunate, and for the most part insupportable. Their cries alone would have sufficed to disorganise a delicate constitution. The noise and joy of these peasants, well-fed and well-clothed as they were, could only find a vent for itself, or believe in its own completeness when they were shouting with all the strength of their lungs.

Now Julien dined alone, or nearly an hour later than the other seminarists. He had a key of the garden and could walk in it when no one else was there.

Julien was astonished to perceive that he was now hated less. He, on the contrary, had been expecting that their hate would become twice as intense. That secret desire of his that he should not be spoken to, which had been only too manifest before, and had earned him so many enemies, was no longer looked upon as a sign of ridiculous haughtiness. It became, in the eyes of the coarse beings who surrounded him, a just appreciation of his own dignity. The hatred of him sensibly diminished, above all among the youngest of his comrades, who were now his pupils, and whom he treated with much politeness. Gradually he obtained his own following. It became looked upon as bad form to call him Martin Luther.

But what is the good of enumerating his friends and his enemies?

The whole business is squalid, and all the more squalid in proportion to the truth of the picture. And yet the clergy supply the only teachers of morals which the people have. What would happen to the people without them? Will the paper ever replace the cure?

Since Julien's new dignity, the director of the seminary made a point of never speaking to him without witnesses. These tactics were prudent, both for the master and for the pupil, but above all it was meant for a test. The invariable principle of that severe Jansenist Pirard was this—"if a man has merit in your eyes, put obstacles in the way of all he desires, and of everything which he undertakes. If the merit is real, he will manage to overthrow or get round those obstacles."

It was the hunting season. It had occurred to Fouqué to send a stag and a boar to the seminary as though they came from Julien's parents. The dead animals were put down on the floor between the kitchen and the refectory. It was there that they were seen by all the seminarists on their way to dinner. They constituted a great attraction for their curiosity. The boar, dead though it was, made the youngest ones feel frightened. They touched its tusks. They talked of nothing else for a whole week.

This gift, which raised Julien's family to the level of that class of society which deserves respect, struck a deadly blow at all jealousy. He enjoyed a superiority, consecrated by fortune. Chazel, the most distinguished of the seminarists, made advances to him, and always reproached him for not having previously apprised them of his parents' position and had thus involved them in treating money without sufficient respect. A conscription took place, from which Julien, in his capacity as seminarist, was exempt. This circumstance affected him profoundly. "So there is just passed for ever that moment which, twenty years earlier, would have seen my heroic life begin. He was walking alone in the seminary garden. He heard the masons who were walling up the cloister walls talking between themselves.

"Yes, we must go. There's the new conscription. When *the other* was alive it was good business. A mason could become an officer then, could become a general then. One has seen such things."

"You go and see now. It's only the ragamuffins who leave for the army. Any one *who has anything* stays in the country here."

"The man who is born wretched stays wretched, and there you are."

"I say, is it true what they say, that the other is dead?" put in the third mason.

"Oh well, it's the '*big men*' who say that, you see. The other one made them afraid."

"What a difference. How the fortification went ahead in his time. And to think of his being betrayed by his own marshals."

This conversation consoled Julien a little. As he went away, he repeated with a sigh:

"Le seul roi dont le peuple a gardé la mémoire."

The time for the examination arrived. Julien answered brilliantly. He saw that Chazel endeavoured to exhibit all his knowledge. On the first day the examiners, nominated by the famous Grand Vicar de Frilair, were very irritated at always having to put first, or at any rate second, on their list, that Julien Sorel, who had been designated to them as the Benjamin of the Abbé Pirard. There were bets in the seminary that Julien would come out first in the final list of the examination, a privilege which carried with it the honour of dining with my Lord Bishop. But at the end of a sitting, dealing with the fathers of the Church, an adroit examiner, having first interrogated Julien on Saint Jerome and his passion for Cicero, went on to speak about Horace, Virgil and other profane authors. Julien had learnt by heart a great number of passages from these authors without his comrades' knowledge. Swept away by his successes, he forgot the place where he was, and recited in paraphrase with spirit several odes of Horace at the repeated request of the examiner. Having for twenty minutes given him enough rope to hang himself, the examiner changed his expression, and bitterly reproached him for the time he had wasted on these profane studies, and the useless or criminal ideas which he had got into his head.

"I am a fool, sir. You are right," said Julien modestly, realising the adroit stratagem of which he was the victim.

This examiner's dodge was considered dirty, even at the seminary, but this did not prevent the abbé de Frilair, that adroit individual who had so cleverly organised the machinery of the Besançon congregation, and whose despatches to Paris put fear into the hearts of judges, prefect, and even the generals of the garrison, from placing with his powerful hand the number 198 against Julien's name. He enjoyed subjecting his enemy, Pirard the Jansenist, to this mortification.

His chief object for the last ten years had been to deprive him of the headship of the seminary. The abbé, who had himself followed the plan which he had indicated to Julien, was sincere, pious, devoted to his duties and devoid of intrigue, but heaven in its anger had given him that bilious temperament which is by nature so deeply sensitive to insults and to hate. None of the insults which were addressed to him was wasted on his burning soul. He would have handed in his resignation a hundred times over, but he believed that he was useful in the place where Providence had set him. "I prevent the progress of Jesuitism and Idolatry," he said to himself.

At the time of the examinations, it was perhaps nearly two months since he had spoken to Julien, and nevertheless, he was ill for eight days when, on receipt of the official letter announcing the result of the competition, he saw the number 198 placed beside the name of that pupil whom he regarded as the glory of his town. This stern character found his only consolation in concentrating all his surveillance on Julien. He was delighted that he discovered in him neither anger, nor vindictiveness, nor discouragement.

Julien felt a thrill some months afterwards when he received a letter. It bore the Paris post-mark. Madame de Rênal is remembering her promises at last, he thought. A gentleman who signed himself Paul Sorel, and who said that he was his relative, sent him a letter of credit for five hundred francs. The writer went on to add that if Julien went on to study successfully the good Latin authors, a similar sum would be sent to him every year.

"It is she. It is her kindness," said Julien to himself, feeling quite overcome. "She wishes to console me. But why not a single word of affection?"

He was making a mistake in regard to this letter, for Madame de Rênal, under the influence of her friend, Madame Derville, was abandoning herself absolutely to profound remorse. She would often think, in spite of herself, of that singular being, the meeting with whom had revolutionized her life. But she carefully refrained from writing to him.

If we were to talk the terminology of the seminary, we would be able to recognise a miracle in the sending of these five hundred francs and to say that heaven was making use of Monsieur de Frilair himself in order to give this gift to Julien. Twelve years previously the abbé de Frilair had arrived in Besançon with an extremely exiguous portmanteau, which, according to the story, contained all his fortune. He was now one of the richest proprietors of the department. In the course of his prosperity, he had bought the one half of an estate, while the other half had been inherited by Monsieur de la Mole. Consequently there was a great lawsuit between these two personages.

M. le Marquis de la Mole felt that, in spite of his brilliant life at Paris and the offices which he held at Court, it would be dangerous to fight at Besançon against the Grand Vicar, who was reputed to make and unmake prefects.

Instead of soliciting a present of fifty thousand francs which could have been smuggled into the budget under some name or other, and of throwing up this miserable lawsuit with the abbé Frilair over a matter of fifty thousand francs, the marquis lost his temper. He thought he was in the right, absolutely in the right. Moreover, if one is permitted to say so, who is the judge who has not got a son, or at any rate a cousin to push in the world?

In order to enlighten the blindest minds the abbé de Frilair took the carriage of my Lord the Bishop eight days after the first decree which he obtained, and went himself to convey the cross of the Legion of Honour to his advocate. M. de la Mole, a little dumbfounded at the demeanour of the other side, and appreciating also that his own advocates were slackening their efforts, asked advice of the abbé Chélan, who put him in communication with M. Pirard.

At the period of our story the relations between these two men had lasted for several years. The abbé Pirard imported into this affair his characteristic passion. Being in constant touch with the Marquis's advocates, he studied his case, and finding it just, he became quite openly the solicitor of M. de la Mole against the all-powerful Grand Vicar. The latter felt outraged by such insolence, and on the part of a little Jansenist into the bargain.

"See what this Court nobility who pretend to be so powerful really are," would say the abbé de Frilair to his intimates. M. de la Mole has not even sent a miserable cross to his agent at Besançon, and will let him be tamely turned out. None the less, so they write me, this noble peer never lets a week go by without going to show off his blue ribbon in the drawing-room of the Keeper of Seal, whoever it may be.

In spite of all the energy of the abbé Pirard, and although M. de la Mole was always on the best of terms with the minister of justice, and above all with his officials, the best that he could achieve after six careful years was not to lose his lawsuit right out. Being as he was in ceaseless correspondence with the abbé Pirard in connection with an affair in which they were both passionately interested, the Marquis came to appreciate the abbé's particular kind of intellect. Little by little, and in spite of the immense distance in their social positions, their correspondence assumed the tone of friendship. The abbé Pirard told the Marquis that they wanted to heap insults upon him till he should be forced to hand in his resignation. In his anger against what, in his opinion, was the infamous stratagem employed against Julien, he narrated his tory to the Marquis.

Although extremely rich, this great lord was by no means miserly. He had never been able to prevail on the abbé Pirard to accept even the reimbursement of the postal expenses occasioned by the lawsuit. He seized the opportunity of sending five hundred francs to his favourite pupil. M. de la Mole himself took the trouble of writing the covering letter. This gave the abbé food for thought. One day the latter received a little note which requested him to go immediately on an urgent matter to an inn on the outskirts of Besançon. He found there the steward of M. de la Mole.

"M. le Marquis has instructed me to bring you his carriage," said the man to him. "He hopes that after you have read this letter you will find it convenient to leave for Paris in four or five days. I will employ the time in the meanwhile in asking you to be good enough to show me the estates of M. le Marquis in the Franche-Comté, so that I can go over them."

The letter was short:—

"Rid yourself, my good sir, of all the chicanery of the provinces and come and breathe peaceful atmosphere of Paris. I send you my carriage which has orders to await your decision for four days. I will await you myself at Paris until Tuesday. You only require to say so, monsieur, to accept in your own name one of the best livings in the environs of Paris. The richest of your future parishioners has never seen you, but is more devoted than you can possibly think: he is the Marquis de la Mole."

Without having suspected it, the stern abbé Pirard loved this seminary, peopled as it was by his enemies, but to which for the past fifteen years he had devoted all his thoughts. M. de la Mole's letter had the effect on him of the visit of the surgeon come to perform a difficult but necessary operation. His dismissal was certain. He made an appointment with the steward for three days later. For forty-eight hours he was in a fever of uncertainty. Finally he wrote to the M. de la Mole, and composed for my Lord the Bishop a letter, a masterpiece of ecclesiastical style, although it was a little long; it would have been difficult to have found more unimpeachable phrases, and ones breathing a more sincere respect. And nevertheless, this letter, intended as it was to get M. de Frilair into trouble with his patron, gave utterance to all the serious matters of complaint, and even descended to the little squalid intrigues which, having been endured with resignation for six years, were forcing the abbé Pirard to leave the diocese.

They stole his firewood, they poisoned his dog, etc., etc.

Having finished this letter he had Julien called. Like all the other seminarists, he was sleeping at eight o'clock in the evening.

"You know where the Bishop's Palace is," he said to him in good classical Latin. "Take this letter to my Lord. I will not hide from you that I am sending you into the midst of the wolves. Be all ears and eyes. Let there be no lies in your answers, but realise that the man questioning you will possibly experience a real joy in being able to hurt you. I am very pleased, my child, at being able to give you this experience before I leave you, for I do not hide from you that the letter which you are bearing is my resignation."

Julien stood motionless. He loved the abbé Pirard. It was in vain that prudence said to him,

"After this honest man's departure the Sacré-Cœur party will disgrace me and perhaps expel me."

He could not think of himself. He was embarrassed by a phrase which he was trying to turn in a polite way, but as a matter of fact he found himself without the brains to do so.

"Well, my friend, are you not going?"

"Is it because they say, monsieur," answered Julian timidly, "that you have put nothing on one side during your long administration. I have six hundred francs."

His tears prevented him from continuing.

"*That also will be noticed,*" said the ex-director of the seminary coldly. "Go to the Palace. It is getting late."

Chance would so have it that on that evening, the abbé de Frilair was on duty in the salon of the Palace. My lord was dining with the prefect, so it was to M. de Frilair himself that Julien, though he did not know it, handed the letter.

Julien was astonished to see this abbé boldly open the letter which was addressed to the Bishop. The face of the Grand Vicar soon expressed surprise, tinged with a lively pleasure, and became twice as grave as before. Julien, struck with his good appearance, found time to scrutinise him while he was reading. This face would have possessed more dignity had it not been for the extreme subtlety which appeared in some features, and would have gone to the fact of actually denoting falseness if the possessor of this fine countenance had ceased to school it for a single minute. The very prominent nose formed a perfectly straight line and unfortunately gave to an otherwise distinguished profile, a curious resemblance to the physiognomy of a fox. Otherwise this abbé, who appeared so engrossed with Monsieur Pirard's resignation, was dressed with an elegance which Julien had never seen before in any priest and which pleased him exceedingly.

It was only later that Julien knew in what the special talent of the abbé de Frilair really consisted. He knew how to amuse his bishop, an amiable old man made for Paris life, and who looked upon Besançon as exile. This Bishop had very bad sight, and was passionately fond of fish. The abbé de Frilair used to take the bones out of the fish which was served to my Lord. Julien looked silently at the abbé who was rereading the resignation when the door suddenly opened with a noise. A richly dressed lackey passed in rapidly. Julien had only time to turn round towards the door. He perceived a little old man wearing a pectoral cross. He prostrated himself. The Bishop addressed a benevolent smile to him and passed on. The handsome abbé followed him and Julien was left alone in the salon, and was able to admire at his leisure its pious magnificence.

The Bishop of Besançon, a man whose spirit had been tried but not broken by the long miseries of the emigration, was more than seventy-five years old and concerned himself infinitely little with what might happen in ten years' time.

"Who is that clever-looking seminarist I think I saw as I passed?" said the Bishop. "Oughtn't they to be in bed according to my regulations."

"That one is very wide-awake I assure you, my Lord, and he brings great news. It is the resignation of the only Jansenist residing in your diocese, that terrible abbé Pirard realises at last that we mean business."

"Well," said the Bishop with a laugh. "I challenge you to replace him with any man of equal worth, and to show you how much I prize that man, I will invite him to dinner for to-morrow."

The Grand Vicar tried to slide in a few words concerning the choice of a successor. The prelate, who was little disposed to talk business, said to him.

"Before we install the other, let us get to know a little of the circumstances under which the present one is going. Fetch me this seminarist. The truth is in the mouth of children."

Julien was summoned. "I shall find myself between two inquisitors," he thought. He had never felt more courageous. At the moment when he entered, two valets, better dressed than M. Valenod himself, were undressing my lord. That prelate thought he ought to question Julien on his studies before questioning him about M. Pirard. He talked a little theology, and was astonished. He soon came to the humanities, to Virgil, to Horace, to Cicero. "It was those names," thought Julien, that earned me my number 198. I have nothing to lose. Let us try and shine. He succeeded. The prelate, who was an excellent humanist himself, was delighted.

At the prefect's dinner, a young girl who was justly celebrated, had recited the poem of the Madeleine. He was in the mood to talk literature, and very quickly forgot the abbé Pirard and his affairs to discuss with the seminarist whether Horace was rich or poor. The prelate quoted several odes, but sometimes his memory was sluggish, and then Julien would recite with modesty the whole ode: the fact which struck the bishop was that Julien never deviated from the conversational tone. He spoke his twenty or thirty Latin verses as though he had been speaking of what was taking place in his own seminary. They talked for a long time of Virgil, or Cicero, and the prelate could not help complimenting the young seminarist. "You could not have studied better."

"My Lord," said Julien, "your seminary can offer you 197 much less unworthy of your high esteem."

"How is that?" said the Prelate astonished by the number.

"I can support by official proof just what I have had the honour of saying before my lord. I obtained the number 198 at the seminary's annual examination by giving accurate answers to the very questions which are earning me at the present moment my lord's approbation.

"Ah, it is the Benjamin of the abbé Pirard," said the Bishop with a laugh, as he looked at M. de Frilair. "We should have been prepared for this. But it is fair fighting. Did you not have to be woken up, my friend," he said, addressing himself to Julien. "To be sent here?"

"Yes, my Lord. I have only been out of the seminary alone once in my life to go and help M. the abbé Chas-Bernard decorate the cathedral on Corpus Christi day.

"Optime," said the Bishop. "So, it is you who showed proof of so much courage by placing the bouquets of feathers on the baldachin. They make me shudder. They make me fear that they will cost some man his life. You will go far, my friend, but I do not wish to cut short your brilliant career by making you die of hunger."

And by the order of the Bishop, biscuits and wine were brought in, to which Julien did honour, and the abbé de Frilair, who knew that his Bishop liked to see people eat gaily and with a good appetite, even greater honour.

The prelate, more and more satisfied with the end of his evening, talked for a moment of ecclesiastical history. He saw that Julien did not understand. The prelate passed on to the moral condition of the Roman Empire under the system of the Emperor Constantine. The end of paganism had been accompanied by that state of anxiety and of doubt which afflicts sad and jaded spirits in the nineteenth century. My Lord noticed Julien's ignorance of almost the very name of Tacitus. To the astonishment of the prelate, Julien answered frankly that that author was not to be found in the seminary library.

"I am truly very glad," said the Bishop gaily, "You relieve me of an embarrassment. I have been trying for the last five minutes to find a way of thanking you for the charming evening which you have given me in a way that I could certainly never have expected. I did not anticipate finding a teacher in a pupil in my seminary. Although the gift is not unduly canonical, I want to give you a Tacitus." The prelate had eight volumes in a superior binding fetched for him, and insisted on writing himself on the title page of the first volume a Latin compliment to Julien Sorel. The Bishop plumed himself on his fine Latinity. He finished by saying to him in a serious tone, which completely clashed with the rest of the conversation.

"Young man, if you are good, you will have one day the best living in my diocese, and one not a hundred leagues from my episcopal palace, but you must be good."

Laden with his volumes, Julien left the palace in a state of great astonishment as midnight was striking.

My Lord had not said a word to him about the abbé Pirard. Julien was particularly astonished by the Bishop's extreme politeness. He had had no conception of such an urbanity in form combined with so natural an air of dignity. Julien was especially struck by the contrast on seeing again the gloomy abbé Pirard, who was impatiently awaiting him.

"Quid tibi dixerunt (What have they said to you)?" he cried out to him in a loud voice as soon as he saw him in the distance. "Speak French, and repeat my Lord's own words without either adding or subtracting anything," said the ex-Director of the seminary in his harsh tone, and with his particularly inelegant manners, as Julien got slightly confused in translating into Latin the speeches of the Bishop.

"What a strange present on the part of the Bishop to a young seminarist," he ventured to say as he turned over the leaves of the superb Tacitus, whose gilt edges seemed to horrify him.

Two o'clock was already striking when he allowed his favourite pupil to retire to his room after an extremely detailed account.

"Leave me the first volume of your Tacitus," he said to him. "Where is my Lord Bishop's compliment? This Latin line will serve as your lightning-conductor in this house after my departure."

Erit tibi, fili mi, successor meus tanquam leo querens quem devoret. (For my successor will be to you, my son, like a ravening lion seeking someone to devour).

The following morning Julien noticed a certain strangeness in the manner in which his comrades spoke to him. It only made him more reserved. "This," he thought, "is the result of M. Pirard's resignation. It is known over the whole house, and I pass for his favourite. There ought logically to be an insult in their demeanour." But he could not detect it. On the contrary, there was an absence of hate in the eyes of all those he met along the corridors. "What is the meaning of this? It is doubtless a trap. Let us play a wary game."

Finally the little seminarist said to him with a laugh,

"Cornelii Taciti opera omnia (complete works of Tacitus)."

On hearing these words, they all congratulated Julien enviously, not only on the magnificent present which he had received from my lord, but also on the two hours' conversation with which he had been honoured. They knew even its minutest details. From that moment envy ceased completely. They courted him basely. The abbé Castanède, who had manifested towards him the most extreme insolence the very day before, came and took his arm and invited him to breakfast.

By some fatality in Julien's character, while the insolence of these coarse creatures had occasioned him great pain, their baseness afforded him disgust, but no pleasure.

Towards mid-day the abbé Pirard took leave of his pupils, but not before addressing to them a severe admonition.

"Do you wish for the honours of the world," he said to them. "For all the social advantages, for the pleasure of commanding pleasures, of setting the laws at defiance, and the pleasure of being insolent with impunity to all? Or do you wish for your eternal salvation? The most backward of you have only got to open your eyes to distinguish the true ways."

He had scarcely left before the devotees of the *Sacré Cœur de Jésus* went into the chapel to intone a Te Deum. Nobody in the seminary took the ex-director's admonition seriously.

"He shows a great deal of temper because he is losing his job," was what was said in every quarter.

Not a single seminarist was simple enough to believe in the voluntary resignation of a position which put him into such close touch with the big contractors.

The abbé Pirard went and established himself in the finest inn at Besançon, and making an excuse of business which he had not got, insisted on passing a couple of days there. The Bishop had invited him to dinner, and in order to chaff his Grand Vicar de Frilair, endeavoured to make him shine. They were at dessert when the extraordinary intelligence arrived from Paris that the abbé Pirard had been appointed to the magnificent living of N.—— four leagues from Paris. The good prelate congratulated him upon it. He saw in the whole affair a piece of good play which put him in a good temper and gave him the highest opinion of the abbé's talents. He gave him a magnificent Latin certificate, and enjoined silence on the abbé de Frilair, who was venturing to remonstrate.

The same evening, my Lord conveyed his admiration to the Marquise de Rubempré. This was great news for fine Besançon society. They abandoned themselves to all kinds of conjectures over this extraordinary favour. They already saw the abbé Pirard a Bishop. The more subtle brains thought M. de la Mole was a minister, and indulged on this day in smiles at the imperious airs that M. the abbé de Frilair adopted in society.

The following day the abbé Pirard was almost mobbed in the streets, and the tradesmen came to their shop doors when he went to solicit an interview with the judges who had had to try the Marquis's lawsuit. For the first time in his life he was politely received by them. The stern Jansenist, indignant as he was with all that he saw, worked long with the advocates whom he had chosen for the Marquis de la Mole, and left for Paris. He was weak enough to tell two or three college friends who accompanied him to the carriage whose armorial bearings they admired, that after having administered the Seminary for fifteen years he was leaving Besançon with five hundred and twenty francs of savings. His friends kissed him with tears in their eyes, and said to each other,

"The good abbé could have spared himself that lie. It is really too ridiculous."

The vulgar, blinded as they are by the love of money, were constitutionally incapable of understanding that it was in his own sincerity that the abbé Pirard had found the necessary strength to fight for six years against Marie Alacoque, the *Sacré Cœur de Jésus*, the Jesuits and his Bishop.

XXX
AN AMBITIOUS MAN

There is only one nobility, the title of duke; a marquis is ridiculous; the word duke makes one turn round.—*Edinburgh Review*.

The Marquis de la Mole received the abbé Pirard without any of those aristocratic mannerisms whose very politeness is at the same time so impertinent to one who understands them. It would have been a waste of time, and the Marquis was sufficiently expeditious in big affairs to have no time to lose.

He had been intriguing for six months to get both the king and people to accept a minister who, as a matter of gratitude, was to make him a Duke. The Marquis had been asking his Besançon advocate for years on end for a clear and precise summary of his Franche-Comté lawsuits. How could the celebrated advocate explain to him what he did not understand himself? The little square of paper which the abbé handed him explained the whole matter.

"My dear abbé," said the Marquis to him, having got through in less than five minutes all polite formulae of personal questions. "My dear abbé, in the midst of my pretended prosperity I lack the time to occupy myself seriously with two little matters which are rather important, my family and my affairs. I manage the fortune of my house on a large scale. I can carry it far. I manage my pleasures, and that is the first consideration in my eyes," he added, as he saw a look of astonishment in the abbé Pirard's eyes. Although a man of common sense, the abbé was surprised to hear a man talk so frankly about his pleasures.

"Work doubtless exists in Paris," continued the great lord, "but it is perched on the fifth story, and as soon as I take anyone up, he takes an apartment on the second floor, and his wife starts a day at home; the result is no more work and no more efforts except either to be, or appear to be, a society man. That is the only thing they bother about, as soon as they have got their bread and butter.

"For my lawsuits, yes, for every single one of them, I have, to put it plainly, advocates who quarrel to death. One died of consumption the day before yesterday. Taking my business all round, would you believe, monsieur, that for three years I have given up all hope of finding a man who deigns, during the time he is acting as my clerk, to give a little serious thought to what he is doing. Besides, all this is only a preliminary.

"I respect you and would venture to add that, although I only see you for the first time to-day, I like you. Will you be my secretary at a salary of eight hundred francs or even double. I shall still be the gainer by it, I swear to you, and I will manage to reserve that fine living for you for the day when we shall no longer be able to agree." The abbé refused, but the genuine embarrassment in which he saw the Marquis suggested an idea to him towards the end of the conversation.

"I have left in the depths of my seminary a poor young man who, if I mistake not, will be harshly persecuted. If he were only a simple monk he would be already *in pace*. So far this young man only knows Latin and the Holy Scriptures, but it is not impossible that he will one day exhibit great talent, either for preaching or the guiding of souls. I do not know what he will do, but he has the sacred fire. He may go far. I thought of giving him to our Bishop, if we had ever had one who was a little of your way of considering men and things."

"What is your young man's extraction?" said the Marquis.

"He is said to be the son of a carpenter in our mountains. I rather believe he is the natural son of some rich man. I have seen him receive an anonymous or pseudonymous letter with a bill for five hundred francs."

"Oh, it is Julien Sorel," said the Marquis.

"How do you know his name?" said the abbé, in astonishment, reddening at his question.

"That's what I'm not going to tell you," answered the Marquis.

"Well," replied the abbé, "you might try making him your secretary. He has energy. He has a logical mind. In a word, it's worth trying."

"Why not?" said the Marquis. "But would he be the kind of man to allow his palm to be greased by the Prefect of Police or any one else and then spy on me? That is only my objection."

After hearing the favourable assurances of the abbé Pirard, the Marquis took a thousand franc note.

"Send this journey money to Julien Sorel. Let him come to me."

"One sees at once," said the abbé Pirard, "that you live in Paris. You do not know the tyranny which weighs us poor provincials down, and particularly those priests who are not friendly to the Jesuits. They will refuse to let Julien Sorel leave. They will manage to cloak themselves in the most clever excuses. They will answer me that he is ill, that his letters were lost in the post, etc., etc."

"I will get a letter from the minister to the Bishop, one of these days," answered the Marquis.

"I was forgetting to warn you of one thing," said the abbé. "This young man, though of low birth, has a high spirit. He will be of no use if you madden his pride. You will make him stupid."

"That pleases me," said the Marquis. "I will make him my son's comrade. Will that be enough for you?"

Some time afterwards, Julien received a letter in an unknown writing, and bearing the Chélon postmark. He found in it a draft on a Besançon merchant, and instructions to present himself at Paris without delay. The letter was signed in a fictitious name, but Julien had felt a thrill in opening it. A leaf of a tree had fallen down at his feet. It was the agreed signal between himself and the abbé Pirard.

Within an hour's time, Julien was summoned to the Bishop's Palace, where he found himself welcomed with a quite paternal benevolence. My lord quoted Horace and at the same time complimented him very adroitly on the exalted destiny which awaited him in Paris in such a way as to elicit an explanation by way of thanks. Julien was unable to say anything, simply because he did not know anything, and my Lord showed him much consideration. One of the little priests in the bishopric wrote to the mayor, who hastened to bring in person a signed passport, where the name of the traveller had been left in blank.

Before midnight of the same evening, Julien was at Fouqué's. His friend's shrewd mind was more astonished than pleased with the future which seemed to await his friend.

"You will finish up," said that Liberal voter, "with a place in the Government, which will compel you to take some step which will be calumniated. It will only be by your own disgrace that I shall have news of you. Remember that, even from the financial standpoint, it is better to earn a hundred louis in a good timber business, of which one is his own master, than to receive four thousand francs from a Government, even though it were that of King Solomon."

Julien saw nothing in this except the pettiness of spirit of a country bourgeois. At last he was going to make an appearance in the atre of great events. Everything was over-shadowed in his eyes by the happiness of going to Paris, which he imagined to be populated by people of intellect, full of intrigues and full of hypocrisy, but as polite as the Bishop of Besançon and the Bishop of Agde. He represented to his friend that he was deprived of any free choice in the matter by the abbé Pirard's letter.'

The following day he arrived at Verrières about noon. He felt the happiest of men for he counted on seeing Madame de Rênal again. He went first to his protector the good abbé Chélan. He met with a severe welcome.

"Do you think you are under any obligation to me?" said M. Chélan to him, without answering his greeting. "You will take breakfast with me. During that time I will have a horse hired for you and you will leave Verrières without seeing anyone."

"Hearing is obeying," answered Julien with a demeanour smacking of the seminary, and the only questions now discussed were theology and classical Latin.

He mounted his horse, rode a league, and then perceiving a wood and not seeing any one who could notice him enter, he plunged into it. At sunset, he sent away the horse. Later, he entered the cottage of a peasant, who consented to sell him a ladder and to follow him with it to the little wood which commands the *Cours de la Fidélité* at Verrières.

"I have been following a poor mutineer of a conscript ... or a smuggler," said the peasant as he took leave of him, "but what does it matter? My ladder has been well paid for, and I myself have done a thing or two in that line."

The night was very black. Towards one o'clock in the morning, Julien, laden with his ladder, entered Verrières. He descended as soon as he could into the bed of the stream, which is banked within two walls, and traverses M. de Rênal's magnificent gardens at a depth of ten feet. Julien easily climbed up the ladder. "How will the watch dogs welcome me," he thought. "It all turns on that." The dogs barked and galloped towards him, but he whistled softly and they came and caressed him. Then climbing from terrace to terrace he easily managed, although all the grills were shut, to get as far as the window of Madame de Rênal's bedroom which, on the garden side, was only eight or six feet above the ground. There was a little heart shaped opening in the shutters which Julien knew well. To his great disappointment, this little opening was not illuminated by the flare of a little night-light inside.

"Good God," he said to himself. "This room is not occupied by Madame de Rênal. Where can she be sleeping? The family must be at Verrières since I have found the dogs here, but I might meet M. de Rênal himself, or even a stranger in this room without a light, and then what a scandal!" The most prudent course was to retreat, but this idea horrified Julien.

"If it's a stranger, I will run away for all I'm worth, and leave my ladder behind me, but if it is she, what a welcome awaits me! I can well imagine that she has fallen into a mood of penitence and the most exalted piety, but after all, she still has some remembrance of me, since she has written to me." This bit of reasoning decided him.

With a beating heart, but resolved none the less to see her or perish in the attempt, he threw some little pebbles against the shutter. No answer. He leaned his long ladder beside the window, and himself knocked on the shutter, at first softly, and then more strongly. "However dark it is, they may still shoot me," thought Julien. This idea made the mad adventure simply a question of bravery.

"This room is not being slept in to-night," he thought, "or whatever person might be there would have woken up by now. So far as it is concerned, therefore, no further precautions are needed. I must only try not to be heard by the persons sleeping in the other rooms."

He descended, placed his ladder against one of the shutters, climbed up again, and placing his hand through the heart-shaped opening, was fortunate enough to find pretty quickly the wire which is attached to the hook which closed the shutter. He pulled this wire. It was with an ineffable joy that he felt that the shutter was no longer held back, and yielded to his effort.

I must open it bit by bit and let her recognise my voice. He opened the shutter enough to pass his head through it, while he repeated in a low voice, "It's a friend."

He pricked up his ears and assured himself that nothing disturbed the profound silence of the room, but there could be no doubt about it, there was no light, even half-extinguished, on the mantelpiece. It was a very bad sign.

"Look out for the gun-shot," he reflected a little, then he ventured to knock against the window with his finger. No answer. He knocked harder. I must finish it one way or another, even if I have to break the window. When he was knocking very hard, he thought he could catch a glimpse through the darkness of something like a white shadow that was crossing the room. At last there was no doubt about it. He saw a shadow which appeared to advance with extreme slowness. Suddenly he saw a cheek placed against the pane to which his eye was glued.

He shuddered and went away a little, but the night was so black that he could not, even at this distance, distinguish if it were Madame de Rênal. He was frightened of her crying out at first in alarm. He heard the dogs prowling and growling around the foot of the ladder. "It is I," he repeated fairly loudly. "A friend."

No answer. The white phantom had disappeared.

"Deign to open to me. I must speak to you. I am too unhappy." And he knocked hard enough to break the pane.

A crisp sound followed. The casement fastening of the window yielded. He pushed the casement and leaped lightly into the room.

The white phantom flitted away from him. He took hold of its arms.

It was a woman. All his ideas of courage vanished. "If it is she, what is she going to say?" What were his emotions when a little cry gave him to understand, that it was Madame de Rênal?

He clasped her in his arms. She trembled and scarcely had the strength to push him away.

"Unhappy man. What are you doing?" Her agonised voice could scarcely articulate the words.

Julien thought that her voice rang with the most genuine indignation.

"I have come to see you after a cruel separation of more than fourteen months."

"Go away, leave me at once. Oh, M. Chélan, why did you prevent me writing to him? I could then have foreseen this horror." She pushed him away with a truly extraordinary strength. "Heaven has deigned to enlighten me," she repeated in a broken voice. "Go away! Flee!"

"After fourteen months of unhappiness I shall certainly not leave you without a word. I want to know all you have done. Yes, I have loved you enough to deserve this confidence. I want to know everything." This authoritative tone dominated Madame de Rênal's heart in spite of herself. Julien, who was hugging her passionately and resisting her efforts to get loose, left off clasping her in his arms. This reassured Madame de Rênal a little.

"I will take away the ladder," he said, "to prevent it compromising us in case some servant should be awakened by the noise, and go on a round."

"Oh leave me, leave me!" she cried with an admirable anger. "What do men matter to me! It is God who sees the awful scene you are now making. You are abusing meanly the sentiments which I had for you but have no longer. Do you hear, Monsieur Julien?"

He took away the ladder very slowly so as not to make a noise.

"Is your husband in town, dear," he said to her not in order to defy her but as a sheer matter of habit.

"Don't talk to me like that, I beg you, or I will call my husband. I feel only too guilty in not having sent you away before. I pity you," she said to him, trying to wound his, as she well knew, irritable pride.

This refusal of all endearments, this abrupt way of breaking so tender a tie which he thought still subsisted, carried the transports of Julien's love to the point of delirium.

"What! is it possible you do not love me?" he said to her, with one of those accents that come straight from the heart and impose a severe strain on the cold equanimity of the listener.

She did not answer. As for him, he wept bitterly.

In fact he had no longer the strength to speak.

"So I am completely forgotten by the one being who ever loved me, what is the good of living on henceforth?" As soon as he had no longer to fear the danger of meeting a man all his courage had left him; his heart now contained no emotion except that of love.

He wept for a long time in silence.

He took her hand; she tried to take it away, and after a few almost convulsive moments, surrendered it to him. It was extremely dark; they were both sitting on Madame de Rênal's bed.

"What a change from fourteen months ago," thought Julien, and his tears redoubled. "So absence is really bound to destroy all human sentiments."

"Deign to tell me what has happened to you?" Julien said at last.

"My follies," answered Madame de Rênal in a hard voice whose frigid intonation contained in it a certain element of reproach, "were no doubt known in the town when you left, your conduct was so imprudent. Some time afterwards when I was in despair the venerable Chélan came to see me. He tried in vain for a long time to obtain a confession. One day he took me to that church at Dijon where I made my first communion. In that place he ventured to speak himself——" Madame de Rênal was interrupted by her tears. "What a moment of shame. I confessed everything. The good man was gracious enough not to overwhelm me with the weight of his indignation. He grieved with me. During that time I used to write letters to you every day which I never ventured to send. I hid them carefully and when I was more than usually unhappy I shut myself up in my room and read over my letters."

"At last M. Chélan induced me to hand them over to him, some of them written a little more discreetly were sent to you, you never answered."

"I never received any letters from you, I swear!"

"Great heavens! Who can have intercepted them? Imagine my grief until the day I saw you in the cathedral. I did not know if you were still alive."

"God granted me the grace of understanding how much I was sinning towards Him, towards my children, towards my husband," went on Madame de Rênal. "He never loved me in the way that I then thought that you had loved me."

Julien rushed into her arms, as a matter of fact without any particular purpose and feeling quite beside himself. But Madame de Rênal repelled him and continued fairly firmly.

"My venerable friend, M. Chélan, made me understand that in marrying I had plighted all my affections, even those which I did not then know, and which I had never felt before a certain fatal attachment ... after the great sacrifice of the letters that were so dear to me, my life has flowed on, if not happily, at any rate calmly. Do not disturb it. Be a friend to me, my best friend." Julien covered her hand with kisses. She perceived he was still crying. "Do not cry, you pain me so much. Tell me, in your turn, what you have been doing," Julien was unable to speak. "I want to know the life you lead at the seminary," she repeated. "And then you will go."

Without thinking about what he was saying Julien spoke of the numberless intrigues and jealousies which he had first encountered, and then of the great serenity of his life after he had been made a tutor.

"It was then," he added, "that after a long silence which was no doubt intended to make me realise what I see only too clearly to-day, that you no longer loved me and that I had become a matter of indifference to you...."

Madame de Rênal wrung her hands.

"It was then that you sent me the sum of five hundred francs."

"Never," said Madame de Rênal.

"It was a letter stamped Paris and signed Paul Sorel so as to avert suspicion."

There was a little discussion about how the letter could possibly have originated.

The psychological situation was altered. Without knowing it Julien had abandoned his solemn tone; they were now once more on the footing of a tender affection. It was so dark that they did not see each other but the tone of their voices was eloquent of everything. Julien clasped his arm round his love's waist. This movement had its dangers. She tried to put Julien's arms away from her; at this juncture he cleverly diverted her attention by an interesting detail in his story. The arm was practically forgotten and remained in its present position.

After many conjectures as to the origin of the five hundred francs letter, Julien took up his story. He regained a little of his self-control as he spoke of his past life, which compared with what he was now experiencing interested him so little. His attention was now concentrated on the final outcome of his visit. "You will have to go," were the curt words he heard from time to time.

"What a disgrace for me if I am dismissed. My remorse will embitter all my life," he said to himself, "she will never write to me. God knows when I shall come back to this part of the country." From this moment Julien's heart became rapidly oblivious of all the heavenly delights of his present position.

Seated as he was close to a woman whom he adored and practically clasping her in his arms in this room, the scene of his former happiness, amid a deep obscurity, seeing quite clearly as he did that she had just started crying, and feeling that she was sobbing from the heaving of her chest, he was unfortunate enough to turn into a cold diplomatist, nearly as cold as in those days when in the courtyard of the seminary he found himself the butt of some malicious joke on the part of one of his comrades who was stronger than he was. Julien protracted his story by talking of his unhappy life since his departure from Verrières.

"So," said Madame de Rênal to herself, "after a year's absence and deprived almost entirely of all tokens of memory while I myself was forgetting him, he only thought of the happy days that he had had in Verrières." Her sobs redoubled. Julien saw the success of his story. He realised that he must play his last card. He abruptly mentioned a letter he had just received from Paris.

"I have taken leave of my Lord Bishop."

"What! you are not going back to Besançon? You are leaving us for ever?"

"Yes," answered Julien resolutely, "yes, I am leaving a country where I have been forgotten even by the woman whom I loved more than anyone in my life; I am leaving it and I shall never see it again. I am going to Paris."

"You are going to Paris, dear," exclaimed Madame de Rênal.

Her voice was almost choked by her tears and showed the extremity of her trouble. Julien had need of this encouragement. He was on the point of executing a manœuvre which might decide everything against him; and up to the time of this exclamation he could not tell what effect he was producing as he was unable to see. He no longer hesitated. The fear of remorse gave him complete control over himself. He coldly added as he got up.

"Yes, madame, I leave you for ever. May you be happy. Adieu."

He moved some steps towards the window. He began to open it. Madame de Rênal rushed to him and threw herself into his arms. So it was in this way that, after a dialogue lasting three hours, Julien obtained what he desired so passionately during the first two hours.

Madame de Rênal's return to her tender feelings and this overshadowing of her remorse would have been a divine happiness had they come a little earlier; but, as they had been obtained by artifice, they were simply a pleasure. Julien insisted on lighting the night-light in spite of his mistress's opposition.

"Do you wish me then," he said to her "to have no recollection of having seen you. Is the love in those charming eyes to be lost to me for ever? Is the whiteness of that pretty hand to remain invisible? Remember that perhaps I am leaving you for a very long time."

Madame de Rênal could refuse him nothing. His argument made her melt into tears. But the dawn was beginning to throw into sharp relief the outlines of the pine trees on the mountain east of Verrières. Instead of going away Julien, drunk with pleasure, asked Madame de

Rênal to let him pass the day in her room and leave the following night.

"And why not?" she answered. "This fatal relapse robs me of all my respect and will mar all my life," and she pressed him to her heart. "My husband is no longer the same; he has suspicions, he believes I led him the way I wanted in all this business, and shows great irritation against me. If he hears the slightest noise I shall be ruined, he will hound me out like the unhappy woman that I am."

"Ah here we have a phrase of M. Chélan's," said Julien "you would not have talked like that before my cruel departure to the seminary; in those days you used to love me."

Julien was rewarded for the frigidity which he put into those words. He saw his love suddenly forget the danger which her husband's presence compelled her to run, in thinking of the much greater danger of seeing Julien doubt her love. The daylight grew rapidly brighter and vividly illuminated the room. Julien savoured once more all the deliciousness of pride, when he saw this charming woman in his arms and almost at his feet, the only woman whom he had ever loved, and who had been entirely absorbed only a few hours before by her fear of a terrible God and her devotion to her duties. Resolutions, fortified by a year's persuasion, had failed to hold out against his courage.

They soon heard a noise in the house. A matter that Madame de Rênal had not thought of began to trouble her.

"That wicked Elisa will come into the room. What are we to do with this enormous ladder?" she said to her sweetheart, "where are we to hide it? I will take it to the loft," she exclaimed suddenly half playfully.

"But you will have to pass through the servants' room," said Julien in astonishment.

"I will leave the ladder in the corridor and will call the servant and send him on an errand."

"Think of some explanation to have ready in the event of a servant passing the ladder and noticing it in the corridor."

"Yes, my angel," said Madame de Rênal giving him a kiss "as for you, dear, remember to hide under the bed pretty quickly if Elisa enters here during my absence."

Julien was astonished by this sudden gaiety—"So" he thought, "the approach of a real danger instead of troubling her gives her back her spirits before she forgets her remorse. Truly a superior woman. Yes, that's a heart over which it is glorious to reign." Julien was transported with delight.

Madame de Rênal took the ladder, which was obviously too heavy for her. Julien went to her help. He was admiring that elegant figure which was so far from betokening any strength when she suddenly seized the ladder without assistance and took it up as if it had been a chair. She took it rapidly into the corridor of the third storey where she laid it alongside the wall. She called a servant, and in order to give him time to dress himself, went up into the dovecot.

Five minutes later, when she came back to the corridor, she found no signs of the ladder. What had happened to it? If Julien had been out of the house she would not have minded the danger in the least. But supposing her husband were to see the ladder just now, the incident might be awful. Madame de Rênal ran all over the house.

Madame de Rênal finally discovered the ladder under the roof where the servant had carried it and even hid it.

"What does it matter what happens in twenty-four hours," she thought, "when Julien will be gone?"

She had a vague idea that she ought to take leave of life but what mattered her duty? He was restored to her after a separation which she had thought eternal. She was seeing him again and the efforts he had made to reach her showed the extent of his love.

"What shall I say to my husband," she said to him. "If the servant tells him he found this ladder?" She was pensive for a moment. "They will need twenty-four hours to discover the peasant who sold it to you." And she threw herself into Julien's arms and clasped him convulsively.

"Oh, if I could only die like this," she cried covering him with kisses. "But you mustn't die of starvation," she said with a smile.

"Come, I will first hide you in Madame Derville's room which is always locked." She went and watched at the other end of the corridor and Julien ran in. "Mind you don't try and open if any one knocks," she said as she locked him in. "Anyway it would only be a frolic of the children as they play together."

"Get them to come into the garden under the window," said Julien, "so that I may have the pleasure of seeing them. Make them speak."

"Yes, yes," cried Madame de Rênal to him as she went away. She soon returned with oranges, biscuits and a bottle of Malaga wine. She had not been able to steal any bread.

"What is your husband doing?" said Julien.

"He is writing out the figures of the bargains he is going to make with the peasants."

But eight o'clock had struck and they were making a lot of noise in the house. If Madame de Rênal failed to put in an appearance, they would look for her all over the house. She was obliged to leave him. Soon she came back, in defiance of all prudence, bringing him a cup of coffee. She was frightened lest he should die of starvation.

She managed after breakfast to bring the children under the window of Madame Derville's room. He thought they had grown a great deal, but they had begun to look common, or else his ideas had changed.

Madame de Rênal spoke to them about Julien. The elder answered in an affectionate tone and regretted his old tutor, but he found that the younger children had almost forgotten him.

M. de Rênal did not go out that morning; he was going up and downstairs incessantly engaged in bargaining with some peasants to whom he was selling potatoes.

Madame de Rênal did not have an instant to give to her prisoner until dinner-time. When the bell had been rung and dinner had been served, it occurred to her to steal a plate of warm soup for him. As she noiselessly approached the door of the room which he occupied, she found herself face to face with the servant who had hid the ladder in the morning. At the time he too was going noiselessly along the corridor, as though listening for something. The servant took himself off in some confusion.

Madame de Rênal boldly entered Julien's room. The news of this encounter made him shudder.

"You are frightened," she said to him, "but I would brave all the dangers in the world without flinching. There is only one thing I fear, and that is the moment when I shall be alone after you have left," and she left him and ran downstairs.

"Ah," thought Julien ecstatically, "remorse is the only danger which this sublime soul is afraid of."

At last evening came. Monsieur de Rênal went to the Casino.

His wife had given out that she was suffering from an awful headache. She went to her room, hastened to dismiss Elisa and quickly got up in order to let Julien out.

He was literally starving. Madame de Rênal went to the pantry to fetch some bread. Julien heard a loud cry. Madame de Rênal came back and told him that when she went to the dark pantry and got near the cupboard where they kept the bread, she had touched a woman's arm as she stretched out her hand. It was Elisa who had uttered the cry Julien had heard.

"What was she doing there?"

"Stealing some sweets or else spying on us," said Madame de Rênal with complete indifference, "but luckily I found a pie and a big loaf of bread."

"But what have you got there?" said Julien pointing to the pockets of her apron.

Madame de Rênal had forgotten that they had been filled with bread since dinner.

Julien clasped her in his arms with the most lively passion. She had never seemed to him so beautiful. "I could not meet a woman of greater character even at Paris," he said confusedly to himself. She combined all the clumsiness of a woman who was but little accustomed to paying attentions of this kind, with all the genuine courage of a person who is only afraid of dangers of quite a different sphere and quite a different kind of awfulness.

While Julien was enjoying his supper with a hearty appetite and his sweetheart was rallying him on the simplicity of the meal, the door of the room was suddenly shaken violently. It was M. de Rênal.

"Why have you shut yourself in?" he cried to her.

Julien had only just time to slip under the sofa.

On any ordinary day Madame de Rênal would have been upset by this question which was put with true conjugal harshness; but she realised that M. de Rênal had only to bend down a little to notice Julien, for M. de Rênal had flung himself into the chair opposite the sofa which Julien had been sitting in one moment before.

Her headache served as an excuse for everything. While her husband on his side went into a long-winded account of the billiards pool which he had won at Casino, "yes, to be sure a nineteen franc pool," he added. She noticed Julien's hat on a chair three paces in front of them. Her self-possession became twice as great, she began to undress, and rapidly passing one minute behind her husband threw her dress over the chair with the hat on it.

At last M. de Rênal left. She begged Julien to start over again his account of his life at the Seminary. "I was not listening to you yesterday all the time you were speaking, I was only thinking of prevailing on myself to send you away."

She was the personification of indiscretion. They talked very loud and about two o'clock in the morning they were interrupted by a violent knock at the door. It was M. de Rênal again.

"Open quickly, there are thieves in the house!" he said. "Saint Jean found their ladder this morning."

"This is the end of everything," cried Madame de Rênal, throwing herself into Julien's arms. "He will kill both of us, he doesn't believe there are any thieves. I will die in your arms, and be more happy in my death than I ever was in my life." She made no attempt to answer her husband who was beginning to lose his temper, but started kissing Julien passionately.

"Save Stanislas's mother," he said to her with an imperious look. "I will jump down into the courtyard through the lavatory window, and escape in the garden; the dogs have recognised me. Make my clothes into a parcel and throw them into the garden as soon as you can. In the meanwhile let him break the door down. But above all, no confession, I forbid you to confess, it is better that he should suspect rather than be certain."

"You will kill yourself as you jump!" was her only answer and her only anxiety.

She went with him to the lavatory window; she then took sufficient time to hide his clothes. She finally opened the door to her husband who was boiling with rage. He looked in the room and in the lavatory without saying a word and disappeared. Julien's clothes were thrown down to him; he seized them and ran rapidly towards the bottom of the garden in the direction of the Doubs.

As he was running he heard a bullet whistle past him, and heard at the same time the report of a gun.

"It is not M. de Rênal," he thought, "he's far too bad a shot." The dogs ran silently at his side, the second shot apparently broke the paw of one dog, for he began to whine piteously. Julien jumped the wall of the terrace, did fifty paces under cover, and began to fly in another direction. He heard voices calling and had a distinct view of his enemy the servant firing a gun; a farmer also began to shoot away from the other side of the garden. Julien had already reached the bank of the Doubs where he dressed himself.

An hour later he was a league from Verrières on the Geneva road. "If they had suspicions," thought Julien, "they will look for me on the Paris road."

XXXI
THE PLEASURES OF THE COUNTRY

O rus quando ego te aspiciam?—*Horace*

"You've no doubt come to wait for the Paris mail, Monsieur," said the host of an inn where he had stopped to breakfast.

"To-day or to-morrow, it matters little," said Julien.

The mail arrived while he was still posing as indifferent. There were two free places.

"Why! it's you my poor Falcoz," said the traveller who was coming from the Geneva side to the one who was getting in at the same time as Julien.

"I thought you were settled in the outskirts of Lyons," said Falcoz, "in a delicious valley near the Rhône."

"Nicely settled! I am running away."

"What! you are running away? you Saint Giraud! Have you, who look so virtuous, committed some crime?" said Falcoz with a smile.

"On my faith it comes to the same thing. I am running away from the abominable life which one leads in the provinces. I like the freshness of the woods and the country tranquillity, as you know. You have often accused me of being romantic. I don't want to hear politics talked as long as I live, and politics are hounding me out."

"But what party do you belong to?"

"To none and that's what ruins me. That's all there is to be said about my political life—I like music and painting. A good book is an event for me. I am going to be forty-four. How much longer have I got to live? Fifteen—twenty—thirty years at the outside. Well, I want the ministers in thirty years' time to be a little cleverer than those of to-day but quite as honest. The history of England serves as a mirror for our own future. There will always be a king who will try to increase his prerogative. The ambition of becoming a deputy, the fame of Mirabeau and the hundreds of thousand francs which he won for himself will always prevent the rich people in the province from going to sleep: they will call that being Liberal and loving the people. The desire of becoming a peer or a gentleman of the chamber will always win over the ultras. On the ship of state every one is anxious to take over the steering because it is well paid. Will there be never a poor little place for the simple passenger?"

"Is it the last elections which are forcing you out of the province?"

"My misfortune goes further back. Four years ago I was forty and possessed 500,000 francs. I am four years older to-day and probably 50,000 francs to the bad, as I shall lose that sum on the sale of my chateau of Monfleury in a superb position near the Rhône.

"At Paris I was tired of that perpetual comedy which is rendered obligatory by what you call nineteenth-century civilisation. I thirsted for good nature and simplicity. I bought an estate in the mountains near the Rhine, there was no more beautiful place under the heavens.

"The village clergyman and the gentry of the locality pay me court for six months; I invite them to dinner; I have left Paris, I tell them, so as to avoid talking politics or hearing politics talked for the rest of my life. As you know I do not subscribe to any paper, the less letters the postman brought me the happier I was.

"That did not suit the vicar's book. I was soon the victim of a thousand unreasonable requests, annoyances, etc. I wished to give two or three hundred francs a year to the poor, I was asked to give it to the Paris associations, that of Saint Joseph, that of the Virgin, etc. I refused. I was then insulted in a hundred ways. I was foolish enough to be upset by it. I could not go out in the morning to enjoy the beauty of our mountain without finding some annoyance which distracted me from my reveries and recalled unpleasantly both men and their wickedness. On the Rogation processions, for instance whose chanting I enjoy (it is probably a Greek melody) they will not bless my fields because, says the clergyman, they belong to an infidel. A cow dies belonging to a devout old peasant woman. She says the reason is the neighbourhood of a pond which belongs to my infidel self, a philosopher coming from Paris, and eight days afterwards I find my fish in agonies poisoned by lime. Intrigue in all its forms envelops me. The justice of the peace, who is an honest man, but frightened of losing his place, always decides against me. The peace of the country proved a hell for me. Once they saw that I was abandoned by the vicar, the head of the village congregation, and that I was not supported by the retired captain who was the head of the Liberals they all fell upon me, down to the mason whom I had supported for a year, down to the very wheel-wright who wanted to cheat me with impunity over the repairing of my ploughs.

"In order to find some support, and to win at any rate some of my law suits I became a Liberal, but, as you say, those damned elections come along. They asked me for my vote."

"For an unknown man?"

"Not at all, for a man whom I knew only too well. I refused. It was terribly imprudent. From that moment I had the Liberals on my hands as well, and my position became intolerable. I believe that if the vicar had got it into his head to accuse me of assassinating my servant, there would be twenty witnesses of the two parties who would swear that they had seen me committing the crime."

"You mean to say you want to live in the country without pandering to the passions of your neighbours, without even listening to their gossip. What a mistake!"

"It is rectified at last. Monfleury is for sale. I will lose 50,000 francs if necessary, but I am over-joyed I am leaving that hell of hypocrisy and annoyance. I am going to look for solitude and rustic peace in the only place where those things are to be found in France, on a fourth storey looking on to the Champs-Elysées; and, moreover, I am actually deliberating if I shall not commence my political career by giving consecrated bread to the parish in the Roule quarter."

"All this would not have happened under Bonaparte," said Falcoz with eyes shining with rage and sorrow.

"Very good, but why didn't your Bonaparte manage to keep his position? Everything which I suffer to-day is his work."

At this point Julien's attention was redoubled. He had realised from the first word that the Bonapartist Falcoz was the old boyhood friend of M. de Rênal, who had been repudiated by him in 1816, and that the philosopher Saint-Giraud must be the brother of that chief of the prefecture of——who managed to get the houses of the municipality knocked down to him at a cheap price.

"And all this is the work of your Bonaparte. An honest man, aged forty, and possessed of five hundred thousand francs however inoffensive he is, cannot settle in the provinces and find peace there; those priests and nobles of his will turn him out."

"Oh don't talk evil of him," exclaimed Falcoz. "France was never so high in the esteem of the nations as during the thirteen years of his reign; then every single act was great."

"Your emperor, devil take him," replied the man of forty-four, "was only great on his battle fields and when he reorganised the finances about 1802. What is the meaning of all his conduct since then? What with his chamberlains, his pomp, and his receptions in the Tuileries, he has simply provided a new edition of all the monarchical tomfoolery. It was a revised edition and might possibly have lasted for a century or two. The nobles and the priests wish to go back to the old one, but they did not have the iron hand necessary to impose it on the public."

"Yes, that's just how an old printer would talk."

"Who has turned me out of my estate?" continued the printer, angrily. "The priests, whom Napoleon called back by his Concordat instead of treating them like the State treats doctors, barristers, and astronomers, simply seeing in them ordinary citizens, and not bothering about the particular calling by which they are trying to earn their livelihood. Should we be saddled with these insolent gentlemen today, if your Bonaparte had not created barons and counts? No, they were out of fashion. Next to the priests, it's the little country nobility who have annoyed me the most, and compelled me to become a Liberal."

The conversation was endless. The theme will occupy France for another half-century. As Saint-Giraud kept always repeating that it was impossible to live in the provinces, Julien timidly suggested the case of M. de Rênal.

"Zounds, young man, you're a nice one," exclaimed Falcoz. "He turned spider so as not to be fly, and a terrible spider into the bargain. But I see that he is beaten by that man Valenod. Do you know that scoundrel? He's the villain of the piece. What will your M. de Rênal say if he sees himself turned out one of these fine days, and Valenod put in his place?"

"He will be left to brood over his crimes," said Saint-Giraud. "Do you know Verrières, young man? Well, Bonaparte, heaven confound him! Bonaparte and his monarchical tomfoolery rendered possible the reign of the Rênals and the Chélans, which brought about the reign of the Valenods and the Maslons."

This conversation, with its gloomy politics, astonished Julien and distracted him from his delicious reveries.

He appreciated but little the first sight of Paris as perceived in the distance. The castles in the air he had built about his future had to struggle with the still present memory of the twenty-four hours that he had just passed in Verrières. He vowed that he would never abandon his mistress's children, and that he would leave everything in order to protect them, if the impertinence of the priests brought about a republic and the persecution of the nobles.

What would have happened on the night of his arrival in Verrières if, at the moment when he had leant his ladder against the casement of Madame de Rênal's bedroom he had found that room occupied by a stranger or by M. de Rênal?

But how delicious, too, had been those first two hours when his sweetheart had been sincerely anxious to send him away and he had pleaded his cause, sitting down by her in the darkness! A soul like Julien's is haunted by such memories for a lifetime. The rest of the interview was already becoming merged in the first period of their love, fourteen months previous.

Julien was awakened from his deep meditation by the stopping of the coach. They had just entered the courtyard of the Post in the Rue Rousseau. "I want to go to La Malmaison," he said to a cabriolet which approached.

"At this time, Monsieur—what for?"

"What's that got to do with you? Get on."

Every real passion only thinks about itself. That is why, in my view, passions are ridiculous at Paris, where one's neighbour always insists on one's considering him a great deal. I shall refrain from recounting Julien's ecstasy at La Malmaison. He wept. What! in spite of those wretched white walls, built this very year, which cut the path up into bits? Yes, monsieur, for Julien, as for posterity, there was nothing to choose between Arcole, Saint Helena, and La Malmaison.

In the evening, Julien hesitated a great deal before going to the theatre. He had strange ideas about that place of perdition.

A deep distrust prevented him from admiring actual Paris. He was only affected by the monuments left behind by his hero.

"So here I am in the centre of intrigue and hypocrisy. Here reign the protectors of the abbé de Frilair." On the evening of the third day his curiosity got the better of his plan of seeing everything before presenting himself to the abbé Pirard. The abbé explained to him coldly the kind of life which he was to expect at M. de la Mole's.

"If you do not prove useful to him at the end of some months you will go back to the seminary, but not in disgrace. You will live in the house of the marquis, who is one of the greatest seigneurs of France. You will wear black, but like a man who is in mourning, and not like an ecclesiastic. I insist on your following your theological studies three days a week in a seminary where I will introduce you. Every day at twelve o'clock you will establish yourself in the marquis's library; he counts on making use of you in drafting letters concerning his lawsuits and other matters. The marquis will scribble on the margin of each letter he gets the kind of answer which is required. I have assured him that at the end of three months you will be so competent to draft the answers, that out of every dozen you hand to the marquis for signature, he will be able to sign eight or nine. In the evening, at eight o'clock, you will tidy up his bureau, and at ten you will be free.

"It may be," continued the abbé Pirard, "that some old lady or some smooth-voiced man will hint at immense advantages, or will crudely offer you gold, to show him the letters which the marquis has received."

"Ah, monsieur," exclaimed Julien, blushing.

"It is singular," said the abbé with a bitter smile, "that poor as you are, and after a year at a seminary, you still have any of this virtuous indignation left. You must have been very blind."

"Can it be that blood will tell," muttered the abbé in a whisper, as though speaking to himself. "The singular thing is," he added, looking at Julien, "that the marquis knows you—I don't know how. He will give you a salary of a hundred louis to commence with. He is a man who only acts by his whim. That is his weakness. He will quarrel with you about the most childish matters. If he is satisfied, your wages may rise in consequence up to eight thousand francs.

"But you realise," went on the abbé, sourly, "that he is not giving you all this money simply on account of your personal charm. The thing is to prove yourself useful. If I were in your place I would talk very little, and I would never talk about what I know nothing about.

"Oh, yes," said the abbé, "I have made some enquiries for you. I was forgetting M. de la Mole's family. He has two children—a daughter and a son of nineteen, eminently elegant—the kind of madman who never knows to-day what he will do to-morrow. He has spirit and valour; he has been through the Spanish war. The marquis hopes, I don't know why, that you will become a friend of the young count Norbert. I told him that you were a great classic, and possibly he reckons on your teaching his son some ready-made phrases about Cicero and Virgil.

"If I were you, I should never allow that handsome young man to make fun of me, and before I accepted his advances, which you will find perfectly polite but a little ironical, I would make him repeat them more than once.

"I will not hide from you the fact that the young count de La Mole is bound to despise you at first, because you are nothing more than a little bourgeois. His grandfather belonged to the court, and had the honour of having his head cut off in the Place de Grève on the 26th April, 1574, on account of a political intrigue.

"As for you, you are the son of a carpenter of Verrières, and what is more, in receipt of his father's wages. Ponder well over these differences, and look up the family history in Moreri. All the flatterers who dine at their house make from time to time what they call delicate allusions to it.

"Be careful of how you answer the pleasantries of M. the count de La Mole, chief of a squadron of hussars, and a future peer of France, and don't come and complain to me later on."

"It seems to me," said Julien, blushing violently, "that I ought not even to answer a man who despises me."

"You have no idea of his contempt. It will only manifest itself by inflated compliments. If you were a fool, you might be taken in by it. If you want to make your fortune, you ought to let yourself be taken in by it."

"Shall I be looked upon as ungrateful," said Julien, "if I return to my little cell Number 108 when I find that all this no longer suits me?"

"All the toadies of the house will no doubt calumniate you," said the abbé, "but I myself will come to the rescue. Adsum qui feci. I will say that I am responsible for that resolution."

Julien was overwhelmed by the bitter and almost vindictive tone which he noticed in M. Pirard; that tone completely infected his last answer.

The fact is that the abbé had a conscientious scruple about loving Julien, and it was with a kind of religious fear that he took so direct a part in another's life.

"You will also see," he added with the same bad grace, as though accomplishing a painful duty, "you also will see Madame the marquise de La Mole. She is a big blonde woman about forty, devout, perfectly polite, and even more insignificant. She is the daughter of the old Duke de Chaulnes so well known for his aristocratic prejudices. This great lady is a kind of synopsis in high relief of all the fundamental characteristics of women of her rank. She does not conceal for her own part that the possession of ancestors who went through the crusades is the sole advantage which she respects. Money only comes a long way afterwards. Does that astonish you? We are no longer in the provinces, my friend.

"You will see many great lords in her salon talk about our princes in a tone of singular flippancy. As for Madame de la Mole, she lowers her voice out of respect every time she mentions the name of a Prince, and above all the name of a Princess. I would not advise you to say in her hearing that Philip II. or Henry VII. were monsters. They were kings, a fact which gives them indisputable rights to the respect of creatures without birth like you and me. Nevertheless," added M. Pirard, "we are priests, for she will take you for one; that being our capacity, she considers us as spiritual valets necessary for her salvation."

"Monsieur," said Julien, "I do not think I shall be long at Paris."

"Good, but remember that no man of our class can make his fortune except through the great lords. With that indefinable element in your character, at any rate I think it is, you will be persecuted if you do not make your fortune. There is no middle course for you, make no mistake about it; people see that they do not give you pleasure when they speak to you; in a social country like this you are condemned to unhappiness if you do not succeed in winning respect."

"What would have become of you at Besançon without this whim of the marquis de la Mole? One day you will realise the extraordinary extent of what he has done for you, and if you are not a monster you will be eternally grateful to him and his family. How many poor abbés more learned than you have lived years at Paris on the fifteen sous they got for their mass and their ten sous they got for their dissertations in the Sorbonne. Remember what I told you last winter about the first years of that bad man Cardinal Dubois. Are you proud enough by chance to think yourself more talented than he was?

"Take, for instance, a quiet and average man like myself; I reckoned on dying in my seminary. I was childish enough to get attached to it. Well I was on the point of being turned out, when I handed in my resignation. You know what my fortune consisted of. I had five hundred and twenty francs capital neither more nor less, not a friend, scarcely two or three acquaintances. M. de la Mole, whom I had never seen, extricated me from that quandary. He only had to say the word and I was given a living where the parishioners are well-to-do people above all crude vices, and where the income puts me to shame, it is so disproportionate to my work. I refrained from talking to you all this time simply to enable you to find your level a bit.

"One word more, I have the misfortune to be irritable. It is possible that you and I will cease to be on speaking terms.

"If the airs of the marquise or the spiteful pleasantries of her son make the house absolutely intolerable for you I advise you to finish your studies in some seminary thirty leagues from Paris and rather north than south. There is more civilisation in the north, and, he added lowering his voice, I must admit that the nearness of the Paris papers puts fear into our petty tyrants.

"If we continue to find pleasure in each other's society and if the marquis's house does not suit you, I will offer you the post of my curate, and will go equal shares with you in what I get from the living. I owe you that and even more, he added interrupting Julien's thanks, for the extraordinary offer which you made me at Besançon. If instead of having five hundred and twenty francs I had had nothing you would have saved me."

The abbé's voice had lost its tone of cruelty, Julien was ashamed to feel tears in his eyes. He was desperately anxious to throw himself into his friend's arms. He could not help saying to him in the most manly manner he could assume:

"I was hated by my father from the cradle; it was one of my great misfortunes, but I shall no longer complain of my luck, I have found another father in you, monsieur."

"That is good, that is good," said the embarrassed abbé, then suddenly remembering quite appropriately a seminary platitude "you must never say luck, my child, always say providence."

The fiacre stopped. The coachman lifted up the bronze knocker of an immense door. It was the Hôtel de la Mole, and to prevent the passers by having any doubt on the subject these words could be read in black marble over the door.

This affectation displeased Julien. "They are so frightened of the Jacobins. They see a Robespierre and his tumbril behind every head. Their panic is often gloriously grotesque and they advertise their house like this so that in the event of a rising the rabble can recognise it and loot it." He communicated his thought to the abbé Pirard.

"Yes, poor child, you will soon be my curate. What a dreadful idea you have got into your head."

"Nothing could be simpler," said Julien.

The gravity of the porter, and above all, the cleanness of the court, struck him with admiration. It was fine sunshine. "What magnificent architecture," he said to his friend. The hotel in question was one of those buildings of the Faubourg Saint-Germain with a flat façade built about the time of Voltaire's death. At no other period had fashion and beauty been so far from one another.

XXXII
ENTRY INTO SOCIETY

Ludicrous and pathetic memory: the first drawing-room
where one appeared alone and without support at the age
of eighteen! the look of a woman sufficed to intimidate me.
The more I wished to please the more clumsy I became. I
evolved the most unfounded ideas about everything. I would
either abandon myself without any reason, or I would regard
a man as an enemy simply because he had looked at me with a
serious air; but all the same, in the middle of the unhappiness
of my timidity, how beautiful did I find a beautiful day—*Kant*.

Julien stopped in amazement in the middle of the courtyard. "Pull
yourself together," said the abbé Pirard. "You get horrible ideas into
your head, besides you are only a child. What has happened to the nil
mirari of Horace (no enthusiasm) remember that when they see you
established here this crowd of lackeys will make fun of you. They will see
in you an equal who has been unjustly placed above them; and, under
a masquerade of good advice and a desire to help you, they will try to
make you fall into some gross blunder."

"Let them do their worst," said Julien biting his lip, and he became as
distrustful as ever.

The salons on the first storey which our gentlemen went through
before reaching the marquis' study, would have seemed to you, my
reader, as gloomy as they were magnificent. If they had been given to
you just as they were, you would have refused to live in them. This was
the domain of yawning and melancholy reasoning. They redoubled
Julien's rapture. "How can any one be unhappy?" he thought, "who lives
in so splendid an abode."

Finally our gentlemen arrived at the ugliest rooms in this superb
suite. There was scarcely any light. They found there a little keen man
with a lively eye and a blonde wig. The abbé turned round to Julien
and presented him. It was the marquis. Julien had much difficulty in
recognising him, he found his manner was so polite. It was no longer the
grand seigneur with that haughty manner of the abbey of Bray-le-Haut.
Julien thought that his wig had much too many hairs. As the result of
this opinion he was not at all intimidated. The descendant of the friend
of Henry III. seemed to him at first of a rather insignificant appearance.
He was extremely thin and very restless, but he soon noticed that the
marquis had a politeness which was even more pleasant to his listener
than that of the Bishop of Besançon himself. The audience only lasted
three minutes. As they went out the abbé said to Julien,

"You looked at the marquis just as you would have looked at a picture. I am not a great expert in what these people here call politeness. You will soon know more about it than I do, but really the boldness of your looks seemed scarcely polite."

They had got back into the fiacre. The driver stopped near the boulevard; the abbé ushered Julien into a suite of large rooms. Julien noticed that there was no furniture. He was looking at the magnificent gilded clock representing a subject which he thought very indecent, when a very elegant gentleman approached him with a smiling air. Julien bowed slightly.

The gentleman smiled and put his hand on his shoulder. Julien shuddered and leapt back, he reddened with rage. The abbé Pirard, in spite of his gravity, laughed till the tears came into his eyes. The gentleman was a tailor.

"I give you your liberty for two days," said the abbé as they went out. "You cannot be introduced before then to Madame de la Mole. Any one else would watch over you as if you were a young girl during these first few moments of your life in this new Babylon. Get ruined at once if you have got to be ruined, and I will be rid of my own weakness of being fond of you. The day after to-morrow this tailor will bring you two suits, you will give the man who tries them on five francs. Apart from that don't let these Parisians hear the sound of your voice. If you say a word they will manage somehow to make fun of you. They have a talent for it. Come and see me the day after to-morrow at noon.... Go and ruin yourself.... I was forgetting, go and order boots and a hat at these addresses."

Julien scrutinised the handwriting of the addresses.

"It's the marquis's hand," said the abbé; "he is an energetic man who foresees everything, and prefers doing to ordering. He is taking you into his house, so that you may spare him that kind of trouble. Will you have enough brains to execute efficiently all the instructions which he will give you with scarcely a word of explanation? The future will show, look after yourself."

Julien entered the shops indicated by the addresses without saying a single word. He observed that he was received with respect, and that the bootmaker as he wrote his name down in the ledger put M. de Sorel.

When he was in the Cemetery of Père La Chaise a very obliging gentleman, and what is more, one who was Liberal in his views, suggested that he should show Julien the tomb of Marshal Ney which a sagacious statecraft had deprived of the honour of an epitaph, but when he left this Liberal, who with tears in his eyes almost clasped him in his arms, Julien was without his watch. Enriched by this experience two days afterwards he presented himself to the abbé Pirard, who looked at him for a long time.

THE RED AND THE BLACK

"Perhaps you are going to become a fop," said the abbé to him severely. Julien looked like a very young man in full mourning; as a matter of fact, he looked very well, but the good abbé was too provincial himself to see that Julien still carried his shoulders in that particular way which signifies in the provinces both elegance and importance. When the marquis saw Julien his opinion of his graces differed so radically from that of the good abbé as he said,

"Would you have any objection to M. le Sorel taking some dancing lessons?"

The abbé was thunderstruck.

"No," he answered at last. "Julien is not a priest."

The marquis went up the steps of a little secret staircase two at a time, and installed our hero in a pretty attic which looked out on the big garden of the hotel. He asked him how many shirts he had got at the linen drapers.

"Two," answered Julien, intimidated at seeing so great a lord condescend to such details.

"Very good," replied the marquis quite seriously, and with a certain curt imperiousness which gave Julien food for thought. "Very good, get twenty-two more shirts. Here are your first quarter's wages."

As he went down from the attic the marquis called an old man. "Arsène," he said to him, "you will serve M. Sorel." A few minutes afterwards Julien found himself alone in a magnificent library. It was a delicious moment. To prevent his emotion being discovered he went and hid in a little dark corner. From there he contemplated with rapture the brilliant backs of the books. "I shall be able to read all these," he said to himself. "How can I fail to like it here? M. de Rênal would have thought himself dishonoured for ever by doing one-hundredth part of what the Marquis de la Mole has just done for me.

"But let me have a look at the copies I have to make." Having finished this work Julien ventured to approach the books. He almost went mad with joy as he opened an edition of Voltaire. He ran and opened the door of the library to avoid being surprised. He then indulged in the luxury of opening each of the eighty volumes. They were magnificently bound and were the masterpiece of the best binder in London. It was even more than was required to raise Julien's admiration to the maximum.

An hour afterwards the marquis came in and was surprised to notice that Julien spelt cela with two "ll" cella. "Is all that the abbé told me of his knowledge simply a fairy tale?" The marquis was greatly discouraged and gently said to him,

"You are not sure of your spelling?"

"That is true," said Julien without thinking in the least of the injustice that he was doing to himself. He was overcome by the kindness of

196

the marquis which recalled to him through sheer force of contrast the superciliousness of M. de Rênal.

"This trial of the little Franc-comtois abbé is waste of time," thought the marquis, "but I had such great need of a reliable man."

"You spell cela with one 'l,'" said the marquis to him, "and when you have finished your copies look the words whose spelling you are not sure of up in the dictionary."

The marquis sent for him at six o'clock. He looked at Julien's boots with manifest pain. "I am sorry for a mistake I made. I did not tell you that you must dress every day at half-past five."

Julien looked at him but did not understand.

"I mean to say put on stockings. Arsène will remind you. To-day I will make your apologies."

As he finished the sentence M. de la Mole escorted Julien into a salon resplendent with gilding. On similar occasions M. de Rênal always made a point of doubling his pace so as to have the privilege of being the first to pass the threshold. His former employer's petty vanity caused Julien to tread on the marquis's feet and hurt him a great deal because of his gout. "So he is clumsy to the bargain," he said to himself. He presented him to a woman of high stature and of imposing appearance. It was the marquise. Julien thought that her manner was impertinent, and that she was a little like Madame de Maugiron, the wife of the sub-prefect of the arrondissement of Verrières when she was present at the Saint-Charles dinner. Rendered somewhat nervous by the extreme magnificence of the salon Julien did not hear what M. de la Mole was saying. The marquise scarcely deigned to look at him. There were several men there, among whom Julien recognised with an inexpressible pleasure the young bishop of Agde who had deigned to speak to him some months before at the ceremony of Bray-le-Haut. This young prelate was doubtless frightened by the tender look which the timidity of Julien fixed on him, and did not bother to recognise "the provincial."

The men assembled in this salon seemed to Julien to have a certain element of gloom and constraint. Conversation takes place in a low voice in Paris and little details are not exaggerated.

A handsome young man with moustaches, came in about half-past six. He was very pale, and had a very small head.

"You always keep us waiting" said the marquise, as he kissed her hand.

Julien realised that it was the Count de la Mole. From the very first he thought he was charming.

"Is it possible," he said to himself "that this is the man whose offensive jests are going to drive me out of the house."

As the result of scrutinising count Norbert, Julien noticed that he was in boots and spurs. "And I have got to be in shoes just like an inferior apparently." They sat down at table, Julien heard the marquise raising her voice a little and saying something severe. Almost simultaneously he noticed an extremely blonde and very well developed young person who had just sat down opposite him. Nevertheless she made no appeal to him. Looking at her attentively he thought that he had never seen such beautiful eyes, although they betokened a great coldness of soul. Subsequently Julien thought that, though they looked bored and sceptical, they were conscious of the duty of being impressive. "Madame de Rênal of course had very fine eyes" he said to himself, "she used to be universally complimented on them, but they had nothing in common with these." Julien did not know enough of society to appreciate that it was the fire of repartee which from time to time gave their brilliancy to the eyes of Mademoiselle Mathilde (for that was the name he heard her called by). When Madame de Rênal's eyes became animated, it was with the fire of passion, or as the result of a generous indignation on hearing of some evil deed. Towards the end of the meal Julien found a word to express Mademoiselle de la Mole's type of beauty. Her eyes are scintillating, he said to himself. Apart from her eyes she was cruelly like her mother, whom he liked less and less, and he ceased looking at her. By way of compensation he thought Count Norbert admirable in every respect. Julien was so fascinated that the idea never occurred to him of being jealous, and hating him because he was richer and of nobler birth than he was himself.

Julien thought that the marquis looked bored.

About the second course he said to his son: "Norbert, I ask all your good offices for M. Julien Sorel, whom I have just taken into my staff and of whom I hope to make a man *si cella se peut.*"

"He is my secretary," said the marquis to his neighbour, "and he spells cela with two ll's." Everybody looked at Julien, who bowed to Norbert in a manner that was slightly too marked, but speaking generally they were satisfied with his expression.

The marquis must have spoken about the kind of education which Julien had received for one of the guests tackled him on Horace. "It was just by talking about Horace that I succeeded with the bishop of Besançon," said Julien to himself. Apparently that is the only author they know. From that instant he was master of himself. This transition was rendered easy because he had just decided that he would never look upon Madamoiselle de la Mole as a woman after his own taste. Since the seminary he had the lowest opinion of men, and was not to be easily intimidated by them. He would have enjoyed all his self-possession if the dining-room had been furnished with less magnificence. It was, as a matter of fact, two mirrors each eight feet high in which he would look from time to time at the man who was speaking to him about

Horace, which continued to impress him. His phrases were not too long for a provincial, he had fine eyes whose brilliancy was doubled by his quavering timidity, or by his happy bashfulness when he had given a good answer. They found him pleasant. This kind of examination gave a little interest to a solemn dinner. The marquis signed to Julien's questioner to press him sharply. "Can he possibly know something?" he thought.

Julien answered and thought out new ideas. He lost sufficient of his nervousness, not indeed to exhibit any wit, for that is impossible for any one ignorant of the special language which is used in Paris, but to show himself possessed of ideas which, though presented out of place and ungracefully, were yet original. They saw that he knew Latin perfectly.

Julien's adversary was a member of the Academy Inscriptions who chanced to know Latin. He found Julien a very good humanist, was not frightened of making him feel uncomfortable, and really tried to embarrass him. In the heat of the controversy Julien eventually forgot the magnificent furniture of the dining-room. He managed to expound theories concerning the Latin poets which his questioner had never read of anywhere. Like an honest man, he gave the young secretary all due credit for them. As luck would have it, they started a discussion on the question of whether Horace was poor or rich, a good humoured and careless voluptuary who made verses to amuse himself, like Chapelle the friend of Molière and de la Fontaine, or a poor devil of a poet laureate who wrote odes for the king's birthday like Southey, the accuser of Lord Byron. They talked about the state of society under Augustus and under George IV. At both periods the aristocracy was all-powerful, but, while at Rome it was despoiled of its power by Maecenas who was only a simple knight, it had in England reduced George IV practically to the position of a Venetian doge. This discussion seemed to lift the marquis out of that state of bored torpor in which he had been plunged at the beginning of the dinner.

Julien found meaningless such modern names as Southey, Lord Byron, and George IV, which he now heard pronounced for the first time. But every one noticed that whenever the conversation dealt with events that had taken place in Rome and about which knowledge could be obtained by a perusal of the works of Horace, Martial or Tacitus, etc., he showed an indisputable superiority. Julien coolly appropriated several ideas which he had learnt from the bishop of Besançon in the historic conversation which he had had with that prelate. These ideas were not the least appreciated.

When every one was tired of talking about poets the marquise, who always made it a rule to admire whatever amused her husband, deigned to look at Julien. "Perhaps an educated man lies hid beneath the clumsy manners of this young abbé," said the Academician who happened to be near the marquise. Julien caught a few words of what he said. Ready-made phrases suited the intellect of the mistress of the house quite well. She adopted this one about Julien, and was very pleased with herself for having invited the academician to dinner. "He has amused M. de la Mole" she thought.

XXXIII
THE FIRST STEPS

> This immense valley, filled with brilliant lights and so many thousands of men dazzles my sight. No one knows me. All are superior to me. I lose my head. *Poemi dell' av. REINA.*

Julien was copying letters in the library very early the next day when Mademoiselle Mathilde came in by a little dummy door very well masked by the backs of the books. While Julien was admiring the device, Mademoiselle Mathilde seemed astonished and somewhat annoyed at finding him there: Julien saw that she was in curl-papers and had a hard, haughty, and masculine expression. Mademoiselle de la Mole had the habit of surreptitiously stealing books from her father's library. Julien's presence rendered this morning's journey abortive, a fact which annoyed her all the more as she had come to fetch the second volume of Voltaire's *Princess of Babylon*, a worthy climax to one of the most eminently monarchical and religious educations which the convent of the Sacred Heart had ever provided. This poor girl of nineteen already required some element of spiciness in order to get up an interest in a novel.

Count Norbert put in an appearance in the library about three o'clock. He had come to study a paper so as to be able to talk politics in the evening, and was very glad to meet Julien, whose existence he had forgotten. He was charming, and offered him a ride on horseback.

"My father will excuse us until dinner."

Julien appreciated the us and thought it charming.

"Great heavens! M. le Comte," said Julien, "if it were a question of felling an eighty-foot tree or hewing it out and making it into planks I would acquit myself all right, I daresay, but as for riding a horse, I haven't done such a thing six times in my life."

"Well, this will be the seventh," said Norbert.

As a matter of fact, Julien remembered the king of ——'s entry into Verrières, and thought he rode extremely well. But as they were returning from the Bois de Boulogne he fell right in the middle of the Rue du Bac, as he suddenly tried to get out of the way of a cabriolet, and was spattered all over with mud. It was lucky that he had two suits. The marquis, wishing to favour him with a few words at dinner, asked him for news of his excursion. Norbert began immediately to answer him in general terms.

"M. le Comte is extremely kind to me," answered Julien. "I thank him for it, and I fully appreciate it. He was good enough to have the quietest and prettiest horse given to me, but after all he could not tie me on to it, and owing to the lack of that precaution, I had a fall right in the middle of that long street near the bridge. Madame Mathilde made a futile effort to hide a burst of laughter, and subsequently was indiscreet enough to ask for details. Julien acquitted himself with much simplicity. He had grace without knowing it.

"I prophesy favourably about that little priest," said the marquis to the academician. "Think of a provincial being simple over a matter like that. Such a thing has never been witnessed before, and will never be witnessed again; and what is more, he describes his misfortune before ladies."

Julien put his listeners so thoroughly at their ease over his misfortune that at the end of the dinner, when the general conversation had gone off on to another subject, Mademoiselle Mathilde asked her brother some questions over the details of the unfortunate occurrence. As she put numerous questions, and as Julien met her eyes several times, he ventured to answer himself, although the questions had not been addressed to him, and all three of them finished up by laughing just as though they had all been inhabitants of some village in the depths of a forest.

On the following day Julien attended two theology lectures, and then came back to copy out about twenty letters. He found a young man, who though very carefully dressed, had a mean appearance and an envious expression, established near him in the library.

The marquis entered, "What are you doing here, M. Tanbeau?" he said severely to the new-comer.

"I thought—" answered the young man, with a base smile.

"No, monsieur, you thought nothing of the kind. This is a try-on, but it is an unfortunate one."

Young Tanbeau got up in a rage and disappeared. He was a nephew of the academician who was a friend of Madame de la Mole, and intended to take up the profession of letters. The academician had induced the marquis to take him as a secretary. Tanbeau used to work in a separate room, but having heard of the favour that was vouchsafed to Julien he wished to share it, and he had gone this morning and established his desk in the library.

At four o'clock Julien ventured, after a little hesitation, to present himself to Count Norbert. The latter was on the point of going riding, and being a man of perfect politeness felt embarrassed.

"I think," he said to Julien, "that you had better go to the riding school, and after a few weeks, I shall be charmed to ride with you."

"I should like to have the honour of thanking you for the kindness which you have shewn me. Believe me, monsieur," added Julien very seriously, "that I appreciate all I owe you. If your horse has not been hurt by the reason of my clumsiness of yesterday, and if it is free I should like to ride it this afternoon."

"Well, upon my word, my dear Sorel, you do so at your own risk and peril; kindly assume that I have put forth all the objections required by prudence. As a matter of fact it is four o'clock, we have no time to lose."

As soon as Julien was on horseback, he said to the young count, "What must one do not to fall off?"

"Lots of things," answered Norbert, bursting into laughter. "Keep your body back for instance."

Julien put his horse to the trot. They were at the Place Louis XVI.

"Oh, you foolhardy youngster," said Norbert "there are too many carriages here, and they are driven by careless drivers into the bargain. Once you are on the ground their tilburies will run over your body, they will not risk spoiling their horses' mouths by pulling up short."

Norbert saw Julien twenty times on the point of tumbling, but in the end the excursion finished without misadventure. As they came back the young count said to his sister,

"Allow me to introduce a dashing dare-devil."

When he talked to his father over the dinner from one end of the table to the other, he did justice to Julien's courage. It was the only thing one could possibly praise about his style of riding. The young count had heard in the morning the men who groomed the horses in the courtyard making Julien's fall an opportunity for the most outrageous jokes at his expense.

In spite of so much kindness Julien soon felt himself completely isolated in this family. All their customs seemed strange to him, and he was cognizant of none of them. His blunders were the delight of the valets.

The abbé Pirard had left for his living. "If Julien is a weak reed, let him perish. If he is a man of spirit, let him get out of his difficulties all alone," he thought.

XXXIV
THE HÔTEL DE LA MOLE

What is he doing here? Will he like it there? Will he try to please?—*Ronsard.*

If everything in the aristocratic salon of the Hotel de la Mole seemed strange to Julien, that pale young man in his black suit seemed in his turn very strange to those persons who deigned to notice him. Madame de la Mole suggested to her husband that he should send him off on some business on those days when they had certain persons to dinner.

"I wish to carry the experiment to its logical conclusion," answered the marquis. "The abbé Pirard contends that we are wrong in crushing the self-respect of the people whom we allow around us. *One can only lean on what resists.* The only thing against this man is his unknown face, apart from that he is a deaf mute."

"If I am to know my way about," said Julien to himself. "I must write down the names of the persons whom I see come to the salon together with a few words on their character."

He put at the head of the list five or six friends of the house who took every opportunity of paying court to him, believing that he was protected by a whim of the marquis. They were poor dull devils. But it must be said in praise of this class of men, such as they are found to-day in the salons of the aristocracy, that every one did not find them equally tame. One of them was now allowing himself to be bullied by the marquis, who was venting his irritation at a harsh remark which had been addressed to him by the marquise.

The masters of the house were too proud or too prone to boredom; they were too much used to finding their only distraction in the addressing of insults, to enable them to expect true friends. But, except on rainy days and in rare moments of savage boredom, they always showed themselves perfectly polite.

If the five or six toadies who manifested so paternal an affection towards Julien had deserted the Hotel de la Mole, the marquise would have been exposed to long spells of solitude, and in the eyes of women of that class, solitude is awful, it is the symbol of *disgrace.*

The marquis was charming to his wife. He saw that her salon was sufficiently furnished, though not with peers, for he did not think his new colleagues were sufficiently noble to come to his house as friends, or sufficiently amusing to be admitted as inferiors.

It was only later that Julien fathomed these secrets. The governing policy of a household, though it forms the staple of conversation in bourgeois families, is only alluded to in families of the class of that of the marquis in moments of distress. So paramount even in this bored century is the necessity of amusing one's self, that even on the days of dinner-parties the marquis had scarcely left the salon before all the guests ran away. Provided that one did not make any jests about either God or the priests or the king or the persons in office, or the artists who enjoyed the favour of the court, or of anything that was established, provided that one did not praise either Béranger or the opposition papers, or Voltaire or Rousseau or anything which involved any element of free speech, provided that above all that one never talked politics, one could discuss everything with freedom.

There is no income of a hundred thousand crowns a year and no blue ribbon which could sustain a contest against such a code of salon etiquette.

The slightest live idea appeared a crudity. In spite of the prevailing good form, perfect politeness, and desire to please, *ennui* was visible in every face. The young people who came to pay their calls were frightened of speaking of anything which might make them suspected of thinking or of betraying that they had read something prohibited, and relapsed into silence after a few elegant phrases about Rossini and the weather.

Julien noticed that the conversation was usually kept alive by two viscounts and five barons whom M. de la Mole had known at the time of the emigration. These gentlemen enjoyed an income of from six to eight hundred thousand francs. Four swore by the *Quotidienne* and three by the *Gazette de France*. One of them had every day some anecdote to tell about the Château, in which he made lavish use of the word *admirable*. Julien noticed that he had five crosses, the others as a rule only had three.

By way of compensation six footmen in livery were to be seen in the ante-room, and during the whole evening ices or tea were served every quarter-of-an-hour, while about midnight there was a kind of supper with champagne.

This was the reason that sometimes induced Julien to stay till the end. Apart from this he could scarcely understand why any one could bring himself to take seriously the ordinary conversation in this magnificently gilded salon. Sometimes he would look at the talkers to see if they themselves were not making fun of what they were saying. "My M. de Maistre, whom I know by heart," he thought, "has put it a hundred times better, and all the same he is pretty boring."

Julien was not the only one to appreciate this stifling moral atmosphere. Some consoled themselves by taking a great quantity of ices, others by the pleasure of saying all the rest of the evening, "I have just come from the Hôtel de la Mole where I learnt that Russia, etc."

Julien learnt from one of the toadies that scarcely six months ago madame de la Mole had rewarded more than twenty years of assiduous attention by promoting the poor baron Le Bourguignon, who had been a sub-prefect since the restoration, to the rank of prefect.

This great event had whetted the zeal of all these gentlemen. Previously there were few things to which they would have objected, now they objected to nothing. There was rarely any overt lack of consideration, but Julien had already caught at meals two or three little short dialogues between the marquis and his wife which were cruel to those who were seated near them. These noble personages did not conceal their sincere contempt for everyone who was not sprung from people who were entitled to ride in the carriages of the king. Julien noticed that the word crusade was the only word which gave their face an expression of deep seriousness akin to respect. Their ordinary respect had always a touch of condescension. In the middle of this magnificence and this boredom Julien was interested in nothing except M. de la Mole. He was delighted to hear him protest one day that he had had nothing to do with the promotion of that poor Le Bourguignon, it was an attention to the marquise. Julien knew the truth from the abbé Pirard.

The abbé was working in the marquis's library with Julien one morning at the eternal de Frilair lawsuit.

"Monsieur," said Julien suddenly, "is dining every day with madame la marquise one of my duties or a special favour that they show to me?"

"It's a special honour," replied the scandalised abbé. "M. the Academician, who has been cultivating the family for fifteen years, has never been able to obtain so much for his M. Tanbeau."

"I find it, sir, the most painful part of my employment. I was less bored at the seminary. Some times I see even mademoiselle de la Mole yawn, and yet she ought to be accustomed to the social charms of the friends of the house. I am frightened of falling asleep. As a favour, obtain permission for me to go and get a forty sous' dinner in some obscure inn."

The abbé who was a true snob, was very appreciative of the honour of dining with a great lord. While he was endeavouring to get Julien to understand this point of view a slight noise made them turn round. Julien saw mademoiselle de la Mole listening. He reddened. She had come to fetch a book and had heard everything. She began to entertain some respect for Julien. "He has not been born servile," she thought, "like that old abbé. Heavens, how ugly he is."

At dinner Julien did not venture to look at mademoiselle de la Mole but she was kind enough to speak to him. They were expecting a lot of visitors that day and she asked him to stay. The young girls of Paris are not at all fond of persons of a certain age, especially when they are slovenly. Julien did not need much penetration to realise that the colleagues of M. le Bourguignon who remained in the salon had the privilege of being the ordinary butt of mademoiselle de la Mole's jokes. On this particular day, whether or not by reason of some affectation on her part, she proved cruel to bores.

Mademoiselle de la Mole was the centre of a little knot which used to form nearly every evening behind the marquise's immense arm-chair. There were to be found there the marquis de Croisenois, the comte de Caylus, the vicomte de Luz and two or three other young officers, the friends of Norbert or his sister. These gentlemen used to sit down on a large blue sofa. At the end of the sofa, opposite the part where the brilliant Mathilde was sitting, Julien sat in silence on a little, rather low straw chair. This modest position was envied by all the toadies; Norbert kept his father's young secretary in countenance by speaking to him, or mentioning him by name once or twice in the evening. On this particular occasion mademoiselle de la Mole asked him what was the height of the mountain on which the citadel of Besançon is planted. Julien had never any idea if this mountain was higher or lower than Montmartre. He often laughed heartily at what was said in this little knot, but he felt himself incapable of inventing anything analagous. It was like a strange language which he understood but could not speak.

On this particular day Matilde's friends manifested a continuous hostility to the visitors who came into the vast salon. The friends of the house were the favoured victims at first, inasmuch as they were better known. You can form your opinion as to whether Julien paid attention; everything interested him, both the substance of things and the manner of making fun of them.

"And there is M. Descoulis," said Matilde; "he doesn't wear a wig any more. Does he want to get a prefectship through sheer force of genius? He is displaying that bald forehead which he says is filled with lofty thoughts."

"He is a man who knows the whole world," said the marquis de Croisenois. "He also goes to my uncle the cardinal's. He is capable of cultivating a falsehood with each of his friends for years on end, and he has two or three hundred friends. He knows how to nurse friendship, that is his talent. He will go out, just as you see him, in the worst winter weather, and be at the door of one of his friends by seven o'clock in the morning.

"He quarrels from time to time and he writes seven or eight letters for each quarrel. Then he has a reconciliation and he writes seven or eight letters to express his bursts of friendship. But he shines most brilliantly in the frank and sincere expansiveness of the honest man who keeps nothing up his sleeve. This manœuvre is brought into play when he has some favour to ask. One of my uncle's grand vicars is very good at telling the life of M. Descoulis since the restoration. I will bring him to you."

"Bah! I don't believe all that, it's professional jealousy among the lower classes," said the comte de Caylus.

"M. Descoulis will live in history," replied the marquis. "He brought about the restoration together with the abbé de Pradt and messieurs de Talleyrand and Pozzo di Borgo."

"That man has handled millions," said Norbert, "and I can't conceive why he should come here to swallow my father's epigrams which are frequently atrocious. 'How many times have you betrayed your friends, my dear Descoulis?' he shouted at him one day from one end of the table to the other."

"But is it true that he has played the traitor?" asked mademoiselle de la Mole. "Who has not played the traitor?"

"Why!" said the comte de Caylus to Norbert, "do you have that celebrated Liberal, M. Sainclair, in your house. What the devil's he come here for? I must go up to him and speak to him and make him speak. He is said to be so clever."

"But how will your mother receive him?" said M. de Croisenois. "He has such extravagant, generous and independent ideas."

"Look," said mademoiselle de la Mole, "look at the independent man who bows down to the ground to M. Descoulis while he grabs hold of his hand. I almost thought he was going to put it to his lips."

"Descoulis must stand better with the powers that be than we thought," answered M. de Croisenois.

"Sainclair comes here in order to get into the academy," said Norbert. "See how he bows to the baron L——, Croisenois."

"It would be less base to kneel down," replied M. de Luz.

"My dear Sorel," said Norbert, "you are extremely smart, but you come from the mountains. Mind you never bow like that great poet is doing, even to God the Father."

"Ah there's a really witty man, M. the Baron Bâton," said mademoiselle de la Mole, imitating a little the voice of the flunkey who had just announced him.

"I think that even your servants make fun of him. What a name Baron Bâton," said M. de Caylus.

"What's in a name?" he said to us the other day, went on Matilde. "Imagine the Duke de Bouillon announced for the first time. So far as I am concerned the public only need to get used to me."

"Julien left the vicinity of the sofa."

Still insufficiently appreciative of the charming subtleties of a delicate raillery to laugh at a joke, he considered that a jest ought to have some logical foundation. He saw nothing in these young peoples' conversation except a vein of universal scandal-mongering and was shocked by it. His provincial or English prudery went so far as to detect envy in it, though in this he was certainly mistaken.

"Count Norbert," he said to himself, "who has had to make three drafts for a twenty-line letter to his colonel would be only too glad to have written once in his whole life one page as good as M. Sainclair."

Julien approached successively the several groups and attracted no attention by reason of his lack of importance. He followed the Baron Bâton from a distance and tried to hear him.

This witty man appeared nervous and Julien did not see him recover his equanimity before he had hit upon three or four stinging phrases. Julien thought that this kind of wit had great need of space.

The Baron could not make epigrams. He needed at least four sentences of six lines each, in order to be brilliant.

"That man argues, he does not talk," said someone behind Julien. He turned round and reddened with pleasure when he heard the name of the comte Chalvet. He was the subtlest man of the century. Julien had often found his name in the *Memorial of St. Helena* and in the portions of history dictated by Napoleon. The diction of comte Chalvet was laconic, his phrases were flashes of lightning—just, vivid, deep. If he talked about any matter the conversation immediately made a step forward; he imported facts into it; it was a pleasure to hear him. In politics, however, he was a brazen cynic.

"I am independent, I am," he was saying to a gentleman with three stars, of whom apparently he was making fun. "Why insist on my having to-day the same opinion I had six weeks ago. In that case my opinion would be my master."

Four grave young men who were standing round scowled; these gentlemen did not like flippancy. The comte saw that he had gone too far. Luckily he perceived the honest M. Balland, a veritable hypocrite of honesty. The count began to talk to him; people closed up, for they realised that poor Balland was going to be the next victim.

M. Balland, although he was horribly ugly and his first steps in the world were almost unmentionable, had by dint of his morals and his morality married a very rich wife who had died; he subsequently married a second very rich one who was never seen in society. He enjoyed, in all humility, an income of sixty thousand francs, and had his own flatterers. Comte Chalvet talked to him pitilessly about all this. There was soon a circle of thirty persons around them. Everybody was smiling, including the solemn young men who were the hope of the century.

"Why does he come to M. de la Mole where he is obviously only a laughing stock?" thought Julien. He approached the abbé Pirard to ask him.

M. Balland made his escape.

"Good," said Norbert, "there is one of the spies of my father gone; there is only the little limping Napier left."

"Can that be the key of the riddle?" thought Julien, "but if so, why does the marquis receive M. Balland?"

The stern abbé Pirard was scowling in a corner of the salon listening to the lackeys announcing the names.

"This is nothing more than a den," he was saying like another Basil, "I see none but shady people come in."

As a matter of fact the severe abbé did not know what constitutes high society. But his friends the Jansenites, had given him some very precise notions about those men who only get into society by reason of their extreme subtlety in the service of all parties, or of their monstrous wealth. For some minutes that evening he answered Julien's eager questions fully and freely, and then suddenly stopped short grieved at having always to say ill of every one, and thinking he was guilty of a sin. Bilious Jansenist as he was, and believing as he did in the duty of Christian charity, his life was a perpetual conflict.

"How strange that abbé Pirard looks," said mademoiselle de la Mole, as Julien came near the sofa.

Julien felt irritated, but she was right all the same. M. Pirard was unquestionably the most honest man in the salon, but his pimply face, which was suffering from the stings of conscience, made him look hideous at this particular moment. "Trust physiognomy after this," thought Julien, "it is only when the delicate conscience of the abbé Pirard is reproaching him for some trifling lapse that he looks so awful; while the expression of that notorious spy Napier shows a pure and tranquil happiness." The abbé Pirard, however, had made great concessions to his party. He had taken a servant, and was very well dressed.

Julien noticed something strange in the salon, it was that all eyes were being turned towards the door, and there was a semi silence. The flunkey was announcing the famous Barron Tolly, who had just become publicly conspicuous by reason of the elections. Julien came forward and had a very good view of him. The baron had been the president of an electoral college; he had the brilliant idea of spiriting away the little squares of paper which contained the votes of one of the parties. But to make up for it he replaced them by an equal number of other little pieces of paper containing a name agreeable to himself. This drastic manœuvre had been noticed by some of the voters, who had made an immediate point of congratulating the Baron de Tolly. The good fellow was still pale from this great business. Malicious persons had pronounced the word galleys. M. de la Mole received him coldly. The poor Baron made his escape.

"If he leaves us so quickly it's to go to M. Comte's,"[4] said Comte Chalvet and everyone laughed.

Little Tanbeau was trying to win his spurs by talking to some silent noblemen and some intriguers who, though shady, were all men of wit, and were on this particular night in great force in M. de la Mole's salon (for he was mentioned for a place in the ministry). If he had not yet any subtlety of perception he made up for it as one will see by the energy of his words.

"Why not sentence that man to ten years' imprisonment," he was saying at the moment when Julien approached his knot. "Those reptiles should be confined in the bottom of a dungeon, they ought to languish to death in gaol, otherwise their venom will grow and become more dangerous. What is the good of sentencing him to a fine of a thousand crowns? He is poor, so be it, all the better, but his party will pay for him. What the case required was a five hundred francs fine and ten years in a dungeon."

"Well to be sure, who is the monster they are speaking about?" thought Julien who was viewing with amazement the vehement tone and hysterical gestures of his colleague. At this moment the thin, drawn, little face of the academician's nephew was hideous. Julien soon learnt that they were talking of the greatest poet of the century.

"You monster," Julien exclaimed half aloud, while tears of generosity moistened his eyes. "You little rascal," he thought, "I will pay you out for this."

"Yet," he thought, "those are the unborn hopes of the party of which the marquis is one of the chiefs. How many crosses and how many sinecures would that celebrated man whom he is now defaming have accumulated if he had sold himself—I won't say to the mediocre ministry of M. de Nerval—but to one of those reasonably honest ministries which we have seen follow each other in succession."

The abbé Pirard motioned to Julien from some distance off; M. de la Mole had just said something to him. But when Julien, who was listening at the moment with downcast eyes to the lamentations of the bishop, had at length got free and was able to get near his friend, he found him monopolised by the abominable little Tanbeau. The little beast hated him as the cause of Julien's favour with the marquis, and was now making up to him.

"*When will death deliver us from that aged rottenness*," it was in these words of a biblical energy that the little man of letters was now talking of the venerable Lord Holland. His merit consisted in an excellent knowledge of the biography of living men, and he had just made a rapid review of all the men who could aspire to some influence under the reign of the new King of England.

The abbé Pirard passed in to an adjacent salon. Julien followed him.

"I warn you the marquis does not like scribblers, it is his only prejudice. Know Latin and Greek if you can manage it, the history of the Egyptians, Persians, etc., he will honour and protect you as a learned man. But don't write a page of French, especially on serious matters which are above your position in society, or he will call you a scribbler and take you for a scoundrel. How is it that living as you do in the hotel of a great lord you don't know the Duke de Castries' epigram on Alembert and Rousseau: 'the fellow wants to reason about everything and hasn't got an income of a thousand crowns'!"

"Everything leaks out here," thought Julien, "just like the seminary." He had written eight or six fairly drastic pages. It was a kind of historical eulogy of the old surgeon-major who had, he said, made a man of him. "The little note book," said Julien to himself, "has always been locked." He went up to his room, burnt his manuscript and returned to the salon. The brilliant scoundrels had left it, only the men with the stars were left.

Seven or eight very aristocratic ladies, very devout, very affected, and of from thirty to thirty-five years of age, were grouped round the table that the servants had just brought in ready served. The brilliant maréchale de Fervaques came in apologising for the lateness of the hour. It was more than midnight: she went and sat down near the marquise. Julien was deeply touched, she had the eyes and the expression of madame de Rênal.

Mademoiselle de la Mole's circle was still full of people. She was engaged with her friends in making fun of the unfortunate comte de Thaler. He was the only son of that celebrated Jew who was famous for the riches that he had won by lending money to kings to make war on the peoples.

The Jew had just died leaving his son an income of one hundred thousand crowns a month, and a name that was only too well known. This strange position required either a simple character or force of will power.

Unfortunately the comte was simply a fellow who was inflated by all kinds of pretensions which had been suggested to him by all his toadies.

M. de Caylus asserted that they had induced him to make up his mind to ask for the hand of mademoiselle de la Mole, to whom the marquis de Croisenois, who would be a duke with a hundred thousand francs a year, was paying his attentions.

"Oh, do not accuse him of having a mind," said Norbert pitifully.

Will-power was what the poor comte de Thaler lacked most of all. So far as this side of his character went he was worthy of being a king. He would take council from everybody, but he never had the courage to follow any advice to the bitter end.

"His physiognomy would be sufficient in itself," mademoiselle de la

Mole was fond of saying, "to have inspired her with a holy joy." It was a singular mixture of anxiety and disappointment, but from time to time one could distinguish gusts of self-importance, and above all that trenchant tone suited to the richest man in France, especially when he had nothing to be ashamed of in his personal appearance and was not yet thirty-six. "He is timidly insolent," M. de Croisenois would say. The comte de Caylus, Norbert, and two or three moustachioed young people made fun of him to their heart's content without him suspecting it, and finally packed him off as one o'clock struck.

"Are those your famous Arab horses waiting for you at the door in this awful weather?" said Norbert to him.

"No, it is a new pair which are much cheaper," said M. de Thaler. "The horse on the left cost me five thousand francs, while the one on the right is only worth one hundred louis, but I would ask you to believe me when I say that I only have him out at night. His trot you see is exactly like the other ones."

Norbert's remark made the comte think it was good form for a man like him to make a hobby of his horses, and that he must not let them get wet. He went away, and the other gentleman left a minute afterwards making fun of him all the time. "So," thought Julien as he heard them laugh on the staircase, "I have the privilege of seeing the exact opposite of my own situation. I have not got twenty louis a year and I found myself side by side with a man who has twenty louis an hour and they made fun of him. Seeing a sight like that cures one of envy."

XXXV
SENSIBILITY AND A GREAT PIOUS LADY

> An idea which has any life in it seems like a crudity, so accustomed are they to colourless expression. Woe to him who introduces new ideas into his conversation!—*Faublas*.

This was the stage Julien had reached, when after several months of probation the steward of the household handed him the third quarter of his wages. M. de la Mole had entrusted him with the administration of his estates in Brittany and Normandy. Julien made frequent journeys there. He had chief control of the correspondence relating to the famous lawsuit with the abbé de Frilair. M. Pirard had instructed him.

On the data of the short notes which the marquis would scribble on the margin of all the various paper which were addressed to him, Julien would compose answers which were nearly all signed.

At the Theology School his professors complained of his lack of industry, but they did not fail to regard him as one of their most distinguished pupils. This varied work, tackled as it was with all the ardour of suffering ambition, soon robbed Julien of that fresh complexion which he had brought from the provinces. His pallor constituted one of his merits in the eyes of his comrades, the young seminarist; he found them much less malicious, much less ready to bow down to a silver crown than those of Besançon; they thought he was consumptive. The marquis had given him a horse.

Julien fearing that he might meet people during his rides on horse-back, had given out that this exercise had been prescribed by the doctors. The abbé Pirard had taken him into several Jansenist Societies. Julien was astonished; the idea of religion was indissolubly connected in his mind with the ideas of hypocrisy and covetousness. He admired those austere pious men who never gave a thought to their income. Several Jansenists became friendly with him and would give him advice. A new world opened before him. At the Jansenists he got to know a comte Altamira, who was nearly six feet high, was a Liberal, a believer, and had been condemned to death in his own country. He was struck by the strange contrast of devoutness and love of liberty.

Julien's relations with the young comte had become cool. Norbert had thought that he answered the jokes of his friends with too much sharpness. Julien had committed one or two breaches of social etiquette and vowed to himself that he would never speak to mademoiselle Mathilde. They were always perfectly polite to him in the Hôtel de la Mole but he felt himself quite lost. His provincial common sense explained this result by the vulgar proverb *Tout beau tout nouveau.*

He gradually came to have a little more penetration than during his first days, or it may have been that the first glamour of Parisian urbanity had passed off. As soon as he left off working, he fell a prey to a mortal boredom. He was experiencing the withering effects of that admirable politeness so typical of good society, which is so perfectly modulated to every degree of the social hierarchy.

No doubt the provinces can be reproached with a commonness and lack of polish in their tone; but they show a certain amount of passion, when they answer you. Julien's self-respect was never wounded at the Hôtel de la Mole, but he often felt at the end of the day as though he would like to cry. A café-waiter in the provinces will take an interest in you if you happen to have some accident as you enter his café, but if this accident has everything about it which is disagreeable to your vanity, he will repeat ten times in succession the very word which tortures you, as he tells you how sorry he is. At Paris they make a point of laughing in secret, but you always remain a stranger.

We pass in silence over a number of little episodes which would have made Julien ridiculous, if he had not been to some extent above ridicule. A foolish sensibility resulted in his committing innumerable acts of bad taste. All his pleasures were precautions; he practiced pistol shooting every day, he was one of the promising pupils of the most famous maîtres d'armes. As soon as he had an instant to himself, instead of employing it in reading as he did before, he would rush off to the riding school and ask for the most vicious horses. When he went out with the master of the riding school he was almost invariably thrown.

The marquis found him convenient by reason of his persistent industry, his silence and his intelligence, and gradually took him into his confidence with regard to all his affairs, which were in any way difficult to unravel. The marquis was a sagacious business man on all those occasions when his lofty ambition gave him some respite; having special information within his reach, he would speculate successfully on the Exchange. He would buy mansions and forests; but he would easily lose his temper. He would give away hundreds of louis, and would go to law for a few hundred francs. Rich men with a lofty spirit have recourse to business not so much for results as for distraction. The marquis needed a chief of staff who would put all his money affairs into clear and lucid order. Madame de la Mole, although of so even a character, sometimes made fun of Julien. Great ladies have a horror of those unexpected incidents which are produced by a sensitive character; they constitute the opposite pole of etiquette. On two or three occasions the marquis took his part. "If he is ridiculous in your salon, he triumphs in his office." Julien on his side thought he had caught the marquise's secret. She deigned to manifest an interest in everything the minute the Baron de la Joumate was announced. He was a cold individual with an expressionless physiognomy. He was tall, thin, ugly, very well dressed, passed his life in his château, and generally speaking said nothing about anything. Such was his outlook on life. Madame de la Mole would have been happy for the first time in her life if she could have made him her daughter's husband.

XXXVI
PRONUNCIATION

If fatuity is pardonable it is in one's first youth, for it is then the exaggeration of an amiable thing. It needs an air of love, gaiety, nonchalance. But fatuity coupled with self-importance; fatuity with a solemn and self-sufficient manner! This extravagance of stupidity was reserved for the XIXth century. Such are the persons who want to unchain the *hydra of revolutions!*—
LE JOHANNISBURG, *Pamphlet.*

Considering that he was a new arrival who was too disdainful to put any questions, Julien did not fall into unduly great mistakes. One day when he was forced into a café in the Rue St. Honoré by a sudden shower, a big man in a beaver coat, surprised by his gloomy look, looked at him in return just as mademoiselle Amanda's lover had done before at Besançon.

Julien had reproached himself too often for having endured the other insult to put up with this stare. He asked for an explanation. The man in the tail-coat immediately addressed him in the lowest and most insulting language. All the people in the café surrounded them. The passers-by stopped before the door. Julien always carried some little pistols as a matter of precaution. His hand was grasping them nervously in his pocket. Nevertheless he behaved wisely and confined himself to repeating to his man "Monsieur, your address, I despise you."

The persistency in which he kept repeating these six words eventually impressed the crowd.

"By Jove, the other who's talking all to himself ought to give him his address," they exclaimed. The man in the tail-coat hearing this repeated several times, flung five or six cards in Julien's face.

Fortunately none of them hit him in the face; he had mentally re-solved not to use his pistols except in the event of his being hit. The man went away, though not without turning round from time to time to shake his fist and hurl insults at him.

Julien was bathed in sweat. "So," he said angrily to himself, "the meanest of mankind has it in his power to affect me as much as this. How am I to kill so humiliating a sensitiveness?"

Where was he to find a second? He did not have a single friend. He had several acquaintances, but they all regularly left him after six weeks of social intercourse. "I am unsociable," he thought, and "I am now cruelly punished for it." Finally it occurred to him to rout out an old lieutenant of the 96th, named Liévin, a poor devil with whom he often used to fence. Julien was frank with him.

"I am quite willing to be your second," said Liévin, "but on one con-dition. If you fail to wound your man you will fight with me straight away."

"Agreed," said Julien quite delighted; and they went to find M. de Beauvoisis at the address indicated on his card at the end of the Faubourg Saint Germain.

It was seven o'clock in the morning. It was only when he was being ushered in, that Julien thought that it might quite well be the young relation of Madame de Rênal, who had once been employed at the Rome or Naples Embassy, and who had given the singer Geronimo a letter of introduction.

Julien gave one of the cards which had been flung at him the previous evening together with one of his own to a tall valet.

He and his second were kept waiting for a good three-quarters of an hour. Eventually they were ushered in to a elegantly furnished apartment. They found there a tall young man who was dressed like a doll. His features presented the perfection and the lack of expression of Greek beauty. His head, which was remarkably straight, had the finest blonde hair. It was dressed with great care and not a single hair was out of place.

"It was to have his hair done like this, that is why this damned fop has kept us waiting," thought the lieutenant of the 96th. The variegated dressing gown, the morning trousers, everything down to the embroidered slippers was correct. He was marvellously well-groomed. His blank and aristocratic physiognomy betokened rare and orthodox ideas; the ideal of a Metternichian diplomatist. Napoleon as well did not like to have in his entourage officers who thought.

Julien, to whom his lieutenant of the 96th had explained, that keeping him waiting was an additional insult after having thrown his card so rudely in his face, entered brusquely M. de Beauvoisis' room. He intended to be insolent, but at the same time to exhibit good form.

Julien was so astonished by the niceness of M. de Beauvoisis' manners and by the combination of formality, self-importance, and self-satisfaction in his demeanour, by the admirable elegance of everything that surrounded him, that he abandoned immediately all idea of being insolent. It was not his man of the day before. His astonishment was so great at meeting so distinguished a person, instead of the rude creature whom he was looking for, that he could not find a single word to say. He presented one of the cards which had been thrown at him.

"That's my name," said the young diplomat, not at all impressed by Julien's black suit at seven o'clock in the morning, "but I do not understand the honour."

His manner of pronouncing these last words revived a little of Julien's bad temper.

"I have come to fight you, monsieur," and he explained in a few words the whole matter.

M. Charles de Beauvoisis, after mature reflection, was fairly satisfied with the cut of Julien's black suit.

"It comes from Staub, that's clear," he said to himself, as he heard him speak. "That waistcoat is in good taste. Those boots are all right, but on the other hand just think of wearing a black suit in the early morning! It must be to have a better chance of not being hit," said the chevalier de Beauvoisis to himself.

After he had given himself this explanation he became again perfectly polite to Julien, and almost treated him as an equal. The conversation was fairly lengthy, for the matter was a delicate one, but eventually Julien could not refuse to acknowledge the actual facts. The perfectly mannered young man before him did not bear any resemblance to the vulgar fellow who had insulted him the previous day.

Julien felt an invincible repugnance towards him. He noted the self-sufficiency of the chevalier de Beauvoisis, for that was the name by which he had referred to himself, shocked as he was when Julien called him simply "Monsieur."

He admired his gravity which, though tinged with a certain modest fatuity, he never abandoned for a single moment. He was astonished at his singular manner of moving his tongue as he pronounced his words, but after all, this did not present the slightest excuse for picking a quarrel.

The young diplomatist very graciously offered to fight, but the ex-lieutenant of the 96th, who had been sitting down for an hour with his legs wide apart, his hands on his thigh, and his elbows stuck out, decided that his friend, monsieur de Sorel, was not the kind to go and pick a quarrel with a man because someone else had stolen that man's visiting cards.

Julien went out in a very bad temper. The chevalier de Beauvoisis' carriage was waiting for him in the courtyard before the steps. By chance Julien raised his eyes and recognised in the coachman his man of the day before.

Seeing him, catching hold of him by his big jacket, tumbling him down from his seat, and horse-whipping him thoroughly took scarcely a moment.

Two lackeys tried to defend their comrade. Julien received some blows from their fists. At the same moment, he cocked one of his little pistols and fired on them. They took to flight. All this took about a minute.

The chevalier de Beauvoisis descended the staircase with the most pleasing gravity, repeating with his lordly pronunciation, "What is this, what is this." He was manifestly very curious, but his diplomatic importance would not allow him to evince any greater interest.

When he knew what it was all about, a certain haughtiness tried to assert itself in that expression of slightly playful nonchalance which should never leave a diplomatist's face.

The lieutenant of the 96th began to realise that M. de Beauvoisis was anxious to fight. He was also diplomatic enough to wish to reserve for his friend the advantage of taking the initiative.

"This time," he exclaimed, "there is ground for duel."

"I think there's enough," answered the diplomat.

"Turn that rascal out," he said to his lackeys. "Let someone else get up."

The door of the carriage was open. The chevalier insisted on doing the honours to Julien and his friend. They sent for a friend of M. de Beauvoisis, who chose them a quiet place. The conversation on their way went as a matter of fact very well indeed. The only extraordinary feature was the diplomatist in a dressing-gown.

"These gentlemen, although very noble, are by no means as boring," thought Julien, "as the people who come and dine at M. de la Mole's, and I can see why," he added a moment afterwards. "They allow themselves to be indecent." They talked about the dancers that the public had distinguished with its favour at the ballet presented the night before. The two gentlemen alluded to some spicy anecdotes of which Julien and his second, the lieutenant of the 96th, were absolutely ignorant.

Julien was not stupid enough to pretend to know them. He confessed his ignorance with a good grace. This frankness pleased the chevalier's friend. He told him these stories with the greatest detail and extremely well.

One thing astonished Julien inordinately. The carriage was pulled up for a moment by an altar which was being built in the middle of the street for the procession of Corpus Christi Day. The two gentlemen indulged in the luxury of several jests. According to them, the curé was the son of an archbishop. Such a joke would never have been heard in the house of M. de la Mole, who was trying to be made a duke. The duel was over in a minute. Julien got a ball in his arm. They bandaged it with handkerchiefs which they wetted with brandy, and the chevalier de Beauvoisis requested Julien with great politeness to allow him to take him home in the same carriage that had brought him. When Julien gave the name of M. de la Mole's hôtel, the young diplomat and his friend exchanged looks. Julien's fiacre was here, but they found these gentlemen's conversation more entertaining than that of the good lieutenant of the 96th.

"By Jove, so a duel is only that," thought Julien. "What luck I found that coachman again. How unhappy I should have been if I had had to put up with that insult as well." The amusing conversation had scarcely been interrupted. Julien realised that the affectation of diplomatists is good for something.

"So ennui," he said himself, "is not a necessary incident of conversation among well-born people. These gentlemen make fun of the Corpus Christi procession and dare to tell extremely obscene anecdotes, and what is more, with picturesque details. The only thing they really lack is the ability to discuss politics logically, and that lack is more than compensated by their graceful tone, and the perfect aptness of their expressions." Julien experienced a lively inclination for them. "How happy I should be to see them often."

They had scarcely taken leave of each other before the chevalier de Beauvoisis had enquiries made. They were not brilliant.

He was very curious to know his man. Could he decently pay a call on him? The little information he had succeeded in obtaining from him was not of an encouraging character.

"Oh, this is awful," he said to his second. "I can't possibly own up to having fought a duel with a mere secretary of M. de la Mole, simply because my coachman stole my visiting cards."

"There is no doubt that all this may make you look ridiculous."

That very evening the chevalier de Beauvoisis and his friend said everywhere that this M. Sorel who was, moreover, quite a charming young man, was a natural son of an intimate friend of the marquis de la Mole. This statement was readily accepted. Once it was established, the young diplomatist and friend deigned to call several times on Julien during the fortnight. Julien owned to them that he had only been to the Opera once in his life. "That is awful," said one, "that is the only place one does go to. Your first visit must be when they are playing the *'Comte Ory.'*"

The chevalier de Beauvoisis introduced him at the opera to the famous singer Geronimo, who was then enjoying an immense success.

Julien almost paid court to the chevalier. His mixture of self-respect, mysterious self-importance, and fatuous youthfulness fascinated him. The chevalier, for example, would stammer a little, simply because he had the honour of seeing frequently a very noble lord who had this defect. Julien had never before found combined in one and the same person the drollery which amuses, and those perfect manners which should be the object of a poor provincial's imitation.

He was seen at the opera with the chevalier de Beauvoisis. This association got him talked about.

"Well," said M. de la Mole to him one day, "so here you are, the natural son of a rich gentleman of Franche-Comté, an intimate friend of mine."

The marquis cut Julien short as he started to protest that he had not in any way contributed to obtaining any credence for this rumour.

"M. de Beauvoisis did not fancy having fought a duel with the son of a carpenter."

"I know it, I know it," said M. de la Mole. "It is my business now to give some consistency to this story which rather suits me. But I have one favour to ask of you, which will only cost you a bare half-hour of your time. Go and watch every opera day at half-past eleven all the people in society coming out in the vestibule. I still see you have certain provincial mannerisms. You must rid yourself of them. Besides it would do no harm to know, at any rate by sight, some of the great personages to whom I may one day send you on a commission. Call in at the box office to get identified. Admission has been secured for you."

XXXVII
AN ATTACK OF GOUT

And I got advancement, not on my merit, but because my
master had the gout.—*Bertolotti.*

The reader is perhaps surprised by this free and almost friendly tone.
We had forgotten to say that the marquis had been confined to his house
for six weeks by the gout.

Mademoiselle de la Mole and her mother were at Hyères near the
marquise's mother. The comte Norbert only saw his father at stray
moments. They got on very well, but had nothing to say to each other.
M. de la Mole, reduced to Julien's society, was astonished to find that he
possessed ideas. He made him read the papers to him. Soon the young
secretary was competent to pick out the interesting passages. There was
a new paper which the marquis abhorred. He had sworn never to read it,
and spoke about it every day. Julien laughed. In his irritation against the
present time, the marquis made him read Livy aloud. The improvised
translation of the Latin text amused him. The marquis said one day in
that tone of excessive politeness which frequently tried Julien's patience,

"Allow me to present you with a blue suit, my dear Sorel. When you
find it convenient to wear it and to come and see me, I shall look upon
you as the younger brother of the comte de Chaulnes, that is to say, the
son of my friend the old Duke."

Julien did not quite gather what it was all about, but he tried a visit in
the blue suit that very evening. The marquis treated him like an equal.
Julien had a spirit capable of appreciating true politeness, but he had
no idea of nuances. Before this freak of the marquis's he would have
sworn that it was impossible for him to have been treated with more
consideration. "What an admirable talent," said Julien to himself. When
he got up to go, the marquis apologised for not being able to accompany
him by reason of his gout.

Julien was preoccupied by this strange idea. "Perhaps he is making
fun of me," he thought. He went to ask advice of the abbé Pirard, who
being less polite than the marquis, made no other answer except to
whistle and change the subject.

Julien presented himself to the marquis the next morning in his black
suit, with his letter case and his letters for signature. He was received in
the old way, but when he wore the blue suit that evening, the marquis's
tone was quite different, and absolutely as polite as on the previous day.

"As you are not exactly bored," said the marquis to him, "by these visits which you are kind enough to pay to a poor old man, you must tell him about all the little incidents of your life, but you must be frank and think of nothing except narrating them clearly and in an amusing way. For one must amuse oneself," continued the marquis. "That's the only reality in life. I can't have my life saved in a battle every day, or get a present of a million francs every day, but if I had Rivarol here by my sofa he would rid me every day of an hour of suffering and boredom. I saw a lot of him at Hamburg during the emigration."

And the marquis told Julien the stories of Rivarol and the inhabitants of Hamburg who needed the combined efforts of four individuals to understand an epigram. M. de la Mole, being reduced to the society of this little abbé, tried to teach him. He put Julien's pride on its mettle. As he was asked to speak the truth, Julien resolved to tell everything, but to suppress two things, his fanatical admiration for the name which irritated the marquis, and that complete scepticism, which was not particularly appropriate to a prospective curé. His little affair with the chevalier de Beauvoisis came in very handy. The marquis laughed till the tears came into his eyes at the scene in the café in the Rue St. Honoré with the coachman who had loaded him with sordid insults. The occasion was marked by a complete frankness between the marquis and the protégé.

M. de la Mole became interested in this singular character. At the beginning he had encouraged Julian's droll blunders in order to enjoy laughing at them. Soon he found it more interesting to correct very gently this young man's false outlook on life.

"All other provincials who come to Paris admire everything," thought the marquis. "This one hates everything. They have too much affectation; he has not affectation enough; and fools take him for a fool."

The attack of gout was protracted by the great winter cold and lasted some months.

"One gets quite attached to a fine spaniel," thought the marquis. "Why should I be so ashamed of being attached to this little abbé? He is original. I treat him as a son. Well, where's the bother? The whim, if it lasts, will cost me a diamond and five hundred louis in my will." Once the marquis had realised his protégé's strength of character, he entrusted him with some new business every day.

Julien noticed with alarm that this great lord would often give him inconsistent orders with regard to the same matter.

That might compromise him seriously. Julien now made a point whenever he worked with him, of bringing a register with him in which he wrote his instructions which the marquis initialled. Julien had now a clerk who would transcribe the instructions relating to each matter in a separate book. This book also contained a copy of all the letters.

This idea seemed at first absolutely boring and ridiculous, but in two months the marquis appreciated its advantages. Julien suggested to him that he should take a clerk out of a banker's who was to keep proper book-keeping accounts of all the receipts and of all the expenses of the estates which Julien had been charged to administer.

These measures so enlightened the marquis as to his own affairs that he could indulge the pleasure of undertaking two or three speculations without the help of his nominee who always robbed him.

"Take three thousand francs for yourself," he said one day to his young steward.

"Monsieur, I should lay myself open to calumny."

"What do you want then?" retorted the marquis irritably.

"Perhaps you will be kind enough to make out a statement of account and enter it in your own hand in the book. That order will give me a sum of 3,000 francs. Besides it's M. the abbé Pirard who had the idea of all this exactness in accounts." The marquis wrote out his instructions in the register with the bored air of the Marquis de Moncade listening to the accounts of his steward M. Poisson.

Business was never talked when Julien appeared in the evening in his blue suit. The kindness of the marquis was so flattering to the self-respect of our hero, which was always morbidly sensitive, that in spite of himself, he soon came to feel a kind of attachment for this nice old man. It is not that Julien was a man of sensibility as the phrase is understood at Paris, but he was not a monster, and no one since the death of the old major had talked to him with so much kindness. He observed that the marquis showed a politeness and consideration for his own personal feelings which he had never found in the old surgeon. He now realised that the surgeon was much prouder of his cross than was the marquis of his blue ribbon. The marquis's father had been a great lord.

One day, at the end of a morning audience for the transaction of business, when the black suit was worn, Julien happened to amuse the marquis who kept him for a couple of hours, and insisted on giving him some banknotes which his nominee had just brought from the house.

"I hope M. le Marquis, that I am not deviating from the profound respect which I owe you, if I beg you to allow me to say a word."

"Speak, my friend."

"M. le Marquis will deign to allow me to refuse this gift. It is not meant for the man in the black suit, and it would completely spoil those manners which you have kindly put up with in the man in the blue suit." He saluted with much respect and went out without looking at his employer.

This incident amused the marquis. He told it in the evening to the abbé Pirard.

"I must confess one thing to you, my dear abbé. I know Julien's birth, and I authorise you not to regard this confidence as a secret."

His conduct this morning is noble, thought the marquis, so I will ennoble him myself.

Some time afterwards the marquis was able to go out.

"Go and pass a couple of months at London," he said to Julien. "Ordinary and special couriers will bring you the letters I have received, together with my notes. You will write out the answers and send them back to me, putting each letter inside the answer. I have ascertained that the delay will be no more than five days."

As he took the post down the Calais route, Julien was astonished at the triviality of the alleged business on which he had been sent.

We will say nothing about the feeling of hate and almost horror with which he touched English soil. His mad passion for Bonaparte is already known. He saw in every officer a Sir Hudson Low, in every great noble a Lord Bathurst, ordering the infamies of St. Helena and being recompensed by six years of office.

At London he really got to know the meaning of sublime fatuity. He had struck up a friendship with some young Russian nobles who initiated him.

"Your future is assured, my dear Sorel," they said to him. "You naturally have that cold demeanour, *a thousand leagues away from the sensation one has at the moment*, that we have been making such efforts to acquire."

"You have not understood your century," said the Prince Korasoff to him. "Always do the opposite of what is expected of you. On my honour there you have the sole religion of the period. Don't be foolish or affected, for then follies and affectations will be expected of you, and the maxim will not longer prove true."

Julien covered himself with glory one day in the Salon of the Duke of Fitz-Folke who had invited him to dinner together with the Prince Korasoff. They waited for an hour. The way in which Julien conducted himself in the middle of twenty people who were waiting is still quoted as a precedent among the young secretaries of the London Embassy. His demeanour was unimpeachable.

In spite of his friends, the dandies, he made a point of seeing the celebrated Philip Vane, the one philosopher that England has had since Locke. He found him finishing his seventh year in prison. The aristocracy doesn't joke in this country, thought Julien. Moreover Vane is disgraced, calumniated, etc.

Julien found him in cheery spirits. The rage of the aristocracy prevented him from being bored. "There's the only merry man I've seen in England," thought Julien to himself, as he left the prison.

"The idea which tyrants find most useful is the idea of God," Vane had said to him.

We suppress the rest of the system as being cynical.

"What amusing notion do you bring me from England?" said M. la Mole to him on his return. He was silent. "What notion do you bring me, amusing or otherwise?" repeated the marquis sharply.

"In the first place," said Julien, "The sanest Englishman is mad one hour every day. He is visited by the Demon of Suicide who is the local God.

"In the second place, intellect and genius lose twenty-five per cent. of their value when they disembark in England.

"In the third place, nothing in the world is so beautiful, so admirable, so touching, as the English landscapes."

"Now it is my turn," said the marquis.

"In the first place, why do you go and say at the ball at the Russian Ambassador's that there were three hundred thousand young men of twenty in France who passionately desire war? Do you think that is nice for the kings?"

"One doesn't know what to do when talking to great diplomats," said Julien. "They have a mania for starting serious discussions. If one confines oneself to the commonplaces of the papers, one is taken for a fool. If one indulges in some original truth, they are astonished and at a loss for an answer, and get you informed by the first Secretary of the Embassy at seven o'clock next day that your conduct has been unbecoming."

"Not bad," said the marquis laughing. "Anyway I will wager Monsieur Deep-one that you have not guessed what you went to do in England."

"Pardon me," answered Julien. "I went there to dine once a week with the king's ambassador, who is the most polite of men."

"You went to fetch this cross you see here," said the marquis to him. "I do not want to make you leave off your black suit, and I have got accustomed to the more amusing tone I have assumed with the man who wears the blue suit. So understand this until further orders. When I see this cross, you will be my friend, the Duke of Chaulne's younger son, who has been employed in the diplomatic service the last six months without having any idea of it. Observe," added the marquis very seriously, cutting short all manifestations of thanks, "that I do not want you to forget your place. That is always a mistake and a misfortune both for patron and for dependent. When my lawsuits bore you, or when you no longer suit me, I will ask a good living like that of our good friend the abbé Pirard's for you, and nothing more," added the marquis dryly. This put Julien's pride at its ease. He talked much more. He did not so frequently think himself insulted and aimed at by those phrases which are susceptible of some interpretation which is scarcely polite, and which anybody may give utterance to in the course of an animated conversation.

This cross earned him a singular visit. It was that of the baron de Valenod, who came to Paris to thank the Minister for his barony, and arrive at an understanding with him. He was going to be nominated mayor of Verrières, and to supersede M. de Rênal.

Julien did not fail to smile to himself when M. Valenod gave him to understand that they had just found out that M. de Rênal was a Jacobin. The fact was that the new baron was the ministerial candidate at the election for which they were all getting ready, and that it was M. de Rênal who was the Liberal candidate at the great electoral college of the department, which was, in fact, very ultra.

It was in vain that Julien tried to learn something about madame de Rênal. The baron seemed to remember their former rivalry, and was impenetrable. He concluded by canvassing Julien for his father's vote at the election which was going to take place. Julien promised to write.

"You ought, monsieur le Chevalier, to present me to M. the marquis de la Mole."

"I ought, as a matter of fact," thought Julien. "But a rascal like that!"

"As a matter of fact," he answered, "I am too small a personage in the Hôtel de la Mole to take it upon myself to introduce anyone." Julien told the marquis everything. In the evening he described Valenod's pretensions, as well as his deeds and feats since 1814.

"Not only will you present the new baron to me," replied de la Mole, very seriously, "but I will invite him to dinner for the day after to-morrow. He will be one of our new prefects."

"If that is the case, I ask for my father the post of director of the workhouse," answered Julien, coldly.

"With pleasure," answered the marquis gaily. "It shall be granted. I was expecting a lecture. You are getting on."

M. de Valenod informed Julien that the manager of the lottery office at Verrières had just died. Julien thought it humorous to give that place to M. de Cholin, the old dotard whose petition he had once picked up in de la Mole's room. The marquis laughed heartily at the petition, which Julien recited as he made him sign the letter which requested that appointment of the minister of finance.

M. de Cholin had scarcely been nominated, when Julien learnt that that post had been asked by the department for the celebrated geometrician, monsieur Gros. That generous man had an income of only 1400 francs, and every year had lent 600 to the late manager who had just died, to help him bring up his family.

Julien was astonished at what he had done.

"That's nothing," he said to himself. "It will be necessary to commit several other injustices if I mean to get on, and also to conceal them beneath pretty, sentimental speeches. Poor monsieur Gros! It is he who deserves the cross. It is I who have it, and I ought to conform to the spirit of the Government which gives it me."

XXXVIII
WHAT IS THE DECORATION WHICH CONFERS DISTINCTION?

"Thy water refreshes me not," said the transformed genie.
"'Tis nevertheless the freshest well in all Diar-Békir"—*Pellico*.

One day Julien had just returned from the charming estate of Ville-quier on the banks of the Seine, which was the especial subject of M. de la Mole's interest because it was the only one of all his properties which had belonged to the celebrated Boniface de la Mole.

He found the marquise and her daughter, who had just come back from Hyères, in the hotel. Julien was a dandy now, and understood the art of Paris life. He manifested a perfect coldness towards mademoiselle de la Mole. He seemed to have retained no recollection of the day when she had asked him so gaily for details of his fall from his horse.

Mademoiselle de la Mole thought that he had grown taller and paler. There was no longer anything of the provincial in his figure or his appearance. It was not so with his conversation. Too much of the serious and too much of the positive element were still noticeable. In spite of these sober qualities, his conversation, thanks to his pride, was destitute of any trace of the subordinate. One simply felt that there were still too many things which he took seriously. But one saw that he was the kind of man to stick to his guns.

"He lacks lightness of touch, but not brains," said mademoiselle de la Mole to her father, as she rallied him on the cross that he had given Julien. "My brother has been asking you for it for sixteen months, and he is a La Mole."

"Yes, but Julien has surprises, and that's what the de la Mole, whom you were referring to, has never been guilty of."

M. the duc de Retz was announced.

Mathilde felt herself seized by an irresistible attack of yawning. She knew so well the old gildings and the old habitués of her father's salon. She conjured up an absolutely boring picture of the life which she was going to take up at Paris, and yet, when at Hyères, she had regretted Paris.

"And yet I am nineteen," she thought. "That's the age of happiness, say all those gilt-edged ninnies."

She looked at eight or ten new volumes of poetry which had accumulated on the table in the salon during her journey in Provence. She had the misfortune to have more brains than M.M. de Croisnois, de Caylus, de Luz, and her other friends. She anticipated all that they were going to tell her about the fine sky of Provence, poetry, the South, etc., etc.

These fine eyes, which were the home of the deepest ennui, and worse still, of the despair of ever finding pleasure, lingered on Julien. At any rate, he was not exactly like the others.

"Monsieur Sorel," she said, in that short, sharp voice, destitute of all femininity, which is so frequent among young women of the upper class.

"Monsieur Sorel, are you coming to-night to M. de Retz's ball?"

"Mademoiselle, I have not had the honour of being presented to M. the duke." (One would have said that these words and that title seared the mouth of the proud provincial).

"He asked my brother to take you there, and if you go, you could tell me some details about the Villequier estate. We are thinking of going there in the spring, and I would like to know if the château is habitable, and if the neighbouring places are as pretty as they say. There are so many unmerited reputations."

Julien did not answer.

"Come to the ball with my brother," she added, very dryly. Julien bowed respectfully.

"So I owe my due to the members of the family, even in the middle of a ball. Am I not paid to be their business man?" His bad temper added, "God knows, moreover, if what I tell the daughter will not put out the plans of the father, brother, and mother. It is just like the court of a sovereign prince. You have to be absolutely negative, and yet give no one any right to complain."

"How that big girl displeases me!" he thought, as he watched the walk of Mademoiselle de la Mole, whom her mother had called to present to several women friends of hers. She exaggerates all the fashions. Her dress almost falls down to her shoulders, she is even paler than before she went away. How nondescript her hair has grown as the result of being blonde! You would say that the light passed through it.

What a haughty way of bowing and of looking at you! What queenly gestures! Mademoiselle de la Mole had just called her brother at the moment when he was leaving the salon.

The comte de Norbert approached Julien.

"My dear Sorel," he said to him. "Where would you like me to pick you up to-night for Monsieur's ball. He expressly asked me to bring you."

"I know well whom I have to thank for so much kindness," answered Julien bowing to the ground.

His bad temper, being unable to find anything to lay hold of in the polite and almost sympathetic tone in which Norbert had spoken to him, set itself to work on the answer he had made to that courteous invitation. He detected in it a trace of subservience.

When he arrived at the ball in the evening, he was struck with the magnificence of the Hôtel de Retz. The courtyard at the entrance was covered with an immense tent of crimson with golden stars. Nothing could have been more elegant. Beyond the tent, the court had been transformed into a wood of orange trees and of pink laurels in full flower. As they had been careful to bury the vases sufficiently deep, the laurel trees and the orange trees appeared to come straight out of the ground. The road which the carriages traversed was sanded.

All this seemed extraordinary to our provincial. He had never had any idea of such magnificence. In a single instant his thrilled imagination had left his bad temper a thousand leagues behind. In the carriage on their way to the ball Norbert had been happy, while he saw everything in black colours. They had scarcely entered the courtyard before the rôles changed.

Norbert was only struck by a few details which, in the midst of all that magnificence, had not been able to be attended to. He calculated the expense of each item, and Julien remarked that the nearer he got to a sum total, the more jealous and bad-tempered he appeared.

As for himself, he was fascinated and full of admiration when he reached the first of the salons where they were dancing. His emotion was so great that it almost made him nervous. There was a crush at the door of the second salon, and the crowd was so great that he found it impossible to advance. The decorations of the second salon presented the Alhambra of Grenada.

"That's the queen of the ball one must admit," said a young man with a moustache whose shoulder stuck into Julien's chest.

"Mademoiselle Formant who has been the prettiest all the winter, realises that she will have to go down to the second place. See how strange she looks."

"In truth she is straining every nerve to please. Just look at that gracious smile now that she is doing the figure in that quadrille all alone. On my honour it is unique."

"Mademoiselle de la Mole looks as if she controlled the pleasure which she derives from her triumph, of which she is perfectly conscious. One might say that she fears to please anyone who talks to her."

"Very good. That is the art of alluring."

Julien vainly endeavoured to catch sight of the alluring woman. Seven or eight men who were taller than he prevented him from seeing her.

"There is quite a lot of coquetry in that noble reserve," said the young man with a moustache.

"And in those big blue eyes, which are lowered so slowly when one would think they were on the point of betraying themselves," answered his neighbour. "On my faith, nothing could be cleverer."

"See the pretty Formant looking quite common next to her," said the first.

"That air of reserve means how much sweetness would I spend on you if you were the man who was worthy of me."

"And who could be worthy of the sublime Mathilde," said the first man. "Some sovereign prince, handsome, witty, well-made, a hero in war, and twenty years old at the most."

"The natural son of the Emperor of Russia ... who would be made a sovereign in honour of his marriage, or quite simply the comte de Thaler, who looks like a dressed-up peasant."

The door was free, and Julien could go in.

"Since these puppets consider her so remarkable, it is worth while for me to study her," he thought. "I shall then understand what these people regard as perfection."

As his eyes were trying to find her, Mathilde looked at him. "My duty calls me," said Julien to himself. But it was only his expression which was bad-humoured.

His curiosity made him advance with a pleasure which the extremely low cut dress on Mathilde's shoulder very quickly accentuated, in a manner which was scarcely flattering for his own self-respect. "Her beauty has youth," he thought. Five or six people, whom Julien recognised as those who had been speaking at the door were between her and him.

"Now, Monsieur, you have been here all the winter," she said to him. "Is it not true that this is the finest ball of the season."

He did not answer.   ·

"This quadrille of Coulon's strikes me as admirable, and those ladies dance it perfectly." The young men turned round to see who was the happy man, an answer from whom was positively insisted on. The answer was not encouraging.

"I shall not be able to be a good judge, mademoiselle, I pass my life in writing. This is the first ball of this magnificence which I have ever seen."

The young men with moustaches were scandalised.

"You are a wise man, Monsieur Sorel," came the answer with a more marked interest. "You look upon all these balls, all these festivities, like a philosopher, like J. J. Rousseau. All these follies astonish without alluring you."

Julien's imagination had just hit upon an epigram which banished all illusions from his mind. His mouth assumed the expression of a perhaps slightly exaggerated disdain.

"J. J. Rousseau," he answered, "is in my view only a fool when he takes it upon himself to criticise society. He did not understand it, and he went into it with the spirit of a lackey who has risen above his station."

"He wrote the *Contrat Social*," answered Mathilde reverently.

"While he preaches the Republic, and the overthrow of monarchical dignities, the parvenu was intoxicated with happiness if a duke would go out of his way after dinner to one of his friends."

"Oh yes, the Duke of Luxembourg at Montmorency, used to accompany a Coindet from the neighbourhood of Paris," went on Mademoiselle de la Mole, with all the pleasure and enthusiasm of her first flush of pedantry. She was intoxicated with her knowledge, almost like the academician who discovered the existence of King Feretrius.

Julien's look was still penetrating and severe. Mathilde had had a moment's enthusiasm. Her partner's coldness disconcerted her profoundly. She was all the more astonished, as it was she who was accustomed to produce that particular effect on others.

At this moment the marquis de Croisenois was advancing eagerly towards mademoiselle de la Mole. He was for a moment three yards away from her. He was unable to get closer because of the crowd. He smiled at the obstacle. The young marquise de Rouvray was near her. She was a cousin of Mathilde. She was giving her arm to her husband who had only married her a fortnight ago. The marquis de Rouvray, who was also very young, had all the love which seizes a man who, having contracted a marriage of convenience exclusively arranged by the notaries, finds a person who is ideally pretty. M. de Rouvray would be a duke on the death of a very old uncle.

While the marquis de Croisenois was struggling to get through the crowd, and smiling at Mathilde she fixed her big divinely blue eyes on him and his neighbours. "Could anything be flatter," she said to herself. "There is Croisenois who wants to marry me, he is gentle and polite, he has perfect manners like M. de Rouvray. If they did not bore, those gentlemen would be quite charming. He too, would accompany me to the ball with that smug limited expression. One year after the marriage I shall have my carriage, my horses, my dresses, my château twenty leagues from Paris. All this would be as nice as possible, and enough to make a Countess de Roiville, for example, die of envy and afterwards—"

Mathilde bored herself in anticipation. The marquis de Croisenois managed to approach her and spoke to her, but she was dreaming and did not listen to him. The noise of his words began to get mixed with the buzz of the ball. Her eye mechanically followed Julien who had gone away, with an air which, though respectful, was yet proud and discontented. She noticed in a corner far from the moving crowd, the comte Altamira who had been condemned to death in his own country and whom the reader knows already. One of his relatives had married a Prince de Conti in the reign of Louis XIV. This torical fact was some protection against the police of the congregation.

"I think being condemned to death is the only real distinction," said Mathilde. "It is the only thing which cannot be bought."

"Why, that's an epigram, I just said, what a pity it did not come at a moment when I could have reaped all the credit for it." Mathilde had too much taste to work into the conversation a prepared epigram but at the same time she was too vain not to be extremely pleased with herself. A happy expression succeeded the palpable boredom of her face. The marquis de Croisenois, who had never left off talking, saw a chance of success and waxed twice as eloquent.

"What objection could a caviller find with my epigram," said Mathilde to herself. "I would answer my critic in this way: The title of baron or vicomte is to be bought; a cross, why it is a gift. My brother has just got one. What has he done? A promotion, why that can be obtained by being ten years in a garrison or have the minister of war for a relative, and you'll be a chief of a squadron like Norbert. A great fortune! That's rather more difficult, and consequently more meritorious. It is really quite funny. It's the opposite of what the books say. Well, to win a fortune why you marry M. Rothschild's daughter. Really my epigram is quite deep. Being condemned to death is still the one privilege which one has never thought of canvassing."

"Do you know the comte Altamira," she said to M. de Croisenois.

Her thoughts seemed to have been so far away, and this question had so little connection with all that the poor marquis had been saying for the last five minutes, that his good temper was ruffled. He was nevertheless a man of wit and celebrated for being so.

"Mathilde is eccentric," he thought, "that's a nuisance, but she will give her husband such a fine social position. I don't know how the marquis de la Mole manages. He is connected with all that is best in all parties. He is a man who is bound to come out on top. And, besides, this eccentricity of Mathilde's may pass for genius. Genius when allied with good birth and a large fortune, so far from being ridiculous, is highly distinguished. She has wit, moreover, when she wants to, that mixture in fact of brains, character, and ready wit which constitute perfection."

As it is difficult to do two things at the same time, the marquis answered Mathilde with a vacant expression as though he were reciting a lesson.

"Who does not know that poor Altamira?" and he told her the history of his conspiracy, abortive, ridiculous and absurd.

"Very absurd," said Mathilde as if she were talking to herself, "but he has done something. I want to see a man; bring him to me," she said to the scandalized marquis.

Comte Altamira was one of the most avowed admirers of mademoiselle de la Mole's haughty and impertinent manner. In his opinion she was one of the most beautiful persons in Paris.

"How fine she would be on a throne," he said to M. de Croisenois; and made no demur at being taken up to Mathilde.

There are a good number of people in society who would like to establish the fact that nothing is in such bad form as a conspiracy, in the nineteenth century; it smacks of Jacobinism. And what could be more sordid than unsuccessful Jacobinism.

Mathilde's expression made fun a little of Altamira and M. de Croisenois, but she listened to him with pleasure.

"A conspirator at a ball, what a pretty contrast," she thought. She thought that this man with his black moustache looked like a lion at rest, but she soon perceived that his mind had only one point of view: *utility, admiration for utility.*

The young comte thought nothing worthy his attention except what tended to give his country two chamber government. He left Mathilde, who was the prettiest person at the ball, with alacrity, because he saw a Peruvian general come in. Desparing of Europe such as M. de Metternich had arranged it, poor Altamira had been reduced to thinking that when the States of South America had become strong and powerful they could restore to Europe the liberty which Mirabeau has given it.

A crowd of moustachised young men had approached Mathilde. She realized that Altamira had not felt allured, and was piqued by his departure. She saw his black eye gleam as he talked to the Peruvian general. Mademoiselle de la Mole looked at the young Frenchmen with that profound seriousness which none of her rivals could imitate, "which of them," she thought, "could get himself condemned to death, even supposing he had a favourable opportunity?"

This singular look flattered those who were not very intelligent, but disconcerted the others. They feared the discharge of some stinging epigram that would be difficult to answer.

"Good birth vouchsafes a hundred qualities whose absence would offend me. I see as much in the case of Julien," thought Mathilde, "but it withers up those qualities of soul which make a man get condemned to death."

At that moment some one was saying near her: "Comte Altamira is the second son of the Prince of San Nazaro-Pimentel; it was a Pimentel who tried to save Conradin, was beheaded in 1268. It is one of the noblest families in Naples."

"So," said Mathilde to herself, "what a pretty proof this is of my maxim, that good birth deprives a man of that force of character in default of which a man does not get condemned to death. I seem doomed to reason falsely to-night. Since I am only a woman like any other, well I must dance." She yielded to the solicitations of M. de Croisenois who had been asking for a gallop for the last hour. To distract herself from her failure in philosophy, Mathilde made a point of being perfectly fascinating. M. de Croisenois was enchanted. But neither the dance nor her wish to please one of the handsomest men at court, nor anything at all, succeeded in distracting Mathilde. She could not possibly have been more of a success. She was the queen of the ball. She coldly appreciated the fact.

"What a blank life I shall pass with a person like Croisenois," she said to herself as he took her back to her place an hour afterwards. "What pleasure do I get," she added sadly, "if after an absence of six months I find myself at a ball which all the women of Paris were mad with jealousy to go to? And what is more I am surrounded by the homage of an ideally constituted circle of society. The only bourgeois are some peers and perhaps one or two Juliens. And yet," she added with increasing sadness, "what advantages has not fate bestowed upon me! Distinction, fortune, youth, everything except happiness. My most dubious advantages are the very ones they have been speaking to me about all the evening. Wit, I believe I have it, because I obviously frighten everyone. If they venture to tackle a serious subject, they will arrive after five minutes of conversation and as though they had made a great discovery at a conclusion which we have been repeating to them for the last hour. I am beautiful, I have that advantage for which madame de Stael would have sacrificed everything, and yet I'm dying of boredom. Shall I have reason to be less bored when I have changed my name for that of the marquis de Croisenois?

"My God though," she added, while she almost felt as if she would like to cry, "isn't he really quite perfect? He's a paragon of the education of the age; you can't look at him without his finding something charming and even witty to say to you; he is brave. But that Sorel is strange," she said to herself, and the expression of her eyes changed from melancholy to anger. "I told him that I had something to say to him and he hasn't deigned to reappear."

XXXIX
THE BALL

> The luxurious dresses, the glitter of the candles; all those
> pretty arms and fine shoulders; the bouquets, the intoxicat-
> ing strains of Rossini, the paintings of Ciceri. I am beside
> myself.—*Journeys of Useri.*

"You are in a bad temper," said the marquise de la Mole to her; "let
me caution you, it is ungracious at a ball."

"I only have a headache," answered Mathilde disdainfully, "it is too
hot here."

At this moment the old Baron Tolly became ill and fell down, as
though to justify mademoiselle de la Mole's remark. They were obliged
to carry him away. They talked about apoplexy. It was a disagreeable
incident.

Mathilde did not bother much about it.

She made a point of never looking at old men, or at anyone who had
the reputation of being bad company.

She danced in order to escape the conversation about the apoplexy,
which was not apoplexy inasmuch as the baron put in an appearance
the following day.

"But Sorel does not come," she said to herself after she had danced.
She was almost looking round for him when she found him in another
salon. Astonishing, but he seemed to have lost that impassive coldness
that was so natural to him; he no longer looked English.

"He is talking to comte Altamira who was sentenced to death," said
Mathilde to herself. "His eye is full of a sombre fire; he looks like a prince
in disguise; his haughtiness has become twice as pronounced."

Julien came back to where she was, still talking to Altamira. She
looked at Altamira fixedly, studying his features in order to trace those
lofty qualities which can earn a man the honour of being condemned to
death.

"Yes," he was saying to comte Altamira as he passed by her, "Danton
was a real man."

"Heavens can he be a Danton?" said Mathilde to herself, "but he has so
noble a face, and that Danton was so horribly ugly, a butcher I believe."
Julien was still fairly near her. She did not hesitate to call him; she had
the consciousness and the pride of putting a question that was unusual
for a young girl.

"Was not Danton a butcher?" she said to him.

"Yes, in the eyes of certain persons," Julien answered her with the most
thinly disguised expression of contempt. His eyes were still ardent from

his conversation with Altamira, "but unfortunately for the people of good birth he was an advocate at Méry-sur-Seine, that is to say, mademoiselle," he added maliciously, "he began like many peers whom I see here. It was true that Danton laboured under a great disadvantage in the eyes of beauty; he was ugly."

These last few words were spoken rapidly in an extraordinary and indeed very discourteous manner.

Julien waited for a moment, leaning slightly forward and with an air of proud humility. He seemed to be saying, "I am paid to answer you and I live on my pay." He did not deign to look up at Mathilde. She looked like his slave with her fine eyes open abnormally wide and fixed on him. Finally as the silence continued he looked at her, like a valet looking at his master to receive orders. Although his eyes met the full gaze of Mathilde which were fixed on him all the time with a strange expression, he went away with a marked eagerness.

"To think of a man who is as handsome as he is," said Mathilde to herself as she emerged from her reverie, "praising ugliness in such a way, he is not like Caylus or Croisenois. This Sorel has something like my father's look when he goes to a fancy dress ball as Napoleon." She had completely forgotten Danton. "Yes, I am decidedly bored to-night." She took her brother's arm and to his great disgust made him take her round the ball-room. The idea occurred to her of following the conversation between Julien and the man who had been condemned to death.

The crowd was enormous. She managed to find them, however, at the moment when two yards in front of her Altamira was going near a dumb-waiter to take an ice. He was talking to Julien with his body half turned round. He saw an arm in an embroidered coat which was taking an ice close by. The embroidery seemed to attract his attention. He turned round to look at the person to whom the arm belonged. His noble and yet simple eyes immediately assumed a slightly disdainful expression.

"You see that man," he said to Julien in a low voice; "that is the Prince of Araceli Ambassador of ——. He asked M. de Nerval, your Minister for Foreign Affairs, for my extradition this morning. See, there he is over there playing whist. Monsieur de Nerval is willing enough to give me up, for we gave up two or three conspirators to you in 1816. If I am given up to my king I shall be hanged in twenty-four hours. It will be one of those handsome moustachioed gentlemen who will arrest me."

"The wretches!" exclaimed Julien half aloud.

Mathilde did not lose a syllable of their conversation. Her ennui had vanished.

"They are not scoundrels," replied Count Altamira. "I talk to you about myself in order to give you a vivid impression. Look at the Prince of Araceli. He casts his eyes on his golden fleece every five minutes; he cannot get over the pleasure of seeing that decoration on his breast. In reality the poor man is really an anachronism. The fleece was a signal honour a hundred years ago, but he would have been nowhere near it in those days. But nowadays, so far as people of birth are concerned, you have to be an Araceli to be delighted with it. He had a whole town hanged in order to get it."

"Is that the price he had to pay?" said Julien anxiously.

"Not exactly," answered Altamira coldly, "he probably had about thirty rich landed proprietors in his district who had the reputation of being Liberals thrown into the river."

"What a monster!" pursued Julien.

Mademoiselle de la Mole who was leaning her head forward with keenest interest was so near him that her beautiful hair almost touched his shoulder.

"You are very young," answered Altamira. "I was telling you that I had a married sister in Provence. She is still pretty, good and gentle; she is an excellent mother, performs all her duties faithfully, is pious but not a bigot."

"What is he driving at?" thought mademoiselle de la Mole.

"She is happy," continued the comte Altamira; "she was so in 1815. I was then in hiding at her house on her estate near the Antibes. Well the moment she learnt of marshall Ney's execution she began to dance."

"Is it possible?" said Julien, thunderstruck.

"It's party spirit," replied Altamira. "There are no longer any real passions in the nineteenth century: that's why one is so bored in France. People commit acts of the greatest cruelty, but without any feeling of cruelty."

"So much the worse," said Julien, "when one does commit a crime one ought at least to take pleasure in committing it; that's the only good thing they have about them and that's the only way in which they have the slightest justification."

Mademoiselle de la Mole had entirely forgotten what she owed to herself and placed herself completely between Altamira and Julien. Her brother, who was giving her his arm, and was accustomed to obey her, was looking at another part of the room, and in order to keep himself in countenance was pretending to be stopped by the crowd.

"You are right," Altamira went on, "one takes pleasure in nothing one does, and one does not remember it: this applies even to crimes. I can show you perhaps ten men in this ballroom who have been convicted of murder. They have forgotten all about it and everybody else as well."

"Many are moved to the point of tears if their dog breaks a paw. When you throw flowers on their grave at Père-la-Chaise, as you say so humorously in Paris, we learn they united all the virtues of the knights of chivalry, and we speak about the noble feats of their great-grandfather who lived in the reign of Henri IV. If, in spite of the good offices of the Prince de Araceli, I escape hanging and I ever manage to enjoy the use of my money in Paris, I will get you to dine with eight or ten of these respected and callous murderers.

"At that dinner you and I will be the only ones whose blood is pure, but I shall be despised and almost hated as a monster, while you will be simply despised as a man of the people who has pushed his way into good society."

"Nothing could be truer," said mademoiselle de la Mole.

Altamira looked at her in astonishment; but Julien did not deign to look at her.

"Observe that the revolution, at whose head I found myself," continued the comte Altamira, "only failed for the one reason that I would not cut off three heads and distribute among our partisans seven or eight millions which happened to be in a box of which I happened to have the key. My king, who is burning to have me hanged to-day, and who called me by my christian name before the rebellion, would have given me the great ribbon of his order if I had had those three heads cut off and had had the money in those boxes distributed; for I should have had at least a semi-success and my country would have had a charta like ——. So wags the world; it's a game of chess."

"At that time," answered Julien with a fiery eye, "you did not know the game; now...."

"You mean I would have the heads cut off, and I would not be a Girondin, as you said I was the other day? I will give you your answer," said Altamira sadly, "when you have killed a man in a duel—a far less ugly matter than having him put to death by an executioner."

"Upon my word," said Julien, "the end justifies the means. If instead of being an insignificant man I had some power I would have three men hanged in order to save four men's lives."

His eyes expressed the fire of his own conscience; they met the eyes of mademoiselle de la Mole who was close by him, and their contempt, so far from changing into politeness seemed to redouble.

She was deeply shocked; but she found herself unable to forget Julien; she dragged her brother away and went off in a temper.

"I must take some punch and dance a lot," she said to herself. "I will pick out the best partner and cut some figure at any price. Good, there is that celebrated cynic, the comte de Fervaques." She accepted his invitation; they danced. "The question is," she thought, "which of us two will be the more impertinent, but in order to make absolute fun of him, I must get him to talk." Soon all the other members of the quadrille were dancing as a matter of formality, they did not want to lose any of Mathilde's cutting reparte. M. de Fervaques felt uneasy and as he could only find elegant expressions instead of ideas, began to scowl. Mathilde, who was in a bad temper was cruel, and made an enemy of him. She danced till daylight and then went home terribly tired. But when she was in the carriage the little vitality she had left, was still employed in making her sad and unhappy. She had been despised by Julien and could not despise him.

Julien was at the zenith of his happiness. He was enchanted without his knowing it by the music, the flowers, the pretty women, the general elegance, and above all by his own imagination which dreamt of distinctions for himself and of liberty for all.

"What a fine ball," he said to the comte. "Nothing is lacking."

"Thought is lacking" answered Altamira, and his face betrayed that contempt which is only more deadly from the very fact that a manifest effort is being made to hide it as a matter of politeness.

"You are right, monsieur the comte, there isn't any thought at all, let alone enough to make a conspiracy."

"I am here because of my name, but thought is hated in your salons. Thought must not soar above the level of the point of a Vaudeville couplet: it is then rewarded. But as for your man who thinks, if he shows energy and originality we call him a cynic. Was not that name given by one of your judges to Courier. You put him in prison as well as Béranger. The priestly congregation hands over to the police everyone who is worth anything amongst you individually; and good society applauds.

"The fact is your effete society prizes conventionalism above everything else. You will never get beyond military bravery. You will have Murats, never Washingtons. I can see nothing in France except vanity. A man who goes on speaking on the spur of the moment may easily come to make an imprudent witticism and the master of the house thinks himself insulted."

As he was saying this, the carriage in which the comte was seeing Julien home stopped before the Hôtel de la Mole. Julien was in love with his conspirator. Altamira had paid him this great compliment which was evidently the expression of a sound conviction. "You have not got the French flippancy and you understand the principle of *utility*." It happened that Julien had seen the day before *Marino Faliero*, a tragedy, by Casmir Delavigne.

"Has not Israel Bertuccio got more character than all those noble Venetians?" said our rebellious plebeian to himself, "and yet those are the people whose nobility goes back to the year seven hundred, a century before Charlemagne, while the cream of the nobility at M. de Ritz's ball to-night only goes back, and that rather lamely, to the thirteenth century.

Well, in spite of all the noble Venetians whose birth makes so great, it is Israel Bertuccio whom one remembers.

"A conspiracy annihilates all titles conferred by social caprice. There, a man takes for his crest the rank that is given him by the way in which he faces death. The intellect itself loses some of its power.

"What would Danton have been to-day in this age of the Valenods and the Rênals? Not even a deputy for the Public Prosecutor.

"What am I saying? He would have sold himself to the priests, he would have been a minister, for after all the great Danton did steal. Mirabeau also sold himself. Napoleon stole millions in Italy, otherwise he would have been stopped short in his career by poverty like Pichegru. Only La Fayette refrained from stealing. Ought one to steal, ought one to sell oneself?" thought Julien. This question pulled him up short. He passed the rest of the night in reading the history of the revolution.

When he wrote his letters in the library the following day, his mind was still concentrated on his conversation with count Altamira.

"As a matter of fact," he said to himself after a long reverie, "If the Spanish Liberals had not injured their nation by crimes they would not have been cleared out as easily as they were.

"They were haughty, talkative children—just like I am!" he suddenly exclaimed as though waking up with a start.

"What difficulty have I surmounted that entitles me to judge such devils who, once alive, dared to begin to act. I am like a man who exclaims at the close of a meal, 'I won't dine to-morrow; but that won't prevent me from feeling as strong and merry like I do to-day.' Who knows what one feels when one is half-way through a great action?"

These lofty thoughts were disturbed by the unexpected arrival in the library of mademoiselle de la Mole. He was so animated by his admiration for the great qualities of such invincibles as Danton, Mirabeau, and Carnot that, though he fixed his eyes on mademoiselle de la Mole, he neither gave her a thought nor bowed to her, and scarcely even saw her. When finally his big, open eyes realized her presence, their expression vanished. Mademoiselle de la Mole noticed it with bitterness.

It was in vain that she asked him for Vély's History of France which was on the highest shelf, and thus necessitated Julien going to fetch the longer of the two ladders. Julien had brought the ladder and had fetched the volume and given it to her, but had not yet been able to give her a single thought. As he was taking the ladder back he hit in his hurry one of the glass panes in the library with his elbow; the noise of the glass falling on the floor finally brought him to himself. He hastened to apologise to mademoiselle de la Mole. He tried to be polite and was certainly nothing more. Mathilde saw clearly that she had disturbed him, and that he would have preferred to have gone on thinking about what he had been engrossed in before her arrival, to speaking to her. After looking at him for some time she went slowly away. Julien watched her walk. He enjoyed the contrast of her present dress with the elegant magnificence of the previous night. The difference between the two expressions was equally striking. The young girl who had been so haughty at the Duke de Retz's ball, had, at the present moment, an almost plaintive expression. "As a matter of fact," said Julien to himself, "that black dress makes the beauty of her figure all the more striking. She has a queenly carriage; but why is she in mourning?"

"If I ask someone the reason for this mourning, they will think I am putting my foot in it again." Julien had now quite emerged from the depth of his enthusiasm. "I must read over again all the letters I have written this morning. God knows how many missed out words and blunders I shall find. As he was forcing himself to concentrate his mind on the first of these letters he heard the rustle of a silk dress near him. He suddenly turned round, mademoiselle de la Mole was two yards from his table, she was smiling. This second interruption put Julien into a bad temper. Mathilde had just fully realized that she meant nothing to this young man. Her smile was intended to hide her embarrassment; she succeeded in doing so.

"You are evidently thinking of something very interesting, Monsieur Sorel. Is it not some curious anecdote about that conspiracy which is responsible for comte Altamira being in Paris? Tell me what it is about, I am burning to know. I will be discreet, I swear it." She was astonished at hearing herself utter these words. What! was she asking a favour of an inferior! Her embarrassment increased, and she added with a little touch of flippancy,

"What has managed to turn such a usually cold person as yourself, into an inspired being, a kind of Michael Angelo prophet?"

This sharp and indiscreet question wounded Julien deeply, and rendered him madder than ever.

"Was Danton right in stealing?" he said to her brusquely in a manner that grew more and more surly. "Ought the revolutionaries of Piedmont and of Spain to have injured the people by crimes? To have given all the places in the army and all the orders to undeserving persons? Would not the persons who wore these orders have feared the return of the king? Ought they to have allowed the treasure of Turin to be looted? In a word, mademoiselle," he said, coming near her with a terrifying expression, "ought the man who wishes to chase ignorance and crime from the world to pass like the whirlwind and do evil indiscriminately?"

Mathilde felt frightened, was unable to stand his look, and retreated a couples of paces. She looked at him a moment, and then ashamed of her own fear, left the library with a light step.

240

XL
QUEEN MARGUERITE

> Love! In what madness do you not manage to make us find pleasure!
> *Letters of a Portuguese Nun.*

Julien reread his letters. "How ridiculous I must have appeared in the eyes of that Parisian doll," he said to himself when the dinner-bell rang. "How foolish to have really told her what I was thinking! Perhaps it was not so foolish. Telling the truth on that occasion was worthy of me. Why did she come to question me on personal matters? That question was indiscreet on her part. She broke the convention. My thoughts about Danton are not part of the sacrifice which her father pays me to make."

When he came into the dining-room Julien's thoughts were distracted from his bad temper by mademoiselle de la Mole's mourning which was all the more striking because none of the other members of the family were in black.

After dinner he felt completely rid of the feeling which had obsessed him all day. Fortunately the academician who knew Latin was at dinner. "That's the man who will make the least fun of me," said Julien to himself, "if, as I surmise, my question about mademoiselle de la Mole's mourning is in bad taste."

Mathilde was looking at him with a singular expression. "So this is the coquetry of the women of this part of the country, just as madame de Rênal described it to me," said Julien to himself. "I was not nice to her this morning. I did not humour her caprice of talking to me. I got up in value in her eyes. The Devil doubtless is no loser by it.

"Later on her haughty disdain will manage to revenge herself. I defy her to do her worst. What a contrast with what I have lost! What charming naturalness? What naivety! I used to know her thoughts before she did herself. I used to see them come into existence. The only rival she had in her heart was the fear of her childrens' death. It was a reasonable, natural feeling to me, and even though I suffered from it I found it charming. I have been a fool. The ideas I had in my head about Paris prevented me from appreciating that sublime woman.

"Great God what a contrast and what do I find here? Arid, haughty vanity: all the fine shades of wounded egotism and nothing more."

They got up from table. "I must not let my academician get snapped up," said Julien to himself. He went up to him as they were passing into the garden, assumed an air of soft submissiveness and shared in his fury against the success of Hernani.

"If only we were still in the days of *lettres de cachet*!" he said.

"Then he would not have dared," exclaimed the academician with a gesture worthy of Talma.

Julien quoted some words from Virgil's Georgics in reference to a flower and expressed the opinion that nothing was equal to the abbé Delille's verses. In a word he flattered the academician in every possible way. He then said to him with the utmost indifference, "I suppose mademoiselle de la Mole has inherited something from some uncle for whom she is in mourning."

"What! you belong to the house?" said the academician stopping short, "and you do not know her folly? As a matter of fact it is strange her mother should allow her to do such things, but between ourselves, they do not shine in this household exactly by their force of character. Mademoiselle's share has to do for all of them, and governs them. To-day is the thirtieth of April!" and the academician stopped and looked meaningly at Julien. Julien smiled with the most knowing expression he could master. "What connection can there be between ruling a household, wearing a black dress, and the thirtieth April?" he said to himself. "I must be even sillier than I thought."

"I must confess...." he said to the academician while he continued to question him with his look. "Let us take a turn round the garden," said the academician delighted at seeing an opportunity of telling a long and well-turned story.

"What! is it really possible you do not know what happened on the 30th April, 1574?"

"And where?" said Julien in astonishment.

"At the place de Grève."

Julien was extremely astonished that these words did not supply him with the key. His curiosity and his expectation of a tragic interest which would be in such harmony with his own character gave his eyes that brilliance which the teller of a story likes to see so much in the person who is listening to him. The academician was delighted at finding a virgin ear, and narrated at length to Julien how Boniface de la Mole, the handsomest young man of this century together with Annibal de Coconasso, his friend, a gentleman of Piedmont, had been beheaded on the 30th April, 1574. La Mole was the adored lover of Queen Marguerite of Navarre and "observe," continued the academician, "that mademoiselle de La Mole's full name is Mathilde Marguerite. La Mole was at the same time a favourite of the Duke d'Alençon and the intimate friend of his mistress's husband, the King of Navarre, subsequently Henri IV. On Shrove Tuesday of that year 1574, the court happened to be at St. Germain with the poor king Charles IX. who was dying. La Mole wished to rescue his friends the princes, whom Queen Catherine of Medici was keeping prisoner in her Court. He advanced two hundred cavalry under the walls of St. Germain; the Duke d'Alençon was frightened and La Mole was thrown to the executioner.

"But the thing which affects mademoiselle Mathilde, and what she has admitted to me herself seven or eight years ago when she was twelve, is a head! a head!—--and the academician lifted up his eyes to the heavens. What struck her in this political catastrophe, was the hiding of Queen Marguerite de Navarre in a house in the place de Grève and her then asking for her lover's head. At midnight on the following day she took that head in her carriage and went and buried it herself in a chapel at the foot of the hill at Montmartre."

"Impossible?" cried Julien really moved.

"Mademoiselle Mathilde despises her brother because, as you see, he does not bother one whit about this ancient history, and never wears mourning on the thirtieth of April. It is since the time of this celebrated execution and in order to recall the intimate friendship of La Mole for the said Coconasso, who Italian that he was, bore the name of Annibal that all the men of that family bear that name. And," added the academician lowering his voice, "this Coconasso was, according to Charles IX. himself, one of the cruellest assassins of the twenty-fourth August, 1572. But how is it possible, my dear Sorel, that you should be ignorant of these things—you who take your meals with the family."

"So that is why mademoiselle de la Mole twice called her brother Annibal at dinner. I thought I had heard wrong."

"It was a reproach. It is strange that the marquise should allow such follies. The husband of that great girl will have a fine time of it."

This remark was followed by five or six satiric phrases. Julien was shocked by the joy which shone in the academician's eyes. "We are just a couple of servants," he thought, "engaged in talking scandal about our masters. But I ought not to be astonished at anything this academy man does."

Julien had surprised him on his knees one day before the marquise de la Mole; he was asking her for a tobacco receivership for a nephew in the provinces. In the evening a little chambermaid of mademoiselle de la Mole, who was paying court to Julien, just as Elisa had used to do, gave him to understand that her mistress's mourning was very far from being worn simply to attract attention. This eccentricity was rooted in her character. She really loved that la Mole, the beloved lover of the most witty queen of the century, who had died through trying to set his friends at liberty—and what friends! The first prince of the blood and Henri IV.

Accustomed as he had been to the perfect naturalness which shone throughout madame de Rênal's whole demeanour, Julien could not help finding all the women of Paris affected, and, though by no means of a morose disposition, found nothing to say to them. Mademoiselle de la Mole was an exception.

He now began to cease taking for coldness of heart that kind of beauty which attaches importance to a noble bearing. He had long conversations with mademoiselle de la Mole, who would sometimes walk with him in the garden after dinner. She told him one day that she was reading the History of D'Aubigné and also Brantôme. "Strange books to read," thought Julien; "and the marquis does not allow her to read Walter Scott's novels!"

She told him one day, with that pleased brilliancy in her eyes, which is the real test of genuine admiration, about a characteristic act of a young woman of the reign of Henry III., which she had just read in the memoirs of L'Étoile. Finding her husband unfaithful she stabbed him.

Julien's vanity was flattered. A person who was surrounded by so much homage, and who governed the whole house, according to the academician, deigned to talk to him on a footing almost resembling friendship.

"I made a mistake," thought Julien soon afterwards. "This is not familiarity, I am simply the confidante of a tragedy, she needs to speak to someone. I pass in this family for a man of learning. I will go and read Brantôme, D'Aubigné, L'Étoile. I shall then be able to challenge some of the anecdotes which madame de la Mole speaks to me about. I want to leave off this rôle of the passive confidanté."

His conversations with this young girl, whose demeanour was so impressive and yet so easy, gradually became more interesting. He forgot his grim rôle of the rebel plebian. He found her well-informed and even logical. Her opinions in the gardens were very different to those which she owned to in the salon. Sometimes she exhibited an enthusiasm and a frankness which were in absolute contrast to her usual cold haughtiness.

"The wars of the League were the heroic days of France," she said to him one day, with eyes shining with enthusiasm. "Then everyone fought to gain something which he desired, for the sake of his party's triumph, and not just in order to win a cross as in the days of your emperor. Admit that there was then less egotism and less pettiness. I love that century."

"And Boniface de la Mole was the hero of it," he said to her.

"At least he was loved in a way that it is perhaps sweet to be loved. What woman alive now would not be horrified at touching the head of her decapitated lover?"

Madame de la Mole called her daughter. To be effective hypocrisy ought to hide itself, yet Julien had half confided his admiration for Napoleon to mademoiselle de la Mole.

Julien remained alone in the garden. "That is the immense advantage they have over us," he said to himself. "Their ancestors lift them above vulgar sentiments, and they have not got always to be thinking about their subsistence! What misery," he added bitterly. "I am not worthy to discuss these great matters. My life is nothing more than a series of hypocrisies because I have not got a thousand francs a year with which to buy my bread and butter."

Mathilde came running back. "What are you dreaming about, monsieur?" she said to him.

Julien was tired of despising himself. Through sheer pride he frankly told her his thoughts. He blushed a great deal while talking to such a person about his own poverty. He tried to make it as plain as he could that he was not asking for anything. Mathilde never thought him so handsome; she detected in him an expression of frankness and sensitiveness which he often lacked.

Within a month of this episode Julien was pensively walking in the garden of the hôtel; but his face had no longer the hardness and philosophic superciliousness which the chronic consciousness of his inferior position had used to write upon it. He had just escorted mademoiselle de la Mole to the door of the salon. She said she had hurt her foot while running with her brother.

"She leaned on my arm in a very singular way," said Julien to himself. "Am I a coxcomb, or is it true that she has taken a fancy to me? She listens to me so gently, even when I confess to her all the sufferings of my pride! She too, who is so haughty to everyone! They would be very astonished in the salon if they saw that expression of hers. It is quite certain that she does not show anyone else such sweetness and goodness."

Julien endeavoured not to exaggerate this singular friendship. He himself compared it to an armed truce. When they met again each day, they almost seemed before they took up the almost intimate tone of the previous day to ask themselves "are we going to be friends or enemies to-day?" Julien had realised that to allow himself to be insulted with impunity even once by this haughty girl would mean the loss of everything. "If I have got to quarrel would it not be better that it should be straight away in defending the rights of my own pride, than in parrying the expressions of contempt which would follow the slightest abandonment of my duty to my own self-respect?"

On many occasions, on days when she was in a bad temper Mathilde, tried to play the great lady with him. These attempts were extremely subtle, but Julien rebuffed them roughly.

One day he brusquely interrupted her. "Has mademoiselle de la Mole any orders to give her father's secretary?" he said to her. "If so he must listen to her orders, and execute them, but apart from that he has not a single word to say to her. He is not paid to tell her his thoughts."

This kind of life, together with the singular surmises which it occasioned, dissipated the boredom which he had been accustomed to experience in that magnificent salon, where everyone was afraid, and where any kind of jest was in bad form.

"It would be humorous if she loved me but whether she loves me or not," went on Julien, "I have for my confidential friend a girl of spirit before whom I see the whole household quake, while the marquis de Croisenois does so more than anyone else. Yes, to be sure, that same young man who is so polite, so gentle, and so brave, and who has combined all those advantages of birth and fortune a single one of which would put my heart at rest—he is madly in love with her, he ought to marry her. How many letters has M. de la Mole made me write to the two notaries in order to arrange the contract? And I, though I am an absolute inferior when I have my pen in my hand, why, I triumph over that young man two hours afterwards in this very garden; for, after all, her preference is striking and direct. Perhaps she hates him because she sees in him a future husband. She is haughty enough for that. As for her kindness to me, I receive it in my capacity of confidential servant.

"But no, I am either mad or she is making advances to me; the colder and more respectful I show myself to her, the more she runs after me. It may be a deliberate piece of affectation; but I see her eyes become animated when I appear unexpectedly. Can the women of Paris manage to act to such an extent. What does it matter to me! I have appearances in my favour, let us enjoy appearances. Heavens, how beautiful she is! How I like her great blue eyes when I see them at close quarters, and they look at me in the way they often do? What a difference between this spring and that of last year, when I lived an unhappy life among three hundred dirty malicious hypocrites, and only kept myself afloat through sheer force of character, I was almost as malicious as they were."

"That young girl is making fun of me," Julien would think in his suspicious days. "She is acting in concert with her brother to make a fool of me. But she seems to have an absolute contempt for her brother's lack of energy. He is brave and that is all. He has not a thought which dares to deviate from the conventional. It is always I who have to take up the cudgels in his defence. A young girl of nineteen! Can one at that age act up faithfully every second of the day to the part which one has determined to play. On the other hand whenever mademoiselle de la Mole fixes her eyes on me with a singular expression comte Norbert always goes away. I think that suspicious. Ought he not to be indignant at his sister singling out a servant of her household? For that is how I heard the Duke de Chaulnes speak about me. This recollection caused anger to supersede every other emotion. It is simply a fashion for old fashioned phraseology on the part of the eccentric duke?"

"Well, she is pretty!" continued Julien with a tigerish expression, "I will have her, I will then go away, and woe to him who disturbs me in my flight."

This idea became Julien's sole preoccupation. He could not think of anything else. His days passed like hours.

Every moment when he tried to concentrate on some important matter his mind became a blank, and he would wake up a quarter of an hour afterwards with a beating heart and an anxious mind, brooding over this idea "does she love me?"

XLI
A YOUNG GIRL'S DOMINION

I admire her beauty but I fear her intellect.—*Mérimée.*

If Julien had employed the time which he spent in exaggerating Matilde's beauty or in working himself up into a rage against that family haughtiness which she was forgetting for his sake in examining what was going on in the salon, he would have understood the secret of her dominion over all that surrounded her.

When anyone displeased mademoiselle de La Mole she managed to punish the offender by a jest which was so guarded, so well chosen, so polite and so neatly timed, that the more the victim thought about it, the sorer grew the wound. She gradually became positively terrible to wounded vanity. As she attached no value to many things which the rest of her family very seriously wanted, she always struck them as self-possessed. The salons of the aristocracy are nice enough to brag about when you leave them, but that is all; mere politeness alone only counts for something in its own right during the first few days. Julien experienced this after the first fascination and the first astonishment had passed off. "Politeness," he said to himself "is nothing but the absence of that bad temper which would be occasioned by bad manners." Mathilde was frequently bored; perhaps she would have been bored anywhere. She then found a real distraction and real pleasure in sharpening an epigram.

It was perhaps in order to have more amusing victims than her great relations, the academician and the five or six other men of inferior class who paid her court, that she had given encouragement to the marquis de Croisenois, the comte Caylus and two or three other young men of the highest rank. They simply represented new subjects for epigrams.

We will admit with reluctance, for we are fond of Mathilde, that she had received many letters from several of them and had sometimes answered them. We hasten to add that this person constitutes an exception to the manners of the century. Lack of prudence is not generally the fault with which the pupils of the noble convent of the Sacred Heart can be reproached.

One day the marquis de Croisenois returned to Mathilde a fairly compromising letter which she had written the previous night. He thought that he was thereby advancing his cause a great deal by taking this highly prudent step. But the very imprudence of her correspondence was the very element in it Mathilde liked. Her pleasure was to stake her fate. She did not speak to him again for six weeks.

She amused herself with the letters of these young men, but in her view they were all like each other. It was invariably a case of the most profound, the most melancholy, passion.

"They all represent the same perfect man, ready to leave for Palestine," she exclaimed to her cousin. "Can you conceive of anything more insipid? So these are the letters I am going to receive all my life! There can only be a change every twenty years according to the kind of vogue which happens to be fashionable. They must have had more colour in them in the days of the Empire. In those days all these young society men had seen or accomplished feats which really had an element of greatness. The Duke of N—— my uncle was at Wagram."

"What brains do you need to deal a sabre blow? And when they have had the luck to do that they talk of it so often!" said mademoiselle de Sainte-Hérédité, Mathilde's cousin.

"Well, those tales give me pleasure. Being in a real battle, a battle of Napoleon, where six thousand soldiers were killed, why, that's proof of courage. Exposing one's self to danger elevates the soul and saves it from the boredom in which my poor admirers seem to be sunk; and that boredom is contagious. Which of them ever thought of doing anything extraordinary? They are trying to win my hand, a pretty business to be sure! I am rich and my father will procure advancement for his son-in-law. Well! I hope he'll manage to find someone who is a little bit amusing."

Mathilde's keen, sharp and picturesque view of life spoilt her language as one sees. An expression of hers would often constitute a blemish in the eyes of her polished friends. If she had been less fashionable they would almost have owned that her manner of speaking was, from the standpoint of feminine delicacy, to some extent unduly coloured.

She, on her side, was very unjust towards the handsome cavaliers who fill the Bois de Boulogne. She envisaged the future not with terror, that would have been a vivid emotion, but with a disgust which was very rare at her age.

What could she desire? Fortune, good birth, wit, beauty, according to what the world said, and according to what she believed, all these things had been lavished upon her by the hands of chance.

So this was the state of mind of the most envied heiress of the faubourg Saint-Germain when she began to find pleasure in walking with Julien. She was astonished at his pride; she admired the ability of the little bourgeois. "He will manage to get made a bishop like the abbé Mouray," she said to herself.

Soon the sincere and unaffected opposition with which our hero received several of her ideas filled her mind; she continued to think about it, she told her friend the slightest details of the conversation, but thought that she would never succeed in fully rendering all their meaning.

An idea suddenly flashed across her; "I have the happiness of loving," she said to herself one day with an incredible ecstasy of joy. "I am in love, I am in love, it is clear! Where can a young, witty and beautiful girl of my own age find sensations if not in love? It is no good. I shall never feel any love for Croisenois, Caylus, and *tutti quanti*. They are unimpeachable, perhaps too unimpeachable; any way they bore me."

She rehearsed in her mind all the descriptions of passion which she had read in *Manon Lescaut*, the *Nouvelle Héloise*, the *Letters of a Portuguese Nun*, etc., etc. It was only a question of course of the grand passion; light love was unworthy of a girl of her age and birth. She vouchsafed the name of love to that heroic sentiment which was met with in France in the time of Henri III. and Bassompierre. That love did not basely yield to obstacles, but, far from it, inspired great deeds. "How unfortunate for me that there is not a real court like that of Catherine de' Medici or of Louis XIII. I feel equal to the boldest and greatest actions. What would I not make of a king who was a man of spirit like Louis XIII. if he were sighing at my feet! I would take him to the Vendée, as the Baron de Tolly is so fond of saying, and from that base he would re-conquer his kingdom; then no more about a charter—and Julien would help me. What does he lack? name and fortune. He will make a name, he will win a fortune.

"Croisenois lacks nothing, and he will never be anything else all his life but a duke who is half 'ultra' and half Liberal, an undecided being who never goes to extremes and consequently always plays second fiddle.

"What great action is not an extreme at the moment when it is undertaken? It is only after accomplishment that it seems possible to commonplace individuals. Yes, it is love with all its miracles which is going to reign over my heart; I feel as much from the fire which is thrilling me. Heaven owed me this boon. It will not then have lavished in vain all its bounties on one single person. My happiness will be worthy of me. Each day will no longer be the cold replica of the day before. There is grandeur and audacity in the very fact of daring to love a man, placed so far beneath me by his social position. Let us see what happens, will he continue to deserve me? I will abandon him at the first sign of weakness which I detect. A girl of my birth and of that mediæval temperament which they are good enough to ascribe to me (she was quoting from her father) must not behave like a fool.

"But should I not be behaving like a fool if I were to love the marquis de Croisenois? I should simply have a new edition over again of that happiness enjoyed by my girl cousins which I so utterly despise. I already know everything the poor marquis would say to me and every answer I should make. What's the good of a love which makes one yawn? One might as well be in a nunnery. I shall have a celebration of the signing of a contract just like my younger cousin when the grandparents all break down, provided of course that they are not annoyed by some condition introduced into the contract at the eleventh hour by the notary on the other side."

XLII
IS HE A DANTON?

The need of anxiety. These words summed up the character of my aunt, the beautiful Marguerite de Valois, who was soon to marry the King of Navarre whom we see reigning at present in France under the name of Henry IV. The need of staking something was the key to the character of this charming princess; hence her quarrels and reconciliations with her brothers from the time when she was sixteen. Now, what can a young girl stake? The most precious thing she has: her reputation, the esteem of a lifetime.
Memoirs of the Duke d' Angoulême.
the natural son of Charles IX.

"There is no contract to sign for Julien and me, there is no notary; everything is on the heroic plane, everything is the child of chance. Apart from the noble birth which he lacks, it is the love of Marguerite de Valois for the young La Mole, the most distinguished man of the time, over again. Is it my fault that the young men of the court are such great advocates of the conventional, and turn pale at the mere idea of the slightest adventure which is a little out of the ordinary? A little journey in Greece or Africa represents the highest pitch of their audacity, and moreover they can only march in troops. As soon as they find themselves alone they are frightened, not of the Bedouin's lance, but of ridicule and that fear makes them mad.

"My little Julien on the other hand only likes to act alone. This unique person never thinks for a minute of seeking help or support in others! He despises others, and that is why I do not despise him.

"If Julien were noble as well as poor, my love would simply be a vulgar piece of stupidity, a sheer mésalliance; I would have nothing to do with it; it would be absolutely devoid of the characteristic traits of grand passion—the immensity of the difficulty to be overcome and the black uncertainty cf the result."

Mademoiselle de la Mole was so engrossed in these pretty arguments that without realising what she was doing, she praised Julien to the marquis de Croisenois and her brother on the following day. Her eloquence went so far that it provoked them.

"You be careful of this young man who has so much energy," exclaimed her brother; "if we have another revolution he will have us all guillotined."

She was careful not to answer, but hastened to rally her brother and the marquis de Croisenois on the apprehension which energy caused them. "It is at bottom simply the fear of meeting the unexpected, the fear of being non-plussed in the presence of the unexpected—"

"Always, always, gentlemen, the fear of ridicule, a monster which had the misfortune to die in 1816."

"Ridicule has ceased to exist in a country where there are two parties," M. de la Mole was fond of saying.

His daughter had understood the idea.

"So, gentlemen," she would say to Julien's enemies, "you will be frightened all your life and you will be told afterwards,

Ce n'était pas un loup, ce n'en était que l'ombre."

Matilde soon left them. Her brother's words horrified her; they occasioned her much anxiety, but the day afterwards she regarded them as tantamount to the highest praise.

"His energy frightens them in this age where all energy is dead. I will tell him my brother's phrase. I want to see what answer he will make. But I will choose one of the moments when his eyes are shining. Then he will not be able to lie to me.

"He must be a Danton!" she added after a long and vague reverie. "Well, suppose the revolution begins again, what figures will Croisenois and my brother cut then? It is settled in advance: Sublime resignation. They will be heroic sheep who will allow their throats to be cut without saying a word. Their one fear when they die will still be the fear of being bad form. If a Jacobin came to arrest my little Julien he would blow his brains out, however small a chance he had of escaping. He is not frightened of doing anything in bad form."

These last words made her pensive; they recalled painful memories and deprived her of all her boldness. These words reminded her of the jests of MM. de Caylus, Croisenois, de Luz and her brother; these gentlemen joined in censuring Julien for his priestly demeanour, which they said was humble and hypocritical.

"But," she went on suddenly with her eyes gleaming with joy, "the very bitterness and the very frequency of their jests prove in spite of themselves that he is the most distinguished man whom we have seen this winter. What matter his defects and the things which they make fun of? He has the element of greatness and they are shocked by it. Yes, they, the very men who are so good and so charitable in other matters. It is a fact that he is poor and that he has studied in order to be a priest; they are the heads of a squadron and never had any need of studying; they found it less trouble.

"In spite of all the handicap of his everlasting black suit and of that priestly expression which he must wear, poor boy, if he isn't to die of hunger, his merit frightens them, nothing could be clearer. And as for that priest-like expression, why he no longer has it after we have been alone for some moments, and after those gentlemen have evolved what they imagine to be a subtle and impromptu epigram, is not their first look towards Julien? I have often noticed it. And yet they know well that he never speaks to them unless he is questioned. I am the only one whom he speaks to. He thinks I have a lofty soul. He only answers the points they raise sufficiently to be polite. He immediately reverts into respectfulness. But with me he will discuss things for whole hours, he is not certain of his ideas so long as I find the slightest objection to them. There has not been a single rifle-shot fired all this winter; words have been the only means of attracting attention. Well, my father, who is a superior man and will carry the fortunes of our house very far, respects Julien. Every one else hates him, no one despises him except my mother's devout friends."

The Comte de Caylus had or pretended to have a great passion for horses; he passed his life in his stables and often breakfasted there. This great passion, together with his habit of never laughing, won for him much respect among his friends: he was the eagle of the little circle.

As soon as they had reassembled the following day behind madame de la Mole's armchair, M. de Caylus, supported by Croisenois and by Norbert, began in Julien's absence to attack sharply the high opinion which Mathilde entertained for Julien. He did this without any provocation, and almost the very minute that he caught sight of mademoiselle de la Mole. She tumbled to the subtlety immediately and was delighted with it.

"So there they are all leagued together," she said to herself, "against a man of genius who has not ten louis a year to bless himself with and who cannot answer them except in so far as he is questioned. They are frightened of him, black coat and all. But how would things stand if he had epaulettes?"

She had never been more brilliant, hardly had Caylus and his allies opened their attack than she riddled them with sarcastic jests. When the fire of these brilliant officers was at length extinguished she said to M. de Caylus,

"Suppose that some gentleman in the Franche-Comté mountains finds out to-morrow that Julien is his natural son and gives him a name and some thousands of francs, why in six months he will be an officer of hussars like you, gentlemen, in six weeks he will have moustaches like you gentlemen. And then his greatness of character will no longer be an object of ridicule. I shall then see you reduced, monsieur the future duke, to this stale and bad argument, the superiority of the court nobility over the provincial nobility. But where will you be if I choose to push you to extremities and am mischievous enough to make Julien's father a Spanish duke, who was a prisoner of war at Besançon in the time of Napoleon, and who out of conscientious scruples acknowledges him on his death bed?" MM. de Caylus, and de Croisenois found all these assumptions of illegitimacy in rather bad taste. That was all they saw in Mathilde's reasoning.

His sister's words were so clear that Norbert, in spite of his submissiveness, assumed a solemn air, which one must admit did not harmonise very well with his amiable, smiling face. He ventured to say a few words.

"Are you ill? my dear," answered Mathilde with a little air of seriousness. "You must be very bad to answer jests by moralizing."

"Moralizing from you! Are you soliciting a job as prefect?"

Mathilde soon forgot the irritation of the comte de Caylus, the bad temper of Norbert, and the taciturn despair of M. de Croisenois. She had to decide one way or the other a fatal question which had just seized upon her soul.

"Julien is sincere enough with me," she said to herself, "a man at his age, in a inferior position, and rendered unhappy as he is by an extraordinary ambition, must have need of a woman friend. I am perhaps that friend, but I see no sign of love in him. Taking into account the audacity of his character he would surely have spoken to me about his love."

This uncertainty and this discussion with herself which henceforth monopolised Mathilde's time, and in connection with which she found new arguments each time that Julien spoke to her, completely routed those fits of boredom to which she had been so liable.

Daughter as she was of a man of intellect who might become a minister, mademoiselle de la Mole had been when in the convent of the Sacred Heart, the object of the most excessive flattery. This misfortune can never be compensated for. She had been persuaded that by reason of all her advantages of birth, fortune, etc., she ought to be happier than any one else. This is the cause of the boredom of princes and of all their follies.

Mathilde had not escaped the deadly influence of this idea. However intelligent one may be, one cannot at the age of ten be on one's guard against the flatteries of a whole convent, which are apparently so well founded.

From the moment that she had decided that she loved Julien, she was no longer bored. She congratulated herself every day on having deliberately decided to indulge in a grand passion. "This amusement is very dangerous," she thought. "All the better, all the better, a thousand times. Without a grand passion I should be languishing in boredom during the finest time of my life, the years from sixteen to twenty. I have already wasted my finest years: all my pleasure consisted in being obliged to listen to the silly arguments of my mother's friends who when at Coblentz in 1792 were not quite so strict, so they say, as their words of to-day."

It was while Mathilde was a prey to these great fits of uncertainty that Julien was baffled by those long looks of hers which lingered upon him. He noticed, no doubt, an increased frigidity in the manner of comte Norbert, and a fresh touch of haughtiness in the manner of MM. de Caylus, de Luz and de Croisenois. He was accustomed to that. He would sometimes be their victim in this way at the end of an evening when, in view of the position he occupied, he had been unduly brilliant. Had it not been for the especial welcome with which Mathilde would greet him, and the curiosity with which all this society inspired him, he would have avoided following these brilliant moustachioed young men into the garden, when they accompanied mademoiselle de La Mole there, in the hour after dinner.

"Yes," Julien would say to himself, "it is impossible for me to deceive myself, mademoiselle de la Mole looks at me in a very singular way. But even when her fine blue open eyes are fixed on me, wide open with the most abandon, I always detect behind them an element of scrutiny, self-possession and malice. Is it possible that this may be love? But how different to madame de Rênal's looks!"

One evening after dinner Julien, who had followed M. de la Mole into his study, was rapidly walking back to the garden. He approached Mathilde's circle without any warning, and caught some words pronounced in a very loud voice. She was teasing her brother. Julien heard his name distinctly pronounced twice. He appeared. There was immediately a profound silence and abortive efforts were made to dissipate it. Mademoiselle de la Mole and her brother were too animated to find another topic of conversation. MM. de Caylus, de Croisenois, de Luz, and one of their friends, manifested an icy coldness to Julien. He went away.

XLIII
A PLOT

> Disconnected remarks, casual meetings, become transformed
> in the eyes of an imaginative man into the most convincing
> proofs, if he has any fire in his temperament.—*Schiller.*

The following day he again caught Norbert and his sister talking about him. A funereal silence was established on his arrival as on the previous day. His suspicions were now unbounded. "Can these charming young people have started to make fun of me? I must own this is much more probable, much more natural than any suggested passion on the part of mademoiselle de La Mole for a poor devil of a secretary. In the first place, have those people got any passions at all? Mystification is their strong point. They are jealous of my poor little superiority in speaking. Being jealous again is one of their weaknesses. On that basis everything is explicable. Mademoiselle de La Mole simply wants to persuade me that she is marking me out for special favour in order to show me off to her betrothed?"

This cruel suspicion completely changed Julien's psychological condition. The idea found in his heart a budding love which it had no difficulty in destroying. This love was only founded on Mathilde's rare beauty, or rather on her queenly manners and her admirable dresses. Julien was still a parvenu in this respect. We are assured that there is nothing equal to a pretty society women for dazzling a peasant who is at the same time a man of intellect, when he is admitted to first class society. It had not been Mathilde's character which had given Julien food for dreams in the days that had just passed. He had sufficient sense to realise that he knew nothing about her character. All he saw of it might be merely superficial.

For instance, Mathilde would not have missed mass on Sunday for anything in the world. She accompanied her mother there nearly every time. If when in the salon of the Hôtel de La Mole some indiscreet man forgot where he was, and indulged in the remotest allusion to any jest against the real or supposed interests of Church or State, Mathilde immediately assumed an icy seriousness. Her previously arch expression re-assumed all the impassive haughtiness of an old family portrait.

But Julien had assured himself that she always had one or two of Voltaire's most philosophic volumes in her room. He himself would often steal some tomes of that fine edition which was so magnificently bound. By moving each volume a little distance from the one next to it he managed to hide the absence of the one he took away, but he soon noticed that someone else was reading Voltaire. He had recourse to a trick worthy of the seminary and placed some pieces of hair on those volumes which he thought were likely to interest mademoiselle de La Mole. They disappeared for whole weeks.

M. de La Mole had lost patience with his bookseller, who always sent him all the spurious memoirs, and had instructed Julien to buy all the new books, which were at all stimulating. But in order to prevent the poison spreading over the household, the secretary was ordered to place the books in a little book-case that stood in the marquis's own room. He was soon quite certain that although the new books were hostile to the interests of both State and Church, they very quickly disappeared. It was certainly not Norbert who read them.

Julien attached undue importance to this discovery, and attributed to mademoiselle de la Mole a Machiavellian rôle. This seeming depravity constituted a charm in his eyes, the one moral charm, in fact, which she possessed. He was led into this extravagance by his boredom with hypocrisy and moral platitudes.

It was more a case of his exciting his own imagination than of his being swept away by his love.

It was only after he had abandoned himself to reveries about the elegance of mademoiselle de la Mole's figure, the excellent taste of he dress, the whiteness of her hand, the beauty of her arm, the *disinvoltura* of all her movements, that he began to find himself in love. Then in order to complete the charm he thought her a Catherine de' Medici. Nothing was too deep or too criminal for the character which he ascribed to her. She was the ideal of the Maslons, the Frilairs, and the Castanèdes whom he had admired so much in his youth. To put it shortly, she represented in his eyes the Paris ideal.

Could anything possibly be more humorous than believing in the depth or in the depravity of the Parisian character?

It is impossible that this *trio* is making fun of me thought Julien. The reader knows little of his character if he has not begun already to imagine his cold and gloomy expression when he answered Mathilde's looks. A bitter irony rebuffed those assurances of friendship which the astonished mademoiselle de la Mole ventured to hazard on two or three occasions.

Piqued by this sudden eccentricity, the heart of this young girl, though naturally cold, bored and intellectual, became as impassioned as it was naturally capable of being. But there was also a large element of pride in Mathilde's character, and the birth of a sentiment which made all her happiness dependent on another, was accompanied by a gloomy melancholy.

Julien had derived sufficient advantage from his stay in Paris to appreciate that this was not the frigid melancholy of ennui. Instead of being keen as she had been on at homes, theatres, and all kinds of distractions, she now shunned them.

Music sung by Frenchmen bored Mathilde to death, yet Julien, who always made a point of being present when the audience came out of the Opera, noticed that she made a point of getting taken there as often as she could. He thought he noticed that she had lost a little of that brilliant neatness of touch which used to be manifest in everything she did. She would sometimes answer her friends with jests rendered positively outrageous through the sheer force of their stinging energy. He thought that she made a special butt of the marquis de Croisenois. That young man must be desperately in love with money not to give the go-by to that girl, however rich she maybe, thought Julien. And as for himself, indignant at these outrages on masculine self-respect, he redoubled his frigidity towards her. Sometimes he went so far as to answer her with scant courtesy.

In spite of his resolution not to become the dupe of Mathilde's signs of interest, these manifestations were so palpable on certain days, and Julien, whose eyes were beginning to be opened, began to find her so pretty, that he was sometimes embarrassed.

"These young people of society will score in the long run by their skill and their coolness over my inexperience," he said to himself. "I must leave and put an end to all this." The marquis had just entrusted him with the administration of a number of small estates and houses which he possessed in Lower Languedoc. A journey was necessary; M. de la Mole reluctantly consented. Julien had become his other self, except in those matters which concerned his political career.

"So, when we come to balance the account," Julien said to himself, as he prepared his departure, "they have not caught me. Whether the jests that mademoiselle de la Mole made to those gentlemen are real, or whether they were only intended to inspire me with confidence, they have simply amused me.

"If there is no conspiracy against the carpenter's son, mademoiselle de la Mole is an enigma, but at any rate, she is quite as much an enigma for the marquis de Croisenois as she is to me. Yesterday, for instance, her bad temper was very real, and I had the pleasure of seeing her snub, thanks to her favour for me, a young man who is as noble and as rich as I am a poor scoundrel of a plebeian. That is my finest triumph; it will divert me in my post-chaise as I traverse the Languedoc plains."

He had kept his departure a secret, but Mathilde knew, even better than he did himself, that he was going to leave Paris the following day for a long time. She developed a maddening headache, which was rendered worse by the stuffy salon. She walked a great deal in the garden, and persecuted Norbert, the marquis de Croisenois, Caylus, de Luz, and some other young men who had dined at the Hôtel de la Mole, to such an extent by her mordant witticisms, that she drove them to take their leave. She kept looking at Julien in a strange way.

"Perhaps that look is a pose," thought Julien, "but how about that hurried breathing and all that agitation? Bah," he said to himself, "who am I to judge of such things? We are dealing with the cream of Parisian sublimity and subtlety. As for that hurried breathing which was on the point of affecting me, she no doubt studied it with Léontine Fay, whom she likes so much."

They were left alone; the conversation was obviously languishing. "No, Julien has no feeling for me," said Mathilde to herself, in a state of real unhappiness.

As he was taking leave of her she took his arm violently.

"You will receive a letter from me this evening," she said to him in a voice that was so changed that its tone was scarcely recognisable.

This circumstance affected Julien immediately.

"My father," she continued, "has a proper regard for the services you render him. You must not leave to-morrow; find an excuse." And she ran away.

Her figure was charming. It was impossible to have a prettier foot. She ran with a grace which fascinated Julien, but will the reader guess what he began to think about after she had finally left him? He felt wounded by the imperious tone with which she had said the words, "you must." Louis XV. too, when on his death-bed, had been keenly irritated by the words "you must," which had been tactlessly pronounced by his first physician, and yet Louis XV. was not a parvenu.

An hour afterwards a footman gave Julien a letter. It was quite simply a declaration of love.

"The style is too affected," said Julien to himself, as he endeavoured to control by his literary criticism the joy which was spreading over his cheeks and forcing him to smile in spite of himself.

At last his passionate exultation was too strong to be controlled. "So I," he suddenly exclaimed, "I, the poor peasant, get a declaration of love from a great lady."

"As for myself, I haven't done so badly," he added, restraining his joy as much as he could. "I have managed to preserve my self-respect. I did not say that I loved her." He began to study the formation of the letters. Mademoiselle de la Mole had a pretty little English handwriting. He needed some concrete occupation to distract him from a joy which verged on delirium.

"Your departure forces me to speak.... I could not bear not to see you again."

A thought had just struck Julien like a new discovery. It interrupted his examination of Mathilde's letter, and redoubled his joy. "So I score over the marquis de Croisenois," he exclaimed. "Yes, I who could only talk seriously! And he is so handsome. He has a moustache and a charming uniform. He always manages to say something witty and clever just at the psychological moment."

Julien experienced a delightful minute. He was wandering at random in the garden, mad with happiness.

Afterwards he went up to his desk, and had himself ushered in to the marquis de la Mole, who was fortunately still in. He showed him several stamped papers which had come from Normandy, and had no difficulty in convincing him that he was obliged to put off his departure for Languedoc in order to look after the Normandy lawsuits.

"I am very glad that you are not going," said the marquis to him, when they had finished talking business. "I like seeing you." Julien went out; the words irritated him.

"And I—I am going to seduce his daughter! and perhaps render impossible that marriage with the marquis de Croisenois to which the marquis looks forward with such delight. If he does not get made a duke, at any rate his daughter will have a coronet." Julien thought of leaving for Languedoc in spite of Mathilde's letter, and in spite of the explanation he had just given to the marquis. This flash of virtue quickly disappeared.

"How kind it is of me," he said to himself, "me ... a plebeian, takes pity on a family of this rank! Yes, me, whom the duke of Chaulnes calls a servant! How does the marquis manage to increase his immense fortune? By selling stock when he picks up information at the castle that there will be a panic of a *coup d'état* on the following day. And shall I, who have been flung down into the lowest class by a cruel providence— I, whom providence has given a noble heart but not an income of a thousand francs, that is to say, not enough to buy bread with, literally not enough to buy bread with—shall I refuse a pleasure that presents itself? A limpid fountain which will quench my thirst in this scorching desert of mediocrity which I am traversing with such difficulty! Upon my word, I am not such a fool! Each man for himself in that desert of egoism which is called life."

And he remembered certain disdainful looks which madame de la Mole, and especially her lady friends, had favoured him with.

The pleasure of scoring over the marquis de Croisenois completed the rout of this echo of virtue.

"How I should like to make him angry," said Julien. "With what confidence would I give him a sword thrust now!" And he went through the segoon thrust. "Up till now I have been a mere usher, who exploited basely the little courage he had. After this letter I am his equal.

"Yes," he slowly said to himself, with an infinite pleasure, "the merits of the marquis and myself have been weighed in the balance, and it is the poor carpenter from the Jura who turns the scale.

"Good!" he exclaimed, "this is how I shall sign my answer. Don't imagine, mademoiselle de la Mole, that I am forgetting my place. I will make you realise and fully appreciate that it is for a carpenter's son that you are betraying a descendant of the famous Guy de Croisenois who followed St. Louis to the Crusade."

Julien was unable to control his joy. He was obliged to go down into the garden. He had locked himself in his room, but he found it too narrow to breathe in.

"To think of it being me, the poor peasant from the Jura," he kept on repeating to himself, "to think of it being me who am eternally condemned to wear this gloomy black suit! Alas twenty years ago I would have worn a uniform like they do! In those days a man like me either got killed or became a general at thirty-six. The letter which he held clenched in his hand gave him a heroic pose and stature. Nowadays, it is true, if one sticks to this black suit, one gets at forty an income of a hundred thousand francs and the blue ribbon like my lord bishop of Beauvais.

"Well," he said to himself with a Mephistophelian smile, "I have more brains than they. I am shrewd enough to choose the uniform of my century. And he felt a quickening of his ambition and of his attachment to his ecclesiastical dress. What cardinals of even lower birth than mine have not succeeded in governing! My compatriot Granvelle, for instance."

Julien's agitation became gradually calmed! Prudence emerged to the top. He said to himself like his master Tartuffe whose part he knew by heart:

> Je puis croire ces mots, un artifice honnête.
> * * * * * * * * * * * *
>
> Je ne me firai point à des propos si doux,
> Qu'un peu de ses faveurs après quoi je soupire
> Ne vienne m'assurer tout ce qu'ils m'ont pudire.

Tartuffe, act iv. Scene v.

"Tartuffe, too, was ruined by a woman, and he was as good as most men.... My answer may be shown.... and the way out of that is this," he added pronouncing his words slowly with an intonation of deliberate and restrained ferocity. "We will begin by quoting the most vivid passages from the letter of the sublime Mathilde."

"Quite so, but M. de Croisenois' lackeys will hurl themselves upon me and snatch the original away."

"No, they won't, for I am well armed, and as we know I am accustomed to firing on lackeys."

"Well, suppose one of them has courage, and hurls himself upon me. He has been promised a hundred napoleons. I kill him, or wound him, good, that's what they want. I shall be thrown into prison legally. I shall be had up in the police court and the judges will send me with all justice and all equity to keep Messieurs Fontan and Magalon company in Poissy. There I shall be landed in the middle of four hundred scoundrels.... And am I to have the slightest pity on these people," he exclaimed getting up impetuously! "Do they show any to persons of the third estate when they have them in their power!" With these words his gratitude to M. de la Mole, which had been in spite of himself torturing his conscience up to this time, breathed its last.

"Softly, gentlemen, I follow this little Machiavellian trick, the abbé Maslon or M. Castanède of the seminary could not have done better. You will take the provocative letter away from me and I shall exemplify the second volume of Colonel Caron at Colmar."

"One moment, gentlemen, I will send the fatal letter in a well-sealed packet to M. the abbé Pirard to take care of. He's an honest man, a Jansenist, and consequently incorruptible. Yes, but he will open the letters.... Fouqué is the man to whom I must send it."

We must admit that Julien's expression was awful, his countenance ghastly; it breathed unmitigated criminality. It represented the unhappy man at war with all society.

"To arms," exclaimed Julien. And he bounded up the flight of steps of the hotel with one stride. He entered the stall of the street scrivener; he frightened him. "Copy this," he said, giving him mademoiselle de la Mole's letter.

While the scrivener was working, he himself wrote to Fouqué. He asked him to take care of a valuable deposit. "But he said to himself," breaking in upon his train of thought, "the secret service of the post-office will open my letter, and will give you gentlemen the one you are looking for ... not quite, gentlemen." He went and bought an enormous Bible from a Protestant bookseller, skillfully hid Mathilde's letter in the cover, and packed it all up. His parcel left by the diligence addressed to one of Fouqué's workmen, whose name was known to nobody at Paris.

This done, he returned to the Hôtel de la Mole, joyous and buoyant.

Now it's our turn he exclaimed as he locked himself into the room and threw off his coat.

"What! mademoiselle," he wrote to Mathilde, "is it mademoiselle de la Mole who gets Arsène her father's lackey to hand an only too flattering letter to a poor carpenter from the Jura, in order no doubt to make fun of his simplicity?" And he copied out the most explicit phrases in the letter which he had just received. His own letter would have done honour to the diplomatic prudence of M. the Chevalier de Beauvoisis. It was still only ten o'clock when Julien entered the Italian opera, intoxicated with happiness and that feeling of his own power which was so novel for a poor devil like him. He heard his friend Geronimo sing. Music had never exalted him to such a pitch.

XLIV
A YOUNG GIRL'S THOUGHTS

What perplexity! What sleepless nights! Great God. Am I going to make myself contemptible? He will despise me himself. But he is leaving, he is going away.
Alfred de Musset.

Mathilde had not written without a struggle. Whatever might have been the beginning of her interest in Julien, it soon dominated that pride which had reigned unchallenged in her heart since she had begun to know herself. This cold and haughty soul was swept away for the first time by a sentiment of passion, but if this passion dominated her pride, it still kept faithfully to the habits of that pride. Two months of struggles and new sensations had transformed, so to speak her whole moral life.

Mathilde thought she was in sight of happiness. This vista, irresistible as it is for those who combine a superior intellect with a courageous soul, had to struggle for a long time against her self respect and all her vulgar duties. One day she went into her mother's room at seven o'clock in the morning and asked permission to take refuge in Villequier. The marquise did not even deign to answer her, and advised her to go back to bed. This was the last effort of vulgar prudence and respect for tradition.

The fear of doing wrong and of offending those ideas which the Caylus's, the de Luz's, the Croisenois' held for sacred had little power over her soul. She considered such creatures incapable of understanding her. She would have consulted them, if it had been a matter of buying a carriage or an estate. Her real fear was that Julien was displeased with her.

"Perhaps he, too, has only the appearance of a superior man?"

She abhorred lack of character; that was her one objection to the handsome young men who surrounded her. The more they made elegant fun of everything which deviated from the prevailing mode, or which conformed to it but indifferently, the lower they fell in her eyes.

They were brave and that was all. "And after all in what way were they brave?" she said to herself. "In duels, but the duel is nothing more than a formality. The whole thing is mapped out beforehand, even the correct thing to say when you fall. Stretched on the turf, and with your hand on your heart, you must vouchsafe a generous forgiveness to the adversary, and a few words for a fair lady, who is often imaginary, or if she does exist, will go to a ball on the day of your death for fear of arousing suspicion."

"One braves danger at the head of a squadron brilliant with steel, but how about that danger which is solitary, strange, unforeseen and really ugly."

"Alas," said Mathilde to herself, "it was at the court of Henri III. that men who were great both by character and by birth were to be found! Yes! If Julien had served at Jarnac or Moncontour, I should no longer doubt. In those days of strength and vigour Frenchmen were not dolls. The day of the battle was almost the one which presented the fewest problems."

Their life was not imprisoned, like an Egyptian mummy in a covering which was common to all, and always the same. "Yes," she added, "there was more real courage in going home alone at eleven o'clock in the evening when one came out of the Hôtel de Soissons where Catherine de' Medici lived than there is nowadays in running over to Algiers. A man's life was then a series of hazards. Nowadays civilisation has banished hazard. There are no more surprises. If anything new appears in any idea there are not sufficient epigrams to immortalise it, but if anything new appears in actual life, our panic reaches the lowest depth of cowardice. Whatever folly panic makes us commit is excused. What a degenerate and boring age! What would Boniface de la Mole have said if, lifting his cut-off head out of the tomb, he had seen seventeen of his descendants allow themselves to be caught like sheep in 1793 in order to be guillotined two days afterwards! Death was certain, but it would have been bad form to have defended themselves and to have killed at least one or two Jacobins. Yes! in the heroic days of France, in the age of Boniface de la Mole, Julien would have been the chief of a squadron, while my brother would have been the young priest with decorous manners, with wisdom in his eyes and reason on his lips." Some months previously Mathilde had given up all hope of meeting any being who was a little different from the common pattern. She had found some happiness in allowing herself to write to some young society men. This rash procedure, which was so unbecoming and so imprudent in a young girl, might have disgraced her in the eyes of M. de Croisenois, the Duke de Chaulnes, his father, and the whole Hôtel de Chaulnes, who on seeing the projected marriage broken off would have wanted to know the reason. At that time Mathilde had been unable to sleep on those days when she had written one of her letters. But those letters were only answers. But now she ventured to declare her own love. She wrote first (what a terrible word!) to a man of the lowest social grade.

This circumstance rendered her eternal disgrace quite inevitable in the event of detection. Who of the women who visited her mother would have dared to take her part? What official excuse could be evolved which could successfully cope with the awful contempt of society.

Besides speaking was awful enough, but writing! "There are some things which are not written!" Napoleon had exclaimed on learning of the capitulation of Baylen. And it was Julien who had told her that epigram, as though giving her a lesson that was to come in useful subsequently.

But all this was comparatively unimportant, Mathilde's anguish had other causes. Forgetting the terrible effect it would produce on society, and the ineffable blot on her scutcheon that would follow such an outrage on her own caste, Mathilde was going to write to a person of a very different character to the Croisenois', the de Luz's, the Caylus's.

She would have been frightened at the depth and mystery in Julien's character, even if she had merely entered into a conventional acquaintance with him. And she was going to make him her lover, perhaps her master.

"What will his pretensions not be, if he is ever in a position to do everything with me? Well! I shall say, like Medea: *Au milieu de tant de périls il me reste Moi.*" She believed that Julien had no respect for nobility of blood. What was more, he probably did not love her.

In these last moments of awful doubt her feminine pride suggested to her certain ideas. "Everything is bound to be extraordinary in the life of a girl like me," exclaimed Mathilde impatiently. The pride, which had been drilled into her since her cradle, began to struggle with her virtue. It was at this moment that Julien's departure precipitated everything.

(Such characters are luckily very rare.)

Very late in the evening, Julien was malicious enough to have a very heavy trunk taken down to the porter's lodge. He called the valet, who was courting mademoiselle de la Mole's chambermaid, to move it. "This manœuvre cannot result in anything," he said to himself, "but if it does succeed, she will think that I have gone." Very tickled by this humorous thought, he fell asleep. Mathilde did not sleep a wink.

Julien left the hôtel very early the next morning without being seen, but he came back before eight o'clock.

He had scarcely entered the library before M. de la Mole appeared on the threshold. He handed her his answer. He thought that it was his duty to speak to her, it was certainly perfectly feasible, but mademoiselle de la Mole would not listen to him and disappeared. Julien was delighted. He did not know what to say.

"If all this is not a put up job with comte Norbert, it is clear that it is my cold looks which have kindled the strange love which this aristocratic girl chooses to entertain for me. I should be really too much of a fool if I ever allowed myself to take a fancy to that big blonde doll." This train of reasoning left him colder and more calculating than he had ever been.

"In the battle for which we are preparing," he added, "pride of birth will be like a high hill which constitutes a military position between her and me. That must be the field of the manœuvres. I made a great mistake in staying in Paris; this postponing of my departure cheapens and exposes me, if all this is simply a trick. What danger was there in leaving? If they were making fun of me, I was making fun of them. If her interest for me was in any way real, I was making that interest a hundred times more intense."

Mademoiselle de la Mole's letter had given Julien's vanity so keen a pleasure, that wreathed as he was in smiles at his good fortune he had forgotten to think seriously about the propriety of leaving.

It was one of the fatal elements of his character to be extremely sensitive to his own weaknesses. He was extremely upset by this one, and had almost forgotten the incredible victory which had preceded this slight check, when about nine o'clock mademoiselle de la Mole appeared on the threshold of the library, flung him a letter and ran away.

"So this is going to be the romance by letters," he said as he picked it up. "The enemy makes a false move; I will reply by coldness and virtue."

He was asked with a poignancy which merely increased his inner gaiety to give a definite answer. He indulged in the pleasure of mystifying those persons who he thought wanted to make fun of him for two pages, and it was out of humour again that he announced towards the end of his answer his definite departure on the following morning.

"The garden will be a useful place to hand her the letter," he thought after he had finished it, and he went there. He looked at the window of mademoiselle de la Mole's room.

It was on the first storey, next to her mother's apartment, but there was a large ground floor.

This latter was so high that, as Julien walked under the avenue of pines with his letter in his hands, he could not be seen from mademoiselle de la Mole's window. The dome formed by the well clipped pines intercepted the view. "What!" said Julien to himself angrily, "another indiscretion! If they have really begun making fun of me, showing myself with a letter is playing into my enemy's hands."

Norbert's room was exactly above his sister's and if Julien came out from under the dome formed by the clipped branches of the pine, the comte and his friend could follow all his movements.

Mademoiselle de la Mole appeared behind her window; he half showed his letter; she lowered her head, then Julien ran up to his own room and met accidentally on the main staircase the fair Mathilde, who seized the letter with complete self-possession and smiling eyes.

"What passion there was in the eyes of that poor madame de Rênal," said Julien to himself, "when she ventured to receive a letter from me, even after six months of intimate relationship! I don't think she ever looked at me with smiling eyes in her whole life."

He did not formulate so precisely the rest of his answer; was he perhaps ashamed of the triviality of the motive which were actuating him?

"But how different too," he went on to think, "are her elegant morning dress and her distinguished appearance! A man of taste on seeing mademoiselle de la Mole thirty yards off would infer the position which she occupies in society. That is what can be called a specific merit."

In spite of all this humorousness, Julien was not yet quite honest with himself; madame de Rênal had no marquis de Croisenois to sacrifice to him. His only rival was that grotesque sub-prefect, M. Charcot, who assumed the name of Maugiron, because there were no Maugirons left in France.

At five o'clock Julien received a third letter. It was thrown to him from the library door. Mademoiselle de la Mole ran away again. "What a mania for writing," he said to himself with a laugh, "when one can talk so easily. The enemy wants my letters, that is clear, and many of them." He did not hurry to open this one. "More elegant phrases," he thought; but he paled as he read it. There were only eight lines.

"I need to speak to you; I must speak to you this evening. Be in the garden at the moment when one o'clock is striking. Take the big gardeners' ladder near the well; place it against my window, and climb up to my room. It is moonlight; never mind."

XLV
IS IT A PLOT?

> Oh, how cruel is the interval between the conception
> and the execution of a great project. What vain fears,
> what fits of irresolution! It is a matter of life and
> death—even more is at stake honour!—*Schiller.*

"This is getting serious," thought Julien, "and a little too clear," he added after thinking a little. "Why to be sure! This fine young lady can talk to me in the library with a freedom which, thank heaven, is absolutely complete; the marquis, frightened as he is that I show him accounts, never sets foot in it. Why! M. de la Mole and the comte Norbert, the only persons who ever come here, are absent nearly the whole day, and the sublime Mathilde for whom a sovereign prince would not be too noble a suitor, wants me to commit an abominable indiscretion.

"It is clear they want to ruin me, or at the least make fun of me. First they wanted to ruin me by my own letters; they happen to be discreet; well, they want some act which is clearer than daylight. These handsome little gentlemen think I am too silly or too conceited. The devil! To think of climbing like this up a ladder to a storey twenty-five feet high in the finest moonlight. They would have time to see me, even from the neighbouring houses. I shall cut a pretty figure to be sure on my ladder!" Julien went up to his room again and began to pack his trunk whistling. He had decided to leave and not even to answer.

But this wise resolution did not give him peace of mind. "If by chance," he suddenly said to himself after he had closed his trunk, "Mathilde is in good faith, why then I cut the figure of an arrant coward in her eyes. I have no birth myself, so I need great qualities attested straight away by speaking actions—money down—no charitable credit."

He spent a quarter-of-an-hour in reflecting. "What is the good of denying it?" he said at last. "She will think me a coward. I shall lose not only the most brilliant person in high society, as they all said at M. the duke de Retz's ball, but also the heavenly pleasure of seeing the marquis de Croisenois, the son of a duke, who will be one day a duke himself, sacrificed to me. A charming young man who has all the qualities I lack. A happy wit, birth, fortune....

"This regret will haunt me all my life, not on her account, 'there are so many mistresses!... but there is only one honour!' says old don Diégo. And here am I clearly and palpably shrinking from the first danger that presents itself; for the duel with M. de Beauvoisis was simply a joke. This is quite different. A servant may fire at me point blank, but that is the least danger; I may be disgraced.

"This is getting serious, my boy," he added with a Gascon gaiety and accent. "Honour is at stake. A poor devil flung by chance into as low a grade as I am will never find such an opportunity again. I shall have my conquests, but they will be inferior ones...."

He reflected for a long time, he walked up and down hurriedly, and then from time to time would suddenly stop. A magnificent marble bust of cardinal de Richelieu had been placed in his room. It attracted his gaze in spite of himself. This bust seemed to look at him severely as though reproaching him with the lack of that audacity which ought to be so natural to the French character. "Would I have hesitated in your age great man?"

"At the worst," said Julien to himself, "suppose all this is a trap, it is pretty black and pretty compromising for a young girl. They know that I am not the man to hold my tongue. They will therefore have to kill me. That was right enough in 1574 in the days of Boniface de la Mole, but nobody today would ever have the pluck. They are not the same men. Mademoiselle de la Mole is the object of so much jealousy. Four hundred salons would ring with her disgrace to-morrow, and how pleased they would all be.

"The servants gossip among themselves about marked the favours of which I am the recipient. I know it, I have heard them....

"On the other hand they're her letters. They may think that I have them on me. They may surprise me in her room and take them from me. I shall have to deal with two, three, or four men. How can I tell? But where are they going to find these men? Where are they to find discreet subordinates in Paris? Justice frightens them.... By God! It may be the Caylus's, the Croisenois', the de Luz's themselves. The idea of the ludicrous figure I should cut in the middle of them at the particular minute may have attracted them. Look out for the fate of Abélard, M. the secretary.

"Well, by heaven, I'll mark you. I'll strike at your faces like Cæsar's soldiers at Pharsalia. As for the letters, I can put them in a safe place."

Julien copied out the two last, hid them in a fine volume of Voltaire in the library and himself took the originals to the post.

"What folly am I going to rush into," he said to himself with surprise and terror when he returned. He had been a quarter of an hour without contemplating what he was to do on this coming night.

"But if I refuse, I am bound to despise myself afterwards. This matter will always occasion me great doubt during my whole life, and to a man like me such doubts are the most poignant unhappiness. Did I not feel like that for Amanda's lover! I think I would find it easier to forgive myself for a perfectly clear crime; once admitted, I could leave off thinking of it.

"Why! I shall have been the rival of a man who bears one of the finest names in France, and then out of pure light-heartedness, declared myself his inferior! After all, it is cowardly not to go; these words clinch everything," exclaimed Julien as he got up ... "besides she is quite pretty."

"If this is not a piece of treachery, what a folly is she not committing for my sake. If it's a piece of mystification, by heaven, gentlemen, it only depends on me to turn the jest into earnest and that I will do.

"But supposing they tie my hands together at the moment I enter the room: they may have placed some ingenious machine there.

"It's like a duel," he said to himself with a laugh. "Everyone makes a full parade, says my *maître d'armes*, but the good God, who wishes the thing to end, makes one of them forget to parry. Besides, here's something to answer them with." He drew his pistols out of his pocket, and although the priming was shining, he renewed it.

There was still several hours to wait. Julien wrote to Fouqué in order to have something to do. "My friend, do not open the enclosed letter except in the event of an accident, if you hear that something strange has happened to me. In that case blot out the proper names in the manuscript which I am sending you, make eight copies of it, and send it to the papers of Marseilles, Bordeaux, Lyons, Brussels, etc. Ten days later have the manuscript printed, send the first copy to M. the marquis de la Mole, and a fortnight after that throw the other copies at night into the streets of Verrières."

Julien made this little memoir in defence of his position as little compromising as possible for mademoiselle de la Mole. Fouqué was only to open it in the event of an accident. It was put in the form of a story, but in fact it exactly described his situation.

Julien had just fastened his packet when the dinner bell rang. It made his heart beat. His imagination was distracted by the story which he had just composed, and fell a prey to tragic presentiments. He saw himself seized by servants, trussed, and taken into a cellar with a gag in his mouth. A servant was stationed there, who never let him out of sight, and if the family honour required that the adventure should have a tragic end, it was easy to finish everything with those poisons which leave no trace. They could then say that he had died of an illness and would carry his dead body back into his room.

Thrilled like a dramatic author by his own story, Julien was really afraid when he entered the dining-room. He looked at all those liveried servants—he studied their faces. "Which ones are chosen for to-night's expedition?" he said to himself. "The memories of the court of Henri III. are so vivid in this family, and so often recalled, that if they think they have been insulted they will show more resolution than other persons of the same rank." He looked at mademoiselle de la Mole in order to read the family plans in her eyes; she was pale and looked quite middle-aged. He thought that she had never looked so great: she was really handsome and imposing; he almost fell in love with her. *"Pallida morte futura,"* he said to himself (her pallor indicates her great plans). It was in vain that after dinner he made a point of walking for a long time in the garden, mademoiselle did not appear. Speaking to her at that moment would have lifted a great weight off his heart.

Why not admit it? he was afraid. As he had resolved to act, he was not ashamed to abandon himself to this emotion. "So long as I show the necessary courage at the actual moment," he said to himself, "what does it matter what I feel at this particular moment?" He went to reconnoitre the situation and find out the weight of the ladder.

"This is an instrument," he said to himself with a smile, "which I am fated to use both here and at Verrières. What a difference! In those days," he added with a sigh, "I was not obliged to distrust the person for whom I exposed myself to danger. What a difference also in the danger!"

"There would have been no dishonour for me if I had been killed in M. de Rênal's gardens. It would have been easy to have made my death into a mystery. But here all kinds of abominable scandal will be talked in the salons of the Hôtel de Chaulnes, the Hôtel de Caylus, de Retz, etc., everywhere in fact. I shall go down to posterity as a monster."

"For two or three years," he went on with a laugh, making fun of himself; but the idea paralysed him. "And how am I going to manage to get justified? Suppose that Fouqué does print my posthumous pamphlet, it will only be taken for an additional infamy. Why! I get received into a house, and I reward the hospitality which I have received, the kindness with which I have been loaded by printing a pamphlet about what has happened and attacking the honour of women! Nay! I'd a thousand times rather be duped."

The evening was awful.

XLVI
ONE O'CLOCK IN THE MORNING

> This garden was very big, it had been planned a few years
> ago in perfect taste. But the trees were more than a century
> old. It had a certain rustic atmosphere.—*Massinger.*

He was going to write a countermanding letter to Fouqué when eleven o'clock struck. He noisily turned the lock of the door of his room as though he had locked himself in. He went with a sleuth-like step to observe what was happening over the house, especially on the fourth storey where the servants slept. There was nothing unusual. One of madame de la Mole's chambermaids was giving an entertainment, the servants were taking punch with much gaiety. "Those who laugh like that," thought Julien, "cannot be participating in the nocturnal expedition; if they were, they would be more serious."

Eventually he stationed himself in an obscure corner of the garden. "If their plan is to hide themselves from the servants of the house, they will despatch the persons whom they have told off to surprise me over the garden wall.

"If M. de Croisenois shows any sense of proportion in this matter, he is bound to find it less compromising for the young person, whom he wishes to make his wife if he has me surprised before I enter her room."

He made a military and extremely detailed reconnaissance. "My honour is at stake," he thought. "If I tumble into some pitfall it will not be an excuse in my own eyes to say, 'I never thought of it.'"

The weather was desperately serene. About eleven o'clock the moon rose, at half-past twelve it completely illuminated the facade of the hôtel looking out upon the garden.

"She is mad," Julien said to himself. As one o'clock struck there was still a light in comte Norbert's windows. Julien had never been so frightened in his life, he only saw the dangers of the enterprise and had no enthusiasm at all. He went and took the immense ladder, waited five minutes to give her time to tell him not to go, and five minutes after one placed the ladder against Mathilde's window. He mounted softly, pistol in hand, astonished at not being attacked. As he approached the window it opened noiselessly.

"So there you are, monsieur," said Mathilde to him with considerable emotion. "I have been following your movements for the last hour."

Julien was very much embarrassed. He did not know how to conduct himself. He did not feel at all in love. He thought in his embarrassment that he ought to be venturesome. He tried to kiss Mathilde.

"For shame," she said to him, pushing him away.

Extremely glad at being rebuffed, he hastened to look round him. The moon was so brilliant that the shadows which it made in mademoiselle de la Mole's room were black. "It's quite possible for men to be concealed without my seeing them," he thought.

"What have you got in your pocket at the side of your coat?" Mathilde said to him, delighted at finding something to talk about. She was suffering strangely; all those sentiments of reserve and timidity which were so natural to a girl of good birth, had reasserted their dominion and were torturing her.

"I have all kinds of arms and pistols," answered Julien equally glad at having something to say.

"You must take the ladder away," said Mathilde.

"It is very big, and may break the windows of the salon down below or the room on the ground floor."

"You must not break the windows," replied Mathilde making a vain effort to assume an ordinary conversational tone; "it seems to me you can lower the ladder by tying a cord to the first rung. I have always a supply of cords at hand."

"So this is a woman in love," thought Julien. "She actually dares to say that she is in love. So much self-possession and such shrewdness in taking precautions are sufficient indications that I am not triumphing over M. de Croisenois as I foolishly believed, but that I am simply succeeding him. As a matter of fact, what does it matter to me? Do I love her? I am triumphing over the marquis in so far as he would be very angry at having a successor, and angrier still at that successor being myself. How haughtily he looked at me this evening in the Café Tortoni when he pretended not to recognise me! And how maliciously he bowed to me afterwards, when he could not get out of it."

Julien had tied the cord to the last rung of the ladder. He lowered it softly and leant far out of the balcony in order to avoid its touching the window pane. "A fine opportunity to kill me," he thought, "if anyone is hidden in Mathilde's room;" but a profound silence continued to reign everywhere.

The ladder touched the ground. Julien succeeded in laying it on the border of the exotic flowers along side the wall.

"What will my mother say," said Mathilde, "when she sees her beautiful plants all crushed? You must throw down the cord," she added with great self-possession. "If it were noticed going up to the balcony, it would be a difficult circumstance to explain."

"And how am I to get away?" said Julien in a jesting tone affecting the Creole accent. (One of the chambermaids of the household had been born in Saint-Domingo.)

"You? Why you will leave by the door," said Mathilde, delighted at the idea.

"Ah! how worthy this man is of all my love," she thought.

Julien had just let the cord fall into the garden; Mathilde grasped his arm. He thought he had been seized by an enemy and turned round sharply, drawing a dagger. She had thought that she had heard a window opening. They remained motionless and scarcely breathed. The moonlight lit up everything. The noise was not renewed and there was no more cause for anxiety.

Then their embarrassment began again; it was great on both sides. Julien assured himself that the door was completely locked; he thought of looking under the bed, but he did not dare; "they might have stationed one or two lackeys there." Finally he feared that he might reproach himself in the future for this lack of prudence, and did look. Mathilde had fallen into all the anguish of the most extreme timidity. She was horrified at her position.

"What have you done with my letters?" she said at last.

"What a good opportunity to upset these gentlemen, if they are eavesdropping, and thus avoiding the battle," thought Julien.

"The first is hid in a big Protestant Bible, which last night's diligence is taking far away from here."

He spoke very distinctly as he went into these details, so as to be heard by any persons who might be concealed in two large mahogany cupboards which he had not dared to inspect.

"The other two are in the post and are bound for the same destination as the first."

"Heavens, why all these precautions?" said Mathilde in alarm.

"What is the good of my lying?" thought Julien, and he confessed all his suspicions.

"So that's the cause for the coldness of your letters, dear," exclaimed Mathilde in a tone of madness rather than of tenderness.

Julien did not notice that nuance. The endearment made him lose his head, or at any rate his suspicions vanished. He dared to clasp in his arms that beautiful girl who inspired him with such respect. He was only partially rebuffed. He fell back on his memory as he had once at Besançon with Armanda Binet, and recited by heart several of the finest phrases out of the *Nouvelle Héloise*.

"You have the heart of a man," was the answer she made without listening too attentively to his phrases; "I wanted to test your courage, I confess it. Your first suspicions and your resolutions show you even more intrepid, dear, than I had believed."

Mathilde had to make an effort to call him "dear," and was evidently paying more attention to this strange method of speech than to the substance of what she was saying. Being called "dear" without any tenderness in the tone afforded no pleasure to Julien; he was astonished at not being happy, and eventually fell back on his reasoning in order to be so. He saw that he was respected by this proud young girl who never gave undeserved praise; by means of this reasoning he managed to enjoy the happiness of satisfied vanity. It was not, it was true, that soulful pleasure which he had sometimes found with madame de Rênal. There was no element of tenderness in the feelings of these first few minutes. It was the keen happiness of a gratified ambition, and Julien was, above all, ambitious. He talked again of the people whom he had suspected and of the precautions which he had devised. As he spoke, he thought of the best means of exploiting his victory.

Mathilde was still very embarrassed and seemed paralysed by the steps which she had taken. She appeared delighted to find a topic of conversation. They talked of how they were to see each other again. Julien extracted a delicious joy from the consciousness of the intelligence and the courage, of which he again proved himself possessed during this discussion. They had to reckon with extremely sharp people, the little Tanbeau was certainly a spy, but Mathilde and himself as well had their share of cleverness.

What was easier than to meet in the library, and there make all arrangements?

"I can appear in all parts of the hôtel," added Julien, "without rousing suspicion almost, in fact, in madame de la Mole's own room." It was absolutely necessary to go through it in order to reach her daughter's room. If Mathilde thought it preferable for him always to come by a ladder, then he would expose himself to that paltry danger with a heart intoxicated with joy.

As she listened to him speaking, Mathilde was shocked by this air of triumph. "So he is my master," she said to herself, she was already a prey to remorse. Her reason was horrified at the signal folly which she had just committed. If she had had the power she would have annihilated both herself and Julien. When for a few moments she managed by sheer will-power to silence her pangs of remorse, she was rendered very unhappy by her timidity and wounded shame. She had quite failed to foresee the awful plight in which she now found herself.

"I must speak to him, however," she said at last. "That is the proper thing to do. One does talk to one's lover." And then with a view of accomplishing a duty, and with a tenderness which was manifested rather in the words which she employed than in the inflection of her voice, she recounted various resolutions which she had made concerning him during the last few days.

She had decided that if he should dare to come to her room by the help of the gardener's ladder according to his instructions, she would be entirely his. But never were such tender passages spoken in a more polite and frigid tone. Up to the present this assignation had been icy. It was enough to make one hate the name of love. What a lesson in morality for a young and imprudent girl! Is it worth while to ruin one's future for moments such as this?

After long fits of hesitation which a superficial observer might have mistaken for the result of the most emphatic hate (so great is the difficulty which a woman's self-respect finds in yielding even to so firm a will as hers) Mathilde became eventually a charming mistress.

In point of fact, these ecstasies were a little artificial. Passionate love was still more the model which they imitated than a real actuality.

Mademoiselle de la Mole thought she was fulfilling a duty towards herself and towards her lover. "The poor boy," she said to herself, "has shewn a consummate bravery. He deserves to be happy or it is really I who will be shewing a lack of character." But she would have been glad to have redeemed the cruel necessity in which she found herself even at the price of an eternity of unhappiness.

In spite of the awful violence she was doing to herself she was completely mistress of her words.

No regret and no reproach spoiled that night which Julien found extraordinary rather than happy. Great heavens! what a difference to his last twenty-four hours' stay in Verrières. These fine Paris manners manage to spoil everything, even love, he said to himself, quite unjustly.

He abandoned himself to these reflections as he stood upright in one of the great mahogany cupboards into which he had been put at the sign of the first sounds of movement in the neighbouring apartment, which was madame de la Mole's. Mathilde followed her mother to mass, the servants soon left the apartment and Julien easily escaped before they came back to finish their work.

He mounted a horse and tried to find the most solitary spots in one of the forests near Paris. He was more astonished than happy. The happiness which filled his soul from time to time resembled that of a young sub-lieutenant who as the result of some surprising feat has just been made a full-fledged colonel by the commander-in-chief; he felt himself lifted up to an immense height. Everything which was above him the day before was now on a level with him or even below him. Little by little Julien's happiness increased in proportion as he got further away from Paris.

If there was no tenderness in his soul, the reason was that, however strange it may appear to say so, Mathilde had in everything she had done, simply accomplished a duty. The only thing she had not foreseen in all the events of that night, was the shame and unhappiness which she had experienced instead of that absolute felicity which is found in novels.

"Can I have made a mistake, and not be in love with him?" she said to herself.

XLVII
AN OLD SWORD

I now mean to be serious; it is time
Since laughter now-a-days is deemed too serious.
A jest at vice by virtues called a crime.
Don Juan, c. xiii.

She did not appear at dinner. She came for a minute into the salon in the evening, but did not look at Julien. He considered this behaviour strange, "but," he thought, "I do not know their usages. She will give me some good reason for all this." None the less he was a prey to the most extreme curiosity; he studied the expression of Mathilde's features; he was bound to own to himself that she looked cold and malicious. It was evidently not the same woman who on the proceeding night had had, or pretended to have, transports of happiness which were too extravagant to be genuine.

The day after, and the subsequent day she showed the same coldness; she did not look at him, she did not notice his existence. Julien was devoured by the keenest anxiety and was a thousand leagues removed from that feeling of triumph which had been his only emotion on the first day. "Can it be by chance," he said to himself, "a return to virtue?" But this was a very bourgeois word to apply to the haughty Mathilde.

"Placed in an ordinary position in life she would disbelieve in religion," thought Julien, "she only likes it in so far as it is very useful to the interests of her class."

But perhaps she may as a mere matter of delicacy be keenly reproaching herself for the mistake which she has committed. Julien believed that he was her first lover.

"But," he said to himself at other moments, "I must admit that there is no trace of naivety, simplicity, or tenderness in her own demeanour; I have never seen her more haughty, can she despise me? It would be worthy of her to reproach herself simply because of my low birth, for what she has done for me."

While Julien, full of those preconceived ideas which he had found in books and in his memories of Verrières, was chasing the phantom of a tender mistress, who from the minute when she has made her lover happy no longer thinks of her own existence, Mathilde's vanity was infuriated against him.

As for the last two months she had no longer been bored, she was not frightened of boredom; consequently, without being able to have the slightest suspicion of it, Julien had lost his greatest advantage.

"I have given myself a master," said mademoiselle de la Mole to herself, a prey to the blackest sorrow. "Luckily he is honour itself, but if I offend his vanity, he will revenge himself by making known the nature of our relations." Mathilde had never had a lover, and though passing through a stage of life which affords some tender illusions even to the coldest souls, she fell a prey to the most bitter reflections.

"He has an immense dominion over me since his reign is one of terror, and he is capable, if I provoke him, of punishing me with an awful penalty." This idea alone was enough to induce mademoiselle de la Mole to insult him. Courage was the primary quality in her character. The only thing which could give her any thrill and cure her from a fundamental and chronically recurring ennui was the idea that she was staking her entire existence on a single throw.

As mademoiselle de la Mole obstinately refused to look at him, Julien on the third day in spite of her evident objection, followed her into the billiard-room after dinner.

"Well, sir, you think you have acquired some very strong rights over me?" she said to him with scarcely controlled anger, "since you venture to speak to me, in spite of my very clearly manifested wish? Do you know that no one in the world has had such effrontery?"

The dialogue of these two lovers was incomparably humourous. Without suspecting it, they were animated by mutual sentiments of the most vivid hate. As neither the one nor the other had a meekly patient character, while they were both disciples of good form, they soon came to informing each other quite clearly that they would break for ever.

"I swear eternal secrecy to you," said Julien. "I should like to add that I would never address a single word to you, were it not that a marked change might perhaps jeopardise your reputation." He saluted respectfully and left.

He accomplished easily enough what he believed to be a duty; he was very far from thinking himself much in love with mademoiselle de la Mole. He had certainly not loved her three days before, when he had been hidden in the big mahogany cupboard. But the moment that he found himself estranged from her for ever his mood underwent a complete and rapid change.

His memory tortured him by going over the least details in that night, which had as a matter of fact left him so cold. In the very night that followed this announcement of a final rupture, Julien almost went mad at being obliged to own to himself that he loved mademoiselle de la Mole.

This discovery was followed by awful struggles: all his emotions were overwhelmed.

Two days later, instead of being haughty towards M. de Croisenois, he could have almost burst out into tears and embraced him.

His habituation to unhappiness gave him a gleam of commonsense, he decided to leave for Languedoc, packed his trunk and went to the post.

He felt he would faint, when on arriving at the office of the mails, he was told that by a singular chance there was a place in the Toulouse mail. He booked it and returned to the Hôtel de la Mole to announce his departure to the marquis.

M. de la Mole had gone out. More dead than alive Julien went into the library to wait for him. What was his emotion when he found mademoiselle de la Mole there.

As she saw him come, she assumed a malicious expression which it was impossible to mistake.

In his unhappiness and surprise Julien lost his head and was weak enough to say to her in a tone of the most heartfelt tenderness. "So you love me no more."

"I am horrified at having given myself to the first man who came along," said Mathilde crying with rage against herself.

"The first man who came along," cried Julien, and he made for an old mediæval sword which was kept in the library as a curiosity.

His grief—which he thought was at its maximum at the moment when he had spoken to mademoiselle de la Mole—had been rendered a hundred times more intense by the tears of shame which he saw her shedding.

He would have been the happiest of men if he had been able to kill her.

When he was on the point of drawing the sword with some difficulty from its ancient scabbard, Mathilde, rendered happy by so novel a sensation, advanced proudly towards him, her tears were dry.

The thought of his benefactor—the marquis de la Mole—presented itself vividly to Julien. "Shall I kill his daughter?" he said to himself, "how horrible." He made a movement to throw down the sword. "She will certainly," he thought, "burst out laughing at the sight of such a melodramatic pose:" that idea was responsible for his regaining all his self-possession. He looked curiously at the blade of the old sword as though he had been looking for some spot of rust, then put it back in the scabbard and replaced it with the utmost tranquillity on the gilt bronze nail from which it hung.

The whole manœuvre, which towards the end was very slow, lasted quite a minute; mademoiselle de la Mole looked at him in astonishment. "So I have been on the verge of being killed by my lover," she said to herself.

This idea transported her into the palmiest days of the age of Charles

IX. and of Henri III.

She stood motionless before Julien, who had just replaced the sword; she looked at him with eyes whose hatred had disappeared. It must be owned that she was very fascinating at this moment, certainly no woman looked less like a Parisian doll (this expression symbolised Julien's great objection to the women of this city).

"I shall relapse into some weakness for him," thought Mathilde; "it is quite likely that he will think himself my lord and master after a relapse like that at the very moment that I have been talking to him so firmly." She ran away.

"By heaven, she is pretty said Julien as he watched her run and that's the creature who threw herself into my arms with so much passion scarcely a week ago ... and to think that those moments will never come back? And that it's my fault, to think of my being lacking in appreciation at the very moment when I was doing something so extraordinarily interesting! I must own that I was born with a very dull and unfortunate character."

The marquis appeared; Julien hastened to announce his departure.

"Where to?" said M. de la Mole.

"For Languedoc."

"No, if you please, you are reserved for higher destinies. If you leave it will be for the North.... In military phraseology I actually confine you in the hotel. You will compel me to be never more than two or three hours away. I may have need of you at any moment."

Julien bowed and retired without a word, leaving the marquis in a state of great astonishment. He was incapable of speaking. He shut himself up in his room. He was there free to exaggerate to himself all the awfulness of his fate.

"So," he thought, "I cannot even get away. God knows how many days the marquis will keep me in Paris. Great God, what will become of me, and not a friend whom I can consult? The abbé Pirard will never let me finish my first sentence, while the comte Altamira will propose enlisting me in some conspiracy. And yet I am mad; I feel it, I am mad. Who will be able to guide me, what will become of me?"

XLVIII
CRUEL MOMENTS

And she confesses it to me! She goes into even the smallest details! Her beautiful eyes fixed on mine, and describes the love which she felt for another.—*Schiller.*

The delighted mademoiselle de la Mole thought of nothing but the happiness of having been nearly killed. She went so far as to say to herself, "he is worthy of being my master since he was on the point of killing me. How many handsome young society men would have to be melted together before they were capable of so passionate a transport."

"I must admit that he was very handsome at the time when he climbed up on the chair to replace the sword in the same picturesque position in which the decorator hung it! After all it was not so foolish of me to love him."

If at that moment some honourable means of reconciliation had presented itself, she would have embraced it with pleasure. Julien locked in his room was a prey to the most violent despair. He thought in his madness of throwing himself at her feet. If instead of hiding himself in an out of the way place, he had wandered about the garden of the hôtel so as to keep within reach of any opportunity, he would perhaps have changed in a single moment his awful unhappiness into the keenest happiness.

But the tact for whose lack we are now reproaching him would have been incompatible with that sublime seizure of the sword, which at the present time rendered him so handsome in the eyes of mademoiselle de la Mole. This whim in Julien's favour lasted the whole day; Mathilde conjured up a charming image of the short moments during which she had loved him: she regretted them.

"As a matter of fact," she said to herself, "my passion for this poor boy can from his point of view only have lasted from one hour after midnight when I saw him arrive by his ladder with all his pistols in his coat pocket, till eight o'clock in the morning. It was a quarter of an hour after that as I listened to mass at Sainte-Valère that I began to think that he might very well try to terrify me into obedience."

After dinner mademoiselle de la Mole, so far from avoiding Julien, spoke to him and made him promise to follow her into the garden. He obeyed. It was a new experience.

Without suspecting it Mathilde was yielding to the love which she was now feeling for him again. She found an extreme pleasure in walking by his side, and she looked curiously at those hands which had seized the sword to kill her that very morning.

After such an action, after all that had taken place, some of the former conversation was out of the question.

Mathilde gradually began to talk confidentially to him about the state of her heart. She found a singular pleasure in this kind of conversation, she even went so far as to describe to him the fleeting moments of enthusiasm which she had experienced for M. de Croisenois, for M. de Caylus——

"What! M. de Caylus as well!" exclaimed Julien, and all the jealousy of a discarded lover burst out in those words, Mathilde thought as much, but did not feel at all insulted.

She continued torturing Julien by describing her former sentiments with the most picturesque detail and the accent of the most intimate truth. He saw that she was portraying what she had in her mind's eye. He had the pain of noticing that as she spoke she made new discoveries in her own heart.

The unhappiness of jealousy could not be carried further.

It is cruel enough to suspect that a rival is loved, but there is no doubt that to hear the woman one adores confess in detail the love which rivals inspires, is the utmost limit of anguish.

Oh, how great a punishment was there now for those impulses of pride which had induced Julien to place himself as superior to the Caylus and the Croisenois! How deeply did he feel his own unhappiness as he exaggerated to himself their most petty advantages. With what hearty good faith he despised himself.

Mathilde struck him as adorable. All words are weak to express his excessive admiration. As he walked beside her he looked surreptitiously at her hands, her arms, her queenly bearing. He was so completely overcome by love and unhappiness as to be on the point of falling at her feet and crying "pity."

"Yes, and that person who is so beautiful, who is so superior to every-thing and who loved me once, will doubtless soon love M. de Caylus."

Julien could have no doubts of mademoiselle de la Mole's sincerity, the accent of truth was only too palpable in everything she said. In order that nothing might be wanting to complete his unhappiness there were moments when, as a result of thinking about the sentiments which she had once experienced for M. de Caylus, Mathilde came to talk of him, as though she loved him at the present time. She certainly put an inflection of love into her voice. Julien distinguished it clearly.

He would have suffered less if his bosom had been filled inside with molten lead. Plunged as he was in this abyss of unhappiness how could the poor boy have guessed that it was simply because she was talking to him, that mademoiselle de la Mole found so much pleasure in recalling those weaknesses of love which she had formerly experienced for M. de

Caylus or M. de Luz.

Words fail to express Julien's anguish. He listened to these detailed confidences of the love she had experienced for others in that very avenue of pines where he had waited so few days ago for one o'clock to strike that he might invade her room. No human being can undergo a greater degree of unhappiness.

This kind of familiar cruelty lasted for eight long days. Mathilde sometimes seemed to seek opportunities of speaking to him and sometimes not to avoid them; and the one topic of conversation to which they both seemed to revert with a kind of cruel pleasure, was the description of the sentiments she had felt for others. She told him about the letters which she had written, she remembered their very words, she recited whole sentences by heart.

She seemed during these last days to be envisaging Julien with a kind of malicious joy. She found a keen enjoyment in his pangs.

One sees that Julien had no experience of life; he had not even read any novels. If he had been a little less awkward and he had coolly said to the young girl, whom he adored so much and who had been giving him such strange confidences: "admit that though I am not worth as much as all these gentlemen, I am none the less the man whom you loved," she would perhaps have been happy at being at thus guessed; at any rate success would have entirely depended on the grace with which Julien had expressed the idea, and on the moment which he had chosen to do so. In any case he would have extricated himself well and advantageously from a situation which Mathilde was beginning to find monotonous.

"And you love me no longer, me, who adores you!" said Julien to her one day, overcome by love and unhappiness. This piece of folly was perhaps the greatest which he could have committed. These words immediately destroyed all the pleasure which mademoiselle de la Mole found in talking to him about the state of her heart. She was beginning to be surprised that he did not, after what had happened, take offence at what she told him. She had even gone so far as to imagine at the very moment when he made that foolish remark that perhaps he did not love her any more. "His pride has doubtless extinguished his love," she was saying to herself. "He is not the man to sit still and see people like Caylus, de Luz, Croisenois whom he admits are so superior, preferred to him. No, I shall never see him at my feet again."

Julien had often in the naivety of his unhappiness, during the previous days praised sincerely the brilliant qualities of these gentlemen; he would even go so far as to exaggerate them. This nuance had not escaped mademoiselle de la Mole, she was astonished by it, but did not guess its reason. Julien's frenzied soul, in praising a rival whom he thought was loved, was sympathising with his happiness.

These frank but stupid words changed everything in a single moment; confident that she was loved, Mathilde despised him utterly.

She was walking with him when he made his ill-timed remark; she left him, and her parting look expressed the most awful contempt. She returned to the salon and did not look at him again during the whole evening. This contempt monopolised her mind the following day. The impulse which during the last week had made her find so much pleasure in treating Julien as her most intimate friend was out of the question; the very sight of him was disagreeable. The sensation Mathilde felt reached the point of disgust; nothing can express the extreme contempt which she experienced when her eyes fell upon him.

Julien had understood nothing of the history of Mathilde's heart during the last week, but he distinguished the contempt. He had the good sense only to appear before her on the rarest possible occasions, and never looked at her.

But it was not without a mortal anguish that he, as it were, deprived himself of her presence. He thought he felt his unhappiness increasing still further. "The courage of a man's heart cannot be carried further," he said to himself. He passed his life seated at a little window at the top of the hôtel; the blind was carefully closed, and from here at any rate he could see mademoiselle de la Mole when she appeared in the garden.

What were his emotions when he saw her walking after dinner with M. de Caylus, M. de Luz, or some other for whom she had confessed to him some former amorous weakness!

Julien had no idea that unhappiness could be so intense; he was on the point of shouting out. This firm soul was at last completely overwhelmed.

Thinking about anything else except mademoiselle de la Mole had become odious to him; he became incapable of writing the simplest letters.

"You are mad," the marquis said to him.

Julien was frightened that his secret might be guessed, talked about illness and succeeded in being believed. Fortunately for him the marquis rallied him at dinner about his next journey; Mathilde understood that it might be a very long one. It was now several days that Julien had avoided her, and the brilliant young men who had all that this pale sombre being she had once loved was lacking, had no longer the power of drawing her out of her reverie.

"An ordinary girl," she said to herself, "would have sought out the man she preferred among those young people who are the cynosure of a salon; but one of the characteristics of genius is not to drive its thoughts over the rut traced by the vulgar.

"Why, if I were the companion of a man like Julien, who only lacks the fortune that I possess, I should be continually exciting attention, I should not pass through life unnoticed. Far from incessantly fearing a revolution like my cousins who are so frightened of the people that they have not the pluck to scold a postillion who drives them badly, I should be certain of playing a rôle and a great rôle, for the man whom I have chosen has a character and a boundless ambition. What does he lack? Friends, money? I will give them him." But she treated Julien in her thought as an inferior being whose love one could win whenever one wanted.

XLIX
THE OPERA BOUFFE

How the spring of love resembleth
The uncertain glory of an April day,
Which now shows all the beauty of the sun,
And by and by a cloud takes all away.—*Shakespeare*.

Engrossed by thoughts of her future and the singular rôle which she hoped to play, Mathilde soon came to miss the dry metaphysical conversations which she had often had with Julien. Fatigued by these lofty thoughts she would sometimes also miss those moments of happiness which she had found by his side; these last memories were not unattended by remorse which at certain times even overwhelmed her.

"But one may have a weakness," she said to herself, "a girl like I am should only forget herself for a man of real merit; they will not say that it is his pretty moustache or his skill in horsemanship which have fascinated me, but rather his deep discussions on the future of France and his ideas on the analogy between the events which are going to burst upon us and the English revolution of 1688."

"I have been seduced," she answered in her remorse. "I am a weak woman, but at least I have not been led astray like a doll by exterior advantages."

"If there is a revolution why should not Julien Sorel play the role of Roland and I the rôle of Madame Roland? I prefer that part to Madame de Stael's; the immorality of my conduct will constitute an obstacle in this age of ours. I will certainly not let them reproach me with an act of weakness; I should die of shame."

Mathilde's reveries were not all as grave, one must admit, as the thoughts which we have just transcribed.

She would look at Julien and find a charming grace in his slightest action.

"I have doubtless," she would say, "succeeded in destroying in him the very faintest idea he had of any one else's rights."

"The air of unhappiness and deep passion with which the poor boy declared his love to me eight days ago proves it; I must own it was very extraordinary of me to manifest anger at words in which there shone so much respect and so much of passion. Am I not his real wife? Those words of his were quite natural, and I must admit, were really very nice. Julien still continued to love me, even after those eternal conversations in which I had only spoken to him (cruelly enough I admit), about those weaknesses of love which the boredom of the life I lead had inspired me for those young society men of whom he is so jealous. Ah, if he only knew what little danger I have to fear from them; how withered and stereotyped they seem to me in comparison with him."

While indulging in these reflections Mathilde made a random pencil sketch of a profile on a page of her album. One of the profiles she had just finished surprised and delighted her. It had a striking resemblance to Julien. "It is the voice of heaven. That's one of the miracles of love," she cried ecstatically; "Without suspecting it, I have drawn his portrait."

She fled to her room, shut herself up in it, and with much application made strenuous endeavours to draw Julien's portrait, but she was unable to succeed; the profile she had traced at random still remained the most like him. Mathilde was delighted with it. She saw in it a palpable proof of the grand passion.

She only left her album very late when the marquise had her called to go to the Italian Opera. Her one idea was to catch sight of Julien, so that she might get her mother to request him to keep them company.

He did not appear, and the ladies had only ordinary vulgar creatures in their box. During the first act of the opera, Mathilde dreamt of the man she loved with all the ecstasies of the most vivid passion; but a love-maxim in the second act sung it must be owned to a melody worthy of Cimarosa pierced her heart. The heroine of the opera said "You must punish me for the excessive adoration which I feel for him. I love him too much."

From the moment that Mathilde heard this sublime song everything in the world ceased to exist. She was spoken to, she did not answer; her mother reprimanded her, she could scarcely bring herself to look at her. Her ecstasy reached a state of exultation and passion analogous to the most violent transports which Julien had felt for her for some days. The divinely graceful melody to which the maxim, which seemed to have such a striking application to her own position, was sung, engrossed all the minutes when she was not actually thinking of Julien. Thanks to her love for music she was on this particular evening like madame de Rênal always was, when she thought of Julien. Love of the head has doubtless more intelligence than true love, but it only has moments of enthusiasm. It knows itself too well, it sits in judgment on itself incessantly; far from distracting thought it is made by sheer force of thought.

On returning home Mathilde, in spite of madame de la Mole's remonstrances, pretended to have a fever and spent a part of the night in going over this melody on her piano. She sang the words of the celebrated air which had so fascinated her:—

Devo punirmi, devo punirmi.
Se troppo amai, etc.

As the result of this night of madness, she imagined that she had succeeded in triumphing over her love. This page will be prejudicial in more than one way to the unfortunate author. Frigid souls will accuse him of indecency. But the young ladies who shine in the Paris salons have no right to feel insulted at the supposition that one of their number might be liable to those transports of madness which have been degrading the character of Mathilde. That character is purely imaginary, and is even drawn quite differently from that social code which will guarantee so distinguished a place in the world's history to nineteenth century civilization.

The young girls who have adorned this winter's balls are certainly not lacking in prudence.

I do not think either that they can be accused of being unduly scornful of a brilliant fortune, horses, fine estates and all the guarantees of a pleasant position in society. Far from finding these advantages simply equivalent to boredom, they usually concentrate on them their most constant desires and devote to them such passion as their hearts possess.

Nor again is it love which is the dominant principle in the career of young men who, like Julien, are gifted with some talent; they attach themselves with an irresistible grip to some côterie, and when the côterie succeeds all the good things of society are rained upon them. Woe to the studious man who belongs to no côterie, even his smallest and most doubtful successes will constitute a grievance, and lofty virtue will rob him and triumph. Yes, monsieur, a novel is a mirror which goes out on a highway. Sometimes it reflects the azure of the heavens, sometimes the mire of the pools of mud on the way, and the man who carries this mirror in his knapsack is forsooth to be accused by you of being immoral! His mirror shows the mire, and you accuse the mirror! Rather accuse the main road where the mud is, or rather the inspector of roads who allows the water to accumulate and the mud to form.

Now that it is quite understood that Mathilde's character is impossible in our own age, which is as discreet as it is virtuous, I am less frightened of offence by continuing the history of the follies of this charming girl.

During the whole of the following day she looked out for opportunities of convincing herself of her triumph over her mad passion. Her great aim was to displease Julien in everything; but not one of his movements escaped her.

Julien was too unhappy, and above all too agitated to appreciate so complicated a stratagem of passion. Still less was he capable of seeing how favourable it really was to him. He was duped by it. His unhappiness had perhaps never been so extreme. His actions were so little controlled by his intellect that if some mournful philosopher had said to him, "Think how to exploit as quickly as you can those symptoms which promise to be favourable to you. In this kind of head-love which is seen at Paris, the same mood cannot last more than two days," he would not have understood him. But however ecstatic he might feel, Julien was a man of honour. Discretion was his first duty. He appreciated it. Asking advice, describing his agony to the first man who came along would have constituted a happiness analogous to that of the unhappy man who, when traversing a burning desert receives from heaven a drop of icy water. He realised the danger, was frightened of answering an indiscreet question by a torrent of tears, and shut himself up in his own room.

He saw Mathilde walking in the garden for a long time. When she at last left it, he went down there and approached the rose bush from which she had taken a flower.

The night was dark and he could abandon himself to his unhappiness without fear of being seen. It was obvious to him that mademoiselle de la Mole loved one of those young officers with whom she had chatted so gaily. She had loved him, but she had realised his little merit, "and as a matter of fact I had very little," Julien said to himself with full conviction. "Taking me all round I am a very dull, vulgar person, very boring to others and quite unbearable to myself." He was mortally disgusted with all his good qualities, and with all the things which he had once loved so enthusiastically; and it was when his imagination was in this distorted condition that he undertook to judge life by means of its aid. This mistake is typical of a superior man.

The idea of suicide presented itself to him several times; the idea was full of charm, and like a delicious rest; because it was the glass of iced water offered to the wretch dying of thirst and heat in the desert.

"My death will increase the contempt she has for me," he exclaimed. "What a memory I should leave her."

Courage is the only resource of a human being who has fallen into this last abyss of unhappiness. Julien did not have sufficient genius to say to himself, "I must dare," but as he looked at the window of Mathilde's room he saw through the blinds that she was putting out her light. He conjured up that charming room which he had seen, alas! once in his whole life. His imagination did not go any further.

One o'clock struck. Hearing the stroke of the clock and saying to himself, "I will climb up the ladder," scarcely took a moment.

It was the flash of genius, good reasons crowded on his mind. "May I be more fortunate than before," he said to himself. He ran to the ladder. The gardener had chained it up. With the help of the cock of one of his little pistols which he broke, Julien, who for the time being was animated by a superhuman force, twisted one of the links of the chain which held the ladder. He was master of it in a few minutes, and placed it against Mathilde's window.

"She will be angry and riddle me with scornful words! What does it matter? I will give her a kiss, one last kiss. I will go up to my room and kill myself ... my lips will touch her cheek before I die."

He flew up the ladder and knocked at the blind; Mathilde heard him after some minutes and tried to open the blind but the ladder was in the way. Julien hung to the iron hook intending to keep the blind open, and at the imminent risk of falling down, gave the ladder a violent shake which moved it a little. Mathilde was able to open the blind.

He threw himself into the window more dead than alive.

"So it is you, dear," she said as she rushed into his arms.

The excess of Julien's happiness was indescribable. Mathilde's almost equalled his own.

She talked against herself to him and denounced herself.

"Punish me for my awful pride," she said to him, clasping him in her arms so tightly as almost to choke him. "You are my master, dear, I am your slave. I must ask your pardon on my knees for having tried to rebel." She left his arms to fall at his feet. "Yes," she said to him, still intoxicated with happiness and with love, "you are my master, reign over me for ever. When your slave tries to revolt, punish her severely."

In another moment she tore herself from his arms, and lit a candle, and it was only by a supreme effort that Julien could prevent her from cutting off a whole tress of her hair.

"I want to remind myself," she said to him, "that I am your handmaid. If I am ever led astray again by my abominable pride, show me this hair and say, 'It is not a question of the emotion which your soul may be feeling at present, you have sworn to obey, obey on your honour.'"

But it is wiser to suppress the description of so intense a transport of delirious happiness.

Julien's unselfishness was equal to his happiness. "I must go down by the ladder," he said to Mathilde, when he saw the dawn of day appear from the quarter of the east over the distant chimneys beyond the garden. "The sacrifice that I impose on myself is worthy of you. I deprive myself of some hours of the most astonishing happiness that a human soul can savour, but it is a sacrifice I make for the sake of your reputation. If you know my heart you will appreciate how violent is the strain to which I am putting myself. Will you always be to me what you are now? But honour speaks, it suffices. Let me tell you that since our last interview, thieves have not been the only object of suspicion. M. de la Mole has set a guard in the garden. M. Croisenois is surrounded by spies: they know what he does every night."

Mathilde burst out laughing at this idea. Her mother and a chamber-maid were woken up, they suddenly began to speak to her through the door. Julien looked at her, she grew pale as she scolded the chamber-maid, and she did not deign to speak to her mother. "But suppose they think of opening the window, they will see the ladder," Julien said to her.

He clasped her again in his arms, rushed on to the ladder, and slid, rather than climbed down; he was on the ground in a moment.

Three seconds after the ladder was in the avenue of pines, and Mathilde's honour was saved. Julien returned to his room and found that he was bleeding and almost naked. He had wounded himself in sliding down in that dare-devil way.

Extreme happiness had made him regain all the energy of his char-acter. If twenty men had presented themselves it would have proved at this moment only an additional pleasure to have attacked them unaided. Happily his military prowess was not put to the proof. He laid the ladder in its usual place and replaced the chain which held it. He did not forget to efface the mark which the ladder had left on the bed of exotic flowers under Mathilde's window.

As he was moving his hand over the soft ground in the darkness and satisfying himself that the mark had entirely disappeared, he felt something fall down on his hands. It was a whole tress of Mathilde's hair which she had cut off and thrown down to him.

She was at the window.

"That's what your servant sends you," she said to him in a fairly loud voice, "It is the sign of eternal gratitude. I renounce the exercise of my reason, be my master."

Julien was quite overcome and was on the point of going to fetch the ladder again and climbing back into her room. Finally reason prevailed.

Getting back into the hôtel from the garden was not easy. He suc-ceeded in forcing the door of a cellar. Once in the house he was obliged to break through the door of his room as silently as possible. In his agitation he had left in the little room which he had just abandoned so rapidly, the key which was in the pocket of his coat. "I only hope she thinks of hiding that fatal trophy," he thought.

Finally fatigue prevailed over happiness, and as the sun was rising he fell into a deep sleep.

The breakfast bell only just managed to wake him up. He appeared in the dining-room. Shortly afterwards Mathilde came in. Julien's pride felt deliciously flattered as he saw the love which shone in the eyes of this beautiful creature who was surrounded by so much homage; but soon his discretion had occasion to be alarmed.

Making an excuse of the little time that she had had to do her hair, Mathilde had arranged it in such a way that Julien could see at the first glance the full extent of the sacrifice that she had made for his sake, by cutting off her hair on the previous night.

If it had been possible to spoil so beautiful a face by anything whatsoever, Mathilde would have succeeded in doing it. A whole tress of her beautiful blonde hair was cut off to within half an inch of the scalp.

Mathilde's whole manner during breakfast was in keeping with this initial imprudence. One might have said that she had made a specific point of trying to inform the whole world of her mad passion for Julien. Happily on this particular day M. de la Mole and the marquis were very much concerned about an approaching bestowal of "blue ribbons" which was going to take place, and in which M. de Chaulnes was not comprised. Towards the end of the meal, Mathilde, who was talking to Julien, happened to call him "My Master." He blushed up to the whites of his eyes.

Mathilde was not left alone for an instant that day, whether by chance or the deliberate policy of madame de la Mole. In the evening when she passed from the dining-room into the salon, however, she managed to say to Julien: "You may be thinking I am making an excuse, but mamma has just decided that one of her women is to spend the night in my room."

This day passed with lightning rapidity. Julien was at the zenith of happiness. At seven o'clock in the morning of the following day he installed himself in the library. He hoped the mademoiselle de la Mole would deign to appear there; he had written her an interminable letter. He only saw her several hours afterwards at breakfast. Her hair was done to-day with the very greatest care; a marvellous art had managed to hide the place where the hair had been cut. She looked at Julien once or twice, but her eyes were polite and calm, and there was no question of calling him "My Master."

Julien's astonishment prevented him from breathing—Mathilde was reproaching herself for all she had done for him. After mature reflection, she had come to the conclusion that he was a person who, though not absolutely commonplace, was yet not sufficiently different from the common ruck to deserve all the strange follies that she had ventured for his sake. To sum up she did not give love a single thought; on this particular day she was tired of loving.

As for Julien, his emotions were those of a child of sixteen. He was a successive prey to awful doubt, astonishment and despair during this breakfast which he thought would never end.

As soon as he could decently get up from the table, he flew rather than ran to the stable, saddled his horse himself, and galloped off. "I must kill my heart through sheer force of physical fatigue," he said to himself as he galloped through the Meudon woods. "What have I done, what have I said to deserve a disgrace like this?"

"I must do nothing and say nothing to-day," he thought as he re-entered the hôtel. "I must be as dead physically as I am morally." Julien saw nothing any more, it was only his corpse which kept moving.

L
THE JAPANESE VASE

His heart does not first realise the full extremity of his un-happiness: he is more troubled than moved. But as reason returns he feels the depth of his misfortune. All the pleasures of life seem to have been destroyed, he can only feel the sharp barbs of a lacerating despair. But what is the use of talking of physical pain? What pain which is only felt by the body can be compared to this pain?—*Jean Paul.*

The dinner bell rang, Julien had barely time to dress: he found Mathilde in the salon. She was pressing her brother and M. de Croisenois to promise her that they would not go and spend the evening at Suresnes with madame the maréchale de Fervaques.

It would have been difficult to have shown herself more amiable or fascinating to them. M. de Luz, de Caylus and several of their friends came in after dinner. One would have said that mademoiselle de la Mole had commenced again to cultivate the most scrupulous conventionality at the same time as her sisterly affection. Although the weather was delightful this evening, she refused to go out into the garden, and insisted on their all staying near the arm-chair where madame de la Mole was sitting. The blue sofa was the centre of the group as it had been in the winter.

Mathilde was out of temper with the garden, or at any rate she found it absolutely boring: it was bound up with the memory of Julien.

Unhappiness blunts the edge of the intellect. Our hero had the bad taste to stop by that little straw chair which had formerly witnessed his most brilliant triumphs. To-day none spoke to him, his presence seemed to be unnoticed, and worse than that. Those of mademoiselle de la Mole's friends who were sitting near him at the end of the sofa, made a point of somehow or other turning their back on him, at any rate he thought so.

"It is a court disgrace," he thought. He tried to study for a moment the people who were endeavouring to overwhelm him with their contempt. M. de Luz had an important post in the King's suite, the result of which was that the handsome officer began every conversation with every listener who came along by telling him this special piece of information. His uncle had started at seven o'clock for St. Cloud and reckoned on spending the night there. This detail was introduced with all the appearance of good nature but it never failed to be worked in. As Julien scrutinized M. de Croisenois with a stern gaze of unhappiness, he observed that this good amiable young man attributed a great influence to occult causes. He even went so far as to become melancholy and out of temper if he saw an event of the slightest importance ascribed to a simple and perfectly natural cause.

"There is an element of madness in this," Julien said to himself. This man's character has a striking analogy with that of the Emperor Alexander, such as the Prince Korasoff described it to me. During the first year of his stay in Paris poor Julien, fresh from the seminary and dazzled by the graces of all these amiable young people, whom he found so novel, had felt bound to admire them. Their true character was only beginning to become outlined in his eyes.

"I am playing an undignified rôle here," he suddenly thought. The question was, how he could leave the little straw chair without undue awkwardness. He wanted to invent something, and tried to extract some novel excuse from an imagination which was otherwise engrossed. He was compelled to fall back on his memory, which was, it must be owned, somewhat poor in resources of this kind.

The poor boy was still very much out of his element, and could not have exhibited a more complete and noticeable awkwardness when he got up to leave the salon. His misery was only too palpable in his whole manner. He had been playing, for the last three quarters of an hour, the rôle of an officious inferior from whom one does not take the trouble to hide what one really thinks.

The critical observations he had just made on his rivals prevented him, however, from taking his own unhappiness too tragically. His pride could take support in what had taken place the previous day. "Whatever may be their advantages over me," he thought, as he went into the garden alone, "Mathilde has never been to a single one of them what, twice in my life, she has deigned to be to me!" His penetration did not go further. He absolutely failed to appreciate the character of the extraordinary person whom chance had just made the supreme mistress of all his happiness.

He tried, on the following day, to make himself and his horse dead tired with fatigue. He made no attempt in the evening to go near the blue sofa to which Mathilde remained constant. He noticed that comte Norbert did not even deign to look at him when he met him about the house. "He must be doing something very much against the grain," he thought; "he is naturally so polite."

Sleep would have been a happiness to Julien. In spite of his physical fatigue, memories which were only too seductive commenced to invade his imagination. He had not the genius to see that, inasmuch as his long rides on horseback over forests on the outskirts of Paris only affected him, and had no affect at all on Mathilde's heart or mind, he was consequently leaving his eventual destiny to the caprice of chance. He thought that one thing would give his pain an infinite relief: it would be to speak to Mathilde. Yet what would he venture to say to her?

He was dreaming deeply about this at seven o'clock one morning when he suddenly saw her enter the library.

"I know, monsieur, that you are anxious to speak to me."

"Great heavens! who told you?"

"I know, anyway; that is enough. If you are dishonourable, you can ruin me, or at least try to. But this danger, which I do not believe to be real, will certainly not prevent me from being sincere. I do not love you any more, monsieur, I have been led astray by my foolish imagination."

Distracted by love and unhappiness, as a result of this terrible blow, Julien tried to justify himself. Nothing could have been more absurd. Does one make any excuses for failure to please? But reason had no longer any control over his actions. A blind instinct urged him to get the determination of his fate postponed. He thought that, so long as he kept on speaking, all could not be over. Mathilde had not listened to his words; their sound irritated her. She could not conceive how he could have the audacity to interrupt her.

She was rendered equally unhappy this morning by remorseful virtue and remorseful pride. She felt to some extent pulverised by the idea of having given a little abbé, who was the son of a peasant, rights over her. "It is almost," she said to herself, in those moments when she exaggerated her own misfortune, "as though I had a weakness for one of my footmen to reproach myself with." In bold, proud natures there is only one step from anger against themselves to wrath against others. In these cases the very transports of fury constitute a vivid pleasure.

In a single minute mademoiselle de la Mole reached the point of loading Julien with the signs of the most extreme contempt. She had infinite wit, and this wit was always triumphant in the art of torturing vanity and wounding it cruelly.

For the first time in his life Julien found himself subjected to the energy of a superior intellect, which was animated against him by the most violent hate. Far from having at present the slightest thought of defending himself, he came to despise himself. Hearing himself overwhelmed with such marks of contempt which were so cleverly calculated to destroy any good opinion that he might have of himself, he thought that Mathilde was right, and that she did not say enough.

As for her, she found it deliciously gratifying to her pride to punish in this way both herself and him for the adoration that she had felt some days previously.

She did not have to invent and improvise the cruel remarks which she addressed to him with so much gusto.

All she had to do was to repeat what the advocate of the other side had been saying against her love in her own heart for the last eight days.

Each word intensified a hundredfold Julien's awful unhappiness. He wanted to run away, but mademoiselle de la Mole took hold of his arm authoritatively.

"Be good enough to remark," he said to her, "that you are talking very loud. You will be heard in the next room."

"What does it matter?" mademoiselle de la Mole answered haughtily. "Who will dare to say they have heard me? I want to cure your miserable vanity once and for all of any ideas you may have indulged in on my account."

When Julien was allowed to leave the library he was so astonished that he was less sensitive to his unhappiness. "She does not love me any more," he repeated to himself, speaking aloud as though to teach himself how he stood. "It seems that she has loved me eight or ten days, but I shall love her all my life."

"Is it really possible she was nothing to me, nothing to my heart so few days back?"

Mathilde's heart was inundated by the joy of satisfied pride. So she had been able to break with him for ever! So complete a triumph over so strong an inclination rendered her completely happy. "So this little gentleman will understand, once and for all, that he has not, and will never have, any dominion over me." She was so happy that in reality she ceased to love at this particular moment.

In a less passionate being than Julien love would have become impossible after a scene of such awful humiliation. Without deviating for a single minute from the requirements of her own self-respect, mademoiselle de la Mole had addressed to him some of those unpleasant remarks which are so well thought out that they may seem true, even when remembered in cold blood.

The conclusion which Julien drew in the first moment of so surprising a scene, was that Mathilde was infinitely proud. He firmly believed that all was over between them for ever, and none the less, he was awkward and nervous towards her at breakfast on the following day. This was a fault from which up to now he had been exempt.

Both in small things as in big it was his habit to know what he ought and wanted to do, and he used to act accordingly.

The same day after breakfast madame de la Mole asked him for a fairly rare, seditious pamphlet which her curé had surreptitiously brought her in the morning, and Julien, as he took it from a bracket, knocked over a blue porcelain vase which was as ugly as it could possibly be.

Madame de la Mole got up, uttering a cry of distress, and proceeded to contemplate at close quarters the ruins of her beloved vase. "It was old Japanese," she said. "It came to me from my great aunt, the abbess of Chelles. It was a present from the Dutch to the Regent, the Duke of Orleans, who had given it to his daughter...."

Mathilde had followed her mother's movements, and felt delighted at seeing that the blue vase, that she had thought horribly ugly, was broken. Julien was taciturn, and not unduly upset. He saw mademoiselle de la Mole quite near him.

"This vase," he said to her, "has been destroyed for ever. The same is the case with the sentiment which was once master of my heart. I would ask you to accept my apologies for all the pieces of madness which it has made me commit." And he went out.

"One would really say," said madame de la Mole, as he went out of the room, "that this M. Sorel is quite proud of what he has just done."

These words went right home to Mathilde's heart. "It is true," she said to herself; "my mother has guessed right. That is the sentiment which animates him." It was only then that she ceased rejoicing over yesterday's scene. "Well, it is all over," she said to herself, with an apparent calm. "It is a great lesson, anyway. It is an awful and humiliating mistake! It is enough to make me prudent all the rest of my life."

"Why didn't I speak the truth?" thought Julien. "Why am I still tortured by the love which I once had for that mad woman?"

Far, however, from being extinguished as he had hoped it would be, his love grew more and more rapidly. "She is mad, it is true," he said to himself. "Is she any the less adorable for that? Is it possible for anyone to be prettier? Is not mademoiselle de la Mole the ideal quintessence of all the most vivid pleasures of the most elegant civilisation?" These memories of a bygone happiness seized hold of Julien's mind, and quickly proceeded to destroy all the work of his reason.

It is in vain that reason wrestles with memories of this character. Its stern struggles only increase the fascination.

Twenty-four hours after the breaking of the Japanese vase, Julien was unquestionably one of the most unhappy men in the world.

LI
THE SECRET NOTE

I have seen everything I relate, and if I may have made a mistake when I saw it, I am certainly not deceiving you in telling you of it.*Letter to the author.*

The marquis summoned him; M. de la Mole looked rejuvenated, his eye was brilliant.

"Let us discuss your memory a little," he said to Julien, "it is said to be prodigious. Could you learn four pages by heart and go and say them at London, but without altering a single word?"

The marquis was irritably fingering, the day's *Quotidienne*, and was trying in vain to hide an extreme seriousness which Julien had never noticed in him before, even when discussing the Frilair lawsuit.

Julien had already learned sufficient manners to appreciate that he ought to appear completely taken in by the lightness of tone which was being manifested.

"This number of the *Quotidienne* is not very amusing possibly, but if M. the marquis will allow me, I shall do myself the honour to-morrow morning of reciting it to him from beginning to end."

"What, even the advertisements?"

"Quite accurately and without leaving out a word."

"You give me your word?" replied the marquis with sudden gravity.

"Yes, monsieur; the only thing which could upset my memory is the fear of breaking my promise."

"The fact is, I forgot to put this question to you yesterday: I am not going to ask for your oath never to repeat what you are going to hear. I know you too well to insult you like that. I have answered for you. I am going to take you into a salon where a dozen persons will he assembled. You will make a note of what each one says.

"Do not be uneasy. It will not be a confused conversation by any means. Each one will speak in his turn, though not necessarily in an orderly manner," added the marquis falling back into that light, subtle manner which was so natural to him. "While we are talking, you will write out twenty pages and will come back here with me, and we will get those twenty pages down to four, and those are the four pages you will recite to me to-morrow morning instead of the four pages of the *Quotidienne*. You will leave immediately afterwards. You must post about like a young man travelling on pleasure. Your aim will be to avoid attracting attention.

You will arrive at the house of a great personage. You will there need more skill. Your business will then be to take in all his entourage, for among his secretaries and his servants are some people who have sold themselves to our enemies, and who spy on our travelling agents in order to intercept them.

"You will have an insignificant letter of introduction. At the moment his Excellency looks at you, you will take out this watch of mine, which I will lend you for the journey. Wear it now, it will be so much done; at any rate give me yours.

"The duke himself will be good enough to write at your dictation the four pages you have learnt by heart.

"Having done this, but not earlier, mind you, you can, if his Excellency questions you, tell him about the meeting at which you are now going to be present.

"You will be prevented from boring yourself on the journey between Paris and the minister's residence by the thought that there are people who would like nothing better than to fire a shot at M. the abbé Sorel. In that case that gentleman's mission will be finished, and I see a great delay, for how are we to know of your death, my dear friend? Even your zeal cannot go to the length of informing us of it.

"Run straight away and buy a complete suit," went on the marquis seriously. "Dress in the fashion of two years ago. To-night you must look somewhat badly groomed. When you travel, on the other hand, you will be as usual. Does this surprise you? Does your suspiciousness guess the secret? Yes, my friend, one of the venerable personages you are going to hear deliver his opinion, is perfectly capable of giving information as the result of which you stand a very good chance of being given at least opium some fine evening in some good inn where you will have asked for supper."

"It is better," said Julien, "to do an extra thirty leagues and not take the direct road. It is a case of Rome, I suppose...." The marquis assumed an expression of extreme haughtiness and dissatisfaction which Julien had never seen him wear since Bray-le-Haut.

"That is what you will know, monsieur, when I think it proper to tell you. I do not like questions."

"That was not one," answered Julien eagerly. "I swear, monsieur, I was thinking quite aloud. My mind was trying to find out the safest route."

"Yes, it seems your mind was a very long way off. Remember that an emissary, and particularly one of your age should not appear to be a man who forces confidences."

Julien was very mortified; he was in the wrong. His vanity tried to find an excuse and did not find one.

"You understand," added monsieur de la Mole, "that one always falls back on one's heart when one has committed some mistake."

An hour afterwards Julien was in the marquis's ante-chamber. He looked quite like a servant with his old clothes, a tie of a dubious white, and a certain touch of the usher in his whole appearance. The marquis burst out laughing as he saw him, and it was only then that Julien's justification was complete.

"If this young man betrays me," said M. de la Mole to himself, "whom is one to trust? And yet, when one acts, one must trust someone. My son and his brilliant friends of the same calibre have as much courage and loyalty as a hundred thousand men. If it were necessary to fight, they would die on the steps of the throne. They know everything—except what one needs in emergency. Devil take me if I can find a single one among them who can learn four pages by heart and do a hundred leagues without being tracked down. Norbert would know how to sell his life as dearly as his grandfathers did. But any conscript could do as much."

The marquis fell into a profound reverie. "As for selling one's life too," he said with a sigh, "perhaps this Sorel would manage it quite as well as he could.

"Let us get into the carriage," said the marquis as though to chase away an unwanted idea.

"Monsieur," said Julien, "while they were getting this suit ready for me, I learnt the first page of to-days *Quotidienne* by heart."

The marquis took the paper. Julien recited it without making a single mistake. "Good," said the marquis, who this night felt very diplomatic. "During the time he takes over this our young man will not notice the streets through which we are passing."

They arrived in a big salon that looked melancholy enough and was partly upholstered in green velvet. In the middle of the room a scowling lackey had just placed a big dining-table which he subsequently changed into a writing-table by means of an immense green inkstained tablecloth which had been plundered from some minister.

The master of the house was an enormous man whose name was not pronounced. Julien thought he had the appearance and eloquence of a man who ruminated. At a sign from the marquis, Julien had remained at the lower end of the table. In order to keep himself in countenance, he began to cut quills. He counted out of the corner of his eye seven visitors, but Julien could only see their backs. Two seemed to him to be speaking to M. de la Mole on a footing of equality, the others seemed more or less respectful.

A new person entered without being announced. "This is strange," thought Julien. "People are not announced in this salon. Is this precaution taken in my honour?" Everybody got up to welcome the new arrival. He wore the same extremely distinguished decoration as three of the other persons who were in the salon. They talked fairly low. In endeavouring to form an opinion of the new comer, Julien was reduced to seeing what he could learn from his features and his appearance. He was short and thick-set. He had a high colour and a brilliant eye and an expression that looked like a malignant boar, and nothing else.

Julien's attention was partly distracted by the almost immediate arrival of a very different kind of person. It was a tall very thin man who wore three or four waistcoats. His eye was caressing, his demeanour polite.

"He looks exactly like the old bishop of Besançon," thought Julien. This man evidently belonged to the church, was apparently not more than fifty to fifty-five years of age, and no one could have looked more paternal than he did.

The young bishop of Agde appeared. He looked very astonished when, in making a scrutiny of those present, his gaze fell upon Julien. He had not spoken to him since the ceremony of Bray-le-Haut. His look of surprise embarrassed and irritated Julien. "What!" he said to himself, "will knowing a man always turn out unfortunate for me? I don't feel the least bit intimidated by all those great lords whom I have never seen, but the look of that young bishop freezes me. I must admit that I am a very strange and very unhappy person."

An extremely swarthy little man entered noisily soon afterwards and started talking as soon as he reached the door. He had a yellow complexion and looked a little mad. As soon as this ruthless talker arrived, the others formed themselves into knots with the apparent object of avoiding the bother of listening to him.

As they went away from the mantelpiece they came near the lower end of the table where Julien was placed. His countenance became more and more embarrassed, for whatever efforts he made, he could not avoid hearing, and in spite of all his lack of experience he appreciated all the moment of the things which they were discussing with such complete frankness, and the importance which the high personages whom he apparently had under his observation must attach to their being kept secret.

Julien had already cut twenty quills as slowly as possible; this distraction would shortly be no longer available. He looked in vain at M. de la Mole's eyes for an order; the marquis had forgotten him.

"What I am doing is ridiculous," he said to himself as he cut his quills, "but persons with so mediocre an appearance and who are handling such great interests either for themselves or for others must be extremely liable to take offence. My unfortunate look has a certain questioning and scarcely respectful expression, which will doubtless irritate them. But if I palpably lower my eyes I shall look as if I were picking up every word they said."

His embarrassment was extreme, he was listening to strange things.

LII
THE DISCUSSION

> The republic:—For one man to day who will sacrifice every-
> thing for the public welfare, there are thousands and millions
> who think of nothing except their enjoyments and their van-
> ity. One is requested in Paris by reason of the qualities not of
> one's self but of one's carriage.
> —NAPOLEON, Memorial.

The footman rushed in saying "Monsieur the duke de ——"

"Hold your tongue, you are just a fool," said the duke as he entered. He spoke these words so well, and with so much majesty, that Julien could not help thinking this great person's accomplishments were limited to the science of snubbing a lackey. Julien raised his eyes and immediately lowered them. He had so fully appreciated the significance of the new arrival that he feared that his look might be an indiscretion.

The duke was a man of fifty dressed like a dandy and with a jerky walk. He had a narrow head with a large nose and a face that jutted forward; it would have been difficult to have looked at the same time more insignificant. His arrival was the signal for the opening of the meeting.

Julien was sharply interrupted in his physiognomical observations by de la Mole's voice. "I present to you M. the abbé Sorel," said the Marquis. "He is gifted with an astonishing memory; it is scarcely an hour ago since I spoke to him of the mission by which he might be honoured, and he has learned the first page of the *Quotidienne* by heart in order to give proof of his memory."

"Ah! foreign news of that poor N—" said the master of the house. He took up the paper eagerly and looked at Julien in a manner rendered humorous by its own self-importance. "Speak, monsieur," he said to him.

The silence was profound, all eyes were fixed on Julien. He recited so well that the duke said at the end of twenty lines, "That is enough." The little man who looked like a boar sat down. He was the president, for he had scarcely taken his place before he showed Julien a card-table and signed to him to bring it near him. Julien established himself at it with writing materials. He counted twelve persons seated round the green table cloth.

"M. Sorel," said the Duke, "retire into next room, you will be called."

The master of the house began to look very anxious. "The shutters are not shut," he said to his neighbour in a semi-whisper. "It is no good looking out of the window," he stupidly cried to Julien—"so here I am more or less mixed up in a conspiracy," thought the latter. "Fortunately it is not one of those which lead to the Place-de-Grève. Even though there were danger, I owe this and even more to the marquis, and should be glad to be given the chance of making up for all the sorrow which my madness may one day occasion him."

While thinking of his own madness and his own unhappiness he regarded the place where he was, in such a way as to imprint it upon his memory for ever. He then remembered for the first time that he had never heard the lackey tell the name of the street, and that the marquis had taken a fiacre which he never did in the ordinary way. Julien was left to his own reflections for a long time. He was in a salon upholstered in red velvet with large pieces of gold lace. A large ivory crucifix was on the console-table and a gilt-edged, magnificently bound copy of M. de Maistre's book *The Pope* was on the mantelpiece. Julien opened it so as not to appear to be eavesdropping. From time to time they talked loudly in the next room. At last the door was opened and he was called in.

"Remember, gentlemen," the president was saying "that from this moment we are talking in the presence of the duke of ——. This gentleman," he said, pointing to Julien, "is a young acolyte devoted to our sacred cause who by the aid of his marvellous memory will repeat quite easily our very slightest words."

"It is your turn to speak, Monsieur," he said pointing to the paternal looking personage who wore three or four waistcoats. Julien thought it would have been more natural to have called him the gentleman in the waistcoats. He took some paper and wrote a great deal.

(At this juncture the author would have liked to have put a page of dots. "That," said his publisher, "would be clumsy and in the case of so light a work clumsiness is death."

"Politics," replies the author, "is a stone tied round the neck of literature which submerges it in less than six months. Politics in the midst of imaginative matter is like a pistol shot in the middle of a concert. The noise is racking without being energetic. It does not harmonise with the sound of any instrument. These politics will give mortal offence to one half of the readers and will bore the other half, who will have already read the ideas in question as set out in the morning paper in its own drastic manner."

"If your characters don't talk politics," replied the publisher, "they cease to be Frenchmen of 1830, and your book is no longer a mirror as you claim?")

Julien's record ran to twenty-six pages. Here is a very diluted extract, for it has been necessary to adopt the invariable practice of suppressing those ludicrous passages, whose violence would have seemed either offensive or intolerable (see the *Gazette des Tribunaux*).

The man with the waistcoats and the paternal expression (he was perhaps a bishop) often smiled and then his eyes, which were surrounded with a floating forest of eyebrows, assumed a singular brilliance and an unusually decided expression. This personage whom they made speak first before the duke ("but what duke is it?" thought Julien to himself) with the apparent object of expounding various points of view and fulfilling the functions of an advocate-general, appeared to Julien to fall into the uncertainty and lack of definiteness with which those officials are so often taxed. During the course of the discussion the duke went so far as to reproach him on this score. After several sentences of morality and indulgent philosophy the man in the waistcoats said,

"Noble England, under the guiding hand of a great man, the immortal Pitt, has spent forty milliards of francs in opposing the revolution. If this meeting will allow me to treat so melancholy a subject with some frankness, England fails to realise sufficiently that in dealing with a man like Buonaparte, especially when they have nothing to oppose him with, except a bundle of good intentions there is nothing decisive except personal methods."

"Ah! praising assassination again!" said the master of the house anxiously.

"Spare us your sentimental sermons," cried the president angrily. His boarlike eye shone with a savage brilliance. "Go on," he said to the man with the waistcoats. The cheeks and the forehead of the president became purple.

"Noble England," replied the advocate-general, "is crushed to-day: for each Englishman before paying for his own bread is obliged to pay the interest on forty milliards of francs which were used against the Jacobins. She has no more Pitt."

"She has the Duke of Wellington," said a military personage looking very important.

"Please, gentlemen, silence," exclaimed the president. "If we are still going to dispute, there was no point in having M. Sorel in."

"We know that monsieur has many ideas," said the duke irritably, looking at the interrupter who was an old Napoleonic general. Julien saw that these words contained some personal and very offensive allusion. Everybody smiled, the turncoat general appeared beside himself with rage.

"There is no longer a Pitt, gentlemen," went on the speaker with all the despondency of a man who has given up all hope of bringing his listeners to reason. "If there were a new Pitt in England, you would not dupe a nation twice over by the same means."

"That's why a victorious general, a Buonaparte, will be henceforward impossible in France," exclaimed the military interrupter.

On this occasion neither the president nor the duke ventured to get angry, though Julien thought he read in their eyes that they would very much like to have done so. They lowered their eyes, and the duke contented himself with sighing in quite an audible manner. But the speaker was put upon his mettle.

"My audience is eager for me to finish," he said vigorously, completely discarding that smiling politeness and that balanced diction that Julien thought had expressed his character so well. "It is eager for me to finish, it is not grateful to me for the efforts I am making to offend nobody's ears, however long they may be. Well, gentlemen, I will be brief.

"I will tell you in quite common words: England has not got a sou with which to help the good cause. If Pitt himself were to come back he would never succeed with all his genius in duping the small English landowners, for they know that the short Waterloo campaign alone cost them a milliard of francs. As you like clear phrases," continued the speaker, becoming more and more animated, "I will say this to you: Help yourselves, for England has not got a guinea left to help you with, and when England does not pay, Austria, Russia and Prussia—who will only have courage but have no money—cannot launch more than one or two campaigns against France.

"One may hope that the young soldiers who will be recruited by the Jacobins will be beaten in the first campaign, and possibly in the second; but, even though I seem a revolutionary in your prejudiced eyes, in the third campaign—in the third campaign I say—you will have the soldiers of 1794 who were no longer the soldiers enlisted in 1792."

At this point interruption broke out simultaneously from three or four quarters.

"Monsieur," said the president to Julien, "Go and make a précis in the next room of the beginning of the report which you have written out."

Julien went out to his great regret. The speaker was just dealing with the question of probabilities which formed the usual subject for his meditations. "They are frightened of my making fun of them," he thought. When he was called back, M. de la Mole was saying with a seriousness which seemed quite humorous to Julien who knew him so well,

"Yes, gentlemen, one finds the phrase, 'is it god, table or tub?' especially applicable to this unhappy people. '*It is god*' exclaims the writer of fables. It is to you, gentlemen, that this noble and profound phrase seems to apply. Act on your own initiative, and noble France will appear again, almost such as our ancestors made her, and as our own eyes have seen her before the death of Louis XVI.

"England execrates disgraceful Jacobinism as much as we do, or at any rate her noble lords do. Without English gold, Austria and Prussia would only be able to give battle two or three times. Would that be sufficient to ensure a successful occupation like the one which M. de Richelieu so foolishly failed to exploit in 1817? I do not think so."

At this point there was an interruption which was stifled by the hushes of the whole room. It came again from the old Imperial general who wanted the blue ribbon and wished to figure among the authors of the secret note.

"I do not think so," replied M. de la Mole, after the uproar had subsided. He laid stress on the "I" with an insolence which charmed Julien.

"That's a pretty piece of acting," he said to himself, as he made his pen almost keep pace with the marquis' words.

M. de la Mole annihilated the twenty campaigns of the turncoat with a well turned phrase.

"It is not only on foreign powers," continued the marquis in a more even tone, "on whom we shall be able to rely for a new military occupation. All those young men who write inflammatory articles in the *Globe* will provide you with three or four thousand young captains among whom you may find men with the genius, but not the good intentions of a Kléber, a Hoche, a Jourdan, a Pichegru."

"We did not know how to glorify him," said the president. "He should have been immortalized."

"Finally, it is necessary for France to have two parties," went on M. de la Mole; "but two parties not merely in name, but with clear-cut lines of cleavage. Let us realise what has got to be crushed. On the one hand the journalists and the electors, in a word, public opinion; youth and all that admire it. While it is stupefying itself with the noise of its own vain words, we have certain advantages of administrating the expenditure of the budget."

At this point there was another interruption.

"As for you, monsieur," said M. de la Mole to the interrupter, with an admirable haughtiness and ease of manner, "you do not spend, if the words chokes you, but you devour the forty thousand francs put down to you in the State budget, and the eighty thousand which you receive from the civil list."

"Well, monsieur, since you force me to it, I will be bold enough to take you for an example. Like your noble ancestors, who followed Saint Louis to the crusade, you ought in return for those hundred and twenty thousand francs to show us at any rate a regiment; a company, why, what am I saying? say half a company, even if it only had fifty men, ready to fight and devoted to the good cause to the point of risking their lives in its service. You have nothing but lackeys, who in the event of a rebellion would frighten you yourselves."

"Throne, Church, Nobility are liable to perish to-morrow, gentlemen, so long as you refrain from creating in each department a force of five hundred devoted men, devoted I mean, not only with all the French courage, but with all the Spanish constancy.

"Half of this force ought to be composed of our children, our nephews, of real gentlemen, in fact. Each of them will have beside him not a little talkative bourgeois ready to hoist the tricolor cockade, if 1815 turns up again, but a good, frank and simple peasant like Cathelineau. Our gentleman will have educated him, it will be his own foster brother if it is possible. Let each of us sacrifice the fifth of his income in order to form this little devoted force of five hundred men in each department. Then you will be able to reckon on a foreign occupation. The foreign soldier will never penetrate even as far as Dijon if he is not certain of finding five hundred friendly soldiers in each department.

"The foreign kings will only listen to you when you are in a position to announce to them that you have twenty thousand gentlemen ready to take up arms in order to open to them the gates of France. The service is troublesome, you say. Gentlemen, it is the only way of saving our lives. There is war to the death between the liberty of the press and our existence as gentlemen. Become manufacturers, become peasants, or take up your guns. Be timid if you like, but do not be stupid. Open your eyes.

"'*Form your battalions*,' I would say to you in the words of the Jacobin songs. Some noble Gustavus Adolphus will then be found who, touched by the imminent peril of the monarchical principle, will make a dash three hundred leagues from his own country, and will do for you what Gustavus did for the Protestant princes. Do you want to go on talking without acting? In fifty years' time there will be only presidents or republics in Europe and not one king, and with those three letters R. O. I. you will see the last of the priests and the gentlemen. I can see nothing but candidates paying court to squalid majorities.

"It is no use your saying that at the present time France has not a single accredited general who is universally known and loved, that the army is only known and organised in the interests of the throne and the church, and that it has been deprived of all its old troopers, while each of the Prussian and Austrian regiments count fifty non-commissioned officers who have seen fire.

"Two hundred thousand young men of the middle classes are spoiling for war—"

"A truce to disagreeable truths," said a grave personage in a pompous tone. He was apparently a very high ecclesiastical dignitary, for M. de la Mole smiled pleasantly, instead of getting angry, a circumstance which greatly impressed Julien.

"A truce to unpleasant truths, let us resume, gentlemen. The man who needs to have a gangrened leg cut off would be ill advised to say to his surgeon, 'this disease is very healthy.' If I may use the metaphor, gentlemen, the noble duke of —— is our surgeon."

"So the great words have at last been uttered," thought Julien. "It is towards the —— that I shall gallop to-night."

LIII
THE CLERGY, THE FORESTS, LIBERTY

> The first law of every being, is to preserve itself and live. You sow hemlock, and expect to see ears of corn ripen.—
> *Machiavelli.*

The great personage continued. One could see that he knew his subject. He proceeded to expound the following great truths with a soft and tempered eloquence with which Julien was inordinately delighted:—

"1. England has not a guinea to help us with; economy and Hume are the fashion there. Even the saints will not give us any money, and M. Brougham will make fun of us.

"2. The impossibility of getting the kings of Europe to embark on more than two campaigns without English gold; two campaigns will not be enough to dispose of the middle classes.

"3. The necessity of forming an armed party in France. Without this, the monarchical principle in Europe will not risk even two campaigns.

"The fourth point which I venture to suggest to you, as self-evident, is this:

"The impossibility of forming an armed party in France without the clergy. I am bold enough to tell you this because I will prove it to you, gentlemen. You must make every sacrifice for the clergy.

"Firstly, because as it is occupied with its mission by day and by night, and guided by highly capable men established far from these storms at three hundred leagues from your frontiers——"

"Ah, Rome, Rome!" exclaimed the master of the house.

"Yes, monsieur, Rome," replied the Cardinal haughtily. "Whatever more or less ingenious jokes may have been the fashion when you were young, I have no hesitation in saying that in 1830 it is only the clergy, under the guidance of Rome, who has the ear of the lower classes.

"Fifty thousand priests repeat the same words on the day appointed by their chiefs, and the people—who after all provide soldiers—will be more touched by the voices of its priests than by all the versifying in the whole world." (This personality provoked some murmurs.)

"The clergy has a genius superior to yours," went on the cardinal raising his voice. "All the progress that has been made towards this essential point of having an armed party in France has been made by us." At this juncture facts were introduced. "Who used eighty thousand rifles in Vendée?" etc., etc.

"So long as the clergy is without its forests it is helpless. At the first war the minister of finance will write to his agents that there is no money to be had except for the curé. At bottom France does not believe, and she loves war. Whoever gives her war will be doubly popular, for making war is, to use a vulgar phrase, the same as starving the Jesuits; making war means delivering those monsters of pride—the men of France—from the menace of foreign intervention."

The cardinal had a favourable hearing. "M. de Nerval," he said, "will have to leave the ministry, his name irritates and to no purpose."

At these words everybody got up and talked at the same time. "I will be sent away again," thought Julien, but the sapient president himself had forgotten both the presence and existence of Julien.

All eyes were turned upon a man whom Julien recognised. It was M. de Nerval, the prime minister, whom he had seen at M. the duc de Retz's ball.

The disorder was at its height, as the papers say when they talk of the Chamber. At the end of a long quarter of an hour a little quiet was established.

Then M. de Nerval got up and said in an apostolic tone and a singular voice:

"I will not go so far as to say that I do not set great store on being a minister.

"It has been demonstrated to me, gentlemen, that my name will double the forces of the Jacobins by making many moderates divide against us. I should therefore be willing to retire; but the ways of the Lord are only visible to a small number; but," he added, looking fixedly at the cardinal, "I have a mission. Heaven has said: 'You will either loose your head on the scaffold or you will re-establish the monarchy of France and reduce the Chambers to the condition of the parliament of Louis XV.,' and that, gentlemen, I shall do."

He finished his speech, sat down, and there was a long silence.

"What a good actor," thought Julien. He made his usual mistake of ascribing too much intelligence to the people. Excited by the debates of so lively an evening, and above all by the sincerity of the discussion, M. de Nerval did at this moment believe in his mission. This man had great courage, but at the same time no sense.

During the silence that followed the impressive words, "I shall do it," midnight struck. Julien thought that the striking of the clock had in it a certain element of funereal majesty. He felt moved.

The discussion was soon resumed with increasing energy, and above all with an incredible naivety. "These people will have me poisoned," thought Julien at times. "How can they say such things before a plebian."

They were still talking when two o'clock struck. The master of the house had been sleeping for some time. M. de la Mole was obliged to ring for new candles. M. de Nerval, the minister, had left at the quarter to two, but not without having repeatedly studied Julien's face in a mirror which was at the minister's side. His departure had seemed to put everybody at their ease.

While they were bringing new candles, the man in the waistcoats, whispered to his neighbour: "God knows what that man will say to the king. He may throw ridicule upon us and spoil our future."

"One must own that he must possess an unusual self-assurance, not to say impudence, to put in an appearance here There were signs of it before he became a minister; but a portfolio changes everything and swamps all a man's interests; he must have felt its effect."

The minister had scarcely left before the general of Buonaparte closed his eyes. He now talked of his health and his wounds, consulted his watch, and went away.

"I will wager," said the man in the waistcoats, "that the general is running after the minister; he will apologise for having been here and pretend that he is our leader."

"Let us now deliberate, gentlemen," said the president, after the sleepy servants had finished bringing and lighting new candles. "Let us leave off trying to persuade each other. Let us think of the contents of the note which will be read by our friends outside in forty-eight hours from now. We have heard ministers spoken of. Now that M. de Nerval has left us, we are at liberty to say 'what we do care for ministers.'"

The cardinal gave a subtle smile of approval.

"Nothing is easier it seems to me than summing up our position," said the young bishop of Agde, with the restrained concentrated fire of the most exalted fanaticism. He had kept silent up to this time; his eye, which Julien had noticed as being soft and calm at the beginning, had become fiery during the first hour of the discussion. His soul was now bubbling over like lava from Vesuvius.

"England only made one mistake from 1806 to 1814," he said, "and that was in not taking direct and personal measures against Napoleon. As soon as that man had made dukes and chamberlains, as soon as he had re-established the throne, the mission that God had entrusted to him was finished. The only thing to do with him was to sacrifice him.

The scriptures teach us in more than one place how to make an end of tyrants" (at this point there were several Latin quotations).

"To-day, gentlemen, it is not a man who has to be sacrificed, it is Paris. What is the use of arming your five hundred men in each department, a hazardous and interminable enterprise? What is the good of involving France in a matter which is personal to Paris? Paris alone has done the evil, with its journals and it salons. Let the new Babylon perish.

"We must bring to an end the conflict between the church and Paris. Such a catastrophe would even be in the worldly interests of the throne. Why did not Paris dare to whisper a word under Buonaparte? Ask the cannon of Saint-Roch?"

Julien did not leave with M. de la Mole before three o'clock in the morning.

The marquis seemed tired and ashamed. For the first time in his life in conversation with Julien, his tone was plaintive. He asked him for his word never to reveal the excesses of zeal, that was his expression, of which chance had just made him a witness. "Only mention it to our foreign friend, if he seriously insists on knowing what our young madmen are like. What does it matter to them if a state is overthrown, they will become cardinals and will take refuge in Rome. As for us, we shall be massacred by the peasants in our châteaus."

The secret note into which the marquis condensed Julien's full report of twenty-six pages was not ready before a quarter to five.

"I am dead tired," said the marquis, "as is quite obvious from the lack of clearness at the end of this note; I am more dissatisfied with it than with anything I ever did in my whole life. Look here, my friend," he added, "go and rest for some hours, and as I am frightened you might be kidnapped, I shall lock you up in your room."

The marquis took Julien on the following day to a lonely château at a good distance from Paris. There were strange guests there whom Julien thought were priests. He was given a passport which was made out in a fictitious name, but indicated the real destination of his journey, which he had always pretended not to know. He got into a carriage alone.

The marquis had no anxiety on the score of his memory. Julien had recited the secret note to him several times but he was very apprehensive of his being intercepted.

"Above all, mind you look like a coxcomb who is simply travelling to kill time," he said affectionately to him when he was leaving the salon. "Perhaps there was more than one treacherous brother in this evening's meeting."

The journey was quick and very melancholy. Julien had scarcely got out of the marquis's sight before he forgot his secret note and his mission, and only thought about Mathilde's disdain.

At a village some leagues beyond Metz, the postmaster came and told him that there were no horses. It was ten o'clock in the evening. Julien was very annoyed and asked for supper. He walked in front of the door and gradually without being noticed passed into the stable-yard. He did not see any horses there.

"That man looked strange though," thought Julien to himself. "He was scrutinizing me with his brutal eyes."

As one sees he was beginning to be slightly sceptical of all he heard. He thought of escaping after supper, and in order to learn at any rate something about the surrounding country, he left his room to go and warm himself at the kitchen fire. He was overjoyed to find there the celebrated singer, signor Geronimo.

The Neopolitan was ensconced in an armchair which he had had brought near the fire. He was groaning aloud, and was speaking more to himself than to the twenty dumbfounded German peasants who surrounded him.

"Those people will be my ruin," he cried to Julien, "I have promised to sing to-morrow at Mayence. Seven sovereign princes have gone there to hear me. Let us go and take the air," he added, meaningly.

When he had gone a hundred yards down the road, and it was impossible to be overheard, he said to Julien:

"Do you know the real truth, the postmaster is a scoundrel. When I went out for a walk I gave twenty sous to a little ragamuffin who told me everything. There are twelve horses in the stable at the other end of the village. They want to stop some courier."

"Really," said Julien innocently.

Discovering the fraud was not enough; the thing was to get away, but Geronimo and his friends could not succeed in doing this.

"Let us wait for daybreak," said the singer at last, "they are mistrustful of us. It is perhaps you or me whom they suspect. We will order a good breakfast to-morrow morning, we will go for a walk while they are getting it ready, we will then escape, we will hire horses, and gain the next station."

"And how about your luggage?" said Julien, who thought perhaps Geronimo himself might have been sent to intercept him. They had to have supper and go to bed. Julien was still in his first sleep when he was woken up with a start by the voices of two persons who were speaking in his room with utmost freedom.

He recognised the postmaster armed with a dark lantern. The light was turned on the carriage-seat which Julien had had taken up into his room. Beside the postmaster was a man who was calmly searching the open seat. Julien could see nothing except the sleeves of his coat which were black and very tight.

"It's a cassock," he said to himself and he softly seized the little pistol which he had placed under his pillow.

"Don't be frightened of his waking up, curé," said the postmaster, "the wine that has been served him was the stuff prepared by yourself."

"I can't find any trace of papers," answered the curé. "A lot of linen and essences, pommades, and vanities. It's a young man of the world on pleasure bent. The other one who effects an Italian accent is more likely to be the emissary."

The men approached Julien to search the pockets of his travelling coat. He felt very tempted to kill them for thieves. Nothing could be safer in its consequences. He was very desirous of doing so.... "I should only be a fool," he said to himself, "I should compromise my mission." "He is not a diplomatist," said the priest after searching his coat. He went away and did well to do so.

"It will be a bad business for him," Julien was saying to himself, "if he touches me in my bed. He may have quite well come to stab me, and I won't put up with that."

The curé turned his head, Julien half opened his eyes. He was inordinately astonished, he was the abbé Castanède. As a matter of fact, although these two persons had made a point of talking in a fairly low voice, he had thought from the first that he recognised one of the voices. Julien was seized with an inordinate desire to purge the earth of one of its most cowardly villains; "But my mission," he said to himself.

The curé and his acolyte went out. A quarter of an hour afterwards Julien pretended to have just woken up. He called out and woke up the whole house.

"I am poisoned," he exclaimed, "I am suffering horribly!" He wanted an excuse to go to Geronimo's help. He found him half suffocated by the laudanum that had been contained in the wine.

Julien had been apprehensive of some trick of this character and had supped on some chocolate which he had brought from Paris. He could not wake Geronimo up sufficiently to induce him to leave.

"If they were to give me the whole kingdom of Naples," said the singer, "I would not now give up the pleasure of sleeping."

"But the seven sovereign princes?"

"Let them wait."

Julien left alone, and arrived at the house of the great personage without other incident. He wasted a whole morning in vainly soliciting an audience. Fortunately about four o'clock the duke wanted to take the air. Julien saw him go out on foot and he did not hesitate to ask him for alms. When at two yards' distance from the great personage he pulled out the Marquis de la Mole's watch and exhibited it ostentatiously. *"Follow me at a distance,"* said the man without looking at him.

At a quarter of a league's distance the duke suddenly entered a little *coffee-house.* It was in a room of this low class inn that Julien had the honour of reciting his four pages to the duke. When he had finished he was told to "*start again and go more slowly.*"

The prince took notes. "Reach the next posting station on foot. Leave your luggage and your carriage here. Get to Strasbourg as best you can and at half-past twelve on the twenty-second of the month (it was at present the tenth) come to this same coffee-house. Do not leave for half-an-hour. Silence!"

These were the only words which Julien heard. They sufficed to inspire him with the highest admiration. "That is the way," he thought, "that real business is done; what would this great statesman say if he were to listen to the impassioned ranters heard three days ago?"

Julien took two days to reach Strasbourg. He thought he would have nothing to do there. He made a great detour. "If that devil of an abbé Castanède has recognised me he is not the kind of man to loose track of me easily.... And how he would revel in making a fool of me, and causing my mission to fail."

Fortunately the abbé Castanède, who was chief of the congregational police on all the northern frontier had not recognised him. And the Strasbourg Jesuits, although very zealous, never gave a thought to observing Julien, who with his cross and his blue tail-coat looked like a young military man, very much engrossed in his own personal appearance.

LIV
STRASBOURG

Fascination! Love gives thee all his love, energy and all his power of suffering unhappiness. It is only his enchanting pleasures, his sweet delights, which are outside thy sphere. When I saw her sleep I was made to say "With all her angelic beauty and her sweet weaknesses she is absolutely mine! There she is, quite in my power, such as Heaven made her in its pity in order to ravish a man's heart."—*Ode of Schiller.*

Julien was compelled to spend eight days in Strasbourg and tried to distract himself by thoughts of military glory and patriotic devotion. Was he in love then? he could not tell, he only felt in his tortured soul that Mathilde was the absolute mistress both of his happiness and of his imagination. He needed all the energy of his character to keep himself from sinking into despair. It was out of his power to think of anything unconnected with mademoiselle de la Mole. His ambition and his simple personal successes had formerly distracted him from the sentiments which madame de Rênal had inspired. Mathilde was all-absorbing; she loomed large over his whole future.

Julien saw failure in every phase of that future. This same individual whom we remember to have been so presumptuous and haughty at Verrières, had fallen into an excess of grotesque modesty.

Three days ago he would only have been too pleased to have killed the abbé Castanède, and now, at Strasbourg, if a child had picked a quarrel with him he would have thought the child was in the right. In thinking again about the adversaries and enemies whom he had met in his life he always thought that he, Julien, had been in the wrong. The fact was that the same powerful imagination which had formerly been continuously employed in painting a successful future in the most brilliant colours had now been transformed into his implacable enemy.

The absolute solicitude of a traveller's life increased the ascendancy of this sinister imagination. What a boon a friend would have been! But Julien said to himself, "Is there a single heart which beats with affection for me? And even if I did have a friend, would not honour enjoin me to eternal silence?"

He was riding gloomily in the outskirts of Kehl; it is a market town on the banks of the Rhine and immortalised by Desaix and Gouvion Saint-Cyr. A German peasant showed him the little brooks, roads and islands of the Rhine, which have acquired a name through the courage of these great generals. Julien was guiding his horse with his left hand, while he held unfolded in his right the superb map which adorns the *Memoirs of the Marshal Saint Cyr*. A merry exclamation made him lift his head.

It was the Prince Korasoff, that London friend of his, who had initiated him some months before into the elementary rules of high fatuity. Faithful to his great art, Korasoff, who had just arrived at Strasbourg, had been one hour in Kehl and had never read a single line in his whole life about the siege of 1796, began to explain it all to Julien. The German peasant looked at him in astonishment; for he knew enough French to appreciate the enormous blunders which the prince was making. Julien was a thousand leagues away from the peasant's thoughts. He was looking in astonishment at the handsome young man and admiring his grace in sitting a horse.

"What a lucky temperament," he said to himself, "and how his trousers suit him and how elegantly his hair is cut! Alas, if I had been like him, it might have been that she would not have come to dislike me after loving me for three days."

When the prince had finished his siege of Kehl, he said to Julien, "You look like a Trappist, you are carrying to excess that principle of gravity which I enjoined upon you in London. A melancholy manner cannot be good form. What is wanted is an air of boredom. If you are melancholy, it is because you lack something, because you have failed in something."

"That means showing one's own inferiority; if, on the other hand you are bored, it is only what has made an unsuccessful attempt to please you, which is inferior. So realise, my dear friend, the enormity of your mistake."

Julien tossed a crown to the gaping peasant who was listening to them.

"Good," said the prince, "that shows grace and a noble disdain, very good!" And he put his horse to the gallop. Full of a stupid admiration, Julien followed him.

"Ah! if I have been like that, she would not have preferred Croisenois to me!" The more his reason was offended by the grotesque affectations of the prince the more he despised himself for not having them. It was impossible for self-disgust to be carried further.

The prince still finding him distinctly melancholy, said to him as they re-entered Strasbourg, "Come, my dear fellow, have you lost all your money, or perhaps you are in love with some little actress.

"The Russians copy French manners, but always at an interval of fifty years. They have now reached the age of Louis XV."

These jests about love brought the tears to Julien's eyes. "Why should I not consult this charming man," he suddenly said to himself.

"Well, yes, my dear friend," he said to the prince, "you see in me a man who is very much in love and jilted into the bargain. A charming woman who lives in a neighbouring town has left me stranded here after three passionate days, and the change kills me."

Using fictitious names, he described to the prince Mathilde's conduct and character.

"You need not finish," said Korasoff. "In order to give you confidence in your doctor, I will finish the story you have confided to me. This young woman's husband enjoys an enormous income, or even more probably, she belongs herself to the high nobility of the district. She must be proud about something."

Julien nodded his head, he had no longer the courage to speak. "Very good," said the prince, "here are three fairly bitter pills that you will take without delay.

"1. See madame ——. What is her name, any way?"

"Madame de Dubois."

"What a name!" said the prince bursting into laughter. "But forgive me, you find it sublime. Your tactics must be to see Madame de Dubois every day; above all do not appear to be cold and piqued. Remember the great principle of your century: be the opposite of what is expected. Be exactly as you were the week before you were honoured by her favours."

"Ah! I was calm enough then," exclaimed Julien in despair, "I thought I was taking pity on her...."

"The moth is burning itself at the candle," continued the prince using a metaphor as old as the world.

"1. You will see her every day.

"2. You will pay court to a woman in her own set, but without manifesting a passion, do you understand? I do not disguise from you that your role is difficult; you are playing a part, and if she realises you are playing it you are lost."

"She has so much intelligence and I have so little, I shall be lost," said Julien sadly.

"No, you are only more in love than I thought. Madame de Dubois is preoccupied with herself as are all women who have been favoured by heaven either with too much pedigree or too much money. She contemplates herself instead of contemplating you, consequently she does not know you. During the two or three fits of love into which she managed to work herself for your especial benefit, she saw in you the hero of her dreams, and not the man you really are.

"But, deuce take it, this is elementary, my dear Sorel, are you an absolute novice?

"Oddslife! Let us go into this shop. Look at that charming black cravat, one would say it was made by John Anderson of Burlington Street. Be kind enough to take it and throw far away that awful black cord which you are wearing round your neck."

"And now," continued the prince as they came out of the shop of the first hosier of Strasbourg, "what is the society in which madame de Dubois lives? Great God, what a name, don't be angry, my dear Sorel, I can't help it.... Now, whom are you going to pay court to?"

"To an absolute prude, the daughter of an immensely rich stocking-merchant. She has the finest eyes in the world and they please me infinitely; she doubtless holds the highest place in the society of the district, but in the midst of all her greatness she blushes and becomes positively confused if anyone starts talking about trade or shops. And, unfortunately, her father was one of the best known merchants in Strasbourg."

"So," said the prince with a laugh, "you are sure that when one talks about trade your fair lady thinks about herself and not about you. This silly weakness is divine and extremely useful, it will prevent you from yielding to a single moment's folly when near her sparkling eyes. Success is assured."

Julien was thinking of madame the maréchale de Fervaques who often came to the Hôtel de la Mole. She was a beautiful foreigner who had married the maréchal a year before his death. The one object of her whole life seemed to be to make people forget that she was the daughter of a manufacturer. In order to cut some figure in Paris she had placed herself at the head of the party of piety.

Julien sincerely admired the prince; what would he not have given to have possessed his affectations! The conversation between the two friends was interminable. Korasoff was delighted: No Frenchman had ever listened to him for so long. "So I have succeeded at last," said the prince to himself complacently, "in getting a proper hearing and that too through giving lessons to my master."

"So we are quite agreed," he repeated to Julien for the tenth time. "When you talk to the young beauty, I mean the daughter of the Strasbourg stocking merchant in the presence of madame de Dubois, not a trace of passion. But on the other hand be ardently passionate when you write. Reading a well-written love-letter is a prude's supremest pleasure. It is a moment of relaxation. She leaves off posing and dares to listen to her own heart; consequently two letters a day."

"Never, never," said Julien despondently, "I would rather be ground in a mortar than make up three phrases. I am a corpse, my dear fellow, hope nothing from me. Let me die by the road side."

"And who is talking about making up phrases? I have got six volumes of copied-out love-letters in my bag. I have letters to suit every variation of feminine character, including the most highly virtuous. Did not Kalisky pay court at Richmond-on-the-Thames at three leagues from London, you know, to the prettiest Quakeress in the whole of England?"

Julien was less unhappy when he left his friend at two o'clock in the morning.

The prince summoned a copyist on the following day, and two days afterwards Julien was the possessor of fifty-three carefully numbered love-letters intended for the most sublime and the most melancholy virtue.

"The reason why there is not fifty-four," said the prince "is because Kalisky allowed himself to be dismissed. But what does it matter to you, if you are badly treated by the stocking-merchant's daughter since you only wish to produce an impression upon madame de Dubois' heart."

They went out riding every day, the prince was mad on Julien. Not knowing how else to manifest his sudden friendship, he finished up by offering him the hand of one of his cousins, a rich Moscow heiress; "and once married," he added, "my influence and that cross of yours will get you made a Colonel within two years."

"But that cross was not given me by Napoleon, far from it."

"What does it matter?" said the prince, "didn't he invent it. It is still the first in Europe by a long way."

Julien was on the point of accepting; but his duty called him back to the great personage. When he left Korasoff he promised to write. He received the answer to the secret note which he had brought, and posted towards Paris; but he had scarcely been alone for two successive days before leaving France, and Mathilde seemed a worse punishment than death. "I will not marry the millions Korasoff offers me," he said to himself, "and I will follow his advice.

"After all the art of seduction is his speciality. He has thought about nothing else except that alone for more than fifteen years, for he is now thirty.

"One can't say that he lacks intelligence; he is subtle and cunning; enthusiasm and poetry are impossible in such a character. He is an attorney: an additional reason for his not making a mistake.

"I must do it, I will pay court to madame de Fervaques.

"It is very likely she will bore me a little, but I will look at her beautiful eyes which are so like those other eyes which have loved me more than anyone in the world.

"She is a foreigner; she is a new character to observe.

"I feel mad, and as though I were going to the devil. I must follow the advice of a friend and not trust myself."

LV
THE MINISTRY OF VIRTUE

> But if I take this pleasure with so much prudence and cir-
> cumspection I shall no longer find it a pleasure.—*Lope de
> Vega.*

As soon as our hero had returned to Paris and had come out of the study of the marquis de La Mole, who seemed very displeased with the despatches that were given him, he rushed off for the comte Altamira. This noble foreigner combined with the advantage of having once been condemned to death a very grave demeanour together with the good fortune of a devout temperament; these two qualities, and more than anything, the comte's high birth, made an especial appeal to madame de Fervaques who saw a lot of him.

Julien solemnly confessed to him that he was very much in love with her.

"Her virtue is the purest and the highest," answered Altamira, "only it is a little Jesuitical and dogmatic.

"There are days when, though I understand each of the expressions which she makes use of, I never understand the whole sentence. She often makes me think that I do not know French as well as I am said to. But your acquaintance with her will get you talked about; it will give you weight in the world. But let us go to Bustos," said Count Altamira who had a methodical turn of mind; "he once paid court to madame la maréchale."

Don Diego Bustos had the matter explained to him at length, while he said nothing, like a barrister in his chambers. He had a big monk-like face with black moustaches and an inimitable gravity; he was, however, a good carbonaro.

"I understand," he said to Julien at last. "Has the maréchale de Fervaques had lovers, or has she not? Have you consequently any hope of success? That is the question. I don't mind telling you, for my own part, that I have failed. Now that I am no more piqued I reason it out to myself in this way; she is often bad tempered, and as I will tell you in a minute, she is quite vindictive.

"I fail to detect in her that bilious temperament which is the sign of genius, and shows as it were a veneer of passion over all its actions. On the contrary, she owes her rare beauty and her fresh complexion to the phlegmatic, tranquil character of the Dutch."

Julien began to lose patience with the phlegmatic slowness of the imperturbable Spaniard; he could not help giving vent to some monosyllables from time to time.

"Will you listen to me?" Don Diego Bustos gravely said to him.

"Forgive the *furia franchese*; I am all ears," said Julien.

"The maréchale de Fervaques then is a great hater; she persecutes ruthlessly people she has never seen—advocates, poor devils of men of letters who have composed songs like Collé, you know?

"J'ai la marotte
D'aimer Marote, etc."

And Julien had to put up with the whole quotation.

The Spaniard was very pleased to get a chance of singing in French.

That divine song was never listened to more impatiently. When it was finished Don Diego said—"The maréchale procured the dismissal of the author of the song:

"Un jour l'amour au cabaret."

Julien shuddered lest he should want to sing it. He contented himself with analysing it. As a matter of fact, it was blasphemous and somewhat indecent.

"When the maréchale become enraged against that song," said Don Diego, "I remarked to her that a woman of her rank ought not to read all the stupid things that are published. Whatever progress piety and gravity may make France will always have a cabaret literature.

"'Be careful,' I said to madame de Fervaques when she had succeeded in depriving the author, a poor devil on half-pay, of a place worth eighteen hundred francs a year, 'you have attacked this rhymster with your own arms, he may answer you with his rhymes; he will make a song about virtue. The gilded salons will be on your side; but people who like to laugh will repeat his epigrams.' Do you know, monsieur, what the maréchale answered? 'Let all Paris come and see me walking to my martyrdom for the sake of the Lord. It will be a new spectacle for France. The people will learn to respect the quality. It will be the finest day of my life.' Her eyes never looked finer."

"And she has superb ones," exclaimed Julien.

"I see that you are in love. Further," went on Don Diego Bustos gravely, "she has not the bilious constitution which causes vindictiveness. If, however, she likes to do harm, it is because she is unhappy, I suspect some secret misfortune. May it not be quite well a case of prude tired of her rôle?"

The Spaniard looked at him in silence for a good minute.

"That's the whole point," he added gravely, "and that's what may give you ground for some hope. I have often reflected about it during the two years that I was her very humble servant. All your future, my amorous sir, depends on this great problem. Is she a prude tired of her rôle and only malicious because she is unhappy?"

"Or," said Altamira emerging at last from his deep silence, "can it be as I have said twenty times before, simply a case of French vanity; the memory of her father, the celebrated cloth merchant, constitutes the unhappiness of this frigid melancholy nature. The only happiness she could find would be to live in Toledo and to be tortured by a confessor who would show her hell wide open every day."

"Altamira informs me you are one of us," said Don Diego, whose demeanour was growing graver and graver to Julien as he went out. "You will help us one day in re-winning our liberty, so I would like to help you in this little amusement. It is right that you should know the maréchale's style; here are four letters in her hand-writing."

"I will copy them out," exclaimed Julien, "and bring them back to you."

"And you will never let anyone know a word of what we have been saying."

"Never, on my honour," cried Julien.

"Well, God help you," added the Spaniard, and he silently escorted Altamira and Julien as far as the staircase.

This somewhat amused our hero; he was on the point of smiling. "So we have the devout Altamira," he said to himself, "aiding me in an adulterous enterprise."

During Don Diego's solemn conversation Julien had been attentive to the hours struck by the clock of the Hôtel d'Aligre.

The dinner hour was drawing near, he was going to see Mathilde again. He went in and dressed with much care.

"Mistake No. 1," he said to himself as he descended the staircase: "I must follow the prince's instructions to the letter."

He went up to his room again and put on a travelling suit which was as simple as it could be. "All I have to do now," he thought, "is to keep control of my expression." It was only half-past five and they dined at six. He thought of going down to the salon which he found deserted. He was moved to the point of tears at the sight of the blue sofa. "I must make an end of this foolish sensitiveness," he said angrily, "it will betray me." He took up a paper in order to keep himself in countenance and passed three or four times from the salon into the garden.

It was only when he was well concealed by a large oak and was trembling all over, that he ventured to raise his eyes at mademoiselle de la Mole's window. It was hermetically sealed; he was on the point of fainting and remained for a long time leaning against the oak; then with a staggering step he went to have another look at the gardener's ladder.

The chain which he had once forced asunder—in, alas, such different circumstances—had not yet been repaired. Carried away by a moment of madness, Julien pressed it to his lips.

After having wandered about for a long time between the salon and the garden, Julien felt horribly tired; he was now feeling acutely the effects of a first success. My eyes will be expressionless and will not betray me! The guests gradually arrived in the salon; the door never opened without instilling anxiety into Julien's heart.

They sat down at table. Mademoiselle de la Mole, always faithful to her habit of keeping people waiting, eventually appeared. She blushed a great deal on seeing Julien, she had not been told of his arrival. In accordance with Prince Korasoff's recommendation, Julien looked at his hands. They were trembling. Troubled though he was beyond words by this discovery, he was sufficiently happy to look merely tired.

M. de la Mole sang his praises. The marquise spoke to him a minute afterwards and complimented him on his tired appearance. Julien said to himself at every minute, "I ought not to look too much at mademoiselle de la Mole, I ought not to avoid looking at her too much either. I must appear as I was eight days before my unhappiness——" He had occasion to be satisfied with his success and remained in the salon. Paying attention for the first time to the mistress of the house, he made every effort to make the visitors speak and to keep the conversation alive.

His politeness was rewarded; madame la maréchale de Fervaques was announced about eight o'clock. Julien retired and shortly afterwards appeared dressed with the greatest care. Madame de la Mole was infinitely grateful to him for this mark of respect and made a point of manifesting her satisfaction by telling madame de Fervaques about his journey. Julien established himself near the maréchale in such a position that Mathilde could not notice his eyes. In this position he lavished in accordance with all the rules in the art of love, the most abject admiration on madame de Fervaques. The first of the 53 letters with which Prince Korasoff had presented him commenced with a tirade on this sentiment.

The maréchale announced that she was going to the Opera-Bouffe. Julien rushed there. He ran across the Chevalier de Beauvoisis who took him into a box occupied by Messieurs the Gentlemen of the Chamber, just next to madame de Fervaques's box. Julien constantly looked at her. "I must keep a siege-journal," he said to himself as he went back to the hôtel, "otherwise I shall forget my attacks." He wrote two or three pages on this boring theme, and in this way achieved the admirable result of scarcely thinking at all about mademoiselle de la Mole.

Mathilde had almost forgotten him during his journey. "He is simply a commonplace person after all," she thought, "his name will always recall to me the greatest mistake in my life. I must honestly go back to all my ideas about prudence and honour; a woman who forgets them has everything to lose." She showed herself inclined to allow the contract with the marquis de Croisenois, which had been prepared so long ago, to be at last concluded. He was mad with joy; he would have been very much astonished had he been told that there was an element of resignation at the bottom of those feelings of Mathilde which made him so proud.

All mademoiselle de la Mole's ideas changed when she saw Julien. "As a matter of fact he is my husband," she said to herself. "If I am sincere in my return to sensible notions, he is clearly the man I ought to marry."

She was expecting importunities and airs of unhappiness on the part of Julien; she commenced rehearsing her answers, for he would doubtless try to address some words to her when they left the dinner table. Far from that he remained stubbornly in the salon and did not even look in the direction of the garden, though God knows what pain that caused him!

"It is better to have this explanation out all at once," thought mademoiselle de la Mole; she went into the garden alone, Julien did not appear. Mathilde went and walked near the salon window. She found him very much occupied in describing to madame de Fervaques the old ruined chateau which crown the banks along the Rhine and invest them with so much atmosphere. He was beginning to acquit himself with some credit in that sentimental picturesque jargon which is called wit in certain salons. Prince Korasoff would have been very proud if he had been at Paris. This evening was exactly what he had predicted.

He would have approved the line of conduct which Julien followed on the subsequent days.

An intrigue among the members of the secret government was going to bestow a few blue ribbons; madame maréchale de Fervaques was insisting on her great uncle being made a chevalier of the order. The marquis de la Mole had the same pretensions for his father-in-law; they joined forces and the maréchale came to the Hôtel de la Mole nearly every day. It was from her that Julien learned that the marquis was going to be a minister. He was offering to the *Camarilla* a very ingenious plan for the annihilation of the charter within three years without any disturbance.

If M. de la Mole became a minister, Julien could hope for a bishopric: but all these important interests seemed to be veiled and hazy. His imagination only perceived them very vaguely, and so to speak, in the far distance. The awful unhappiness which was making him into a madman could find no other interest in life except the character of his relations with mademoiselle de la Mole. He calculated that after five or six careful years he would manage to get himself loved again.

This cold brain had been reduced, as one sees, to a state of complete disorder. Out of all the qualities which had formerly distinguished him, all that remained was a little firmness. He was literally faithful to the line of conduct which prince Korasoff had dictated, and placed himself every evening near madame Fervaques' armchair, but he found it impossible to think of a word to say to her.

The strain of making Mathilde think that he had recovered exhausted his whole moral force, and when he was with the maréchale he seemed almost lifeless; even his eyes had lost all their fire, as in cases of extreme physical suffering.

As madame de la Mole's views were invariably a counterpart of the opinions of that husband of hers who could make her into a Duchess, she had been singing Julien's praises for some days.

LVI
MORAL LOVE

There also was of course in Adeline
That calm patrician polish in the address,
Which ne'er can pass the equinoctial line
Of anything which Nature would express;
Just as a Mandarin finds nothing fine.
At least his manner suffers not to guess
That anything he views can greatly please.
Don Juan, c. xiii. st. 84.

"There is an element of madness in all this family's way of looking at things," thought the maréchale; "they are infatuated with their young abbé, whose only accomplishment is to be a good listener, though his eyes are fine enough, it is true."

Julien, on his side, found in the maréchale's manners an almost perfect instance of that patrician calm which exhales a scrupulous politeness; and, what is more, announces at the same time the impossibility of any violent emotion. Madame de Fervaques would have been as much scandalised by any unexpected movement or any lack of self-control, as by a lack of dignity towards one's inferiors. She would have regarded the slightest symptom of sensibility as a kind of moral drunkenness which puts one to the blush and was extremely prejudicial to what a person of high rank owed to herself. Her great happiness was to talk of the king's last hunt; her favourite book, was the Memoirs of the Duke de Saint Simon, especially the genealogical part.

Julien knew the place where the arrangement of the light suited madame de Fervaques' particular style of beauty. He got there in advance, but was careful to turn his chair in such a way as not to see Mathilde.

Astonished one day at this consistent policy of hiding himself from her, she left the blue sofa and came to work by the little table near the maréchale's armchair. Julien had a fairly close view of her over madame de Fervaques' hat.

Those eyes, which were the arbiters of his fate, frightened him, and then hurled him violently out of his habitual apathy. He talked, and talked very well.

He was speaking to the maréchale, but his one aim was to produce an impression upon Mathilde's soul. He became so animated that eventually madame de Fervaques did not manage to understand a word he said.

This was a prime merit. If it had occurred to Julien to follow it up by some phrases of German mysticism, lofty religion, and Jesuitism, the maréchale would have immediately given him a rank among the

323

superior men whose mission it was to regenerate the age.

"Since he has bad enough taste," said mademoiselle de la Mole, "to talk so long and so ardently to madame de Fervaques, I shall not listen to him any more." She kept her resolution during the whole latter part of the evening, although she had difficulty in doing so.

At midnight, when she took her mother's candle to accompany her to her room, madame de la Mole stopped on the staircase to enter into an exhaustive eulogy of Julien. Mathilde ended by losing her temper. She could not get to sleep. She felt calmed by this thought: "the very things which I despise in a man may none the less constitute a great merit in the eyes of the maréchale."

As for Julien, he had done something, he was less unhappy; his eyes chanced to fall on the Russian leather portfolio in which prince Korasoff had placed the fifty-three love letters which he had presented to him. Julien saw a note at the bottom of the first letter: No. 1 is sent eight days after the first meeting.

"I am behind hand," exclaimed Julien. "It is quite a long time since I met madame de Fervaques." He immediately began to copy out this first love letter. It was a homily packed with moral platitudes and deadly dull. Julien was fortunate enough to fall asleep at the second page.

Some hours afterwards he was surprised to see the broad daylight as he lent on his desk. The most painful moments in his life were those when he woke up every morning to realise his unhappiness. On this particular day he finished copying out his letter in a state verging on laughter. "Is it possible," he said to himself, "that there ever lived a young man who actually wrote like that." He counted several sentences of nine lines each. At the bottom of the original he noticed a pencilled note. "These letters are delivered personally, on horseback, black cravat, blue tail-coat. You give the letter to the porter with a contrite air; expression of profound melancholy. If you notice any chambermaid, dry your eyes furtively and speak to her."

All this was duly carried out.

"I am taking a very bold course!" thought Julien as he came out of the Hôtel de Fervaques, "but all the worse for Korasoff. To think of daring to write to so virtuous a celebrity. I shall be treated with the utmost contempt, and nothing will amuse me more. It is really the only comedy that I can in any way appreciate. Yes, it will amuse me to load with ridicule that odious creature whom I call myself. If I believed in myself, I would commit some crime to distract myself."

The moment when Julien brought his horse back to the stable was the happiest he had experienced for a whole month. Korasoff had expressly forbidden him to look at the mistress who had left him, on any pretext whatsoever. But the step of that horse, which she knew so well, and

Julien's way of knocking on the stable door with his riding-whip to call a man, sometimes attracted Mathilde to behind the window-curtain. The muslin was so light that Julien could see through it. By looking under the brim of his hat in a certain way, he could get a view of Mathilde's figure without seeing her eyes. "Consequently," he said to himself, "she cannot see mine, and that is not really looking at her."

In the evening madame de Fervaques behaved towards him, exactly as though she had never received the philosophic mystical and religious dissertation which he had given to her porter in the morning with so melancholy an air. Chance had shown Julien on the preceding day how to be eloquent; he placed himself in such a position that he could see Mathilde's eyes. She, on her side, left the blue sofa a minute after the maréchale's arrival; this involved abandoning her usual associates. M. de Croisenois seemed overwhelmed by this new caprice: his palpable grief alleviated the awfulness of Julien's agony.

This unexpected turn in his life made him talk like an angel, and inasmuch as a certain element of self-appreciation will insinuate itself even into those hearts which serve as a temple for the most august virtue, the maréchale said to herself as she got into her carriage, "Madame de la Mole is right, this young priest has distinction. My presence must have overawed him at first. As a matter of fact, the whole tone of this house is very frivolous; I can see nothing but instances of virtue helped by oldness, and standing in great need of the chills of age. This young man must have managed to appreciate the difference; he writes well, but I fear very much that this request of his in his letter for me to enlighten him with my advice, is really nothing less than an, as yet, unconscious sentiment.

"Nevertheless how many conversions have begun like that! What makes me consider this a good omen is the difference between his style and that of the young people whose letters I have had an opportunity of seeing. One cannot avoid recognising unction, profound seriousness, and much conviction in the prose of this young acolyte; he has no doubt the sweet virtue of a Massillon."

LVII
THE FINEST PLACES IN THE CHURCH

Services! talents! merits! bah! belong to a côterie.
Télémaque.

The idea of a bishopric had thus become associated with the idea of Julien in the mind of a woman, who would sooner or later have at her disposal the finest places in the Church of France. This idea had not struck Julien at all; at the present time his thoughts were strictly limited to his actual unhappiness. Everything tended to intensify it. The sight of his room, for instance, had become unbearable. When he came back in the evening with his candle, each piece of furniture and each little ornament seemed to become articulate, and to announce harshly some new phase of his unhappiness.

"I have a hard task before me today," he said to himself as he came in with a vivacity which he had not experienced for a long time; "let us hope that the second letter will be as boring as the first."

It was more so. What he was copying seemed so absurd that he finished up by transcribing it line for line without thinking of the sense.

"It is even more bombastic," he said to himself, "than those official documents of the treaty of Munster which my professor of diplomacy made me copy out at London."

It was only then that he remembered madame de Fervaque's letters which he had forgotten to give back to the grave Spaniard Don Diego Bustos. He found them. They were really almost as nonsensical as those of the young Russian nobleman. Their vagueness was unlimited. It meant everything and nothing. "It's the Æolian harp of style," thought Julien. "The only real thing I see in the middle of all these lofty thoughts about annihilation, death, infinity, etc., is an abominable fear of ridicule."

The monologue which we have just condensed was repeated for fifteen days on end. Falling off to sleep as he copied out a sort of commentary on the Apocalypse, going with a melancholy expression to deliver it the following day, taking his horse back to the stable in the hope of catching sight of Mathilde's dress, working, going in the evening to the opera on those evenings when madame de Fervaques did not come to the Hôtel de la Mole, such were the monotonous events in Julien's life. His life had more interest, when madame la Fervaques visited the marquise; he could then catch a glimpse of Mathilde's eyes underneath a feather of the maréchale's hat, and he would wax eloquent. His picturesque and sentimental phrases began to assume a style, which was both more striking and more elegant.

He quite realised that what he said was absurd in Mathilde's eyes, but he wished to impress her by the elegance of his diction. "The falser my speeches are the more I ought to please," thought Julien, and he then had the abominable audacity to exaggerate certain elements in his own character. He soon appreciated that to avoid appearing vulgar in the eyes of the maréchale it was necessary to eschew simple and rational ideas. He would continue on these lines, or would cut short his grand eloquence according as he saw appreciation or indifference in the eyes of the two great ladies whom he had set out to please.

Taking it all round, his life was less awful than when his days were passed in inaction.

"But," he said to himself one evening, "here I am copying out the fifteenth of these abominable dissertations; the first fourteen have been duly delivered to the maréchale's porter. I shall have the honour of filling all the drawers in her escritoire. And yet she treats me as though I never wrote. What can be the end of all this? Will my constancy bore her as much as it does me? I must admit that that Russian friend of Korasoff's who was in love with the pretty Quakeress of Richmond, was a terrible man in his time; no one could be more overwhelming."

Like all mediocre individuals, who chance to come into contact with the manœuvres of a great general, Julien understood nothing of the attack executed by the young Russian on the heart of the young English girl. The only purpose of the first forty letters was to secure forgiveness for the boldness of writing at all. The sweet person, who perhaps lived a life of inordinate boredom, had to be induced to contract the habit of receiving letters, which were perhaps a little less insipid than her everyday life.

One morning a letter was delivered to Julien. He recognised the arms of madame la Fervaques, and broke the seal with an eagerness which would have seemed impossible to him some days before. It was only an invitation to dinner.

He rushed to prince Korasoffs instructions. Unfortunately the young Russian had taken it into his head to be as flippant as Dorat, just when he should have been simple and intelligible! Julien was not able to form any idea of the moral position which he ought to take up at the maréchale's dinner.

The salon was extremely magnificent and decorated like the gallery de Diane in the Tuileries with panelled oil-paintings.

There were some light spots on these pictures. Julien learnt later that the mistress of the house had thought the subject somewhat lacking in decency and that she had had the pictures corrected. "What a moral century!" he thought.

He noticed in this salon three of the persons who had been present at the drawing up of the secret note. One of them, my lord bishop of ----

the maréchale's uncle had the disposition of the ecclesiastical patronage, and could, it was said, refuse his niece nothing. "What immense progress I have made," said Julien to himself with a melancholy smile, "and how indifferent I am to it. Here I am dining with the famous bishop of ——."

The dinner was mediocre and the conversation wearisome.

"It's like the small talk in a bad book," thought Julien. "All the greatest subjects of human thought are proudly tackled. After listening for three minutes one asks oneself which is greater—the speaker's bombast, or his abominable ignorance?"

The reader has doubtless forgotten the little man of letters named Tanbeau, who was the nephew of the Academician, and intended to be professor, who seemed entrusted with the task of poisoning the salon of the Hôtel de la Mole with his base calumnies.

It was this little man who gave Julien the first inkling that though, madame de Fervaques did not answer, she might quite well take an indulgent view of the sentiment which dictated them. M. Tanbeau's sinister soul was lacerated by the thought of Julien's success; "but since, on the other hand, a man of merit cannot be in two places at the same time any more than a fool," said the future professor to himself, "if Sorel becomes the lover of the sublime maréchale, she will obtain some lucrative position for him in the church, and I shall be rid of him in the Hôtel de la Mole."

M. the abbé Pirard addressed long sermons to Julien concerning his success at the hotel de Fervaques. There was a sectarian jealousy between the austere Jansenist and the salon of the virtuous maréchale which was Jesuitical, reactionary, and monarchical.

LVIII
MANON LESCAUT

> Accordingly once he was thoroughly convinced of the asinine
> stupidity of the prior, he would usually succeed well enough
> by calling white black, and black white. *Lichtenberg.*

The Russian instructions peremptorily forbade the writer from ever contradicting in conversation the recipient of the letters. No pretext could excuse any deviation from the rôle of that most ecstatic admiration. The letters were always based on that hypothesis.

One evening at the opera, when in madame de Fervaques' box, Julien spoke of the ballet of *Manon Lescaut* in the most enthusiastic terms. His only reason for talking in that strain was the fact that he thought it insignificant.

The maréchale said that the ballet was very inferior to the abbé Prévost's novel.

"The idea," thought Julien, both surprised and amused, "of so highly virtuous a person praising a novel! Madame de Fervaques used to profess two or three times a week the most absolute contempt for those writers, who, by means of their insipid works, try to corrupt a youth which is, alas! only too inclined to the errors of the senses."

"*Manon Lescaut*" continued the maréchale, "is said to be one of the best of this immoral and dangerous type of book. The weaknesses and the deserved anguish of a criminal heart are, they say, portrayed with a truth which is not lacking in depth; a fact which does not prevent your Bonaparte from stating at St. Helena that it is simply a novel written for lackeys."

The word Bonaparte restored to Julien all the activity of his mind. "They have tried to ruin me with the maréchale; they have told her of my enthusiasm for Napoleon. This fact has sufficiently piqued her to make her yield to the temptation to make me feel it." This discovery amused him all the evening, and rendered him amusing. As he took leave of the maréchale in the vestibule of the opera, she said to him, "Remember, monsieur, one must not like Bonaparte if you like me; at the best he can only be accepted as a necessity imposed by Providence. Besides, the man did not have a sufficiently supple soul to appreciate masterpieces of art."

"When you like me," Julien kept on repeating to himself, "that means nothing or means everything. Here we have mysteries of language which are beyond us poor provincials." And he thought a great deal about madame de Rênal, as he copied out an immense letter destined for the maréchale.

"How is it," she said to him the following day, with an assumed indifference which he thought was clumsily assumed, "that you talk to me about London and Richmond in a letter which you wrote last night, I think, when you came back from the opera?"

Julien was very embarrassed. He had copied line by line without thinking about what he was writing, and had apparently forgotten to substitute Paris and Saint Cloud for the words London and Richmond which occurred in the original. He commenced two or three sentences, but found it impossible to finish them. He felt on the point of succumbing to a fit of idiotic laughter. Finally by picking his words he succeeded in formulating this inspiration: "Exalted as I was by the discussion of the most sublime and greatest interests of the human soul, my own soul may have been somewhat absent in my letter to you."

"I am making an impression," he said to himself, "so I can spare myself the boredom of the rest of the evening." He left the Hôtel de Fervaques at a run. In the evening he had another look at the original of the letter which he had copied out on the previous night, and soon came to the fatal place where the young Russian made mention of London and of Richmond. Julien was very astonished to find this letter almost tender.

It had been the contrast between the apparent lightness of his conversation, and the sublime and almost apocalyptic profundity of his letters which had marked him out for favour. The maréchale was particularly pleased by the longness of the sentences; this was very far from being that sprightly style which that immoral man Voltaire had brought into fashion. Although our hero made every possible human effort to eliminate from his conversation any symptom of good sense, it still preserved a certain anti-monarchical and blasphemous tinge which did not escape madame de Fervaques. Surrounded as she was by persons who, though eminently moral, had very often not a single idea during a whole evening, this lady was profoundly struck by anything resembling a novelty, but at the same time she thought she owed it to herself to be offended by it. She called this defect: Keeping the imprint of the lightness of the age.

But such salons are only worth observing when one has a favour to procure. The reader doubtless shares all the ennui of the colourless life which Julien was leading. This period represents the steppes of our journey.

Mademoiselle de la Mole needed to exercise her self-control to avoid thinking of Julien during the whole period filled by the de Fervaques episode. Her soul was a prey to violent battles; sometimes she piqued herself on despising that melancholy young man, but his conversation captivated her in spite of herself. She was particularly astonished by his absolute falseness. He did not say a single word to the maréchale which was not a lie, or at any rate, an abominable travesty of his own way of thinking, which Mathilde knew so perfectly in every phase. This Machiavellianism impressed her. "What subtlety," she said to herself. "What a difference between the bombastic coxcombs, or the common rascals like Tanbeau who talk in the same strain."

Nevertheless Julien went through awful days. It was only to accomplish the most painful of duties that he put in a daily appearance in the maréchale's salon.

The strain of playing a part ended by depriving his mind of all its strength. As he crossed each night the immense courtyard of the Hôtel de Fervaques, it was only through sheer force in character and logic that he succeeded in keeping a little above the level of despair.

"I overcame despair at the seminary," he said, "yet what an awful prospect I had then. I was then either going to make my fortune or come to grief just as I am now. I found myself obliged to pass all my life in intimate association with the most contemptible and disgusting things in the whole world. The following spring, just eleven short months later, I was perhaps the happiest of all young people of my own age."

But very often all this fine logic proved unavailing against the awful reality. He saw Mathilde every day at breakfast and at dinner. He knew from the numerous letters which de la Mole dictated to him that she was on the eve of marrying de Croisenois. This charming man already called twice a day at the Hôtel de la Mole; the jealous eye of a jilted lover was alive to every one of his movements. When he thought he had noticed that mademoiselle de la Mole was beginning to encourage her intended, Julien could not help looking tenderly at his pistols as he went up to his room.

"Ah," he said to himself, "would it not be much wiser to take the marks out of my linen and to go into some solitary forest twenty leagues from Paris to put an end to this atrocious life? I should be unknown in the district, my death would remain a secret for a fortnight, and who would bother about me after a fortnight?"

This reasoning was very logical. But on the following day a glimpse of Mathilde's arm between the sleeve of her dress and her glove sufficed to plunge our young philosopher into memories which, though agonising, none the less gave him a hold on life. "Well," he said to himself, "I will follow this Russian plan to the end. How will it all finish?"

"So far as the maréchale is concerned, after I have copied out these fifty-three letters, I shall not write any others.

"As for Mathilde, these six weeks of painful acting will either leave her anger unchanged, or will win me a moment of reconciliation. Great God! I should die of happiness." And he could not finish his train of thought.

After a long reverie he succeeded in taking up the thread of his argument. "In that case," he said to himself, "I should win one day of happiness, and after that her cruelties which are based, alas, on my lack of ability to please her will recommence. I should have nothing left to do, I should be ruined and lost for ever. With such a character as hers what guarantee can she give me? Alas! My manners are no doubt lacking in elegance, and my style of speech is heavy and monotonous. Great God, why am I myself?"

LIX
ENNUI

Sacrificing one's self to one's passions, let it pass; but sacrificing one's self to passions which one has not got! Oh!
melancholy nineteenth century!
Girodet.

Madame de Fervaques had begun reading Julien's long letters without
any pleasure, but she now began to think about them; one thing, however,
grieved her. "What a pity that M. Sorel was not a real priest! He could
then be admitted to a kind of intimacy; but in view of that cross, and that
almost lay dress, one is exposed to cruel questions and what is one to
answer?" She did not finish the train of thought, "Some malicious woman
friend may think, and even spread it about that he is some lower middle-
class cousin or other, a relative of my father, some tradesman who has
been decorated by the National Guard." Up to the time which she had
seen Julien, madame de Fervaque's greatest pleasure had been writing
the word maréchale after her name. Consequently a morbid parvenu
vanity, which was ready to take umbrage at everything, combatted the
awakening of her interest in him. "It would be so easy for me," said the
maréchale, "to make him a grand vicar in some diocese near Paris! but
plain M. Sorel, and what is more, a man who is the secretary of M. de la
Mole! It is heart-breaking."

For the first time in her life this soul, which was afraid of everything,
was moved by an interest which was alien to its own pretensions to rank
and superiority. Her old porter noticed that whenever he brought a
letter from this handsome young man, who always looked so sad, he was
certain to see that absent, discontented expression, which the maréchale
always made a point of assuming on the entry of any of her servants,
immediately disappear. The boredom of a mode of life whose ambitions
were concentrated on impressing the public without her having at heart
any real faculty of enjoyment for that kind of success, had become
so intolerable since she had begun to think of Julien that, all that was
necessary to prevent her chambermaids being bullied for a whole day,
was that their mistress should have passed an hour in the society of this
strange young man on the evening of the preceding day. His budding
credit was proof against very cleverly written anonymous letters. It was
in vain that Tanbeau supplied M. de Luz, de Croisenois, de Caylus, with
two or three very clever calumnies which these gentlemen were only too
glad to spread, without making too many enquiries of the actual truth of
the charges. The maréchale, whose temperament was not calculated to
be proof against these vulgar expedients related her doubts to Mathilde,

and was always consoled by her.

One day, madame de Fervaques, after having asked three times if there were any letters for her, suddenly decided to answer Julien. It was a case of the triumph of ennui. On reaching the second letter in his name the maréchale almost felt herself pulled up sharp by the unbecomingness of writing with her own hand so vulgar an address as to M. Sorel, care of M. le Marquis de la Mole.

"You must bring me envelopes with your address on," she said very drily to Julien in the evening. "Here I am appointed lover and valet in one," thought Julien, and he bowed, amused himself by wrinkling his face up like Arsène, the old valet of the marquis.

He brought the envelopes that very evening, and he received the third letter very early on the following day: he read five or six lines at the beginning, and two or three towards the end. There were four pages of a small and very close writing. The lady gradually developed the sweet habit of writing nearly every day. Julien answered by faithful copies of the Russian letters; and such is the advantage of the bombastic style that madame de Fervaques was not a bit astonished by the lack of connection between his answers and her letters. How gravely irritated would her pride have been if the little Tanbeau who had constituted himself a voluntary spy on all Julien's movements had been able to have informed her that all these letters were left unsealed and thrown haphazard into Julien's drawer.

One morning the porter was bringing into the library a letter to him from the maréchale. Mathilde met the man, saw the letter together with the address in Julien's handwriting. She entered the library as the porter was leaving it, the letter was still on the edge of the table. Julien was very busy with his work and had not yet put it in his drawer.

"I cannot endure this," exclaimed Mathilde, as she took possession of the letter, "you are completely forgetting me, me your wife, your conduct is awful, monsieur."

At these words her pride, shocked by the awful unseemliness of her proceeding, prevented her from speaking. She burst into tears, and soon seemed to Julien scarcely able to breathe.

Julien was so surprised and embarrassed that he did not fully appreciate how ideally fortunate this scene was for himself. He helped Mathilde to sit down; she almost abandoned herself in his arms.

The first minute in which he noticed this movement, he felt an extreme joy. Immediately afterwards, he thought of Korasoff: "I may lose everything by a single word."

The strain of carrying out his tactics was so great that his arms stiffened. "I dare not even allow myself to press this supple, charming frame to my heart, or she will despise me or treat me badly. What an awful character!" And while he cursed Mathilde's character, he loved her a hundred times more. He thought he had a queen in his arms.

Julien's impassive coldness intensified the anguished pride which was lacerating the soul of mademoiselle de la Mole. She was far from having the necessary self-possession to try and read in his eyes what he felt for her at that particular moment. She could not make up her mind to look at him. She trembled lest she might encounter a contemptuous expression.

Seated motionless on the library divan, with her head turned in the opposite direction to Julien, she was a prey to the most poignant anguish that pride and love can inflict upon a human soul. What an awful step had she just slipped into taking! "It has been reserved for me, unhappy woman that I am, to see my most unbecoming advances rebuffed! and rebuffed by whom?" added her maddened and wounded pride; "rebuffed by a servant of my father's! That's more than I will put up with," she said aloud, and rising in a fury, she opened the drawer of Julien's table, which was two yards in front of her.

She stood petrified with horror when she saw eight or ten unopened letters, completely like the one the porter had just brought up. She recognised Julien's handwriting, though more or less disguised, on all the addresses.

"So," she cried, quite beside herself, "you are not only on good terms with her, but you actually despise her. You, a nobody, despise madame la maréchale de Fervaques!"

"Oh, forgive me, my dear," she added, throwing herself on her knees; "despise me if you wish, but love me. I cannot live without your love." And she fell down in a dead faint.

"So our proud lady is lying at my feet," said Julien to himself.

LX
A BOX AT THE BOUFFES

As the blackest sky
Foretells the heaviest tempest
Don Juan, c. 1. st.76.

In the midst of these great transports Julien felt more surprised than happy. Mathilde's abuse proved to him the shrewdness of the Russian tactics. "'Few words, few deeds,' that is my one method of salvation." He picked up Mathilde, and without saying a word, put her back on the divan. She was gradually being overcome by tears.

In order to keep herself in countenance, she took madame de Fervaques' letters in her hands, and slowly broke the seals. She gave a noticeable nervous movement when she recognised the maréchale's handwriting. She turned over the pages of these letters without reading them. Most of them were six pages.

"At least answer me," Mathilde said at last, in the most supplicatory tone, but without daring to look at Julien: "You know how proud I am. It is the misfortune of my position, and of my temperament, too, I confess. Has madame de Fervaques robbed me of your heart? Has she made the sacrifices to which my fatal love swept me?"

A dismal silence was all Julien's answer. "By what right," he thought, "does she ask me to commit an indiscretion unworthy of an honest man?" Mathilde tried to read the letters; her eyes were so wet with tears that it was impossible for her to do so. She had been unhappy for a month past, but this haughty soul had been very far from owning its own feelings even to itself. Chance alone had brought about this explosion. For one instant jealousy and love had won a victory over pride. She was sitting on the divan, and very near him. He saw her hair and her alabaster neck. For a moment he forgot all he owed to himself. He passed his arm around her waist, and clasped her almost to his breast.

She slowly turned her head towards him. He was astonished by the extreme anguish in her eyes. There was not a trace of their usual expression.

Julien felt his strength desert him. So great was the deadly pain of the courageous feat which he was imposing on himself.

"Those eyes will soon express nothing but the coldest disdain," said Julien to himself, "if I allow myself to be swept away by the happiness of loving her." She, however, kept repeatedly assuring him at this moment, in a hushed voice, and in words which she had scarcely the strength to finish, of all her remorse for those steps which her inordinate pride had dictated.

"I, too, have pride," said Julien to her, in a scarcely articulate voice, while his features portrayed the lowest depths of physical prostration.

Mathilde turned round sharply towards him. Hearing his voice was a happiness which she had given up hoping. At this moment her only thought of her haughtiness was to curse it. She would have liked to have found out some abnormal and incredible actions, in order to prove to him the extent to which she adored him and detested herself.

"That pride is probably the reason," continued Julien, "why you singled me out for a moment. My present courageous and manly firmness is certainly the reason why you respect me. I may entertain love for the maréchale."

Mathilde shuddered; a strange expression came into her eyes. She was going to hear her sentence pronounced. This shudder did not escape Julien. He felt his courage weaken.

"Ah," he said to himself, as he listened to the sound of the vain words which his mouth was articulating, as he thought it were some strange sound, "if I could only cover those pale cheeks with kisses without your feeling it."

"I may entertain love for the maréchale," he continued, while his voice became weaker and weaker, "but I certainly have no definite proof of her interest in me."

Mathilde looked at him. He supported that look. He hoped, at any rate, that his expression had not betrayed him. He felt himself bathed in a love that penetrated even into the most secret recesses of his heart. He had never adored her so much; he was almost as mad as Mathilde. If she had mustered sufficient self-possession and courage to manœuvre, he would have abandoned all his play-acting, and fallen at her feet. He had sufficient strength to manage to continue speaking: "Ah, Korasoff," he exclaimed mentally, "why are you not here? How I need a word from you to guide me in my conduct." During this time his voice was saying,

"In default of any other sentiment, gratitude would be sufficient to attach me to the maréchale. She has been indulgent to me; she has consoled me when I have been despised. I cannot put unlimited faith in certain appearances which are, no doubt, extremely flattering, but possibly very fleeting."

"Oh, my God!" exclaimed Mathilde.

"Well, what guarantee will you give me?" replied Julien with a sharp, firm intonation, which seemed to abandon for a moment the prudent forms of diplomacy. "What guarantee, what god will warrant that the position to which you seem inclined to restore me at the present moment will last more than two days?"

"The excess of my love, and my unhappiness if you do not love me," she said to him, taking his hands and turning towards him.

The spasmodic movement which she had just made had slightly displaced her tippet; Julien caught a view of her charming shoulders. Her slightly dishevelled hair recalled a delicious memory....

He was on the point of succumbing. "One imprudent word," he said to himself, "and I have to start all over again that long series of days which I have passed in despair. Madame de Rênal used to find reasons for doing what her heart dictated. This young girl of high society never allows her heart to be moved except when she has proved to herself by sound logic that it ought to be moved."

He saw this proof in the twinkling of an eye, and in the twinkling of an eye too, he regained his courage. He took away his hands which Mathilde was pressing in her own, and moved a little away from her with a marked respect.

Human courage could not go further. He then busied himself with putting together madame de Fervaque's letters which were spread out on the divan, and it was with all the appearance of extreme politeness that he cruelly exploited the psychological moment by adding,

"Mademoiselle de la Mole will allow me to reflect over all this." He went rapidly away and left the library; she heard him shut all the doors one after the other.

"The monster is not the least bit troubled," she said to herself. "But what am I saying? Monster? He is wise, prudent, good. It is I myself who have committed more wrong than one can imagine."

This point of view lasted. Mathilde was almost happy today, for she gave herself up to love unreservedly. One would have said that this soul had never been disturbed by pride (and what pride!)

She shuddered with horror when a lackey announced madame le Fervaques into the salon in the evening. The man's voice struck her as sinister. She could not endure the sight of the maréchale, and stopped suddenly. Julien who had felt little pride over his painful victory, had feared to face her, and had not dined at the Hôtel de la Mole.

His love and his happiness rapidly increased in proportion to the time that elapsed from the moment of the battle. He was blaming himself already. "How could I resist her?" he said to himself. "Suppose she were to go and leave off loving me! One single moment may change that haughty soul, and I must admit that I have treated her awfully."

In the evening he felt that it was absolutely necessary to put in an appearance at the Bouffes in madame de Fervaques' box. She had expressly invited him. Mathilde would be bound to know of his presence or his discourteous absence. In spite of the clearness of this logic, he could not at the beginning of the evening bring himself to plunge into society. By speaking he would lose half his happiness. Ten o'clock struck and it was absolutely necessary to show himself. Luckily he found the maréchale's box packed with women, and was relegated to a place near the door where he was completely hidden by the hats. This position saved him from looking ridiculous; Caroline's divine notes of despair in the *Matrimonio Segreto* made him burst into tears. Madame de Fervaques saw these tears. They represented so great a contrast with the masculine firmness of his usual expression that the soul of the old-fashioned lady, saturated as it had been for many years with all the corroding acid of parvenu haughtiness, was none the less touched. Such remnants of a woman's heart as she still possessed impelled her to speak: she wanted to enjoy the sound of his voice at this moment.

"Have you seen the de la Mole ladies?" she said to him. "They are in the third tier." Julien immediately craned out over the atre, leaning politely enough on the front of the box. He saw Mathilde; her eyes were shining with tears.

"And yet it is not their Opera day," thought Julien; "how eager she must be!"

Mathilde had prevailed on her mother to come to the Bouffes in spite of the inconveniently high tier of the box, which a lady friend of the family had hastened to offer her. She wanted to see if Julien would pass the evening with the maréchale.

LXI
FRIGHTEN HER

So this is the fine miracle of your civilisation; you have turned love into an ordinary business.—*Barnave.*

Julien rushed into madame de la Mole's box. His eyes first met the tearful eyes of Mathilde; she was crying without reserve. There were only insignificant personages present, the friend who had leant her box, and some men whom she knew. Mathilde placed her hand on Julien's; she seemed to have forgotten all fear of her mother. Almost stifled as she was by her tears, she said nothing but this one word: "Guarantees!"

"So long as I don't speak to her," said Julien to himself. He was himself very moved, and concealed his eyes with his hand as best he could under the pretext of avoiding the dazzling light of the third tier of boxes. "If I speak she may suspect the excess of my emotion, the sound of my voice will betray me. All may yet be lost." His struggles were more painful than they had been in the morning, his soul had had the time to become moved. He had been frightened at seeing Mathilde piqued with vanity. Intoxicated as he was with love and pleasure he resolved not to speak.

In my view this is one of the finest traits in his character, an individual capable of such an effort of self-control may go far si *fata sinant.*

Mademoiselle de la Mole insisted on taking Julien back to the hôtel. Luckily it was raining a great deal, but the marquise had him placed opposite her, talked to him incessantly, and prevented him saying a single word to her daughter. One might have thought that the marquise was nursing Julien's happiness for him; no longer fearing to lose everything through his excessive emotion, he madly abandoned himself to his happiness.

Shall I dare to say that when he went back to his room Julien fell on his knees and covered with kisses the love letters which prince Korasoff had given him.

"How much I owe you, great man," he exclaimed in his madness. Little by little he regained his self-possession. He compared himself to a general who had just won a great battle. "My advantage is definite and immense," he said to himself, "but what will happen to-morrow? One instant may ruin everything."

With a passionate gesture he opened the *Memoirs* which Napoleon had dictated at St. Helena and for two long hours forced himself to read them. Only his eyes read; no matter, he made himself do it. During this singular reading his head and his heart rose to the most exalted level and worked unconsciously. "Her heart is very different from madame de Rênal's," he said to himself, but he did not go further.

"Frighten her!" he suddenly exclaimed, hurling away the book. "The enemy will only obey me in so far as I frighten him, but then he will not dare to show contempt for me."

Intoxicated with joy he walked up and down his little room. In point of fact his happiness was based rather on pride than on love.

"Frighten her!" he repeated proudly, and he had cause to be proud.

"Madame de Rênal always doubted even in her happiest moments if my love was equal to her own. In this case I have to subjugate a demon, consequently I must subjugate her." He knew quite well that Mathilde would be in the library at eight o'clock in the morning of the following day. He did not appear before nine o'clock. He was burning with love, but his head dominated his heart.

Scarcely a single minute passed without his repeating to himself. "Keep her obsessed by this great doubt. Does he love me?" Her own brilliant position, together with the flattery of all who speak to her, tend a little too much to make her reassure herself.

He found her sitting on the divan pale and calm, but apparently completely incapable of making a single movement. She held out her hand,

"Dear one, it is true I have offended you, perhaps you are angry with me."

Julien had not been expecting this simple tone. He was on the point of betraying himself.

"You want guarantees, my dear, she added after a silence which she had hoped would be broken. Take me away, let us leave for London. I shall be ruined, dishonoured for ever." She had the courage to take her hand away from Julien to cover her eyes with it.

All her feelings of reserve and feminine virtue had come back into her soul. "Well, dishonour me," she said at last with a sigh, "that will be a guarantee."

"I was happy yesterday, because I had the courage to be severe with myself," thought Julien. After a short silence he had sufficient control over his heart to say in an icy tone,

"Once we are on the road to London, once you are dishonoured, to employ your own expression, who will answer that you will still love me?

that my very presence in the post-chaise will not seem importunate? I am not a monster; to have ruined your reputation will only make me still more unhappy. It is not your position in society which is the obstacle, it is unfortunately your own character. Can you yourself guarantee that you will love me for eight days?"

"Ah! let her love me for eight days, just eight days," whispered Julien to himself, "and I will die of happiness. What do I care for the future, what do I care for life? And yet if I wish that divine happiness can commence this very minute, it only depends on me."

Mathilde saw that he was pensive.

"So I am completely unworthy of you," she said to him, taking his hand.

Julien kissed her, but at the same time the iron hand of duty gripped his heart. If she sees how much I adore her I shall lose her. And before leaving her arms, he had reassumed all that dignity which is proper to a man.

He managed on this and the following days to conceal his inordinate happiness. There were moments when he even refused himself the pleasure of clasping her in his arms. At other times the delirium of happiness prevailed over all the counsels of prudence.

He had been accustomed to station himself near a bower of honey-suckle in the garden arranged in such a way so as to conceal the ladder when he had looked up at Mathilde's blind in the distance, and lamented her inconstancy. A very big oak tree was quite near, and the trunk of that tree prevented him from being seen by the indiscreet.

As he passed with Mathilde over this very place which recalled his excessive unhappiness so vividly, the contrast between his former despair and his present happiness proved too much for his character. Tears inundated his eyes, and he carried his sweetheart's hand to his lips: "It was here I used to live in my thoughts of you, it was from here that I used to look at that blind, and waited whole hours for the happy moment when I would see that hand open it."

His weakness was unreserved. He portrayed the extremity of his former despair in genuine colours which could not possibly have been invented. Short interjections testified to that present happiness which had put an end to that awful agony.

"My God, what am I doing?" thought Julien, suddenly recovering himself. "I am ruining myself."

In his excessive alarm he thought that he already detected a diminution of the love in mademoiselle de la Mole's eyes. It was an illusion, but Julien's face suddenly changed its expression and became overspread by a mortal pallor. His eyes lost their fire, and an expression of haughtiness touched with malice soon succeeded to his look of the most genuine and unreserved love.

"But what is the matter with you, my dear," said Mathilde to him, both tenderly and anxiously.

"I am lying," said Julien irritably, "and I am lying to you. I am reproaching myself for it, and yet God knows that I respect you sufficiently not to lie to you. You love me, you are devoted to me, and I have no need of praises in order to please you."

"Great heavens! are all the charming things you have been telling me for the last two minutes mere phrases?"

"And I reproach myself for it keenly, dear one. I once made them up for a woman who loved me, and bored me—it is the weakness of my character. I denounce myself to you, forgive me."

Bitter tears streamed over Mathilde's cheeks.

"As soon as some trifle offends me and throws me back on my meditation," continued Julien, "my abominable memory, which I curse at this very minute, offers me a resource, and I abuse it."

"So I must have slipped, without knowing it, into some action which has displeased you," said Mathilde with a charming simplicity.

"I remember one day that when you passed near this honeysuckle you picked a flower, M. de Luz took it from you and you let him keep it. I was two paces away."

"M. de Luz? It is impossible," replied Mathilde with all her natural haughtiness. "I do not do things like that."

"I am sure of it," Julien replied sharply.

"Well, my dear, it is true," said Mathilde, as she sadly lowered her eyes. She knew positively that many months had elapsed since she had allowed M. de Luz to do such a thing.

Julien looked at her with ineffable tenderness, "No," he said to himself, "she does not love me less."

In the evening she rallied him with a laugh on his fancy for madame de Fervaques. "Think of a bourgeois loving a parvenu, those are perhaps the only type of hearts that my Julien cannot make mad with love. She has made you into a real dandy," she said playing with his hair.

During the period when he thought himself scorned by Mathilde, Julien had become one of the best dressed men in Paris. He had, moreover, a further advantage over other dandies, in as much as once he had finished dressing he never gave a further thought to his appearance.

One thing still piqued Mathilde, Julien continued to copy out the Russian letters and send them to the maréchale.

LXII
THE TIGER

Alas, why these things and not other things?—*Beaumarchais.*

An English traveller tells of the intimacy in which he lived with a tiger. He had trained it and would caress it, but he always kept a cocked pistol on his table.

Julien only abandoned himself to the fulness of his happiness in those moments when Mathilde could not read the expression in his eyes. He scrupulously performed his duty of addressing some harsh word to her from time to time.

When Mathilde's sweetness, which he noticed with some surprise, together with the completeness of her devotion were on the point of depriving him of all self-control, he was courageous enough to leave her suddenly.

Mathilde loved for the first time in her life.

Life had previously always dragged along at a tortoise pace, but now it flew.

As, however, her pride required to find a vent in some way or other, she wished to expose herself to all the dangers in which her love could involve her. It was Julien who was prudent, and it was only when it was a question of danger that she did not follow her own inclination; but submissive, and almost humble as she was when with him, she only showed additional haughtiness to everyone in the house who came near her, whether relatives or friends.

In the evening she would call Julien to her in the salon in the presence of sixty people, and have a long and private conversation with him.

The little Tanbeau installed himself one day close to them. She requested him to go and fetch from the library the volume of Smollet which deals with the revolution of 1688, and when he hesitated, added with an expression of insulting haughtiness, which was a veritable balm to Julien's soul, "Don't hurry."

"Have you noticed that little monster's expression?" he said to her.

"His uncle has been in attendance in this salon for ten or twelve years, otherwise I would have had him packed off immediately."

Her behaviour towards MM. de Croisenois, de Luz, etc., though outwardly perfectly polite, was in reality scarcely less provocative. Mathilde keenly reproached herself for all the confidential remarks about them which she had formerly made to Julien, and all the more so since she did not dare to confess that she had exaggerated to him the, in fact, almost absolutely innocent manifestations of interest of which these gentlemen had been the objects. In spite of her best resolutions her womanly pride invariably prevented her from saying to Julien, "It was because I was talking to you that I found a pleasure in describing my weakness in not drawing my hand away, when M. de Croisenois had placed his on a marble table and had just touched it."

But now, as soon as one of these gentlemen had been speaking to her for some moments, she found she had a question to put to Julien, and she made this an excuse for keeping him by her side.

She discovered that she was *enceinte* and joyfully informed Julien of the fact.

"Do you doubt me now? Is it not a guarantee? I am your wife for ever."

This announcement struck Julien with profound astonishment. He was on the point of forgetting the governing principle of his conduct. How am I to be deliberately cold and insulting towards this poor young girl, who is ruining herself for my sake. And if she looked at all ill, he could not, even on those days when the terrible voice of wisdom made itself heard, find the courage to address to her one of those harsh remarks which his experience had found so indispensable to the preservation of their love.

"I will write to my father," said Mathilde to him one day, "he is more than a father to me, he is a friend; that being so, I think it unworthy both of you and of myself to try and deceive him, even for a single minute."

"Great heavens, what are you going to do?" said Julien in alarm.

"My duty," she answered with eyes shining with joy.

She thought she was showing more nobility than her lover.

"But he will pack me off in disgrace."

"It is his right to do so, we must respect it. I will give you my arm, and we will go out by the front door in full daylight."

Julien was thunderstruck and requested her to put it off for a week.

"I cannot," she answered, "it is the voice of honour, I have seen my duty, I must follow it, and follow it at once."

"Well, I order you to put it off," said Julien at last. "Your honour is safe for the present. I am your husband. The position of us will be changed by this momentous step. I too am within my rights. To-day is Tuesday, next Tuesday is the duke de Retz's at home; when M. de la Mole comes home in the evening the porter will give him the fatal letter. His only thought is to make you a duchess, I am sure of it. Think of his unhappiness."

"You mean, think of his vengeance?"

"It may be that I pity my benefactor, and am grieved at injuring him, but I do not fear, and shall never fear anyone."

Mathilde yielded. This was the first occasion, since she had informed Julien of her condition, that he had spoken to her authoritatively. She had never loved him so much. The tender part of his soul had found happiness in seizing on Mathilde's condition as an excuse for refraining from his cruel remarks to her. The question of the confession to M. de la Mole deeply moved him. Was he going to be separated from Mathilde? And, however grieved she would be to see him go, would she have a thought for him after his departure?

He was almost equally horrified by the thought of the justified reproaches which the marquis might address to him.

In the evening he confessed to Mathilde the second reason for his anxiety, and then led away by his love, confessed the first as well.

She changed colour. "Would it really make you unhappy," she said to him, "to pass six months far away from me?"

"Infinitely so. It is the only thing in the world which terrifies me."

Mathilde was very happy. Julien had played his part so assiduously that he had succeeded in making her think that she was the one of the two who loved the more.

The fatal Tuesday arrived. When the marquis came in at midnight he found a letter addressed to him, which was only to be opened himself when no one was there:—

"My father,

"All social ties have been broken between us, only those of nature remain. Next to my husband, you are and always will be the being I shall always hold most dear. My eyes are full of tears, I am thinking of the pain that I am causing you, but if my shame was to be prevented from becoming public, and you were to be given time to reflect and act, I could not postpone any longer the confession that I owe you. If your affection for me, which I know is extremely deep, is good enough to grant me a small allowance, I will go and settle with my husband anywhere you like, in Switzerland, for instance. His name is so obscure that no one would recognize in Madame Sorel, the daughter-in-law of a Verrières carpenter, your daughter. That is the name which I have so much difficulty in writing. I fear your wrath against Julien, it seems so justified. I shall not be a duchess, my father; but I knew it when I loved him; for I was the one who loved him first, it was I who seduced him. I have inherited from you too lofty a soul to fix my attention on what either is or appears to be vulgar. It is in vain that I thought of M. Croisenois with a view to pleasing you. Why did you place real merit under my eyes? You told me yourself on my return from Hyères, 'that young Sorel is the one person who amuses me,' the poor boy is as grieved as I am if it is possible, at the pain this letter will give you. I cannot prevent you being irritated as a father, but love me as a friend.

"Julien respected me. If he sometimes spoke to me, it was only by reason of his deep gratitude towards yourself, for the natural dignity of his character induces him to keep to his official capacity in any answers he may make to anyone who is so much above him. He has a keen and instinctive appreciation of the difference of social rank. It was I (I confess it with a blush to my best friend, and I shall never make such a confession to anyone else) who clasped his arm one day in the garden.

"Why need you be irritated with him, after twenty-four hours have elapsed? My own lapse is irreparable. If you insist on it, the assurance of his profound respect and of his desperate grief at having displeased you, can be conveyed to you through me. You need not see him at all, but I shall go and join him wherever he wishes. It is his right and it is my duty. He is the father of my child. If your kindness will go so far as to grant us six thousand francs to live on, I will receive it with gratitude; if not, Julien reckons on establishing himself at Besançon, where he will set up as a Latin and literature master. However low may have been the station from which he springs, I am certain he will raise himself. With him I do not fear obscurity. If there is a revolution, I am sure that he will play a prime part. Can you say as much for any of those who have asked for my hand? They have fine estates, you say. I cannot consider that circumstance a reason for admiring them. My Julien would attain a high position, even under the present régime, if he had a million and my father's protection...."

Mathilde, who knew that the marquis was a man who always abandoned himself to his first impulse, had written eight pages.

"What am I to do?" said Julien to himself while M. de la Mole was reading this letter. "Where is (first) my duty; (second) my interest? My debt to him is immense. Without him I should have been a menial scoundrel, and not even enough of a scoundrel to be hated and persecuted by the others. He has made me a man of the world. The villainous acts which I now have to do are (first) less frequent; (second) less mean. That is more than as if he had given me a million. I am indebted to him for this cross and the reputation of having rendered those alleged diplomatic services, which have lifted me out of the ruck.

"If he himself were writing instructions for my conduct, what would he prescribe?"

Julien was sharply interrupted by M. de la Mole's old valet. "The marquis wants to see you at once, dressed or not dressed." The valet added in a low voice, as he walked by Julien's side, "He is beside himself: look out!"

LXIII
THE HELL OF WEAKNESS

A clumsy lapidary, in cutting this diamond, deprived it of some of its most brilliant facets. In the middle ages, nay, even under Richelieu, the Frenchman had *force of will.—Mirabeau.*

Julien found the marquis furious. For perhaps the first time in his life this nobleman showed bad form. He loaded Julien with all the insults that came to his lips. Our hero was astonished, and his patience was tried, but his gratitude remained unshaken.

"The poor man now sees the annihilation, in a single minute, of all the fine plans which he has long cherished in his heart. But I owe it to him to answer. My silence tends to increase his anger." The part of Tartuffe supplied the answer;

"I am not an angel.... I served you well; you paid me generously.... I was grateful, but I am twenty-two.... Only you and that charming person understood my thoughts in this household."

"Monster," exclaimed the marquis. "Charming! Charming, to be sure! The day when you found her charming you ought to have fled."

"I tried to. It was then that I asked permission to leave for Languedoc."

Tired of stampeding about and overcome by his grief, the marquis threw himself into an arm-chair. Julien heard him whispering to himself, "No, no, he is not a wicked man."

"No, I am not, towards you," exclaimed Julien, falling on his knees. But he felt extremely ashamed of this manifestation, and very quickly got up again.

The marquis was really transported. When he saw this movement, he began again to load him with abominable insults, which were worthy of the driver of a fiacre. The novelty of these oaths perhaps acted as a distraction.

"What! is my daughter to go by the name of madame Sorel? What! is my daughter not to be a duchess?" Each time that these two ideas presented themselves in all their clearness M. de la Mole was a prey to torture, and lost all power over the movements of his mind.

Julien was afraid of being beaten.

In his lucid intervals, when he was beginning to get accustomed to his unhappiness, the marquis addressed to Julien reproaches which were reasonable enough. "You should have fled, sir," he said to him. "Your duty was to flee. You are the lowest of men."

Julien approached the table and wrote:

"I have found my life unbearable for a long time; I am putting an end to it. I request monsieur the marquis to accept my apologies (together with the expression of my infinite grati-tude) for any embarrassment that may be occasioned by my death in his hôtel."

"Kindly run your eye over this paper, M. the marquis," said Julien. "Kill me, or have me killed by your valet. It is one o'clock in the morning. I will go and walk in the garden in the direction of the wall at the bottom."

"Go to the devil," cried the marquis, as he went away.

"I understand," thought Julien. "He would not be sorry if I were to spare his valet the trouble of killing me....

"Let him kill me, if he likes; it is a satisfaction which I offer him.... But, by heaven, I love life. I owe it to my son."

This idea, which had not previously presented itself with so much definiteness to his imagination, completely engrossed him during his walk after the first few minutes which he had spent thinking about his danger.

This novel interest turned him into a prudent man. "I need advice as to how to behave towards this infuriated man.... He is devoid of reason; he is capable of everything. Fouqué is too far away; besides, he would not understand the emotions of a heart like the marquis's."

"Count Altamira ... am I certain of eternal silence? My request for advice must not be a fresh step which will raise still further complications. Alas! I have no one left but the gloomy abbé Pirard. His mind is crabbed by Jansenism.... A damned Jesuit would know the world, and would be more in my line. M. Pirard is capable of beating me at the very mention of my crime."

The genius of Tartuffe came to Julien's help. "Well, I will go and confess to him." This was his final resolution after having walked about in the garden for two good hours. He no longer thought about being surprised by a gun shot. He was feeling sleepy.

Very early the next day, Julien was several leagues away from Paris and knocked at the door of the severe Jansenist. He found to his great astonishment that he was not unduly surprised at his confidence.

"I ought perhaps to reproach myself," said the abbé, who seemed more anxious than irritated. "I thought I guessed that love. My affection for you, my unhappy boy, prevented me from warning the father."

"What will he do?" said Julien keenly.

At that moment he loved the abbé, and would have found a scene between them very painful.

"I see three alternatives," continued Julien.

"M. de la Mole can have me put to death," and he mentioned the suicide letter which he had left with the Marquis; (2) "He can get Count Norbert to challenge me to a duel, and shoot at me point blank."

"You would accept?" said the abbé furiously as he got up.

"You do not let me finish. I should certainly never fire upon my benefactor's son. (3) He can send me away. If he says go to Edinburgh or New York, I will obey him. They can then conceal mademoiselle de la Mole's condition, but I will never allow them to suppress my son."

"Have no doubt about it, that will be the first thought of that depraved man."

At Paris, Mathilde was in despair. She had seen her father about seven o'clock. He had shown her Julien's letter. She feared that he might have considered it noble to put an end to his life; "and without my permission?" she said to herself with a pain due solely to her anger.

"If he dies I shall die," she said to her father. "It will be you who will be the cause of his death.... Perhaps you will rejoice at it but I swear by his shades that I shall at once go into mourning, and shall publicly appear as *Madame the widow Sorel*, I shall send out my invitations, you can count on it.... You will find me neither pusillanimous nor cowardly."

Her love went to the point of madness. M. de la Mole was flabbergasted in his turn.

He began to regard what had happened with a certain amount of logic. Mathilde did not appear at breakfast. The marquis felt an immense weight off his mind, and was particularly flattered when he noticed that she had said nothing to her mother.

Julien was dismounting from his horse. Mathilde had him called and threw herself into his arms almost beneath the very eyes of her chambermaid. Julien was not very appreciative of this transport. He had come away from his long consultation with the abbé Pirard in a very diplomatic and calculating mood. The calculation of possibilities had killed his imagination. Mathilde told him, with tears in her eyes, that she had read his suicide letter.

"My father may change his mind; do me the favour of leaving for Villequier this very minute. Mount your horse again, and leave the hôtel before they get up from table."

When Julien's coldness and astonishment showed no sign of abatement, she burst into tears.

"Let me manage our affairs," she exclaimed ecstatically, as she clasped him in her arms. "You know, dear, it is not of my own free will that I separate from you. Write under cover to my maid. Address it in a strange hand-writing, I will write volumes to you. Adieu, flee."

This last word wounded Julien, but he none the less obeyed. "It will be fatal," he thought "if, in their most gracious moments these aristocrats manage to shock me."

Mathilde firmly opposed all her father's prudent plans. She would not open negotiations on any other basis except this. She was to be Madame Sorel, and was either to live with her husband in poverty in Switzerland, or with her father in Paris. She rejected absolutely the suggestion of a secret accouchement. "In that case I should begin to be confronted with a prospect of calumny and dishonour. I shall go travelling with my husband two months after the marriage, and it will be easy to pretend that my son was born at a proper time."

This firmness though at first received with violent fits of anger, eventually made the marquis hesitate.

"Here," he said to his daughter in a moment of emotion, "is a gift of ten thousand francs a year. Send it to your Julien, and let him quickly make it impossible for me to retract it."

In order to obey Mathilde, whose imperious temper he well knew, Julien had travelled forty useless leagues; he was superintending the accounts of the farmers at Villequier. This act of benevolence on the part of the marquis occasioned his return. He went and asked asylum of the abbé Pirard, who had become Mathilde's most useful ally during his absence. Every time that he was questioned by the marquis, he would prove to him that any other course except public marriage would be a crime in the eyes of God.

"And happily," added the abbé, "worldly wisdom is in this instance in agreement with religion. Could one, in view of Mdlle. de la Mole's passionate character, rely for a minute on her keeping any secret which she did not herself wish to preserve? If one does not reconcile oneself to the frankness of a public marriage, society will concern itself much longer with this strange *mésalliance*. Everything must be said all at once without either the appearance or the reality of the slightest mystery."

"It is true," said the marquis pensively.

Two or three friends of M. de la Mole were of the same opinion as the abbé Pirard. The great obstacle in their view was Mathilde's decided character. But in spite of all these fine arguments the marquis's soul could not reconcile itself to giving up all hopes of a coronet for his daughter.

He ransacked his memory and his imagination for all the variations of knavery and duplicity which had been feasible in his youth. Yielding to necessity and having fear of the law seemed absurd and humiliating for a man in his position. He was paying dearly now for the luxury of those enchanting dreams concerning the future of his cherished daughter in which he had indulged for the last ten years.

"Who could have anticipated it?" he said to himself. "A girl of so proud a character, of so lofty a disposition, who is even prouder than I am of the name she bears? A girl whose hand has already been asked for by all the cream of the nobility of France."

"We must give up all faith in prudence. This age is made to confound everything. We are marching towards chaos."

LXIV
A MAN OF INTELLECT

The prefect said to himself as he rode along the highway on horseback, "why should I not be a minister, a president of the council, a duke? This is how I should make war.... By these means I should have all the reformers put in irons."—*The Globe*.

No argument will succeed in destroying the paramount influence of ten years of agreeable dreaming. The marquis thought it illogical to be angry, but could not bring himself to forgive. "If only this Julien could die by accident," he sometimes said to himself. It was in this way that his depressed imagination found a certain relief in running after the most absurd chimæras. They paralysed the influence of the wise arguments of the abbé Pirard. A month went by in this way without negotiations advancing one single stage.

The marquis had in this family matter, just as he had in politics, brilliant ideas over which he would be enthusiastic for two or three days. And then a line of tactics would fail to please him because it was based on sound arguments, while arguments only found favour in his eyes in so far as they were based on his favourite plan. He would work for three days with all the ardour and enthusiasm of a poet on bringing matters to a certain stage; on the following day he would not give it a thought.

Julien was at first disconcerted by the slowness of the marquis; but, after some weeks, he began to surmise that M. de La Mole had no definite plan with regard to this matter. Madame de La Mole and the whole household believed that Julien was travelling in the provinces in connection with the administration of the estates; he was in hiding in the parsonage of the abbé Pirard and saw Mathilde every day; every morning she would spend an hour with her father, but they would sometimes go for weeks on end without talking of the matter which engrossed all their thoughts.

"I don't want to know where the man is," said the marquis to her one day. "Send him this letter." Mathilde read:

"The Languedoc estates bring in 20,600 francs. I give 10,600 francs to my daughter, and 10,000 francs to M. Julien Sorel. It is understood that I give the actual estates. Tell the notary to draw up two separate deeds of gift, and to bring them to me to-morrow, after this there are to be no more relations between us. Ah, Monsieur, could I have expected all this? The marquis de La Mole."

"I thank you very much," said Mathilde gaily. "We will go and settle in the Château d'Aiguillon, between Agen and Marmande. The country is said to be as beautiful as Italy."

This gift was an extreme surprise to Julien. He was no longer the cold, severe man whom we have hitherto known. His thoughts were engrossed in advance by his son's destiny. This unexpected fortune, substantial as it was for a man as poor as himself, made him ambitious. He pictured a time when both his wife and himself would have an income of 36,000 francs. As for Mathilde, all her emotions were concentrated on her adoration for her husband, for that was the name by which her pride insisted on calling Julien. Her one great ambition was to secure the recognition of her marriage. She passed her time in exaggerating to herself the consummate prudence which she had manifested in linking her fate to that of a superior man. The idea of personal merit became a positive craze with her.

Julien's almost continuous absence, coupled with the complications of business matters and the little time available in which to talk love, completed the good effect produced by the wise tactics which Julien had previously discovered.

Mathilde finished by losing patience at seeing so little of the man whom she had come really to love.

In a moment of irritation she wrote to her father and commenced her letter like Othello:

"My very choice is sufficient proof that I have preferred Julien to all the advantages which society offered to the daughter of the marquis de la Mole. Such pleasures, based as they are on prestige and petty vanity mean nothing to me. It is now nearly six weeks since I have lived separated from my husband. That is sufficient to manifest my respect for yourself. Before next Thursday I shall leave the paternal house. Your acts of kindness have enriched us. No one knows my secret except the venerable abbé Pirard. I shall go to him: he will marry us, and an hour after the ceremony we shall be on the road to Languedoc, and we will never appear again in Paris except by your instructions. But what cuts me to the quick is that all this will provide the subject matter for piquant anecdotes against me and against yourself. May not the epigrams of a foolish public compel our excellent Norbert to pick a quarrel with Julien, under such circumstances I know I should have no control over him. We should discover in his soul the mark of the rebel plebian. Oh father, I entreat you on my knees, come and be present at my marriage in M. Pirard's church next Thursday. It will blunt the sting of malignant scandal and will guarantee the life's happiness of your only daughter, and of that of my husband, etc., etc."

This letter threw the marquis's soul into a strange embarrassment. He must at last take a definite line. All his little habits: all his vulgar friends had lost their influence.

In these strange circumstances the great lines of his character, which had been formed by the events of his youth, reassumed all their original force. The misfortunes of the emigration had made him into an imaginative man. After having enjoyed for two years an immense fortune and all the distinctions of the court, 1790 had flung him into the awful miseries of the emigration. This hard schooling had changed the character of a spirit of twenty-two. In essence, he was not so much dominated by his present riches as encamped in their midst. But that very imagination which had preserved his soul from the taint of avarice, had made him a victim of a mad passion for seeing his daughter decorated by a fine title.

During the six weeks which had just elapsed, the marquis had felt at times impelled by a caprice for making Julien rich. He considered poverty mean, humiliating for himself, M. de la Mole, and impossible in his daughter's husband; he was ready to lavish money. On the next day his imagination would go off on another tack, and he would think that Julien would read between the lines of this financial generosity, change his name, exile himself to America, and write to Mathilde that he was dead for her. M. de la Mole imagined this letter written, and went so far as to follow its effect on his daughter's character.

The day when he was awakened from these highly youthful dreams by Mathilde's actual letter after he had been thinking for along time of killing Julien or securing his disappearance he was dreaming of building up a brilliant position for him. He would make him take the name of one of his estates, and why should he not make him inherit a peerage? His father-in-law, M. the duke de Chaulnes, had, since the death of his own son in Spain, frequently spoken to him about his desire to transmit his title to Norbert....

"One cannot help owning that Julien has a singular aptitude for affairs, had boldness, and is possibly even brilliant," said the marquis to himself ... "but I detect at the root of his character a certain element which alarms me. He produces the same impression upon everyone, consequently there must be something real in it," and the more difficult this reality was to seize hold of, the more it alarmed the imaginative mind of the old marquis.

"My daughter expressed the same point very neatly the other day (in a suppressed letter).

"Julien has not joined any salon or any côterie. He has nothing to support himself against me, and has absolutely no resource if I abandon him. Now is that ignorance of the actual state of society? I have said to him two or three times, the only real and profitable candidature is the candidature of the salons.

"No, he has not the adroit, cunning genius of an attorney who never loses a minute or an opportunity. He is very far from being a character like Louis XL. On the other hand, I have seen him quote the most ungenerous maxims ... it is beyond me. Can it be that he simply repeats these maxims in order to use them as a *dam* against his passions?

"However, one thing comes to the surface; he cannot bear contempt, that's my hold on him.

"He has not, it is true, the religious reverence for high birth. He does not instinctively respect us.... That is wrong; but after all, the only things which are supposed to make the soul of a seminary student impatient are lack of enjoyment and lack of money. He is quite different, and cannot stand contempt at any price."

Pressed as he was by his daughter's letter, M. de la Mole realised the necessity for making up his mind. "After all, the great question is this:— Did Julien's audacity go to the point of setting out to make advances to my daughter because he knows I love her more than anything else in the world, and because I have an income of a hundred thousand crowns?"

Mathilde protests to the contrary.... "No, monsieur Julien, that is a point on which I am not going to be under any illusion.

"Is it really a case of spontaneous and authentic love? or is it just a vulgar desire to raise himself to a fine position? Mathilde is far-seeing; she appreciated from the first that this suspicion might ruin him with me—hence that confession of hers. It was she who took upon herself to love him the first.

"The idea of a girl of so proud a character so far forgetting herself as to make physical advances! To think of pressing his arm in the garden in the evening! How horrible! As though there were not a hundred other less unseemly ways of notifying him that he was the object of her favour.

"*Qui s'excuse s'accuse*; I distrust Mathilde." The marquis's reasoning was more conclusive to-day than it was usually. Nevertheless, force of habit prevailed, and he resolved to gain time by writing to his daughter, for a correspondence was being carried on between one wing of the hôtel and the other. M. de la Mole did not dare to discuss matters with Mathilde and to see her face to face. He was frightened of clinching the whole matter by yielding suddenly.

"Mind you commit no new acts of madness; here is a commission of lieutenant of Hussars for M. the chevalier, Julien Sorel de la Vernaye. You see what I am doing for him. Do not irritate me. Do not question me. Let him leave within twenty-four hours and present himself at Strasbourg where his regiment is. Here is an order on my banker. Obey me."

Mathilde's love and joy were unlimited. She wished to profit by her victory and immediately replied.

"If M. de la Vernaye knew all that you are good enough to do for him, he would be overwhelmed with gratitude and be at your feet. But amidst all this generosity, my father has forgotten me; your daughter's honour is in peril. An indiscretion may produce an everlasting blot which an income of twenty thousand crowns could not put right. I will only send the commission to M. de la Vernaye if you give me your word that my marriage will be publicly celebrated at Villequier in the course of next month. Shortly after that period, which I entreat you not to prolong, your daughter will only be able to appear in public under the name of Madame de la Vernaye. How I thank you, dear papa, for having saved me from the name of Sorel, etc., etc."

The reply was unexpected:

"Obey or I retract everything. Tremble, you imprudent young girl. I do not yet know what your Julien is, and you yourself know less than I. Let him leave for Strasbourg, and try to act straightly. I will notify him from here of my wishes within a fortnight."

Mathilde was astonished by this firm answer. *I do not know Julien.* These words threw her into a reverie which soon finished in the most fascinating suppositions; but she believed in their truth. My Julien's intellect is not clothed in the petty mean uniform of the salons, and my father refuses to believe in his superiority by reason of the very fact which proves it.

All the same, if I do not obey this whim of his, I see the possibility of a public scene; a scandal would lower my position in society, and might render me less fascinating in Julien's eyes. After the scandal ... ten years of poverty; and the only thing which can prevent marrying for merit becoming ridiculous is the most brilliant wealth. If I live far away from my father, he is old and may forget me.... Norbert will marry some clever, charming woman; old Louis XIV. was seduced by the duchess of Burgundy.

She decided to obey, but refrained from communicating her father's letter to Julien. It might perhaps have been that ferocious character driven to some act of madness.

Julien's joy was unlimited when she informed him in the evening that he was a lieutenant of Hussars. Its extent can be imagined from the fact that this had constituted the ambition of his whole life, and also from the passion which he now had for his son. The change of name struck him with astonishment.

"After all," he thought, "I have got to the end of my romance, and I deserve all the credit. I have managed to win the love of that monster of pride," he added, looking at Mathilde. "Her father cannot live without her, nor she without me."

LXV
A STORM

My God, give me mediocrity.—*Mirabeau*.

His mind was engrossed; he only half answered the eager tenderness that she showed to him. He remained gloomy and taciturn. He had never seemed so great and so adorable in Mathilde's eyes. She was apprehensive of some subtle twist of his pride which would spoil the whole situation.

She saw the abbé Pirard come to the hôtel nearly every morning. Might not Julien have divined something of her father's intentions through him? Might not the marquis himself have written to him in a momentary caprice. What was the explanation of Julien's stern manner following on so great a happiness? She did not dare to question.

She did not *dare*—she—Mathilde! From that moment her feelings for Julien contained a certain vague and unexpected element which was almost panic. This arid soul experienced all the passion possible in an individual who has been brought up amid that excessive civilisation which Paris so much admires.

Early on the following day Julien was at the house of the abbé Pirard. Some post-horses were arriving in the courtyard with a dilapidated chaise which had been hired at a neighbouring station.

"A vehicle like that is out of fashion," said the stern abbé to him morosely. "Here are twenty thousand francs which M. de la Mole makes you a gift of. He insists on your spending them within a year, but at the same time wants you to try to look as little ridiculous as possible." (The priest regarded flinging away so substantial a sum on a young man as simply an opportunity for sin).

"The marquis adds this: 'M. Julien de la Vernaye will have received this money from his father, whom it is needless to call by any other name. M. de la Vernaye will perhaps think it proper to give a present to M. Sorel, a carpenter of Verrières, who cared for him in his childhood....' I can undertake that commission," added the abbé. "I have at last prevailed upon M. de la Mole to come to a settlement with that Jesuit, the abbé de Frilair. His influence is unquestionably too much for us. The complete recognition of your high birth on the part of this man, who is in fact the governor of B—— will be one of the unwritten terms of the arrangement." Julien could no longer control his ecstasy. He embraced the abbé. He saw himself recognised.

"For shame," said M. Pirard, pushing him away. "What is the meaning of this worldly vanity? As for Sorel and his sons, I will offer them in my own name a yearly allowance of five hundred francs, which will be paid to each of them as long as I am satisfied with them."

Julien was already cold and haughty. He expressed his thanks, but in the vaguest terms which bound him to nothing. "Could it be possible," he said to himself, "that I am the natural son of some great nobleman who was exiled to our mountains by the terrible Napoleon?" This idea seemed less and less improbable every minute.... "My hatred of my father would be a proof of this.... In that case, I should not be an unnatural monster after all."

A few days after this soliloquy the Fifteenth Regiment of Hussars, which was one of the most brilliant in the army, was being reviewed on the parade ground of Strasbourg. M. the chevalier de La Vernaye sat the finest horse in Alsace, which had cost him six thousand francs. He was received as a lieutenant, though he had never been sub-lieutenant except on the rolls of a regiment of which he had never heard.

His impassive manner, his stern and almost malicious eyes, his pallor, and his invariable self-possession, founded his reputation from the very first day. Shortly afterwards his perfect and calculated politeness, and his skill at shooting and fencing, of which, though without any undue ostentation, he made his comrades aware, did away with all idea of making fun of him openly. After hesitating for five or six days, the public opinion of the regiment declared itself in his favour.

"This young man has everything," said the facetious old officers, "except youth."

Julien wrote from Strasbourg to the old curé of Verrières, M. Chélan, who was now verging on extreme old age.

"You will have learnt, with a joy of which I have no doubt, of the events which have induced my family to enrich me. Here are five hundred francs which I request you to distribute quietly, and without any mention of my name, among those unfortunate ones who are now poor as I myself was once, and whom you will doubtless help as you once helped me."

Julien was intoxicated with ambition, and not with vanity. He nevertheless devoted a great part of his time to attending to his external appearance. His horses, his uniform, his orderlies' liveries, were all kept with a correctness which would have done credit to the punctiliousness of a great English nobleman. He had scarcely been made a lieutenant as a matter of favour (and that only two days ago) than he began to calculate that if he was to become commander-in-chief at thirty, like all the great generals, then he must be more than a lieutenant at twenty-three at the latest. He thought about nothing except fame and his son.

It was in the midst of the ecstasies of the most reinless ambition that he was surprised by the arrival of a young valet from the Hôtel de la Mole, who had come with a letter.

"All is lost," wrote Mathilde to him: "Rush here as quickly as possible, sacrifice everything, desert if necessary. As soon as you have arrived, wait for me in a fiacre near the little garden door, near No. — — of the street — — I will come and speak to you: I shall perhaps be able to introduce you into the garden. All is lost, and I am afraid there is no way out; count on me; you will find me staunch and firm in adversity. I love you."

A few minutes afterwards, Julien obtained a furlough from the colonel, and left Strasbourg at full gallop. But the awful anxiety which devoured him did not allow him to continue this method of travel beyond Metz. He flung himself into a post-chaise, and arrived with an almost incredible rapidity at the indicated spot, near the little garden door of the Hôtel de la Mole. The door opened, and Mathilde, oblivious of all human conventions, rushed into his arms. Fortunately, it was only five o'clock in the morning, and the street was still deserted.

"All is lost. My father, fearing my tears, left Thursday night. Nobody knows where for? But here is his letter: read it." She climbed into the fiacre with Julien.

"I could forgive everything except the plan of seducing you because you are rich. That, unhappy girl, is the awful truth. I give you my word of honour that I will never consent to a marriage with that man. I will guarantee him an income of 10,000 francs if he will live far away beyond the French frontiers, or better still, in America. Read the letter which I have just received in answer to the enquiries which I have made. The impudent scoundrel had himself requested me to write to madame de Rênal. I will never read a single line you write concerning that man. I feel a horror for both Paris and yourself. I urge you to cover what is bound to happen with the utmost secrecy. Be frank, have nothing more to do with the vile man, and you will find again the father you have lost."

"Where is Madame de Rênal's letter?" said Julien coldly.

"Here it is. I did not want to shew it to you before you were prepared for it."

LETTER

"My duties to the sacred cause of religion and morality, oblige me, monsieur, to take the painful course which I have just done with regard to yourself: an infallible principle orders me to do harm to my neighbour at the present moment, but only in order to avoid an even greater scandal. My sentiment of duty must overcome the pain which I experience. It is only too true, monsieur, that the conduct of the person about whom you ask me to tell you the whole truth may seem incredible or even honest. It may possibly be considered proper to hide or to disguise part of the truth: that would be in accordance with both prudence and religion. But the conduct about which you desire information has been in fact reprehensible to the last degree, and more than I can say. Poor and greedy as the man is, it is only by the aid of the most consummate hypocrisy, and by seducing a weak and unhappy woman, that he has endeavoured to make a career for himself and become someone in the world. It is part of my painful duty to add that I am obliged to believe that M. Julien has no religious principles. I am driven conscientiously to think that one of his methods of obtaining success in any household is to try to seduce the woman who commands the principal influence. His one great object, in spite of his show of disinterestedness, and his stock-in-trade of phrases out of novels, is to succeed in doing what he likes with the master of the household and his fortune. He leaves behind him unhappiness and eternal remorse, etc., etc., etc."

This extremely long letter, which was almost blotted out by tears, was certainly in madame de Rênal's handwriting; it was even written with more than ordinary care.

"I cannot blame M. de la Mole," said Julien, "after he had finished it. He is just and prudent. What father would give his beloved daughter to such a man? Adieu!" Julien jumped out of the fiacre and rushed to his post-chaise, which had stopped at the end of the street. Mathilde, whom he had apparently forgotten, took a few steps as though to follow him, but the looks she received from the tradesmen, who were coming out on the thresholds of their shops, and who knew who she was, forced her to return precipitately to the garden.

Julien had left for Verrières. During that rapid journey he was unable to write to Mathilde as he had intended. His hand could only form illegible characters on the paper.

He arrived at Verrières on a Sunday morning. He entered the shop of the local gunsmith, who overwhelmed him with congratulations on his recent good fortune. It constituted the news of the locality.

Julien had much difficulty in making him understand that he wanted a pair of pistols. At his request the gunsmith loaded the pistols.

The three peals sounded; it is a well-known signal in the villages of France, and after the various ringings in the morning announces the immediate commencement of Mass.

Julien entered the new church of Verrières. All the lofty windows of the building were veiled with crimson curtains. Julien found himself some spaces behind the pew of madame de Rênal. It seemed to him that she was praying fervently The sight of the woman whom he had loved so much made Julien's arm tremble so violently that he was at first unable to execute his project. "I cannot," he said to himself. "It is a physical impossibility."

At that moment the young priest, who was officiating at the Mass, rang the bell for the elevation of the host. Madame de Rênal lowered her head, which, for a moment became entirely hidden by the folds of her shawl. Julien did not see her features so distinctly: he aimed a pistol shot at her, and missed her: he aimed a second shot, she fell.

LXVI
SAD DETAILS

Do not expect any weakness on my part. I have avenged myself. I have deserved death, and here I am. Pray for my soul.—*Schiller*

Julien remained motionless. He saw nothing more. When he recovered himself a little he noticed all the faithful rushing from the church. The priest had left the altar. Julien started fairly slowly to follow some women who were going away with loud screams. A woman who was trying to get away more quickly than the others, pushed him roughly. He fell. His feet got entangled with a chair, knocked over by the crowd; when he got up, he felt his neck gripped. A gendarme, in full uniform, was arresting him. Julien tried mechanically to have recourse to his little pistol; but a second gendarme pinioned his arms.

He was taken to the prison. They went into a room where irons were put on his hands. He was left alone. The door was doubly locked on him. All this was done very quickly, and he scarcely appreciated it at all.

"Yes, upon my word, all is over," he said aloud as he recovered himself. "Yes, the guillotine in a fortnight ... or killing myself here."

His reasoning did not go any further. His head felt as though it had been seized in some violent grip. He looked round to see if anyone was holding him. After some moments he fell into a deep sleep.

Madame de Rênal was not mortally wounded. The first bullet had pierced her hat. The second had been fired as she was turning round. The bullet had struck her on the shoulder, and, astonishing to relate, had ricocheted from off the shoulder bone (which it had, however, broken) against a gothic pillar, from which it had loosened an enormous splinter of stone.

When, after a long and painful bandaging, the solemn surgeon said to madame de Rênal, "I answer for your life as I would for my own," she was profoundly grieved.

She had been sincerely desirous of death for a long time. The letter which she had written to M. de la Mole in accordance with the injunctions of her present confessor, had proved the final blow to a creature already weakened by an only too permanent unhappiness. This unhappiness was caused by Julien's absence; but she, for her own part, called it remorse. Her director, a young ecclesiastic, who was both virtuous and enthusiastic, and had recently come to Dijon, made no mistake as to its nature.

"Dying in this way, though not by my own hand, is very far from being a sin," thought madame de Rênal. "God will perhaps forgive me for rejoicing over my death." She did not dare to add, "and dying by Julien's hand puts the last touch on my happiness."

She had scarcely been rid of the presence of the surgeon and of all the crowd of friends that had rushed to see her, than she called her maid, Elisa. "The gaoler," she said to her with a violent blush, "is a cruel man. He will doubtless ill-treat him, thinking to please me by doing so.... I cannot bear that idea. Could you not go, as though on your own account, and give the gaoler this little packet which contains some louis. You will tell him that religion forbids him to treat him badly, above all, he must not go and speak about the sending of this money."

It was this circumstance, which we have just mentioned, that Julien had to thank for the humanity of the gaoler of Verrières. It was still the same M. Noiraud, that ideal official, whom he remembered as being so finely alarmed by M. Appert's presence.

A judge appeared in the prison. "I occasioned death by premeditation," said Julien to him. "I bought the pistols and had them loaded at so-and-so's, a gunsmith. Article 1342 of the penal code is clear. I deserve death, and I expect it." Astonished at this kind of answer, the judge started to multiply his questions, with a view of the accused contradicting himself in his answers.

"Don't you see," said Julien to him with a smile, "that I am making myself out as guilty as you can possibly desire? Go away, monsieur, you will not fail to catch the quarry you are pursuing. You will have the pleasure to condemn me. Spare me your presence."

"I have an irksome duty to perform," thought Julien. "I must write to mademoiselle de la Mole:—"

"I have avenged myself," he said to her. "Unfortunately, my name will appear in the papers, and I shall not be able to escape from the world incognito. I shall die in two months' time. My revenge was ghastly, like the pain of being separated from you. From this moment I forbid myself to write or pronounce your name. Never speak of me even to my son; silence is the only way of honouring me. To the ordinary commonplace man, I shall represent a common assassin. Allow me the luxury of the truth at this supreme moment; you will forget me. This great catastrophe of which I advise you not to say a single word to a single living person, will exhaust, for several years to come, all that romantic and unduly adventurous element which I have detected in your character. You were intended by nature to live among the heroes of the middle ages; exhibit their firm character. Let what has to happen take place in secret and without your being compromised. You will assume a false name, and you will confide in no one. If you absolutely need a friend's help, I bequeath the abbé Pirard to you.

"Do not talk to anyone else, particularly to the people of your own class—the de Luz's, the Caylus's.

"A year after my death, marry M. de Croisenois; I command you as your husband. Do not write to me at all, I shall not answer. Though in my view, much less wicked than Iago, I am going to say, like him: 'From this time forth, I never will speack word.'[5]

"I shall never be seen to speak or write again. You will have received my final words and my final expressions of adoration.

"J. S."

It was only after he had despatched this letter and had recovered himself a little, that Julien felt for the first time extremely unhappy. Those momentous words, I shall die, meant the successive tearing out of his heart of each individual hope and ambition. Death, in itself, was not horrible in his eyes. His whole life had been nothing but a long preparation for unhappiness, and he had made a point of not losing sight of what is considered the greatest unhappiness of all.

"Come then," he said to himself; "if I had to fight a duel in a couple of months, with an expert duellist, should I be weak enough to think about it incessantly with panic in my soul?"

He passed more than an hour in trying to analyze himself thoroughly on this score.

When he saw clear in his own soul, and the truth appeared before his eyes with as much definiteness as one of the pillars of his prison, he thought about remorse.

"Why should I have any? I have been atrociously injured; I have killed—I deserve death, but that is all. I die after having squared my account with humanity. I do not leave any obligation unfulfilled. I owe nothing to anybody; there is nothing shameful about my death, except the instrument of it; that alone, it is true, is simply sufficient to disgrace me in the eyes of the bourgeois of Verrières; but from the intellectual standpoint, what could be more contemptible than they? I have one means of winning their consideration; by flinging pieces of gold to the people as I go to the scaffold. If my memory is linked with the idea of gold, they will always look upon it as resplendent."

After this chain of reasoning, which after a minute's reflection seemed to him self-evident, Julien said to himself, "I have nothing left to do in the world," and fell into a deep sleep.

About 9 o'clock in the evening the gaoler woke him up as he brought in his supper.

"What are they saying in Verrières?"

"M. Julien, the oath which I took before the crucifix in the 'Royal Courtyard,' on the day when I was installed in my place, obliges me to silence."

He was silent, but remained. Julien was amused by the sight of this vulgar hypocrisy. I must make him, he thought, wait a long time for the five francs which he wants to sell his conscience for.

When the gaoler saw him finish his meal without making any attempt to corrupt him, he said in a soft and perfidious voice:

"The affection which I have for you, M. Julien, compels me to speak. Although they say that it is contrary to the interests of justice, because it may assist you in preparing your defence. M. Julien you are a good fellow at heart, and you will be very glad to learn that madame de Rênal is better."

"What! she is not dead?" exclaimed Julien, beside himself.

"What, you know nothing?" said the gaoler, with a stupid air which soon turned into exultant cupidity. "It would be very proper, monsieur, for you to give something to the surgeon, who, so far as law and justice go, ought not to have spoken. But in order to please you, monsieur, I went to him, and he told me everything."

"Anyway, the wound is not mortal," said Julien to him impatiently, "you answer for it on your life?"

The gaoler, who was a giant six feet tall, was frightened and retired towards the door. Julien saw that he was adopting bad tactics for getting at the truth. He sat down again and flung a napoleon to M. Noiraud.

As the man's story proved to Julien more and more conclusively that madame de Rênal's wound was not mortal, he felt himself overcome by tears. "Leave me," he said brusquely.

The gaoler obeyed. Scarcely had the door shut, than Julien exclaimed: "Great God, she is not dead," and he fell on his knees, shedding hot tears.

In this supreme moment he was a believer. What mattered the hypocrisies of the priests? Could they abate one whit of the truth and sublimity of the idea of God?

It was only then that Julien began to repent of the crime that he had committed. By a coincidence, which prevented him falling into despair, it was only at the present moment that the condition of physical irritation and semi-madness, in which he had been plunged since his departure from Paris for Verrières came to an end.

His tears had a generous source. He had no doubt about the condemnation which awaited him.

"So she will live," he said to himself. "She will live to forgive me and love me."

Very late the next morning the gaoler woke him up and said, "You must have a famous spirit, M. Julien. I have come in twice, but I did not want to wake you up. Here are two bottles of excellent wine which our curé, M. Maslon, has sent you."

"What, is that scoundrel still here?" said Julien.

"Yes, monsieur," said the gaoler, lowering his voice. "But do not talk so loud, it may do you harm."

Julien laughed heartily.

"At the stage I have reached, my friend, you alone can do me harm in the event of your ceasing to be kind and tender. You will be well paid," said Julien, changing his tone and reverting to his imperious manner. This manner was immediately justified by the gift of a piece of money.

M. Noiraud related again, with the greatest detail, everything he had learnt about madame de Rênal, but he did not make any mention of mademoiselle Elisa's visit.

The man was as base and servile as it was possible to be. An idea crossed Julien's mind. "This kind of misshapen giant cannot earn more than three or four hundred francs, for his prison is not at all full. I can guarantee him ten thousand francs, if he will escape with me to Switzerland. The difficulty will be in persuading him of my good faith." The idea of the long conversation he would need to have with so vile a person filled Julien with disgust. He thought of something else.

In the evening the time had passed. A post-chaise had come to pick him up at midnight. He was very pleased with his travelling companions, the gendarmes. When he arrived at the prison of Besançon in the morning they were kind enough to place him in the upper storey of a Gothic turret. He judged the architecture to be of the beginning of the fourteenth century. He admired its fascinating grace and lightness. Through a narrow space between two walls, beyond the deep court, there opened a superb vista.

On the following day there was an interrogation, after which he was left in peace for several days. His soul was calm. He found his affair a perfectly simple one. "I meant to kill. I deserve to be killed."

His thoughts did not linger any further over this line of reasoning. As for the sentence, the disagreeableness of appearing in public, the defence, he considered all this as slight embarrassment, irksome formalities, which it would be time enough to consider on the actual day. The actual moment of death did not seize hold of his mind either. "I will think about it after the sentence." Life was no longer boring, he was envisaging everything from a new point of view, he had no longer any ambition. He rarely thought about mademoiselle de la Mole. His passion of remorse engrossed him a great deal, and often conjured up the image of madame de Rênal, particularly during the silence of the night, which in this high turret was only disturbed by the song of the osprey.

He thanked heaven that he had not inflicted a mortal wound. "Astonishing," he said to himself, "I thought that she had destroyed my future happiness for ever by her letter to M. de la Mole, and here am I, less than a fortnight after the date of that letter, not giving a single thought to all the things that engrossed me then. An income of two or three thousand francs, on which to live quietly in a mountain district, like Vergy.... I was happy then.... I did not realise my happiness."

At other moments he would jump up from his chair. "If I had mortally wounded madame de Rênal, I would have killed myself.... I need to feel certain of that so as not to horrify myself."

"Kill myself? That's the great question," he said to himself. "Oh, those judges, those fiends of red tape, who would hang their best citizen in order to win the cross.... At any rate, I should escape from their control and from the bad French of their insults, which the local paper will call eloquence."

"I still have five or six weeks, more or less to live.... Kill myself. No, not for a minute," he said to himself after some days, "Napoleon went on living."

"Besides, I find life pleasant, this place is quiet, I am not troubled with bores," he added with a smile, and he began to make out a list of the books which he wanted to order from Paris.

LXVII
A TURRET

The tomb of a friend.—*Sterne.*

He heard a loud noise in the corridor. It was not the time when the gaoler usually came up to his prison. The osprey flew away with a shriek. The door opened, and the venerable curé Chélan threw himself into his arms. He was trembling all over and had his stick in his hands.

"Great God! Is it possible, my child—I ought to say monster?"

The good old man could not add a single word. Julien was afraid he would fall down. He was obliged to lead him to a chair. The hand of time lay heavy on this man who had once been so active. He seemed to Julien the mere shadow of his former self.

When he had regained his breath, he said, "It was only the day before yesterday that I received your letter from Strasbourg with your five hundred francs for the poor of Verrières. They brought it to me in the mountains at Liveru where I am living in retirement with my nephew Jean. Yesterday I learnt of the catastrophe.... Heavens, is it possible?" And the old man left off weeping. He did not seem to have any ideas left, but added mechanically, "You will have need of your five hundred francs, I will bring them back to you."

"I need to see you, my father," exclaimed Julien, really touched. "I have money, anyway."

But he could not obtain any coherent answer. From time to time, M. Chélan shed some tears which coursed silently down his cheeks. He then looked at Julien, and was quite dazed when he saw him kiss his hands and carry them to his lips. That face which had once been so vivid, and which had once portrayed with such vigour the most noble emotions was now sunk in a perpetual apathy. A kind of peasant came soon to fetch the old man. "You must not fatigue him," he said to Julien, who understood that he was the nephew. This visit left Julien plunged in a cruel unhappiness which found no vent in tears. Everything seemed to him gloomy and disconsolate. He felt his heart frozen in his bosom.

This moment was the cruellest which he had experienced since the crime. He had just seen death and seen it in all its ugliness. All his illusions about greatness of soul and nobility of character had been dissipated like a cloud before the hurricane.

This awful plight lasted several hours. After moral poisoning, physical remedies and champagne are necessary. Julien would have considered himself a coward to have resorted to them. "What a fool I am," he exclaimed, towards the end of the horrible day that he had spent entirely in walking up and down his narrow turret. "It's only, if I had been going to die like anybody else, that the sight of that poor old man would have had any right to have thrown me into this awful fit of sadness: but a rapid death in the flower of my age simply puts me beyond the reach of such awful senility."

In spite of all his argumentation, Julien felt as touched as any weak-minded person would have been, and consequently felt unhappy as the result of the visit. He no longer had any element of rugged greatness, or any Roman virtue. Death appeared to him at a great height and seemed a less easy proposition.

"This is what I shall take for my thermometer," he said to himself. "To-night I am ten degrees below the courage requisite for guillotine-point level. I had that courage this morning. Anyway, what does it matter so long as it comes back to me at the necessary moment?" This thermometer idea amused him and finally managed to distract him.

When he woke up the next day he was ashamed of the previous day. "My happiness and peace of mind are at stake." He almost made up his mind to write to the Procureur-General to request that no one should be admitted to see him. "And how about Fouqué," he thought? "If he takes it upon himself to come to Besançon, his grief will be immense." It had perhaps been two months since he had given Fouqué a thought. "I was a great fool at Strasbourg. My thoughts did not go beyond my coat-collar. He was much engrossed by the memory of Fouqué, which left him more and more touched. He walked nervously about. Here I am, clearly twenty degrees below death point.... If this weakness increases, it will be better for me to kill myself. What joy for the abbé Maslon, and the Valenods, if I die like an usher."

Fouqué arrived. The good, simple man, was distracted by grief. His one idea, so far as he had any at all, was to sell all he possessed in order to bribe the gaoler and secure Julien's escape. He talked to him at length of M. de Lavalette's escape.

"You pain me," Julien said to him. "M. de Lavalette was innocent—I am guilty. Though you did not mean to, you made me think of the difference...."

"But is it true? What? were you going to sell all you possessed?" said Julien, suddenly becoming mistrustful and observant.

Fouqué was delighted at seeing his friend answer his obsessing idea, and detailed at length, and within a hundred francs, what he would get for each of his properties.

"What a sublime effort for a small country land-owner," thought Julien. "He is ready to sacrifice for me the fruits of all the economies, and all the little semi-swindling tricks which I used to be ashamed of when I saw him practice them."

"None of the handsome young people whom I saw in the Hôtel de la

Mole, and who read René, would have any of his ridiculous weaknesses: but, except those who are very young and who have also inherited riches and are ignorant of the value of money, which of all those handsome Parisians would be capable of such a sacrifice?"

All Fouqué's mistakes in French and all his common gestures seemed to disappear. He threw himself into his arms. Never have the provinces in comparison with Paris received so fine a tribute. Fouqué was so delighted with the momentary enthusiasm which he read in his friend's eyes that he took it for consent to the flight.

This view of the sublime recalled to Julien all the strength that the apparition of M. Chélan had made him lose. He was still very young; but in my view he was a fine specimen. Instead of his character passing from tenderness to cunning, as is the case with the majority of men, age would have given him that kindness of heart which is easily melted ... but what avail these vain prophecies.

The interrogations became more frequent in spite of all the efforts of Julien, who always endeavoured by his answers to shorten the whole matter.

"I killed, or at any rate, I wished to occasion death, and I did so with premeditation," he would repeat every day. But the judge was a pedant above everything. Julien's confessions had no effect in curtailing the interrogations. The judge's conceit was wounded. Julien did not know that they had wanted to transfer him into an awful cell, and that it was only, thanks to Fouqué's efforts, that he was allowed to keep his pretty room at the top of a hundred and eighty steps.

M. the abbé de Frilair was one of the important customers who entrusted Fouqué with the purveying of their firewood. The good tradesmen managed to reach the all powerful grand vicar. M. de Frilair informed him, to his unspeakable delight, that he was so touched by Julien's good qualities, and by the services which he had formerly rendered to the seminary, that he intended to recommend him to the judges. Fouqué thought he saw a hope of saving his friend, and as he went out, bowing down to the ground, requested M. the grand vicar, to distribute a sum of ten louis in masses to entreat the acquittal of the accused.

Fouqué was making a strange mistake. M. de Frilair was very far from being a Valenod. He refused, and even tried to make the good peasant understand that he would do better to keep his money. Seeing that it was impossible to be clear without being indiscreet, he advised him to give that sum as alms for the use of the poor prisoners, who, in point of fact, were destitute of everything.

"This Julien is a singular person, his action is unintelligible," thought M. de Frilair, "and I ought to find nothing unintelligible. Perhaps it will be possible to make a martyr of him.... In any case, I shall get to the bottom of the matter, and shall perhaps find an opportunity of putting fear into the heart of that madame de Rênal who has no respect for us, and at the bottom detests me.... Perhaps I might be able to utilise all this as a means of a brilliant reconciliation with M. de la Mole, who has a weakness for the little seminarist."

The settlement of the lawsuit had been signed some weeks previously, and the abbé Pirard had left Besançon after having duly mentioned Julien's mysterious birth, on the very day when the unhappy man tried to assassinate madame de Rênal in the church of Verrières.

There was only one disagreeable event between himself and his death which Julien anticipated. He consulted Fouqué concerning his idea of writing to M. the Procureur-General asking to be exempt from all visits. This horror at the sight of a father, above all at a moment like this, deeply shocked the honest middle-class heart of the wood merchant.

He thought he understood why so many people had a passionate hatred for his friend. He concealed his feelings out of respect for misfortune.

"In any case," he answered coldly, "such an order for privacy would not be applied to your father."

LXVIII
A POWERFUL MAN

But her proceedings are so mysterious and her figure is so elegant! Who can she be?—*Schiller.*

The doors of the turret opened very early on the following day.

"Oh! good God," he thought, "here's my father! What an unpleasant scene!"

At the same time a woman dressed like a peasant rushed into his arms. He had difficulty in recognising her. It was mademoiselle de la Mole.

"You wicked man! Your letter only told me where you were. As for what you call your crime, but which is really nothing more or less than a noble vengeance, which shews me all the loftiness of the heart which beats within your bosom, I only got to know of it at Verrières."

In spite of all his prejudices against mademoiselle de la Mole, prejudices moreover which he had not owned to himself quite frankly, Julien found her extremely pretty. It was impossible not to recognise both in what she had done and what she had said, a noble disinterested feeling far above the level of anything that a petty vulgar soul would have dared to do? He thought that he still loved a queen, and after a few moments said to her with a remarkable nobility both of thought and of elocution,

"I sketched out the future very clearly. After my death I intended to remarry you to M. de Croisenois, who will officially of course then marry a widow. The noble but slightly romantic soul of this charming widow, who will have been brought back to the cult of vulgar prudence by an astonishing and singular event which played in her life a part as great as it was tragic, will deign to appreciate the very real merit of the young marquis. You will resign yourself to be happy with ordinary worldly happiness, prestige, riches, high rank. But, dear Mathilde, if your arrival at Besançon is suspected, it will be a mortal blow for M. de la Mole, and that is what I shall never forgive myself. I have already caused him so much sorrow. The academician will say that he has nursed a serpent in his bosom.

"I must confess that I little expected so much cold reason and so much solicitude for the future," said mademoiselle de la Mole, slightly annoyed. "My maid who is almost as prudent as you are, took a passport for herself, and I posted here under the name of madam Michelet."

"And did madame Michelet find it so easy to get to see me?"

"Ah! you are still the same superior man whom I chose to favour. I started by offering a hundred francs to one of the judge's secretaries, who alleged at first that my admission into this turret was impossible. But once he had got the money the worthy man kept me waiting, raised objections, and I thought that he meant to rob me—" She stopped.

"Well?" said Julien.

"Do not be angry, my little Julien," she said, kissing him. "I was obliged to tell my name to the secretary, who took me for a young working girl from Paris in love with handsome Julien. As a matter of fact those are his actual expressions. I swore to him, my dear, that I was your wife, and I shall have a permit to see you every day."

"Nothing could be madder," thought Julien, "but I could not help it. After all, M. de la Mole is so great a nobleman that public opinion will manage to find an excuse for the young colonel who will marry such a charming widow. My death will atone for everything;" and he abandoned himself with delight to Mathilde's love. It was madness, it was greatness of soul, it was the most remarkable thing possible. She seriously suggested that she should kill herself with him.

After these first transports, when she had had her fill of the happiness of seeing Julien, a keen curiosity suddenly invaded her soul. She began to scrutinize her lover, and found him considerably above the plane which she had anticipated. Boniface de La Mole seemed to be brought to life again, but on a more heroic scale.

Mathilde saw the first advocates of the locality, and offended them by offering gold too crudely, but they finished by accepting.

She promptly came to the conclusion that so far as dubious and far reaching intrigues were concerned, everything depended at Besançon on M. the abbé de Frilair.

She found at first overwhelming difficulties in obtaining an interview with the all-powerful leader of the congregation under the obscure name of madame Michelet. But the rumour of the beauty of a young dress-maker, who was madly in love, and had come from Paris to Besançon to console the young abbé Julien Sorel, spread over the town.

Mathilde walked about the Besançon streets alone: she hoped not to be recognised. In any case, she thought it would be of some use to her cause if she produced a great impression on the people. She thought, in her madness, of making them rebel in order to save Julien as he walked to his death. Mademoiselle de la Mole thought she was dressed simply and in a way suitable to a woman in mourning, she was dressed in fact in such a way as to attract every one's attention.

She was the object of everyone's notice at Besançon when she obtained an audience of M. de Frilair after a week spent in soliciting it.

In spite of all her courage, the idea of an influential leader of the congregation, and the idea of deep and calculating criminality, were so associated with each other in her mind, that she trembled as she rang the bell at the door of the bishop's palace. She could scarcely walk when she had to go up the staircase, which led to the apartment of the first grand Vicar. The solitude of the episcopal palace chilled her. "I might sit down in an armchair, and the armchair might grip my arms: I should then disappear. Whom could my maid ask for? The captain of the gendarmerie will take care to do nothing. I am isolated in this great town."

After her first look at the apartment, mademoiselle de la Mole felt reassured. In the first place, the lackey who had opened the door to her had on a very elegant livery. The salon in which she was asked to wait displayed that refined and delicate luxury which differs so much from crude magnificence, and which is only found in the best houses in Paris. As soon as she noticed M. de Frilair coming towards her with quite a paternal air, all her ideas of his criminality disappeared. She did not even find on his handsome face the impress of that drastic and somewhat savage courage which is so anti-pathetic to Paris society. The half-smile which animated the features of the priest, who was all-powerful at Besançon, betokened the well-bred man, the learned prelate, the clever administrator. Mathilde felt herself at Paris.

It was the work of a few minutes for M. de Frilair to induce Mathilde to confess to him that she was the daughter of his powerful opponent, the marquis de la Mole.

"As a matter of fact, I am not Madame Michelet," she said, reassuming all the haughtiness of her natural demeanour, "and this confession costs me but little since I have come to consult you, monsieur, on the possibility of procuring the escape of M. de la Vernaye. Moreover, he is only guilty of a piece of folly; the woman whom he shot at is well; and, in the second place, I can put down fifty-thousand francs straight away for the purpose of bribing the officials, and pledge myself for twice that sum. Finally, my gratitude and the gratitude of my family will be ready to do absolutely anything for the man who has saved M. de la Vernaye."

M. de Frilair seemed astonished at the name. Mathilde shewed him several letters from the Minister of War, addressed to M. Julien Sorel de la Vernaye.

"You see, monsieur, that my father took upon himself the responsibility of his career. I married him secretly, my father was desirous that he should be a superior officer before the notification of this marriage, which, after all, is somewhat singular for a de la Mole."

Mathilde noticed that M. de Frilair's expression of goodwill and mild cheerfulness was rapidly vanishing in proportion as he made certain important discoveries. His face exhibited a subtlety tinged with deep perfidiousness, the abbé had doubts, he was slowly re-reading the official documents.

"What can I get out of these strange confidences?" he said to himself. "Here I am suddenly thrown into intimate relations with a friend of the celebrated maréchale de Fervaques, who is the all-powerful niece of my lord, bishop of —— who can make one a bishop of France. What I looked upon as an extremely distant possibility presents itself unexpectedly. This may lead me to the goal of all my hopes."

Mathilde was at first alarmed by the sudden change in the expression of this powerful man, with whom she was alone in a secluded room. "But come," she said to herself soon afterwards. "Would it not have been more unfortunate if I had made no impression at all on the cold egoism of a priest who was already sated with power and enjoyment?"

Dazzled at the sight of this rapid and unexpected path of reaching the episcopate which now disclosed itself to him, and astonished as he was by Mathilde's genius, M. de Frilair ceased for a moment to be on his guard. Mademoiselle de la Mole saw him almost at her feet, tingling with ambition, and trembling nervously.

"Everything is cleared up," she thought. "Madame de Fervaques' friend will find nothing impossible in this town." In spite of a sentiment of still painful jealousy she had sufficient courage to explain that Julien was the intimate friend of the maréchale, and met my lord the bishop of —— nearly every day.

"If you were to draw by ballot four or five times in succession a list of thirty-six jurymen from out the principal inhabitants of this department," said the grand Vicar, emphasizing his words, and with a hard,

ambitious expression in his eyes, "I should not feel inclined to congratulate myself, if I could not reckon on eight or ten friends who would
be the most intelligent of the lot in each list. I can always manage in
nearly every case to get more than a sufficient majority to secure a condemnation, so you see, mademoiselle, how easy it is for me to secure a
conviction." The abbé stopped short as though astonished by the sound
of his own words; he was admitting things which are never said to the
profane. But he in his turn dumbfounded Mathilde when he informed
her that the special feature in Julien's strange adventure which astonished and interested Besançon society, was that he had formerly inspired
Madame de Rênal with a grand passion and reciprocated it for a long
time. M. de Frilair had no difficulty in perceiving the extreme trouble
which his story produced.

"I have my revenge," he thought. "After all it's a way of managing
this decided young person. I was afraid that I should not succeed."
Her distinguished and intractable appearance intensified in his eyes the
charm of the rare beauty whom he now saw practically entreating him.
He regained all his self-possession—and he did not hesitate to move the
dagger about in her heart.

"I should not be at all surprised," he said to her lightly, "if we were to
learn that it was owing to jealousy that M. Sorel fired two pistol shots at
the woman he once loved so much. Of course she must have consoled
herself and for some time she has been seeing extremely frequently a
certain abbé Marquinot of Dijon, a kind of Jansenist, and as immoral as
all Jansenists are."

M. de Frilair experienced the voluptuous pleasure of torturing at his
leisure the heart of this beautiful girl whose weakness he had surprised.

"Why," he added, as he fixed his ardent eyes upon Mathilde, "should
M. Sorel have chosen the church, if it were not for the reason that his rival
was celebrating mass in it at that very moment? Everyone attributes an
infinite amount of intelligence and an even greater amount of prudence
to the fortunate man who is the object of your interest. What would
have been simpler than to hide himself in the garden of M. de Rênal
which he knows so well. Once there he could put the woman of whom
he was jealous to death with the practical certainty of being neither seen,
caught, nor suspected."

This apparently sound train of reasoning eventually made Mathilde
loose all self-possession. Her haughty soul steeped in all that arid prudence, which passes in high society for the true psychology of the human
heart, was not of the type to be at all quick in appreciating that joy of
scorning all prudence, which an ardent soul can find so keen. In the high
classes of Paris society in which Mathilde had lived, it is only rarely that
passion can divest itself of prudence, and people always make a point of

throwing themselves out of windows from the fifth storey.

At last the abbé de Frilair was sure of his power over her. He gave Mathilde to understand (and he was doubtless lying) that he could do what he liked with the public official who was entrusted with the conduct of Julien's prosecution. After the thirty-six jurymen for the sessions had been chosen by ballot, he would approach at least thirty jurymen directly and personally.

If M. de Frilair had not thought Mathilde so pretty, he would not have spoken so clearly before the fifth or sixth interview.

LXIX
THE INTRIGUE

Castres 1676—A brother has just murdered his sister in the house next to mine. This gentleman had already been guilty of one murder. His father saved his life by causing five-hundred crowns to be distributed among the councillors.—
Locke: Journey in France.

When she left the bishop's palace, Mathilde did not hesitate to despatch a courier to madame de Fervaques. The fear of compromising herself did not stop her for a moment. She entreated her rival to obtain for M. de Frilair an autograph letter from the bishop of ——. She went as far as to entreat her to come herself to Besançon with all speed. This was an heroic act on the part of a proud and jealous soul.

Acting on Fouqué's advice, she had had the discretion to refrain from mentioning the steps she had taken for Julien. Her presence troubled him enough without that. A better man when face to face with death than he had ever been during his life, he had remorse not only towards M. de la Mole, but also towards Mathilde.

"Come," he said to himself, "there are times when I feel absent-minded and even bored by her society. She is ruining herself on my account, and this is how I reward her. Am I really a scoundrel?" This question would have bothered him but little in the days when he was ambitious. In those days he looked upon failure as the only disgrace.

His moral discomfort when with Mathilde was proportionately emphasized by the fact that he inspired her at this time with the maddest and most extraordinary passion. She talked of nothing but the strange sacrifices that she was ready to make in order to save him.

Exalted as she was by a sentiment on which she plumed herself, to the complete subordination of her pride, she would have liked not to have let a single minute of her life go by without filling it with some extraordinary act. The strangest projects, and ones involving her in the utmost danger, supplied the topics of her long interviews with Julien. The well-paid gaolers allowed her to reign over the prison. Mathilde's ideas were not limited by the sacrifice of her reputation. She would have thought nothing of making her condition known to society at large. Throwing herself on her knees before the king's carriage as it galloped along, in order to ask for Julien's pardon, and thus attracting the attention of the prince, at the risk of being crushed a thousand times over, was one of the least fantastic dreams in which this exalted and courageous imagination chose to indulge. She was certain of being admitted into the reserved portion of the park of St. Cloud, through those friends of hers who were employed at the king's court.

Julien thought himself somewhat unworthy of so much devotion. As a matter of fact, he was tired of heroism. A simple, naïve, and almost timid tenderness was what would have appealed to him, while Mathilde's haughty soul, on the other hand, always required the idea of a public and an audience.

In the midst of all her anguish and all her fears for the life of that lover whom she was unwilling to survive, she felt a secret need of astonishing the public by the extravagance of her love and the sublimity of her actions.

Julien felt irritated at not finding himself touched by all this heroism. What would he have felt if he had known of all the mad ideas with which Mathilde overwhelmed the devoted but eminently logical and limited spirit of the good Fouqué?

He did not know what to find fault with in Mathilde's devotion. For he, too, would have sacrificed all his fortune, and have exposed his life to the greatest risks in order to save Julien. He was dumbfounded by the quantity of gold which Mathilde flung away. During the first days Fouqué, who had all the provincial's respect for money, was much impressed by the sums she spent in this way.

He at last discovered that mademoiselle de la Mole's projects frequently varied, and he was greatly relieved at finding a word with which to express his blame for a character whom he found so exhausting. She was changeable. There is only a step from this epithet to that of wrongheaded, the greatest term of opprobrium known to the provinces.

"It is singular," said Julien to himself, as Mathilde was going out of his prison one day, "that I should be so insensible at being the object of so keen a passion! And two months ago I adored her! I have, of course, read that the approach of death makes one lose interest in everything, but it is awful to feel oneself ungrateful, and not to be able to change. Am I an egoist, then?" He addressed the most humiliating reproaches to himself on this score.

Ambition was dead in his heart; another passion had arisen from its ashes. He called it remorse at having assassinated madame de Rênal.

As a matter of fact, he loved her to the point of distraction. He experienced a singular happiness on these occasions when, being left absolutely alone, and without being afraid of being interrupted, he could surrender himself completely to the memory of the happy days which he had once passed at Verrières, or at Vergy. The slightest incidents of these days, which had fleeted away only too rapidly, possessed an irresistible freshness and charm. He never gave a thought to his Paris successes; they bored him.

These moods, which became intensified with every succeeding day, were partly guessed by the jealous Mathilde. She realised very clearly that she had to struggle against his love of solitude. Sometimes, with terror in her heart, she uttered madame de Rênal's name.

She saw Julien quiver. Henceforth her passion had neither bounds nor limit.

"If he dies, I will die after him," she said to herself in all good faith. "What will the Paris salons say when they see a girl of my own rank carry her adoration for a lover who is condemned to death to such a pitch as this? For sentiments like these you must go back to the age of the heroes. It was loves of this kind which thrilled the hearts of the century of Charles IX. and Henri III."

In the midst of her keenest transports, when she was clasping Julien's head against her heart, she would say to herself with horror, "What! is this charming head doomed to fall? Well," she added, inflamed by a not unhappy heroism, "these lips of mine, which are now pressing against this pretty hair, will be icy cold less than twenty-four hours afterwards."

Thoughts of the awful voluptuousness of such heroic moments gripped her in a compelling embrace. The idea of suicide, absorbing enough in itself, entered that haughty soul (to which, up to the present it had been so utterly alien), and soon reigned over it with an absolute dominion.

"No, the blood of my ancestors has not grown tepid in descending to me," said Mathilde proudly to herself.

"I have a favour to ask of you," said her lover to her one day. "Put your child out to nurse at Verrières. Madame de Rênal will look after the nurse."

"Those words of yours are very harsh." And Mathilde paled.

"It is true, and I ask your pardon a thousand times," exclaimed Julien, emerging from his reverie, and clasping her in his arms.

After having dried his tears, he reverted to his original idea, but with greater tact. He had given a twist of melancholy philosophy to the conversation. He talked of that future of his which was so soon going to close. "One must admit, dear one, that passions are an accident in life, but such accidents only occur in superior souls.... My son's death would be in reality a happiness for your own proud family, and all the servants will realize as much. Neglect will be the lot of that child of shame and unhappiness. I hope that, at a time which I do not wish to fix, but which nevertheless I am courageous enough to imagine, you will obey my last advice: you will marry the marquis de Croisenois."

"What? Dishonoured?"

"Dishonour cannot attach to a name such as yours. You will be a widow, and the widow of a madman—that is all. I will go further—my crime will confer no dishonour, since it had no money motive. Perhaps when the time comes for your marriage, some philosophic legislator will have so far prevailed on the prejudice of his contemporaries as to have secured the suppression of the death penalty. Then some friendly voice will say, by way of giving an instance: 'Why, madame de la Mole's first husband was a madman, but not a wicked man or a criminal. It was absurd to have his head cut off.' So my memory will not be infamous in any way—at least, after a certain time.... Your position in society, your fortune, and, if you will allow me to say so, your genius, will make M. de Croisenois, once he is your husband, play a part which he would have never managed to secure unaided. He only possesses birth and bravery, and those qualities alone, though they constituted an accomplished man in 1729, are an anachronism a century later on, and only give rise to unwarranted pretensions. You need other things if you are to place yourself at the head of the youth of France."

"You will take all the help of your firm and enterprising character to the political party which you will make your husband join. You may be able to be a successor to the Chevreuses and the Longuevilles of the Fronde—but then, dear one, the divine fire which animates you at present will have grown a little tepid. Allow me to tell you," he added, "after many other preparatory phrases, that in fifteen years' time you will look upon the love you once had for me as a madness, which though excusable, was a piece of madness all the same."

He stopped suddenly and became meditative. He found himself again confronted with the idea which shocked Mathilde so much: "In fifteen years, madame de Rênal will adore my son and you will have forgotten him."

LXX
TRANQUILITY

It is because I was foolish then that I am wise to-day. Oh
thou philosopher who seest nothing except the actual instant.
How short-sighted are thy views! Thine eye is not adapted to
follow the subterranean work of the passions.—*M. Goethe.*

This conversation was interrupted by an interrogation followed by
a conference with the advocate entrusted with the defence. These moments were the only absolutely unpleasant ones in a life made up of
nonchalance and tender reveries.

"There is murder, and murder with premeditation," said Julien to the
judge as he had done to the advocate, "I am sorry, gentlemen, he added
with a smile, that this reduces your functions to a very small compass."

"After all," said Julien to himself, when he had managed to rid himself
of those two persons, "I must really be brave, and apparently braver than
those two men. They regard that duel with an unfortunate termination,
which I can only seriously bother myself about on the actual day, as the
greatest of evils and the arch-terror."

"The fact is that I have known a much greater unhappiness," continued
Julien, as he went on philosophising with himself. "I suffered far more
acutely during my first journey to Strasbourg, when I thought I was
abandoned by Mathilde—and to think that I desired so passionately that
same perfect intimacy which to-day leaves me so cold—as a matter of
fact I am more happy alone than when that handsome girl shares my
solitude."

The advocate, who was a red-tape pedant, thought him mad, and
believed, with the public, that it was jealousy which had lead him to take
up the pistol. He ventured one day to give Julien to understand that this
contention, whether true or false, would be an excellent way of pleading.
But the accused man became in a single minute a passionate and drastic
individual.

"As you value your life, monsieur," exclaimed Julien, quite beside
himself, "mind you never put forward such an abominable lie." The
cautious advocate was for a moment afraid of being assassinated.

He was preparing his case because the decisive moment was drawing
near. The only topic of conversation in Besançon, and all the department,
was the *cause célèbre*. Julien did not know of this circumstance. He had
requested his friends never to talk to him about that kind of thing.

On this particular day, Fouqué and Mathilde had tried to inform him
of certain rumours which in their view were calculated to give hope.
Julien had stopped them at the very first word.

"Leave me my ideal life. Your pettifogging troubles and details of practical life all more or less jar on me and bring me down from my heaven. One dies as best one can: but I wish to chose my own way of thinking about death. What do I care for other people? My relations with other people will be sharply cut short. Be kind enough not to talk to me any more about those people. Seeing the judge and the advocate is more than enough."

"As a matter of fact," he said to himself, "it seems that I am fated to die dreaming. An obscure creature like myself, who is certain to be forgotten within a fortnight, would be very silly, one must admit, to go and play a part. It is nevertheless singular that I never knew so much about the art of enjoying life, as since I have seen its end so near me."

He passed his last day in promenading upon the narrow terrace at the top of the turret, smoking some excellent cigars which Mathilde had had fetched from Holland by a courier. He had no suspicion that his appearance was waited for each day by all the telescopes in the town. His thoughts were at Vergy. He never spoke to Fouqué about madame de Rênal, but his friend told him two or three times that she was rapidly recovering, and these words reverberated in his heart.

While Julien's soul was nearly all the time wholly in the realm of ideas, Mathilde, who, as befits an aristocratic spirit, had occupied herself with concrete things, had managed to make the direct and intimate correspondence between madame de Fervaques and M. de Frilair progress so far that the great word bishopric had been already pronounced. The venerable prelate, who was entrusted with the distribution of the benefices, added in a postscript to one of his niece's letters, "This poor Sorel is only a lunatic. I hope he will be restored to us."

At the sight of these lines, M. de Frilair felt transported. He had no doubts about saving Julien.

"But for this Jacobin law which has ordered the formation of an unending panel of jurymen, and which has no other real object, except to deprive well-born people of all their influence," he said to Mathilde on the eve of the balloting for the thirty-six jurymen of the session, "I would have answered for the verdict. I certainly managed to get the curé N—— acquitted."

When the names were selected by ballot on the following day, M. de Frilair experienced a genuine pleasure in finding that they contained five members of the Besançon congregation and that amongst those who were strangers to the town were the names of MM. Valenod, de Moirod, de Cholin. I can answer for these eight jurymen he said to Mathilde. The first five are mere machines, Valenod is my agent: Moirod owes me everything: de Cholin is an imbecile who is frightened of everything.

The journal published the names of the jurymen throughout the department, and to her husband's unspeakable terror, madame de Rênal wished to go to Besançon. All that M. de Rênal could prevail on her to promise was that she would not leave her bed so as to avoid the unpleasantness of being called to give evidence. "You do not understand my position," said the former mayor of Verrières. "I am now said to be disloyal and a Liberal. No doubt that scoundrel Valenod and M. de Frilair will get the procureur-general and the judges to do all they can to cause me unpleasantness."

Madame de Rênal found no difficulty in yielding to her husband's orders. "If I appear at the assize court," she said to herself, "I should seem as if I were asking for vengeance." In spite of all the promises she had made to the director of her conscience and to her husband that she would be discreet, she had scarcely arrived at Besançon before she wrote with her own hand to each of the thirty-six jurymen:—

"I shall not appear on the day of the trial, monsieur, because my presence might be prejudicial to M. Sorel's case. I only desire one thing in the world, and that I desire passionately—for him to be saved. Have no doubt about it, the awful idea that I am the cause of an innocent man being led to his death would poison the rest of my life and would no doubt curtail it. How can you condemn him to death while I continue to live? No, there is no doubt about it, society has no right to take away a man's life, and above all, the life of a being like Julien Sorel. Everyone at Verrières knew that there were moments when he was quite distracted. This poor young man has some powerful enemies, but even among his enemies, (and how many has he not got?) who is there who casts any doubt on his admirable talents and his deep knowledge? The man whom you are going to try, monsieur, is not an ordinary person. For a period of nearly eighteen months we all knew him as a devout and well behaved student. Two or three times in the year he was seized by fits of melancholy that went to the point of distraction. The whole town of Verrières, all our neighbours at Vergy, where we live in the fine weather, my whole family, and monsieur the sub-prefect himself will render justice to his exemplary piety. He knows all the Holy Bible by heart. Would a blasphemer have spent years of study in learning the Sacred Book. My sons will have the honour of presenting you with this letter, they are children. Be good enough to question them, monsieur, they will give you all the details concerning this poor young man which are necessary to convince you of how barbarous it would be to condemn him. Far from revenging me, you would be putting me to death.

"What can his enemies argue against this? The wound, which was the result of one of those moments of madness, which my children themselves used to remark in their tutor, is so little dangerous than in less than two months it has allowed me to take the post from Verrières to Besançon. If I learn, monsieur, that you show the slightest hesitation in releasing so innocent a person from the barbarity of the law, I will leave my bed, where I am only kept by my husband's express orders, and I will go and throw myself at your feet. Bring in a verdict, monsieur, that the premeditation has not been made out, and you will not have an innocent man's blood on your head, etc."

LXXI
THE TRIAL

The country will remember this celebrated case for a long time. The interest in the accused amounted to an agitation. The reason was that his crime was astonishing, and yet not atrocious. Even if it had been, this young man was so handsome. His brilliant career, that came to an end so early in his life, intensified the pathos. "Will they condemn him?" the women asked of the men of their acquaintance, and they could be seen to grow pale as they waited for the answer.—
Sainte Beuve.

The day that madame de Rênal and Mathilde feared so much arrived at last.

Their terror was intensified by the strange appearance of the town, which had its emotional effect even upon Fouqué's sturdy soul. All the province had rushed to Besançon to see the trial of this romantic case.

There had been no room left in the inns for some days. M. the president of the assizes, was besieged by requests for tickets; all the ladies in the town wanted to be present at the trial. Julien's portrait was hawked about the streets, etc., etc.

Mathilde was keeping in reserve for this supreme moment a complete autograph letter from my lord, bishop of ——. This prelate, who governed the Church of France and created its bishops, was good enough to ask for Julien's acquittal. On the eve of the trial, Mathilde took this letter to the all-powerful grand vicar.

When she was going away in tears at the end of the interview, M. de Frilair at last emerged from his diplomatic reserve and almost shewed some emotion himself. "I will be responsible for the jury's verdict," he said to her. "Out of the twelve persons charged with the investigation of whether your friend's crime is made out, and above all, whether there was premeditation, I can count six friends who are devoted to my fortunes, and I have given them to understand that they have it in their power to promote me to the episcopate. Baron Valenod, whom

I have made mayor of Verrières, can do just as he likes with two of his officials, MM. de Moirod, and de Cholin. As a matter of fact, fate has given us for this business two jurymen of extremely loose views; but, although ultra-Liberals, they are faithful to my orders on great occasions, and I have requested them to vote like M. Valenod. I have learnt that a sixth juryman, a manufacturer, who is immensely rich, and a garrulous Liberal into the bargain, has secret aspirations for a contract with the War Office, and doubtless he would not like to displease me. I have had him told that M. de Valenod knows my final injunctions."

"And who is this M. Valenod?" said Mathilde, anxiously.

"If you knew him, you could not doubt our success. He is an audacious speaker, coarse, impudent, with a natural gift for managing fools. 1814 saw him in low water, and I am going to make a prefect of him. He is capable of beating the other jurymen if they do not vote his way."

Mathilde felt a little reassured.

Another discussion awaited her in the evening. To avoid the pro-longation of an unpleasant scene, the result of which, in his view, was absolutely certain, Julien had resolved not to make a speech.

"My advocate will speak," he said to Mathilde. "I shall figure too long anyway as a laughing-stock to all my enemies. These provincials have been shocked by the rapidity of my success, for which I have to thank you, and believe me, there is not one of them who does not desire my conviction, though he would be quite ready to cry like an idiot when I am taken to my death."

"They desire to see you humiliated. That is only too true," answered Mathilde, "but I do not think they are at all cruel. My presence at Be-sançon, and the sight of my sufferings have interested all the women; your handsome face will do the rest. If you say a few words to your judges, the whole audience will be on your side, etc., etc."

At nine o'clock on the following day, when Julien left his prison for the great hall of the Palais de Justice, the gendarmes had much difficulty in driving away the immense crowd that was packed in the courtyard. Julien had slept well. He was very calm, and experienced no other sentiment except a sense of philosophic pity towards that crowd of jealous creatures who were going to applaud his death sentence, though without cruelty. He was very surprised when, having been detained in the middle of the crowd more than a quarter of an hour, he was obliged to admit that his presence affected the public with a tender pity. He did not hear a single unpleasant remark. "These provincials are less evil than I thought," he said to himself.

As he entered the courtroom, he was struck by the elegance of the architecture. It was real Gothic, with a number of pretty little columns hewn out of stone with the utmost care. He thought himself in England.

But his attention was soon engrossed by twelve or fifteen pretty women, who sat exactly opposite the prisoner's seat and filled the three balconies above the judges and the jury. As he turned round towards the public, he saw that the circular gallery that dominated the amphitheatre was filled with women, the majority were young and seemed very pretty, their eyes were shining and full of interest. The crowd was enormous throughout the rest of the room. People were knocking against the door, and the janitors could not obtain silence.

When all the eyes that were looking for Julien observed where he was, and saw him occupying the slightly raised place which is reserved for the prisoner, he was greeted by a murmur of astonishment and tender interest.

You would have taken him for under twenty on this day. He was dressed very simply, but with a perfect grace. His hair and his forehead were charming. Mathilde had insisted on officiating personally at his toilette. Julien's pallor was extreme. Scarcely was he seated in this place than he heard people say all over the room, "Great heavens! how young he is!... But he's quite a child!... He is much better than his portrait."

"Prisoner," said the gendarme who was sitting on his right, "do you see those six ladies in that balcony?" The gendarme pointed out a little gallery that jutted out over the amphitheatre where the jury were placed. "That's madame, the prefect's wife," continued the gendarme. "Next to her, madame the marquise de M——. She likes you well: I have heard her speak to the judge of first instance. Next to her is madame Derville."

"Madame Derville!" exclaimed Julien, and a vivid blush spread over his forehead. "When she leaves here," he thought, "she will write to madame de Rênal." He was ignorant of madame de Rênal's arrival at Besançon. The witnesses were quickly heard. After the first words of the opening of the prosecution by the advocate-general, two of the ladies in the little balcony just opposite Julien burst into tears. Julien noticed that madame Derville did not break down at all. He remarked, however, that she was very red.

The advocate-general was indulging in melodrama in bad French over the barbarity of the crime that had been perpetrated. Julien noticed that madame Derville's neighbours seemed to manifest a keen disapproval. Several jurors, who were apparently acquainted with the ladies, spoke to them and seemed to reassure them. "So far as it goes, that is certainly a good omen," thought Julien.

Up to the present, he had felt himself steeped in an unadulterated contempt for all the persons who were present at the trial. This sentiment of disgust was intensified by the stale eloquence of the advocate-general. But the coldness of Julien's soul gradually disappeared before the marks of interest of which he was evidently the object.

He was satisfied with the sturdy demeanour of his advocate. "No phrases," he said to him in a whisper, as he was about to commence his speech.

"All the bombast which our opponent has stolen from Bossuet and lavished upon you," said the advocate, "has done you good."

As a matter of fact, he had scarcely spoken for five minutes before practically all the women had their handkerchiefs in their hands. The advocate was encouraged, and addressed some extremely strong remarks to the jury. Julien shuddered. He felt on the point of breaking into tears. "My God," he thought, "what would my enemies say?"

He was on the point of succumbing to the emotion which was overcoming him, when, luckily for him, he surprised an insolent look from M. the baron de Valenod.

"That rogue's eyes are gleaming," he said to himself "What a triumph for that base soul! If my crime had only produced this one result, it would be my duty to curse it. God knows what he will say about it to madame de Rênal."

This idea effaced all others. Shortly afterwards Julien was brought back to reality by the public's manifestation of applause. The advocate had just finished his speech. Julien remembered that it was good form to shake hands with him. The time had passed rapidly.

They brought in refreshments for the advocate and the prisoner. It was only then that Julien was struck by the fact that none of the women had left the audience to go and get dinner.

"Upon my word, I am dying of hunger," said the advocate. "And you?"

"I, too," answered Julien.

"See, there's madame, the prefect's wife, who is also getting her dinner," said the advocate, as he pointed out the little balcony. "Keep up your courage; everything is going all right." The court sat again.

Midnight struck as the president was summing up. The president was obliged to pause in his remarks. Amid the silence and the anxiety of all present, the reverberation of the clock filled the hall.

"So my last day is now beginning," thought Julien. He soon felt inflamed by the idea of his duty. Up to the present he had controlled his emotion and had kept his resolution not to speak. When the president of the assizes asked him if he had anything to add, he got up. He saw in front of him the eyes of madame Derville, which seemed very brilliant in the artificial light. "Can she by any chance be crying?" he thought.

"Gentlemen of the jury!

"I am induced to speak by my fear of that contempt which I thought, at the very moment of my death, I should be able to defy. Gentlemen, I have not the honour of belonging to your class. You behold in me a peasant who has rebelled against the meanness of his fortune.

"I do not ask you for any pardon," continued Julien, with a firmer note in his voice. "I am under no illusions. Death awaits me; it will be just. I have brought myself to make an attempt on the life of the woman who is most worthy of all reverence and all respect. Madame de Rênal was a mother to me. My crime was atrocious, and it was premeditated. Consequently, I have deserved death, gentlemen of the jury. But even if I were not so guilty, I see among you men who, without a thought for any pity that may be due to my youth, would like to use me as a means for punishing and discouraging for ever that class of young man who, though born in an inferior class, and to some extent oppressed by poverty, have none the less been fortunate enough to obtain a good education, and bold enough to mix with what the pride of the rich calls Society.

"That is my crime, gentlemen, and it will be punished with even more severity, inasmuch as, in fact, I am very far from being judged by my peers. I do not see on the jury benches any peasant who has made money, but only indignant bourgeois...."

Julien talked in this strain for twenty minutes. He said everything he had on his mind. The advocate-general, who aspired to the favours of the aristocracy, writhed in his seat. But in spite of the somewhat abstract turn which Julien had given to his speech, all the women burst out into tears. Even madame Derville put her handkerchief to her eyes. Before finishing, Julien alluded again to the fact of his premeditation, to his repentance, and to the respect and unbounded filial admiration which, in happier days, he had entertained for madame de Rênal.... Madame Derville gave a cry and fainted.

One o'clock was striking when the jury retired to their room. None of the women had left their places; several men had tears in their eyes. The conversations were at first very animated, but, as there was a delay in the verdict of the jury, their general fatigue gradually began to invest the gathering with an atmosphere of calm. It was a solemn moment; the lights grew less brilliant. Julien, who was very tired, heard people around him debating the question of whether this delay was a good or a bad omen. He was pleased to see that all the wishes were for him. The jury did not come back, and yet not a woman left the court.

When two o'clock had struck, a great movement was heard. The little door of the jury room opened. M. the baron de Valenod advanced with a slow and melodramatic step. He was followed by all the jurors. He coughed, and then declared on his soul and conscience that the jury's unanimous verdict was that Julien Sorel was guilty of murder, and of murder with premeditation. This verdict involved the death penalty, which was pronounced a moment afterwards. Julien looked at his watch, and remembered M. de Lavalette. It was a quarter past two. "To-day is

Friday," he thought.

"Yes, but this day is lucky for the Valenod who has got me convicted.... I am watched too well for Mathilde to manage to save me like madame de Lavalette saved her husband.... So in three days' time, at this very hour, I shall know what view to take about the great perhaps."

At this moment he heard a cry and was called back to the things of this world. The women around him were sobbing: he saw that all faces were turned towards a little gallery built into the crowning of a Gothic pilaster. He knew later that Mathilde had concealed herself there. As the cry was not repeated, everybody began to look at Julien again, as the gendarmes were trying to get him through the crowd.

"Let us try not to give that villain Valenod any chance of laughing at me," thought Julien. "With what a contrite sycophantic expression he pronounced the verdict which entails the death penalty, while that poor president of the assizes, although he has been a judge for years and years, had tears in his eyes as he sentenced me. What a joy the Valenod must find in revenging himself for our former rivalry for madame de Rênal's favors! ... So I shall never see her again! The thing is finished.... A last good-bye between us is impossible—I feel it.... How happy I should have been to have told her all the horror I feel for my crime!

"Mere words. I consider myself justly convicted."

LXXII

[There is no heading to this and the following chapters in the original.—TRANSL.]

When Julien was taken back to prison he had been taken into a room intended for those who were condemned to death. Although a man who in the usual way would notice the most petty details, he had quite failed to observe that he had not been taken up to his turret. He was thinking of what he would say to madame de Rênal if he had the happiness of seeing her before the final moment. He thought that she would break into what he was saying and was anxious to be able to express his absolute repentance with his very first words. "How can I convince her that I love her alone after committing an action like that? For after all, it was either out of ambition, or out of love for Mathilde, that I wanted to kill her."

As he went to bed, he came across sheets of a rough coarse material. "Ah! I am in the condemned cell, he said to himself. That is right.

"Comte Altamira used to tell me that Danton, on the eve of his death, would say in his loud voice: 'it is singular but you cannot conjugate the verb guillotine in all its tenses: of course you can say, I shall be guillotined, thou shalt be guillotined, but you don't say, I have been guillotined.'

"Why not?" went on Julien, "if there is another life.... Upon my word, it will be all up with me if I find the God of the Christians there: He is a tyrant, and as such, he is full of ideas of vengeance: his Bible speaks of nothing but atrocious punishment. I never liked him—I could never get myself to believe that anyone really liked him. He has no pity (and he remembered several passages in the Bible) he will punish me atrociously.

"But supposing I find Fénelon's God: He will perhaps say to me: 'Much forgiveness will be vouchsafed to thee, inasmuch as thou hast loved much.'

"Have I loved much? Ah! I loved madame de Rênal, but my conduct has been atrocious. In that, as in other cases, simple modest merit was abandoned for the sake of what was brilliant.

"But still, what fine prospects? Colonel of Hussars, if we had had a war: secretary of a legation during peace: then ambassador ... for I should soon have picked up politics ... and even if I had been an idiot, would the marquis de la Mole's son-in-law have had any rivalry to fear? All my stupidities have been forgiven, or rather, counted as merits. A man of merit, then, and living in the grandest style at Vienna or London.

"Not exactly, monsieur. Guillotined in three days' time."

Julien laughed heartily at this sally of his wit. "As a matter of fact, man has two beings within him, he thought. Who the devil can have thought of such a sinister notion?"

"Well, yes, my friend: guillotined in three days," he answered the interruptor. "M. de Cholin will hire a window and share the expense with the abbé Maslon. Well, which of those two worthy personages will rob the other over the price paid for hiring that window?" The following passage from Rotrou's "Venceslas" suddenly came back into his mind:—

LADISLAS

...............Mon âme est toute prête.

THE KING, *father of Ladislas*.

L'échafaud l'est aussi: portez-y-votre tête.

"A good repartee" he thought, as he went to sleep. He was awakened in the morning by someone catching hold of him violently.

"What! already," said Julien, opening his haggard eyes. He thought he was already in the executioner's hands.

It was Mathilde. "Luckily, she has not understood me." This reflection restored all his self possession. He found Mathilde as changed as though she had gone through a six months' illness: she was really not recognisable.

"That infamous Frilair has betrayed me," she said to him, wringing her hands. Her fury prevented her from crying.

"Was I not fine when I made my speech yesterday?" answered Julien. "I was improvising for the first time in my life! It is true that it is to be feared that it will also be the last."

At this moment, Julien was playing on Mathilde's character with all the self-possession of a clever pianist, whose fingers are on the instrument.... "It is true," he added, "that I lack the advantage of a distinguished birth, but Mathilde's great soul has lifted her lover up to her own level. Do you think that Boniface de la Mole would have cut a better figure before his judges?"

On this particular day, Mathilde was as unaffectedly tender as a poor girl living in a fifth storey. But she failed to extract from him any simpler remark. He was paying her back without knowing it for all the torture she had frequently inflicted on him.

"The sources of the Nile are unknown," said Julien to himself: "it has not been vouchsafed to the human eye to see the king of rivers as a simple brook: similarly, no human eye shall see Julien weak. In the first place because he is not so. But I have a heart which it is easy to touch. The most commonplace words, if said in a genuine tone, can make my voice broken and even cause me to shed tears. How often have frigid characters not despised me for this weakness. They thought that I was asking a favour: that is what I cannot put up with.

"It is said that when at the foot of the scaffold, Danton was affected by the thought of his wife: but Danton had given strength to a nation of coxcombs and prevented the enemy from reaching Paris.... I alone know what I should have been able to do.... I represent to the others at the very outside, simply A PERHAPS.

"If madame de Rênal had been here in my cell instead of Mathilde, should I have been able to have answered for myself? The extremity of my despair and my repentance would have been taken for a craven fear of death by the Valenods and all the patricians of the locality. They are so proud, are those feeble spirits, whom their pecuniary position puts above temptation! 'You see what it is to be born a carpenter's son,' M. de Moirod and de Cholin doubtless said after having condemned me to death! 'A man can learn to be learned and clever, but the qualities of the heart—the qualities of the heart cannot be learnt.' Even in the case of this poor Mathilde, who is crying now, or rather, who cannot cry," he said to himself, as he looked at her red eyes.... And he clasped her in his arms: the sight of a genuine grief made him forget the sequence of his logic.... "She has perhaps cried all the night," he said to himself, "but how ashamed she will be of this memory on some future day! She will regard herself as having been led astray in her first youth by a plebeian's low view of life.... Le Croisenois is weak enough to marry her, and upon my word, he will do well to do so. She will make him play a part."

"Du droit qu'un esprit ferme et vaste en ses desseins
A sur l'esprit grossier des vulgaires humaines."

"Ah! that's really humorous; since I have been doomed to die, all the verses I ever knew in my life are coming back into my memory. It must be a sign of demoralisation."

Mathilde kept on repeating in a choked voice: "He is there in the next room." At last he paid attention to what she was saying. "Her voice is weak," he thought, "but all the imperiousness of her character comes out in her intonation. She lowers her voice in order to avoid getting angry."

"And who is there?" he said, gently.

"The advocate, to get you to sign your appeal."

"I shall not appeal."

"What! you will not appeal," she said, getting up, with her eyes sparkling with rage. "And why, if you please?"

"Because I feel at the present time that I have the courage to die without giving people occasion to laugh too much at my expense. And who will guarantee that I shall be in so sound a frame of mind in two months' time, after living for a long time in this damp cell? I foresee interviews with the priests, with my father. I can imagine nothing more unpleasant. Let's die."

This unexpected opposition awakened all the haughtiness of Mathilde's character. She had not managed to see the abbé de Frilair before the time when visitors were admitted to the cells in the Besançon prison. Her fury vented itself on Julien. She adored him, and nevertheless she exhibited for a good quarter of an hour in her invective against his, Julien's, character, and her regret at having ever loved him, the same haughty soul which had formerly overwhelmed him with such cutting insults in the library of the Hôtel de la Mole.

"In justice to the glory of your stock, Heaven should have had you born a man," he said to her.

"But as for myself," he thought, "I should be very foolish to go on living for two more months in this disgusting place, to serve as a butt for all the infamous humiliations which the patrician party can devise,[6] and having the outburst of this mad woman for my only consolation.... Well, the morning after to-morrow I shall fight a duel with a man known for his self-possession and his remarkable skill ... his very remarkable skill," said the Mephistophelian part of him; "he never makes a miss. Well, so be it—good." (Mathilde continued to wax eloquent). "No, not for a minute," he said to himself, "I shall not appeal."

Having made this resolution, he fell into meditation....

"The courier will bring the paper at six o'clock as usual, as he passes; at eight o'clock, after M. de Rênal has finished reading it, Elisa will go on tiptoe and place it on her bed. Later on she will wake up; suddenly, as she reads it she will become troubled; her pretty hands will tremble; she will go on reading down to these words: *At five minutes past ten he had ceased to exist.*

"She will shed hot tears, I know her; it will matter nothing that I tried to assassinate her—all will be forgotten, and the person whose life I wished to take will be the only one who will sincerely lament my death.

"Ah, that's a good paradox," he thought, and he thought about nothing except madame de Rênal during the good quarter of an hour which the scene Mathilde was making still lasted. In spite of himself, and though he made frequent answers to what Mathilde was saying, he could not take his mind away from the thought of the bedroom at Verrières. He saw the Besançon Gazette on the counterpane of orange taffeta; he saw that white hand clutching at it convulsively. He saw madame de Rênal cry…. He followed the path of every tear over her charming face.

Mademoiselle de la Mole, being unable to get anything out of Julien, asked the advocate to come in. Fortunately, he was an old captain of the Italian army of 1796, where he had been a comrade of Manuel.

He opposed the condemned man's resolution as a matter of form. Wishing to treat him with respect, Julien explained all his reasons.

"Upon my word, I can understand a man taking the view you do," said M. Felix Vaneau (that was the advocate's name) to him at last. "But you have three full days in which to appeal, and it is my duty to come back every day. If a volcano were to open under the prison between now and two months' time you would be saved. You might die of illness," he said, looking at Julien.

Julien pressed his hand—"I thank you, you are a good fellow. I will think it over."

And when Mathilde eventually left with the advocate, he felt much more affection for the advocate than for her.

LXXIII

When he was deep asleep an hour afterwards, he was woken up by feeling tears flow over his hand. "Oh, it is Mathilde again," he thought, only half awake. "She has come again, faithful to her tactics of attacking my resolution by her sentimentalism." Bored by the prospect of this new scene of hackneyed pathos he did not open his eyes. The verses of Belphgor, as he ran away from his wife, came into his mind. He heard a strange sigh. He opened his eyes. It was madame de Rênal.

"Ah, so I see you again before I die, or is it an illusion," he exclaimed as he threw himself at her feet.

"But, forgive me, madame, you must look upon me as a mere murderer," he said, immediately, as he recovered himself.

"Monsieur, I have come to entreat you to appeal; I know you do not want to...." her sobs choked her; she was unable to speak.

"Deign to forgive me."

"If you want me to forgive you," she said to him, getting up and throwing herself into his arms, "appeal immediately against your death sentence."

Julien covered her with kisses.

"Will you come and see me every day during those two months?"

"I swear it—every day, unless my husband forbids me."

"I will sign it," exclaimed Julien.

"What! you really forgive me! Is it possible?"

He clasped her in his arms; he was mad. She gave a little cry.

"It is nothing," she said to him. "You hurt me."

"Your shoulder," exclaimed Julien, bursting into tears. He drew back a little, and covered her hands with kisses of fire. "Who could have prophesied this, dear, the last time I saw you in your room at Verrières?"

"Who could have prophesied then that I should write that infamous letter to M. de la Mole?"

"Know that I have always loved you, and that I have never loved anyone but you."

"Is it possible?" cried Madame de Rênal, who was delighted in her turn. She leant on Julien, who was on his knees, and they cried silently for a long time.

Julien had never experienced moments like this at any period of his whole life.

"And how about that young madame Michelet?" said Madame de Rênal, a long time afterwards when they were able to speak. "Or rather, that mademoiselle de la Mole? for I am really beginning to believe in that strange romance."

"It is only superficially true," answered Julien. "She is my wife, but she is not my mistress."

After interrupting each other a hundred times over, they managed with great difficulty to explain to each other what they did not know. The letter written to M. de la Mole had been drafted by the young priest who directed Madame de Rênal's conscience, and had been subsequently copied by her, "What a horrible thing religion has made me do," she said to him, "and even so I softened the most awful passages in the letter."

Julien's ecstatic happiness proved the fulness of her forgiveness. He had never been so mad with love.

"And yet I regard myself as devout," madame de Rênal went on to say to him in the ensuing conversation. "I believe sincerely in God! I

equally believe, and I even have full proof of it, that the crime which I
am committing is an awful one, and yet the very minute I see you, even
after you have fired two pistol shots at me—" and at this point, in spite
of her resistance, Julien covered her with kisses.

"Leave me alone," she continued, "I want to argue with you, I am
frightened lest I should forget.... The very minute I see you all my duties
disappear. I have nothing but love for you, dear, or rather, the word love
is too weak. I feel for you what I ought only to feel for God; a mixture
of respect, love, obedience.... As a matter of fact, I don't know what
you inspire me with.... If you were to tell me to stab the gaoler with a
knife, the crime would be committed before I had given it a thought.
Explain this very clearly to me before I leave you. I want to see down
to the bottom of my heart; for we shall take leave of each other in two
months.... By the bye, shall we take leave of each other?" she said to him
with a smile.

"I take back my words," exclaimed Julien, getting up, "I shall not
appeal from my death sentence, if you try, either by poison, knife, pistol,
charcoal, or any other means whatsoever, to put an end to your life, or
make any attempt upon it."

Madame de Rênal's expression suddenly changed. The most lively
tenderness was succeeded by a mood of deep meditation.

"Supposing we were to die at once," she said to him.

"Who knows what one will find in the other life," answered Julien,
"perhaps torment, perhaps nothing at all. Cannot we pass two delicious
months together? Two months means a good many days. I shall never
have been so happy."

"You will never have been so happy?"

"Never," repeated Julien ecstatically, "and I am talking to you just as I
should talk to myself. May God save me from exaggerating."

"Words like that are a command," she said with a timid melancholy
smile.

"Well, you will swear by the love you have for me, to make no attempt
either direct or indirect, upon your life ... remember," he added, "that
you must live for my son, whom Mathilde will hand over to lackeys as
soon as she is marquise de Croisenois."

"I swear," she answered coldly, "but I want to take away your notice
of appeal, drawn and signed by yourself. I will go myself to M. the
procureur-general."

"Be careful, you will compromise yourself."

"After having taken the step of coming to see you in your prison,
I shall be a heroine of local scandal for Besançon, and the whole of
Franche-Comté," she said very dejectedly. "I have crossed the bounds of
austere modesty.... I am a woman who has lost her honour; it is true that

it is for your sake...."

Her tone was so sad that Julien embraced her with a happiness which was quite novel to him. It was no longer the intoxication of love, it was extreme gratitude. He had just realised for the first time the full extent of the sacrifice which she had made for him.

Some charitable soul, no doubt informed M. de Rênal of the long visits which his wife paid to Julien's prison; for at the end of three days he sent her his carriage with the express order to return to Verrières immediately.

This cruel separation had been a bad beginning for Julien's day. He was informed two or three hours later that a certain intriguing priest (who had, however, never managed to make any headway among the Jesuits of Besançon) had, since the morning, established himself in the street outside the prison gates. It was raining a great deal, and the man out there was pretending to play the martyr. Julien was in a weak mood, and this piece of stupidity annoyed him deeply.

In the morning, he had already refused this priest's visit, but the man had taken it into his head to confess Julien, and to win a name for himself among the young women of Besançon by all the confidences which he would pretend to have received from him.

He declared in a loud voice that he would pass the day and the night by the prison gates. "God has sent me to touch the heart of this apostate ..." and the lower classes, who are always curious to see a scene, began to make a crowd.

"Yes, my brothers," he said to them, "I will pass the day here and the night, as well as all the days and all the nights which will follow. The Holy Ghost has spoken to me. I am commissioned from above; I am the man who must save the soul of young Sorel. Do you join in my prayers, etc."

Julien had a horror of scandal, and of anything which could attract attention to him. He thought of seizing the opportunity of escaping from the world incognito; but he had some hope of seeing madame de Rênal again, and he was desperately in love.

The prison gates were situated in one of the most populous streets. His soul was tortured by the idea of this filthy priest attracting a crowd and creating a scandal—"and doubtless he is repeating my name at every single minute!" This moment was more painful than death.

He called the turnkey who was devoted to him, and sent him two or three times at intervals of one hour to see if the priest was still by the prison gates.

"Monsieur," said the turnkey to him on each occasion, "he is on both his knees in the mud; he is praying at the top of his voice, and saying litanies for your soul.

"The impudent fellow," thought Julien. At this moment he actually heard a dull buzz. It was the responses of the people to the litanies. His patience was strained to the utmost when he saw the turnkey himself move his lips while he repeated the Latin words.

"They are beginning to say," added the turnkey, "that you must have a very hardened heart to refuse the help of this holy man."

"Oh my country, how barbarous you still are!" exclaimed Julien, beside himself with anger. And he continued his train of thought aloud, without giving a thought to the turn-key's presence.

"The man wants an article in the paper about him, and that's a way in which he will certainly get it.

"Oh you cursed provincials! At Paris I should not be subjected to all these annoyances. There they are more skilled in their charlatanism.

"Show in the holy priest," he said at last to the turnkey, and great streams of sweat flowed down his forehead. The turnkey made the sign of the cross and went out rejoicing.

The holy priest turned out to be very ugly, he was even dirtier than he was ugly. The cold rain intensified the obscurity and dampness of the cell. The priest wanted to embrace Julien, and began to wax pathetic as he spoke to him. The basest hypocrisy was only too palpable; Julien had never been so angry in his whole life.

A quarter of an hour after the priest had come in Julien felt an absolute coward. Death appeared horrible to him for the first time. He began to think about the state of decomposition which his body would be in two days after the execution, etc., etc.

He was on the point of betraying himself by some sign of weakness or throwing himself on the priest and strangling him with his chain, when it occurred to him to beg the holy man to go and say a good forty franc mass for him on that very day.

It was twelve o'clock, so the priest took himself off.

LXXIV

As soon as he had gone out Julien wept desperately and for a long time. He gradually admitted to himself that if madame de Rênal had been at Besançon he would have confessed his weakness to her. The moment when he was regretting the absence of this beloved woman he heard Mathilde's step.

"The worst evil of being in prison," he thought "is one's inability to close one's door." All Mathilde said only irritated him.

She told him that M. de Valenod had had his nomination to the prefectship in his pocket on the day of his trial, and had consequently dared to defy M. de Frilair and give himself the pleasure of condemning him to death.

"Why did your friend take it into his head," M. de Frilair just said to me, "to awaken and attack the petty vanity of that bourgeois aristocracy. Why talk about caste? He pointed out to them what they ought to do in their own political interest; the fools had not been giving it a thought and were quite ready to weep. That caste interest intervened and blinded their eyes to the horror of condemning a man to death. One must admit that M. Sorel is very inexperienced. If we do not succeed in saving him by a petition for a reprieve, his death will be a kind of suicide."

Mathilde was careful not to tell Julien a matter concerning which she had now no longer any doubts; it was that the abbé de Frilair seeing that Julien was ruined, had thought that it would further his ambitious projects to try and become his successor.

"Go and listen to a mass for me," he said to Mathilde, almost beside himself with vexation and impotent rage, and leave me a moment in peace. Mathilde who was already very jealous of madame de Rênal's visits and who had just learned of her departure realised the cause of Julien's bad temper and burst into tears.

Her grief was real; Julien saw this and was only the more irritated. He had a crying need of solitude, and how was he to get it?

Eventually Mathilde, after having tried to melt him by every possible argument, left him alone. But almost at the same moment, Fouqué presented himself.

"I need to be alone," he said, to this faithful friend, and as he saw him hesitate: "I am composing a memorial for my petition for pardon ... one thing more ... do me a favour, and never speak to me about death. If I have need of any especial services on that day, let me be the first to speak to you about it."

When Julien had eventually procured solitude, he found himself more prostrate and more cowardly than he had been before. The little force which this enfeebled soul still possessed had all been spent in concealing his condition from mademoiselle de la Mole.

Towards the evening he found consolation in this idea.

"If at the very moment this morning, when death seemed so ugly to me, I had been given notice of my execution, the public eye would have acted as a spur to glory, my demeanour would perhaps have had a certain stiffness about it, like a nervous fop entering a salon. A few penetrating people, if there are any amongst these provincial might have managed to divine my weakness.... But no one would have seen it."

And he felt relieved of part of his unhappiness. "I am a coward at this very moment," he sang to himself, "but no one will know it."

An even more unpleasant episode awaited him on the following day. His father had been announcing that he would come and see him for some time past: the old white-haired carpenter appeared in Julien's cell before he woke up.

Julien felt weak, he was anticipating the most unpleasant reproaches. His painful emotion was intensified by the fact that on this particular morning he felt a keen remorse for not loving his father.

"Chance placed us next to each other in the world," he said to himself, while the turnkey was putting the cell a little in order, "and we have practically done each other all the harm we possibly could. He has come to administer the final blow at the moment of my death."

As soon as they were without witnesses, the old man commenced his stern reproaches.

Julien could not restrain his tears. "What an unworthy weakness," he said to himself querulously. "He will go about everywhere exaggerating my lack of courage: what a triumph for the Valenod, and for all the fatuous hypocrites who rule in Verrières! They are very great in France, they combine all the social advantages. But hitherto, I could at any rate say to myself, it is true they are in receipt of money, and that all the honours lavished on them, but I have a noble heart.

"But here is a witness whom everyone will believe, and who will testify to the whole of Verrières that I shewed weakness when confronted with death, and who will exaggerate it into the bargain! I shall be taken for a coward in an ordeal which comes home to all!"

Julien was nearly desperate. He did not know how to get rid of his father. He felt it absolutely beyond his strength to invent a ruse capable of deceiving so shrewd an old man.

His mind rapidly reviewed all the alternatives. "I have saved some money," he suddenly exclaimed.

This inspiration produced a change in the expression of the old man and in Julien's own condition.

"How ought I to dispose of it?" continued Julien more quietly. The result had freed him from any feeling of inferiority.

The old carpenter was burning not to let the money slip by him, but it seemed that Julien wanted to leave part of it to his brothers. He talked at length and with animation. Julien felt cynical.

"Well, the Lord has given me a message with regard to my will. I will give a thousand francs to each of my brothers and the rest to you."

"Very good," said the old man. "The rest is due to me: but since God has been gracious enough to touch your heart, your debts ought to be paid if you wish to die like a good Christian. There are, moreover, the expenses of your board and your education, which I advanced to you, but which you are not thinking of."

"Such is paternal love," repeated Julien to himself, dejectedly, when he was at last alone. Soon the gaoler appeared.

"Monsieur, I always bring my visitors a good bottle of champagne after near relations have come to see them. It is a little dear, six francs a bottle, but it rejoices the heart."

"Bring three glasses," said Julien to him, with a childish eagerness, "and bring in two of the prisoners whom I have heard walking about in the corridor." The gaoler brought two men into him who had once been condemned to the gallows, and had now been convicted of the same offence again, and were preparing to return to penal servitude. They were very cheerful scoundrels, and really very remarkable by reason of their subtlety, their courage, and their coolness.

"If you give me twenty francs," said one of them to Julien, "I will tell you the story of my life in detail. It's rich."

"But you will lie," said Julien.

"Not me," he answered, "my friend there, who is jealous of my twenty francs will give me away if I say anything untrue."

His history was atrocious. It was evidence of a courageous heart which had only one passion—that of money.

After their departure Julien was no longer the same man. All his anger with himself had disappeared. The awful grief which had been poisoned and rendered more acute by the weakness of which he had been a victim since madame de Rênal's departure had turned to melancholy.

"If I had been less taken in by appearances," he said to himself, "I would have had a better chance of seeing that the Paris salons are full of honest men like my father, or clever scoundrels like those felons. They are right. The men in the salons never get up in the morning with this poignant thought in their minds, how am I going to get my dinner? They boast about their honesty and when they are summoned on the jury, they take pride in convicting the man who has stolen a silver dish because he felt starving.

"But if there is a court, and it's a question of losing or winning a portfolio, my worthy salon people will commit crimes exactly similar to those, which the need of getting a dinner inspired those two felons to perpetrate.

"There is no such thing as natural law, the expression is nothing more than a silly anachronism well worthy of the advocate-general who harried me the other day, and whose grandfather was enriched by one of the confiscations of Louis XIV. There is no such thing as right, except when there is a law to forbid a certain thing under pain of punishment.

"Before law existed, the only natural thing was the strength of the lion, or the need of a creature who was cold or hungry, to put it in one word, need. No, the people whom the world honours are merely villains who have had the good fortune not to have been caught red-handed. The prosecutor whom society put on my track was enriched by an infamous act. I have committed a murder, and I am justly condemned, but the Valenod who has condemned me, is by reason alone of that very deed, a hundred times more harmful to society.

"Well," added Julien sadly but not angrily, "in spite of his avarice, my father is worth more than all those men. He never loved me. The disgrace I bring upon him by an infamous death has proved the last straw. That fear of lacking money, that distorted view of the wickedness of mankind, which is called avarice, make him find a tremendous consolation and sense of security in a sum of three or four hundred louis, which I have been able to leave him. Some Sunday, after dinner, he will shew his gold to all the envious men in Verrières. 'Which of you would not be delighted to have a son guillotined at a price like this,' will be the message they will read in his eyes."

This philosophy might be true, but it was of such a character as to make him wish for death. In this way five long days went by. He was polite and gentle to Mathilde, whom he saw was exasperated by the most violent jealousy. One evening Julien seriously thought of taking his own life. His soul was demoralised by the deep unhappiness in which madame de Rênal's departure had thrown him. He could no longer find pleasure in anything, either in real life or in the sphere of the imagination. Lack of exercise began to affect his health, and to produce in him all the weakness and exaltation of a young German student. He began to lose that virile disdain which repels with a drastic oath certain undignified ideas which besiege the soul of the unhappy.

"I loved truth.... Where is it? Hypocrisy everywhere or at any rate charlatanism. Even in the most virtuous, even in the greatest," and his lips assumed an expression of disgust. "No, man cannot trust man."

"Madame de —— when she was making a collection for her poor orphans, used to tell me that such and such a prince had just given ten louis, a sheer lie. But what am I talking about. Napoleon at St. Helena ... Pure charlatanism like the proclamation in favour of the king of Rome.

"Great God! If a man like that at a time when misfortune ought to summon him sternly to his duty will sink to charlatanism, what is one to expect from the rest of the human species?"

"Where is truth? In religion. Yes," he added, with a bitter smile of utter contempt. "In the mouth of the Maslons, the Frilairs, the Castanèdes—perhaps in that true Christianity whose priests were not paid any more than were the apostles. But St. Paul was paid by the pleasure of commanding, speaking, getting himself talked about."

"Oh, if there were only a true religion. Fool that I am. I see a Gothic cathedral and venerable stained-glass windows, and my weak heart conjures up the priest to fit the scene. My soul would understand him, my soul has need of him. I only find a nincompoop with dirty hair. About as comforting as a chevalier de Beauvoisis.

"But a true priest, a Massillon, a Fénelon. Massillon sacrificed Dubois. Saint-Simon's memoirs have spoilt the illusion of Fénelon, but he was a true priest anyway. In those days, tender souls could have a place in the world where they could meet together. We should not then have been isolated. That good priest would have talked to us of God. But what God? Not the one of the Bible, a cruel petty despot, full of vindictiveness, but the God of Voltaire, just, good, infinite."

He was troubled by all the memories of that Bible which he knew by heart. "But how on earth, when the deity is three people all at the same time, is one to believe in the great name of GOD, after the frightful way in which our priests have abused it."

"Living alone. What a torture."

"I am growing mad and unreasonable," said Julien to himself, striking his forehead. "I am alone here in this cell, but I have not lived alone on earth. I had the powerful idea of duty. The duty which rightly or wrongly I laid down for myself, has been to me like the trunk of a solid tree which I could lean on during the storm, I stumbled, I was agitated. After all I was only a man, but I was not swept away.

"It must be the damp air of this cell which made me think of being alone.

"Why should I still play the hypocrite by cursing hypocrisy? It is neither death, nor the cell, nor the damp air, but madame de Rênal's absence which prostrates me. If, in order to see her at Verrières, I had to live whole weeks at Verrières concealed in the cellars of her house, would I complain?"

"The influence of my contemporaries wins the day," he said aloud, with a bitter laugh. "Though I am talking to myself and within an ace of death, I still play the hypocrite. Oh you nineteenth century! A hunter fires a gun shot in the forest, his quarry falls, he hastens forward to seize it. His foot knocks against a two-foot anthill, knocks down the dwelling place of the ants, and scatters the ants and their eggs far and wide. The most philosophic among the ants will never be able to understand that black, gigantic and terrifying body, the hunter's boot, which suddenly invaded their home with incredible rapidity, preceded by a frightful noise, and accompanied by flashes of reddish fire."

"In the same way, death, life and eternity, are very simple things for anyone who has organs sufficiently vast to conceive them. An ephemeral fly is born at nine o'clock in the morning in the long summer days, to die at five o'clock in the evening. How is it to understand the word 'night'?"

"Give it five more hours of existence, and it will see night, and understand its meaning."

"So, in my case, I shall die at the age of twenty-three. Give me five more years of life in order to live with madame de Rênal."

He began to laugh like Mephistopheles. How foolish to debate these great problems.

"(1). I am as hypocritical as though there were someone there to listen to me.

"(2). I am forgetting to live and to love when I have so few days left to live. Alas, madame de Rênal is absent; perhaps her husband will not let her come back to Besançon any more, to go on compromising her honour."

"That is what makes me lonely, and not the absence of a God who is just, good and omnipotent, devoid of malice, and in no wise greedy of vengeance."

"Oh, if He did exist. Alas I should fall at His feet. I have deserved death, I should say to Him, but oh Thou great God, good God, indulgent God, give me back her whom I love!"

By this time the night was far advanced. After an hour or two of peaceful sleep, Fouqué arrived.

Julien felt strongly resolute, like a man who sees to the bottom of his soul.

LXXV

"I cannot play such a trick on that poor abbé Chas-Bernard, as to summon him," he said to Fouqué: "it would prevent him from dining for three whole days.—But try and find some Jansenist who is a friend of M. Pirard."

Fouqué was impatiently waiting for this suggestion. Julien acquitted himself becomingly of all the duty a man owes to provincial opinion. Thanks to M. the abbé de Frilair, and in spite of his bad choice of a confessor, Julien enjoyed in his cell the protection of the priestly congregation; with a little more diplomacy he might have managed to escape. But the bad air of the cell produced its effect, and his strength of mind diminished. But this only intensified his happiness at madame de Rênal's return.

"My first duty is towards you, my dear," she said as she embraced him; "I have run away from Verrières."

Julien felt no petty vanity in his relations with her, and told her all his weaknesses. She was good and charming to him.

In the evening she had scarcely left the prison before she made the priest, who had clung on to Julien like a veritable prey, go to her aunt's:

as his only object was to win prestige among the young women who belonged to good Besançon society, madame de Rênal easily prevailed upon him to go and perform a novena at the abbey of Bray-le-Haut.

No words can do justice to the madness and extravagance of Julien's love.

By means of gold, and by using and abusing the influence of her aunt, who was devout, rich and well-known, madame de Rênal managed to see him twice a day.

At this news, Mathilde's jealousy reached a pitch of positive madness. M. de Frilair had confessed to her that all his influence did not go so far as to admit of flouting the conventions by allowing her to see her sweetheart more than once every day. Mathilde had madame de Rênal followed so as to know the smallest thing she did. M. de Frilair exhausted all the resources of an extremely clever intellect in order to prove to her that Julien was unworthy of her.

Plunged though she was in all these torments, she only loved him the more, and made a horrible scene nearly every day.

Julien wished, with all his might, to behave to the very end like an honourable man towards this poor young girl whom he had so strangely compromised, but the reckless love which he felt for madame de Rênal swept him away at every single minute. When he could not manage to persuade Mathilde of the innocence of her rival's visits by all his thin excuses, he would say to himself: "at any rate the end of the drama ought to be quite near. The very fact of not being able to lie better will be an excuse for me."

Mademoiselle de La Mole learnt of the death of the marquis de Croisenois. The rich M. de Thaler had indulged in some unpleasant re-marks concerning Mathilde's disappearance: M. de Croisenois went and asked him to recant them: M. de Thaler showed him some anonymous letters which had been sent to him, and which were full of details so artfully put together that the poor marquis could not help catching a glimpse of the truth.

M. de Thaler indulged in some jests which were devoid of all taste. Maddened by anger and unhappiness, M. de Croisenois demanded such unqualified satisfaction, that the millionaire preferred to fight a duel. Stupidity triumphed, and one of the most lovable of men met with his death before he was twenty-four.

This death produced a strange and morbid impression on Julien's demoralised soul.

"Poor Croisenois," he said to Mathilde, "really behaved very reason-ably and very honourably towards us; he had ample ground for hating me and picking a quarrel with me, by reason of your indiscretion in your mother's salon; for the hatred which follows on contempt is usually frenzied."

M. de Croisenois' death changed all Julien's ideas concerning Mathilde's future. He spent several days in proving to her that she ought to accept the hand of M. de Luz. "He is a nervous man, not too much of a Jesuit, and will doubtless be a candidate," he said to her. "He has a more sinister and persevering ambition than poor Croisenois, and as there has never been a dukedom in his family, he will be only too glad to marry Julien Sorel's widow."

"A widow, though, who scorns the grand passions," answered Mathilde coldly, "for she has lived long enough to see her lover prefer to her after six months another woman who was the origin of all their unhappiness."

"You are unjust! Madame de Rênal's visits will furnish my advocate at Paris, who is endeavouring to procure my pardon, with the subject matter for some sensational phrases; he will depict the murderer honoured by the attention of his victim. That may produce an impression, and perhaps some day or other, you will see me provide the plot of some melodrama or other, etc., etc."

A furious and impotent jealousy, a prolonged and hopeless unhappiness (for even supposing Julien was saved, how was she to win back his heart?), coupled with her shame and anguish at loving this unfaithful lover more than ever had plunged mademoiselle de la Mole into a gloomy silence, from which all the careful assiduity of M. de Frilair was as little able to draw her as the rugged frankness of Fouqué.

As for Julien, except in those moments which were taken up by Mathilde's presence, he lived on love with scarcely a thought for the future.

"In former days," Julien said to her, "when I might have been so happy, during our walks in the wood of Vergy, a frenzied ambition swept my soul into the realms of imagination. Instead of pressing to my heart that charming arm which is so near my lips, the thoughts of my future took me away from you; I was engaged in countless combats which I should have to sustain in order to lay the foundations of a colossal fortune. No, I should have died without knowing what happiness was if you had not come to see me in this prison."

Two episodes ruffled this tranquil life. Julien's confessor, Jansenist though he was, was not proof against an intrigue of the Jesuits, and became their tool without knowing it.

He came to tell him one day that unless he meant to fall into the awful sin of suicide, he ought to take every possible step to procure his pardon. Consequently, as the clergy have a great deal of influence with the minister of Justice at Paris, an easy means presented itself; he ought to become converted with all publicity.

"With publicity," repeated Julien. "Ha, Ha! I have caught you at it—I

401

have caught you as well, my father, playing a part like any missionary."

"Your youth," replied the Jansenist gravely, "the interesting appearance which Providence has given you, the still unsolved mystery of the motive for your crime, the heroic steps which mademoiselle de la Mole has so freely taken on your behalf, everything, up to the surprising affection which your victim manifests towards you, has contributed to make you the hero of the young women of Besançon. They have forgotten everything, even politics, on your account. Your conversion will reverberate in their hearts and will leave behind it a deep impression. You can be of considerable use to religion, and I was about to hesitate for the trivial reason that in a similar circumstance the Jesuits would follow a similar course. But if I did, even in the one case which has escaped their greedy clutches they would still be exercising their mischief. The tears which your conversation will cause to be shed will annul the poisonous effect of ten editions of Voltaire's works."

"And what will be left for me," answered Julien, coldly, "if I despise myself? I have been ambitious; I do not mean to blame myself in any way. Further, I have acted in accordance with the code of the age. Now I am living from day to day. But I should make myself very unhappy if I were to yield to what the locality would regard as a piece of cowardice...."

Madame de Rênal was responsible for the other episode which affected Julien in quite another way. Some intriguing woman friend or other had managed to persuade this naïve and timid soul that it was her duty to leave for St. Cloud, and go and throw herself at the feet of King Charles X.

She had made the sacrifice of separating from Julien, and after a strain as great as that, she no longer thought anything of the unpleasantness of making an exhibition of herself, though in former times she would have thought that worse than death.

"I will go to the king. I will confess freely that you are my lover. The life of a man, and of a man like Julien, too, ought to prevail over every consideration. I will tell him that it was because of jealousy that you made an attempt upon my life. There are numerous instances of poor young people who have been saved in such a case by the clemency of the jury or of the king."

"I will leave off seeing you; I will shut myself up in my prison," exclaimed Julien, "and you can be quite certain that if you do not promise me to take no step which will make a public exhibition of us both, I will kill myself in despair the day afterwards. This idea of going to Paris is not your own. Tell me the name of the intriguing woman who suggested it to you.

"Let us be happy during the small number of days of this short life. Let us hide our existence; my crime was only too self-evident. Mademoiselle de la Mole enjoys all possible influence at Paris. Take it from me that she has done all that is humanly possible. Here in the provinces I have all the men of wealth and prestige against me. Your conduct will still further aggravate those rich and essentially moderate people to whom life comes so easy.... Let us not give the Maslons, the Valenods, and the thousand other people who are worth more than they, anything to laugh about."

Julien came to find the bad air of the cell unbearable. Fortunately, nature was rejoicing in a fine sunshine on the day when they announced to him that he would have to die, and he was in a courageous vein. He found walking in the open air as delicious a sensation as the navigator, who has been at sea for a long time, finds walking on the ground. "Come on, everything is going all right," he said to himself. "I am not lacking in courage."

His head had never looked so poetical as at that moment when it was on the point of falling. The sweet minutes which he had formerly spent in the woods of Vergy crowded back upon his mind with extreme force.

Everything went off simply, decorously, and without any affectation on his part.

Two days before he had said to Fouqué: "I cannot guarantee not to show some emotion. This dense, squalid cell gives me fits of fever in which I do not recognise myself, but fear?—no! I shall not be seen to flinch."

He had made his arrangements in advance for Fouqué to take Mathilde and madame de Rênal away on the morning of his last day.

"Drive them away in the same carriage," he had said. "Do you see that the post-horses do not leave off galloping. They will either fall into each other's arms, or manifest towards each other a mortal hatred. In either case the poor women will have something to distract them a little from their awful grief."

Julien had made madame de Rênal swear that she would live to look after Mathilde's son.

"Who knows? Perhaps we have still some sensations after our death," he had said one day to Fouqué. "I should like to rest, for rest is the right word, in that little grotto in the great mountain which dominates Verrières. Many a time, as I have told you, I have spent the night alone in that grotto, and as my gaze would plunge far and wide over the richest provinces of France, ambition would inflame my heart. In those days it was my passion.... Anyway, I hold that grotto dear, and one cannot dispute that its situation might well arouse the desires of the philosopher's soul.... Well, you know! those good priests of Besançon will make money out of everything. If you know how to manage it, they will sell you my mortal remains."

Fouqué succeeded in this melancholy business. He was passing the night alone in his room by his friend's body when, to his great surprise, he saw Mathilde come in. A few hours before he had left her ten leagues from Besançon. Her face and eyes looked distraught.

"I want to see him," she said.

Fouqué had not the courage either to speak or get up. He pointed with his finger to a big blue cloak on the floor; there was wrapped in it all that remained of Julien.

She threw herself on her knees. The memory of Boniface de la Mole, and of Marguerite of Navarre gave her, no doubt, a superhuman courage. Her trembling hands undid the cloak. Fouqué turned away his eyes.

He heard Mathilde walking feverishly about the room. She lit several candles. When Fouqué could bring himself to look at her, she had placed Julien's head on a little marble table in front of her, and was kissing it on the forehead.

Mathilde followed her lover to the tomb which he had chosen. A great number of priests convoyed the bier, and, alone in her draped carriage, without anyone knowing it, she carried on her knees the head of the man whom she had loved so much.

When they arrived in this way at the most elevated peak of the high mountains of the Jura, twenty priests celebrated the service of the dead in the middle of the night in this little grotto, which was magnificently illuminated by a countless number of wax candles. Attracted by this strange and singular ceremony, all the inhabitants of the little mountain villages which the funeral had passed through, followed it.

Mathilde appeared in their midst in long mourning garments, and had several thousands of five-franc pieces thrown to them at the end of the service.

When she was left alone with Fouqué, she insisted on burying her lover's head with her own hands. Fouqué nearly went mad with grief.

Mathilde took care that this wild grotto should be decorated with marble monuments that had been sculpted in Italy at great expense.

Madame de Rênal kept her promise. She did not try to make any attempt upon her life; but she died embracing her children, three days after Julien.

THE END.

*   *   *   *   *   *   *   *   *   *

The inconvenience of the reign of public opinion is that though, of course, it secures liberty, it meddles with what it has nothing to do with—private life, for example. Hence the gloominess of America and England. In order to avoid infringing on private life, the author has invented a little town—Verrières, and when he had need of a bishop, a jury, an assize court, he placed all this in Besançon, where he has never been.

Made in the USA
Middletown, DE
22 February 2020

85177184R10243